THE

CURATE'S DAUGHTERS;

OR,

THE TWIN ROSES OF ARUNDALE.

𝔄 𝔇𝔬𝔪𝔢𝔰𝔱𝔦𝔠 𝔖𝔱𝔬𝔯𝔶.

BY HANNAH MARIA JONES.

. . . . : . . . . . Beauty is their own.
The feeling heart, simplicity of life,
And elegance, and taste; the faultless form,
Shaped by the hand of harmony; the cheek,
Where the live crimson, through the native white
Soft-shoo'ing. o'er the face diffuses bloom,
And every nameless grace; the parted lip,
Like the red rose-bud moist with morning dew,
Breathing delight; and under flowing jet,
Or sunny ringlets, or of circling brown,
The neck, slight-shaded, and the swelling breast;
The look, resistless, piercing to the soul,
And, by the soul inform'd when drest in love,
She sits high smiling in the conscious eye.—THOMSON.

LONDON:

E. LLOYD, 12, SALISBURY-SQUARE, FLEET-STREET.

PREFACE.

In the following pages will be found nothing so extraordinary but what the reader may find a parallel for within the sphere of his own knowledge. Who is there, even at the present day, who does not know of some poor curate who is striving harder than the most resolute tradesman strives for success in business, to keep in the ranks of gentility on a scanty pittance that society does not deem a sufficient remuneration for the working artisan, while the incumbent is enjoying the incomes of the living on the continent, or wasting the products of parishes in profligacy. Yet in spite of the obstacles by which they are surrounded, we find many such curates as Mr. Leslie, who quietly proceed in the good work before them, and realise a much greater share of happiness than those placed above them. In the quiet, meek and gentle Mrs. Leslie and her amiable daughter, Bess, our readers will find characters which when imitated by many of us will produce like results. Of Bell we will say but little; an inordinate ambition, discontentment with her station and associates, fed and encouraged very foolishly, if not culpably, by Lady Jane Bevington, paved the way to her ultimate ruin.

London, 1863.

THE
CURATE'S DAUGHTERS;
OR, THE
TWIN ROSES OF ARUNDALE.

CHAPTER I.

——Have I then no tears for thee?
Can I forget thy cares, from helpless years
Thy tenderness for me? An eye still beam'd
With love? A brow that never knew a frown?
Nor a harsh word thy tongue? Shall I for these
Repay thy stooping, venerable age
With shame, disquiet, anguish, and dishonour?
THOMSON.

In the month of August, 1823, a hackney coach drew up to the corner of a quiet street, of humble but respectable appearance, in the "pleasant suburban village of Islington," at five o'clock in the morning, the inhabitants were still buried in slumber. Even the *watchful* guardian of the night, whose box — fortunately for the purposes of those whose acts we are about to record—was situated at the other end of the street, was sleeping on his post. A gentleman, tall, of elegant proportions and distinguished appearance, though somewhat past the heyday of youth, alighted from the vehicle, and cast an anxious reconnoitring glance towards the second-floor windows of a house a few doors from the corner. The sash of one of those windows was precisely at that moment raised, as noiselessly as possible, and the head of a youthful female for a moment protruded, and was as instantaneously drawn back again. A smile of doubtful meaning passed over the handsome countenance of the gentleman at that moment. Could that unfortunate girl, his destined victim, have seen that equivocal smile, that expression of triumph, of sensual passion, of——No, we will not attempt to describe the hateful feelings which were depicted in that momentary expression.

"Get on the box, Jarvey," said the gentleman, "and be ready to drive off without a moment's delay. If you manage cleverly——"

He held up a piece of gold between his thumb and forefinger, which he seemed to think rendered any further explanation unnecessary, and then walked quickly up the street. The coachman, however, looked by no means satisfied, though he obeyed the command.

"I shall jest see what you're arter, my kiddy," he observed, looking after his employer. "If you think as how Bill P—— is a-goin' to be draw'd in to run the ri— of being sent over the herrin'-pond ——lly of that 'ere yaller boy, ye've —— rong pig by the tail. I'll have my —— or I won't have nothin', and

—— oliloquy was interrupted, or rather con——ded, by a long low whistle.

"—ew! that's all, is it? Who'd ha' thought he'd bin upon that lay?" he added, gathering up the reins, and, in his own language, preparing for a start.

That which had so suddenly altered the coachman's opinion of his employer was the sight of a young female, who at the moment the gentleman had reached the house already indicated, appeared at the door with a large bundle in her hand, which she delivered to him, and then passing her arm through his, hurried towards the coach, as if afraid to look behind her, or even to bestow a moment's reflection on the irrevocable step she was taking.

On the following morning the annexed advertisement appeared in the front column of every morning paper in London—

"If this should meet the eye of B. L. who quitted her home at Islington yesterday morning, she is earnestly implored to return to her distracted mother and sister, by whom she will be received with the utmost kindness,, and everything within their power done to secure her future comfort and happiness."

How many such advertisements meet the public eye during the course of a year! How few who read them reflect on the amount of misery which they comprise! Apparently, this either did not fall under the observation of the person to whom it was addressed, or failed to have the wished-for effect; for, two days after, in the same papers, and in several provincial ones—the Bath, Cheltenham, Brighton, Margate, Dover, &c.—might be seen another, to the following effect—

"TWENTY POUNDS REWARD.

"Left her home at Islington, on Friday, the 16th, a young female. She is about seventeen, rather above the middle size, slender figure, of dark complexion, deep blue eyes, long dark eye-lashes, Grecian nose, and a remarkable dimple in her left cheek; her hair, a bright chestnut, curls naturally, and in extreme profusion. She is supposed to have been dressed in a lilac muslin morning dress, a large Leghorn bonnet, with white feather, white satin ribbon, and Brussels lace veil; a light Cachemere shawl, and reticule of the same material. Had also with her a pale primrose and a light blue silk dress, and a black satin shawl embroidered in colours; a gold watch and neck-chain, the former ciphered in brilliants B. L.; a pearl necklace, earrings, and hair ornament, an arrow of gold feathered with pearls; several rings, diamond, pearl, ruby, and turquoise, together with a locket set round with brilliants, and containing three shades of hair—one, a silvery white, a dark brown, and the third the colour of her own hair—and bearing the initials H. M. B. L. It is hoped this minute description will enable some one to recognise her, and relieve her agonised mother and sister by communicating her present situation, when the above reward will be cheerfully and most gratefully paid. Apply to Mrs. Rachel Mytton, ——— Street, Islington.—N. B. It is suspected that the young person was taken away by a gentleman in a hackney-coach. Ten guineas will be given to the driver, if he will come forward and give information whither he conveyed his fare, and the whole of the reward if the persons are eventually traced through the medium of his information."

For three days this advertisement was repeated, and many were the observation to which it gave rise ; for the description of the young lady and her jewels was such as to prove that it was no *common* person (to use a common phrase) who was the subject of it. On the third day, the public curiosity, which had been so strongly excited, was somewhat relieved by the following paragraph, which ran through all the papers, among the other news and occurrences of the day.

"THE LATE ELOPEMENT AT ISLINGTON. —The young lady whose mysterious disappearance has plunged a most respectable family into the utmost distress and misery, is Miss B. L., a most superlatively beautiful girl, the daughter of a deceased clergyman, and the niece of a highly respected, wealthy, and influential merchant, the M. P. for ——shire. A great sensation was produced in the fashionable world, last season, by the introduction into society of this young lady and her twin sister by their aunt, Lady Jane B——. The exact resemblance of the two lovely sisters, which was said to puzzle even their most intimate relatives, and their fresh and blooming beauty, gained for them the soubriquet of the 'Twin Roses of ——dale,' the romantic and secluded valley of ——dale having been honoured by their birth. The young ladies were the presumptive co-heiresses of the countless thousands of their maternal uncle, M——w B——n, Esq., and, as such, excited universal attention and admiration. Contrary to all expectation, or calculation, within the last few months the Lady J——n B——n has presented her lawful lord with a son and heir ; an event which has, of course, had a very material effect upon the fortunes of the Twin Roses, who, it is said, were sent back rather abruptly to the obscurity from which they had been prematurely drawn, there 'to blush unseen, and,' probably, 'waste their sweetness on the desert air.' Of the circumstances of the elopement, by which it appears the young lady in question has desperately attempted to mend her fortunes, we know little, except that her companion is said to be a certain *roué* of the highest rank beneath royalty, and from whose well known opinions of matrimony no hope can ever be entertained that she will share a better fate than the numerous female favourites who have been to him the toys of a day. The much to be pitied and most respected mother of the young lady is said to be in a state which leaves little hope of her life."

The subject, like every other nine days'

wonder, died away, and was succeeded by others which probably had banished from the minds of the public all interest in the fate of the blighted Rose of Arundale, when the general sympathy, which is so easily excited when the objects of it belong to what is called the higher classes of society, was again aroused by the following statement appearing in the same papers—

"An inquest was held on Wednesday, at the Windmill, Lower Road, Deptford, on the body of a young female, which was taken out of the Surrey Canal, on Monday last, and which was identified by a respectable-looking elderly female, named Mytton, as the remains of Miss Bell Leslie, daughter of the late Rev. Horace Leslie, rector of Arundale, ——shire. The body, which was in a dreadful state of decomposition, was supposed to have been more than a fortnight in the water, and was only identified by the clothes, the initials B. L. on the linen, and an empty purse in the pocket of the deceased, which was recognised by the witness as having been her own gift, on the last birthday of the unfortunate deceased.

"Rachel Mytton, who appeared overwhelmed with grief, and was obliged to be supported into the jury-room, deposed that she was servant to the late Reverend Horace Leslie, and nursed the deceased Bell Leslie and her twin-sister from the hour of her birth. The deceased left her mother's residence in ——Street, Islington, on Friday morning, the 18th of August, and nothing had been heard of her since by her distressed family. She had been traced, by means of a hackney coachman who had been hired by a gentleman that morning, to have accompanied that gentleman to the ——Hotel, Covent Garden, but no farther traces of her could be found. Witness never saw her since the night preceding her quitting her mother's house, when she assisted her to undress. The young lady then appeared in her usual spirits. Had no suspicion of any unfair means having been adopted to induce her to leave her home, and could form no idea as to her death. Mrs. Leslie was supposed to be at the point of death, in consequence of the loss of her daughter. Came to identify the body in consequence of seeing the account of its being found, and the description of the dress, &c. The deceased was just turned seventeen, and was a most beautiful, accomplished girl.

"The coroner pointed out to the jury that there was no evidence to prove how the deceased came into the water, and it would be advisable, therefore, to return an open verdict. The jury, after a few moments' consultation, returned a verdict of 'Found drowned, but how there is no evidence to show;' and the coroner immediately gave his warrant for the removal of the body to the residence of the family."

Thus apparently ended this tragedy, but in reality this was only the first act. A long, long tale of mystery, of misery and woe remained—

"Thus bad begins, and worse remains behind,"

CHAPTER II.

—— Like two artificial gods,
Created with our needles both one flower,
Both on one sampler, sitting on one cushion ;
Both warbling of one song, both in one key,
As if our hands, our sides, voices and minds
Had been incorp'rate. So we grew together,
Like to a double cherry, seeming parted,
But yet in union in partition.—SHAKSPEARE.

MBOSOMED in a deep romantic valley is situated the lovely and picturesque town of Arundale. Except where a few tradesmen have congregated together for conveniency in the immediate vicinity of the little market-place, such as the shoemaker, the saddler, &c. &c., nearly every house stands separate, surrounded with gardens and orchards, and in the spring and summer it has the appearance of a town roofed in with leaves. The traveller journeying either on foot or by the solitary stage-coach which, three times a-week, is seen slowly toiling up the sandy road that crosses the adjacent hill, and on the alternate days descending it, would scarcely discover the existence of habitations in that leafy and secluded spot. A bird, it has been said, might fly over the town, and not suspect it was there, were it not for the high spire of the church that towers above the foliage. At a short distance from that ancient edifice, and, like it, shrouded even to the very roof with ivy and other climbers, stands the Parsonage—a modest, unassuming dwelling ; and yet, from the various indications of taste in the disposal of its rich and elegantly tinted glass, and the well-kept lawn with its velvety surface studded with clumps of the brightest flowering shrubs, maintaining a certain air of superiority over the other dwellings, illustrative of the rank its inhabitants held in the estimation of their owners. And yet Mr. Leslie was but an humble curate. The rector, for the greater part of the year,

resided on a distant and richer living, and the Parsonage, as it was called, was given up to Leslie, as part payment for his indefatigable attention to the arduous duties of his situation.

It was in this lovely and peaceful scene that Bess and Bell Leslie first saw the light. They were twins, the elder, Bess, claiming one hour's seniority over her sister Bell ; an advantage which, from the exact resemblance of the children from the hour of their birth, it would have been difficult to have secured to the elder, had it not occurred to the wise woman who officiated as nurse to Mrs. Leslie to mark the difference by tying a ribbon round the fat little chubby arm of the elder-born. But old Rachel had scarcely completed this operation before she discovered that Nature herself had affixed a mark more imperishable, though not so immediately cognisable, to distinguish the sisters.

"Dear ma'am, I do believe it's a strawberry here, on the dear little angel's neck," she whispered to Mrs. Leslie's maiden sister, pointing to a deep red spot, or, rather, a cluster of spots, which stained the snowy skin of the last comer. "Well, to be sure, that is lucky, for there can be no mistakes made now, any how."

Many mistakes, however, were made, not only during the infancy of the sisters, but as they grew up. They were truly like—

"Twin cherries on one stalk,"

Not even by the parents of the two lovely girls could the difference be seen at a glance ; and by casual acquaintances, or their neighbours, the townsfolk of Arundale, it was utterly undiscoverable. To Bess it was often a subject of infinite diversion to be addressed as Bell; but to the latter it was not altogether a matter of pleasantry. Bell, there is no concealing the fact, was vain, very vain. She had no objection to the general appellation of the "Twin Roses of Arudale;" but her glass told her, or at least she fancied so, that on the score of personal charms she had considerably the advantage of her sister.

Bessie's eyes were a shade lighter, though certainly her long dark eye-lashes somewhat disguised this fact; but moreover they, the eyes, were not so brilliant, and Bell wondered how any one could be so stupid as not to discover that important difference. Then, Bessie's skin was not so transparently fair, and her hair was a shade darker, and the *tournure* of her shoulders was less graceful, and her air altogether not so *distingue*; and, in short, Bell was convinced that people were either obstinately blind, or determinately stupid, who could not discover, at a single glance, her infinite superiority over her sister. There was one satisfaction—Bess herself never disputed this superiority. In her eyes, indeed, her sister Bell was the most beautiful creature in existence; and she was fully inclined to agree with the latter, that it was strange people should be so stupid as not to see how great a difference existed between them. It was a sore subject with Bell, the constant mistakes that were made in their identity; and even to old Rachel's stories of the difficulty in knowing one from the other in the cradle—and how, when they were taken to be christened, she was obliged to open the shawls in which they were wrapped, to look for the strawberry on the neck of the youngest, before she gave either of them into the arms of their father, lest Bess should be named Bell, and Bell named Bess, which would have angered her dear master—even to this simple proof of their striking resemblance Bell listened with an expression of impatience and contempt that certainly did not increase her claims to superior beauty. There was another subject, too, which was never alluded to without exciting a sensation of discontent in the bosom of the younger born.

"What could possess my father to give us such ridiculous names, mamma?" she one day inquired. "Miss Bess and Miss Bell! I declare I'm sometimes quite provoked at hearing the odious monosyllables."

"What's in a name," observed the laughing Bess; "the rose by any other name would smell as sweet, and ——"

"Oh, I didn't ask your opinion," interrupted her sister, scornfully. "I believe you would be contented, as long as papa did it; but why was it, mamma? I'm sure you did not choose ——"

"No, my love, I had nothing to do with it," returned Mrs. Leslie, smiling, "but I believe I can satisfy you as to your father's reason. He had often, with some degree of dissatisfaction, remarked that all our plain, old-fashioned English names were gradually disappearing in Arundale, and that the rising generation, whom he was called to make Christians, were all Clementinas, Adelaides, Cecilias, and suchlike romantic and affected names. Look at Tomkins the butcher's five girls, for instance, Bell, and tell me if your simple name is not much more distinctive and pleasing than their Evelinas, Lavinias, and the rest of them? And then your father will have it that those names have an influence on their wearers, and that they are sure to be as lack-a-daisical and affected as——"

"Well, then, I wonder what he thinks Bell is to make of me," returned the young lady, discontentedly.

"Why, a sweet, harmonious, cheerful, merry darling, as you are," observed Bess, throwing her arms around her sister's neck, "I'm sure I love the sound."

Bell, however, looked anything but sweet or harmonious at this minute, for to her the unpretending nature of the patronymic her father had bestowed upon her was a source of serious vexation.

Mrs. Leslie was a gentle, kind-hearted, sensitive woman, rather disposed to consult her own personal ease and quiet too much to have the sole conduct and direction of two lively, high-spirited, and it must be confessed in some measure wilful, and, especially as regarded the younger, obstinate and self-willed girls. It was true that their father, a plain sensible man, watched sedulously over them, and on all occasions studied to counteract the evils of his wife's unlimited indulgence of her children. The twins were nearly ten years old when an event took place that materially altered the prospects and situation of the family.

Mrs. Leslie's brother was a merchant of immense fortune. The marriage of his sister to Mr. Leslie, the poor curate, had at the time greatly offended her brother, Mr. Bevington, and having paid over into the hands of the former the few hundred pounds that had been left to her by her father, he had since rigidly adhered to the resolution he had then rudely expressed, that he would have nothing more to do with the parson or his wife. This resolution had given but little pain to Mr. Leslie, who thoroughly despised the narrow-minded and purse-proud Bevington. Mrs. Leslie, though she at first shed some natural tears at her brother's estrangement from her, was too happy in her marriage ever to regret the exchange she had made from the ostentatiously furnished house, and troublesome establishment, of which she had been the ostensible mistress (Mr. Bevington having been at that time unmarried), to the comparatively humble dwelling, the Parsonage of Arundale; and though Bevington Hall, her brother's splendid seat, was only a few miles distant from the Vale of Arundale, it was to her as if they were at the opposite confines of the world. They never met, and one or two conciliatory letters, which she had sent soon after her marriage, having been returned in blank covers, she had ceased even to hope or wish for any renewal of the intercourse between her and her inexorable relative. It must be confessed that, after the birth of the twins, she thought much oftener of the wealthy owner of Bevington Hall than she had done for many years previous. Bess and Bell were not born until their father and mother had passed the middle period of life, and had ceased to expect or hope for any increase of family. Mr. Leslie's income, though fully adequate to his limited desires, and indeed enabling him and his wife to enjoy all the comforts and many of the luxuries of life, was still such as the wealthy inhabitants of Bevington Hall would have looked upon, or rather did look upon, with contempt.

"A poor miserable pittance," he had been heard to say, "not as much as I appropriate to the maintenance of my dog-kennel; but as they made their bed, so may they lie in it. The parson shall find himself mistaken, if he thought of making a stepping stone of fortune in me. My sister, with the recommendations she possessed, and my introduction, might have married well; she has chosen, in spite of my advice, to wed herself to poverty and obscurity, and let her reap the benefit of it."

There were not wanting, of course, gossips to repeat to Mrs. Leslie her brother's unfeeling remarks. Gossip is the besetting sin of small secluded towns, where every family live in the closest relations to each other, as in our sweet little town of Arundale.

"What a fine thing it would be for the dear young ladies, if their uncle could but be persuaded to look upon them," observed one of these busy people who sometimes found toleration for a few hours at the Parsonage, though discouraged by the little interest which either the master or mistress of it ever evinced in the subjects which afforded them topics for conversation.

Mrs. Leslie felt that it might indeed be very desirable that her brother should regard her children with affection, or, at least, with natural kindness. Mr. Leslie's income would not admit of any saving, so his wife thought, who shrunk from the exertion necessary for a purpose that yet lay near her heart—that of making a provision for the beloved beings who, in event of their father's death, would be left friendless and helpless. She trembled, shuddered to think of such a possibility; and yet, still all went on the same, though perhaps, in the bosoms of both Mr. and Mrs. Leslie, lurked the unrevealed hope that, though unacknowleged and unnoticed by Mr. Bevington, the natural rights of his nieces would not be entirely overlooked. He was still single, and had not another near relation in the world.

This source of inward gratulation vanished. The girls were not more than seven years old when the whole country was in excitement with the fetes, balls, dejeauers, &c., &c., which were given at Bevington Hall, on the occasion of the marriage of its proprietor to Lady Jane Aylmer, the sister of the Earl of Woodchester. Oxen were roasted whole in the park; hogsheads of porter flowed like water. The whole population of Arundale deserted their homes for days, either to see or to share in the festivities consequent upon this great event, and poor Mrs. Leslie was left to her sad cogitations on the sad disappointment to the hopes which she had allowed to gain but too much ascendancy in her mind."

"It was but natural to expect that he would marry," she observed to the good-natured friends who thought proper to offer their condolements rather than their congratulations. "Mr. Bevington was only fifty; and, though the world had chosen to consider him as a decided bachelor, she had never been of that opinion; in fact, from her knowledge of his nature and disposition, she had always believed he would marry, whenever a suitable match offered."

And yet she sighed heavily, as she looked upon her two beautiful and unconscious children, and wished that Matthew her brother had but seen them, could but have known what sweet creatures they were. Mr. Leslie said nothing, but his countenance certainly became more thoughtful and melancholy. The project of a pony-chaise, which had been talked of as an addition to their establishment, for the sake of the children's health, was quietly relinquished; the curate talked seriously of applying to the rector for some addition to his very moderate stipend, and determined firmly henceforth to devote a part even of the little he possessed to secure his children from the probability of absolute want and beggary, by insuring his life for a thousand pounds; and what is still more he persevered in these good intentions, though the rector declared it to be utterly impossible he could spare more than the hundred and twenty pounds Mr. Leslie received, and hinted that there were hundreds of learned and deserving men who would gladly accept less; and Mrs. Leslie, to enable her husband to persevere in his prudent and commendable undertaking, was obliged to limit her own and her children's wardrobe, and to renounce all thoughts of the master's lessons in dancing and music, and the grand pianoforte, which she had, "in her mind's eye," seen replacing her own old-fashioned square one. It is but justice to say, that all were relinquished without a murmur. She would have done much more to secure her children from the possibility of want. She did do more; for, still hoping that Matthew's naturally kindly nature might be awakened, even now, in behalf of her children, she humbled herself; and, unknown to Mr. Leslie, almost the only secret she had kept since their marriage, she wrote a letter of congratulation to her brother on his marriage, though her cheeks burned, while she wrote, with the consciousness of her insincerity. But it was for the sake of her children, who now ran the risk of being entirely forgotten by their uncle, (it was a question if he had ever remembered them), and what would she not do, for the sake of those dear objects of her love!

The letter remained unanswered; and Mrs. Leslie, more humbled than ever she had been before in her own estimation, carefully concealed the whole affair from her husband.

Every year, for the first four after Mr. Bevington's marriage, Mrs. Leslie regularly received intimation from some of the gossips of Arundale that Lady Jane was in the way that "ladies wish to be who love their lords;" and the vast preparations that were making to receive the expected heir of the immense wealth of Squire Bevington formed a regular subject of conversation among those who pretended to be in the secret; but the four years passed away, and Lady Jane still continued childless, and it began now to be whispered in confidence that the family physician had given his decided opinion that her ladyship was too delicate to hope ever to present her husband with the wished-for heir.

"Too old, he should have said," observed Rachel, Mrs. Leslie's nurse, who now held the situation of confidential servant and friend in the family; "I told you, ma'am, that when I saw her in the coach going to Frampton church, where Lucy, my sister, lives, she looked near fifty, in spite of all her paint and jewels."

This was a relief for which Mrs. Leslie was duly grateful, though the castles in the air she again began to build were, she sometimes herself feared, destitute of any more substantial foundation.

Bess and Bell were nearly ten years old, and beautiful as Houris, when their mother was persuaded to entrust them to the care of a neighbour, whose husband was going to take her and his family over in a chaise cart to the races on the Downs, which had been newly instituted in a great measure by the interest and interference of Matthew Bevington, Esquire. Mrs. Leslie had heard of the style in which Lady Jane and Mr. Bevington had appeared on the grounds on the first day of the races. This was the second day, and the tears came into the mother's eyes as she beheld her children mounting by the aid of a wooden chair into the humble vehicle, though, as the kind-hearted mistress of it observed, the seats were stuffed and quite easy, and her children could stand and give the young ladies their places; and the springs made it as easy as the best carriage going. Bess and Bell were dressed in their best white frocks and tippets, and their cottage bonnets were very becoming. Dress, indeed, could add little to their rare beauty; and yet their mother was not satisfied with their appearance. She fancied the coarse materials spoke of their father's poverty, and she imagined what the proud Lady Jane would say, if the children were pointed out to her as her husband's nieces. And yet it must be confessed that her chief inducement in letting them go without Mr. Leslie's permission (he was absent, at the bedside of a dying parishioner) was the hope that they might catch the eyes of their rich relations.

This, in fact, happened, though in a very different way to which she could have expected or wished. It was a beautiful day, and the Downs were crowded to behold he sight. As Mrs. Franklin, the carpenter's wife, and *chaperone* to the curate's two little girls—an office of which she was not a little proud—observed, "All the world and his wife were there;" and Bess and Bell, who had never witnessed anything approaching to such a scene, were completely bewildered with the various noises and sights that surrounded them.

"And whose is that beautiful carriage, and those ladies on horseback, and that, and that?" they had demanded, and had received answers as near the truth as Mrs. Franklin could frame them. But now the horses were going to start, and the driver of the chaise-cart drew up as close as he could to the course; and the two sisters, hand-in-hand, mounted upon the stuffed seat which Mrs. Franklin's own children were not allowed to profane with their thick shoes.

"Draw back there, you sir—draw back!" exclaimed a corpulent gentleman with a whip in his hand, who seemed to take upon himself the dictatorship of the whole affair. "You ought to have known very well that your cart had no business here."

Mr. Franklin, who knew very well that this was Squire Bevington, glanced back at the two girls.

"If he knew who they were," observed the good-natured man to his jolly spouse, "I don't think he'd hinder their stopping to get a good sight; and now, if we draw off to where the carts stand, the poor things will see nothing."

Mr. Bevington was not used to have his commands disputed—indeed, to meet with a moment's hesitation. He had turned away to speak to some one after issuing his peremptory order to Franklin, and did not observe the man's appealing look to the children. Perhaps if he had, it would have made no difference; but, be that as it might, he turned round again, saw that the cart was not moved, and without a moment's reflection or hesitation he seized the bridle and struck the horse with the whip, and by the sudden jerk the two sisters, who were still standing on the seat, were thrown over. Bess was caught by the skirt of her frock by Mrs. Franklin, but Bell was less fortunate; she fell under the feet of a horse that was passing, and shrieks of "She's killed!—she's killed!" resounded on every side.

"And you own sister's child, too—your own niece, Mr. Bevington," shouted Mrs. Franklin to the unhappy man, who had been the cause of the accident. "Oh, what shall I say to Mrs. Leslie?"

"Leslie, my God!—Is this Leslie's child?" exclaimed the horror-struck Bevington, who had been the first to raise the insensible girl from the ground.

"Yes; and this is their's, too," returned Mrs. Franklin, who was holding the terrified Bess in her arms, to prevent her jumping out among the crowd to the assistance of her sister. "This is their other child," she repeated; "and it was only that they might have a better sight that we drew up here among the gentlefolks; I'm sure we should never have thought of it on our own account; but blood is blood, and we thought ——"

Mr. Bevington did not attend to what she thought.

"Go, and bring up my carriage," he exclaimed to the bystanders, "and take care not to alarm Lady Jane, but ask her for her smelling-bottle; I hope, I pray, the child is not seriously hurt; but that one will faint. Take care of her."

He was gazing on Bess's pale countenance, from which terror had banished almost the appearance of life.

"And some of you run for a surgeon, and send him up to the hall; for a dozen, if you can find them. I'll pay them all. My God! I would not that this should have happened for ten thousand pounds!"

"All the money in the world couldn't pay Mr. and Mrs. Leslie for their beautiful children," muttered Mrs. Franklin, who was holding Bess in her arms, and fanning her with a pocket-handkerchief, while her own tears fell on her pale face. She could not, did not dare look at Bell, as she afterwards said, for fear she should see her beautiful face disfigured.

The carriage was brought, and Lady Jane was almost as soon at the side of her husband, asking a thousand questions in a breath, and uttering as many more exclamations of surprise and horror, among which not the least intelligible was—

"In a cart—Mr. Leslie's children—Mr. Bevington's sister's children in a common cart!"

"Their relations might find them a better carriage, certainly," muttered Franklin, who was by no means pleased at the contempt thus thrown on what he considered a very creditable set-out.

Bell was lifted into the coach, into which Lady Jane condescended to follow Mr. Bevington, whose anxiety for the child had evidently driven away all his interest in the race, though the horses were waiting only for his appearance to order the bell to be rung; but at the moment the carriage was moving away, Bess recovered her voice, and her shrieks for her sister—her dear, dear Bell—were so overpowering, that it stopped.

"Bring her here. Let her come with us," said Mr. Bevington, putting his head out.

Franklin alighted, and Bess was carefully lifted into the carriage; and then Mr. Bevington, seeming suddenly to recollect himself, observed to the former—

"You had better follow us; I shall want, of course, to send some message to my——to Mrs. Leslie; and you can explain matters better than any one else."

It was a source of self-gratulation in after times to Mrs. Franklin, when she related the history of this untoward, but in the end, lucky accident, to her friends, that though she missed seeing the race, and never had another chance (because next year Mr. Bevington withdrew his patronage, and the affair fell to the ground), she had no right to complain, for she had the opportunity of seeing all the grandeur and splendour at the hall, and was treated like a lady in the housekeeper's room; and Franklin got all the work for the future for Mr. Bevington; so that it made good the old saying, that "it's an ill wind that blows nobody good," setting aside that it was the means of bringing her and Mrs. Leslie together again, and making them better friends than ever; and, after all, Miss Bell was not seriously hurt, and her sweet face had not a mark on it, though she (Mrs. Franklin), could have

taken her oath that she saw the horse put his great nasty foot right upon her face.

Within three or four hours of the accident on the Downs, Mr. and Mrs. Leslie were seated at Lady Jane's tea-table, with their children between them, with hearts throbbing with gratitude to that Almighty Providence which had thus brought out of evil, good.

By the management of Mr. Bevington, the parents had been saved all alarm with respect to their children, until the sight of them safe and smiling, though a little paler than usual, convinced them there was nothing now to tremble at.

A polite and friendly note, written by Lady Jane, had informed her and Mrs. Leslie that their daughters were her guests, and that they only required the presence of their father and mother to make them quite happy and contented.

Mr. Bevington having wisely detained the Franklins, and sent a house-servant with the note, who knew nothing of what had happened, the parents were spared all unnecessary alarm, and the surgeon having declared that the child had received no injury, (a fact, indeed, which was soon evident from the manner in which Bell began to survey the grandeur with which she found herself surrounded) every trace of agitation and terror had vanished before Mr. and Mrs. Leslie arrived, and all went "merry as a marriage bell."

CHAPTER III.

We were as twinn'd lambs, that did frisk i' th' sun,
And bleat the one at th' other; what we chang'd,
Was innocence for innocence; we knew not
The doctrine of ill doing: no, nor dream'd
That any did.—SHAKSPEARE.

HE surpassing beauty of the twin-sisters, and the still more surprising resemblance, which made it so difficult to distinguish one from the other, was a source of endless amusement and interest to Lady Jane Bevington. She was, for days, never weary of admiring and talking of them; and Mr. and Mrs. Leslie, who had never since their birth been absent from them three consecutive hours, were compelled reluctantly to yield to their newly introduced relative, and suffer the children to remain with her at the hall. Mr. Bevington, too, seemed to make up for his former coldness and indifference by kindness to his nieces; and Mrs. Leslie, feeling that now, indeed, all her cares were at an end, returned home quite happy.

Striking, however, as their personal resemblance was, the girls soon gave sufficient evidence that their dispositions were very different. To Bell, the change from the plain fare and comparatively humble mode of living of her parental home, seemed to sit quite easy upon her, as if she were "to the manner born;" and while her more timid sister betrayed constraint and diffidence in every look and movement —while Bess blushed and hesitated when spoken to, and sat silent and pensive when not the object of attention—Bell's little person seemed to swell with conscious dignity. Her speech was free and unrestrained; and the admiration that was bestowed but too openly upon her, she seemed to take as her due. In Lady Jane Bevington's eyes all this was highly estimable; and the sisters had passed very few hours at the hall before Bell was her decided favourite.

"I foresee," she observed to Mr. Bevington, "that Bell will make a figure in the world. I am not so sanguine of her sister —I am afraid she is a little, a very little bit stupid."

"Stupid!" repeated Mr. Bevington, "with that face, that speaking face, stupid? I must take leave to differ from you. She is timid, certainly, but——"

"I hate timid, blushing young ladies," rejoined her ladyship with quickness.

"Hate!—that is rather a strong expression to apply to a child of ten years of age, is it not, my dear?" replied Mr. Bevington, smiling.

Lady Jane looked rather confused.

"Oh, I only meant that as a general remark," she observed, "certainly not to apply to Miss Leslie. She is the elder, you know, so we may give her that title. I detest to utter the vulgar name her father has given her. Bess, indeed! Oh, how glad I am it is not my sweet little favourite that bears it; I should have been quite miserable. Bell is not exactly what I like—but then it may be considered only a pet name for Isabel or Arabella, and so it will pass—but Bess! oh, it's horrible!"

"You forget, my dear Lady Jane, that Bess was a pet name, applied even to royalty," observed Mr. Bevington. "Our great and good Queen Elizabeth——"

"Oh, don't talk of it—I always connect everything that was gross and vulgar with the great and good queen you speak of," returned Lady Jane.

Mr. Bevington only smiled in reply, and the subject was dropped, though from that time it became a decided matter with the visitors, as well as the establishment at Bevington Hall, that Miss Leslie, as Lady Jane persevered in calling Bess, was her uncle's favourite niece, and Bell the pet and protegé of her aunt.

Bell was now the happiest of the happy —the gayest of the gay. The white muslin frocks which were all that their scanty wardrobe supplied, were as speedily as possible discarded for the richest silks. The milliners and dress-makers of the neighbourhood were all set to work to render the appearance of the curate's daughters suitable to the fortune and station of their wealthy and noble relatives; and Bell entered as deeply as Lady Jane herself into all the merits and demerits of the colours and trimmings, and make and shape of the various and elegant materials and patterns that were submitted for their examination and approval. It is not to be supposed that Bess was indifferent to all this finery and display—no, the sparkle of her bright eyes, and the deepened colour on her cheek, as she surveyed herself, in her new array, in the splendid mirrors which reflected her whole figure from head to foot, betrayed that she was not at all insensible to the advantage of dress; but still she sometimes showed a strange indifference to the trivial details which her sister and Lady Jane discussed with such interest and energy. She would decide very readily whether she preferred apple-green to peach-blossom, or primrose to orange colour; but the trimmings or the shape of the sleeves or bodies—all the fiddle-faddle, as she once profanely called it, in Lady Jane's absence, were all referred to the taste of her sister or aunt, or even the dress-maker herself, or any one who would take the trouble to think or decide for her.

Poor Bess indeed began soon to feel that all this devotion to appearance was very tiresome, and that her occupations at home, her books, and birds, and flowers, or even a game of romps, either with papa, who was an excellent romp, or her young companions, was far preferable to being shut up all the morning in Lady Jane's dressing-room, surrounded with silks, satins, gauzes, and laces, and all the rest of what she in her heart called frippery. Nay, she privately thought that even teaching Rachel's parrot to sing "Home, sweet home," her pretty French poodle to dance a *pas seul*, which had been her latest occupations at home when her lessons were learned, and she had practised the set time on mamma's pianoforte, ay, even the lessons themselves were infinitely pleasanter than listening to the endless discussions upon camails and mantelets, crepelisse, gouffres, and half a thousand other things, which Bess felt quite sure she never could understand, nor even would try to learn so to do. Lady Jane became every hour more convinced that her first impression was correct; and the milliner, the dress-maker, and the lady's maid, all confirmed it. Miss Bell was a paragon of taste. They had never seen a young lady of her age have such correct ideas as to the becoming, and tasteful, and fashionable. It was quite a pleasure to work for her ; and then everything sat so well on her ; while Miss Leslie was really quite difficult to fit, she was so impatient of standing still, and looked so miserable when her corsets were drawn tight, thought it was quite impossible that any dress could look well without the waist was confined, so as to make the shoulders look as wide as possible.

"But I cannot breathe, dear aunt, if I am pinched in," sighed Bess, "and I am afraid to move my arms in these tight sleeves, for fear I should burst them."

"Your sister finds no difficulty in accommodating herself to the present style of dress, Miss Leslie," observed Lady Jane, "though, of course, she is as little used to it as you are ; but it is plain you do not think it worth while to submit to the slightest inconvenience to oblige me. There, what have I said to call for tears ? Really you are a very incomprehensible young lady. However, I shall not take any trouble about your appearance for the future. Have the goodness, Mrs. Chapman, to take Miss Leslie's own directions for the frock. I should be very sorry that she should be pinched, or rendered any way uncomfortable, to please me."

"Oh, Bess, how can you be so ungrateful," whispered Bell ; but Bess felt she was not ungrateful ; and though her ready tears had rushed to her eyes, at the severity of the tone Lady Jane had assumed, she calmly and quietly pointed out, in reply to Mrs. Chapman's questions, what she thought the necessary alterations, to enable her to move with ease and comfort.

"She is neither so stupid nor apathetic as I thought her," reflected Lady Jane, "but a great deal too decisive and independent for her age. My sweet little Bell tells me that her sister is the father's favourite ; and I suppose he teaches her all these ridiculous airs of being superior to the frivolities of dress. I declare she made me feel, for a minute, just as I do when he fixes his calm grave eye upon me; and yet I can't dislike him either, though he does make one feel his superiority."

The visit to Bevington Hall, which was originally intended only to last for a week, was extended to a month. Bess, although she saw her father and mother several times, and though she found that she became every day a greater favourite with her uncle, and was no longer expected even to join in the dressing-room *coterie*, began to long for the return to her dear home—her birds, her flowers, her delightful rambles and conversations with her father—and, in short, everything that she had been from infancy accustomed to, and which, in her eyes, seemed the more endeared by absence. Bell, on the contrary, looked forward with dismay to the moment that she should be compelled to relinquish the grandeur of her present mode of life. Mr. Bevington and Lady Jane were going to London for some months, and Bell felt miserable at the thought that she should be compelled to return to the dull domestic life of the Parsonage. No carriage drives —no evening parties—no servants ready to execute her slightest wishes—no indulgent aunt to administer to her vanity, always but too evident, and now rendered quite inordinate by Lady Jane's weak indulgence and flattery.

Bess, however, did not suspect the true state of her sister's feelings ; and when she saw her sister throw herself into Lady Jane's arms, drowned in tears, and telling her that she should never be happy till she came back again to the hall, Bess attributed it all to Bell's affectionate disposition, and her gratitude for the kindness and attachment which her aunt had shown towards her. Not a spark of envy existed, or could find place in Bessie's pure mind. She was quite convinced that, in spite of all people said of the wonderful resemblance between them, Bell was much handsomer and attractive than herself ; and she felt neither vexed nor surprised that Lady Jane, or Lady Jane's friends, should make such a marked distinction between her and her sister.

"Oh, here is our own dear little bedroom, once more," said Bess, when the sisters retired for the night. "I don't know how it was, Bell, but it seemed to me that I never slept so sweetly, or so sound, at the hall ; though the curtains were satin damask, and the bed was down. I suppose it was that I was feverish with sitting up so late, and eating suppers."

Bell burst into a fit of tears. She had suppressed her discontent, and put on a calm, if not a pleased look and manner in the presence of her father and mother; and she felt really happy and gratified while she was displaying to Rachel and Sarah, the two domestics, and to Mrs. Franklin, who, with her usual kind homely feelings, had stepped in to welcome the young ladies home, all the treasures which Lady Jane had lavished upon her; but now that she had no longer anything to display, and that instead of being waited upon to bed by Mad'moiselle, Lady Jane's French waiting-woman—wax candles on the superb toilette, and surrounded with everything that could minister to luxury and ease, she found herself in her own plain little chamber, with one little tallow candle, in a bright brass flat candlestick, placed before the old-fashioned swing-glass, the casement windows shaded with plain white calico, and the bed furniture of the same material, with only her sister to untie her clothes, and expecting from her the same service, the contrast was so great that she could no longer suppress her feelings, and pushing Bess angrily away she continued, in spite of the latter's affectionate and surprised inquiries and remonstrances, to sob as if her heart would break.

"What can be the matter? What can make you unhappy, dear, dear Bell? Do, pray, tell me what it is, there's a dear girl? I haven't offended you?—what can it be that makes you cry?" was repeated over and over again, before Bell could command her voice.

"What can it be?" she at length angrily replied. "Only look at this mean, wretched-looking little room, that Lady Jane would scorn to use even for a closet. And everything about the house seems to have grown older and shabbier since we have been away; and the paltry supper-table, and mamma sending Sarah away to the kitchen, and telling her she need not wait because she must be tired with washing all day ; even papa and mamma seem to have grown less genteel since we have seen such superior people at——"

"I never saw papa and mamma's superiors yet, Bell," interrupted Bess, with warmth ; "and, really, if you have nothing of more importance to cry for than this, I cannot feel any great pity for you."

"No, I dare say not," retorted Bell, angrily; "as my aunt says, you are just fitted to creep and grovel through life, without spirit to aspire to be anything above the situation in which mamma's impruden has placed herself and her children in marrying a poor curate without——"

"If my aunt said that, Bell, and you listened to it with patience—" exclaimed Bess, her eyes darting fire. "But I will not quarrel with you," she added, bursting into tears; "I will try to forget that you could hear, or could repeat, a disrespectful word of our dear, dear father. The best, the kindest—and, after all, Bell, can you, from your heart, say that Lady Jane Bevington, with all the splendour she is surrounded with, and all the riches that are at her command, is half so happy, so contented, or so cheerful as our dear mother? Look how fretful she is, when not surrounded with company—hear her ever-lasting complaints of the torment of servants—and then how petulant she is if my uncle offers the slightest contradiction to her wishes. See how ill-tempered and disagreeable she was for two whole days, because my uncle found it necessary to go to London a week or two earlier than she had fixed upon, because she had fixed her mind upon giving some foolish fete champetre, as she called it, to outdo the masked ball and private theatricals at Lady Charlier's, though she knew that my uncle's duty obliged him to attend the House of Commons."

"Well, and it was provoking and vexatious," interrupted Bell.

"Everything is provoking and vexatious that interferes when people set their whole heart and happiness on trifling amusements," observed Bess, with a gravity far beyond her years.

"Ah, aunt is right," replied Bell, sneeringly; "she says that it is a thousand pities you were not a boy, that your papa might make a parson of you, like himself."

"Aunt never paid me a higher compliment, though she did not intend it as such, my dear sister," returned Bess, smiling. "But I have not yet said all that I intended to say, before you interrupted my sermon—as I suppose you would call it—for I meant to ask you whether you can deny that our dear mother is happier, ten times happier, better, and more respected than Lady Jane?"

"Yes—because she is like you—such an easy, unambitious disposition, that she would——"

"I won't hear another word after that, dear Bell, for I feel that it is a compliment," interrupted her sister, stopping her mouth with a kiss ; and, to prevent her sister's renewing the subject, the sweet and right-thinking girl threw herself on her knees by the side of the bed, to offer up her innocent prayers; to which, this night, was added a fervent petition that her sister might be restored to contentment and peace.

At Bell Leslie's age it might have been expected that any impression, however forcible at the time, would soon wear away; but this was not the case in the present instance; and Mrs. Leslie, who soon discovered the source of her daughter's discontent and gloom, felt almost inclined to regret that which she had, at the time, considered a most fortunate event for her children—namely, their recognition by her brother, and the sudden *penchant* towards them which had been exhibited by Lady Jane. Bell's naturally high spirits, indeed, had completely fled. She would sit in her bed-room for hours during the day, sullen and silent, or drowned in tears; and the only times that she seemed to feel anything like satisfaction or pleasure, was when she had an opportunity of displaying some of her newly-acquired finery to those of their young neighbours who had not previously seen it.

Several weeks had passed since their departure from the Hall, and nothing had been heard of Mr. Bevington and Lady Jane by the curate's family, except that, from the servants who were left in charge of the former, Rachel, Mr. Leslie's confidential domestic, heard when she met with one or other of them in the market, that their master and mistress were quite well, and had been giving a series of splendid entertainments, at their new mansion in Cavendish Square.

Bell, who had listened with eagerness to this information, disappeared the moment she heard the conclusion of it; and Mrs. Leslie, who had marked with extreme pain the change in her daughter's countenance, followed her to her chamber, and found her in a paroxysm of hysterical tears. It was in vain that the grieved mother represented the folly and unreasonableness of Bell's expectations. Lady Jane had forgotten her already—had treated her cruelly after raising her hopes, and in fact (this was the first time Mrs. Leslie had heard of any allusion to it) had promised that she (Lady Jane) would persuade her uncle to send for her to London.

" But, even if you were with your aunt, my dear Bell," observed Mrs. Leslie, " you cannot suppose that at your age you would be allowed to join in these parties. Do you think that your father and I would permit it, even if Lady Jane's partiality for you induced her to overlook the impropriety of initiating such a mere child into such scenes? Do you think, I say, that we should be so blind to your welfare, as to consent to it? No, no, Bell—be assured that we are too solicitous for your real happiness, to allow your health to be sacrificed to London hours, or your mind perverted by the frivolities of London manners and fashions. Let me, therefore, prevail upon you, at once, to relinquish all expectations of the sort, and return cheerfully to those simple habits that become your age and situation, and which I sincerely regret should have ever been broken in upon. Believe me, Bell, not even your

father as yet scarcely suspects the weak folly in which you have indulged since you have returned from the Hall; but he complains of your growing inattention and indifference to your studies, and you know well that I have even more cause to complain—for it appears to me, that one of the evil results of your visit has been to teach you to despise such accomplishments as I have attempted to teach you. Certainly, it cannot be expected that I——"

Mr. Leslie's voice was heard at this moment, calling on Bell cheerfully to join Bess and him in a walk ; but Bell's eyes were swollen with weeping, and her mother undertook to excuse her.

All Mrs. Leslie's kind remonstrances and efforts to screen her daughter from the resentment of her father proved, however, in vain ; and, as day after day passed over without any communication from Lady Jane, her petulance, and carelessness and indifference to all that had formerly given her pleasure, increased. Bitterly, bitterly did Mrs. Leslie regret that her daughter had ever seen Lady Jane, to whose influence she could not but attribute this sad change.

" Even if my brother were to leave her the half of his fortune," she observed to Rachel, who was her only confidant, " it could not compensate for the loss of her affection—the introduction into her mind of such mistaken views, as it is plain have taken possession of her."

" Mamma—mamma !" exclaimed Bell, rushing into the room, her eyes sparkling, and her cheeks glowing with pleasure. " Here is a letter from aunt to you, and another to papa from my uncle—I thought —I was sure——"

" Bell, before I open it," returned Mrs Leslie, gravely, " I must tell you that if it contains the invitation you have been expecting, my mind is made up to refuse it. I will give you my reasons hereafter; but of this be assured, nothing can induce me to alter my determination."

Bell turned pale as death, and sank into a chair, while her mother proceeded deliberately to open and read the letter to herself.

" Oh, Miss Bell," remonstrated Rachel, in a low voice, " how sorry I am to see you so ungrateful for all your mother's love and kindness to you, as to want to leave her for strangers—for they are strangers, as one may say."

Bell drew herself up with a haughty look of contempt and displeasure at Rachel's interference, which, but for her fear of her mother, she would have resented in more than looks.

"I am very glad to say," observed Mrs. Leslie, folding the letter, "that Lady Jane makes no allusion to the promise you spoke of, Bell—except, indeed, it is contained in the observation that your uncle considers it necessary that you should have advantages afforded to you in the way of education, superior to those you now possess; and makes a proposition, which I must consult your father upon before I communicate it to you. Stop, Bell," (the young lady had turned silently away,) "I forgot—there are a few lines on the other page addressed to you."

She tore them off, and Bell, with eyes blinded with tears of vexation and disappointment, retired to read them.

The proposition to which Mrs. Leslie alluded was, that the sisters should be placed, at Mr. Bevington's expense, at one of the most fashionable boarding-schools in the neighbourhood of London, where they would be under the eye of Lady Jane, the latter unequivocally observing that, from the intentions of Mr. Bevington to introduce his nieces into society suited to the expectations they might reasonably indulge, it was highly necessary that they should acquire accomplishments and manners superior to what it was possible to obtain in such an *obscure* and secluded place as Arundale. Though referring, in the most courteous terms, the decision to Mrs. Leslie on this subject, so important to her daughters' welfare, it was very plain that Lady Jane's mind was quite made up that it would be impossible that the former should refuse to assent to so reasonable and advantageous a proposition; and the tender mother, who had maintained so calm a demeanour in the presence of her daughter, burst into a fit of agonised tears as soon as she was alone, and, wringing her hands, exclaimed—

"Both my children—both my dear, dear little ones to be taken from me—to be taught to despise their humble, insignificant mother—to forget, perhaps, all that has been done to secure their happiness here and hereafter—to be made heartless, mindless, fine ladies! But I am—oh, yes, I am wrong—ungrateful! I will hope, still hope that the lessons their dear father has engrafted on their hearts—the principles which his example as well as precepts, and my humble efforts, have inculcated will not be wholly lost. And yet already the mischief has begun. Bell, poor unhappy girl—the poison is already at work in her bosom. Her heart is estranged from us, and that one plague spot, vanity, which for years we have been labouring to extirpate, is already tainting the whole system, to the exclusion of every healthful, every proper feeling."

Painful and agitating had been Mrs. Leslie's sensations; but long before her husband returned she had subdued all outward expression of them, and no one could have suspected the anguish that was rankling at her heart, as she put into his hand her brother's letter addressed to him, and containing, as she supposed, of course, a repetition of Lady Jane's proposal.

"By his decision it shall stand or fall," was her resolution. "He has his children's welfare as much at heart as I have, and is far more competent than I am to judge what is fitting and proper for them."

How surprised was she to see his eyes light up with an expression of pleasure and satisfaction that it was impossible to mistake.

"This is, indeed, noble and unexpected on the part of your brother, my beloved," he observed; "and his acknowledgment that he has hitherto wronged me is even more creditable to his heart than the exertions he has made to compensate for it. But I forget; you are as yet unacquainted with what he has done for us."

Mrs. Leslie suppressed a heavy sigh as she took the letter.

"How different men—even the best, the most amiable of men—think on the subject, from an anxious, fearful woman," she thought to herself. But she was speedily convinced that she was wrong in this instance. There was not a word in the letter relative to Lady Jane's proposal—the only mention made of the children was a hope that they were quite well, and that he should soon see them. The purport of the letter was to inform Mr. Leslie that he had, through a nobleman with whom he had some influence, procured for Mr. Leslie the reversion of a living in Yorkshire, the incumbent of which, a very aged man, was supposed to be on his death-bed.

"The living, my dear sir," concluded Mr. Bevington, "is, I understand, worth nearly a thousand a year; but were it ten times that sum, I am convinced it could not be better bestowed; and I hope it will prove only a stepping-stone to higher and better things. Let me know if I can be useful to you in any way in making the necessary arrangements for your removal, which there can be no doubt will be speedy."

Mrs. Leslie's tears were tears of joy; for her husband was happy, and how could she refuse to share in his happiness? And yet, to quit the place where she had so long enjoyed all that was necessary to her pure and simple tastes and wishes, to go among utter strangers, and enter into a new mode of life.

There is no felicity unmixed in this transitory world, she thought, for she felt that to quit Arundale would be like tearing up by the roots a flourishing flower, long habituated to the soil, to plant it where there was a chance, but only a chance, that it might take root, mingled with a fear that it might fade for ever. In Mr. Leslie's bosom, however, no fears for the future intruded. He felt that his sphere of usefulness would be enlarged by the change, and that he should be enabled to indulge now, on a large scale, those benevolent feelings which had hitherto been circumscribed by his limited, even narrow means, and he rejoiced as much for others as for himself that it would be so.

"And our dear children, too," he observed.

Mrs. Leslie started. She had been so wholly engrossed by this unexpected communication, that she had almost forgotten Lady Jane's proposition.

"You have often said that pure, unmixed happiness seldom, if ever, falls to the lot of mortals, dear Horace, that it can only be hoped for, or expected, on the other side of the grave."

"What is the drawback now, dearest, that you think this preparation necessary?" he demanded, with a look of anxiety.

Mrs. Leslie explained; but to her great surprise her husband seemed by no means to regard Lady Jane's proposal in the formidable light that she did. And yet, until now, he had never seemed to consider his daughters' deficiency in fashionable accomplishments as of any importance.

"But they will be differently situated, my love, now," he observed, when she hinted this. "As the poor curate's daughters, the education we could give them ourselves was sufficient; but, as the heiresses of Matthew Bevington, Esquire, it will be absolutely necessary that they should be placed on an equality with the sort of folks with whom they will be chiefly associated."

"And they will learn, perhaps," observed the apprehensive mother, "to look down upon--to despise the simple habits, the——"

"I hope not, most sincerely I hope not," interrupted Mr. Leslie, with emotion, and in a tone almost of regret "They have been happy—we have been happy—very, very happy, hitherto. It is but natural, certainly, to dread the consequences of such a sudden change, and yet I hope their dispositions—our dear children's dispositions and principles are too good to——"

"I fear nothing for Bess," interrupted Mrs. Leslie, hastily.

"And why more for Bell?" demanded Mr. Leslie, who, of course, had had less opportunity than the quick-sighted and anxious mother of observing the change that had been wrought in the manners and feelings of his second daughter.

Mrs. Leslie was silent—she could not bear to breathe a word that sounded like an unkind estimation of Bell, who, if there was the slightest difference in the father's feelings towards his children, had enjoyed that shade of a preference. The termination of this conference, however, as might have been expected, resulted in unconditional acquiescence in Lady Jane Bevington's plans. Bess and Bell were placed wholly at her ladyship's disposal, and the mother compelled herself to stifle every feeling of regret, and declare her readiness to part with her two dear girls, whenever Lady Jane should have made the necessary arrangements. Notwithstanding, however, this apparent perfect resignation on her part, it was like a death-blow when, a few days after she had despatched her answer to her condescending sister-in-law, a postchaise drew up to the gate of the parsonage, and Mademoiselle Dupere, Lady Jane's own maid, announced herself as having come to conduct the *demoiselles* Leslie, in the first place, to *Miladi leur chere tante* in London; and from thence, to the *pension* (boarding school) of Madame Deville, at Guines, near Calais; an establishment which, Mademoiselle Dupere assured Mrs. Leslie, was, beyond all comparison, the most superb, elegant, and fashionable that could be selected even in France itself.

France !—were her children to be banished to France? The sea to separate them from her, who had never been one whole day apart from them since the hour of their birth? Mrs. Leslie was in agonies; and even Mr. Leslie seemed not a little staggered at the total and unconditional surrender of his children, which was thus required of him. He did not like France —he liked nothing French—and least of all did he like the painted, frippery, artificial Mademoiselle Dupere, whom Lady Jane had deputed to be her representative. Yet, on the other hand, should he now draw back—should he even demur to the plan Lady Jane had marked out—it might be fatal to all his new-born hopes and prospects. Could he sink back—could he see his children sink back into that obscurity, that comparative poverty, from which Lady Jane's patronage and their uncle's fortune was to rescue them? And, himself, could he be content to remain the humble curate of Arundale, when fortune, distinction awaited but his acceptance? Alas, alas! as but too often, where wealth and dignity are arrayed against the dictates of reason and of conscience, the wordly motives prevailed, and Bess and Bell, in spite of the mother's tears of agony, and the father's ill-suppressed foreboding's, departed under the care of Mademoiselle Dupere—never again to revisit the peaceful vale of Arundale, where their early years had passed in unclouded happiness.

CHAPTER IV.

My sister, my sweet sister's clear glad voice,
  At last I heard it fill the sunny air,
Is sounding near—and she, my bosom's choice,
  The hallowed idol of my soul is there
And yet, mayhap, this very hour, her heart
  Bounds to the music of its own delight,
Framing new joys in which I bear a part,
  Joys all, alas, too fair and overbright!—Anon.

 FEW months only after the departure of his children, Mr. Leslie was removed from the curacy of Arundale to the rich living of Upton Barton. The tasteful, though comparatively humble and limited Parsonage House of Arundale, gave place to a substantial modern mansion, much too large and rambling to suit Mrs. Leslie's ideas of comfort; and good old Rachel and her single hand-maiden were succeeded by a regular establishment of servants, whose habits and manners were so different to the quit, orderly way of life to which the curate's family had been accustomed, that nothing but complaints occurred, which Mrs. Leslie was quite powerless to remedy.

Mr. Leslie, too, was not without his discomforts. He had quitted a simple, unsophisticated people, to whom he was endeared by his long life of usefulness and kindness among them, who had looked up to him as their pastor, their friend, and adviser, and who had, with few exceptions, striven to repay his labours of love by a thousand acts of kindness, and on every occasion the testimonial of their affection and esteem; and now, in the midst of the crowded population of a manufacturing town, he found himself a stranger, and powerless to carry into effect those plans of usefulness with which his mind was fraught, to benefit the afflicted, and amend the dissolute among those over whom he considered he was placed in charge, and for whose well-doing he felt himself responsible. Among the upper classes he found his efforts either repulsed or treated with indifference—the utmost consideration afforded him being that accorded to an amiable but mistaken enthusiasm; while others, whose apathy and lukewarmness stood rebuked by his zeal, regarded him with dislike, and maligned his motives in his absence.

How often are we cursed in the fruition of our own wishes! The rich rector of Upton Barton felt this to the bottom of his heart, and sighed as he looked back to his happy peaceful life as the poor curate of Arundale.

During two whole years the fond parents languished in vain for a sight of their children. Lady Jane Bevington, in the course of her summer tours, twice visited the establishment of Madame Deville, and she considered her report of the girls' supreme happiness and astonishing acquirements and improvement as quite sufficient to satisfy the most anxious parents. She would not, however, deceive them—Miss Leslie (by which title she always designated Bess) was in every respect inferior to her sister. She did not possess the tact, the—in short, she was still, in spite of everything that had been done to erase the evil effects of her early habits, a complete awkward English country-girl, while Bell was *tout-a-fait Française* from head to toe.

"Sweet creature," wrote Lady Jane, "were it not that the extraordinary resemblance between them still remains undiminished, it might be doubted whether they were sisters who had possessed the same advantages of education. Miss Leslie was all flutter, blushes, tears, and trepidation in her reception of us. I do really believe we had been a full half-hour in the room before she had uttered an intelligible sentence. Mamma and pappa were the only words I could comprehend, as if she had been a mere child out of the nursery; while Bell's reception of us was all I could wish—elegant, self-possessed, everything in short that could gratify me, and do honour to her instructress. And yet, Madame Deville assures me, that Miss Leslie is by no means behindhand with her sister in her school acquirements. But then, as I say, what is the use of it, if she plays, and sings, and dances like an angel, if that intolerable *mauvaise honte* (which is the curse of our English girls) is to obscure everything? It was entirely to get rid of that, that I preferred a French to an English establishment; but for any good that it has done with Miss Leslie, as far as regards manners, she might as well have remained at home, or at some second rate boarding-school in the country."

" My dear, dear Bess," ejaculated Mrs. Leslie, " I always thought that even a French school couldn't corrupt her."

She returned to the letter which was intended to produce so different an effect upon her mind.

"Were it not," continued Lady Jane, "that Mr. Bevington obstinately opposes the idea of separating the two girls, and indeed that I myself have set my heart upon bringing them out together, and enjoying the effect their extraordinary beauty and perfect similitude to each other will produce, I really should have felt inclined to listen to Miss Leslie's evident desire to return home, before the period which I and Mr. Bevington have assigned for their residence abroad. What motive can actuate her in such perverse, and I must say ungrateful feelings, it is impossible for me to divine; but as Madame Deville herself says, Miss Leslie's heart has always seemed closed to every one except her own relatives. To her sister she certainly displays affection; but otherwise, as madame says, she is *froid comme la glace.* I am really quite ashamed to have said so much on this subject to you, as her mother, for it cannot be pleasant to hear only censure where one has a right to expect only praise. However, I hope still that my dear Bell's example, and the consciousness Miss Leslie must feel that I have a right to be dissatisfied, will rouse her to exertion—I do not mean as to her scholastic duties,

for even madame herself declares she has no cause for complaint on that head; and, indeed, that Miss Leslie is wonderfully quick in acquiring whatever she chooses to bend her mind to. So that it is very evident that it is not stupidity that keeps her from being all that we could wish—but this renders her faults the more unpardonable. However, there is yet time to rectify all; and I will hope that by the time she returns to England, she will equal our most sanguine wishes."

" And if she only returns as pure and uncontaminated as she went—if she brings back the same warm heart, the unsophisticated principles, the gentle mind, the unselfish disposition, that she carried with her, her mother's hopes and wishes will be realised," observed Mrs. Leslie. "Dear girl, still longing for her home—still thinking only of her parents—and yet, in all her letters, studiously concealing that she is not—never has been happy since she left. Dear Bess, ever more thoughtful, more regardful of the happiness of others than her own, she would not add to my regret and uneasiness at her absence, and so has affected to be quite happy and contented. But I knew she was not—I knew her heart yearned for her mother and her home. And Lady Jane thinks her cold, apathetic. Ah, little does she know the rich mine of feeling that is buried in that heart.—No, Bess never was, never will be, what Lady Jane essays to make her. Her sphere is home—her empire that of affections, and she may well afford to let her sister outshine her. Poor Bell —poor Bell!"

What were the thoughts which prompted this maternal exclamation of pity towards the daughter, who, according to Lady Jane's estimation, was more a subject for pride and exultation than sorrow and despondency, it would be difficult to say; but, certainly, Mrs. Leslie could not at all enter into Lady Jane's feelings with regard to the sisters.

Months, weeks, nay even days began to be counted by Mrs. Leslie, for the stipulated period of Bess and Bell's return was approaching. At last, it arrived—but again the parents' hopes and anxieties were kept on the stretch. Bevington Hall was undergoing a complete ornamental repair and refurnishing; it was not yet fit for the reception of the family, and Lady Jane had resolved to pass a month at Brighton, before she returned home. Of course, her nieces would remain with her, and then she would have the pleasure of bringing them to Upton Barton, on her way to the Hall. Mr. Leslie seemed to feel the disappointment more than his wife. His health had been for some time declining, though he persisted that nothing ailed him. It was to Mrs. Leslie a source of satisfaction that there was no longer the (to her) formidable sea between her and her children. Lady Jane's letter had assured her that they were well, and impatient for the pleasure of seeing "dear mamma and papa." Bess, indeed, had repeated this in a postscript which she had been allowed to add to her aunt's letter. A month would soon pass away, and with the certainty that then she should be re-united to her children, Mrs. Leslie soothed herself into contentment, and tried to soothe the drooping spirits of her partner, who could not conceal the bitterness of his disappointment.

"A month," he observed, as he folded Lady Jane's letter, "a month is an age to me now."

Mrs. Leslie's affection took the alarm—she had for some time felt uneasy at the alteration in his looks and spirits; but she believed him, when he attributed it merely to the vexation and disappointments which were attendant on his situation; and while, in her secret heart, she acknowledged how little, hitherto, their increase in wealth and advancement in station had done for their happiness, she consoled herself with the hope that time would reconcile all things; that her husband's merits and exertions would eventually be acknowledged by those who now neglected or maligned him; that he would cease to regret the rural shades of Arundale, and its simple, kind-hearted inhabitants; that his children would occupy those hours which now hung so heavily on his hands; and that they should be quite happy.

Mrs. Leslie was, in fact, one of those calm, quiet dispositions so much to be envied, whose happiness, independent of all place and station, exists only in the exercise of the gentler affections. Devoted to her husband and children, she could have been contented with them in the humblest cottage; and for their sakes only did she rejoice in the change that had taken place in their situation. But Mr. Leslie's despondent tone, as he uttered these words, struck terror to her heart, though he tried to explain them away by saying, "that he only meant that disappointment *now* made a month appear an age."

"Hope deferred, maketh the heart sick, you know, my dear," he observed, with a melancholy smile; "but, as you properly say, a month will soon pass away, and I must try to be content."

Notwithstanding this attempt at explanation, however, Mrs. Leslie felt that more was meant than met the ear in his first observation; and Rachel, to whom she communicated her uneasiness, rather confirmed than abated it by her own honest remarks.

"I have seen for a long time, ever since the first bustle of moving here was over," she observed, "that master is not what he used to be; and if we, that are always with him, can see the alteration, he must look worse to them that don't see him often. And he tries to hide it, too; but it won't do. Oh, dear, dear, I wish we were back at our own pleasant Arundale, and the sweet children about us, as they used to be, even if they never got their uncle's fortune—for what is all the money in the world to health and contentment? I do think, the sight of his children would restore his spirits, though; and if he was once easy in his mind——"

"He shall not be long without that, at any rate," interrupted Mrs. Leslie, with sudden resolution. "Lady Jane cannot be angry, and if she is, my husband's health and comfort must not, shall not be sacrificed to her unreasonable requirements."

The very next day, under the pretext of paying a visit to her relations in London, which Rachel had long talked of, when she could be spared for a week or two, the latter departed for Brighton, armed with full credentials from her mistress to represent to Lady Jane the precarious state of Mr. Leslie's health, and to bring the children, as she still called them, home with her. Mrs. Leslie knew, had she proposed this to her husband, he would have decidedly objected to it, as likely to injure the interest of his daughters with their uncle and aunt.

Two days after Rachel's departure, a post-chaise drew up to the door of the Rectory at Upton Barton, and in another instant a lovely girl rushed into the arms of her father, and then, speechless with joy and agitation, threw her fair arms around the neck of her mother.

"It is Bess—my heart tells me it is my own girl," exclaimed Mrs. Leslie; "but where is your sister?"

"She will be here soon—soon, dear mother," returned the trembling girl. "My aunt could not be persuaded to part with her, but I——Oh, dear, dear papa, why did you not send for me before: the whole world should not have kept me away from you if I had known——"

Again she threw herself into her father's arms, and wept tears of mingled agony at his wan, altered form and features, and happiness at being restored to him.

It was some time before Mr. Leslie fully understood to what he was indebted for this unexpected pleasure ; but when he did, he was far from expressing any anger at the deception Mrs. Leslie and Rachel had practised ; though, it was evident, he felt some uneasiness, lest Lady Jane should resent Bess's having left her with such precipitancy. He tried by several indirect questions to ascertain what had been the feelings of the lady on the subject; and heard, to his great satisfaction, both from his daughter and Rachel, that so far from having opposed her departure, her ladyship had herself instantly proposed that Miss Leslie should accompany Rachel.

"It is no use concealing it from you, dear papa," observed Bess, her cheeks crimsoning ; "I am not a favourite with my aunt ; nor can I wonder at it, for our dear Bell is so superior to me, that——'"

"Superior !" murmured Mrs. Leslie, her eyes fixed on her daughter's glowing countenance. "Oh, if she is only——but tell me, dear girl, is not Bell impatient to see her father, and me ? Did she——"

"Oh, yes, dear mamma, and she would willingly have come with me and Rachel, only she saw that to persist in doing so would have given offence to her aunt, and——"

"She is prudent—very prudent for her age," observed Mr. Leslie, with somewhat of bitterness in the tones of his voice ; while Mrs. Leslie turned away her head to conceal her tears and quivering lip.

"But she does not know how altered papa is," observed Bess, with a pleading look. "She thought that nurse Rachel, and you, dear mamma, fancied him worse than he is ; and so, indeed, Lady Jane said, when she heard he was not confined to his room, and preached twice on Sunday ; but if she had known——"

"Yet you came, on the very first indication that I was ill," said Mr. Leslie.

"Oh, dear papa, do not think hardly of poor Bell," exclaimed the generous girl, " if she has been willing to yield to her hopes rather than her fears; and then, too, Lady Jane's fondness for her is so flattering, and—and—Oh, you will love her so, when you see her—she is the most beautiful, fascinating creature that ever you beheld, and she is as sweet-tempered and good-hearted as ever."

" Good-hearted," muttered Rachel, who was fidgetting about the room, with evident dissatisfaction in her looks.

The imploring look which Bess cast towards the old and faithful domestic did not escape Mrs. Leslie, though the agitated father saw it not. His eyes were fixed on the ground, and he appeared deeply reflecting on what Bess had said.

Mrs. Leslie followed Rachel from the room.

"Tell me the truth, Rachel—you are dissatisfied with Bell. Was she—did she —tell. me all that passed—what did she say ?"

"Say ! nothing," returned Rachel, " nothing that I could understand. She seems to have lost the use of her native tongue ; for while Bess was hugging me and crying as if her heart would break— between sorrow at the news I brought, and joy at seeing her old nurse again, Miss Bell was jabbering French to her aunt, and looking at herself all the while in the mirror opposite. She didn't know me either, or she wouldn't—for that was most likely ; and when she did condescend to speak to me, she held out one of her delicate little white fingers, as if she were afraid my coarse hand would contaminate her. Lord—lord ! that ever I should live to see the day that one of my dear master and mistress' children should turn the cold shoulder to one who ever loved her as her own. But, never mind, we have got one dear girl that they couldn't spoil—one that will be your pride and comfort, let what will happen. Let Lady Jane keep her favourite, if she will—it won't fret me."

It did fret Mrs. Leslie, however. Every proof of Bess's undeviating affection, gratifying as it was, served but to remind her of the coldness and neglect of her other daughter, and in secret she regretted that she had ever suffered worldly interest to induce her to run the risk of the alienation of her children's love.

Cheered by the presence and unremitting attention of his darling Bess, and diverted from the melancholy lassitude that had so long preyed upon both his mental and bodily health by her intelligent and vivacious descriptions and remarks upon all she had seen and heard during their separation, Mr. Leslie, for a week or two, seemed in a fair way to recover his pristine health and spirits ; but the insidious disease, which had been so long secretly undermining his constitution, was too deeply rooted, and before the arrival of his second, and once favourite daughter, he was confined to a bed of sickness.

Prepared as she had been by Rachel's remarks to see a being very different from the warm-hearted and ingenuous Bess, Mrs. Leslie yet found her previous conception fell far beneath the manners and appearance of the elegant and self-possessed companion of Lady Jane Bevington, as extending both her hands, with the most winning smile, Bell observed, in the softest voice—

"Dear mamma, how happy I am to see you once more. I hope papa is better; and that my sister's ardent imagination has led her to exaggerate his illness."

The words fell as coldly from the rose-bud lips which were just parted to emit those musical sounds, as if the speaker had been uttering a well-conned lesson; and Mrs. Leslie, who, at first sight of her beautiful daughter, had forgotten everything but the pride and pleasure of gratified maternal love, sank back in the chair without returning the formal kiss with which the former had greeted her, after a separation of nearly three years; while Bell retreated to a sofa, to give place to Lady Jane's dignified recognition of her sister-in-law, and studiously polite inquiries into the state of Mr. Leslie's health.

Mrs. Leslie's lip quivered as she replied to the latter; to her daughter she had, as yet, been unable to utter one word, so completely were her feelings chilled by her automaton-like address.

"Mr. Leslie," she (Mrs. Leslie) said, "had appeared better the last two days; and she hoped, now, that his most anxious desire would be satisfied." She glanced at Bell, without the power of continuing the sentence; but the latter neither observed the look, nor the emotion that suppressed her mother's voice. Her eyes were evidently employed in scanning the dimensions of the drawing-room, and scrutinizing its furniture, which, handsome as it was, probably fell short of what her refined taste would have suggested in some of its appointments; for there was something of an equivocal smile on her countenance as her eyes met those of Lady Jane, between whom and herself there evidently existed a perfect understanding, for the smile was returned, and an almost imperceptible shrug of the shoulders confirmed the correctness of the young lady's impressions.

Bess entered, and Mrs. Leslie's heart leaped with pleasure, for the hitherto inanimate and statue-like features of her sister for a moment lighted up with pleasure, and then, and not till then, Mrs. Leslie seemed to recognise in the new comer her own darling Bell.

"Papa is impatient to see you," whispered Bess, who had affectionately returned her sister's greeting; Bell looked at Lady Jane as if to solicit, and graciously received permission to accompany her sister.

Had Mrs. Leslie accompanied her daughters to this interview with their father, it would have tended still farther to soften her feelings towards Bell, and convince her, that tutored as she had been into that apparent calmness and seeming indifference, which Lady Jane considered so essential to the character of perfect good-breeding and lady-like manners in her favourite, the heart of the beautiful girl still retained some traces of its natural feelings, and disdained not to show them, when she feared no reprehension. Bell, indeed, was shocked when she beheld the ravages that illness had already effected in the person and countenance of her father. She wept long and bitterly in his arms; and Mr. Leslie, convinced that he had wronged his darling child, in believing her cold and insensible, felt that at this moment she was dearer to him than ever.

"I shall get well now, my dear, dear girl," he observed; "with such nurses as you and Bess, how can I fail to get well? Yes, yes, all will be right now you are come. I shall soon be able to leave my room; and though this is not our beloved Arundale, which I regret I ever left—But never mind, my children's society will make even Upton a paradise. I feel already as if my strength were returning. In a few days I hope to be able to quit this irksome chamber, and, till then, I will have patience, for my children will be my companions. Bess, indeed, has confined herself too much already; but Bell will now share her kind attentions; and relieve her too close attendance; will you not, dearest?"

Bell's countenance did not correspond with the ready "Yes, papa," which she uttered; and her sister's searching eye instantly discovered her uneasiness.

"Lady Jane surely cannot be so unreasonable as to wish to take you away with her, dear Bell?" she whispered, when they together quitted, at Mr. Leslie's desire, his bed-room, to return to the drawing-room.

"Let me go with you and bathe my eyes with some cold water, and make myself fit to be seen before we go back to aunt, and then we will talk about what is to be done," replied Bell.

Bess led the way to her own bed-room.

"Now, tell me, what shall I do, Bess?" observed her sister, having made the requisite application to her eyes, and now standing before the dressing-glass, re-arranging the luxuriant ringlets which her father's warm embraces had considerably discomposed. "You know, I am sure, that I should be very happy to stay with papa, and, as he says, share your labours; but you know, too, how Lady Jane hates to have any of her plans discomposed, and, to tell you the truth, I was obliged to promise, before she would consent to my coming here, that I would not ask to prolong my stay beyond the few hours that she intends to remain here. Dear Bess, what shall I do? I know I shall give her mortal offence if I propose that she should leave me behind. Indeed, to tell you the truth, she has set her heart on taking you, too, away with her."

"I will not go," exclaimed Bess, impetuously. "Not for any inducement the world could offer would I quit my dear father now. Oh, Bell, surely she can never be so cruel and unfeeling as to wish you——"

"My dear girl, she is not cruel or unfeeling," interrupted Bell, "but you know she is so little used to be thwarted or contradicted; and there is to be a large party of all the nobility and gentry for miles around Bevington Hall, on the day after our arrival; and one of the pleasures she proposes is the introduction of the "Twin Roses," as she flatteringly calls us. I know she anticipates a thousand pretty compliments and speeches on the occasion, and, indeed, to tell you the truth, dear Bess, I must confess——"

"Bell, Bell, I cannot bear to even hear you speak of enjoying pleasure, when the life of our dear father is trembling in the balance," interrupted Bess, in faltering accents. "You must not—cannot leave him."

"I do not wish it," said Bell, almost pettishly; "but I do want you to advise me how I can get off from going with my aunt without offending her. I am sure, even my dear father would not wish me to do that."

"No, he has already sacrificed too much to conciliate her," returned Bess, with a heavy sigh; "but there is nothing to be done in this case, that I can see, but to state the plain case, and say, that you are convinced it would be dangerous to oppose my dear father's wishes in his present precarious state."

"It will never do," returned Bell, shaking her head. "She will accuse me of ingratitude, want of consideration for her, and a whole host of offences, if I originate the proposal. I will tell you how we must manage. I will return to the room alone, and appear unconscious of my father's wishes, and you must strive to consult with mamma, so that it may come

from her. My aunt cannot, of course, blame me, if mamma is decisive; and I must contrive to make her believe that I unwillingly yield up my own inclinations in obedience to the will of my parents."

"She never can believe you so unnatural as to wish to leave your father," remonstrated Bess, to whom this manœuvring and management appeared repulsive and unnecessary.

"Never mind what she believes, dear Bess," returned her sister. "I know her better than you do; and know, too, how she is to be managed; so let me have my own way, there's a dear girl, for I should ruin myself for ever with her if she were to think I prefer——"

How could Bess suspect that in reality Bell was secretly praying for the very contrary of what she appeared anxious to effect! That she would, in fact, be dreadfully disappointed if she were to be left behind by Lady Jane in accordance with her father's wish, while, in appearance, she was willing to do anything in her power, even to practise deception, which Bess abhorred, in order to induce her aunt to yield to her parent's request.

"Evil should never be done that good may result," observed Bess, as they were descending the stairs together.

"Pooh, you are a little fool," returned her sister. "It cannot be evil, if good results. Recollect, if you take your own headstrong way, Bess, and offend Lady Jane, you will not only irrevocably injure us, but grieve my poor father, who will, when too late, repent that the indulgence of a mere whim has undone the work of years. Why has he so long consented to our absence from him, but with the view and hope of securing my uncle's fortune to his girls? and do you think he would feel indebted to you now, if you let your foolish scruples overturn all that has been done? No, no; I tell you Lady Jane must be managed; and the only way is, to let the proposition come from mamma, and appear quite passive myself. You can excuse me to mamma; and I am sure she will be rather disposed to commend than blame me for not hazarding my aunt's displeasure."

Where had Bell acquired this worldly wisdom, was a question which naturally occurred to Bess, as she saw the former, with her usual sweet complacency, cross the room, and seat herself by the side of Lady Jane. The result of all this may be anticipated. Lady Jane carried off her favourite niece in triumph, graciously compromising with the disappointed parents by extending her stay at the Rectory three days, to allow them to enjoy the society of the daughter from whom they had been so long estranged. During that time Mr. Leslie's penetration had discovered sufficient of Bell's character to lessen, perhaps, his regret that she was not allowed to remain with him, while it increased his sorrow at having ever parted with her, and thus allowed the prevailing follies and faults of her disposition to be fostered and encouraged by the weak and superficial people among whom she had been thrown.

"Bell's talent does not lie in domestic life," he observed, with a deep sigh, when she quitted him with expressions of regret and affection on her lips, and ill-concealed triumph and pleasure in the glance of her sparkling eye. "She would have been miserable in the privacy and confinement of a sick chamber. It is better, therefore, for all parties that she is gone."

From this time Bell was seldom mentioned by her parents; never, by her father, without a sigh, or her mother without an expression of anger at her evident deficiency in filial affection and duty. On these occasions Bess was ever the mediator. She was sure her dear Bell was neither so thoughtless nor so selfish as they believed her to be; and then she would suggest a thousand excuses for her sister, though her own heart told her that she could not act so.

Three months after Bell's visit Mr. Leslie died, blessing with his last breath the tender and dutiful child who had soothed with her constant presence and attention his bed of sickness, and praying for the absent, and, as he pathetically called her, "lost one," who, immersed in a round of pleasures, had scarcely from time to time leisure to bestow even to make the common inquiries which decency dictated; but callous, indeed, must the heart be which the irreparable loss of a parent does not awaken. Bell, in the first impulse of grief, wrote to her sister, in language which showed that she was for the moment deeply impressed with sorrow for her neglect and thoughtlessness. She was, no doubt, sincere when she said, that she would give worlds if she could recal the last three months, that her heart smote her for her cruel neglect of one of the best of parents; and yet that very letter concluded with an excuse for not immediately complying with her sister's intimation, that it would be a consolation to their afflicted mother if she, Bell, would get permission from Lady Jane to pass a week or two at Upton Barton.

"I would have you do this, dear Bell," wrote her sister, "not as if it were in compliance with any solicitation on my part, but your own spontaneous inclination. My poor dear mother suspects you, I know, unjustly, of not feeling so warm an affection for her as before you became attached to Lady Jane. I am sure she is wrong; but my assurances would not go half so far in convincing her, as one act of yours. Do come, then, dear Bell. Lady Jane cannot refuse you so trifling a tribute to the feelings of the most exemplary and affectionate mother that ever existed."

Bell's reply to this was, as usual, full of tender protestations and expressions of affection to her mother.

"Nothing in the world," she wrote, "could give her more heartfelt pleasure than to embrace her dear mother, to whom she would devote every hour of her future life."

"But, my dear sister," she continued, "to leave Lady Jane at this time would expose me to the charge of the basest ingratitude; and that, I am sure, dear mamma would, of all things, wish me to avoid. The fact is, dear Bess, my aunt has been for some weeks suffering from a dreadful nervous attack. The physician has recommended quiet, and change of air and scene. We have lived a sad racketty life lately, for the house has been filled with company ever since we came down. We have had the most delightful private theatricals you can imagine; and only that I am afraid you would think me vain, I could fill a whole sheet with the compliments I have received. Even now, I am doubtful whether my forte lies in tragedy or comedy; for my *Juliet*, and *Cora* (in *Pizarro*), you know, were pronounced equal to that of Miss —— the first living actress of the English stage; while my *Miss Peggy* in the *Country Girl*, and my *Nell* in the *Devil to Pay*, were said to excel any of the modern actresses; and even my uncle, who was, at first rather inclined to oppose my taking such prominent parts at my age, acknowledged that I strongly reminded him of his former favourite, Mrs. Jordan, especially in the songs, which I got through wonderfully, though I was dreadfully frightened at first. We have got the sweetest, most elegant little theatre you ever saw, fitted up at the hall. But, of course, that's all done with now; though, next year, Lady Jane purposes to have everything on a much superior scale. Some of our performers, indeed, were sad muffs, and my dear aunt was worried almost into a fever with the difficulty of managing to avoid offending some who were so insufferably conceited as to think themselves capable of taking first parts, when, in reality, they were hardly fit even to deliver messages. I had a delightful Romeo, in the Marquis of Ledbury. Oh, such an elegant man, Bess. Such an incomparable lover. There was not a female present who did not envy me. I must tell you, dear Bess, what he said when he was receiving the compliments of the company after the performance. Somebody observed how very perfect he was in the text, and he replied, looking at me, 'That there was no merit in that, for he learnt it by *heart*, not by *rote*.'

"You will think me a sad giddy girl, I am afraid, my dear sister, for writing all this nonsense; but, indeed, I am so low-spirited, that I am glad to catch at anything that can beguile my melancholy thoughts. Bevington Hall is quite deserted now; and poor, dear Lady Jane is so dreadfully nervous, it is quite a misery to be with her; but, then, as I said before, it would be the height of ingratitude in me to desert her. You cannot think how deeply she was affected by poor papa's death. We were denied to everybody for a whole fortnight; and her mourning is as deep as if it were for her own brother. She fancies she looks well in mourning; but between you and me, it is very unbecoming to her. As for myself, I look horrid in black. I shall be so glad when we change for second mourning; though everything we have had is the most elegant and expensive that could be procured. My uncle has paid the greatest respect to my dear father's memory. All the men servants have new black liveries, and the females two suits of handsome mourning. As my uncle said, it was the least he could do to show his respect to a truly worthy and honourable man. This will be very gratifying, I am sure, to dear mamma. Lady Jane is talking of going to Bath for three or four weeks; for, she says, she is sure she shall never recover her spirits while we remain at the hall. She wishes to know what mamma has finally resolved on. Of course you will be obliged soon to give up the rectory to the new rector. My uncle desires me to say, that he will willingly assist mamma in any plan she may devise for her future comfort. He says he knows poor papa could not have had time to make such provision for her as he would have done. As to us—you and I—we are, of course, provided for. My uncle makes no secret, that he looks upon us as his heiresses. Are we not lucky girls, dear Bess? My aunt, of course, would not think, at present, of depriving mamma of your society; but next season, that is to say, the London season, she says that it will be indispensable that we should both be properly brought out. I begin to fancy already the sensation that we shall make. Only fancy, Bess, in the newspaper, details of the queen's birthday—'The two beautiful Miss Leslie's, co-heiresses of Matthew Bevington, Esq. (by-the-by, uncle has a prospect of being created a baronet if the Tories get into power again) were introduced by their aunt, Lady Jane Bevington.' Then fancy the paragraph eulogising our beauty, the splendour of our dresses, and the value of our jewels. Lady Jane talks of having her diamonds reset for me; and my uncle will not, I know, let you be behindhand in appearance. To tell the truth, Bess, you are decidedly my uncle's favourite. But do not think I am jealous, my dear girl; quite the reverse. I am satisfied with my place in Lady Jane's affections, and do not envy you my uncle's praises. By-the-by, I often think I owe a great deal of her favour to that very circumstance; for I don't know how it is, she and Mr. Bevington seem to make it a principle to oppose each other on every subject. And yet Lady Jane contrives, somehow, always to have her own way in the end; and now, whenever I know she has set her mind on carrying a point I always consider it settled, though it is very uncomfortable sometimes to be a witness of their storms and squabbles. Mr. Bevington has got a fit of the sulks now, because Lady Jane persists in going to Bath. He says it would be more decorous, and contribute more to the restoration of her health, if she would remain a few weeks in quiet seclusion at the hall; but surely, as my aunt says, she is the best judge of what will do her good, and she detests seclusion and the hall, too, without company to fill it. Was it not a pity, dear Bess—we were in the midst of preparations, and two hundred cards were issued for a fancy ball, when the sad news arrived, and obliged my aunt to countermand it all. I had such a love of a dress just arrived from London. I was to have been a Circassian, and the Marquis of Ledbury a Turk. Oh, such a splendid figure he would have looked, for we had tried on our dresses and rehearsed together. Lady Jane was to have been a sultana, and my uncle a greak slave. But it's no use to talk of it now. My uncle said one of the most cruel things to me that I ever heard on the occasion ; but, there, I won't vex myself, or you, by repeating it, though I have never forgotten it, or my aunt either.

" ' Had it been your favourite niece, Miss Leslie,' she observed, ' you would not have thought of such a thing, Mr. Bevington.'

" ' No,' he replied, ' Bess would not have given me the opportunity to say it.'

" This was making bad worse, as Lady Jane remarked ; and, really, I was frightened at the storm that took place, never having seen any one in such a terrible passion as she was. Such dreadful hysterics, I thought to be sure she would die, and quite hated my uncle, he was so cool, and seemed not in the least alarmed. Really, it is very annoying and disagreeable to be a third person in matrimonial quarrels ; but it is soon over with Lady Jane, I will say that for her ; she is not sullen, but my uncle is, very. I have known him to be a whole week without exchanging a word with my aunt ; so miserable, isn't it ? And yet I can scarcely help laughing sometimes, to see how polite and complaisant they are to each other before company. ' Quite patterns of domestic happiness,' said old Lady Burbage, the other day. If she could but have known what I knew ! I suppose, though, as my aunt says, they are only like the rest of the world—the fashionable world, I mean. But when I think how different it was with my dear father and mother—heigho, I must not begin to think of that—Bess, suppose, after all, I should be Marchioness of Ledbury, Duchess of Presteigne—that will be his title when his father dies. My aunt says, more unlikely things have happened, but that I must not set my heart upon it, because it is generally believed that he is not what is called a marrying man. I am afraid he is a sad rake. My uncle says, that no woman of delicacy ought to countenance him ; but, as my aunt says, it would be quite ridiculous to pretend to such rigid morality. If all rakes were to be excluded from society, we should soon have empty drawing-rooms ; and, after all, reformed rakes make the best husbands. However, it is time enough yet for me to trouble my head about men's morals and characters ; for, of course, I cannot expect to marry for two or three years yet. Lady Jane says, a young woman is foolish who gives up her liberty before she has seen anything of the world, that is, before she is three or four-and-twenty, I'm sure if I wait till that time, I shall never be Marchioness of Ledbury, for he is notorious for fickleness. I don't think he is

capable of such a lasting passion. *Entre nous.* I suspect Lady Jane only so because, as all the world knows, she did not get married till she was long past the years of discretion. I declare I've made a bon mot without intending it ; and so I think I had better conclude this long scrawl, which, I dare say, has heartily tired you."

Tired ! How little did that word express Bess's feelings. She was indignant, alarmed, incredulous. Could this farrago of levity, folly, affectation be the deliberate production of her sister ? Could she have thus seriously recorded her own want of feeling, delicacy, the utter absence of all right principle ?

" God forbid !" ejaculated Bess, as her eye again rested on the paragraph in which Bell had mentioned her hopes respecting the Marquis of Ledbury, and then, with seeming unconsciousness of the disgrace it reflected on herself, had proceeded to delineate in such hateful colours his character.

" God forbid !" repeated Bess, with fervency, " that ever I should behold my dear Bell the wife of such a man. Of what avail would be the possession of rank and wealth with such a companion as that for life? And yet Bell seemed to speak of the possibility of such an event as if it were the very summit of her wishes.

" She cannot mean it. Oh, no, she cannot mean it," repeated Bess ; " and if she were weak and foolish enough—if it were possible she could be so blind as to be willing to incur such hopeless misery, surely Lady Jane and my uncle would oppose such a sacrifice."

Again and again, with cheeks glowing with indignation, and tears of sorrow almost obscuring her sight, Bess returned to the perusal of her sister's letter. But the oftener she read it the more inexcusable in all its bearings did it appear. Her mother must not see it. Oh, no; bitterly indeed would it aggravate the sufferings of that affectionate parent, to behold her child's reckless avowal of sentiments for which she ought to blush.

" Is all the counsel we two have shared," said Bess in the words of the immortal bard, " oh, and is it come to this?"

The letter was consigned to the fire, as the only certain method of preventing its falling into the hands of Mrs. Leslie. Fortunately the good lady had not risen when the letter arrived, and Rachel, who was the only person who knew that Bess had received it, was easily persuaded to be silent on the subject, when convinced that it was not such a letter as would conduce to her mistress's happiness.

Rachel shook her head with a sorrowful look as she gazed on Bess's swollen eyes and agitated countenance.

"Ah, my dear child, it is just as I have always feared," she observed, "and the trouble is only beginning now, but if she has already secrets which must be kept from her mother——"

"No—no, Rachel, no secrets," returned Bess, anxiously. "Do not believe it. Bell has said nothing that she is conscious is wrong. It is only that I fear that my mother would think [that she is unfeeling, that is to say, that she is not sufficiently impressed with the irreparable loss we have met with, and that—Oh, how I wish that Bell were at home with us, never—never to part again," she added, with a burst of irrepressible emotion, the tears flowing down her flushed cheeks, which she in vain tried to conceal.

"I wish she had never left her home," returned Rachel; "but the mischief is done, my dear child, and it is now too late to regret it. God grant that my dear mistress may not have bitter, bitter reason to repent that she ever parted with her children. My dear master, I know, in his last moments felt that all Mr. Bevington's fortune could not compensate for the loss of his child's love; but even he did not foresee——"

Rachel paused; she felt indeed she was only adding to the affliction of the beloved girl for whom she would have given her life, and she listened in silence, though not with conviction, to Bess's earnest and warm defence of her sister from all imputation but that of thoughtlessness, and a naturally gay and volatile disposition.

CHAPTER V.

Gentle, shy, and fond,
My eldest born, first hope, and dearest treasure,
Faithful and true, with sense beyond thy years,
And natural piety that lean'd to Heaven;
Wrung by a harsh word suddenly to tears,
Yet patient of rebuke when justly given—
Obedient—easy to be reconciled—
And meekly cheerful—such wert thou, my child!—MRS. NORTON.

THREE months had passed away since the death of Mr. Leslie, and Bess had been allowed undisturbed to remain with her mother, and by her filial affection and duty to soothe the grief which else would have perhaps been insupportable. But this comparative happiness was now to be disturbed. Mrs. Leslie, after long consideration, had resolved to fix her permanent residence in the neighbourhood of London. She had at first thought of returning to Arundale, the scene of her former happiness, and had even written to her humble friends, the Franklins, to procure her, if possible, a small house there; but to this plan Mr. Bevington and Lady Jane decidedly objected. It could only foster melancholy thoughts and unavailing regrets, they observed; besides, there was no society in the immediate neighbourhood of Arundale. If, indeed, Mrs. Leslie were in a situation to keep a carriage, it would be a different affair, because the circle then within her reach was genteel and fashionable; but as it was, they could see nothing at all desirable in Arundale. The thousand pounds for which Mr. Leslie had insured his life was nearly all that the widow possessed, to provide for the comfort of her declining years, for the Rector of Upton Barton had, during the comparatively short period which he had held his benefice, found it quite as impossible to save any part of his income as he had been when he was the poor curate of Arundale. All anxiety, however, on this subject was prevented by the generosity and fraternal feeling of Mr. Bevington, who, as soon as he had ascertained the circumstances in which his sister was left, hastened to remove that source of uneasiness by presenting her with a deed, by which he had settled a hundred-and-fifty pounds upon her for life. This, however, grateful and obliged as she was for his kindness, at one time so unexpected from that source, Mrs. Leslie felt rivetted but the firmer the chains of dependance on her brother. How could she venture to have an opinion of her own, in opposition to him to whom she was indebted, if not for the actual means of existence, at least for the enjoyment of them. This was certainly a wrong view of their respective situations, and Bess tried to convince her mother it was so, and persuade her to exercise her right of opinion, at least so far as regarded the welfare of her children; but Mrs. Leslie was naturally of a yielding, quiescent disposition.

"And besides, my dear child," she would observe, "although there is little doubt that your uncle will eventually fulfil all the expectations he has raised in your and dear Bell's favour, I can never forget that nothing is yet secured to you, and that Lady Jane, on whom, I suspect, principally all depends, is very capricious, and easily offended. If, after all that has been done, Bess, I were to act contrary to her wishes, I tremble to think what might be the consequences to you, if I were taken from you."

"For myself I have no fears," returned the weeping Bess. "With the education, or rather the accomplishments they—I mean my uncle and Lady Jane—have been the means of my acquiring, and the determination I feel I possess of exerting them to the best advantage, should I be called upon so to do, I am certain I should be able to support myself in respectability; but for Bell, with her high-raised expectations——"

"And her love of great folks and grand doings," interrupted Rachel, who, busily engaged with her knitting, was seated in her accustomed corner, maintaining by her own wish what she consider a proper and respectful distance from her mistress and Bess, whom she nevertheless treated with the same confidence and affection as if she had been in reality what she always called her, "her dear child." "Yes—yes," continued the old woman, "it would be a death blow to Bell, if after all—And as to you, my dear child," and she pushed up her spectacles on her furrowed brow and gazed upon Bess with tears standing in her light grey eyes—"God forbid that ever I should see the day that you should be driven to depend upon your accomplishments for a living, though I know you would do your best and would deserve to thrive and prosper; but what a wearisome life it is, and how little rich and great people think of poor governesses.

"When I was a very young girl, my dear, nothing would suit me but that I must see more of the world than I could

by staying in service in the country, and so I never rested till an aunt of mine, that was house-keeper in a gentleman's family in London, got me a place as under-house-maid at Lady Springtown's, in Grosvenor Square. There were nine women servants, and fourteen men, and a fine, merry, thoughtless, lazy life we led ; and the only grave, miserable-looking face in the house was that of the governess. Poor thing— it was my place to wait upon her, and she —that is, the first one (the one that was there when I went)—was a pale, delicate-looking, gentle creature, that seemed as if she were heart-broken. And so she was —she had left her happy home in the country, and all the pleasant music of birds and running streams, and the beautiful flowers and green fields and lanes, and her poor widowed mother, who was pining away her life in a lone cottage, as she told me, without a friend in her old age. And there—let her be sick or sorry, and it was seldom, poor thing, she was otherwise—there she was, in the great, dismal-looking school-room, toiling hour after hour to teach three great gawky, upstart, stupid girls, that always looked as if they thought the whole world was made for them; and never spoke to the servants but as if they thought them so many clods of dirt, to be trodden upon and kicked about at their pleasure. And, worse than that, she, the poor young governess—she was under twenty—had to attend, in the long holiday times, to the Latin and French lessons of the great saucy booby of a son, the young lord, for his father was dead, and such a *my-lording* as there was at every word that was spoke to him by the men servants, it was quite sickening to hear. As to the women—but I am not going to tell you what I have seen— and yet he was a mere child, only between twelve and thirteen, but such a one as I hope there are not many like him. As for me, I was but two years older than himself, but I was a strong, sturdy, healthy, rosy-cheeked girl then, and he was a poor pale-faced, unhealthy stripling, and I soon made him afraid of the weight of my hands. Many's the time I've longed to give him a good cuffing, when I've seen him bring the beautiful bright crimson blush into the cheeks of the poor governess, when I've been waiting upon them at dinner—for she always dined with her pupils—and such dinners—my goodness !

"My lady—that is, Lady Springtown— was one that thought that children could not be kept upon too low and spare diet, and so I suppose the governess was expected to set her pupils the example, and to be content with the potatoes and flour dumplings, and toast and water, and such messes that we poor servants, that were on board-wages, would have turned up our noses at. Poor young creature—she never uttered a word of complaint, but often and often I've seen her sit at the table, and have taken away her plate, without her having tasted a mouthful of the coarse, unsavoury stuff that I knew her stomach turned against, and I would have given the world if I had dared to have carried her up my share of our good dinner in the kitchen. For, let people be ever so refined and delicate, it is no trifling evil to go not only from day to day, or even from month to month, as she did, without the comfort of a good and sufficient meal. But somehow—gentle as she was, and kindly as she talked to me when she had an opportunity, (which was only when her pupils had been sent for into the dining-parlour with the dessert, when they made themselves amends for their bad dinners by stuffing all the fruit and pastry they could get), I say, gentle as she was, there was that about her that always kept up the distance between the servants and her, and I could as soon, or, indeed, much sooner, have made free to offer Lady Springtown part of my dinner than her, lest I should hurt her feelings.

"Well, my dear, it's no use dwelling on this dismal story. The poor young lady dwined and dwined away till she was a skeleton, and nobody ever thought even of asking her if she was ill, except me. I saw she was, for she never said so, and sometimes when I was let into the housekeeper's room, to help the old lady to make jellies and preserves, and prepare other things for the grand dinners and balls, and so forth, that Lady Springtown used to give in the season, I used to beg some nice dainty, and sometimes even a glass of wine, when Mrs. Shrimpton, the housekeeper, was in good humour, and carry it up slily to the poor sinking governess that nobody thought nor cared about, and always as if it were by my lady's orders. And it was a treat to me, though it brought tears in my eyes, too, to see how grateful she would look even for such trifling marks of attention, and how for a while she would seem refreshed and cheerful; but she wanted that which she could not have—constant attention and nourishment—and to be free for a time from the harassing school lessons, and the more harassing duty of trying to put hearts and proper feelings into bosoms that—God forgive me, for saying so—I often thought had been created without

any; and so at last she sank, and could no longer rise from her bed. The doctor was sent for then: he ought to have been consulted weeks before, if doctors could mend broken hearts. However, I saw in a minute, from his looks and manner, that he knew it was too late. He was a kind hearted man, and he tried, as delicately as possible, to find out how her friends were situated, and whether, if he suggested to Lady Springtown that she should go home for change of air and rest for a few weeks, she could hope for proper attention and nourishment at home. Poor thing, she seemed at once to long for such a blessed change, and yet to be alarmed at the thought, and then the truth came out. Her poor mother was living on such a trifling annuity—she was an officer's widow —that it was barely sufficient to maintain her, even with all the dutiful affectionate daughter had spared from her paltry salary of thirty pounds a year. My lady gave her French man-cook, a creature more resembling a monkey than a man, two hundred a year——

" ' It would put my dear mother to such inconvenience, sir,' observed the poor girl, raising herself up in bed with eagerness, ' and the expense of travelling so many miles would be very great. If you think it is likely I shall get well enough in a short time to resume my duties, and Lady Springtown would kindly allow me to remain here, I——'

"She seemed all at once to read the doctor's thoughts, for she sank down upon the pillow, and after a few moments' silence, removing the fair hand, that was so thin and transparent that you could almost see through it, from the large blue eyes it shaded, she murmured—

" ' God's will be done. I only pray now that I may live to die in her arms.'

" Then she burst into such grief that it was heartrending to hear her, though it was not for herself, but only the dear mother that would be left alone in the world when she was gone.

"Well, my dear, the doctor said all he could to comfort her, and he told her that she was yet young, and there was no knowing what a powerful effect her native air and change of scene would produce, and that he would go at once and represent to Lady Springtown her situation and his opinion; and he bade her keep up her spirits, for that he would take care that everything should be done that was necessary for her comfort.

"She thanked him very gratefully; but I could see that her expectations from my lady's kindness were not much, and that now her only thoughts and anxieties were to be enabled to reach her home.

"I followed the doctor out of the room —he saw that I was crying, and he said— as if to himself—

"'Poor young creature, I am afraid she has led too confined a life, and has been overworked. I am glad to see she has so kind a nurse in you, my good girl. What do you give her—I mean in the way of diet. Medicine will not do much for her.'

"My heart was full, and I could not help speaking the truth, though I ran the risk of being perhaps turned out of my place, if he spoke of it; the doctor was too prudent and humane. He seemed quite shocked when I told him the truth, that up to that hour she had had nothing but the coarse fare allowed for the children, except the few trifles that I could get, often at my own expense, though I had deceived her into thinking they were sent by my lady's orders.

"He only shook his head, however, for I suppose he was afraid to trust me by saying anything to condemn my lady that might be repeated.

"'I will take care, my good girl,' he said, at last, 'that the patient shall have all that is necessary for the little time she will be here; but, if there is anything particular that she expresses a wish for, or you may think of, to tempt her, when it does not happen to be comeatable in the house, take this, and get it, without saying anything, either to her or any one else.'

"It was a guinea he put into my hand; but, poor thing, she did not live to want it."

"But did she not live to see her mother?" demanded Bess, in a voice choked by tears.

"No, my dear child," returned Rachel, who had paused, evidently to recover from the emotion which these reminiscences had excited. "No," she continued, "Lady Springtown paid her a visit in form the next morning. It was the first time, I suspect, that her ladyship had ever crossed the threshold of the close, uncomfortable chamber that the governess had been removed to by the housekeeper, when it was found that she was too ill any longer to remain in the large, well-furnished, double-bedded chamber, where she had been used to sleep with the young ladies—thus preventing her having even one hour to herself. Well, what was I saying—Oh, I remember, that my lady looked rather ashamed when she saw what sort of a place Dr. Southwood had been introduced to, as the only apartment that could be given up to the sole use and accommodation of a lady. A lady by birth and breeding, certainly, Miss Seymour was, if not by fortune. But what of that, if the last was wanting? So thought Mrs. Shrimpton, Lady Springtown's housekeeper; and so, my dear Bess, you will find, not, I hope, by experience, as poor Miss Seymour did, the world in general both speaks and acts.

"I was not in the room while my lady stayed with the poor sick governess," continued Rachel. "Lady Springtown hardly knew, I imagine, that there were such creatures in her establishment as under housemaids; at least, I know, that all except the ladies-maid and upper house-maid, whose services were at times required in the principal chambers, were expressly ordered never to go up or down the grand staircase; and never, if we could help it, come at all in my lady's sight on any occasion, without orders. I don't think all the time I was in the house I ever saw my lady more than three times —except I caught a glimpse of her from the kitchen windows or the area, as she was getting in or out of the carriage at the house-door. But that has nothing to do with my story, except that it explains why, when I answered the tap at Miss Seymour's chamber-door, the morning after the doctor's visit, and saw that it was Lady Springtown that the housekeeper was showing into the sick room, I hardly knew whether I stood on my head or my heels, but dropping half-a-dozen curtsies, which she—my lady, I mean—took no notice of, but by a frown and a stare intended to pierce me, I sneaked down the back stairs into the kitchen. I declare I didn't come to myself for half-an hour after, and then I was roused by Miss Seymour's bell ringing. Well, my dear, I went up directly, for, poor thing, she'd been left altogether to my care, and I remember very well that I was proud enough of being called the governess's nurse, though my fellow-servants did it more in the way of jeering than anything else. When I went into the room, the poor thing was sitting up in the bed, and her before pale cheeks were burning like coals of fire, and her eyes looked so bright and wild, brighter than ever I saw them in health.

"'I am going home, Rachel,' she said, 'my good, kind Rachel. Lady Springtown thinks it best that I should go at once, for she says I shall not get stronger by lying here, and she has removed all obstacles by paying up my half-year's salary, though there is little more than three months due, and she has been pleased to say that she is so well satisfied with my exertions that she shall not engage any one, until I have tried what effect the journey has upon my health; and, if I find that I am likely to get well again, I am to write and say so, and—— Oh, I hope I shall get well again, for my dear mother's sake. I hope—I hope——'

"She clasped her poor thin hands together, and I never saw anything so beautiful as her look upwards, as she said this. She was praying, I saw, to live—but God knew what was best for her. She died that night."

It was long before another word was uttered by either of the auditors or the narrator of this melancholy tale. Bess threw her arms around her mother's neck, and sobbed as if she realised at that moment the feelings of that affectionate and dutiful child, who had thus yielded up her last breath among strangers, at the very moment that her heart was throbbing with anticipation of being once more re-united to the beloved parent, for whose sake she had struggled with and conquered every selfish feeling, and borne unrepiningly with the difficulties, the coldness, the privations, which had crushed her young and tender frame, even to the grave.

"And did the poor girl know her prayers had not been answered, as she hoped and expected, but which, we know, it was the merciful dispensation of her creator to reject?" inquired Mrs. Leslie. "Was she aware, Rachel, that she was dying?"

"No, ma'am," returned Rachel, wiping away the tears that had been silently stealing down her withered cheeks, "I tried to persuade her to lie down, and try to get a little rest, while I went down to the housekeeper for some arrow-root and wine, which the doctor had ordered for her, but she said—

"'No, no, Rachel, I must not think of sleep now. I shall have plenty of time for rest when I get home to my own dear little room, which I have not slept in these three years. Three years—only think, Rachel, what a time to be away from one's home! I have seen my mother, to be sure, every year, for she has contrived to come up to London to see her poor Lucy every year; but then I grudged myself the indulgence, because I knew that the expense of the journey would sadly curtail her few comforts for some months; and, besides, I could only pass a few hours with her, for of course I could not neglect my pupils—but now—Oh, how happy I shall be!'

"She turned very pale when she was

speaking, and lay down as if she were exhausted, but presently she roused up again.

"'Rachel,' she said, 'this will not do. I must not yield to this weakness. I think if I were to get up and dress, I could help you to pack my clothes up. It is the last trouble I shall give you for some time, my kind friend, except to go with me to the coach and see me off. I asked leave for you, of Mrs. Shrimpton, for I knew you would like to be with me till the last minute. Oh, how I wish I was rich enough to take you down with me, and how glad my dear mother would be to see the kind friend who has done so much when all the world beside seemed to have forgotten me.'

"I could hardly speak for crying," continued Rachel, "when she said this, for she seemed all at once to have forgotten that there was any difference between us— that I was only a poor, ignorant servant-girl, and she—I can't describe what she was—but this I can say, that I have seen many ladies of rank and title, and that have been talked of as great ladies, but never, in my life, did I see a truer lady in all her looks, and ways, and manners—ay, in her very thoughts—for you could read her thoughts in her sweet face—than poor Lucy Seymour.

"Well, my dear, I learned that the Herefordshire coach, by which it was proposed she should go, would start from the White Horse Cellar, in Piccadilly, at six o'clock, and that I was to go there with her, in a hackney-coach; but when I looked at her, so weak, and trembling, and exhausted that she could scarcely sit upright in the bed five minutes together, and thought of her jolting all night long in a rough stage-coach, without anyone to attend to her, my heart sunk—I could not believe that she could live to the end of the journey.

"'Hadn't you better put it off for a week or so, my dear miss?' I said; 'you will then, perhaps, be stronger.'

"Oh, no—no, Rachel, not for a day," she replied, so eagerly, 'besides, I promised Lady Springtown that I would go this evening. She is going down to Cheltenham to-morrow, or next day, for a few weeks—and she told me it would be very inconvenient that I should stay here, as she cannot spare a servant, of course, to attend to me. Besides, only consider, dear Rachel, how miserable I should be here, if you were gone.'

"'I will not go, if you will stay,' said I, firmly. "My lady, I am sure, could not refuse me, if I spoke to her myself. Let me go now, and try and see her before she goes out to dinner. Mrs. Mansel (that was the lady's maid) is very good-natured, and if I ask her, she will contrive, I know, for me to see my lady, without saying anything to that cross, unfeeling old housekeeper.'

"Poor girl, she wavered for a minute— 'I am very weak, to be sure,' she observed, 'but no——' and she suddenly lighted up again, as if with fresh strength. 'No, Rachel, my mind will support me, and—and my God will enable me to bear up and meet my mother. No, I will go at once. Dr. Southwood, you know, said the change might do wonders for me.'

"I saw it was useless to say more, but I did persuade her to lie still, while I packed her things. There was little, gracious knows, to do—for her stock of clothes was very scanty, and yet she always looked genteel and well-dressed. I was soon finished, and then I sat down to wait till she should awake, that I might make her some tea before I went for the hackney coach. She had never spoken from the time I shook up her pillow and drew the curtains round the bed, and I had moved about the room on tiptoes, and hardly breathing, lest I should disturb the sleep that I thought was to refresh her, and prepare her for the toils of her journey. Four o'clock struck just after I had finished and sat down. I was young then, and, like most girl, heavy to sleep if I sat still. The room, too, was close and warm, and being at the top of the house, no noise could reach it—in short, I fell off into a sound sleep. When I awoke, it was getting dusk, and the first thought that struck me was, that it was too late to get my poor patient any tea. At that moment the hall-clock struck six, and I felt almost glad that her journey must be put off till the next day; and yet I dreaded that she would be vexed at my neglect. At all events I determined to steal down and get her tea ready before I awoke her.

"As I passed, I softly opened the bed-curtains. There was just light enough to see that she was lying in the same composed posture that she had gone to sleep in, with her head resting on one arm, and the other outside the bed clothes. The dark heavy curls shaded her face that was whither than the pillow-case it rested on. All at once, the dreadful thought came into my head that this was the sleep of death. I stooped over and listened—not a breath—oh, how awful that silence was, and yet I could not break it. I tried to speak—to utter her name—but my voice was gone—I could not move. At last, a

faint light gleamed through the half-opened door of the room—I started, and screamed. It was one of the maids, who wondering I had not come down to tea, had come in search of me. She had a light in her hand, and, as I pointed to the bed, she came close.

"'Poor young creature,' she said, after looking steadfastly at the beautiful image that lay there, as calm as if it had been cut out of marble. 'Poor young creature—all her troubles are over.'

"And so they were—Lucy Seymour had died in her sleep, without a sigh, or the movement even of a curl of her hair."

"And her poor mother," said Bess, as soon as she could command her voice. "Oh, if she could but have seen her!"

"So, my dear child, I said, over and over again, when I found that she was gone," returned Rachel; "but I was soon taught how little we poor mortals can judge what is for the best. It was a merciful Providence that prevented the poor girl's journey—for, as I learned afterwards, her mother was then on her deathbed. She had caught a fever in attending some poor people in the neighbourhood of her cottage, and, had Lucy lived to reach home, a most dreadful shock would have awaited her; for the clergyman, who wrote in answer to the letter that was sent to say that Lucy was dead, said that Mrs. Seymour died in a state of delirium, and never knew that her daughter had gone before her to Heaven. The only thing that grieved me, then, and that did grieve me, was, that the poor girl was buried in a crowded churchyard in London. If I could have had my way, she should have been taken down to the place where she had lived so happily, and where her mother could have been laid in the same grave. It might then have been truly said— 'They were lovely in their lives, and in death they were not divided.' But it was not to be. My lady was so dreadfully shocked at the thoughts of having a corpse in the house, that she would not return to it—(she had just gone to a dinner party, and the news was sent after her that Miss Seymour was dead)—until it was removed to an undertaker's to be buried. Fortunately, at least so I thought, the news had spread that the young lady had died suddenly, and that she had not had proper advice and attention, so there was obliged to be a coroner's inquest, and the body could not be removed till after it. So my lady and the family set off at once for Cheltenham, leaving only me and two or three of the other servants, who, as

the doctor said, would be all that was necessary as witnesses, as he could prove
that she died of diseased heart. He ought
to have said, broken heart—for that was
the real truth. However, all passed off
very quietly. Of course, the jury could
know nothing of the slights and coldness
that had worn down her spirits, and
broken her health ; and as it was proved
that she was not neglected after she took
to her bed—for I had hardly ever left her
from that time—and that she had been
supplied with all the doctor ordered—
when it was too late ; and Mrs. Shrimpton
proved how handsome my lady had behaved in supplying her with the means of
going into the country for change of air—
when she was absolutely dying ; why, of
course, the verdict was that Lucy Seymour
died a natural death, and everybody—
except those who were in the secret—was
convinced that Lady Springtown was a
very feeling, charitable, kind-hearted lady.

"The only good of all this was, that I
was left to manage the funeral as I liked,
the housekeeper setting off to Cheltenham,
after her mistress, as soon as the inquest
was over ; and so, you may be sure, my
dear child, that I took care she was buried
with all proper respect, and as far as possible in a manner that suited her birth and
education as a lady. And as Lady Springtown got all the credit of having bestowed
so handsome a funeral upon the poor
governess, she found no fault with what
was done, except that when she came back
from Cheltenham, and I was, for the first
time in my life, called into her presence
to give my account how I had managed,
her ladyship said, in a very sharp tone,
that she saw no necessity for my having
provided myself with such deep mourning.
I answered by laying the balance of the
poor young lady's money and the undertaker's bill on the table before her, and
then, with an humble curtsey, I replied
that if her ladyship would be pleased to
look, she would find that I had not spent
one shilling, except in the necessary expenses. I had certainly given Anne, the
other housemaid, money to buy a black
gown, as I thought her ladyship would
expect her to attend the funeral—but my
own mourning I had bought myself.

"She looked, I thought, rather ashamed
for a minute, but then she drew up as
proud and stately as ever.

"'You appear to be a very independent
young person, I think, for your station in
life,' she said, with a frown.

"I trembled from head to foot—I was a
mere girl then, you know, my dear child—
however I managed to say I hoped I had

not displeased her ladyship. I had tried
my best to do what was right—And then,
little fool as I was, I burst out a-crying,
and she told me I might go and send up
Shrimpton.

"'I expected nothing else,' continued
Rachel, "when the housekeeper came
down, but that I should get a reprimand,
or perhaps my discharge—but, to my
great surprise, Mrs. Shrimpton came down
in a very good humour, and told me that
my lady said, as I had had all the trouble,
I was justly entitled to what Miss Seymour had left behind, both in clothes and
money, as it seemed she had not a relation
or friend to claim them.

"I was at first very unwilling to accept
this. It seemed like paying me for my
services—but the housekeeper got angry,
and said, like my lady, that I was a vast
deal too lofty and independent for a
servant, and that if I refused, my lady
would consider it as an affront to her ; and
so, my dear, I was compelled to take it,
though I never made use of the money, or
even opened the box that held the clothes,
for I should have thought it an insult to
poor Miss Seymour's memory, that a common servant-girl like me should have presumed to wear them. Some time or
another, my dear child, I will tell you how
I disposed of them, two or three years
afterwards ; but that is a dismal story, too,
and we have had enough of that at present.
So, dry your eyes, and then I will tell you
about the next governess—the one that
came in poor Lucy Seymour's place—but
oh, how different!

"'Well, my dear,' resumed Rachel,
having taken up her knitting again, and
put on her spectacles, which had been laid
aside in the deep interest she had both felt
and excited in her last story. "Well, in
a few weeks came a new governess. My
fellow servants, who were not very feeling,
threw out many jeers, or what they meant
for such, about Rachel's getting a new
friend—for, of course, I still had the job of
waiting on the governess and the young
ladies ; but the very first glance I had of
her, told me she would never be to me
what Miss Seymour had been ; and I
thought, too, that she would never want an
humble friend like me. She was a tall,
fine, dashing-looking young woman,
dressed in the first style of fashion—
French fashion I should have said—for
she had just come from France ; and it
seemed, or at least I heard among the
servants, that her great recommendation to
my lady had been, that she had spent the
last five years of her life abroad. I soon
saw she was not one to be humbled or put

upon like poor Lucy Seymour, and I did not blame her for that—though I was nettled not a little at the way she began to treat me, at first. I was bashful, to be sure, and, I dare say, awkward enough, though I had never been called so by Miss Seymour; but now, I could do nothing right, and then she fixed her great black eyes upon me with such a stare, and though I couldn't understand the names she called me in her French gibberish (for she was one, too, my dear, who seemed to think her own English wasn't good enough for her——)"

Poor Bess coloured; she knew too well that this homely sarcasm was levelled at her sister, one of whose great offences in Rachel's eyes had been her affectation of French phrases.

"Where was I?" said Rachel, after a pause of a moment or two. "Oh, describing Miss Fitzmorris, that was the name the lady chose to be called, though her proper name was Morris—the Fitz was added, I suppose, because it sounded fine. Well, the first week I led a wretched life enough. Nothing pleased the new governess —she seemed determined to turn the house upside down, and, what was very strange, my lady gave up to her in everything she chose to ask. So much for boldness and assurance. I no longer led an idle life, for she wanted as much waiting on as a princess, and yet, in my heart, I often said to myself—this is no lady, for all her airs and graces. Let her be what she might, however, her pupils soon grew quite fond of her. I soon found out the secret of that was, that she let them do just as they liked, and instead of keeping them steadily to their lessons like poor patient Miss Seymour, who used to worry her poor heart out to make them clever and accomplished, she just did nothing but coax and flatter them to keep them in good humour, and save herself trouble. One of the pretty ways she had to divert them was turning me into ridicule, mocking my walk and my countrified talk, which I had not got rid of, though I had been nearly two years in London, and asking me questions that I could not answer, to expose my ignorance, that they might laugh at me. I bore it all as quiet as I could—but at last she got hold of the story about my fondness for Miss Seymour. I couldn't bear to hear her unfeeling jokes on that subject, and I was, I am almost ashamed to remember now how saucy I was. At first she seemed in a terrible passion, and the young ladies threatened to complain to their mamma, and get me turned out of the house. I did not say a word to them, for I felt they were not to blame, when they had such an example set them; but to my great surprise, all at once she interfered in my favour, and forced them to promise that they would say nothing about it; and then the first opportunity, when they were not present, she asked me to forgive her, and said, she had only done it to try the strength of my attachment to the poor young lady, whose fate she heartily pitied, and that she was sure I was a good, faithful girl who was to be trusted and depended upon. I was puzzled to make out what all this could mean," continued Rachel, "for I somehow couldn't believe she was sincere; however, I was very ready to make it up and shake hands when she asked, though it was the last thing I should have expected from her who had ordered that I should never even lay the cloth for her dinner, or bring in the tea things without gloves on, as the sight of my coarse red hands, she said, made her sick; but now, all at once, she grew just as familiar with me as she had been proud and insolent before—but I soon found out what it all meant. Lady Springtown was very strict indeed, both about going out and having visitors at home. Miss Fitzmorris had beforehand agreed to all my lady laid down as rules for the governess as well as us servants. Miss Fitzmorris was to have a week, twice a year, to visit her friends— poor Miss Seymour was denied even that —but no visitors were allowed; and she was expected that she would not go out, except when she went with the young ladies for an airing. The governess was tired already of this confinement—but this was one of the things that, with all her assurance and managent of my lady, she couldn't get over. Mrs. Shrimpton told me afterwards that Lady Springtown had had good reason from the conduct of her first governess—she had one before Miss Lucy—for being so particular; and, indeed, as the housekeeper said, that had made it so bad for my poor young friend. Well, my dear, the truth soon peeped out. The young ladies always went to bed at eight o'clock in the winter. Miss Lucy, poor thing, was obliged to go at the same time, whether she liked it or not, because she slept in the same room with her pupils, and they must not be disturbed by her coming after them—but Miss Fitzmorris would not submit to this. She had a separate chamber, and she took care to choose one as far from my lady's room as she could get, and her supper-tray was always carried up there at ten o'clock, for she wouldn't live upon the miserable fare

THE TWIN ROSES.

the other governess had submitted to; and, indeed, I fancy Dr. Southwood had said something to my lady on that subject at the time of Miss Seymour's death, and very properly too, for the school-room dinners were very different afterwards to what they had been before that. Instead of the one continued round of the coarse and scanty fare, there was now plenty, and that of very good quality indeed. The more than hint of the doctor respecting poor Lucy's death had made Lady Springtown rather alarmed for the consequences of her acts towards that poor obedient, suffering governess; and now that atonement for her fault was out of her reach, she was determined not to have a repetition of it in the person of Miss Fitzmorris, but she might have spared herself the trouble, for Miss Fitzmorris was not at all a likely person to submit to much from Lady Springtown Of course, it was my place to carry up the governess's tray, and then Miss Fitzmorris began to sound me, talking to me quite free about the misery of being so confined, and having no one to keep her company all the long winter evenings, and telling me how she envied me that had cheerful companions and liberty to go out when I wanted, and to see my friends. I told her she was mistaken—and that we were looked after very sharply by the house-keeper—were not allowed to have any followers—and only had our day out in turn, once a month.

"'Ay,' she said, laughing, 'those are very fine rules, no doubt; but don't tell me that you girls cannot cheat the old housekeeper, if you want to have a ramble for an hour or two, or that you can't manage, if you have a mind, to smuggle in your sweethearts to have a comfortable chat and a bit of supper sometimes.'

"You may be sure I was astonished to hear a lady talk in such a manner, and then again a thought struck me that she was playing the spy with me, and wanted to draw me in to say something about my fellow-servants that she might tell my lady, to gain her favour with her; and so I told her, very gravely, that possibly such things might be done in some gentlemen's houses, but I did not think any one would venture to try it at Lady Spring———. I could see she was disappointed at my answer, but she only put on a laugh and told me I was a sly, demure little chit, and knew how to keep a secret.

"I did not expect to hear anything more of this sort after what I had said; but, the very next night, she began to talk in the same free way, and at last, to cut the matter short, she went to her drawers, and took out a very nice French silk shawl, and asked my opinion of it. Of course I admired it, and then, throwing it over my shoulders, she said—

"'There, then, I will make you a present of it, on condition that you wear it the next time you go to see your lover; and, if he asks where you got it, tell him it was a poor forlorn young lady gave it you who is cooped up like a bird in a cage, and dying broken-hearted, because she is cruelly separated from the object of her affections. Oh, Rachel, that's a dear, dear girl, do not refuse what I am going to ask,' she added, taking my two hands in hers and pressing them against her bosom.

"I was so petrified, that I couldn't speak, but I guessed what was coming, and in an instant made up my mind I would have nothing to do with it. I dare say you guess, but no—you could hardly think she would have been so daring.

There was a gentleman, she said, that she had been engaged to for three years; but, as yet, they dared not marry, because he had a rich uncle, who would cut him off with a shilling if he married a girl without fortune. Of course, she had not been able to see him ever since she had been at our house, and what she wanted of me was, that I should bring him into the house, under pretence that he was coming to see me.

"'Or else,' said she, 'perhaps you might be able———'

"I didn't intend to let her go on—I had taken the shawl off and folded it up, and laid it on her drawers, and now said, at once, that I could not do it. I had nothing but my character to depend upon for a livelihood, and I could not—would not run such a risk for any one.

"She was very mild, at first, and cried and took on, but when she found that I stood firm, I saw her countenance change, and, when I left her, I happened to turn round to ask if I should bring up the supper-tray, and I caught her eyes fixed on me with such a look that it made me tremble again. How foolish, I thought to myself afterwards, she can do me no harm. She is in my power, not me in hers; and so I need not be afraid of her. Two or three weeks passed. How she managed it, I don't know, but somehow or another she had contrived to get hold of one of the housemaids, named Anne, who was rather a flighty girl, and had very nearly two or three times got into trouble with Mrs. Shrimpton for staying out too late, and gossiping with the foot-men at the next door, from the top of the area-steps. Ever so many times I caught Jane in Miss Fitzmorris's room, when she could have no business there, and I saw two or three bits of finery in her, Jane's, possession, that I knew had belonged to the governess. I did not know what to do, and yet I thought it a pity the foolish and giddy girl should be drawn into her own ruin by that bad, artful woman—for I was sure Miss Fitzmorris was such. I gave Jane some gentle hints, but she only laughed at my prudery, and told me not to be concerned for her, she knew how to take care of herself; and I knew she told the governess what I had said, for I could see that she could hardly bring herself to speak to me with common civility when I went into the school-room. But I little thought how deep was the black scheme she was planning to get rid of me, and have her revenge at the same time. There were whispers going on, I soon found, among the servants, of the game, as they called it, that was being carried on between Jane and the governess; and, indeed, it seemed the foolish girl scarcely made any secret that she was only a cover for the fine dashing visitor to Miss Fitzmorris. As far as winks, and nods, and laughs went, she confirmed all that was said about him and the governess; and as ever so many times she produced a guinea for the *gentlemen* and *ladies* of the servants' hall to drink her beau's health, as she called him, they were all very willing to keep the secret. I would never join in these merry-makings, though, as I told them, I would never turn informer. The housekeeper was laid up with the rheumatic gout, so they thought all was safe, and I found that Miss Fitzmorris was even grown bold enough to leave home for hours and hours, when Lady Springtown was gone to evening parties. It was no business of mine, and yet I was miserable at the thought, that some time or other it would all come out, and that her imprudence would perhaps bring ruin upon so many; for I knew Mrs. Shrimpton wouldn't have hesitated to turn every one out of the house that was concerned in such a plot. When once a person lets themselves down from their proper station, only one step, how soon they are brought to the very bottom! I could scarcely believe my eyes, when coming in one night from my usual monthly holiday, rather before my time, I found Miss Fitzmorris seated at the supper-table in the servants' hall—the companion of footmen, &c., and seeming quite at her ease until she saw me. I soon found that she was mistress of the feast, which had been provided at her expense. She tried to be civil, and asked me to sit beside her; but I said I was tired with my long walk, which was the truth, and went up to bed. That night, as I have reason to believe, she determined on my ruin. I slept very sound. There were two beds in the room, and four of us girls slept in them. It was very late, I know, when I was half awoke by Jane and the others coming to bed. They were laughing and romping, and I remembered afterwards having a faint idea that Miss Fitzmorris was in the room; but I was so sleepy that I never looked up. I could not, of course, if I had thought about it, have been surprised at anything she did, after what I had seen down stairs. The next day the governess was very ill, and kept her bed with a sick head-ache. Jane waited on her, and made her gruel, and I was very glad of it, for I quite hated to look at her.

"It was the next day, I shall never forget it, one of the young ladies came into the room, while I was laying the breakfast table.

" 'Rachel,' said she, 'have you seen, or do you know anything of the gold chain and locket mamma gave me? You have seen me wear it?'

" 'Yes, miss, I have seen you wear it,' I replied; 'but I do not know anything about it. Have you mislaid it?'

" 'I don't know anything about mislaying,' she answered very sharply, 'but I know the last time I took it off my neck, when I came home from my aunt's, was the night before last, and then I put it in the red leather case on the toilette, and I think I left it there, though Georgina (that was her youngest sister) says she remembers I put the case in my drawer, where I keep my trinkets. However, whether or not, it is gone, the case is empty; and, what is more, Rachel,' she added, looking at me with such a look, 'Georgina has lost a silk purse with some money in it.'

"You do not think *I* have taken it, miss?" said I, in amazement, and more angry than frightened.

"Miss Fitzmorris came into the room at that minute, quite unconcerned as it seemed.

" 'What is the matter, love?' she asked carelessly; 'has Rachel offended you, or you offended Rachel?'

" 'I don't know, ma'am,' replied the young lady, 'who has a right to be offended. I was only telling Rachel that I have lost my gold chain and locket, with papa's hair in it, out of my bed-room, and Rachel——'

" 'Lost it?' said the governess, 'impossible! You must have mislaid it, dear, and haven't looked carefully for it. Recollect,' she added, in a low voice, though quite loud enough for me to hear, 'recollect, it is a very serious thing to a poor servant to bring any charge of that kind.'

" 'I did not charge her with anything,' said the young lady, 'but she chose to take it to herself; and as to mislaying, ma'am, if I have mislaid my chain, it is not likely that Georgina has mislaid her purse that you netted for her—and that is gone, too, and the seventeen and sixpence that was in it, and the gold Spanish piece that grandmamma gave her.'

"Miss Fitzmorris sat down on the nearest chair, as if she were quite overcome. She looked at me, and I returned her look boldly. I felt my innocence, and I had no fear.

" 'Where is Miss Georgina?' she said, at last.

"At this moment the young lady came running into the room.

" 'I am quite sure now, Matilda,' she said to her sister, 'for I have emptied every drawer, and put everything away, singly, and they are not there. There must have been a thief in the room.'

" ' What is to be done?" said Miss Fitz-morris, looking at me; 'Mrs. Shrimpton must be told of this. Do not be alarmed, Rachel, I think I could answer with my life for your honesty.'

" ' I can answer or it myself, ma'am,' said I, very composedly, 'and, therefore, I am not alarmed.'

" And yet, to confess the truth. my dear," continued Rachel, "my legs trembled so I could scarcely stand. I knew Miss Fitzmorris was not sincere—that she was not my friend, and I did not like her looks nor her pretences. I had a fear of something, and I knew not what.

" ' We will all go to Mrs. Shrimpton, together,' said the governess. 'She is not able to come here, is she, Rachel?'

" *She* knew that, well enough, artful as she was—for if the poor old lady had not been confined to her sofa, with the rheumatic gout, *she* would never have been able to play the tricks she had been doing for the last three weeks.

" Well, away we all went, the young ladies and all, to the housekeeper's room. Poor old lady, she was sadly put out—for though she was cross and passionate, and strict with the servants, she was a very just, honest woman. As to suspecting me, she said she would as soon believe that she committed the robbery herself, as that I did it.

" ' No, no, nobody accuses Rachel,' said Miss Fitzmorris; 'only as she is most about the young ladies, it was natural they should speak to her first.'

" At last it was agreed that my lady should be informed of what had happened, and I stayed with the housekeeper while Miss Fitzmorris went to my lady's dressing-room. They came back together—the governess and Lady Springtown. All this while none of the other servants knew anything of what had happened. My lady asked me several questions, and I fancied that she was not inclined to think so well of me as the housekeeper and Miss Fitzmorris; but I was bold in my innocence, and I answered her truly and firmly, I and Jane together had made the young ladies' bed, and cleaned the room out the day before, when the chain and purse were supposed to have been stolen; and the upper-housemaid, Anne, was the only other person that to my knowledge had been in the room that day. She had come in once or twice and put a clean toilet cloth on the table, and she could speak to what was on the table at that time. Anne and Jane were sent for; but they could say no more than I did. The end of it was, that after the bed room had been

horoughly searched, and nothing found, he servants were all called together and old what had happened. There was, of course, great surprise and consternation among them; but everybody declared their innocence, and their readiness to have their rooms and boxes searched.

" ' If my lady thinks proper,' said the butler, 'the best way will be to have an officer sent for, and let him make the search; then there can be no mistakes, nor no favour shown.'

" This was accordingly done, and every one of us, except the butler, who went himself for the officer, stayed in the house-keeper's room till he came. If there was any one among us that seemed more uneasy than the other—of course none of us were very comfortable—it was Jane. I could see that she turned pale and red, and pale again, and seemed two or three times to be in deep thought, and once I caught her eyes fixed on Miss Fitzmorris with such a strange look, I fancied it meant to say—'It is you that have brought all this trouble upon me.' But that was not the meaning, as you shall hear.

" The officer was not long before he came. He was a keen, sharp man, and his eyes seemed to go through one as he asked a question. Miss Fitzmorris took upon herself to be spokeswoman—for my lady was too proud to have anything to do with such people. The young ladies told their story, and then he asked which were the young women who were known to have been in the room last. Anne, and Jane, and I stood forward directly.

" ' Well, then, my girls,' said he, 'of course you have no objection to have your boxes searched, first of all, and if we don't find anything there——'

" We all drew out our keys in a minute, and I felt great relief when I saw Jane was as ready as either of us.

" ' Stop a moment,' said he, 'there is something to be done first. Let all the men leave the room with me. It will be necessary that these young women prove that they haven't the property secreted about them. When that's done, they can show me their boxes.'

" The examination was soon made, in the presence of my lady, the governess, and the housekeeper. Jane coloured sadly when, from among the contents of her pocket, which were turned out upon the table, the housekeeper took up a little bit of brown paper screwed up, and opened it. In it there was a very smart pair of coral ear-rings.

" ' Where did this finery come from, pray?' said the old lady, looking sharply in Jane's face. 'Not very situable, I think, for a servant-girl. Where, and when did you buy them?'

"'I did not buy them, ma'am, they were given me,' said Jane; and I saw her steal a look at Miss Fitzmorris that explained in a minute, to me, where they came from. At the same time I heard one of the young ladies say something to the governess in a whisper, to which she replied—

"'Oh, dear no, my love, they are quite different, I assure you.'

"Miss Matilda, however, did not seem satisfied of this; she went to the table, and was going to take up the ear-rings which Mrs. Shrimpton had laid down, when my lady, in her severe voice, said—

"'What are you thinking of, Matilda? You are not going to touch the *things*, are you?'

" I'm making a long story of it, my dear child," continued Rachel; "but everything that happened, and every word that was said, is so printed on my mind, I often look back and shudder, and think what might have been my fate if a merciful Providence had not brought the truth to light." Tears of gratitude and thankfulness stole down the old woman's withered cheeks, and it was some minutes before she proceeded.

"Of course there was nothing about any of us that could cause any suspicion. As to Jane's ear-rings I knew very well, if she was pressed, that she could explain where they came from—so away we all went— the females I mean,—all except my lady and poor Mrs. Shrimpton, who could not walk—to our bed-room.

"'Now, young woman,' said the officer to Jane—I could see, somehow, he suspected her most—'Now please to unlock your boxes.'

"She did so in a minute.

"'Now stand back,' said he, 'and let me look over your rattletraps.'

"Poor Jane looked very angry at his calling her finery by such a vulgar name, and his tossing it on the ground; and I was glad to see she did, for I knew by that that she had no reason to be afraid— and so it proved. There was nothing there but what was her own.

"'There,' said he, 'you may put 'em all back now,' getting up from his knees 'I'm sorry to have offended such a pretty young woman, and made her so ill-natured; but we're sad rough fellows, and can't help it. Now, miss,' and he turned to Anne, 'you next, if you please.'

"Anne pointed out her trunk, and produced her keys, and the search there was as unsuccessful as before. It was my turn now. I gave him my keys. I had two

boxes. He put the key of the largest into the keyhole, but he could not turn it. 'Is this the right one?' he asked.

"'Yes, sir,' said I, very readily; 'shall I unlock it for you?'

"'Yes, my girl, if you can,' said he, and he looked at me with his cunning eyes, from under his bent brows, with such a strange look, I shall never forget it. And yet I couldn't understand what he meant.

"I tried and tried again, and I twisted my apron round the key to give me a better hold, but all would not do.

"'Something's the matter with the lock,' said the man. 'Was it ever so before, my girl?'

"'Never, sir,' said I, 'it was a very easy lock, wasn't it?' and I turned round to Anne and Jane.

"Never shall I forget Jane's look—her lips and cheeks were as white as a corpse, and her hands trembled so, that she could not put the clothes she held into her box. I stood quite bewildered, looking at her, and that drew every one's attention to her.

"'The poor girl is faint,' said Miss Fitzmorris, hastily going to her. 'She had better go into the air. I suppose there is no occasion for her staying here any longer, sir?'

"'I don't know,' said the officer slowly, looking at her all the time. 'I would rather no one should leave the room. Throw up the window if she wants air.'

"Miss Fitzmorris herself supported her to the window, and Jane recovered in a minute or two.

"'Now then, about this lock,' said the officer, turning to me. 'It's plain to me it has been hampered—when did you open it last, my girl?'

"'Not since Monday night, sir, when I put the clothes away—you know, Anne,' said I, 'that I wore when I was out for my holiday.'

"'So you did,' said Anne, 'and the lock was all right then, I can swear.'

"'Well, it is all wrong now, that's plain,' said the man. 'Go down stairs, my dear,' said he to Anne, 'and see if there is such a thing as a chisel or screwdriver to be had among the men. If not, bring a strong table-knife.' Anne was soon back with what he wanted, and he soon had the box open.

"'Some one has been at my box,' said I, the moment it was opened. 'I did not leave it in that manner.'

"'No,' said Anne, 'that you never did, for you are always so particular about your clothes, and never put your shawl in rumpled up in that manner.'

"The man never said a word, but he

looked up at both of us with that strange look, that I never saw anything like it in my life. It was just as if he was reading our hearts as he would a printed book, and then I saw he glanced at Jane, who was stooping over her box as if she would hide her face in it. For my own part I seemed as if I was in a dream, and yet, somehow, I was prepared for what was to come."

Again Rachel paused, almost beathless and gasping, at the recollection of the scene she was portraying ; while Bess's agitated countenance, and the pressure of her hands, as she held the old woman's withered ones between them, expressed the sympathy which her faltering lips could not utter.

"The man did not throw the things about as he had done Jane and Anne's," continued Rachel, "but he took everything out, one by one, shook them out, and laid them aside; but he had not far to look. There was a coloured muslin gown that was quite new. I had never worn it, because I went into mourning for Miss Seymour directly after I had bought it, and I was still, you know, in black. I saw the minute he took it out that it was not folded as I had left it, and one of the sleeves was pinned up in a strange way. The man's sharp eyes saw that in a moment. He felt it between his fingers— looked at me—took the pin out, and shook it, and the green silk purse that was missing fell on the ground. Miss Georgina rushed forward to seize it.

"'That's my purse,' she cried out. 'Oh, Rachel !'

"The man caught it up before she touched it.

"'How much was in it, miss?' said he to her.

"She told him.

"'That's right,' said he, turning the contents of one end into his hand, and then putting it back.

"'And this?' said he, holding up the gold chain which he had taken out of the other end.

"'That is my chain,' said Miss Matilda; 'but it was not in the purse when——''

"'Never mind where it was, miss, that's nothing at present. You own it, that's sufficient.'

"He put it in his pocket, and then turned to me.

"'Now, Rachel,' said he, 'what have you got to say about this matter?'

"'Only that I never put those things there,' said I, 'that they have been placed there by some one who wishes to ruin me. God forgive them—they are more misera-ble at this moment than I am—for I am innocent.'

"'Well, I wish you may be able to prove yourself so, my girl,' he replied ; 'but I am afraid this is a poor story to tell a jury. However, you must look to that. I have nothing now but to do my duty. Put on your bonnet and shawl, and let one of the young women tie up what you want to take with you in a bundle—for you'll have three weeks to lie in gaol before your trial comes on.'

"The maid-servants were all in tears as soon as he said this; but I did not shed one. Miss Fitzmorris hid her face in her handkerchief. As to Jane, she sat on the ground, rocking herself backwards and forwards, and seeming quite in agony.

"'Come, why don't you stir yourselves, some of you young women, to help your fellow-servant,' said the officer. 'You must know what she will want—for she is sure to be committed. Here you, my dear,' and he laid hold of Jane with his strong arm, and lifted her up on her feet so as to make her face me. 'She was your bed-fellow, wasn't she?' said he ; "I'll be bound she's done you many a kind office, and sure you're not going to turn your back upon her directly she's got into trouble? It's a shocking thing, to be sure, to be thrown into goal and transported, but I hope it will be a warning to you, Susan, Martha, Jenny or whatever your name is.'

"I don't know how it was, my dear," continued Rachel, "this was not a very, pleasant or feeling speech, and yet I felt at that moment as if I had no reason to fear. As if, indeed, that I was certain that the man knew I was innocent, and knew, too, who was the guilty party.

"I looked at Jane, firmly, as she raised her eyes to mine.

"'I've made up my mind,' said she, in a faltering voice, 'you shall not go to prison, Rachel.'

"'Your mind!' said the officer, with pretended surprise. 'What have you to do with it?'

"Miss Fitzmorris, who was standing close to the door at this moment, glided out of the room. I don't think anybody saw her but me—but I was watching her —for I was well aware she was at the bottom of it all. I did not attempt to stop her, however; indeed, I didn't know what to do, until I should hear what Jane had to say.

"It was a long time, however, before she could say anything—for she now downright fainted away, and vinegar and water, and sal volatile, were obliged to be sent for, before she came to, and could speak.

"The news that the things had been found in my box had by this time reached my lady and Mrs. Shrimpton; and all the men servants were in consternation—for though I say it, my dear, I was well-liked among them. One of the footmen brought up my ladies commands that I should be brought down to the housekeeper's room.

"'I don't know,' said the officer, doubtfully. 'The young woman is my prisoner now, and it's my duty to take her at once before a magistrate, when she is sure to be sent to Newgate.'

"'Oh, no—no—no,' interrupted Jane, eagerly, 'she is not guilty—indeed she is not.'

"'Not guilty!' he repeated. 'Well, then, who is? Did you put the articles in her box, then?'

"Jane shook her head.

"'Do you know who did, then?' said he.

"'I think I do,' replied Jane, in a low voice.

"'Think?' he repeated. 'Thoughts won't do in the law. We must have facts. However, as I see you have a story to tell, we may as well go down stairs and hear it—so come along, my girl, I must not lose sight of my prisoner.'

"He took hold of my arm, but I could see it was rather in a jeering way than in earnest—and as we were going down stairs he whispered to me to keep up my spirits, for he could see how matters would turn out.

"'You've had some quarrel, I suppose,' he added, 'with this young woman, or there is some jealousy—a sweetheart, or something in the case.'

"I said 'No, I never quarrelled with any one in the house in my life, and as to sweethearts I never had thought of such a thing.'

"He seemed surprised.

"'You must know,' said he, 'that this girl has a spite against you. I'm sure you did know it from the first, because I noticed your look at her.'

"'Yes; I did suspect she had a hand in it,' I said. 'But there is another person who has made a tool of her.'

"'Ah! indeed—is that it,' said he. 'Who is it—one of the men?'

"I said—'No. He would hear presently,' and just then we entered the housekeeper's room.

"I looked round to see if Miss Fitzmorris was there—but she wasn't. The men were all standing in the lobby, look-ing very serious and concerned. Mrs. Shrimpton was crying, and my lady herself seemed quite hurt.

"'Oh, Rachel, Rachel,' said the old housekeeper. 'Oh! could I believe that you——'

"'Don't believe anything, ma'am, yet,' said the officer. 'Here we've got a witness to examine, and if you please, we'll allow her a seat, as she seems rather poorly yet.'

"He placed Jane in a chair.

"'Now then, my girl, tell us your story; but, remember, none of your thoughts. Stick to facts.'

"'Well then, sir, you've got the chain in the purse in your pocket,' said Jane.

"'Yes; I have,' he replied, putting his hand on the outside of his waistcoat pocket.

"'There was a locket to it, wasn't there, miss, when you lost it?' said Jane to Miss Georgina.

"'Oh, yes; I forgot to look. Is it not there now, sir?' said the young lady.

"The man took it out and looked at it —there was no locket.

"'Ay, I thought so,' said Jane.

"'D—n it, you're at your thoughts again,' said the officer, in a passion. 'Why can't you say at once what you know about the locket? Where is it?'

"'I shall come to that in time, if you'll let me speak, sir,' said Jane, sullenly.

"The officer grumbled something about obstinate women and fools, and then he told her to go on.

"Jane began her story with what Miss Fitzmorris had said to her first about Rachel.

"'Who's Miss Fitzmorris?' interrupted the man, looking about. 'Is she here? because, we must not listen to what people said, if they're not present.'

"'Where is Miss Fitzmorris?' inquired my lady, who seemed to forget her pride for a moment; she was so eager to hear the tale Jane had to tell.

"Nobody could answer the question. She had gone down stairs in a hurry, somebody said, as soon as she heard Jane declare she would tell the truth.

"'I hope,' added Jane, 'she hasn't found the locket, and made away with it, because——'

"The officer interrupted her by swearing at her for not saying at once, when she saw the locket was missing, where it was to be found, and what she knew about it; and Anne was sent to the governess's room, to desire her to come to my lady.

"The maid was no sooner gone, however, than the man insisted on Jane's telling instantly where the locket was to be found. Threatening he would else take her into custody.

"'I put it into the left-hand drawer of the dressing-glass in Miss Fitzmorris's room,' returned Jane.

"'*You* put it there—then you are the thief, after all,' said the officer; 'but come and show me where it is, and some of you young women come and witness where it is found. You stay where you are, my girl; the truth's coming out, I can see.'

"These words were addressed to me. Jane, however, would not go until she had declared that she was not a thief. She had found the locket, she said, in Miss Fitzmorris's bed, when she made it, that very morning. She knew it was the same Miss Matilda wore, but she had never thought about how it came in the governess's bed. She put it in the drawer for safety, intending to tell Miss Fitzmorris, but had forgot—but the minute she saw the chain she thought——'

"'*Thought* again,' said the man. 'It seems to me you have no thought at all, or you would not have got yourself into this hobble—but come along.'

"In a few minutes he came back with the locket in his hand. He had found it where she said it was. Before he and Jane came back, however, Anne had run breathless into the room to say that Miss Fitzmorris had left the house.

"'I saw her pink satin bonnet and Cashmere shawl were gone, my lady, as soon as I went into the room, for the band-box stood open on the floor, so I ran to the porter in the hall, and he said—

"'Yes, she went out in a great hurry, more than ten minutes ago, and said, as she passed, that she was going to consult Sir Robert Stanstead (that was my lady's own brother, my dear,) what was best to be done in this affair.'

"Well, to be sure, my lady was thunderstruck, and the man—the officer—seemed terribly vexed, and he rated poor Jane preciously, declaring he would have her locked up for not telling in time to stop the woman—meaning Miss Fitzmorris. I saw he blamed himself, too, for his oversight; but he excused himself by saying that he thought, from the authority she assumed, that the governess was one of my lady's own family.

"'Your *thoughts*, then, can be wrong, as well as mine, sir,' said Jane, who was always a pert girl, and was now beginning to get her spirits up again.

"I saw he could hardly help smiling.

"'Come, go on with your story, if you please, from the beginning, and don't be saucy,' he said.

"Well, my dear, Jane told the whole truth—how Miss Fitzmorris had bribed, and flattered, and inveigled her into her schemes, and how the gentleman that the governess said she was going to be married to had been let into the house by her, Jane. Poor girl, she tried to keep everybody else out of trouble; for, though the officer questioned and cross-questioned her, she wouldn't own that any of her fellow-servants knew anything about it. Poor Mrs. Shrimpton, what a way *she* was in; but then, as she said to my lady, 'It was the nasty rheumatism that was to blame—if she could have walked about, it couldn't have happened.'

"The officer jumped up when he heard that a strange man had been let secretly into the house.

"'Are you sure, my lady, that you haven't been robbed?' he cried. 'Where's the butler? Is the plate all safe?'

"The butler was listening at the door, so he came forward directly.

"Everything was right, he said, for he had just finished looking over it.

"'Then you're a lucky fellow, Mr. Butler,' said the officer; 'for ninety-nine times out of a hundred these pretended love-affairs are only a plant. That is, my lady, a cloak for a robbery, you know. You are sure, my lady, your jewels are safe?'

"My lady was sure, she said; but, however, Mrs. Mansell was sent to see that they were.

"Jane went on to tell how Miss Fitzmorris was always abusing me, and telling her that I was a spy upon them all, and that I was only waiting for an opportunity to ruin everybody.

"'And then,' said Jane, 'she hinted that if we could only plan to get Rachel out of the house, we should be safe, and could manage everything quite comfortable. I said I didn't see how it was to be done, for Rachel was so prudent and careful, and such a favourite with Mrs. Shrimpton and my lady.'

"'Only as she deserved,' said Mrs. Shrimpton, eagerly. 'I never made favourites, my lady, I assure you, of any of the servants.'

"'Pray don't interrupt the witness, ma'am,' said the man, very cross.

"Jane went on to say that Miss Fitzmorris hinted ever so many times, that if there could be some temptation thrown in Rachel's way, without her seeming to have anything to do with it, and she, Rachel, could be proved dishonest, it would be all over with her, and even if she peached upon us she would not be believed.

"'But I told her,' continued Jane, 'that I verily believed Rachel might be trusted with untold gold, she wouldn't touch it. She didn't believe it, she said. Rachel was an artful wretch, and was no better in her heart than other people. And then she went on to say, that she had a scheme in her head that would do the

BESSY LESLIE MOURNING OVER THE LOSS OF HER FATHER.

business, if I would help her. She dropt two or three more words,' said Jane, 'that gave me a hint what she meant, but I wouldn't take them. I'm sure I wouldn't have hurt you, Rachel,' said the girl, looking at me, 'though certainly I did wish you out of the house, because she per- suaded me that you were my enemy, and I thought——'

"'We shall never get to the truth this way,' said the officer, impatiently. 'Let me ask you two or three questions. Did you ever see this Miss Fitzmorris in the room were the articles were found?'

"'Yes, two or three times,' said Jane.

"'Two or three won't do. How many, exactly,' asked the man.

"'Three, then,' said Jane. 'Once when Rachel was in bed——'

"'I heard her though, Jane,' said I, 'though she did not know it. I was——'

"'Never mind what *you* heard, I'm not talking to you,' interrupted the officer. 'Did she say anything about Rachel's box, or boxes?'

"'Not then,' replied Jane; 'but the next day she stole up while I was cleaning myself, to give me a new lace collar, and then she asked me which was the governess's box. That was the one, ma'am, which belonged to poor Miss Seymour, and was given to Rachel. And I said, that underneath one, and then she said—'Oh, then those belong to Rachel, do they?' I said yes, and then she tried to lift up the lid, but it was locked, and then she said, 'I should like to have a peep at the fine legacy she got from her idol, Miss Seymour, but I suppose she's too careful of her keys.' I said I didn't believe Rachel ever even looked into the box herself, and I was sure she would never forgive anybody that pulled them about. She didn't say any more then, but I saw she was examining Rachel's own box very particularly, and 'specially the lock.'

"'And did you leave her in the room?' said the officer.

"'No, she went down before me,' replied Jane.

"'Well, when was the next time,' said he.

"'Yesterday,' replied Jane. 'You know, ma'am,' said she, to the housekeeper, 'I came and asked you for a bottle of soda water for Miss Fitzmorris, who was ill a-bed.'"

"Mrs. Shrimpton nodded.

"'Well she took it,' Jane went on, 'and I left her. Two or three times I went into her room in the day with gruel, and one thing or the other, and I noticed that every time she asked me where was Rachel, and what was she doing. The last time was just after tea-time, that is, our tea-time in the kitchen, and then I told her Rachel was gone out, I believed, to the druggist's, for Mrs. Shrimpton's gout physic, and I saw directly by her eyes that Miss Fitzmorris had some reason for asking so particular—but it didn't strike me then what it was. However I went down to the kitchen again, and about three quarters of an hour afterwards I happened to go up to our room for a bit of muslin I wanted to make some borders. On my way I thought I'd look in and see if Miss Fitzmorris

wanted anything; but when I went in, the bed was empty.

"'At first I thought she had dressed herself, and was gone down to the schoolroom; but when I looked about I saw her clothes were all folded as I left them, and she could only have her flannel dressing-gown on. I was going at first to surprise her, by making the bed before she came back, and I'd begun to pull the clothes off, when, all at once, something came over me—a fright, like—and up-stairs I ran to our room in the attics. I suppose she heard me coming—for before I got to the door, out she came, and, though it was dusk, I could see her face was as white as snow, and she could hardly get her words out.

"'Lor, Jane, how you frightened me,' said she, 'I thought it was that devil, Rachel, and I wouldn't have had her catch me out of bed for the world—I want to speak with you.'

"'When we'd got back to her room and she'd got into bed, she told me she knew what would cure her headache in a moment, and as she fancied she heard me go up to my own room a few minutes before, she thought she'd go after me and ask me to get a little brandy if I could, for she was all of a shiver. And so she was, sure enough,' said Jane, 'as cold as ice, and, as I said to her, she seemed as if she had been out of bed a long time, and I couldn't think how she could run such a risk to get out of a warm bed and go up stairs without shoes or stockings—it was enough to kill her.

"'Never mind, my dear girl,' said she, 'take a shilling out of my reticule, and try if you can get out and bring a shilling's-worth of brandy, and make me a strong glass of hot brandy and water, and I shall be well.'

"'When I went to get the shilling, however,' said Jane, 'I found her reticule was locked up in her drawers, and then I looked for her bunch of keys where I knew I'd left them, on the table, when I was in the room last. 'Oh, here they are,' said Miss Fitzmorris, when she found what I was looking for. She'd got them in her hand, inside the bed, and then I knew I was right when I thought I heard the jingle of keys in our room when I ran up stairs and met her.'

"'And pray,' said Mrs. Shrimpton, 'did you go and get the brandy? you good-for-nothing, deceitful——'

"'Never mind that, ma'am, said the officer. 'To be sure she did, and drink her share of it, too, or else she was a fool for her pains—for a little drop, in reason, goes a great way to help to get at the truth.

I don't think it would do me any harm in the present case.'

"Mrs. Shrimpton took the hint, and ordered Anne to make him a glass.

"'Now, go on, young woman,' said he to Jane. 'Is there anything more about the keys?'

"'Only, sir, that when Miss Fitzmorris gave me the bunch I saw there was one bent, as if some great force had been used with it,' said Jane.

"'And did the lady say nothing more to you? Recollect now, because if you don't tell the whole truth ——'

"'I want to tell the whole truth,' said Jane, crying. 'After she drank the brandy and water,' she continued, 'Miss Fitzmorris got quite bold again, and very chatty; but as she was sitting up in bed she suddenly missed a blue silk handkerchief, that she had had round her neck, in bed. We looked all about for it, and at last she said, 'Run up stairs, Jane, I must have dropped it there.' I went, but couldn't find it, and she seemed sadly vexed and puzzled. After a bit she said—

"'Now mind, Jane, whatever happens, whatever you hear or see, or whatever questions you're asked, keep close. Don't own to anything, and whatever Rachel may say, deny it boldly, and leave me to get through it all.'

"'I asked her what she meant, and she said, 'Never mind, you know nothing, that's all. I only tell you to be prepared for this. I know, that if we don't get rid of that sly, artful, undermining hussy, Rachel, she'll ruin us all. But, as I told you before, you have nothing to do but to be on your guard, and hold your tongue, whatever happens.' I was very uneasy and unhappy,' continued Jane. 'for I thought, all along, that with all Miss Fitzmorris's cleverness, she would be found out at last, and I should get into trouble; but she promised me faithfully that if any harm came to me, that is, if I lost my place, I should live with her till she was married, and that Mr. Beaumaris, that's the gentleman's name, had said I should be their housekeeper when he got his fortune, and should never want all my life long.'

"'Housekeeper, indeed," muttered Mrs. Shrimpton. 'Poor fool!'

"'Well—but how about the blue handkerchief,' said the officer, 'did you find it?'

"'Yes, sir, I found it on the ground, in the young ladies' room, when I went in to turn down the beds,' replied Jane, 'after I left Miss Fitzmorris, and I wondered what in the world she had been in there

for; but when I carried it to her she said, though she looked very foolish about it, that she remembered, now, she had been in there for a minute, because she thought I might be there.'

"'A likely story, that,' said Mrs. Shrimpton; 'the young ladies' room, sir,' said she, 'is three rooms off Miss Fitzmorris, on the same floor, and she goes first there, and then up to the attic to——'

"'That is just what I was going to ask, ma'am, said the officer; 'but I will go, if you please, and look at the situation of the rooms myself presently. Well, Miss Jane, have you anything more to add to this pretty story?'

"Jane said no, that was all she could remember. She was very sorry that she had had any hand in it, and she made up her mind, as soon as she heard that Rachel was to go to gaol, that she would tell the truth.

"'I only wish you had, as you ought to have done, told the truth in time,' said the officer; 'but it seems you took care to let the guilty party get off first.'

"Jane, however, declared that she did not intend any such thing, and I believe she told the truth," continued Rachel; "but the fact was, the governess had got such a power over her, poor foolish creature, that till the last minute, when she thought I was going to be dragged off to gaol, she had not the courage to utter a word.

"Well, my dear, the upshot of all this was, that everybody was sent out of the room, but my lady, Mrs. Shrimpton, me, and the officer; the butler was told to take care that Jane did not leave the house—and then he told us that though he was as well convinced that I was innocent as if he had seen Miss Fitzmorris take the chain and the purse out of the young lady's drawer, and put it in my box, yet still it was absolutely necessary that I should go before a magistrate, and that even then he was afraid the case must go before a jury, though there was no doubt I should be acquitted.

"'I was thunderstruck at this, and, somehow, the thoughts of the magistrate and the gaol frightened me more now than when I was in real danger. Lady Springtown—I never saw her forget her pride and consequence so entirely as she did then—she quite got into a passion, with what she thought the ignorance and obstinacy of the man. I should not be taken out of the house—she would order her servants to turn him, the officer, into the street, if he offered to lay a hand on me. After all, she was a good-hearted and upright woman, dear Bess, only, in general, it is wrapped up in so much pride and dignity.

"The officer threatened her with the vengeance of the law if she interfered, and pointed out if the affair was hushed up, Miss Fitzmorris would get off without any punishment. This my lady could not, or would not believe. Luckily, Mrs. Shrimpton was a sensible, cool-headed woman, and knew the world. She persuaded my lady to leave the room, and sent me into her stone closet, where I could be seen by the officer, who would not let me go out of his sight, but where I could not hear what passed. I have no doubt in my own mind that she paid him handsomely for all the trouble that he had been at. At any rate, I was called after a little while, and told that the *gentleman* had agreed to accept my lady's security that I should be forthcoming if I was wanted, and having made a proper acknowledgment for this *kindness* on his part, I was allowed to return to my fellow-servants, who, to do them justice, seemed not less rejoiced on my account than they were on their own, at the narrow escape they had had of losing their places and characters, which would have been the case had either Jane or I betrayed that they were so deep in Miss Fitzmorris's secrets. And so, my dear, ended my adventures with the second governess."

"But was nothing heard of the infamous woman?" demanded Mrs. Leslie, who, though she had heard from Rachel some particulars of her narrow escape, now for the first time learned the full detail.

"Yes, ma'am," returned Rachel. "It turned out that through some of her former connexions she had succeeded in getting off to France, after she left Lady Springtown's; and some months afterwards my lady received an order to deliver up her clothes, and pay what money was due to her, to a person who called himself her solicitor. At first my lady thought of resisting this demand—as far as the money; but she found that it would, perhaps, bring about an exposure of what had happened in the family—and the very idea of the young ladies being obliged to appear at a public office was enough to frighten her into anything. So for that time, at least, the wicked wretch got off with colours flying."

"And poor Jane," inquired Bess. "I cannot help pitying her, though she certainly acted very wrong."

"Everybody pitied her, my dear," returned Rachel; "and I do think my lady would have forgiven her, and let her stayed in her place, but Mrs. Shrimpton said she should lose all her authority over the other servants if she kept her, and so poor Jane was sent away. But I believe—indeed, I know—Mrs. Shrimpton was very good to her while she was out of place, and I fancy, at last, helped her to another; and when I last saw Jane, she was doing very well—for, as she said, Miss Fitzmorris had been a lesson to her that had driven all her giddiness and wildness out of her for life. So you see, my dear, out of evil came good."

CHAPTER VI.

But gaunt famine doth not stride
By the proud and wealthy's side;
There ye see not little feet
Press upon the frozen street,
While the infant's tearful eye
Tells its tale of misery.
When in curtain'd, lighted hall,
What to you that snow-flakes fall?
When beside the blazing log,
What to you is frost or fog?
When on down your limbs ye stretch,
Think ye of the houseless wretch?—CAMILLA TOULMIN.

YOU promised, dear Rachel, to tell me a tale connected with that poor young lady, Miss Seymour's legacy to you, or, rather, what became your property at her death," said Bess Leslie, the first time they were again quietly seated together at their work. "We were interrupted, you know, just as you were going to relate the story; but I have thought so much about the poor girl who met so melancholy a fate, that I am anxious to hear of anything that had the most distant connection with her."

Rachel smiled approvingly.

" Well, love, it is not quite such a long tale as the others, though this, too, relates to a governess—and in the same family. I never lived in any other, indeed, as I believe you know, till I came to your dear mother, whom I had often nursed when I was a young girl—for though I look so much older, dear Bess, there is only fourteen years between me and your mamma. I was, as I may say, born and brought up in the Bevington family, for my mother was servant to your grandfather Bevington ; and though she married out of the family, she went back after I was born, to be wet-nurse to Mr. Bevington's third child, who did young, and if I had not taken it into my foolish head to go to London, I need never have left your grandfather's family. However, we must all buy wisdom at some price. I had like, you see, to have paid very dear; and I have reason to be truly grateful for the mercy that suffered not the guilty to triumph, or the innocent to fall beneath the oppressor. But you have heard this before, my dear child, and so I will tell you my last story.

" After finding out how she had been deceived by Miss Fitzmorris, Lady Springtown resolved that she would not again have a governess to live in the house, especially as the young ladies were now getting old enough to sit at table, and go with their mamma upon family visits. So after a little time a daily governess was found, to come from ten o'clock in the morning till three, and teach everything —music, dancing, drawing—and all for a weekly sum; less, as Mrs. Shrimpton said, than a common working man would get for as many hours' work. But there were so many applications, she said, that Lady Springtown could pick and choose at any price, and as it could not be denied that she was very avaricious, of course she took the cheapest.

" Mrs. Lytham, the new governess, (my lady would not have anything more to do with the *misses*, she said,) was not very young, or very pretty, and somehow, though she was genteel, she was not so much of the lady as Miss Seymour, though I took to her from the first—I suppose because she looked melancholy and careworn, like my poor Miss Lucy. It was the latter end of autumn when she began to come to our house, and very wet, cold weather, and I used to pity her when I went to help her off with her cloak and clogs, and take her umbrella, and espe-

cially when she told me one day, when she was all in a flutter at being half an hour beyond her time, that she had to walk from Somers' Town, which was full two miles from our house. There was no refreshment ever sent into the school-room, now that the young ladies dined with their mamma, and often when I passed the door and heard her singing with her scholars, or playing the piano to their dancing, I used to think it was hard work after her long walk, and then to have to walk back again, without any thing to keep up her strength. She was very free in her manner with me, when we were together in the little back parlour, where the cloaks and umbrellas were kept—not to say chatty—but not timid or reserved, like my poor friend Lucy—and so, one day when she looked paler, and more careworn than usual, I said to her, that I was afraid the exertion was almost too much for her.

" She smiled, but I saw the tears stood in her eyes, and hardly knowing what I was saying, I remarked that I dare say she was very glad when the time came to get home to dinner. It is a great many hours, said I, to wait, and, of course, ma'am, you are obliged to breakfast early to get off in time.

" She said, yes, and I saw a faint blush come in her cheek. It put me so in mind of poor Miss Lucy. But still, thought I, she *is* better off than that poor thing was —for, of course, she has rest, and has got a comfortable home—when she does go home—but Miss Seymour had no comfort, night or day. Well, my dear, everything went on as usual for four or five weeks, only the weather, of course, got colder and colder, and I noticed that Mrs. Lytham looked thinner and thinner, and her clothes did not improve in appearance—she still wore only the same thin scanty washed silk gown, that was enough to make one cold to look at it, and her little kid slippers, when I took her clogs off, looked almost worn off her feet. There was one good thing, she had a nice warm cloak, and when she was wrapped in that, with her large bonnet and thick black veil, she looked so genteel and comfortable, nobody would have dreamt how scantily she was clothed under it. But at last, one day,—and a bitter day it was, too—she came without the cloak, nothing but a threadbare, faded, silk shawl to cover her. How my heart ached for her, and she caught my eyes, I know, fixed on the shawl as she hastily took it off, and such a deep colour came in her cheeks. I felt ashamed for myself, and for those who paid so poor a pittance for her services, as to compel her to such a sacrifice—for I knew, in my own mind, that nothing but bitter necessity could have made her part with the comfortable article of dress she seemed to have in her possession. After she was gone into the school-room, I sat down and pondered what I should do. There was a nice, large, thick whittle in Miss Seymour's chest, and I thought to myself, it could not be better disposed of, if I knew how to offer it to this poor lady without offending her. It began to snow heavily, long before her time for coming down-stairs, and that decided me. I ran up and fetched the whittle, and put it all ready in the cloak-room. Oh, how wan and woe-begone she looked when the bell was rung, and I went up to wait upon her. I saw her cast a look up at the skies, and then I said, you will have a sad walk home, ma'am.

"'I shall indeed,' she said, with a deep sigh.

"Well, my dear, then I brought forward the whittle, and I told her, I hoped she would not be offended, that I would not have taken the liberty of offering anything I wore myself to a lady like her, but that this had belonged to a lady, Miss Seymour, who I knew she had heard mentioned by the young ladies as having died in the house, and if she would accept of it, she would make me happy. You know I was very young, my dear, then," continued Rachel, "and, I dare say, I looked as I felt, foolish and awkward enough—but I shall never forget her, she stood and struggled with her feelings, and at last she sank down in a chair and leaned her head against my bosom, and gave way to such a passionate burst of tears I was afraid she would have gone into hysterics, and I should have been so sorry that she should have been exposed to the servants. As good luck would have it, Mrs. Shrimpton happened at that moment to open the room door, and immediately asked what was the matter. I was, as you already know, my dear, a bit of a favourite with the old lady, so I said, bold enough, that the lady was faint and overcome—and well she might be, walking such a distance in the cold, and exerting herself so many hours, without so much as being offered a crust of bread.

"'I believe, indeed,' muttered the old woman, 'my lady thinks governesses ought to live upon air—but come to my room, ma'am, if you are better, and have a glass of wine and a crust before you go into the cold air.'

"'Don't refuse, for my sake—don't re-fuse, my dear lady,' I whispered, as the housekeeper hobbled away.

"Mrs. Lytham seemed surprised at my eagerness, but I threw the whittle over her shoulders. She took my arm, and away we went. Poor woman—again I thought of Miss Lucy, when I saw what a change a glass of wine and a bit of plum cake made in her.

"'You look nicely now, ma'am, said I; 'it's only your having to wait so many hours between your breakfast and dinner, after your long walk, that overcomes you.'

"The old lady took the hint. She happened to be in a very good humour, or perhaps I should have been scolded for my officiousness; but now, she said, if she had known it before, Mrs. Lytham should not have gone so.

"'And so, for the future, ma'am,' said she, 'when the young ladies go for their half-hour to lunch with my lady, do you come down here. I can't always promise you wine—but a crust of bread and cheese or a sandwich with a glass of porter I can command.'

"Mrs. Lytham expressed her thanks, but I saw that she felt much more than her lips uttered.

"Who knows, I thought to myself, perhaps, poor lady, even at home she may not be able to get such nourishment as her delicate health and hard work require.

"I longed to know more of her circumstances, but I was too bashful to ask any questions; however, I took care as soon as ever my lady's bell rang at one o'clock next day, for the young ladies to go to their lunch, in the best drawing-room, to run up and fetch poor Mrs. Lytham down to hers, with the housekeeper. She had consented to keep the whittle till, she said, in a low voice, she could get her cloak back again; but, my dear Bess, how I felt, when at last she owned to me, that she had been compelled to part with it because my lady, who had agreed to pay her weekly, had for the last fortnight, as she said, forgotten her.

"'But I dare say,' she added, 'she will pay me altogether next week, and then, my dear, good Rachel, I will return your shawl.'

"I told her, what was the truth, I had made up my mind never to take it back again—that it would only have laid by and spoiled, if I had not found some one worthy to wear it—as I should think it a sin and a shame any common person should put them on.

"Poor woman! Mrs. Lytham shed tears as she said, there were few in the world who could feel like me.

"After she was gone it struck me how remiss I had been, for I thought to myself who knows, perhaps, poor thing, she is badly in want of money, and there is the balance that was left of poor Miss Seymour's, that my lady forced me to take. I have never used it, nor never shall—for it would deprive me of all satisfaction, to think I had been, as it were, paid for all I had done. Dear soul, if she could look out of her grave, I'm sure her gentle spirit would be rejoiced at her money being made the means of cheering that poor woman's heart. Then all at once I began to think, whether her husband was living. I knew she was married, because, from the first, I noticed the wedding-ring on her finger. All that night I could not sleep for thinking of the poor governess. It was Saturday night, and I thought to myself, who knows, she might not have the means even to go to market for her Sunday's dinner. Well, love, luckily it was my Sunday out, and so I thought to myself, if I could find out where poor Mrs. Lytham lives, I would make bold to call with some excuse, and then I shall see, perhaps, how matters are with her.

"I remembered, at last, that once or twice notes had been sent by one of the footmen from my lady, to alter Mrs. Lytham's hours to suit her convenience, so I went to him and ask for her direction.

"'Oh, I suppose you are invited to dinner with your friend, the governess,' said he, with a sneering laugh. 'A grand entertainment you'll meet with, if one may judge by the elegance of her residence—I mean, outside—for I've never had the honour to be admitted over the threshold, for though it's plain she's as poor as a church mouse, the lady governess, like most of them, can put on all the airs of a duchess.'

"It must only be to them that forget the respect due to her, I thought to myself, and was near saying it, only it came into my head, that if I affronted the pert footman, perhaps he wouldn't give me the direction I wanted, so I said I didn't know anything about either her pride or her poverty, but I wanted to call on Mrs. Lytham, because I had something in my possession belonging to her, which I was afraid she might want.

"'You're a comical one, Rachel,' said he, laughing, 'to think of spending your time in going hunting up the governess, merely to return her some trifle—a pocket handkerchief, I suppose, or something of that sort—for, I'm sure, she's not over-burdened—but don't frown so, I'm really sorry for the poor woman, and so will you be, when you see what a poor, miserable hut she's sheltered in. I was an hour before I could find it out, though I was all the time within a stone's throw of the place; but it seemed nobody knew them in the neighbourhood, they keep so aloof from the poor devils they live among. However, if you're determined to go, I'll write her address on a bit of paper, so that you shan't have as much trouble as I had.'

"I was very glad of this offer; but somehow, though Richard's account made me still more anxious to see Mrs. Lytham as soon as I could, yet I was more timid than ever, because I thought, poor thing, may be her feelings would be hurt at seeing me there. However, I got the direction, put the money in my pocket, which had never seen the light of day since I locked it up in the trunk, the morning my lady gave it me, and away I set of for Somers' Town, the first thing after breakfast. It was a bitter cold morning, though the snow that had been falling for two or three days was now thawing, and the ground was miserably wet and slushy. I made my way, as Richard had directed, straight through Somers' Town, and then turned out of the high road up a back lane that was nothing but deep ruts and hillocks, and scarcely could I get along, for at times I was almost up to my ancles, and I wondered how she, poor thing, who was so weak and delicate, could ever manage. At last, standing by itself, in a little garden that, I dare say, looked pretty enough in the summer, I spied out the humble cottage which, as Richard had said, was indeed little better than a hut, it was so roughly built—so low and small, and had such a desolate look, though it was clean white-washed, and the bits of muslin curtains that shaded the two little casement windows showed an attempt at decency that convinced me I was right that this was poor Mrs. Lytham's home. Oh, how my heart beat, when I opened the little wicket gate. I almost wished I hadn't come, I was so afraid she would be hurt and offended; but though she looked surprised when she came out to me, and her colour went and came, and her voice faltered as she said, 'Dear Rachel, this is an unexpected visit,' yet I saw she was rather pleased than vexed at seeing me; but oh, how surprised I was, my dear, when two pretty children, though looking so pale and thin that it was easy to be seen they lived very poorly, crept out of the door behind her, and looking earnestly at me, the elder whispered, loud enough for me to hear—

"'Mamma, mamma, is that the lady that is to bring you money to buy us bread and butter?'

"Poor little dear, I could hardly help crying, and the poor mother seemed ready to drop, till I said—

"'Yes, dear, I have brought the money, and for cakes, too, and if mamma will tell me which way I must go to find a shop, we will go and buy some.'

"'Has Lady Springtown been so kind and considerate as to send the money?' said Mrs. Lytham, her voice faltering, and looking doubtfully in my face.

"'My lady gave me this, ma'am,' said I, putting poor Miss Seymour's purse, with the money in it, into her hand—for, somehow, I was afraid to tell the downright truth, lest I should offend her, and this, you know, dear Bessie, was only an equivocation. My dear mother used to say an equivocation was worse than a lie—but in this case, I made an excuse to my conscience, that it was for a good purpose.

"'Come, love, where's your bonnet? well go and buy cakes,' said I to the little girl, just to give poor Mrs. Lytham time to recover herself, for she seemed quite overcome like. Poor little dear, she flew for her bonnet and the little boy's hat, and I took him up in my arms, and away I went, before the mother could say a word.

"Oh, Miss Bess, what a heartrending tale did I hear from that dear little chattering girl as we went along looking out for a shop. Papa was ill in bed, and mamma could not give him any breakfast because she had no fire, nor bread and butter, and mamma cried so, and some cruel, wicked man had come yesterday when mamma was out, and said he would take papa's bed away and turn him and poor Clara and William, herself and brother, into the street, and they might go to the workhouse. 'But you won't let him, will you?' said the little prattler, looking up with her tearful blue eyes in my face.

"Oh, how I wished at that minute that I was but as rich as Lady Springtown, and to think, too, that all, or at least a great part of this misery, was all through my lady's carelessness and thoughtlessness, in not paying the poor governess her just due. How rejoiced I was that I had come—and how my heart ached when I saw the eagerness with which the poor children devoured the biscuits I got for them. I got a plentiful stock of tea and sugar and other necessaries from the shop, for I thought it would not offend Mrs. Lytham, because I could easily say I had only done t to save her the trouble and unpleasant-

ness of coming out on a Sunday morning, and the dear little thoughtful Clara's eyes sparkled with joy as she clapped her little hands and said—'Oh, now papa will get better when he has some tea.' Even the woman of the shop seemed to feel it, and said, 'Ah, poor things, it's sad to see people that's known better days so put about, I'm sure. I'm sorry for them, but I'm but a poor, struggling woman myself, and can't afford to let my goods go out of the shop without the money, or else I should be out of house and home myself; but I'm glad to my heart to see the poor lady's got some friends willing and able to help her.'

"This I found afterwards was an excuse for having refused to give Mrs. Lytham trust for a few necessaries on Saturday night, though the poor lady had, for the sake of her sick husband and the dear children, humbled herself to tell their distress, and promised to pay the moment she got her salary from Lady Springtown. Ah, my dear, how easy it is to talk of pity—how few there are who act up to what is so ready on their lips. When I got back to the cottage, I found Mrs. Lytham sitting down with the purse still in her hand, and the tears streaming down her cheeks. I heard her voice before I lifted the latch. It seemed she was conferring with her poor husband, who was in bed, in the little place that was parted off from the outer room to make a bedroom, for that was the whole of the cottage.

"'Tell me, my dear, good Rachel,' said she, holding up the purse, 'what does this mean? Here is more money than is due to me from Lady Springtown. I fear that it is your own hard earnings that you are bringing to me, and poor and distressed as I acknowledge myself to be, I cannot consent——'

"I interrupted her by assuring her that she was mistaken; but she would not be satisfied until I told her the whole truth, and begged of her to use it freely, as I felt it was the best respect I could show to Miss Seymour's memory. I will not tell you, my dear, all she said, and the poor gentleman, her husband, said to me—He would insist that I should come to his bedside, that he might see her that he called his guardian angel, the preserver of his dear wife and children.

"I tried all I could to persuade him not to give way to such agitation, which, I was sure, must hurt him, in his weak state. Poor man, my heart bled when I looked at him—for I saw, plainly, he was not long for this world. He was in the last stage of consumption—and to think that my lady's neglect should have been the means of so cruelly increasing his sufferings. He told me, with his own lips, Bessie, that none of them had tasted food since breakfast-time on the day before, and he had been, as he said, driven almost to desperation, at hearing the poor children vainly asking for bread. It was the great and merciful God, he said, that put it into my heart to come to them, and never again would he despair. Never

SIR MATTHEW SEALS THE DEED OF GIFT TO THE TWIN ROSES.

shall I forget that breakfast as long as I live. Money, in London, will do anything; and so with the help of one of the poor neighbours, I contrived to get coals and wood, though it was Sunday, and I bustled about, and the dear little things, how they enjoyed the warm fire—for they had suffered almost as much from cold as hunger. Oh, how often have I thought, how little the rich can know of the real sufferings of the poor and destitute. Well, my dear, you may be sure I gave up all thoughts of any other pleasure that day, than staying and making myself as useful as I could to poor Mrs. Lytham and her husband—she couldn't rally her spirits all day; but he was quite cheerful, and said he had not felt so well and happy for months, and he would get up and come to the comfortable fire-side ; and, indeed, when the place was shut in, and everything to rights, and a nice bright fire burning, and the tea-things on the table, and the dear little smiling children sitting up to it, even that poor humble cottage did look comfortable, though, gracious knows, it was a poor place for such as them to call their home. And to think, that even that they had trembled at the thought of being turned out of—for it seemed they owed a month's rent—ten shillings, which they knew they could pay as soon as Lady Springtown should pay them; but the landlord was a harsh man, and wouldn't listen to the truth. ' It was a likely thing, he said, that a lady of quality should be keeping poor people out of their money. He didn't believe a word of it, and if the money wasn't forthcoming on Monday morning, out they must and should go.'

"'But now,' said Mr. Lytham, 'thanks to our dear good friend, we shall be able to pay him, and I shall have a good night's rest. I only want strength to get well again, and able to exert myself, and I shall, I am sure, get some occupation. We have learned to live upon so little, that a sum which I used to think too trifling to be spoken of as a reward for my services will appear a little fortune to us; and then, my dear Clara,' and he looked so affectionately at his wife, ' will no longer lead such a harassing life, but be able to stay at home with her children.'

"Would you believe it, dear Bessie, I found out that all Mrs. Lytham received from my lady—when she did receive it—was eighteen shillings a week.

"'But we could make shift to live upon that,' said the governess, 'if I could get a few evening pupils, as I had when we lived in the city; but Mr. Lytham's health was so injured by confinement, and the physician said a removal into a better air was the only remedy, that I was obliged to give them up.'

"It seemed they had at first taken lodgings at Hampstead, and he had for a time appeared to have got better, but, as she said, they could not live upon the air, and so they were obliged to come nearer town ; and this place—humble as it was—in the summer time, when the flowers were all in bloom, looked very pretty ; and Mr.

Lytham found pleasure and occupation—and he fancied health, too—in digging and attending to the garden. By degrees, I learned their whole history. Mrs. Lytham was the daughter of a merchant in the city, and was brought up as the heiress to a large fortune—for her father was believed to be a very rich man. Her husband, William Lytham, was her own first cousin, her mother and his being sisters. He lost his parents while he was quite young ; and Clara's father took charge of him and the two thousand pounds which his father had left him. Clara and he, therefore, were brought up together ; and Mr. Maynard, her father, always seemed to intend that his nephew should marry Clara, and succeed him in business, if he were so inclined—though it was thought by many people that the old gentleman had money enough to prevent his son-in-law's having any occasion to meddle with business. However, at a proper time, when the young gentleman was of a proper age, and had finished his education, he was taken into his uncle's counting-house, and it was understood, that in a year or two, if he continued to give Mr. Maynard satisfaction, no objection would be made to his marriage with Clara ; but, in the meantime, the young people were forbid to look upon one another in any other light than as friends and near relations. For, as the old gentleman said, there was no knowing what might happen before that time, to render it desirable that they should both be free. And so, it seemed, it did happen--at least, as far as Mr. Maynard's wishes and opinions were concerned—for, before Clara was nineteen, and just as William was twenty-one, a very rich baronet fell desperately in love with her, and proposed himself for her husband. He was a good many years older than Miss Maynard, and not to compare— in her eyes—to her cousin William ; but all the young people could say, made no impression upon the old gentleman. He insisted that he had never made any promises or engagement to his nephew, and forbid his daughter to give any encouragement to him, declaring that he was determined she should marry no one but the baronet. He even threatened, it seems, to turn Mr. Lytham adrift, and leave him to make his own way in the world how he could, if he did not give up all thoughts of his cousin being his wife. The consequence of this was, that the young man, William Lytham, persuaded Clara—who had no mother to persuade or direct her—to consent to a private marriage ; and when, at last, Mr. Maynard, who had made sure of conquering his daughter's objections, insisted upon her naming the time for her marriage, she was obliged to own the truth, that she had put it out of her power to comply with his wishes, as she had been three months the wife of her cousin.

"Poor lady, as she said to me, she was prepared for her father's rage and reproaches when she made this discovery, though she flattered herself—and so did her husband—that after the first burst of passion was over, and he knew that what was done couldn't be undone, he would be brought to acknowledge that he had been to blame himself, and would forgive them—especially as in every other respect he had always shown the greatest affection for his nephew; but she was dreadfully frightened when, instead of breaking out into a fit of rage as she expected, he turned as pale as death, and staggering back into a chair, seemed as if he were struck with death. She went on her knees to him, begging him to speak to her, and say that he forgave her the only act of disobedience she had ever committed.

"'Forgive you, poor, unhappy, miserable girl?' he said, at last, when he could get power to speak. 'How will you forgive yourself and me—for it is all my doing, when I tell you that you have brought ruin on yourself and me, and your unfortunate husband.'

"The explanation of all this was, my dear," continued Rachel, "that Mr. Maynard, whom the world thought so rich, was a bankrupt. He had failed in some great speculation to a greater amount than his whole fortune, and had been kept above water, as the saying is, by the help of his intended son-in-law, who, if I recollect right, was a great banker. The worst part, perhaps, of the whole story was, or at least it seemed so to me, that Mr. Maynard, not content to bring ruin on himself, and trying to sacrifice his daughter, had reduced poor Lytham to beggary, having spent every farthing of the two thousand pounds —his nephew's whole fortune.

"The upshot of this was, that as soon as ever Miss Maynard's marriage was made public, and it couldn't be kept secret for the reason that she was in the way to increase her family, the creditors all came down upon the unfortunate merchant, and the most hard-hearted of them all was the baronet, who considered that he had been shamefully used and deceived by both father and daughter, though that was not the case, as far as Clara was concerned, as she had never given him any encouragement. Poor Mr. Maynard was thrown into prison. All their property was seized and sold off, both in town and country. Mr. Maynard's business all went into other hands, and, of course, his nephew turned out of employment, and the poor young couple brought up in the midst of luxury were, as Mrs. Lytham said, thrown upon the world, with scarcely enough in their pockets to provide even common necessaries against the time that she was to become a mother. She had not a single relation in the world to help or advise her, and to add to her grief and sorrow, her father's mind became deranged by the sight of the misery and distress his imprudence had brought on those who were so dear to him, and he was only removed from prison to die in a mad-house. From that time, it seemed, the life of Mr. and Mrs. Lytham had been a constant struggle with poverty. I fancy, though I never heard it from her, poor thing, for she thought there wasn't such a man in the world as her husband; but, I do fancy myself, that Mr. Lytham wasn't much of a man of business, or fitted to get on in the world. You understand me, dear Bessie, though I am not scholar enough to explain my meaning very clear."

Bess smiled.

"It is quite clear enough, dear Rachel," she replied. "You mean that, although Mr. Lytham was an amiable and honourable man, he did not possess that firmness and energy which is necessary to enable a man, thrown out of his proper sphere, to contend with difficulties, and by perseverance, conquer them. Your friend, his poor wife, however seems to have been more happily constituted."

"You are right, my love," returned Rachel. "She was, indeed, a noble-minded woman—one who never wearied with exertion, nor let pride stand in the way, when she could spare either herself or husband from suffering."

"And what was the end of her history?" demanded Bess. "Of course, after proving yourself so true a friend, you did not lose sight of her."

"Not while I could be of any service to her, you may be sure, my dear," replied Rachel, "though many years have passed since I heard of her. I hope, however, that she is as happy as she deserves to be; but I must tell you all that remains in my own homely, old-fashioned way, if it does not tire you."

"Tire me, dear Rachel? I could listen to you for ever," returned Bess, "you seem almost to have brought every scene before my eyes, and I could almost fancy, even, that the people you speak of were well-known to me—poor Miss Seymour, especially ; but, go on, I am impatient for the rest of the story. I hope you shamed Lady Springtown, by letting her know the misery she had occasioned by her neglect, and the different conduct you——"

"I am afraid that would not have been much to my advantage," returned Rachel. "Great ladies don't like to be made look little in their own eyes. No, no, I was prudent enough to keep secret all that I had seen and heard at the cottage ; but I managed to get leave from Mrs. Shrimpton to go as often as possible to see them, by telling her that I had a friend lying dangerously ill, who had no friends or relations in London but me. Luckily, the old lady never asked me any particular questions ; and, many a time, when I got leave to go for a few hours to see my sick relation, as she called poor Mr. Lytham, she would give me some nice little dainty to take with me. Poor man, he lingered on till May, still talking of getting well, and of the happy times he fancied were still in store for him. I knew from the first he would never recover, but I had not the heart to tell his wife so. I think I see him now—how his pale face would light up when the dear children would dart out to meet me, and hurry in, holding me by the hands, one on one side, and one on the other, and calling out—' Oh, papa, papa, here she is, dear aunt Rachel is come.' People used to talk of their pride —but neither Mr. Lytham nor his wife had any pride to me. I was always their dear sister Rachel, and the children would have broken their hearts if I had told them I was not their aunt, but only a poor servant girl. But I never forgot it. Well, dear, matters went on pretty smooth for a time, the weather got fine, and Mrs. Lytham's walks were no longer so wearisome. She was an excellent manager, and Miss Seymour's money went a long way in making them comfortable. I contrived, too, to make her take all the clothes, which were only spoiling by lying by ; and the dear little ones, how proud they were of the new frocks and tippets, and bonnets, that their mamma and aunt Rachel contrived to make out of the stores. Lady Springtown paid pretty regularly for a time, and the housekeeper, the more she saw of the poor governess, the kinder she was ; but I foresaw that a time was coming, when more would be wanted than I could supply, though I managed to persuade her that Miss Seymour's legacy wasn't all gone yet —for I knew what a grief it would be to her, if she thought that she was trespass-

ing on my own poor earnings for the little extras that were necessary for the poor invalid. He had all along refused to have a doctor—for, he said, he had no complaint but weakness, and that he should get over it, as soon as spring-time came, and he could get about in his garden again ; but poor thing, she began to take alarm, when she found that the nasty hacking cough, as he called it, increased, instead of lessening, as the fine weather advanced. She tried to persuade him to let her call in a doctor, but he would not hear of it. He could not bear the thoughts of a charity doctor, and as to paying a physician's fee—that was quite out of the question. Luckily, for it proved lucky, my lady was taken very poorly, and, of course, Dr. Southwood was sent for. He it was, you know, my dear, who attended poor Lucy Seymour, though too late. I was a great favourite with the doctor from that time, and he would always stop to talk to me when I chanced to come in his way. One day he happened to see me letting Mrs. Lytham out, just as he came up to the door, and he stood back for a minute while she was shaking hands with me, as she always did, and begging me if I could get out to come up in the evening, for poor Mr. Lytham was longing to see me. She went away without observing how earnestly he was looking at her ; but I coloured as red as fire, for he was so used to joke me. Now, however, he looked very serious as he came into the hall, and while he was rubbing his shoes on the mat, for he was a nice particular man, he said—

"'Who was that lady, Rachel, who seemed on such intimate terms with you?' and I coloured still more, as I said—

"'It is the young ladies' daily governess, sir.'

"'Ay—but her name,' said he. 'I fancy I have seen her before—and yet I should hardly think it can be.'

"I told him her name was Lytham.

"'Lytham — Lytham.' he repeated, 'surely I have heard that name   Is she a married lady?'

"Something struck me in a moment that if anybody could do Mr. Lytham good, it would be him, and I well knew he was a very kind-hearted man, though a fashionable doctor.

"So I said—

"'Yes, sir, she is married, poor lady ; but I am afraid it will not be long before she is a widow, for her husband——' and then something put it into my head to say—'Her maiden name was Maynard, sir ; perhaps you might have known—'

"'Maynard—you are right, I perfectly remember. Yes—she married her cousin —but come in here, my good girl, you must tell me more about this.'

"We went into the little back parlour, and there I told him all about them, and he wrote down their direction in his memorandum book, and how glad was I to hear him say he would go and see what he could do for Mr. Lytham.

"I found afterwards he had been a friend of Mr. Maynard, Mrs. Lytham's father, had attended her mother, and, indeed, all the family for years, and received what now would have been a fortune to her, poor thing—he was a kind man, for many in his situation would have thought no more about their patients, when they could no longer afford to pay them. Like as it was with poor Miss Seymour, however, it was too late for the doctor to do any good with the patient, but his visit did do good for Mrs. Lytham and her children—for, in the first place, his plain speaking, and the tale he told my lady of her governess's distress, had the effect of getting her a better salary ; and when Mr. Lytham died, the doctor exerted himself so among those who had known Mr. Maynard in his prosperity, that a sum was raised sufficient not only to pay all the expenses of the funeral, but to place the widow in a respectable house, where she opened a school ; and the last time I saw her, when I quitted London to come to your mamma, she was as comfortably situated as could be, as she said, after having lost him for whose sake she had borne all her troubles and toils, and changes of fortune with cheerfulness. Poor dear lady, if ever a wife was devoted to a husband, she was. And here, dear Bessie, ended my acquaintance with the governesses ; and you will allow, I am sure, that I have reason to say, that I hope and pray that I may never live to see you in that ill-used class."

"And yet all are not Lady Springtowns," thought Bess. "Surely there must be some, I hope many, among the titled and wealthy, who can appreciate the merits and sympathise with the feelings of those who fill such an important station."

Alas ! Bess Leslie knew little of the world.

CHAPTER VII.

They say that later years
Will sometimes change a parent's hope for bitter grief and tears.
But *thou*, so innocent ! canst thou be aught but what thou art,
And all this bloom of feeling with the bloom of face depart ?
Canst thou this tabernacle fair, where God reigns bright within,
Profane, like Judah's children, with the pagan rites of sin ?—Anon

RS. LESLIE was now comfortably settled in a pretty unpretending cottage at Highgate, which was as near London as was consistent with her love of the green fields and the fresh air, and near enough, too, she hoped, to satisfy her brother and Lady Jane, who, with their protege, Bell, were yet on the wing from watering-place to watering-place, passing occasionally a week or two at Bevington Hall, but always so immersed in pleasure that Bell could, as she declared, scarcely snatch time to reply to her sister's letters. The gentle hint, however, which Bess had thought it her duty to give her sister respecting the Marquis of Ledbury, seemed to have taken due effect, for his name never now occurred in their correspondence, though in most of her letters Bell still betrayed her prevailing foible, vanity, to be as predominant as ever, recording the triumphs of her beauty, the splendour of her dresses, and the compliments that were paid her, with a zest and minuteness of detail, that to any one else would have appeared insufferably egotistical ; and even to Bess, partial and affectionate as she was to her sister, was often so offensive as to raise a burning blush in her cheek, and induce her to throw aside the letter with a sigh.

"And yet she is so good-hearted," she would say to herself, "so kind and affectionate, and so clever, that if she were away from the frivolous society that fosters this (her only) fault, she would soon learn to see it in its proper light, and become all we could wish her."

The necessity of keeping these letters from her mother was a most painful circumstance attendant upon their receipt; but Bess could not bring herself to inflict the pain she knew they would give to her plain, right-minded and unassuming parent. She knew the evil was one that was beyond Mrs. Leslie's power to cure, and she feared that even the reproofs that they would not fail to draw forth from the latter might do more mischief than good, by rendering Bell more cautious in her communications, without lessening the evil. It was, perhaps, an unfortunate circumstance that Bess's characteristic diffidence had always induced her to consider herself as inferior to her sister, not only in beauty but in intellect. Bell certainly possessed a shrewdness and quickness in comprehension that was superior, if it could be properly called superiority, to her more calmly judging and reflective sister. She had also striking decision of manner, assumption it might be called by the impartial and unprejudiced observer, but be it what it might, it had succeeded in fixing in Bess's mind a habit of deference to Bell, that even now restrained her from the full expression of her feelings, and led her to put the most favourable construction possible on her conduct. A slight hint, however, that her letters were not such as were likely to please her mother was taken by Bell, and the answer to her sister was written in a very different style. She was now, according to her account, all impatient to see her dear mother and sister, whose society was, she said, infinitely preferable to all the heartless, insincere pleasures of the gay world. In a fortnight from that time, she hoped to enjoy this anxiously longed-for happiness, and till then, she assured her dear mother she should count every hour with impatience.

Bess placed the letter in her mother's hand, without a word of comment, and she sighed, unconsciously, as she beheld the flush of pleasure that animated the countenance, and sparkled in the eyes of the gratified and affectionate parent. That letter had lowered her sister more in Bess's estimation than all the previous levity, frivolity and vanity which had been so conspicuous in Bell's former epistles, for she felt that it was artful, hollow, and insincere. In one, written but a week or two previous, Bell had expressed her surprise how her sister could exist in such a seclusion as the latter had described her mother's residence.

"I would as soon be out of the world at once, dear Bess," she had written in that letter, "as lead such a humdrum life. Society—company, if you will have it, is as necessary to me as the air I breathe. Do not, for goodness' sake, frighten me with the prospect of having nothing to waste my glances upon, when I come to see you, but flowers and fine prospects. I confess to you, that the garland of ful, blown carnations, scented *a la nature* which has just been sent home from Madame Latour's, and which I am to wear to-night at the Rooms, has infinitely more charms to me than all the flowers in your garden; and that the finest prospect in the world, to my sight, is a crowded ball-room, especially when there are more beaux than belles present, and I am well satisfied that I outshine all of them. No, no, Bess, no retirement for me. I was never made to blossom in the shade, or waste my sweetness on the desert air. One, week such as you describe your life to be might be borne, because I shall have so much to do when we meet—but longer than that—oh, *mon dieu*—the very thought of family parties gives me the horrors. I tell you beforehand, dear Bess, if you expect me to stay with you beyond the time that our mutual confidences will be exhausted, you must contrive some scheme for amusement—but, *entre nous*—I do not expect that Lady Jane will part with me for more than a few days, though I am very well pleased to think that when the season actually commences, we shall be within a reasonable distance of each other. I do not understand exactly what my aunt's plans are respecting you. Some time ago, you know, she talked of bringing us both together; but after reading one or two of your letters to me——She is much too curious and abitrary on this point, I must say—I mean in opening all letters addressed to me—apropos, thereby hangs a tale, which you shall hear the first opportunity, even at the risk of making you prim up your mouth and look grave; but as I was saying, since she has read your sentimental descriptions of the happiness you enjoy in your rural retirement, I suspect she begins to think that it would be a thousand pities to disturb it. Give me credit for candour, dear Bess. I do acknowledge and confess that I should not be *very* inconsolable, if you were to continue in your present retirement for a year or two, that is to say, until I have achieved that glorious end to which all my aunt's thoughts and wishes are directed —that is to say, I don't want you to 'come out until I have made sure of the brilliant match which Lady Jane believes must reward my personal qualifications, and the *pose* I am enabled to take in society as the co-heiress of Matthew Bevington, Esquire. The 'Twin Roses of Arundale,' by which pretty sentimental title my aunt is still very desirous we should be distinguished, may *divide* attention and admiration too much for me, who am ambitious of reigning alone. Seriously—and I don't mean it in the way of compliment to you, *ma chère*—I shall tremble for my empire, if you are to be brought forward at the same time as I am. As yet I have had every reason to be satisfied with myself, and I often read in my aunt's complacent looks that, as yet, she dreads no rival near the throne, in all our widely-extended circle of acquaintances; but when I think of our juxta-position, Bess, (as my uncle would say) I own I sometimes feel very aguish, and secretly breathe a wish that you may still continue to bloom and blossom in the rural shades of your cottage residence. I am sadly afraid, however, both for your sake and mine—that is, if you are sincere—that there will be a formidable opposition raised to this, however, in the person of my uncle, who, when thoroughly determined on any point, is, as Lady Jane says, the most obstinate, impracticable man in the world—which, between ourselves, means that in one, perhaps, out of one hundred cases in which Lady Jane and he differ, she fails in getting her own way. Now it strikes me very forcibly, that this will prove a case in point—that is to say, I am *afraid*—yes, it's the truth, Bess—I am actually afraid that my dear, good, obstinate uncle will be unconvinceable of the propriety of bringing his niece, Bell, out without his niece, Bess, seeing especially that the last mentioned is decidedly his favourite. Well, I must submit to my fate, if it is so; but I give you warning, I shall make a hard struggle to outshine you, if I can. We come to town—as far as Lady Jane's resolutions and intentions are to be depended upon—which, by-the-bye, is about as much as the gilded vane that is now glittering in my sight from the steeple of the church—the middle of next month. One week, one little week, Bess. I have let the secret out, though I did not intend it. Yes—one week is to be devoted to mamma—and then, one of the Twin Roses, if not both, will be launched out into the full stream. Not very appropriate, you will say—Roses swimming— Well, then, my dear, they, or it, as the case may be, will be seen expanding their beauties in the full sunshine of fashion."

Bess re-read this letter, and then she returned to the perusal of the more recent one which had been evidently written by Bell for her mother's satisfaction.

"How can I ever trust in one who can with such seeming sincerity assume such opposite characters?" thought Bess. "But which is the true one?"

Alas! there needed very little reflection to assure her that the former one spoke her sister's real sentiments. Had not Bess thought and judged with partiality, she would have felt convinced that Bell's letter was but a feeble transcript of the weakness, vanity and frivolity that directed all her actions, and clouded all the better parts of her natural disposition.

"Here they are, at last, dear mamma," exclaimed Bess, springing from the table at which she was drawing from memory the old Rectory House at Arundale to the window, as the cracking of whips, and the unusual sound of carriage wheels were heard rattling round the limited circular road which swept the lawn in front of the cottage. In another minute she was in the porch, and before she had time to recollect Lady Jone's oft-repeated reprehensions of any display of natural feelings, had clasped Bell in her arms, and with a, voice faltering with emotion, welcomed, her *home*.

"Oh, my dear Bell," she added "mamma will be so rejoiced—come to her she——"

But Bell's significant look, and the manner in which she gently and gracefully withdrew herself from her sister's warm embrace, reminded the latter of the error she had committed, while it heightened to painfulness the crimson blushes which had been kindled by pleasure in her fair cheeks. Lady Jane, however, was at this moment more engaged in scanning Bess's person than criticising her manners. The tranquil life she had led for some months past—early hours, a regular mode of living and freedom from all disquietude, had indeed wonderfully improved Bess's appearance. The traces, indeed, of grief for the loss of her father might still be discovered in her softened voice and subdued manner, except when, as at the present moment, she was temporarily excited; but still the afflicting remembrance of that sad event had yielded, as grief always does in young minds, to time, and, in Bess's case, the consolatory reflection that only for a comparatively short period was she separated from her beloved and exemplary parent; and neither pale cheeks, nor the dimmed lustre of those sparkling eyes now betrayed the ravages of the sorrow with which she had mourned the loss of her father. It would be too much, perhaps, to say that Lady Jane felt mortified at the comparison she was making "in her mind's eye" between the sisters; but, certainly, she was compelled, secretly, to acknowledge that whatever advantage her protege, Bell, had gained in point of, as her ladyship would have herself expressed it, *les graces de maniere et tournure*, however fascinating and irresistible might be the *stamp of fashion* she vaunted so much as having been acquired by her niece's late associations, there was a freshness in the bloom of her sister rose—a simple elegance in her form and manner that was very captivating. Bell was a hot-house plant, forced prematurely into the very perfection of splendour—but exhibiting but too evident tokens of fragility. Bess, a simple flower, nursed with the wholesome dews of heaven, and deriving strength and beauty from its native soil. The sisters were now just turned sixteen, and, though twins, which is generally supposed to deteriorate their growth, had reached the full standard in height that is considered desirable for females. Bell, however, from being rather slighter than her sister, would, apart from her, perhaps, been pronounced the taller of the two, but in reality there was not a hair's-breadth between. Exquisitely formed, and graceful in every step and motion they both were. Their eyes of the same deep blue, shaded with long, dark eye-lashes, which, unless fully raised, gave the brilliant orbs the hue of black. Both could boast skins of such transparent fairness, that the hackneyed comparison of the lily and the rose would have fallen short of depicting its purity and brilliancy. Despite of the striking similarity in their classically beautiful features, a critical observer must have acknowledged that Bell's were the most regular and faultless, though this was, perhaps, more than compensated for by the sweet, ingenuous expression of Bess's countenance. It was not that Bell's also was not a smiling face—on the contrary, she smiled, perhaps, oftener, or rather more constantly than her sister—but the expression was not so heartfelt. It seemed confined to the lips alone, or the dimples which it brought into existence; while Bess's whole countenance seemed to light up with pleasureable emotion, and it might be said her very eyes appeared to laugh in sympathy. Both sisters possessed in perfection that most beautiful ornament of woman—a luxuriant head of glossy hair

but at present it depended on the taste of the beholder which was most to be admired, Bess's auburn ringlets hanging below her ivory shoulders in the unstudied negligence of nature, or Bell's, a shade or two darker, approximating to chestnut, but plaited, braided and arranged with the utmost attention to becomingness of effect and fashion. To this array of personal beauties, so equally balanced, it may be added that Bell, though she acknowledged her sister's foot and ancle to be faultless in their shape and proportions, piqued herself not a little in the fact that her slipper was required to be a degree smaller than Bessie's—an advantage, however, which the partisans of the latter considered more than compensated by the circumstance that Bell's hands and arms, white and small, and rounded as they were, became mere common-place, everyday sort of hands and arms when compared with the polished ivory ones of Bess, which, but for the rose-tinted palms, might have been taken for the *chef d'œuvres* of a sculptor. Beautiful, however, exceedingly beautiful were both sisters; and to the eye of the common observer it would, perhaps, have been difficult to say to which the palm of beauty should be given.

The naturally kind, affectionate disposition of Bell broke, for once, through all the restraints which Lady Jane's precepts and example had enforced. The sight of her mother, pale and agitated—the widow's sombre dress, so forcibly reminding the too-thoughtless girl of her irreparable loss, triumphed over all artificial forms—and for some minutes she sobbed on her mother's neck an irrepressible sorrow and regret, while Mrs. Leslie, in broken accents, could only murmur—" My dear, dear child! Thank God, at last we meet;" and Bess, holding her sister's hand and pressing it to her lips, and then to her heart, gave free vent to her tears, which had their source almost equally in joy as grief.

"Bell, my love," said Lady Jane, in her usual calm, unmoved tone, "this is very wrong, very foolish of you, indeed. I was in hopes that you had acquired more self-control. Miss Leslie, excuse my saying, that from your avowed devotion to your mamma, and your *superior* understanding, I expected you had by this time subdued these violent and unavailing regrets. Death is a debt which, sooner or later, all must pay; and our regard and duty for the living, should teach us the folly of inordinate grief. No one, I am sure, could be more sincerely sorry for the irreparable loss you have sustained than

myself. It was, indeed, my dear Mrs. Leslie, quite a shock to both Mr. Bevington and I, for when we last saw poor Mr. Leslie, neither of us had the slightest idea of his being so near the termination of his valuable life; and he was in the prime of life, too, poor dear creature—not more, I suppose, than forty-five or six, was he, Mrs. Leslie?"

Mrs. Leslie tried to reply, but sobs choked her voice, while Bess trembled, as much from indignation at the total want of proper feeling which Lady Jane's manner betrayed, even the more than common-place observations to which she had given utterance, as sorrow for her mother, whose acquired calmness and equanimity were thus in a moment destroyed by her relative's ill-judged and ill-timed attempt at consolation.

Lady Jane's attention, however, was already so completely withdrawn from the subject which had seemed but a moment before to occupy all her thoughts, that she did not require an answer to her question. "You have chosen a very pretty little box, here, my dear Mrs. Leslie," she observed, glancing her eyes around; "rather of the smallest, though, this apartment. It would be a great improvement if you could throw the two rooms into one, occasionally, by means of folding doors, which is generally the case, I think, in houses of this description."

Mrs. Leslie observed, in a low tone, that she considered the room was large enough for her occupation, adding, "that except on occasions like the present, it was not probable that she should have guests to entertain, and therefore——"

"Why, certainly, as you say," returned her ladyship, quickly; "as there will be only yourself, when Miss Leslie leaves you, and as you are resolved not to enter into society, it would be scarcely worth while to make any alterations."

Poor Bess—the look which she exchanged with her mother spoke volumes on both sides. She waited a moment to see whether her mother would speak, and then seeing that the latter could not apparently get courage, or command her voice to do so, she observed, "that she hoped it would be a long time before she should leave her mother."

Lady Jane opened her large unmeaning grey eyes to their fullest extent, in apparent surprise at this remark.

"I thought, Miss Leslie," she observed, "that it was fully understood by both you and your mamma that it was intended by Mr. Bevington that you were to be placed under my care, and introduced into society, with the same advantages as your sister. If, indeed, you have formed plans of your own and mean to decline——"

"Oh, no, madam," interrupted Mrs. Leslie, evidently alarmed at the resentment which her ladyship's manner betrayed. "Oh, no, Bess would not—does not presume to form any plans which are not honoured by your approbation."

"My approbation has very little to do with it, madam, I assure you," returned Lady Jane, with an equivocal glance at her favourite niece, Bell, who had left her mother's side, and with an air of languor and indifference thrown herself on a sofa, and seemed totally occupied in caressing a pet poodle dog, which was Lady Jane's constant companion, and which gratefully returned the notice bestowed upon it by keeping up a succession of sharp barks and snarls, not a little annoying to the nerves of an invalid like Mrs. Leslie. The latter, however, saw that Bell was not so entirely occupied by her play-fellow as not to attend to what was passing, though the significant compression of her lips with which she replied to her aunt's look was equally unintelligible to both Mrs. Leslie and Bess.

"I assure——" recommenced Lady Jane, in her usual monotonous, unimpassioned tone. "I do assure you, my dear Mrs. Leslie, that if it depended upon me, I should be inclined to leave Miss Leslie to the full enjoyment of the obscurity which she evidently considers so much more desirable than the brilliant destiny which Mr. Bevington's partiality has marked out for her. You are well aware, however, I dare say, that your brother is not accustomed to have his will disputed, and it is in obedience to that, and not my own inclinations, I candidly confess, that I undertook to announce to you his intention that Miss Leslie should take up her residence with us, at once."

Had Lady Jane, or her protege, either of them, spoken their full sentiments they would have avowed that this resolution of Mr. Bevington's was quite as unwelcome to them as it could possibly be to either Bess or her mother, but, although her ladyship felt a secret uneasiness at the prospect of Bess more than sharing the admiration which had been, hitherto, exclusively bestowed on her more favoured niece, her pride and consequence were piqued at the former's presuming to have an opinion of her own, and daring to avow that she considered anything preferable to her ladyship's patronage. On Mrs. Leslie's part, sad experience had convinced her how dangerous it was to oppose her brother's wishes, to dare, in fact, to have an opinion contrary to his on such a subject. Already, in imagination, she beheld Bess deserted and discarded by him, and she, herself, too—on her would, perhaps, be visited her daughter's disobedience. The motive, amiable as it was, would, she knew, weigh nothing in his estimation against the crime of daring to judge for herself where he had already decided, and all the consequences rushed at once into her mind which would result from his anger. Subduing, therefore, every feeling of repugnance to the parting with her beloved and affectionate child, Mrs. Leslie at once declared her entire deference to her brother's will, adding, "that she would undertake to answer also for Bess's cheerful compliance."

"And, after all, you know, dear Bessie," she observed, "the separation, for a time at least, will be only nominal; you will be within a short distance of me, and my brother and Lady Jane will, I am sure, allow you to devote all your disengaged hours to your mother. Besides, in a very little time I shall get accustomed to this place, and shall find many new pleasures and occupations."

Bess saw how deeply her mother was interested in reconciling her, at least in appearance, to this painful separation, and though her heart sunk at the thoughts of leaving her kind, affectionate parent to utter solitude, she tried to emulate her fortitude and affect a resignation to her uncle's will that she was far from feeling. For the remainder of that evening almost the sole topic of conversation was the splendid entertainments by which Lady Jane intended to introduce her nieces into the world of fashion, in which she predicted they would be the brightest stars that had for many seasons shone in that horizon. The elegance of the new carriage-horses, liveries, &c., which were already in preparation, and were to be expressly devoted to their accommodation—the splendid suite of rooms, which were nearly completed at the town residence of Mr. Bevington—the dresses—the jewels—all the appointments for which Mr. Bevington had given her *carte blanche* as to expense—these, and similar discussions occupied and animated both Lady Jane and Bell into a good humour and high spirits, and seemed entirely to banish that *ennui*, which Bell had anticipated must be the attendant of even one evening family party. Mrs. Leslie constrained herself to appear pleased and interested; but Bess involuntarily sighed as she heard her sister expressing her delight that the period of throwing aside her odious mourning dresses was so near.

"I declare I quite hate to look at myself in the glass, since I have been in black," observed Bell, at the very moment that she was stealing—for, at least, the twentieth time, since she had entered that room—a self-satisfied glance at herself in the mirror, opposite to which she had contrived to seat herself. "I cannot think how it is, Bessie," she continued, "that black is so becoming to you, while I look absolutely frightful in it. And yet yours is much deeper and plainer than mine. You would look quite lovely in bugle trimmings—and that sleeve is very old-fashioned. What a wretch of a dress-maker you must employ—who would ever think of making such a sleeve now?—why it is, at least, six months behind the fashion. How could you put up with it?"

"I thought little of make or shape, or fashion, when this was made," said Bess,

sighing, and looking down at her black dress.

Bell coloured. She felt the reproof her sister's words conveyed, and as she glanced at her mother she read in her tearful eyes a still deeper reprehension of her thoughtlessness and levity.

"I am sorry—very sorry, my dear Bell," observed Mrs. Leslie, in a faltering voice, "that you should be so anxious to get rid of your mourning; but, certainly, if the heart does not feel its loss, it is hypocrisy to assume the outward semblance of woe."

"My dear Mrs. Leslie," observed Lady Jane, remonstratively, "that is really very harsh towards poor Bell, who, I am sure, does not deserve it. It is so natural to be glad to get rid of a dress which one is aware is unbecoming. Not that I think she does not look well in black—but then, you know, nobody now thinks of such long mournings. The court itself has set the fashion."

"Fashion?" repeated Mrs. Leslie, in a low voice, and with a deep sigh, "the word seems so inconsistent to me with—"

"My dear madam, forgive me," hastily interrupted Lady Jane, in a tone of decision, "living, as you have done, out of the world, as I may say, for so many years, you cannot judge of these matters. *We* are obliged to make many sacrifices that you would never think of, or comprehend the necessity; and now I never think of, or comprehend the necessity; and now I hope this subject is at an end, for it has made poor Bess look so miserable, it is quite distressing to *me*."

It was far more distressing, however, to Bess, to find that it would be expected of her that she should so soon lay aside the outward tribute of regret and respect for her father; but it was evident Lady Jane would brook no contradiction, either on this or any other subject; and in pursuance of the system which she saw her mother was determined to adopt, of sacrificing all her own feelings and inclinations, rather than give the imperious lady offence, the remonstrance Bess was about to utter was stifled on her lips. This, however, serious as it appeared in her eyes, was less painful than the discovery which immediately followed. Lady Jane's visit, so long expected and looked forward to by both Mrs. Leslie and Bess, was to be terminated the very next day; and thus the poor desolate widow was to be not only defrauded of the long-promised indulgence of Bell's society, but without any previous warning to give her, as she said, time to accustom herself to the thought—to prepare herself for giving up her last treasure, Bess, the kind, affectionate girl, whose attention and soothing had so long been her only consolation. But Lady Jane was already tired of what she called the dull monotony of her sister-in-law's conversation and household, and though she had originally intended to pass a week with her, before she retired for the night she announced the change in her plans.

"She had considered," she said, " that her presence at her town residence would expedite the alterations and improvements that were making there, and then, too, previous to her throwing open her house for the reception of company, there would be so much time gained for the dress-maker and other tradespeople to attend the young ladies."

This was, of course, a quite convincing reason. Mrs. Leslie bowed in silent acquiescence, and Bess feigned an excuse for suddenly quitting the room, that she might give vent in private to her overwhelming sorrow at the approaching separation.

CHAPTER VIII.

There is an absent one, with whose dear name
All happy memories of the past are twined.

"Good angels ! guard her with your tenderest care ;
Fence her from this rough world—she ill can bear
To have her gentle form hurt by too rude an air !"

MONTH after the event which had left Mrs. Leslie's house desolate, the mother's pride and maternal affection were gratified by the elaborate description, which occupied nearly half a column in the most fashionable morning papers of the time, of the dress, equipage, jewels, &c., of the two Miss Leslies, co-heiresses of Sir Matthew Bevington—her brother had been raised to the dignity of a baronet—who were presented at the drawing-room of St. James's, held on occasion of the queen's birthday, by their aunt, Lady Jane Bevington. Nothing, it was said, could exceed the surpassing beauty, grace and elegance of the 'Twin Roses,' while their dresses were described as being distinguished alike for richness, novelty and taste.

Unsophisticated and ignorant of the petty stratagems employed by those who would fain acquire distinction, in what Lady Jane so emphatically called the fashionable world, Mrs. Leslie imagined all this was a spontaneous tribute to the beauty and attractions of her daughters. How could she imagine that the paragraph was the carefully constructed product of Lady Jane's own pen, paid for, and no doubt regarded by those who were *au fait* to such affairs, as a mere advertisement. To the fond and now ambitious mother, however, it acted as a cordial that revived her drooping spirits, and though it could not supply the loss of her children, induced her to bear the deprivation without murmuring.

And what felt the twins themselves under these circumstances ? It is not in human nature for a young and beautiful girl to be insensible to the homage paid to her charms, or to view with indifference the advantages of dress and ornament. Bess could not but acknowledge to herself that the figure her glass reflected, arrayed in white satin silver and blonde trimmings, looked much more attractive than it had done in black bombazine and crape ; nor could she deny that her glossy hair braided with the rich and chaste pearls which her uncle had presented her with, looked at least *as well* as when hanging uncoufined in its natural ringlets, "in most admired disorder." But, though Bessie's eyes sparkled with pleasure and animation, they bore no comparison with the exultation, the gratified consciousness of her own superiority, which gave tenfold lustre to Bell's beauty, and but added grace and elegance to her symmetrical form. Bess, had she been as vain as she was decidedly the reverse, would have been compelled to acknowledge that she was completely outshone by her sister's brilliant appearance ; but fortunately for Bessie's peace, this conviction gave her not a moment's uneasiness. Not even Lady Jane's exulting remarks upon Bell's manifest superiority, could excite a single unpleasant thought in her bosom, or ruffle, for an instant, the calm serenity of Bessie's lovely countenance.

"The girl is absolutely a stoic or a fool," observed Lady Jane to her intimate friend and toady, Miss Moulsey. "Could any one but herself keep her temper, and see herself so completely cut out?"

"Perhaps she don't see it, your ladyship," replied Miss Moulsey. "It was quite plain that she did not comprehend the difference between her pearls and the dear Bell's diamonds. Any one but herself would have known that there was no comparison to be drawn between them, and yet she looked as delighted as——"

"I don't know—I rather suspect that was art, not folly," interrupted Lady Jane. "They were her uncle's present, you know, and it is her cue, I observe, to lay siege to her uncle."

"Dear me, is it possible? Well, I declare, your ladyship is so penetrating," exclaimed Miss Moulsey, "you see through every thing in a moment, while my poor stupid head is wool gathering, and sees nothing. She must be shockingly artful, though, for such a very young girl; but I suppose she has been tutored on the subject. It is a pity, though, that Sir Matthew is not aware of her real character, for I do really think that he shows great preference to her, over our dear, ingenuous, open-hearted Bell."

Lady Jane was silent. Probably her conscience reproached her in sanctioning these unjust remarks, for she was well aware that many artifices had with her concurrence been practised by the *ingenuous* Bell to conciliate her uncle, and turn towards herself the current of favour which had, ever since the introduction of the sisters, decidedly set towards Bess on the part of Sir Matthew.

Miss Moulsey, however, either did not or would not understand the motive of Lady Jane's silence, and, before many hours had passed, the tale had been whispered in the ears of half Lany Jane Bevington's acquaintances—"How unhappily that dear lady was living with Sir Matthew, in consequence of the influence his artful niece, Miss Bess Leslie, had acquired over him, and which she turned to the basest purposes, creating differences between Sir Matthew and his lady, and secretly undermining her sister, in the hope of getting the greater part of his fortune."

"Shocking—oh, dreadful—quite unnatural—and so young, too, and apparently so artless and innocent," were the exclamations which this confidential communication elicited. But none thought of doubting the truth of it—none offered a word in defence of the innocent girl thus vilely aspersed. It might be supposed that the implicit belief which was accorded to Miss Moulsey's representations had the effect of rendering Bessie's reception, in the circle of her aunt's acquaintance, somewhat less warm than that of the sister towards whom, according to the representations, she was acting so unfairly. But how stood the fact? Bess, who had hitherto been rather thrown into the shade by the superior polish and brilliancy her sister had acquired, as much from natural confidence as greater intercourse with the world, and her aunt's solicitous instructions—Bess, all at once, found herself the object of universal attraction and attention.

The whisper had circulated that she was Sir Matthew's decided favourite, in opposition to Lady Jane, who had from the first adopted Bell as hers; and from its being merely hinted that Sir Matthew's preference was likely to materially advance *Miss Leslie's* future prospects, the report gradually grew into a positive assertion that the whole of Sir Matthew's fortune would be Miss Leslie's, and that the younger twin would have no provision but that which Lady Jane's separate fortune would enable her to bestow upon her favourite, and which was, in comparison with Sir Matthew's wealth, a mere trifle.

But to return to the birthday, and that which, according to the fashionable world, is to be considered as the *debut* of the "Twin Roses of Arundale"—their introduction to royalty. Nothing could exceed the gracious reception they met with, or the universal buzz of admiration which their appearance excited. Wherever they moved a crowd of gentlemen attended their steps, and amidst the congratulations which were showered upon Lady Jane, as soon as she retired with her nieces from the circle, nothing was heard on all sides but importunate petitions for introduction to the Twin Roses.

Bell's eye glistened with almost supernatural brilliancy. It was a scene of triumph and gratified vanity which she could have wished prolonged for ever; but Lady Jane was becoming fatigued. So many hours' excitement had been too much for her, and she began to feel that she required rest and refreshment. Bess was the first to discover this, and with her usual thoughtfulness and attention to the comforts of others, rather than her own gratification, she whispered to her sister—

"I hope it will not be long, Bell, before the carriage is announced—Lady Jane looks dreadfully pale. I was afraid, before we came, that she was not well enough to bear this bustle, and——"

"Don't try to persuade her that she is ill," returned Bell, hastily, "or we shall have a scene. And it will be no use, either," she added, "for we cannot get away till our turn comes."

Bess did not reply, but she pressed up closer to her aunt, and affectionately drew the arm of the latter through hers, observing, with a smile,—

"You will not be sorry, dear aunt, any more than myself, I suspect, to exchange this crowd, and glitter, and bustle, for our own quiet home."

"So soon!" exclaimed a gentleman, who at this moment approached them, and who had evidently only caught the concluding words of the sentence Bess had uttered. "Oh, no, surely Lady Jane would not have the cruelty so soon to withdraw our splendid luminary, and leave us in gloom and darkness."

Bess turned away her blushing face from the dauntless gaze of the speaker, and pressed still nearer to her aunt, without attempting to utter any reply to his rhodomontade, which to her bore rather the appearance of ridicule than compliment. Bell, who was standing at a little distance from her friends, was temporarily separated from them by a group of gentleman who had taken advantage of, in some respects, a very slight acquaintance with Lady Jane Bevington to get introduced to the new beauty, and were now vying with each other in administering to her vanity. It seemed, however, that the voice of the gentleman who had so hyperbolically addressed Lady Jane, or rather, through her, her niece Bess, had reached Bell's ear, and at once dissipated her attention to, and satisfaction at, the compliments she was receiving from the circle who was surrounding her; for, abruptly breaking from them, she returned to the side of her aunt, her colour heightened, and her sparkling eyes assuming a still deeper lustre as they glanced, with a pretty assumed look of disdain, at the stranger, who starting back with a theatrical air and accent, exclaimed—

"Good heavens, what a miracle! Are there two suns in one firmament?"

"Oh, I had forgotten, my lord," interposed Lady Jane. "You have not before seen my twin rose. Miss Leslie—the Marquis of Ledbury."

Bess curtsied coldly in return to the studied bow of the marquis. The sight of him had at once confirmed, or rather strengthened the prejudice she had felt against him from the first introduction of his name in her sister's letters. The Marquis of Ledbury, however, was not one to be daunted or abashed by the coldness, reserve, and hauteur which Bess adopted towards him. On the contrary, his tone and manner became more familiar and assured, in proportion as she receded from his advances, and Bess with sorrow and indignation saw that not only her sister, but Lady Jane herself, encouraged, and even seemed to consider his notice as an honour and distinction. But, in this respect, Bess soon discovered that her aunt and sister were not singular. Wherever the Marquis turned his eyes, it appeared they were greeted with the sweetest smiles. None, not even the highest born, or most gifted by Nature and fortune, shrank from him, or attempted to repress his self-confidence and assurance. No, the Marquis of Ledbury was the fashion, and it would have been death to the pretensions of any of those who moved within the charmed circle of which he was so conspicuous a member, to have been unnoticed or disregarded by him, who, in the eyes of the pure, unsophisticated Bess Leslie, appeared a wretch, whom every modest and right-thinking female should avoid and discountenance.

And what said or thought the gay and giddy Bell?

Bess could only read her sister's countenance, but those flushed cheeks, those dazzlingly bright eyes, the tremulous accents, the flutter which had taken place of her former easy self-possession, all spoke volumes even to the unsuspecting and inexperienced Bess Leslie.

And what, after all, was the bewitching charm which apparently rendered the Marquis of Ledbury irresistible to all but her?

"He is certainly neither very young, nor very handsome," thought Bess, as she stole a scrutinising glance of him, while gaily conversing with Lady Jane.

Except a pair of brilliant black eyes, teeth unexceptionably white and regular, and what the ladies pronounced splendid dark whiskers, there was nothing particularly striking in the face of the marquis. His complexion was swarthy, his forehead low and narrow, and his chin so prominent as to be quite disproportioned to the other features, which were of the most commonplace order. His smile, however, was considered by his admirers irresistibly fascinating, and his address and manner, when he chose it to be so, most graceful, polished, and insinuating. In person he was manly and elegant, though even in that respect there was nothing, as Bess thought, very strikingly superior to the generality of his class. There were many, indeed, at that moment present (and Bess thought so, as she timidly glanced around her) who had decidedly the advantage over the Marquis of Ledbury in personal qualifications. Many whose features were not only handsomer, but irradiated with an intelligence and feeling to which his were utter strangers. And yet, among all, it might have been questioned whether there was one who could have successfully competed with the marquis, where the latter chose to select any lady as the especial object of his attention. What, then, was the secret magic which rendered him so irresistible? What the infatuation which made the lovely, the young, the modest, the delicate, all anxious rivals for the honour—the dishonour, in Bessie's simple estimation—of a smile, a look, a word of compliment, from a man who ought to have been banished from the society of all who had any claims to modesty or delicacy? He was the fashion. It was the fashion to regard his notorious vices with a gentle smile of indulgence, as mere peccadilloes; his low-bred propensities, his street brawls, his encouragement and association with gamblers, prize-fighters, and horse-jockeys —his open violation of decency in his amours — the outrageous and extravagantly luxurious manner in which he maintained and paraded the unfortunate and short-lived objects of his transitory likings on the public eye—were all passed over as eccentricities. Mothers, who should have spurned him, contended and manœuvred for his society, and daughters, to whom his very breath was contamination, languished and smiled, and envied each other even the most temporary attention from the polluted idol of their worship. Even Lady Jane Bevington who, weak and frivolous as she was, on general matters connected with the delicacy of her sex was so rigidly punctilious and severe as to have acquired the designation of a prude—even she was conveniently blind and deaf to the dictates of prudence when it related to the Marquis of Ledbury, whose taste was unerring, his authority on all matters of *ton* unquestioned, and whose very nod could confer distinction, and fix the standard of those on whom it was bestowed. It might have been questioned whether Bell or her aunt felt most exultation when, on the announcement— "Sir Matthew Bevington's carriage stops the way," the marquis drew an arm of

each through his, and, followed by the downcast Bess, conducted them from the waiting-room. And not even here did the proud distinction end.

"May I intrude upon your ladyship to set me down ?" he demanded, when they were seated. "It would be positive misery to return, now that the brightest ornaments of the circle are withdrawn," he added, bowing to Lady Jane, but looking at Bell, as he threw himself into the corner of the carriage opposite to her.

Bell's eloquent eyes betrayed how highly she appreciated this compliment, and Lady Jane testified her satisfaction by saying, in a pretty affected tone—

"Oh, you flatterer ! Do you think we can possibly believe that you are indifferent to the bevy of bright beauties we have left behind ?"

"You have the very best security of my sincerity in my presence here," he replied, "for I assure your ladyship I am too idle ever to play the hypocrite, and, moreover, too much accustomed to follow the impulse of the moment, to put the slightest restraint on myself. I confess, however, that, in independent of my desire to prolong for a few short moments the inexpressible gratification of such society as the present, I was actuated a little by malice towards those who I saw were dying for the pleasure which my more fortunate stars have secured to me."

"Rather your assurance and impertinence," thought Bess, whose dislike to the intrusive and self-conceited marquis momentarily increased, and with it her anxiety for Bell, who made no effort to disguise the different light in which she regarded him. Most grateful, indeed, was the relief to Bess, when the carriage stopped at the door of the hotel at which the marquis resided; but here, another cause of vexation and mortification arose; for she learned that he was to form one of the party to the ball at the palace that night, and she heard, with an uneasiness she could not have disguised, had not her companions been too much occupied to attend to her, that Bell's hand for the first two dances was asked and secured by the marquis, who observed, that on this occasion he should certainly lay aside his customary idleness, which generally led him to be a mere spectator on such occasions.

"But it would be death to me," she heard him whisper to her sister, "to see any one in possession of that fair hand, and enjoying those smiles which I would give the world were they mine alone."

Scarcely had he left them before Lady Jane's triumph and gratification burst forth in the warmest congratulations to her favourite niece, and Bell received them, "nothing loath." On the contrary, she seemed to consider that she had achieved a most signal triumph in subjugating one who was notorious for more than indifference, for actual rudeness and inattention to what he classed as *marriageable* young ladies, of whom he avowed a perfect horror, and whose pretentions and attractions he treated with unsparing ridicule and contempt.

"It will be such an advantage to you, too, Miss Leslie," observed her ladyship, seeming for the first time to remember Bessie's presence; "as the sister of the Marchioness of Ledbury you cannot fail to secure a suitable alliance, and I shall have the pleasure of seeing——but, good heavens, what ails the girl? She is looking the image of misery and woe—tears, too—well, really, Miss Leslie, this is quite unaccountable. Do, pray, dry your eyes, child, and behave like a reasonable being, or people will be apt to think that you envy your sister."

"Envy?" repeated Bess, with emphasis; "oh, no, no, far from envying, I shudder at the thought that my sister should become the wife of that man."

"That man!" repeated Lady Jane indignantly; "do you know whom you are speaking of, Miss Leslie—that the person you designate so contemptuously is the heir to a dukedom—that he possesses already a princely fortune—and that the woman who becomes his wife will be the envy of her own sex, and——"

"If he could confer a diadem on the object of his choice," observed Bess, with spirit, "I should think her situation to be pitied, rather than envied, and I do hope—I pray that Bell will never suffer herself to be dazzled into an alliance with one who, if I had never heard his character, I should pronounce the last man in the world to be the voluntary choice of a delicate, right-thinking, and right-principled woman."

"Really, this is very extraordinary, and very insulting to me, Miss Leslie," returned Lady Jane, while Bell tittered contemptuously; "but you will also allow me to remark," continued her ladyship, "that I think your presumption in setting yourself up as a censor of one so much your superior as the Marquis of Ledbury——"

"Superior?" softly articulated Bess.

"Yes, superior," repeated Lady Jane, growing still more angry. "For, whatever your sentimental and high-flown notions may induce you to think of the matter, I fancy you will find few who will not acknowledge the superiority of a peer of the realm—the heir to one of the oldest as well as wealthiest houses in the united kingdom—to a poor, obscure curate's daughters, whose beauty and personal accomplishments are their only dower and title to distinction. But let me hear no more of this nonsense, I beg. It is fortunate that your sister has more sense than you, or I should bitterly repent having taken such a charge upon myself."

Bess was silenced but not convinced. It would have been difficult, indeed, to convince her that Bell's happiness could be secured by her being united to such a man as the Marquis of Ledbury; but the thoughts of the whole party were soon turned in another direction by Lady Jane's increased indisposition. She had struggled against it while there existed any excitement to her spirits, but that being over, she became completely exhausted, and when the carriage stopped was obliged to be lifted from it, and conveyed at once to her room.

For the first time, Bess gave her sister credit for extreme sensibility and kindheartedness, qualities in which, especially since she had been under the tuition of Lady Jane, the latter had often appeared extremely deficient. But now Bess herself could not be exceeded in tenderness and attention to the invalid. Bell's dress was hurried off, with a single glance at herself in the glass, and she was at her aunt's bedside with tears in her eyes, and grief and anxiety depicted in her features, almost as soon as Bess herself, though the latter had dispensed with the ceremony of going to her own dressing-room, and would, indeed, have forgotten the necessity of disencumbering herself of her stately robes, had she not been rather ungraciously reminded of it by the invalid herself, whose first words, after she was placed on a couch in her dressing-room, were—

"If you really wish to be of service, Miss Leslie, you will take off that dress. Satin and spangles will cut but a poor figure in a sick-room, besides the danger of spoiling it."

Bess had, therefore, instantly arrayed herself in a dressing-gown belonging to her ladyship, and when Bell with tearful eyes, and a haste which showed how deeply she was affected by her aunt's illness, entered the room, she found her sister already occupied in administering to Lady Jane such restoratives as her previous experience with her mother suggested would be proper.

"Oh, dear—dear aunt, are you so ill as to be obliged to go to bed?" was Bell's first

exclamation. "I thought—I was in hopes that when you had rested a little, and taken something, you would have been better. And you have such a horror, too, of being confined to bed. It is enough, I know, to make you ill."

Bess felt that the look of dissatisfaction with which this was uttered was levelled at her, but she was saved all attempt at vindication by mademoiselle, Lady Jane's attendant, who observed that she had never before seen her dear lady give up so, for both she and Mademoiselle Leslie had tried to persuade "miladi" to try to rest on the couch.

"I am very ill—much' worse than you think I am, Bell," observed the invalid, faintly. "I felt ill this morning, though I struggled against it on your account; but I found it impossible to continue the effort any longer."

Bell burst into a passionate fit of tears, and threw herself on the bed by the side of her aunt, as if overcome with grief; but from this she was roused by a message from Sir Matthew, who had just returned and heard of his lady's indisposition, and had sent to know whether he might be admitted to see her.

Bell quickly arose, and passing her arm through her sister's drew her with her into the adjoining dressing-room, and closed the door after her.

"Was there ever anything so provoking, so *mal-apropos* as this illness," she exclaimed, as soon as they were out of hearing. "My uncle will persuade her, I know, that she is ten times worse than even she fancies herself, and there will be an end to all hopes of the ball to-night."

Until that moment Bess had forgotten the engagement for the evening. The court ball, albeit of no little importance in the eyes of a lively young girl, who had never witnessed such a scene of splendour, had, in consequence of Lady Jane's illness, as completely vanished from her memory as if her going there had never been contemplated. Now, however, she comprehended in an instant the cause of her sister's extreme sorrow, which she had, in the innocence and unsuspiciousness of her own nature, attributed to the more amiable source of grief and anxiety for her aunt's illness.

Scarcely knowing what to say, unwilling to reprehend, and yet unable to dissemble her want of sympathy in this, to Bell, all-absorbing cause of grief, Bess could only after some moments of silence observe, that she was sorry to see her sister take such a disappointment to heart, adding, that if it should prove, as she feared, that Lady Jane's illness was of a serious nature, they should have much deeper cause for regret and sorrow than the mere loss of a few hours' amusement.

"Serious!" repeated Bell, with fury in her looks. "If you knew her as well as I do, her whims and affectations and caprices, you would think as I do, that there is nothing the matter with her but what she could easily shake off, if she would. But it seems as if fate itself were against me. This is the second time that I have been engaged to the Marquis of Ledbury, and have been compelled to disappoint him, though he is such an enthusiastic admirer of dancing, that——"

"If there were no other cause to regret than the breaking of that engagement," interrupted Bess, with energy, "I should, I confess, rejoice. Oh, Bell, can it be possible that you have forgotten the counsels and precepts of our dear parents——"

"Pshaw, you talk like an ignorant, inexperienced, romantic fool, Bess," exclaimed her sister, passionately. "No one but yourself but would say I should be mad to refuse such an offer. And, after all, depend upon it, the marquis is no worse than hundreds of others, only they are sly, while he scorns to play the hypocrite."

"I am very, very sorry to hear you say so, Bell," returned her sister, "and I should be still more sorry if I thought your assertion true; but, even if it were so, it would be better that he should be a hypocrite than that he should thus boldly and openly outrage decency. Oh, Bell, how miserable would my poor mother be, if she knew——"

"Don't tease me, Bess," interrupted Bell, petulantly. "It is quite enough, I think, to meet with such a disappointment, without being obliged to listen to such methodistical prosing. What is it to me what the Marquis of Ledbury has done? Besides, I don't believe half the stories that are told about him, and, even if they were true, that is no reason that I should not be very happy as his wife, if I were fortunate enough to be chosen; but it seems as if——"

Sir Matthew interrupted her by knocking at the dressing-room door. He came to say that he was fearful Lady Jane's illness was more serious than she was willing to allow, and that he should send for the family physician without delay.

Bell's tears broke out afresh, but her sister saw, not without pain and confusion, that she was artful enough to mislead Sir Matthew as to the cause of her grief, and he left the room in the full conviction that Bell was much more warm-hearted and attached to her aunt than he had previously thought her.

"I knew it would be so," exclaimed Bell, the moment he quitted the room. "One would think he delighted in seeing everybody miserable; but with his own will, I do believe he would keep the physician in constant attendance. By to-morrow I suppose we shall be having the knocker tied up, straw before the door, and nothing but long faces, and——"

"But this will not be unless it be necessary," interrupted Bess, angry and ashamed of her sister's selfishness.

Ere Bell could reply, the two girls were summoned to Lady Jane's bedside.

"I have been thinking, my dears," observed the invalid, "that it will be a serious disappointment if you should not attend the ball to-night, and I very much fear that it will be quite impossible I can accompany you."

"Oh, my dear aunt," exclaimed Bell,

bursting into a fresh paroxysm of tears, "do not talk of our disappointment. How trifling is that consideration compared to your illness. If I could but see you well again, I would not care for all the balls in the world."

"I know that, my love—I am quite sure of it," replied Lady Jane.

Bess turned away in silence, blushing at her sister's duplicity.

"I cannot expect, however, that Miss Leslie should feel equally indifferent to such a disappointment," continued Lady Jane, "and, therefore——"

Bess was about warmly to profess that it would be no disappointment at all to her, and to beg that her aunt would think no more about it; but she was prevented by a most significant gesture from her sister, imploring silence; and before she could recollect herself, or utter what was really dictated by her heart, Lady Jane proceeded to say that there would be no necessity for her nieces remaining at home, for she was very sure her friend Mrs. Balcombe would willingly act as *chaperone* to them.

"Oh, my dear aunt, I should never forgive myself, if I were to leave you and you were to be worse. No, no, indeed, you must not think of it—not, at least, until we have heard Dr. Burnett's opinion. I should be miserable, and fancy a thousand dreadful things, without I were assured there was no danger, and even then——"

"You are a dear good girl, I know, Bell," returned her aunt, "but, my dear child, we must sometimes sacrifice feelings to necessity. We must write to Mrs. Balcombe in time, for she is very ceremonious, you know, and if we put it off till the last moment she may plead some engagement. She cannot very well otherwise refuse me, because I once did a similar service for her, on the occasion of her daughter's *debut*—though I believe her rheumatism then, in reality, was that her diamonds were not forthcoming. She is, or rather was, a shocking gambler, and it was whispered that she had been obliged to raise a large sum of money on her jewels—so she had a very convenient fit of the rheumatism, and I went in her place."

And this is the woman, thought Bess, whom my aunt considers a fit person to entrust with the protection of her nieces, and such are the friendships of that world in which I am expected to find my happiness?

Bell's ready smile, however, proved in how different a light she viewed her aunt's observations; but it was very evident that she was impatient to make the trial at once, whether Mrs. Balcombe would accept the charge intended for her; and as Lady Jane remained silent, she quickly brought the subject forward, by observing—

"I think, aunt, you told me once that Mrs. Balcome is related to the Marquis of Ledbury?"

"Yes, my dear, they are second cousins, and that, by the bye, is another reason why I should wish you to accompany her. She is rather a favourite with the marquis. He likes those bold, free-spoken woman, though, for my part, she is quite a horror. However, I would have you, my dear, pay her great attention, for I can assure you her opinion is of great weight in a certain quarter. At the same time do not be afraid of her, Bell. She is very sarcastic, but the best of her is, she will give and take; and she will think all the better of you, if you can meet her at her own weapons ; for of all things in the world, I know she hates your namby-pampy misses, who seem afraid to open their lips, and have no opinion of their own. I need not, however, tell you all this, Bell, for you know her; and Miss Leslie will pardon me if I give her a gentle hint on the subject."

"I thank you for your intended kindness, my dear aunt," returned Bess, smiling, "but you must forgive my saying the lesson is useless. I shall not put Mrs. Balcombe's patience to the test on my account."

"What do you mean, Miss Leslie?" "What can you mean, Bessie?" were simultaneously uttered by the aunt and niece.

"Only that, with your permission, madam, I will remain with you this evening," returned Bess, "and, by so doing, at once gratify myself and remove all difficulty to Bell's perfect enjoyment, for she will, I know, give me credit for being a good nurse."

"But, my dear, I cannot think of your making so great a sacrifice on my account," observed Lady Jane, with more kindness of manner than she usually expressed towards her elder niece.

Bess, however, assured her, and with truth, that so far from considering it a sacrifice, it would be conferring a favour on her to allow her to stay at home.

"The fact, is, aunt," continued Bess, with her usual candour, "if I were ever so anxious to go, and your illness did not otherwise afford me a sufficient reason for staying at home, your description of Mrs. Balcombe is quite enough to frighten me out of all wish to be her companion ; for I am quite conscious I am one of the young woman who would be obnoxious. I do not think," and she laughed as she made the admission, "I do not think that I ever said a clever or satirical thing in my life."

"I deny that, Miss Leslie," observed Lady Jane, coldly, "at least, I have seen you look satirically, and what the eyes can express so forcibly, the lips must have power to utter, though motives of prudence, or some other feeling, may induce you to suppress the expression. However, I assure you, I am very sincerely sorry if anything I have said has induced you to form an unfavourable opinion of Mrs. Balcombe, from whom, I am sure, you may rely on meeting the most friendly consideration on my account, if not on your own. My advising your sister to cultivate her friendship is quite another thing. It related entirely to a matter in which you are not concerned."

Bessie's eyes filled with tears. Not concerned—was she not concerned in that which was to decide the happiness or misery of her dear sister's life? Lady Jane's cold and austere manner, however, awed her into silence, and Bell, who had been scarcely able to conceal her impatience to have the affair finally settled, now observed, rather petulantly,—

"Well, Bessie, you must make up your mind at once, whether you intend to go or not; for, as my aunt says, the communication to Mrs. Balcombe must not be delayed; and as it certainly will not be right or proper that we should both leave my aunt—for my own part, I am sure I should be much happier——"

Bess interrupted the absolute falsehood her sister was about to utter, by observing, quietly, "that she *had* all along made up her mind. With Lady Jane's permission, she would remain with her. She had only said what she did because she was not willing to assume the merit of making a sacrifice, when in fact she was only consulting her own inclinations."

"You are a very extraordinary girl, certainly, Miss Leslie," observed Lady Jane; but whether this was meant as commendation, or really expressed what it appeared, namely, that the latter was unable to comprehend her niece's motives, Bess did not trouble herself to understand.

A note was hastily written by Bell, for her aunt, to the intended lady-chaperon, and Bess looked even more grave than usual as she listened to the fulsome expressions of flattery towards Mrs. Balcombe with which her sister had thought proper to accompany her aunt's request. Could it be her own, unsophisticated, innocent

sister, thus transformed into a paltry, mean, equivocating time-server, glorying in her dexterity, and receiving, as applause due to merit, her aunt's smiling observations that "Mrs. Balcombe must be more than mortal, if she could resist such a missive as that."

"Miss Leslie is shocked at our insincerity, Bell," observed Lady Jane, laughing. "Ah, my dear, you will soon learn, as *we* have done, that it is impossible to get through the world without a little dexterous manœuvring. It is only the price we are obliged to pay for the accomplishment of our wishes."

"It is a very heavy price," replied Bess, with a deep sigh.

Lady Jane and her favourite niece exchanged glances, but they were evidently equally willing to let the subject drop.

Mrs. Balcombe returned a gracious answer to Lady Jane's request, and all Bell's fears and apprehensions being removed, it was with difficulty she could subdue her exuberant spirits, and appear properly anxious as to her aunt's situation. Lady Jane herself, indeed, seemed so fully to enter into Bell's feelings as at times almost to forget her own indisposition; and even Bess, when she saw her aunt sitting up in bed, giving directions, suggesting alterations and additions, and busying herself in the decorations of her favourite, as if her whole fortune depended on that night's appearance, began to think that her sister was a better judge than herself of Lady Jane's indisposition, and she felt that her respect for the latter did not increase, when, upon the arrival of Mrs. Balcombe, she again sank down upon her pillow, with every symptom of comple exhaustion, and in faint accents expressed her gratitude for her dear friend's kindness.

Mrs. Balcombe, a tall, masculine woman, with the eyes and forehead of a Juno or a Minerva, and the mouth and chin of a Hecate, received all these expressions as a mere matter of course, without either replying to, or attempting to stop them, and then looking at Bess, who indeed seemed from the first to excite considerable attention from her, she observed—

"How is it, Lady Jane, that this young lady does not go? It ought to be no trifling matter that should prevent her enjoying such a distinction as an invitation to a court-ball."

"Miss Leslie does not think my illness a trifling matter, madam," replied Lady Jane, evidently offended at the remark.

"Oh, I beg your pardon, it is on your account," returned Mrs. Balcombe.

"Well, I give Miss Leslie credit for a degree of fortitude and forbearance that I believe few of her sex and age could practise."

"I am fortunate then, it seems," replied Lady Jane, "for I assure you that it was with some difficulty I could persuade Bell to leave me."

Mrs. Balcombe uttered the word "Indeed!" accompanied with a look at Bell that spoke volumes; but, though Bess blushed for her sister, the latter appeared not in the slightest degree disconcerted.

"Well, Miss Leslie," demanded Lady Jane, when they were gone, "what do you think now of my friend, Mrs. Balcombe? Did she prove as formidable as you had pre-conceived her to be?"

"It would be presumption in me to judge from so short an interview, madam," returned Bess; "but, though I should certainly tremble to incur her censure, from the certainty that she would not spare the lash, yet——"

"You are right, neither to friends nor foes," observed Lady Jane, hastily.

"Still," continued Bess, "I should think she would be just, as well as severe; that is to say ——"

"That she complimented you, child, and therefore you think she must be a woman of great penetration," interrupted Lady Jane, with an ill-natured sneer.

"I could not take it as a compliment, aunt," returned Bess, with her usual candour, "because I felt there was no necessity for my exercising fortitude or forbearance, when I am happier with you than I should have been at the ball."

Lady Jane looked earnestly at her.

"Is this really from your heart, my dear?" she demanded, in a tone of kindness.

Bess looked, as she felt, surprised as well as hurt at this question.

"My dear aunt," she replied, "why should you doubt my sincerity? What possible motive could I have for affecting what I did not feel? You would not, I am sure, have been either surprised or vexed had I shown an anxiety to go."

"No, I should have considered it very natural that you should have done so, child," replied Lady Jane. "At your age, I am sure, I should have considered it the greatest misfortune that could have befallen me; and it is your strange indifference that puzzles me. I cannot help, I acknowledge, thinking that you must have some motive that I am not aware of."

Tears stood in Bessie's eyes. She felt that her aunt was incapable of appreciating her rightly; but she attempted no further vindication of herself than merely quietly observing—

"Indeed, madam, you wrong me. I told you the plain truth at first, that I should be happier at home with you, and contributing, as I hope I can do, to your comfort, than I should have been in the ball-room."

"After all," observed Lady Jane to Bell, on the following morning, "I suspect that your sister is not quite so stupid, or so indifferent to appearances, as she affects to be. I think I found out, last night, the secret of her readiness to give up the ball."

Bell looked surprised.

"And what was it then, aunt? I did not think she had any other reason than her good nature towards me—for certainly Bess is good-natured in the extreme; and she knew I should be miserable if you were left alone. I have known her many times to give up her own pleasure to gratify me."

"That may be, my love—I am not disposed to deny your sister's merits," returned Lady Jane; "but I confess, in this instance, I do not think she was quite so disinterested, for I contrived to draw from her an acknowledgment that she was conscious that your appearance quite eclipsed hers, and that diamonds were infinitely superior, in appearance as well as intrinsic value, to pearls.

"'Diamonds,' she said, very truly, 'give additional lustre to beauty, and set off the very plainest person, while pearls really require beauty in the wearer to make them ornamental.'

"'And yet I thought, my dear,' I observed, 'that you seemed quite delighted with your uncle's present.'

"'I should have been very ungrateful, dear aunt, if I had not been so,' she replied; 'and, indeed,' she added, smiling, 'though I dare say you will think me very vain, after what I have said, I must acknowledge the truth, I was very well satisfied with my own looks in my pearl ornaments, though, as I said before, generally speaking, their purity is very trying to the complexion, and they do not give that lustre and brilliancy to the eyes, or set off the features, like diamonds. The poet Thomson, you know, aunt, says—

"Beauty needs not the foreign aid of ornament,
But is when unadorn'd adorned the most."

But I am sure, if he had seen Bell this morning, before she was dressed, and afterwards glittering in her diamonds, he would have acknowledged that it is not always so, for I never saw her look so beautiful before.'

"I should think this all very pretty, my

dear Bell," continued Lady Jane, "and have considered it a proof of what you have always asserted, that your sister is totally destitute of vanity or envy, but I could not be mistaken as to her feelings, when she added, with a deep sigh, ' Bell always, in our childish plays, would assume the part of a fine lady, and I remember that once she made my dear father angry with her by saying that she felt convinced that she was born to be a duchess.'

" ' I hope it will prove a true prophecy, my dear,' I observed, but, so far from joining cordially in my wish, my dear Bell, as I might have expected from your representations of her character, your sister's gay spirits seemed all to vanish at the prospect of such a fortunate event. She sank into a deep silence, while I (to tease her) went on talking of the marquis's wealth, his beautiful seats, and so on, and at last I actually detected the tears stealing silently down her cheeks."

Bell could not cordially join in the laugh with which Lady Jane concluded, nor could she conscientiously encourage the conclusion to which Lady Jane had come, that envy was the source of her sister's feelings, although Bess and herself had had a more serious difference on the marquis's account than had ever happened between them from their birth.

Bell had returned from the ball, perfectly intoxicated with the admiration she had excited, and Bess had listened with patience, though not without secret sorrow and vexation of spirit, to her sister's repetitions of the compliments she had received, and the remarks that had reached her ear respecting her beauty, her grace, and the superior style of her dancing; but when Bell proceeded to relate with undisguised pleasure the Marquis of Ledbury's rapturous expressions, his undeviating attention, having scarcely quitted her side the whole evening, and to exult in the envy and malice which she said were depicted in the countenances of more than half of the ladies present, Bess could no longer keep silent. From the first moment she had beheld the marquis in her sister's company, a presentiment that he would be the cause of unhappiness to her had weighed on Bessie's spirits, and every word that Bell now uttered, every expression of his that she repeated, tended to confirm this impression. Even if his views were honourable—if he were really resolved to relinquish his well-known and publicly avowed determination never to enthral himself with the chains of matrimony, was he the man who could render her sister happy? Was he such a one as she (Bess)

could respect and treat as a brother, whom her mother could regard and lean upon as a son? Bessie's heart returned a decided negative to these self-inquiries, but she did not believe that the marquis had any such intentions; neither his looks, his manners, nor his language towards Bell, were such as in Bessie's estimation, as a man of common understanding (and the marquis's was undisputed), let his principles be what they might, would assume towards the female whom he intended to make his wife. Besides, as Bess remarked, in expostulating with her sister, "Why did he not take the proper and obvious course, and at once avow his wishes and intentions to her friends and natural guardians?" Two months or more had already passed since his first introduction to Bell, and all that time, according to her own account, he had eagerly profited by every opportunity of breathing the most passionate professions of love in her ear.

"But has he ever talked clearly, and without mystery, of making you his wife?" demanded Bess, on that eventful night, when, after her return from the ball, Bell had kept her sister awake for two or three hours, recapitulating all that had passed; and the conversation had insensibly glided into a discussion of the merits and recommendations of the Marquis of Ledbury, and the flattering prospects, which the former fancied were now certain of being realized, of being raised to rank and affluence, beyond what even her most ambitious dreams could have suggested.

"I will own to you, Bell," continued her sister, finding the latter hesitated to reply to her question, "I will acknowledge that I should be very sorry to see you the wife of the marquis—for I am firmly convinced that, after the first dazzle had worn off, you would be a miserable woman; but do not be angry, my dear sister, at my telling you that I do not believe—nay, more, I am firmly convinced that marriage has no place in that man's thoughts or intentions towards you."

"And what then," said Bell, indignantly, " do you pretend to suppose are his intentions? You will not—you dare not, Bess, presume to imagine that he has the insolence to indulge dishonourable views, that he——"

" God forbid !" ejaculated Bess, emphatically. "Not in the sense you use the word dishonourable. Again I say, oh, God forbid that even he, licentious and unprincipled as he is, should dare to regard my sister with——Oh, I cannot bear to think of it. But no, Bell, it is not so—it cannot be so—though I will speak the truth. I believe him capable of any baseness."

"Bess, this is shameful," exclaimed Bell, angrily. "What do you know of him, except by common report, and that you ought to know always exaggerates and misrepresents."

"I do not speak merely from common report, Bell. Listen to me, and do not turn so angrily away, while I relate what came under my own observation. A few weeks only before my dear father was taken from us, he one day received a note—it was beautifully written, and the purport of it was to implore him to visit the writer, and administer to her the consolations of religion, she being confined to her bed and in the utmost distress of body and mind. To his great surprise the address given was in one of the poorest streets in Upton Barton, one that was notorious as the refuge of the lowest and most degraded of the population of that place; but this, far from deterring, made him only the more anxious to hasten to the relief of the poor sufferer. He went, Bell, and there, in a miserable cellar, destitute even of the commonest articles of furniture, he found a delicate and still beautiful young woman, whose emaciated frame at once convinced him that she was fast approaching the termination of all her sorrows, and by her side lay an infant, a lovely though sickly boy, who was vainly trying to draw from the unhappy mother that nourishment which her state refused to supply. I need not say that my dear father, without inquiring into the cause of her fearful destitution, so inconsistent with her looks, her manners, or her language, hastened instantly to administer all the comfort and consolation in his power. He soothed her mind with those hopes of pardon and peace which are promised to the truly contrite in heart, whatever may have been the nature and sum of their offences; and then he hastened home to make arrangements with my mother for the bodily comfort of the unhappy woman. A room was taken for her in an airy, clean cottage, and my mother sent a bed and everything necessary, and she was removed——"

"Well, I can see the end of all this," interrupted Bell, "and so there is no use in swelling it out into a long melancholy story. I can foresee that this elegant, accomplished young lady was one who had been ruined, as it is called, by the marquis, or, at least, chose to attribute her ruin to him; though, very probably, if the real truth were known, her own vanity and folly were more to blame than he."

"Oh, Bell, Bell, do not talk so, it is unjust, unfeminine," exclaimed Bess. "I cannot bear to hear you espousing the cause of a libertine against one of your own sex, and that, too, without knowing any of the circumstances; which, though they certainly could not exonerate her from blame, must plead in excuse for——"

"Oh, there is no doubt that, of course, she could make her story good," interrupted Bell, contemptuously; "but I will own the truth, however much it may offend you, who are predetermined to condemn the marquis. I have very little, or, indeed, no pity for young ladies who, like your friend, are weak and silly, or very often, as I verily believe, wicked enough to act in such a manner as to bring disgrace upon themselves, and their families and friends, and then try to throw the whole blame upon the man, though they must have known very well, if they had had common sense, or common reflection, the consequences of such conduct, and that there is not one man in five thousand who does not think himself right in taking advantage of women's credulity. For my own part, as I said before, I never pity a woman in such circumstances; and as to the marquis and this interesting, accomplished young lady, I dare say, if he had failed in making a proper provision for her—which was the utmost she had a right to expect after forfeiting her character—I will be bound that her conduct had some way or other deserved that he should discard her."

"Discard her?" repeated Bess. "Oh, Bell, how little you can appreciate that poor girl's feelings when you use such an expression. No, no, she had fled from him when she had discovered how cruelly she had been betrayed. Not only from him, but from all who could reproach her, she had hidden herself and her disgrace. She had submitted to the bitterest privations, and laboured incessantly to support herself and her child, rather than stoop to the humiliation of receiving assistance from the man who had betrayed her. I am not going to force upon you, Bell, the particulars of a long story, to which I see you are unwilling to listen, and which I fear would have very little influence with you, under your present infatuation, but I will repeat to you what I heard from my dear father's lips after he had returned from the melancholy office of reading the burial service over the remains of poor Mrs. Ross, as she was always called, her real name, I believe, was Anna Rossiter; but she was desirous, even to the last moment, of shielding her family from the disgrace it had been, I verily believe, more her misfortune than her fault to have brought upon them. This, I know, that my dear father, who never judged with harshness of ——"

"I do not want to hear any more about it, Bess," interrupted Bell, with increasing anger. "My father, like you, was a well-meaning enthusiast who knew nothing of the world, or he would, perhaps, have judged and decided very differently. There is only one thing I want to know. The young woman you say is dead—what became of the child?"

"It is in heaven, I hope, with its mother," returned Bess, her voice choked almost with emotion.

"Oh, it did die, then," replied Bell, in a tone of evident satisfaction. "Well, that is the best thing that could have happened for it."

"It was, indeed," observed Bess, warmly. "Deprived of its mother, and with such a father——"

"Oh, pooh, nonsense, Bess," exclaimed her sister, with affected liveliness. "I dare say he would have made a very good papa, if he had been tried. It's very plain that it was not his fault if he did not, for if the mother had acted with a little more common sense, or—But I can't talk any more, my dear girl, positively. I have been more than half asleep ever since you began your dismal story. So good-night. God bless you, and make your foolish little heart easy ; for, depend upon it, I do not need any such gloomy examples to teach me to defend myself against the snares and wiles of this terrible man, if he dared practise them against me."

Bess, however, though thus enjoined, was far from indulging in such security ; but it was not only her fears and apprehensions as to the intentions of the Marquis of Ledbury towards her sister, that rendered her nights sleepless, and watered her pillow with tears — she was grieved, astonished, and indignant at the sentiments Bell had expressed—the tone of levity and indulgence towards positive vice which she had assumed, and her evident obstinate determination to persevere in her present course, of giving encouragement to the Marquis of Ledbury, even under the full conviction of his utter and complete worthlessness.

CHAPTER IX.

Where be the bending peers that flatter'd thee ?
Where be the thronging troops that follow'd thee ?
Decline all this, and see what now thou art.

Thus hath the course of justice wheel'd about,
And left thee but a very prey to time ;
Having no more but thought of what thou wert,
To torture thee the more, being what thou art.—SHAKSPEARE.

ADY JANE'S indisposition still continued, and, to the extreme mortification and disappointment of Bell Leslie, the parties, balls, routs, &c., in which they—the Bevington family—had been engaged knee-deep, as Miss Moulsey not very elegantly, though perhaps expressively observed, were all perforce postponed *sine die.* Bell, indeed, in her private conferences with her sister, which were not very frequent, but which she sometimes sought as the only opportunity of unbosoming her griefs without reserve, persisted in asserting that in reality there was nothing the matter with her aunt, that her complaints and apparent suffering were all affectation—fancy, the love of being waited upon, and exciting interest ; and sometimes even she went so far as to aver that Lady Jane was actuated merely by the spirit of contradiction and ill-humour, which took a delight in upsetting every previously concerted plan, and proving her own consequence by disconcerting and disappointing every one of their promised pleasures, and though while in the sick chamber she contrived in general tolerably to disguise her discontent, it was visible, even to Lady Jane herself, that the confinement was irksome to her, and her attentions bestowed with a very ill-grace. To Bess, on the contrary, it appeared undeniable that her aunt, however whim-

sical and exacting she might be, was really suffering. It was impossible not to see the alteration in her person and spirits, and under this impression Bessie's attentions and care were unremitting, though even she sometimes failed in giving satisfaction to the invalid, whose whims and fretfulness seemed to increase every hour. A week passed away, and Bess remained in close attendance upon her aunt, seldom quitting her room from morning till night, and even sleeping on a sofa in the adjoin-

ing dressing-room, that she might be ready to attend her call even in the hours that should have been devoted to repose. For a day or two Bell shared these cares, but a visit from Mrs. Balcombe, her *chaperone* on the night of the ball, to her great satisfaction, though to the increase of Bessie's uneasiness, in a great measure relieved her.

"Bell, dear girl, is not at all at home in a sick room," observed Lady Jane. "Poor thing, she is so sensitive that she becomes completely unnerved, and I am really fearful that the solitude and confinement will have a serious effect upon her health and spirits. She was positively almost as hysterical last night as I am myself."

"It is fortunate for your ladyship," observed Mrs. Balcombe, "that Miss Leslie possesses stronger nerves."

"Oh, yes, Miss Leslie is an excellent nurse. I do not know, indeed, what would become of me if I had not her with me, for as to my own maid, she is not fit for anything in the world, if she is put out of her regular course, and she is so attached to me that she frightens herself to death at every little occurrence. Sir Matthew bores me sadly to have a regular nurse, but I have such a horror of having strangers about me, I am sure I should die if Miss Leslie were to leave me; but as to Bell, poor thing, really it would be quite a relief if I could get rid of her for a few days, for it makes me more nervous than ever when I see her looking so pale and desponding. I am sure it would be quite a charity, both to me and her, if any one would take charge of her for a short time, and endeavour to divert her mind from dwelling so continually on my suffer——

Mrs. Balcombe had her own private reasons for wishing to conciliate Lady Jane's favour, and though perhaps it was very far from her wish or intention to encourage or forward the plans which she had penetration enough to discover her ladyship had formed for the advancement of her favourite niece, she thought it advisable for her own sake, in this instance at least, to appear to fall into Lady Jane's views.

"If you will entrust Miss Bell to my care," she observed, "and she can be prevailed upon to quit you for a few days, I shall be very happy to entertain her in Harley Street. Sophia, too, will be very glad of her company, for her sister, Louisa, goes to Hastings with her old schoolfellow, Lady Beechcroft, to-morrow, for a fortnight, and poor Sophy is quite *au desespoir* at the loss of her sister."

Lady Jane expressed a world of gratitude (to use her own phrase) at this obliging offer, which, she said, "would relieve her spirits of a heavy load. There was only one difficulty now to be got over. She was afraid Bell would be unwilling to quit her."

Bess, who had been a silent auditor of this conversation, felt her cheeks crimson at the tone, but still more the look with which Mrs. Balcombe observed, "that she dared to say they, Lady Jane and herself,

should be able to find some means of conquering the young lady's repugnance."

"Will you go, my dear, and ask your sister to come here?" said Lady Jane. "Do not tell her, though, of Mrs. Balcombe's offer, for that will give her time to —Stay, it will be better, perhaps, to ring for mademoiselle, and send her for Bell. The proposal will come best from me, before she is prepared with objections."

"Can my aunt," thought Bess, "really believe that Bell would, for a moment hesitate to accept an invitation which at once releases her from the dulness and confinement that is so hateful to her, and places her within reach of——"

She did not finish the sentence even in her mind, but a heavy sigh betrayed the feelings that were excited by the train of thoughts that followed.

Mrs. Balcombe's keen eyes were fixed on her as if she would fain have read those thoughts.

"It is hardly fair towards you, either, my dear," she observed, "to rob you of your companion, and leave the whole duty of attending your aunt upon your shoulders."

"Oh, she will not, I am sure, feel it any hardship," observed Lady Jane, quickly. "Will you, my love? Indeed, I do assure you," she continued, addressing Mrs. Balcombe, "without in the least disparaging Bell, she has, I am sure, every wish and inclination to be serviceable, she is the most unfit person in the world to be about an invalid, and especially one so nervous and irritable as myself. She is so timid, so terrified, and loses all presence of mind so, that we have been obliged sometimes to send her away from us. Have we not, my dear?"

Bess, of course, assented to this. She had, indeed, more than once been compelled to request Bell to leave the room; but, in reality, it had been more from the fear that the latter would betray the petulance and impatience her aunt's complaints excited, than any other motive.

Bell entered, and Bess would have given worlds to have been absent during the scene of mutual dissimulation and affectation that ensued. Bell would not hear of leaving her dear, dear aunt. She threw herself on her knees by the side of the couch on which the invalid was lying, and hid her face on the pillow, while Lady Jane was uttering her soft persuasions to her dear niece, to accept Mrs. Balcombe's kind and considerate invitation.

"What pleasure can I possibly enjoy, dear aunt," she observed, "and know that you are suffering? I know, indeed, that I am not so good a nurse as Bessie, and that you will have every comfort and attendance while she is with you; but still it looks so selfish and heartless in me to leave you; and my uncle, too, I am afraid he will——"

"Leave me to manage with your uncle, my love. I will undertake to convince him that you are neither selfish nor heartless," returned Lady Jane. "I will tell him that it was entirely in obedience to my wishes that you leave me. Besides, I know that he has so high an opinion of your sister, while she is with me, he will be perfectly satisfied. You know he said this morning that it was almost worth while to be ill to have such a gentle, clever, and patient nurse as Bessie; and, indeed, I confess that I am very grateful to Miss Leslie, who, I am sure, I can never repay for her attention."

"Ah, but you must not let her supplant your poor Bell in your affection," whispered the latter, entwining her arms around her aunt, and looking coaxingly in her face. "If you will not promise to love me as you have always done, I will not go."

Lady Jane whispered something in a lower tone than even Bell had uttered the last sentence, but, whatever it was, it brought a smile to the lips, and a bright blush to Bell's cheeks, though she shook her head, as if in playful denial of what her aunt had said,

"Come, Miss Bell," observed Mrs. Balcombe, with a satirical smile, "I trust that your aunt has vanquished your objections now, and that you will no longer refuse me the honour of your company; so, as I am rather pressed for time, perhaps you will have the goodness to make your preparations as speedily as possible, and go with me, or, as I have one or two calls to make on my way home, maybe, you would prefer that I should send the carriage for you after it has taken me to Harley-street."

"Oh, no, my dear Mrs. Balcombe, I cannot consent to your having so much trouble," observed Lady Jane, who had previously learned that one of Mrs. Balcombe's intended calls was to be upon Lady Barbara Presteigne, the Marquis of Ledbury's unmarried sister, who, being many years older than him, resided with him, or rather presided as mistress at his elegant mansion in Portman Square, although he generally lived at an hotel, the free and easy habits of which suited him better than the regularity of a family residence. It was an opportunity Lady Jane considered too favourable to be lost, of Bell's getting an introduction to another member of the marquis's family. She had

heard, indeed, that Lady Barbara was insufferably proud and intolerant to those whom she considered her inferiors, especially if they were at all remarkable for youth and beauty, of which she could no longer boast the possession; but she trusted to Bell's tact and address to surmount even these difficulties. At all events, it was worth while to run any risk, even of being treated with the coldness and hauteur, verging upon insolence, of which, she had heard Lady Barbara was quite capable.

"Bell will be ready in a few minutes to accompany you," she observed. "Mademoiselle can select and pack up what is necessary to be sent after you, love. Your Leghorn, with the white feather," added her ladyship in a half whisper, "and the green silk pelisse, to go in——"

The favourite looked dissatisfied.

"I have been told, aunt," she replied, in the same under tone, and with a meaning look, "that pink is so becoming to my complexion that I ought never to wear any other colour. I have never worn my pink drawn bonnet, and the laced scarf, lined with rose colour, will suit admirably with it."

"Oh, by all means, my dear," returned Lady Jane, nodding significantly, as if to say that she perfectly comprehended who it was that had thought pink so becoming to her niece.

"The Marquis of Ledbury is, I believe, gone down to Melton for a few days; we shall find Lady Presteigne, therefore, alone," observed Mrs. Balcombe, compressing her lips with one of her peculiar smiles.

It was impossible not to see instantly the meaning of this abrupt remark; but Bessie's ingenuous countenance was the only one that betrayed that it excited any particular sensation. Lady Jane and her favourite were both too practised in the art of concealing their emotions, whether of pain or pleasure. That her words conveyed a keen disappointment to the two last, Mrs. Balcombe had not the slightest doubt; but she was puzzled to account for, or comprehend the ray of pleasure that lighted up the elder sister's eyes, and seemed at once to infuse new life and alacrity into her whole manner.

"Shall I go with, and assist you, dear Bell?" she asked, while Lady Jane, with well-affected indifference, uttered some observation respecting the exclusive pleasure gentlemen enjoyed in their hunting establishments, especially, as she heard, at Melton.

In the petulant tone in which Bell replied to her sister's offer might easily be discovered the effects of her disappointment. She saw and knew, "none so well as her," the effect which the announcement of the marquis's absence had had upon Bess, and all the anger felt at this inopportune circumstance was transferred to her sister, whose offer of assistance she rejected with a tartness by no means in accordance with her previously assumed gentleness and amiability, or even with the *sweet* smile with which, as she quitted the room, she assured Mrs. Balcombe that she would not detain her many minutes.

"Yes," observed the latter, as if resuming the conversation, "as your ladyship was observing, these exclusive establishments among the gentlemen are a sad hindrance in the way of young women who are laying out for husbands and establishments. The marquis, for instance, I do not believe that he will ever have a serious thought of matrimony, so long as he finds so much enjoyment at the different clubs of which he is a member, and especially at Melton, where I have heard they make it quite a point to decry matrimony, and turn into ridicule all who are so foolish as to be, according to their phrase, caught in the trap."

Lady Jane could with difficulty dissemble that this subject was not a pleasant one, but she did manage to maintain a tone of indifference.

"Oh, indeed," she observed, with a yawn. "Well, I confess my ignorance on this subject, for do you know I was not aware, or at least I fancied that there were many of the Melton gentlemen who were married men. I certainly have some sort of recollection of Sir Matthew being solicited to become a member, and his declining on account of (I think) its interfering with his parliamentary duties—but I suppose I must be wrong."

"Oh, no, not at all," returned Mrs. Balcombe, "your ladyship, I dare say, is perfectly right ; but then, you know, Sir Matthew was previously caught, as they saucily phrase it ; and that of course is quite a different thing. All I meant to say was, that while the younger members, who are bachelors, uphold each other in their contempt and ridicule of the fetters of Hymen, it——"

"But the marquis, though a bachelor, can scarcely be enrolled among the youthful members," observed Lady Jane, tartly.

Mrs. Balcombe laughed.

"You, like me, my dear friend, then begin to think that it is almost time he laid aside his youthful follies, and began to think of living soberly. Ah, I am afraid, though *we* think so, there is very

little hope of bringing him to look upon it in the same light. I fear, in spite of all our grave counsels, he will persevere in the same gay course, until old age and infirmity come upon him ; and then, as I tell him, he will, if he does not make a worse fool of himself, barter his wealth and title with some poor girl or another who will be willing, for their sakes, to become his nurse, and repay herself, after she has got rid of him, by buying a younger husband. Here is Miss Leslie, for instance—if, which I acknowledge is very unlikely, she should remain single for ten years or so (I do not allow him a longer course, at the rate he runs), but if she should, I say, be then disengaged, I think the best thing I could do for him would be to recommend him to her. What do you say, my dear ; don't you think that the title of duchess and a handsome jointure would reconcile you to the gout and flannels for a few years ? Your aunt says you are the best nurse in the world, and so I think——"

"If I did not know, madam, that this is all mere badinage——" returned Bess.

"Badinage ! Oh, no, indeed," replied Mrs. Balcombe, quickly. "I am sure I should think the marquis a very happy man if he possessed such a prospect in reverson. I do really believe that I should begin to try to persuade him very seriously to think of shortening the probation by some years, and fancying that he has a much earlier necessity for a nurse than he is at present willing to think."

"Miss Leslie is certainly indebted to your good opinion, madam," observed Lady Jane, who seemed by no means pleased at her friend's remark. "I should hope, however, that she has somewhat higher qualities to recommend her to a husband than merely being a good nurse."

"*I* do not doubt it, I assure your ladyship," returned Mrs. Balcombe, emphatically. "Indeed, if I were not well convinced that she has very superior qualities to those of a mere domestic drudge, however estimable and useful she might be in that light, I should be very sorry to see her the wife of my nephew, who——"

"My dear Mrs. Balcombe," exclaimed Lady Jane, opening her eyes to their very utmost extent in utter amazement. "My dear Mrs, Balcombe, what in the world can have put such an idea in your head? You speak of such a thing as if there were really some serious foundation for it—but it cannot be. I think I can answer for Miss Leslie that such a preposterous, absurb, ridiculous thought never entered her mind."

"Mrs. Balcombe is quite convinced of that, dear aunt, without any assurances, either on your part or mine," observed Bess, smiling at Lady Jane's eagerness. "If she were not—and Bess fixed her eyes with a peculiar meaning on Mrs. Balcombe—quite convinced that such a preposterous, absurd idea has never, nor is likely ever to enter my mind, she would not have said what she has done."

"You are right, my dear," said Mrs. Balcombe, nodding, and returning Bessie's significant look; "though I am not altogether inclined to admit that it would be so very preposterous and absurd."

"*I* should think it so," replied Bess, gently, but decidedly; "but let us talk of something else, if you please."

Lady Jane's thoughts, however, were evidently too pre-occupied by what had passed to dismiss it so easily.

"My dear Mrs. Balcombe," she observed, "I know you seldom speak at random—you must have some reason for what you have said."

Mrs. Balcombe only smiled significantly, and her friend forgetting her usual caution and coolness was about to give utterance to a more direct interrogation, when the entrance of Bell seemed suddenly to recal to her aunt's mind the prudence of not pursuing the subject in her presence.

"Oh, you have adopted my recommendation, I see, my dear," she observed, raising herself on the sofa to survey her favourite niece.

The Leghorn bonnet and green pelisse, as at first advised, had been substituted for the pink satin and lace scarf—Bell's own, or rather according to her previous whisper, the Marquis of Ledbury's taste.

"Yes, of course, aunt," returned Bell, significantly; but it might have been doubted whose cheeks were dyed the deepest crimson, Bessie's or hers, as Mrs. Balcombe, with one of her peculiarly sly smiles, repeated the words—

"Of course."

The longest and most verbose sentence in which she could have clothed her thought, could not more emphatically have betrayed how fully she comprehended the motives that had actuated Bell in this change from her original intention. Even Lady Jane herself for a moment seemed startled at this proof of Mrs. Balcombe's penetration into motives which she had thought hidden from all but herself and Bell. Bessie's blush was one of pure ingenuous shame for her sister, and indignation at what she could not consider otherwise than impertinence and want of feeling on the part of Mrs. Balcombe, who, while professing the warmest friendship towards Lady Jane, and kindness and interest for Bell, thus eagerly seized upon an opportunity to humiliate them both.

"Of course, my dear," continued the former, repeating her words after a pause. "Your aunt is a better judge than you of the becoming and suitable, and it is a proof of your good sense that you are so ready to yield your own opinions in such an important matter as dress."

Bess felt that this seeming explanation of her observation on the part of Mrs. Balcombe was at the best very equivocal; but to her sister and aunt it appeared quite satisfactory, and Bell departed with her friend in the full conviction that her designs, or rather Lady Jane's designs on the marquis were still unsuspected.

Whatever might be Lady Jane's fancied security on this point, however, she was far from feeling equally at her ease respecting Mrs. Balcombe's strange, as she called them, observations to Bess. It might have appeared to most persons a matter of indifference which of her nieces was to be *ennobled* by an alliance with the marquis, or at least, that if she were convinced that Bess was his choice, she would have been satisfied with the prospect that Bell might be equally fortunate, and have been willing to forward Bessie's elevation by every means in her power. But this was not the case. She had decided in her own mind that Bell was to be the favoured one who was to be raised to wealth and dignity, and that Bess's elevation was to follow, of course; or rather, in fact, that it was comparatively of little moment even if Bess never attained to the high station for which her sister, in her own opinion, as well as her aunt's, was predestined, and the very possibility which Mrs. Balcombe's mysterious observations had awakened a suspicion of, that, after all, Bess might be the favoured one, was as unreasonable to her, Lady Jane, as though the latter had been a perfect stranger, in whom she had no interest. Under this impression she attacked Bess the moment they were left together, in a manner that perfectly astonished and alarmed the innocent and undesigning girl, who, though she had felt a vague suspicion that Mrs. Balcombe had some motive beyond mere raillery in the remarks she had made, and had herself felt vexed that her aunt should have betrayed so much interest in the subject, had never dreamt how deeply it had galled the latter. What was her astonishment then to hear herself accused of a deep-laid plan to circumvent her *artless*, unsuspecting sister. To become, in fact, the Marchioness of Ledbury. Bess could not at first believe that Lady Jane was serious. She could scarcely credit her own senses when she heard herself accused of being deep, artful, treacherous, designing; but Lady Jane's accusation, though at first veiled in ironical congratulations on the conquest Miss Leslie had made, and her good fortune in having secured so valuable an anxuiliary as Mrs. Balcombe, became too pointed to be mistaken or misunderstood, and her indignation was scarcely exceeded by her astonishment at such an unfounded accusation.

She have designs upon the Marquis of Ledbury—a man with whom she had scarcely exchanged half-a-dozen sentences —whom she had never seen but twice; but whom, from his character, and especially from circumstances that had come under her own immediate observation, she despised and contemned; towards whom she felt, she might say, almost personal hatred. A man from whom, ever since she had heard his name in connexion with her sister's, she had anticipated evil, and had prayed that her sister might be delivered from!

"Yes, madam," she continued, her fine face glowing with emotion, and her beautiful hands clasped and upraised with intense devotion to the Great God who knows the secrets of all hearts, "I do now offer my fervent prayers that she may be saved even from the misery of becoming the wife of that profligate and unprincipled man, whom I should shame to own as a brother, whom my mother, I am well assured, would never acknowledge as a son. But I will tell you even more, aunt. I feel indeed that, however painful the circumstances are that give me the opportunity of uttering my thoughts upon the subject to you—still I say, I feel that it is a welcome relief to me to be able to tell you that I have still more dreadful fears from the acquaintance of my sister with the marquis. I will speak plainly, however painful it may be to you, who have encouraged — who are promoting that intimacy, however dreadful and degrading it is to me and to my poor sister, I will avow the truth—that I do not believe the marquis has any other intentions towards her than such as will bring ruin, misery, and disgrace upon her and her family. Oh, aunt, how I have longed to tell you this—to implore you not to encourage my poor sister in——"

"It cannot be," interrupted Lady Jane, upon whom it was plain that Bess's ardent and pathetic representations had made a considerable impression, and who

eemed, under these new feelings, to have entirely lost sight of her suspicions of Bessie's double-dealing. It was impossible, indeed, for the most determined and suspicious to doubt that the Marquis of Ledbury was to her an object of the greatest horror and contempt—but it was not equally easy to convince Lady Jane that Bessie's feelings towards him and her suspicions were correct and well-founded. Even the history of poor Anna Ross, which Bess related more at large to her aunt than her sister had allowed her to do to her, failed to make that impression on the latter which Bess had hoped that it would.

It was a sad story, certainly, Lady Jane allowed, and the marquis was very greatly to blame, if the girl's account were all true —but still, great allowances were to be made. It was very natural that she should try to shift as much of the guilt off her own shoulders as possible; and then, too, the usages of the world, and especially of the fashionable world, allowed so much latitude to men of rank and fortune. It would not do to be too extreme in searching into the private history of gentlemen, especially those who, like the marquis, had been left in early youth to their own guidance, and with unlimited means at his command to indulge his passions. A young romantic girl like her (Bess) of course saw things in a very different light to what men of the world did. It was quite right that she should feel an abhorrence of such conduct —but still she would find that it was not only prudent, but absolutely necessary, as society is constituted, to make allowances, and, in fact, to shut our eyes to what we cannot amend. As to the Marquis of Ledbury daring to indulge dishonourable views towards the niece of Sir Matthew Bevington, that was quite out of the question; and, even if he were daring and insolent enough, Bell was too well taught, too prudent and guarded for any fears on that ground. Oh, no, Lady Jane had no fears on that head.

"I have heard," said Bess, in a subdued voice, indeed, suited to the depressed and melancholy feelings which her aunt's time-serving and wordly observations had excited in her bosom—"I have heard that there is, even now, an unhappy woman in existence who, gifted with beauty, fortune, and rank—the wife of one of his dearest friends, or, I should rather say, his most intimate associates, for of the sacred tie of friendship, of course, such a man can know nothing—but I have heard, I say, that even with her, moving in the same sphere as himself, and wanting nothing that ought to render a reasonable woman happy, even to a family of beautiful children——"

"Oh, I know what you allude to, my dear," Lady Jane hastily interrupted, "but really, in the case of Mrs. Pomeroy, there were many who considered that the marquis was not so much to blame ; and, indeed, I really believe that he would have made her the proper reparation by marrying her, but that her husband obstinately resisted putting it in his power by refusing to sue for a divorce. You know, I suppose, that the marquis and Mr. Pomeroy met, and that he, the marquis, was wounded, and very honourably fired in the air."

"It was honourable, certainly, not to add the murder of the husband to the ruin of the wife, and the eternal disgrace of her family," observed Bess ; "but there is another circumstance, which is not, perhaps, known to you, aunt, but which I remember hearing my dear father speak of, at the time the sad fate of poor Mrs. Ross came under our notice, and that was, that the unfortunate Mr. Pomeroy became a wretched lunatic, and that his family were thus deprived of both their parents."

"It was a sad thing, my dear, I do not deny it," returned Lady Jane, "but I believe madness was hereditary in the Pomeroy family. His mother I have heard, died mad—so that, after all, Ledbury could hardly be considered responsible for that ; and, indeed, it did not look as if Pomeroy were in his sober senses from the first, or he would have hardly refused to have adopted the regular course and divorced her, when, of course, the marquis would have married her ; but it was a lucky escape for him—for it is said she has turned out quite an abandoned woman, and dissipates the handsome allowance he settled upon her in the lowest vices."

"Heaping coals on the head of her destroyer," murmured Bess with a shudder.

Lady Jane appeared disconcerted by this remark. She saw that she had not only totally failed in her object—that of vindicating, or at least extenuating the conduct of the marquis, but had also lowered herself in the opinion of her single-minded, firm-principled niece.

"What a provoking thing it is to have to deal with self-opinionated, obstinate young women, especially the over-righteous and correct," observed her ladyship to Miss Moulsey, who, extremely to Bessie's satisfaction, put an end to the discussion of the marquis's merits and demerits by her sudden entrance, and unexpected announcement that she had come to pass a few

hours with her "dear Lady Jane," who she was sure must be quite miserable, now she had lost "that dear Bell."

Whatever Lady Jane might have thought proper to reply to this, had Bess been absent, she could not very well avoid in her presence observing that Miss Leslie's constant attentions left her very little room for regret.

Miss Moulsey seemed to take this as a hint to try another course, and she immediately commenced an elaborate compliment to Miss Leslie on her superiority to most of the frivolous young women of the present day, "who, like butterflies," she said, "were only fit to glitter and shine—"

Lady Jane rather petulantly interruped this original simile.

"You will be glad, I dare say, Miss Leslie, to have two or three hours' liberty, for I am sure you have been quite a prisoner here, and Sir Matthew will no doubt be glad of your company at his tea-table in the drawing-room, as my friend Miss Moulsey is kind enough to offer to remain with me."

Bess gladly accepted the permission. She affected no reluctance to leave her "dear aunt," and that perhaps added bitterness to the observation of the latter, as soon as the door closed upon her.

Miss Moulsey was no longer in doubt whether praise or blame of her niece was the course that would please Lady Jane.

"Well, really," she observed, "but that I was afraid of displeasing your ladyship, I should long ago have said that I wondered how you could put up with Miss Leslie's overbearing affectation of superior morality and virtue. I declare, I have heard two or three of our friends declare, that if they were in your ladyship's situation they would not have a young person about them to be setting herself up for a pattern."

"Indeed?" returned Lady Jane, rather incredulously. "Well now, do you know, I did not think anybody ever suspected such a thing, for Miss Leslie is in general so silent and diffident——"

"Yes, my dear Lady Jane," interrupted Miss Moulsey, with quickness, "but as the Marquis of Ledbury in my hearing observed this morning to our dear Bell, Miss Leslie speaks in a single glance—"

The marquis—Bell—Bess, and all her faults, were in a moment forgotten, and Lady Jane was only anxious to hear about the marquis and her favourite niece. When and where Miss Moulsey had seen them, what passed, with a thousand et ceteras; which were all crowded into a succession of questions, and uttered with a rapidity and eagerness so unlike Lady Jane's usual assumption of nonchalance and quiet indifference, that even Miss Moulsey was surprised.

"She had seen Mrs. and Miss Balcombe, Miss Bell and the marquis, at Granger's, in Bond Street, and had learned that the latter was to be of Mrs. Balcombe's party to dinner and to the opera at night."

"If the marquis were a marrying man," continued Moulsey significantly, "and Mrs. Balcombe at all a match maker, I should consider it a settled affair that a certain young lady would be the marchioness—but as it is I hardly know what to think, for our friend Mrs. B. bears the character of having broken many matches, and never made one, (even her daughter Louisa, you know, made a runaway match) and as to the chance of the marquis marrying, I have heard that only within a few days, in a mixed party, he declared himself so decidedly against matrimony, that the married ladies present took it as a personal insult, and one or two decided upon shutting their doors to him. So that——'

"I really wonder, my dear Moulsey, where you contrive to pick up such incorrigible stuff," interrupted Lady Jane. "As to my friend Mrs. Balcombe—by the bye, that is a sad vulgar habit, I must tell you, you have acquired of using the initial letter for the full name——"

"The Duchess of Lennox always abbreviates," observed Miss Moulsey, snappishly. "She never calls me anything but my dear M."

"Very possibly," returned Lady Jane, coolly, "but that does not disprove my assertion."

Miss Moulsey was silenced, and Lady Jane was satisfied, for she had revenged herself for her dear friend's unwelcome insinuations respecting Bell's chance of becoming the Marchioness of Ledbury.

As if by mutual compact the offensive subjects were not again alluded to by either party, and Lady Jane and Miss Moulsey parted as *sincere* friends as they met—the former assuring Bess, when she returned to the chamber, that she was positively bored to death with the little, tiresome, gossiping, scandalising old maid; and Miss Moulsey departing with the full intention of exposing, wherever she had an opportunity, Lady Jane's presumptuous and arrogant expectations of seeing her niece a peeress.

Whatever was Lady Jane's private opinion on this subject, it was certain that Bell's narrative of all that had occurred between herself and the marquis, when,

on the following morning, she visited her aunt, was not calculated to diminish those hopes. Even Mrs. Balcombe acknowledged that she was infinitely indebted to Lady Jane for having procured her the honour and pleasure or her noble relative's constant society ; for that it was easy to see what was the magnet that drew him to Harley Street. But it was strange, unaccountable, so Bell thought, and so it appeared even to Bess, that their aunt seemed all at once to have cooled upon the subject of her niece's hoped-for elevation. To Bell, indeed, in private, she attributed this revulsion of feeling to what Miss Moulsey had repeated of the marquis's recent expression of sentiments ; but, as Bell argued, in the first place, her aunt knew too well Miss Moulsey's malicious, envious, lying disposition to give the smallest credit to what she said ; and, in the second, she (Bell) was very certain that Lady Jane would not be in such exuberant good spirits, if she had really given up all hopes of seeing her favourite project brought to bear. Bess herself was puzzled to account, not only for many expressions of absolute indifference, as to the success or failure of that which had formerly seemed to occupy her every thought, but also for a wonderful accession of spirits in her aunt, although her complaints seemed to remain unabated. But the mystery was soon explained. Bell returned from her visit to Mrs. Balcombe, that lady having been unexpectedly summoned to Bath, to her married daughter, who was seriously indisposed. According to Bell's account she had every reason to be satisfied with what had passed during that visit. Mrs. Balcombe and Sophia had treated her as one who at no distant period was to become a valued member of their family, and the marquis had, without reserve, spoken of his intended union with her, in their presence, as only delayed for a short time from some difficulties which were in a fair way of settlement.

Bess looked silent and grave at hearing this—but she had learned by experience that her remonstrances or opposition availed nothing ; and as to consulting her mother (though to Bess it seemed indispensable), Bell never appeared for a moment to consider it necessary. It was with no little surprise and gratification, therefore, the former heard Lady Jane observe to her favourite niece, that she thought if the *affaire* was really so far advanced, it would be but proper and respectfully to Mrs. Leslie that she should be made acquainted with it.

Bell was visibly disconcerted. She

nanged colour, glanced reproachfully at her sister, whose expressive countenance betrayed her satisfaction at her aunt's observation, and then, in a low tone, remarked,—

"I am sure, dear aunt, I can have no objection to mamma's being consulted, because, of course, it is impossible she can have any objection to a marriage so much above my hopes and expectations—ah, you may shake your head, Bess, but——"

"Never mind your sister's expressive gestures, my dear—though, undoubtedly, they are wonderfully becoming," observed Lady Jane, sneeringly, "but proceed and tell me what are your objections to my letting your mother know——"

"Oh, no, aunt, I have no objections, if *you* will do it," returned Bell, eagerly; "but I was afraid that you wished me to tell mamma, and, really, she has so many prejudices and old-fashioned notions, like Bess, that I do not think I could bring myself even to hint such a matter to her.

And besides, the marquis seemed to think, though he did not positively say so, that it would be as well that nothing should be mentioned to my family, until he had satisfactorily arranged the——I will tell you candidly, aunt, what I suspect is the obstacle to our immediate settlement. As to Bess, I know she will look more dismal than ever," (and Bell forced a laugh) " but you and I know too much of the world, dear aunt, to condemn the marquis for a folly in which he is countenanced by the example of the highest in the realm, and which he is now, I know, seriously determined to reform. The truth is, then, for I heard it from Sophia Balcombe, that Ledbury has been foolish enough to form a *liason* with the celebrated Signora D—— of the Italian Opera—She with whose divine voice Bess was so enraptured, on her first visit to the King's Theatre. Ha, ha, ha! Look how Bessie blushes, aunt, actually as if she——"

" Oh, Bell, Bell, if I blush," interrupted her sister, " it is at hearing you thus coolly and composedly speak of vices which——"

" Of course ought to make me foreswear mankind, and vow to live a vestal," observed Bell, laughing still more heartily. " Never mind, child, you'll know better by and by. But, as I was saying, aunt, it is the difficulty of getting rid of this signora, who is a most dreadful virago, Sophia says, and would not mind using the stiletto, or poisoning him, if she were driven to desperation."

" Well, certainly, this is a horrid affair, my dear," observed Lady Jane, " and I scarcely wonder at Miss Leslie's looking so shocked. However, if you can bear it with such magnanimity, Bell, I do not see that any one else ought to make themselves unhappy about it. At the same time, I would not advise you, my dear, to be quite so communicative to Mrs. Leslie as you have been to me."

" Certainly not, dear aunt," replied Bell, " indeed, I only mentioned it now, to leave to your consideration whether it would not be advisable to keep the whole affair a secret from mamma, until Ledbury shall be at liberty to request an introduction to her, which he hinted would, he hoped, be in the course of a week or two. The Opera season, you know, is nearly over, and the signora will of course be forming fresh engagements.—Look at Bessie's indignant face, aunt—Is it not enough to make one die with laughing? Why, Bess, you will never get a husband, child, if you are so prudishly intolerant."

" God forbid I ever should," returned Bess, warmly, " if, as the price of a husband, I am to renounce every feeling of delicacy, every principle, every——"

Bell's loud laugh again interrupted her sister, but Lady Jane did not now laugh with her. She did not, even by a look, acknowledge that she approved of her favourite's levity. On the contrary, after a long pause, which Bell herself seemed to feel awkward and ominous, Lady Jane observed—

" After all, Bell, I have made up my mind that your mother must be made acquainted with your proposed alliance. It is taking too great a responsibility on myself, to conceal it from her. I have other reasons, too, for wishing to see Mrs. Leslie, and as Dr. Burnet strongly recommends fresh air and carriage exercise, I have determined that we will drive over to the cottage, and have a quiet day with her, the day after to-morrow. It will be as well, perhaps, that you write a note to your mother, Miss Leslie, to apprise her of my intention."

The first faint indications of a smile since the commencement of this conversation irradiated Jane's lovely face, as she hastened to obey this command. More than three weeks had passed since she had visited her mother, and in the happy prospect of spending one quiet day with her, as Lady Jane had expressed it, she almost forgot the painful purport of the intended visit. Bell's silence and disturbed looks, however, betrayed that she was not equally, or, indeed, at all delighted with her aunt's proposition, though she knew not how to object to it ; but both she and her sister were rather curious to know what were the other motives to which Lady Jane more than once emphatically alluded, as inducing her to seek an interview with Mrs. Leslie.

A very short conference between the ladies when they met, however, revealed to Mrs. Leslie a circumstance which at once put an end to the security she indulged as to the provision for her daughters. " The Twin Roses" were no longer the certain or even presumptive heiresses of Sir Matthew Bevington, for Lady Jane was at last, beyond a doubt, " in the way that ladies wish to be who love their lords," and she announced it to Mrs. Leslie with an exultation which the latter felt might have been a little softened.

" Nevertheless, my dear Mrs. Leslie," she continued, " as Sir Matthew observes, the girls must and shall be well provided for. We have been so long accustomed to consider and treat them as our own children, and they have unfortunately been led to consider themselves so secure, that I really have not yet had courage to announce to them that their prospects are so considerably altered."

Mrs. Leslie faltered out an assurance that her children were not so mercenary as to grieve at an event which would confer so much happiness on their kind uncle and aunt.

"I should be a hypocrite, my dear Lady Jane," she continued, "if I were to pretend that my feelings are those of unalloyed pleasure. I do, indeed, most sincerely congratulate you and my brother, yet you must forgive my saying that I wish now my girls had not been taught——You look angry—forgive me—I only meant to say that it would have been happier for them, if they had never been withdrawn from their obscurity, and given tastes and ——"

"But, my dear Mrs. Leslie, you do not suppose that Sir Matthew or I mean to be so unjust as to withdraw our countenance and protection from them? Oh, no—I assure you, they will remain with us on the same footing as ever, and, rely upon it, we shall exert ourselves to establish them well in the world. Indeed, on that point I have a communication to make, respecting Bell, that will, I trust, relieve you from all uneasiness on her account; because I do not think that the loss of the fortune it was expected Sir Matthew would have given, will be at all considered by the Marquis of Ledbury."

"The Marquis of Ledbury!" Mrs. Leslie repeated, starting with horror and amazement.

But we will not repeat the discussion to which this was a prelude, since Lady Jane's arguments—if the sophistries she uttered could be so called—were precisely the same by which both she and Bell had attempted to convince Bess, while Mrs. Leslie's determined opposition was grounded on the same feelings and principles as had actuated the remonstrances of the latter.

"If her father had lived, Lady Jane," she concluded, "to have seen her even speak to that man would have been a grief to him; but to suppose that ever a child of his could listen to his polluted addresses—could seriously purpose to become his wife —Oh, never, never! Sooner would I see her in her coffin—for she is as yet innocent, I trust, of all but thoughtlessness in suffering herself to be dazzled by the sounding title which would confer, in my eyes, only disgrace upon her! And does Bess, too—pardon me, my lady—does Bess countenance this man? Does she

see, and that in the same light as does her sister——?"

"Really, Mrs. Leslie, I have scarcely thought it worth while to consult Miss Leslie on the subject," returned Lady Jane, disdainfully, though conscious of her shameful evasion of the anxious mother's question. "As I told you at first," she added, "I leave the affair entirely in your hands to decide."

"Thank God—thank God!" repeated Mrs. Leslie, hurriedly, "Thank God that I have the power left to decide—painful as it is in this, the first instance, to oppose my child! Oh, I am sure, I am certain that your ladyship, if you knew the character of the Marquis of Ledbury, would not blame me for saying that I would sooner see Bell dead than behold her his wife. You will feel this, Lady Jane, when you are a mother yourself," she added, as she beheld the sneering smile which passed over the countenance of the latter. "Your child may prove a daughter, and then—"

"And then I should be quite satisfied, if she should meet with as good and eligible an offer *your* daughter has, madam," hastily interrupted Lady Jane; "but I beg the subject may drop here—I can make every allowance for your mistaken feelings, but any further remarks I shall consider as reflecting on myself."

Mrs. Leslie was silenced—she felt the necessity of conciliating Lady Jane, for her children's sake, though she could not repress a look of anguish, when the two girls, arm-in-arm, entered from the garden.

The clear, open, yet sympathising glance which Bess returned, at once satisfied the anxious mother that all was still right with the latter, and her heart gloried in her child; but oh, how different was the result when her eyes rested on Bell. Anger, impatience, obstinacy were written in legible characters on her countenance, and Mrs. Leslie inwardly prayed for strength to encounter the trial which she foresaw awaited her.

The quiet day Lady Jane had bespoken turned out, as is too often the case, anything but that which was intended. Her ladyship's temper, never particularly amiable, was thoroughly ruffled and discomposed, and she vented it in satirical observations and ineundos upon Mrs. Leslie and Bess, whenever she could make an opportunity. The latter were sympathetically silent and sorrowful. Forbidden to speak on the subject nearest her heart, Mrs. Leslie found it impossible to sustain indifferent conversation, while Bess dreaded too much the malice which she saw lurking in Lady Jane's eyes to feel any inclination to break the silence which she had indeed, though naturally lively and animated, learned habitually to practise, whenever her aunt was out of humour. Bell was the only one who even affected to be at ease, but an observant eye could have easily detected that her high spirits were feigned, and that, in reality, she was the most miserable of the party. The long tiresome day, as in her heart Bell called it, at length drew to a close, and she began to anticipate with inward satisfaction her release from the observant and regretful glances of her mother, without any open explanation on the subject which she was quite conscious had given rise to those glances. What, then, was her astonishment and consternation when Lady Jane, in reply to a hint she threw out that she was fearful her aunt would feel the ill effects of the night air, replied with a forced smile——

"Tell the truth, Bell—you want to get rid of me as soon as possible."

"Rid of you, aunt—I do not understand you," replied Bell.

"Do you not, child—then you are more dull of comprehension than I ever knew you to be," replied her ladyship. "I mean, of course, that you are anxious I should go, that you may enjoy your confidential communications with mamma."

"Am I not, then, to return with you?" inquired Bell, in a faltering voice, that showed how unwelcome was the alternative.

"That certainly was not my intention, my dear, in bringing you hither," observed her aunt. "I thought," and she turned to Bess, "that I had fully explained to Miss Leslie that I intended to leave her and her sister with their mother for a few days. I am sorry if there has been any mistake, and it will at all inconvenience Mrs. Leslie, because, to tell the truth, I have promised my friend, Miss Moulsey——"

"Inconvenience?" repeated Mrs. Leslie. "My dear Lady Jane, it can never be other than a pleasure to me ——"

"I am sure, Bess never hinted such a thing to me," interrupted Bell, with a glance of anger at her sister. "I am much obliged to her, I am sure, for treating me like a child, whom it is thought necessary to cheat into——"

She paused, conscious that what she was going to add was improper, while Bess, quite conscious that Lady Jane's intention was an after-thought, observed—

"I could not tell you, Bell, what I did not know. Believe me, I should have been too much rejoiced, and too grateful for the indulgence, if I had understood my aunt's intention, not to have immediately acknowledged it."

"Ah, well, I suppose, with my usual thoughtlessness, I omitted the principal part of what I meant to communicate," observed Lady Jane. "I am thankful, however, that, as your mamma says, your company cannot put her to inconvenience, however unexpected, and I trust my dear Bell will not appreciate the favour the less, because it is unexpected."

Bell felt, in its full force, the sarcasm of this observation; but, whatever resentment she felt, it was confined to her own bosom, and she mildly observed—

"I am sure mamma will not think that I am unwilling to remain with her, because I felt unhappy at the thought of my aunt's returning home alone."

"I should be sorry, indeed, Bell, if I thought your love for me inconsistent with the gratitude due to your aunt."

Neither Bell nor her aunt thought proper to make any reply to this, and Lady Jane, after abundance of embraces and reiterations of their impatience to see each other again, between her and her favourite niece, bade them farewell.

Convinced that something more was meant than she yet understood, by Lady Jane's sudden determination of leaving her and her sister behind, Bell was yet totally unprepared for the communication Mrs. Leslie had to make of the probable overthrow of all their expectations, as the heiresses of their uncle. That it was not a disappointment to Bess, would be too much to aver, for she felt very keenly the vast difference of being the uncontrolled possessor of an immense fortune, and of being left, as was but too probable, from what she had seen of Lady Jane, with little dependance but on her own exertions. But Bess, after the first shock, soon recovered her usual equanimity. She even began to rejoice in the prospect of being entirely freed from what she now acknowledged to be galling fetters—her attendance upon, and forced subserviency to Lady Jane's whims and caprices. Bell, on the contrary, gave way alternately to violent fits of hysterical tears, and resentment against her aunt, whom she accused of already planning to shake her and Bess entirely off.

"And, after all," she observed with bitterness, "they may be disappointed. The child may die, and, even if it lives, if it be a daughter, I suspect my uncle will be so vexed that it will not be a source of much happiness to them. I have heard Lady Jane say, that when she had a prospect of bringing him an heir, soon after their marriage, he was so bent on having a boy, that he said, if it proved the contrary sex, he should never like it. I do, from the bottom of my heart, hope it will be a girl."

Mrs. Leslie gently reproved this uncharitable wish, but her thoughts were too much occupied by a subject which she considered of infinitely more importance to Bell's future welfare, than even the loss of Sir Matthew's fortune, to dwell long upon that subject. But what was her grief and surprise when, on mentioning the intelligence she had received from Lady Jane respecting the Marquis of Ledbury, Bell without reserve avowed her intention to accept his offer, in spite of all persuasion, entreaties, or commands on the part of her mother.

"I am prepared for all the arguments you can use, my dear mamma," she observed ; "but they will be of no avail, because I know they are founded on a wrong view of the case. I know, in the first place, you are unjustly prejudiced against the marquis, who is not half so bad as he is represented ; and even if he were, it is never too late to mend, and I have too good an opinion of, and confidence in myself, not to be thoroughly convinced that, as my husband, he will become quite an altered man. No, no, mamma, do not ask me to give up such a splendid prospect, for I will candidly tell you I cannot. It would be no use to deceive you, by promising what I could not perform. If the marquis still perseveres in his intentions—and I will do him the justice to say that I do not believe the loss of my uncle's fortune will make any difference to him—I shall be the Marchioness of Ledbury, and, I will venture to predict, a happy woman."

"A lost, miserable one," returned Mrs. Leslie, with emphasis. "Oh, Bell, my child—my child, be not tempted by that empty title to peril your immortal soul. The Marquis of Ledbury is not only an abandoned and shameless profligate, but an avowed infidel—a disbeliever in all that you have been taught to revere ; and can you then conscientiously promise at the holy altar to love, honour, and obey such a man?"

A satirical smile dimpled the cheek of Bell, as she replied—

"As to the mere ceremony of marriage, mamma, I regard it as, indeed, all sensible people, now-a-days, do. The world is becoming too enlightened, my dear mamma, to look upon it in any other light than a mere form of words, which custom and the usages of society render necessary, but which——"

"No more, if you wish me to preserve my senses, Bell. Let me hear no more of this," exclaimed Mrs. Leslie, clasping her hands in agony. "Already has poison transformed my once good, dutiful, and obedient child into a presumptuous—Oh, Bell, my heart will break !"

Mrs. Leslie sank back into her chair, and, but that a violent fit of tears came to her relief, would have fainted, while Bess, who by sad experience knew how vain were any remonstrances on this subject, or indeed any other, could only weep over, without being able to offer a single word of consolation to her afflicted mother.

"I should, indeed, be a fool," observed Bell, when she with her sister retired for the night ; "the world would, I am sure, pronounce me mad, if I were *now* to refuse the marquis, whatever they might say when, as co-heiress to Sir Matthew Bevington, I might, with my other advantages, perhaps, have been entitled to expect even a better offer. But now only look at it, Bessie, in a fair light, setting aside all romantic nonsense, and those over-pious sentiments, which, though they are very proper and becoming in the mouth of a clergyman or his widow, are not at all calculated for the every-day wear of the world."

"No," replied Bess, mildly, "they may not be, my dear sister, but they raise us above it, and fit us for a better."

"Psha ! this would be all very fine, if we were grey-headed old women, tottering down the hill of life," replied Bell, petulantly, "but the case is different—now, hold your tongue, Bess, and keep remonstrances until I have set the case fairly before you. On the one hand, then, here is the Marquis of Ledbury, offering a title, for you know, if he lives, he will succeed to the dukedom of Presteigne eventually. Then, a title only one degree below royalty, riches almost unbounded, respect, the power of commanding compliance to every wish, and what, I know, you will regard as still more valuable, the power of doing almost unlimited good ; and, on the other hand, is poverty, with all its countless train of evils—dependance, neglect, obscurity, and

' All the ills that patient merit of the unworthy takes.'

Is it not enough to make one's very blood chill to think of it ? No, no, Bess, all the arguments in the world will not induce me to believe that it is my duty to reject so many advantages, and sit down contented to be poor and miserable."

"But, my dear sister," mildly remonstrated Bess, "there ——"

"But me no buts," interrupted Bell, disguising her anger and impatience of remonstrance in assumed playfulness. "The die is cast—it is your sister's vocation to be a duchess, and it shall not be her fault if her twin rose shall not climb as high as herself. There, now, not another word, for I am determined to go to sleep with that pretty prospect before my eyes. Two full-blown roses, topping over all the meaner flowers, pre-eminent in beauty, and dispensing fragrance all around. Would not that delight my aunt, if she heard it, Bess? No, no, I forgot," and she sighed heavily, "the rose is no longer her favourite flower, though I predict that the bud who is destined to supersede them will turn out a poor little weakly thing, that will not be worth the rearing. Ha, ha, ha! Am I not poetical to-night, Bess? I must try to preserve that idea, and put it in rhyme, for the benefit of Lady Jane, if matters turn out as I suspect they will."

Bess did not attempt to reply. She had no spirits to enter into her sister's raillery, neither could she bring herself to believe that there was any foundation for the conclusion her sister had so hastily come to, that their uncle and aunt would entirely desert them. On Lady Jane, indeed, Bess was secretly compelled to acknowledge very little dependance could be placed. Ever fickle, capricious, and unsteady, she had lately appeared to become doubly so; though Bess could now account for, and understand much that within a few weeks had appeared inexplicable and mysterious. From Sir Matthew, however, she hoped better things. She was sure that, independent of his sense of justice, which would of course prevent his totally abandoning those who for some years he had treated and considered as the heiresses to his immense wealth, he really felt as much affection for herself and Bell as it was in his nature to feel. They were the children, too, of his only sister.

"Oh, no, no," reflected Bess, "he cannot, he will not leave us to all the evils that my sister predicates. He will secure us from poverty and neglect—and happier, far happier, shall I be in what Bell calls obscurity, than in the false, hollow, heartless society that forms my poor sister's world."

CHAPTER X.

Oh, fairest of creation, last and best
Of all God's works, Creature in whom excell'd
Whatever can to sight or thought be form'd,
How art thou lost, how on a sudden lost,
Defaced, defloured, and now to death devote?—MILTON.

THE subsequent conduct of Sir Matthew proved that the opinion which Bess had formed of him was well founded. The very second evening of the sisters' residence with their mother beheld him an unexpected but most welcome guest at their tea-table.

Bell received him with an exuberant display of pleasure, although in general her manners towards him were, in imitation of her aunt, studiously polite and attentive, but nothing more. Now, however, he was her "dear, dear uncle," and she threw her white arms around his neck, and pressed her rose-bud lips to his cheek with a warmth so different from the studied prettiness of her usual salutations to him that it was quite astonishing to the good man when he became convinced that it was really Bell and not Bess, as he had at first imagined—their striking resemblance even yet making it difficult, to their nearest relatives, to distinguish one from the other.

"You are a coaxing little gipsy, I perceive, Miss Bell, when you choose to be so," he at length observed, "but, really, I am quite at a loss to imagine how I have deserved these unusual marks of favour. Bessie, indeed," and he pulled his favourite niece on the other knee, Bell having established herself on one, "your sister and I have always been sworn friends, and she has never seemed to forget that she had an uncle, who, though not quite so refined and fashionable as some of her friends, had a claim to her affection, and——"

"Oh, dear, dear uncle," and Bell's ready tears came to her aid, "do not say that I do not—have not always loved you as well as Bess does—but you know that aunt disapproves of young women showing their feelings—and—and——"

"Well, well, child, say no more about it," observed Sir Matthew. "Your aunt is right, I dare say, and, at any rate, I will do you the justice to say that she has had every reason to be satisfied with you."

This was but an equivocal compliment after all, and Bell felt it was so. But, though the remark brought a slight blush to her cheek, it did not deter her from pursuing her new system of tactics, that of endeavouring, by every means in her power, to conciliate her uncle's favour. On all wordly subjects, Bell, as her sister had often occasion to remark, evinced a degree of foreknowledge and penetration which seemed almost like intuition; and, in the present instance, this faculty, if it might be so called, did not fail her. From the instant she learned the real truth of Lady Jane's situation, she considered her reign of favouritism with that lady—all her reliance on her, either for the present or the future, at an end.

"She will take the first opportunity, depend upon it, Bess, of shaking us both off," observed Bell. "Even now, I should not be at all surprised if she is planning, or has planned, some scheme to prevent our returning home."

"Home?" repeated Bess, calmly. "I have never considered my uncle's residence as *my* home, my dear sister. Thank heaven, we have a home that Lady Jane's influence cannot make otherwise than a happy one."

"Happy?" exclaimed Bell, looking round her with an undisguised expression of contempt. "Happy, indeed, in such a paltry, confined, dismal place as this! I'm sure, if I thought I was to pass the rest of my life here, I should—but it is of no use talking about it—I cannot bear even to think of the possibility of such a thing."

Bess with difficulty suppressed an indignant reply to this observation; but she mildly remarked that, under all circumstances, they might perhaps have cause to look back even to their present situation with regret.

Bell tossed her head with an air of contemptuous credulity, which provoked Bess to observe, that if she (Bell) were right in her conjectures respecting Lady Jane's intention of withdrawing her patronage from them, they would certainly have cause to be thankful, if they were able to retain their present position in society.

"Yes," returned Bell, her eyes sparkling with some sudden recollection, "yes, it might be so, I acknowled, if I had no other dependance than Lady Jady—but, fortunately, that is not the case; and I trust the time is not far distant when I may look down with contempt on Lady Jane and her patronage."

Gladly did Bess avail herself of an opportunity to change the subject. She could not approve of her sister's feelings, or rather total want of feeling, towards her aunt, for whom and to whom she had so lately professed the most ardent affection; and yet, whom she now spoke of as undeserving even of common respect; and still less was Bess disposed to enter on the subject of those hopes her sister alluded to, the fruition of which was to raise her to an eminence which, she thought, even Lady Jane might envy.

Time, however, proved that Bell's estimation of her aunt's character was a just one. Lady Jane's absence from London was protracted for nearly two months—her companion being the ductile, complacent, and ultra-convenient Miss Moulsey, who, it appeared, had completely superseded the favourite niece as a general associate, and was, as her ladyship in one of her letters remarked, only second to Miss Leslie as a nurse. One of her letters, we have said—but the fact was, Lady Jane only wrote twice. The first time in answer to a most impassioned epistle from Bell, describing her misery and despair, at being separated from her "dear, dear aunt;" and the second time, requesting of Bell to execute some commissions, which her unexpected stay in the country rendered necessary. But, in neither of these letters, was the slightest allusion made to Bell, or her sister, again becoming permanent residents in the family of Sir Matthew and Lady Jane Bevington. Lady Jane, indeed, reiterated all Bell's expressions of fondness; she was still her "dear, dear niece," and she assured her that no one in the world would rejoice more than herself to see her dear Bell attain the height of her ambition; but there was none of that confidential tone that her ladyship had been accustomed to preserve towards the latter, and especially did her ladyship cautiously avoid even a word of encouragement or advice on the subject which had but so lately seemed to occupy her every thought. Bell might have imagined that her aunt had forgotten there existed such a person as the Marquis of

Ledbury, but for the postscript of her letter, which (as usual) was the most important part of the epistle.

"I saw," wrote her ladyship, "in a Cheltenham paper of last week, among other arrivals, that of the Marquis of Ledbury. So, if I keep in my present humour, of spending a week or two there, before I return home, I suppose I shall meet with his lordship. I should have been surprised at his having left town, just now, but I see that he belongs to the Cheltenham Hunt, as it is called—so that accounts for it. Have you seen anything of the Balcombes? Tell me, when you write, who you *have* seen, and all about everything."

"The Balcombes, or anybody else, dear aunt," wrote Bell, in reply, "are little likely to seek me in this obscure place. I have seen nobody, heard of nobody. Mamma does not even take in a newspaper, except some vile thing of a weekly paper, which gives no information whatever on the subjects in which alone I feel any interest. But everything is alike here —all dulness and stagnation. I do believe I shall become as mere a piece of still life as the wax figures in Westminster, if I stay here long; or else I shall grow desperate, and break into some wild freaks that will frighten my mild, equable sister and mamma out of their senses. I have never been in town but once, dear aunt, since you left. Mamma had some purchases to make, and I contrived to prove beyond a doubt that she would save two or three pounds by going to town, instead of buying in the neighbourhood; and as, fortunately, her oracle Rachel was of the same opinion, it was agreed that we should all go. But, dear aunt, only conceive my mortification when I found that we were all to be packed into the Highgate stage-coach, which was to set us down at the end of Oxford-street, from whence, as wise sister Miss Bess observed, it would be but a pleasant walk to the various shops mamma had occasion to visit. I had a great mind to draw back and stay at home, but the temptation to be once more among reasonable civilised beings was too great to be resisted, and so I went. The coach drove round and took us up at our own door, so that I was spared the pain of being seen to get into such a vehicle. There was one *gentleman* passenger already inside. Fancy a *gentleman*, aunt, inside a Highgate stage. For my own part, I scarcely looked at the man; but oracle Rachel declared he was the handsomest gentleman she ever saw in her life, though he looked in ill health. Mamma is con-

vinced he was polite and well-behaved, because he told her who inhabited one or two pretty enough places that we passed, and enlightened her as to the hours at which our conveyance returned from town, (which, by-the-by, she could just as well have learned from the coachman), and my demure sister turned her head away to hide a blush, and said nothing when I (provoked at so much being said about such an insignificant person as a stage-coach *gentleman*) observed that I dare say he was some paltry tradesman or another, who slept out at Highgate, and went back to his shop in the morning, adding, that to my fancy he had the very look of a shoemaker or tailor. You may be sure, dear aunt, that I had a fine lecture from mamma upon my aristocratic pride; and, what vexed me still more, I could see that Bess approved of every word that was said to me, though she herself coloured with indignation at my suggestions as to the rank of their stage-coach companion. You will think all this very trifling to write about, dear aunt, but I suspect it will not turn out so in the end; for, whatever the man may be, I am certain he was greatly struck with Bess. I do actually believe he dodged round so as to meet us in Oxford-street, just as we came out of the carpet warehouse, and, though I will not have it that he can be a gentleman, I must own, between you and me, that he is a fine tall young man, with something of a military look and walk, but as I said (perhaps a little maliciously) to Bess, three parts of the swindlers in London contrive to assume both the title and appearance of military men.

"'Or shoemakers or tailors,' said she quietly, in allusion of course to what I had said before, when he got out in the Tottenham Court Road. But what I intended to tell you, dear aunt, and to which all this is but a prelude, is that I have a strong suspicion that it was a preconcerted affair this man's being in the coach that morning. I mean—that he, somehow, had gained intelligence that mamma had sent to take places in the coach which called for us at the cottage; for every morning since, or at least at some part of the day, I have seen him ride on horseback; and sometimes, I am convinced, he is watching our windows, though he pretends not to look up when he is near enough for me to see his eyes. Bess—I beg your pardon, aunt, for calling her by that name, which I know you hate, but I hear it now so constantly I cannot help it—Bess, then, I say, pretended at first not to recognise him; and then, when I reproached her plainly for her

decei.., she got very indignant, and removed her embroidery frame from that window, which is the only one that commands a full view of the road ; and I have had two or three gentle hints since, from her, that it would be as well if I did not pass so much of my time at that window ; and, yesterday, mamma took up the cudgels, quoting some musty old writer on female propriety, who has said that nothing is so striking a proof of vacuity of mind in a young female as her being seen continu-ally at a window, which must be either for the blameable purpose of exhibiting herself, or watching her neighbours.

"I replied, saucily enough, that really I could not help wishing that we had some neighbours to watch. 'As to exhibiting myself,' I observed, 'nobody, I am sure, can accuse me of that—for I really believe not one of the persons who pass ever lift their eyes to the window, unless it is Bessie's beau, the shoemaker or tailor, or whatever he is, and how he ——'

"'My beau!' exclaimed Bess, with her cheeks like scarlet; 'nay, Bell, quite as likely, I should think, to be your beau as mine—but it is nonsensical of me to be vexed about words that can have no meaning.'

"'Well, I am sure, if you disclaim the conquest, I am very willing to accept of it,' said I, 'for anything, even an *affaire de cœur* with a shoemaker or a tailor, is something in the humdrum life we lead; and as I believe the poor man is strangely puzzled to ascertain which is his real inamorata, it will be no very difficult matter for me to appropriate him to myself.'

"I fancied—I don't know whether I am right—but I certainly did think that Bess gave me a saucy glance from the corner of her eye, that bade me defiance. And yet I cannot understand it. She does not think anything about the man, or she would not so determinately avoid the only possible opportunity she can have of seeing him, and suffer me so quietly to occupy her place.

"After all, aunt, wouldn't it be curious, if Bess has really made a conquest worth having? You will see, I daresay, that this letter has been written at different times. Yesterday, I set off to walk with mamma and Bess over to Hampstead. It is now too late in the season for the cockney *canaille* to resort to the heath; and, therefore, the few we do meet there are tolerably decent people. Mamma is grown a most determined walker—she thinks nothing of three or four miles of a morning, and therefore I, who have never, as I tell her, been accustomed to such robust exercise, seldom accept her invitations to accompany her. Bess, of course, always does as mamma does, and they are, I do believe, happier without me than with me. However, as it happened, I was tempted by the prospect of a stroll on the heath, and away we went.

"There is a very beautiful house stands at the south side of—but it is no use my attempting to describe the situation to you, for I recollect hearing you say, when you were here, that you had never been to Hampstead, or any other of the cockney resorts about London. However, the house I am speaking of is such a one as you cannot doubt belongs to a person of wealth and distinction. Marble colonnades, plate-glass windows, draperies of the richest satin damask, extensive grounds, greenhouses, hothouses, &c., &c., all in the most superb style; and on the opposite side of the road stand the coach-houses, stables, and their accompaniments. From the gate opening to the latter, just as we came near enough to discern him, came out a gentleman who crossed the road without observing us, though not unseen by any of our party, and sauntered in at the house-gate, with all the ease of either an inhabitant or a regular visitor. You have guessed, I know already, that this was our stage-coach companion. You are right—for, as if not to leave a doubt on my mind, just as we came up close to the spot, a groom led from the stable the beautiful bay horse that I had seen so many times within the last few days. It was all plain to me that the master was just going to mount for his usual morning ride, but had previously gone back into the house for something. In a few minutes, no doubt, he would be cantering leisurely past a certain cottage, and slily reconnoitring a certain window.

"'But he will be disappointed,' I murmured to myself, 'the bird has flown. After all,' I thought, 'I wonder if it is Bessie—or does he know one from the other?' I do not know whether he ever looked at me in the coach—I know I never looked at him but once, I was in such an ill-humour, and that was when he replied to mamma's question. I confess that I should have been rather struck with his voice, had he been anywhere but where he was. But in a Highgate stage, you know, aunt—however, to return to the second meeting, if so it might be called. After my first surprise, I turned to look at Bess. She was, as usual, quite calm, 'mild as the moonbeams,' as my uncle used to say of her. I was really doubtful that she did not recognise the gentleman, but she smiled as she met my inquiring glance.

"'You did know him, then, Bessie?' said I.

"'Yes, my dear—the tailor or shoemaker—which is it?' she replied, with pretended seriousness.

"'Oh, nonsense,' I replied; 'but what do you think of him, now?'

"'Why, I dare say he has been to measure the groom, either for new jackets or boots,' she replied, with provoking gravity, 'and now he has gone to——'

"I would not listen to her any longer, but went round to the other side of mamma; but, whether she did not or would not know what was the subject of conversation between Bess and I, she did not utter a word, and the matter was dropped.

"All the time we were on the heath, I was on the fidget—I wanted to find out who was the owner of that elegant residence, and whether it is likely that Bessie —if it be her who is the attraction—could reasonably indulge any expectations. I thought it just possible that we might make some discovery, as we returned and passed the mansion, when, as if they read my thoughts, and were determined to disappoint me, mamma and Bess agreed, without even consulting me, to return across the fields by a way I had never been, and which I could make no objection to, because they said it was much shorter, and I had complained of being tired. The abominable stiles, however, gave me a good opportunity of venting my ill-humour all the way home.

"I have tried in vain to make our stupid gardener understand what house I mean. He was *borned*, as he says, in Highgate, and knows the names of all the houses about, but they change and chop owners so, that he can't *purtend* to say who they belong to, except a few of the very *old ancient* families. And then he goes on to enumerate half-a-dozen titles, and about twice as many squires and maiden ladies, who are what he calls the old standards.

"'Do you know a tall pale gentleman that rides a bright bay horse past here of a morning?' I demanded, for I was determined to go any lengths to satisfy my curiosity.

"'I 'spose it be Squire Truman you mean, miss,' he replied, after a long scratch of his head, to assist, I suppose, his memory and comprehension. 'He have got rather a cast in his eye, and a sort of a comical twist of his mouth. It's a nice house that, through ——'

"'Psha, that is not the person I mean,' I replied, but whether *Samiwel*, as he calls himself, is or pretends to be so stupid as not to comprehend who I meant, I don't know. I could get no satisfactory answer from him, though I made the description, I am sure, as clear as noonday, and I left him in a pet that seemed quite to astonish the old man.

"Yours, dear aunt,
            BELL LESLIE.

"P.S. Dear aunt, I have just found out that the house belongs to the Earl of St. Aldwyn, and that there are three sons. I suspect, *our* beau is the youngest—the Honourable Lewis Charles Cheverton. Our laundress, it seems, is occasionally at Raby House, which is the name of the lovely mansion I mentioned. An accident betrayed this to me, and I hastened to get all the information I could on the subject. Bes showed more anger and vexation than I thought her capable of feeling, at what she called laying myself open to the surmises and observations of an ignorant gossiping woman, by making such particular inquiries, but I determined to run all risks to ascertain the truth. The earl is a very good sort of man, says my informant, but the countess is a very proud, violent woman, and governs her husband as well as her family. Lord Raby, the heir, is a cripple, from an accident in childhood, but is 'shocking wild.' The Honourable Horatio, the second son, is to be a clergyman, and is at Oxford—so that it is pretty certain that our friend is Lewis, who is '*summut* in the navy,' and is now on leave of absence, having been severely wounded in some sea-fight. Mrs. Hopkins, our *blanchisseuse*, believes that the younger sons have not got much money of their own, but the countess has got a sister living, an old maid, as proud and as stiff as herself, and they *do* say that Mr. Lewis is her favourite, and will have all her money when she dies; and nobody knows what she is worth, but the servants say she's as rich as a Jew, and as mean too, and cares for nobody nor anything but her young nephew Lewis. This is but a poor prospect, I guess, for our Bess, aunt —if it be her the young man is looking after. As to me, I shall not bestow another thought upon the Honourable Lewis Charles Cheverton, now that my curiosity is gratified. I cannot help telling you that Bessie's sparkling eye betrayed a much deeper interest in the history of the St. Aldwyn family than her lips would acknowledge—and yet she pertinaciously avoids the window. No matter—I am a very good substitute, and I do not believe, at the distance he is obliged to keep, Mr. Cheverton can discover the difference."

Lady Jane's reply to this letter gave very little encouragement to Bell to pursue the subject which had engrossed so much of her thoughts. Her ladyship, indeed, evinced no desire to hear anything more about it. The only notice she took of Bell's diffuse communication respecting the St. Aldwyn family being contained in a concise remark—"I have more than once met the Countess of St. Aldwyn and her sister, Miss Berlingham, in company. They are two of the most arrogant, conceited, disagreeable women I know, and your sister's chance there is not worth a doit."

A deep blush suffused Bessie's transparently fair cheek when Bell maliciously, having first carefully folded down Lady Jane's letter, so that her sister should not read more than what concerned herself, laid it before her, pointing at the same time with her finger to the paragraph in question.

"Oh, Bell, how could you be so thoughtless—so silly—I ought, perhaps, to say so cruel, as to mention to Lady Jane that which, after all, has no foundation but your own fanciful surmises," she observed. "It is plain," she continued, "that your aunt looks upon it in a serious light. You know how unrestrained she is in her confidential communications, as she calls them, and perhaps by this time my name is bandied about by that garrulous—worse than garrulous Miss Moulsey, connected with that of a man with whom I have never exchanged three sentences, and those of merely common civility, as between utter strangers. Oh, Bell, Bell, I should die with shame and mortification if it were to come to the ears of Mr. Cheverton."

"Nonsense, Bessie—now, don't cry so, without you want to make me go and hang myself, or jump into the fish-pond," exclaimed Bell, "which, I assure you, I am more than half tempted to do, from my own private vexations, setting aside this folly, which I should indeed heartily repent, if I thought it could do you any harm. But what a simpleton you are, child, not to know that the very way to enhance your value in the eyes of the world, is to be talked about. What else is the meaning of all those paragraphs which we daily see, or at least used to see, in the fashionable journals? Such as, 'We understand that a marriage is on the tapis between So-and-so, and So-and-so,' or 'It is whispered that Lord Somebody is about to lead to the hymeneal altar the beautiful and accomplished Miss Somebody?' Why, you foolish thing, nine times out of ten, there is as little truth or foundation for such reports, nay infinitely less, than there is if the Honourable Lewis Cheverton and the lovely Bess Leslie were the parties named; because frequently those alluded to had never even thought of each other, whereas, in the present instance, we know that, as far as thoughts and Love's messengers, the eyes, can interpret ——"

"Bell, I cannot bear this raillery," interrupted Bess. "If you love me, you will never mention the subject again, either to me or to any one else."

"Why, then, you are farther gone in the tender passion, Bess, than even I suspected," rejoined her incorrigible tormentor; "but there—don't look so formidably angry at me, and I will not only put a bridle on my tongue, but I will, in my next letter, undeceive my aunt, and assure her that ——"

"Only forbear to speak of me at all, Bell—that is all I require—that I beg—entreat," interrupted Bess, with energy. "The subject will, I hope and trust, fade entirely from Lady Jane's mind, if you do not keep it alive."

"Yes, as everything else does, that is not immediately connected with herself, or her own selfish gratifications," observed Bell, with bitterness. "You are right there, Bessie—Lady Jane no longer feels sufficient interest in the Twin Roses to care what becomes of them, whether they flourish or fade, whether they are trodden under foot, or left to pine and whither unnoticed. But I shall live yet to see her repent her heartless conduct to us. Oh, yes, I know I shall be able to show her that we were not quite so dependant on her high and mighty patronage as I know she thinks we were; and that there were those in the world capable of estimating our value, although it is no longer gilded with Sir Matthew Bevington's paltry gold, or trumpeted into notoriety by his weak vain, heartless wife!"

Exhausted by the violence of the passion which had dictated this *tirade*, Bell threw herself on the sofa, and hiding her face on the pillow, gave way to a burst of tears, pushing away almost fiercely her gentle, tender-hearted sister, who in vain attempted to offer some words of consolation.

They were in this position, Bessie's pale face betraying at once distress and alarm, at her sister's unexpected violence, and Bell sobbing hysterically from her still unsubdued passion, when the door of the little room in which, from its containing all their small store of books, was distinguished by the somewhat assuming name of "the library," was thrown open, and the housemaid Susan, unused to the task of announcing company, without uttering a word ushered in a gentleman, and then closing the door, departed to go in search of Mrs. Leslie, for whom the visitor, it afterwards appeared, had asked, and who, as Susan well knew, was at that moment engaged in some domestic arrangements with Rachel in the kitchen.

The Honourable Lewis Charles Cheverton—(yes it was he himself)—stood for a moment in utter surprise and consternation at the scene to which he had thus abruptly been introduced, while Bess regarded him with equal astonishment and confusion, and her sister, after a glance at their unexpected visitor, concealed her swollen and flushed face again in the pillow of the sofa.

"I am afraid I am a very unwelcome

intruder, madam," observed the gentleman, addressing Bess. "It is Miss Leslie, I believe, I have the honour of speaking to ——"

Bess bowed, as collectedly as she could, but her eyes were again turned on her sister, with a look in which distress and confusion were blended.

"Pray forgive me—I hope, I—If there is any service I can render—I trust nothing has happened to ——"

Mr. Cheverton paused. It was very evident he was as much confused and embarrassed as even Bess herself could be, and yet there was a warmth and kindness in his offer of service that did not sound like the mere words, of course, of a stranger Before Bess could utter a word, however, Bell started up from her reclining posture, and shaking back her luxuriant curls, which had fallen in disorder over her face, she dashed away the tears from her eyes.

"It is I who ought to be ashamed, and to apologise," she observed, with a winning smile, "for having given way to my feeling on such an unworthy subject—but it is all over now. My dear, dear Bessie, how shall I ever make you amends, for having so alarmed and distressed you?"

The grace with which she threw her arms around the neck of the frightened, puzzled, and perplexed Bessie, was quite irresistible. So, at least, the stranger's eyes seemed to say, for they dwelt upon her face and figure with a look of undisguised admiration, which made Bessie's heart throb even quicker than it had done before.

That the latter recovered her self-possession, and was enabled to listen to Mr. Cheverton's explanation of his abrupt appearance—that the gentleman himself resumed his natural, easy, open and frank manners—and that, in short, before the entrance of Mrs. Leslie, the trio in the little library were upon the best possible terms, and scarcely a vestige remaining of the disorder which had characterised their first meeting, was almost entirely owing to the tact, presence of mind, and address of Bell, who, with inimitable grace, contrived to "soothe all discordant elements into peace." With the most frank and candid humility and penitence she acknowledged that she had suffered her feelings to be excited almost to frenzy by an unlooked-for discovery that "a female friend—one with whom her own very heart and existence had been, as it were, bound up—was false, cold, unfeeling; possessed not, in short, any of those qualities for which she (Bell Leslie) had all but idolized her."

"But I will dismiss from this moment, her very memory," she continued. "I will have no friend but my dear sister, my own Bessie, whose cooler judgment and deeper penetration would long ago have taught me distrust, had I not been headstrong, and blindly infatuated by the acts of one whom I foolishly thought as warm-hearted and sincere as I was to her. There," she continued, as, rising and advancing to the fire-side, she threw Lady Jane's letter into the flames, "thus perish the record of her falsehood, and my silly, trusting confidence in one who never deserved it. And now," she added, turning to their visitor with a bright smile and sparkling eyes, "Now, Richard's himself again."

There was something in the whole of this exhibition but too much in character with the concluding theatrical exclamation, not to strike the calm, penetrating Cheverton with the conviction that it was unreal. But, had he been inclined to doubt that it was, for at least the greater part of it, got up to serve the exigency of the moment, Bessie's blushing, conscious face would have at once obliterated those doubts. He saw that there was something behind the curtain, which would have explained much more naturally, though perhaps not quite so creditably for Bell, the scene he had beheld on his entrance; but it would have distressed her lovely ingenuous sister had it been exposed, and he was content to let it pass. Nay, more, to enter so completely into the spirit of the part Bell had assumed, as to appear deceived, and exert himself to the utmost to set both sisters at rest under the conviction that he was so.

"I have forgotten, all this time," he at length observed, "that while I am assuming the enviable privilege of talking to you ladies, as a friend, I am in reality a nameless individual, who——"

"Oh, dear, no," interrupted Bell, with an affectation of childish simplicity, "we know you very well, Mr. Cheverton. That is, I mean, my sister—at least, I and my sister—" Bell put on the prettiest look of confusion imaginable, as if she were conscious of betraying what should be concealed, while she added with a laugh, "I hope it will not make you vain, when I tell you that after we met you in that horrid stage-coach, we could not rest, Bessie and I, till we found out who you were."

The young man laughed in his turn, but there was a slight degree of confusion in his manner as he observed—

"I hope, however, that I am not indebted to the name of Cheverton for my flattering reception, because I am compelled to avow that it is one to which I have no claim. My name is Leicester—Ronald Leicester. I sent a card to Mrs. Leslie, but——"

"Then you are not the son of the Earl of St. Aldwyn, sir?" said Bell, with a look and in a tone that expressed not only disappointment, but something more. It sounded, indeed, so harsh in Bessie's ear that she hastened to soften it by observing—

"Mr. Leicester is not, I hope he will feel, less welcome on that account. We know nothing at all of the St. Aldwyn family, and the mistake originated——"

Bess paused. She felt that it was an awkward affair to explain how it originated, for it would not have been quite pleasant to have named Mrs. Hopkins, the washerwoman, as their authority.

Mr. Leicester smiled.

"Probably from my being for a short time the guest of the earl," he observed, "who is my mother's brother."

"Oh, then, you are a relative of Lord St. Aldwyn," observed Bell, the smiles, which his renunciation of the name of Cheverton had banished from her face, quickly returning.

Leicester bowed assent—Bess thought not with the cordiality which had before marked his manner; but the slight unpleasant feeling was soon banished, for he almost immediately observed—

"I do hope that, in reality, my name will be a better passport to your favour than even that of Cheverton. To Mrs. Leslie, I am sure, it will—for she will recognise it as one born by a very sincere and attached friend of her respected husband."

"Oh, dear, how strangely forgetful I have been," exclaimed Bess, with warmth, "not to have instantly recognised the name, which was so frequently on my dear father's lips, and ever connected with some gentle or pleasant recollection of his youthful days."

The young man's eyes beamed animation and delight as he gazed on the expressive features of the speaker; but "a change came o'er her mood," and her eyes filled with tears.

"You, too, Mr. Leicester, have suffered the irreparable loss of a father," she observed, in a tone that showed how deeply she still felt the bereavement she thus pathetically alluded to.

Mr. Leicester's eyes were cast down, and his manly chest heaved with emotion as in a faltering voice he replied—

"I have been even more unfortunate than you, Miss Leslie—for in little more than one year I have lost father, mother, and an only sister—an amiable, beautiful being, in the very spring time of life—and am now, indeed, alone in the world. But I cannot talk of this—Forgive me, I——"

He arose suddenly and walked to the window, evidently unable to control the painful feelings this explanation of his situation had excited in his bosom, while the big tear-drops of sympathy in silence coursed each other adown Bessie's fair cheeks.

"Where in the world can mamma be?" observed Bell, suddenly. "That stupid Susan must certainly have neglected to inform her that Mr. Leicester is here."

She rang the bell with a violence which betrayed, even more than her words, or the tone in which they were uttered, her impatience and dislike of the serious turn the conversation had taken.

Mr. Leicester started, and turned a piercing look of surprise and almost reproach upon Bell, who was, however, totally unconscious of it. She had stolen the opportunity, as she thought, when his back was towards her, and his attention otherwise engaged, to adjust her ringlets at the chimney-glass.

"What a horrible fright I have made of myself," she whispered to her sister. "If it had been any one who was worth caring about, I should go mad at their seeing me with these swollen eyes and reddened nose; but as I have no ambition to captivate——"

Bess was in agonies lest her sister's words, which were but too audible, should reach the ear of their guest, and she abruptly interrupted them by rising to mend the fire, making as much noise as she possibly could with the fire-irons, and at the same time inquiring of Mr. Leicester whether Lord St. Aldwyn had any daughters.

"Why, you know very well, Bessie, he has not," observed Bell, before the gentleman could utter a word in reply to the question. "Did not our friend, Mrs. H." (and she nodded significantly at her sister) "tell us that there were only three sons living, though the countess, she believed, had had several daughters."

"Yes, our family have been particularly unfortunate in the female branches," observed Mr. Leicester, sighing.

"I wonder, though," rejoined Bell, resuming her smiles, though to her sister they bore a mischievous meaning that made her almost tremble at the coming sentence—"I wonder Mrs. H, who pretended to be so *au fait* to all concerning the St. Aldwyn family, should have omitted to mention so important a member of it as the earl's nephew, Mr. Leicester."

It was now Mr. Leicester's turn to smile, though his companions could not comprehend the meaning of the peculiar archness of that smile

"If there is no very important motive for concealing the name of your lady informant under the initial by which you designate her," he observed, looking at Bell, "will you allow me to hazard a guess that it was your neighbour, Mrs. Hopetoun, in whose good graces I, unfortunately, do not rank very high."

"Oh, indeed," returned Bell, playfully, "is that the case? Then the omission is accounted for."

This was an evasion, or rather an equivocation on the part of her sister, which Bess felt little less degrading to the former than a direct falsehood. Neither Bess nor herself were, in reality, aware that there was such a person in the neighbourhood as Mrs. Hopetoun, though, after a moment's reflection, they guessed that the name appertained to a remarkably tall, ungainly, sour-looking old Scotch lady, who inhabited a very small but pretty cottage, the nearest to their own residence. Vexed, however, as Bess was at her sister's reckless disregard of truth, she she could not but feel a satisfaction that Mr. Leicester had not, nor was likely now to discover the mortifying fact that Bell had descended to question Mrs. Hopkins, the Countess St. Aldwyn's laundress, and quote her authority under the familiar assumption of Mrs. H. And yet, how often had Bess blushed for, and been surprised at the easy indifference with which Lady Jane—the proud, assuming, Lady Jane Bevington, the daughter and sister of an earl, as she frequently designated herself —would give as her authority, for any disputed news or doubted scandal, her own maid, Madamoiselle—who had it direct, she would observe, from some other equally dignified personage — the own maid, or own footman, or other servant in the family to which the news or scandal, as the case might be, related. With such an example fresh in her recollection, it would not have been very surprising if Bell had boldly avowed the source from which she had derived her information, but Bess was spared this mortification, this degradation in Mr. Leicester's eyes, and most truly thankful did she feel when the subject was entirely dismissed, as she hoped, by the entrance of Mrs. Leslie, who, ever attentive to the maintenance of respectability, had been detained so long

from her guest by her having considered it necessary to exchange her every-day suit for her very best black. But again poor Bessie was in tribulation—Mr. Leicester's card had, in Susan's "flustration," as she called it, escaped from her hand, while she was hastily pulling off her coarse apron, as not being a fit attire to precede a gentleman to her young ladies, and Susan having somehow happened to imbibe the same belief as her mistresses, that the gentleman who rode by every day on the bright bay horse was named Cheverton, and was a lord's son, she had announced the visitor by that name to Mrs. Leslie, and sent the good lady off at a tangent to make herself fit to receive so distinguished a guest.

Again, therefore, there was an explanation of the mistake to be made, but Bess now took it upon herself, and again the evil she so much dreaded was averted, and in this instance fortunately without having recourse to deception or equivocation. Mrs. Leslie's emotion and pleasure at beholding the son of her husband's dearest friend, effectually, indeed, occupied all parties, with the exception, it may be said, of Bell—whose countenance expressed rather impatience and vexation at an excess of feeling for which she saw no cause. Indeed, although she had affected total forgetfulness of even the name of Leicester, she had from the moment she heard it employed herself in recalling to her mind some particulars connected with the history of her father's early friend, which had the effect of rendering her very indifferent to the renewal of the intercourse between her family and the son of that friend.

Mr. Leicester (the father), she remembered hearing, was the son of an eminent banker, and had been brought up with the expectation of inheriting a very large fortune. He was scarcely of age when he became attached to Lady Sarah Cheverton, the daughter of the last and sister of the present Earl of St. Aldwyn, a beautiful girl, not more than eighteen, whose birth and talents were nearly her only dowry.

The consent of the parents on both sides was easily obtained, for Mr. Leicester's fortune was considered by the lady's family an equivalent for his want of rank. The marriage day was fixed, and everything was in preparation, when a dreadful blow was given to the happiness of the youthful pair. The senior Mr. Leicester had, it appeared, entered into some speculations to an immense amount. One after the other they had failed, and unable to bear up against the disgrace and poverty that awaited him and his family, the unhappy man destroyed himself. The act, of course, accelerated the ruin of the firm of which Mr. Leicester and his son were the principal partners; but, next to the shock which his father's death under such dreadful circumstances inflicted, was the conduct of the St. Aldwyn family to young Leicester. Lady Sarah was hurried off to the country by her parents, and forbade to think any more of him to whom her whole heart was given. He was represented to her as equally, if not more guilty than his father, in having sought to prop the fortunes of their falling house by an alliance with the St. Aldwyn family, though, in point of fact, to none had the catastrophe which had plunged him into ruin been more unexpected than to the unfortunate young man, who had never been allowed to take any active share in the business. Lady Sarah, however, was not of an age or disposition to listen to the dictates of prudence, or desert the man of her choice for no other fault than his having been, by no act or error of his own, reduced at once from affluence to poverty. She contrived to let her lover know her real sentiments, and to raise him from utter despair to immediate exertion by an assurance that she was determined to fulfil her engagements and share his fate, whenever he chose to require it. For four long years Leicester toiled before he could procure even a provision which would have been thought scarcely sufficient by one of his own rank in life—but to the object of his choice, reared in every luxury and indulgence, was comparative poverty. But Lady Sarah, who had disdained concealment of her sentiments towards Leicester, was now harassed with the continued importunity of her father and mother to accept an offer made her by a young nobleman whom they considered an unexceptionable match. She was now of age, and though Leicester trembled at the prospect of the privations to which his beautiful high-bred Sarah would be exposed in her union with one who depended on the labour of his hands for the comparatively paltry pittance of two hundred a year, he having, by careful attention to business and unremitting exertion, risen to a clerkship in a mercantile house, in which his situation at first had not been equal to half that sum. But he could not resist her entreaties to remove her from a scene which was rendered unbearable by the constant reproaches of her parents, and the solicitations of her new lover, who was ungenerous enough to persist in his suit, and

take advantage of her friends' interference in his favour, although she had candidly confessed to him that her heart was given, and her hand pledged, to one who had once been the favoured object of her parents' choice, as well as her own.

"If you love me—if all your professions have not been false," she wrote to Leicester, "you will no longer hesitate to take that final step, which will at once remove me from a life of utter misery to that of perfect happiness."

It was not in man—or, at least, in one so attached as Leicester—to resist this appeal. In a few days, a still-youthful couple stood at the altar, whose plain appearance, and want of all the paraphernalia and attendants that are usual on such occasions, contrasted strangely with their noble and dignified bearing and persons. Mr. Leslie, then just in orders, was the officiating clergyman—for an humble curate was now thought good enough to perform that ceremony for which a bishop's attendance had once been engaged—and from the church, the high-bred beauty, who had been used to have carriages and a train of servants at her command, retired in an humble hackney-coach to a furnished lodging in a cheap suburb of London.

"And soon learned to repent her having thrown herself away so, I suppose, papa," Bell had observed, when Mr. Leslie had related this story, in consequence of his daughter having gaily questioned him one evening as to who the first pair were that he had united in the bonds of matrimony.

"I hope she never had reason to repent it, Bell," returned Mr. Leslie, after a thoughtful pause. "She was, I could almost say, an angel on earth; and most beautiful it was to see her effort to sustain my friend Leicester's drooping spirits, and to prove to him how little of happiness was really dependant on those superfluities which he, for her sake, so bitterly regretted the want of. For the two or three years that I, still poorer than themselves, was their only and a happy, honoured guest at their tea-table, after Leicester returned from the fatigues of the day, I never saw a cloud upon her countenance. She sank as naturally into the station of her husband as though she were 'to the manner born;' and yet was as completely the lady of high birth and refined breeding, in her own scantily but neatly furnished parlour, presiding at the plain and frugal meals which her own hands had assisted to prepare, as when she was the admired of all beholders in the brilliant drawing or ball room of her father's mansion. One thing alone, I believe, sometimes cast a shade

over her else perfect happiness. That was, the continued enmity of her parents, by whom, from the moment she was married, she was utterly discarded. But, satisfied that she had not deserved their resentment, in having preferred her own happiness, and that of her husband's, to the realisation of their ambitious schemes, she at length relinquished her attempts to conciliate them, and trusted to time, and her husband's exemplary conduct and character, eventually to plead successfully with them.

"'For the sake of my children,' (she had then two—a lovely girl and a boy), 'to whom their countenance and protection might be desirable,' she would observe, while tears, the only ones I ever saw her shed, would force themselves into her eyes—'for their sakes, I would submit to anything to conciliate my father and mother, except that which I understand they are unjust enough to require as the price of their favour—namely, an avowal that I repent the step by which I forfeited it. No, they must be just to him, as well as kind to me."

"And were her hopes eventually realized, dear papa?" inquired Bess, eagerly.

"I do not know, my dear. Circumstances separated me from my friends. Leicester was persuaded upon to accept an agency in the West Indies, for the house in which he was employed. It was a great advantage to him, in point of emolument, and it also held out to him the prospect of increasing to a great degree his power of benefiting a large number of his fellow-creatures, in the persons of the poor degraded slaves, of whom there were, I understood, more than seven hundred on the estates to which he was appointed agent."

"And did Lady Sarah consent to go out with him, and live among those horrid blacks?" demanded Bell.

"Mrs. Leicester did, my dear—she was no longer Lady Sarah—indeed, she was before only a lady by courtesy, as it is called, but even that she relinquished by her marriage. Yes, it was her persuasion determined Leicester," continued Mr. Leslie, "and the last I ever saw of her or my friend was on board the vessel in which they had taken their passage; and then she was, as usual, cheering his too-sensitive mind by all sorts of bright and beautiful anticipations of the life they were to lead in Demerara, and the good they should be able to achieve. I believe those hopes were fully realized, at least for some time," added Mr. Leslie, "for Leicester's letters to me were full of hope and gratitude; but circumstances occurred, too long to relate now, that interrupted our correspondence. I contracted other ties," (and he glanced affectionately at his wife) "that engrossed all my thoughts, and most of my affections; my being removed to a distance was also an impediment to my hearing of Leicester, and it is now some years since I have known anything of his fate."

All these particulars, though they had not made a deep impression, at the time they were related, on Bell's mind, were yet recalled to her memory with wonderful accuracy, now that she found herself so unexpectedly in company with the son of her father's friend. He had himself avowed that his parents were both dead, and in all probability——Oh, yes, she, Bell, was quite sure that this young man, in spite of his imposing appearance, and that easy, independent air and manner which would so well become a better fortune, was now nothing more than a

dependant, a mere hanger-on, on the score of relationship, of the Earl of St. Aldwyn's.

Bell's manner towards their visitor was now quite suited to her impression of his situation in life. She neither joined in, nor seemed to take any interest in the animated conversation which, at the end of several hours, found her mother, sister, and Mr. Leicester, almost as well acquainted with each other as though they had been associates for as many months. It was not worth Bell's while to attempt to shine. Besides, the subjects they conversed upon were not such as she could take any interest in, and she returned to the vexatious contemplation of Lady Jane's letter — a contemplation which neither added beauty to her countenance, nor pleasantness to her manners. By degrees, Mr. Leicester's attention, which had at first been equally divided between the sisters, became totally centred in Bess, whose radiant features had never looked more beautiful. She had totally forgotten, or, at least, disregarded, the threatened evil which had so dreadfully agitated her sister, although the clouded brow and disdainful silence of the latter would have forcibly reminded Bess of it, had she been less happy and interested than she was in her present society.

Two or three times Bell's significant consultation of the small time-piece that was placed on a marble slab in a recess, close to Mr. Leicester's elbow, reminded him, as expressively as if she had spoken her thoughts, that she at any rate considered it time he should depart. But, though he could not help comprehending this indirect hint, he did not see any corroboration of it in either the looks of Bess or her mother, until at last the latter, in reply to a whispered remonstrance from Bell, delivered with no very gentle looks or tones, observed—

"Is it, my dear? I was not aware of it—time passes so pleasantly with one who seems to recal happier times. My daughter tells me, my dear Mr. Leicester," she added, smiling, "it is near our dinner hour."

"Passed more than half an hour," murmured Bell, sullenly.

"We are very unfashionably early, I know," continued Mrs. Leslie, "but if you will do us the honour to dine with us, if you have not any other engagement—"

"And if Mr. Leicester has," observed Bess, smilingly, "it will only be lunch for him."

If Mr. Leicester had even predetermined to decline the offer, Bessie's smiles would have most probably induced him to rescind that determination; but the fact was, he had been for the last half-hour secretly hoping that Mrs. Leslie would not consider it necessary to treat him with the formality of a new acquaintance, and most gladly he assured her that he had no other engagements, and should be most happy to avail himself of her offer.

Bell's looks were not improved by this frank invitation and its acceptance.

"Was there ever anything so ridiculous," she muttered to her sister, while Mrs. Leslie was engaged in showing Mr. Leicester a beautiful plant, which she was rearing in the recessed window of the room; "mamma knows very well we have a make-up dinner to-day, and to ask a stranger, who is used to such a table as the Earl of St. Aldwyn's."

Bess laughed.

"Never mind, Bell," she observed, "he did not come, I dare say, expecting we could vie with the earl; and, besides, if I have any skill in judging of persons, Mr. Leicester is not one who places his enjoyment in a good dinner, if he does ——"

"And we shall not have a moment, I suppose, to change our dresses," interrupted Bell, glancing at her plain merino and black silk apron with dissatisfaction.

"I do not think our new friend would consider us more estimable," replied Bess, "if we were ——"

"Oh, do not suppose I want to recommend myself to him," observed Bell, disdainfully. "I assure you, I am perfectly indifferent to what he thinks of me, but I do hate to be looked down upon—to be considered inferior to anybody; and it would be so easy for mamma to keep up a little more style in her arrangements. For instance, what will this man think of us, when he sees nobody but a stupid servant-girl waiting at table? I declare, I never myself eat my dinner with any satisfaction, after being used to the attentions of proper servants."

"I am sorry to hear it," replied Bess, with a sigh; "for my own part, I think our quiet, social meals, infinitely preferable to dining in public, as I may call it, with half-a-dozen liveried attendants watching every look and ——"

Mrs. Leslie and Mr. Leicester returned to the sofa, and the former quitted the room for a few minutes, leaving the young people together. Mr. Leicester talked to them of the books which he saw around him, but Bell's silence told him this was a subject which possessed no interest for her, and Bessie appeared rather inclined to listen to his opinions than to give her own. He then spoke of music, observing he had been more than once gratified with the sound of voices accompanied by a pianoforte, as he passed their cottage at night. He was an enthusiastice admirer of music. So was Bell. She was, indeed, fully conscious of her own superiority to most private performers, and indifferent as she had professed herself, and really was, as to Mr. Leicester's opinion, she condescended to speak on this subject, so as to convince him she was no mere pretender, but deeply (for a young lady of seventeen) skilled in the science. The conversation naturally diverged to the discussion of the merits of the most popular and fashionable singers of the day, and Mr. Leicester seemed somewhat surprised at the intimate acquaintance Bell had with their respective styles—the points in which they were defective, or most excelled—but still more at her evident familiarity with all the tittle-tattle, scandal, and private histories of the signors and signoras, &c., of the King's Theatre, or Italian Opera House. Still greater was his astonishment when Bell spoke of *our* box, and betrayed a perfect acquaintance with all the mysteries appertaining to a place which, from the unpretending appearance of Mrs. Leslie's household and mode of living, he did not suppose her daughters had ever visited. The mystery, however, was soon explained—Bell had got upon a subject now that she could talk upon, and she became more and more animated, as she found that Mr. Leicester, if not so *au fait* to the operatic arrangements as herself, was acquainted with most of the fashionable patrons and patronesses, and was himself a frequent visitant.

"The St. Aldwyn family have not a box this year?" she observed.

"No, they have not," replied Leicester, "they have been this last year in Italy, and, when they returned, the season was far advanced."

"Ah, I thought I was right in my recollection," returned Bell. "Their box was next to my aunt's, Lady Jane Bevington. I remember her telling me what fine young men the Chevertons were, and regretting that that disagreeable old fright, Lady Almar, and her five, ugly, old-maidish daughters, with their long crane necks, sallow skins, and everlasting black velvets and paste ornaments, occupied their places. The Almars are fixtures there; I used to expect to see them as regularly as the old shabby curtain."

"My cousins, certainly, are indebted to Lady Jane for the preference," observed

Mr. Leicester, smiling, "but you are not aware, perhaps, that the Miss Almars are accomplished musicians, and go merely to enjoy the music, not to see, or be seen. Their appearance there, I suppose, is a matter of indifference to them; and that which you say so uniformly distinguishes them is assumed as the most convenient. If their ornaments are false, of which I confess myself no judge, it cannot be from their inability to procure others, because I believe it is generally known that Sir George Almar died immensely rich."

"You are acquainted with the family, I see," returned Bell, not without some trace of confusion, at her having been so unguarded in her remarks.

"Lady Almar was my mother's cousin and intimate friend," he replied, "almost the only female friend she retained after her marriage; and, I assure you, if her face is 'frightful,' it is no index to her mind—for she is truly good and amiable, and the same epithets are strictly applicable to her daughters. I do not know, indeed, a more united, happier family than the Almars; and I am sure," he added, with an arch smile, "that if I were only to give them a hint that their uniformity of attire renders them obnoxious to Miss Leslie, they——"

"Oh, for goodness' sake, Mr. Leicester, I am quite sufficiently mortified for my foolishness, in having made such remarks," exclaimed Bell, with a pretty affectation of confusion and penitence, which greatly improved the expression of her beautiful features. "But, really," she added, "I was not the originator of those observations. It was—yes, I perfectly remember now—it was the Marquis of Ledbury, who said one evening, in my aunt's box, that he really believed the Miss Almars slept in their black velvets, to be ready for the first note of the overture; and I remember, too, that my impression respecting their diamonds being false, arose from his or somebody saying—

"Pardon me, I am not desirous of hearing anything for which the Marquis of Ledbury's authority is quoted," interrupted Leicester, his fine face glowing, and both his voice and look expressing undisguised contempt towards the nobleman in question.

Bell's eyes flashed fire—but Leicester, either not noticing, or pretending not to notice her agitation, calmly and quietly continued—

"I am quite certain that Miss Bell Leslie is unacquainted with the character of the man who, it appears, had inad-vertently, I am sure, on the part of Lady Jane Bevington, been admitted to sufficient terms of familiarity to give utterance to his impertinent observations on a family so much his superiors that I am convinced he would not dare——"

"You are mistaken, sir, I assure you," interrupted Bell, haughtily. "The Marquis of Ledbury is the most intimate friend of Sir Matthew and Lady Jane, and I cannot hear him slandered, in his absence. If what he said was impertinence, it was only a repetition of what I have heard many times about the Miss Almars' appearance. I remember, indeed, somebody saying—that was not the marquis——"

"My dear Bell," interposed Bess, "you forget that it is Mr. Leicester's friends and relatives of whom you are repeating remarks that must be disagreeable to hear, though they only prove the emptiness, and I hope the thoughtlessness of those who uttered them."

Leicester's eyes betrayed his thankfulness for, and the approval of this interposition; but Bell, though at first she appeared disposed to reply angrily to her sister's mild reproof, suddenly burst into an apparently uncontrollable fit of laughter.

"You must excuse me, you must indeed, Mr. Leicester," she observed as soon as she could speak. "Bess, did you ever see the five Miss Almars? But I suppose you have not,—for I believe you have never been but twice to the opera, and then I know, as my aunt remarked, your attention was so riveted to the stage that you were hardly conscious that there was an audience. Bess is an enthusiast, too, for music, Mr. Leicester, and, I assure you, she looked the first night as if she could have beaten Lady Jane and me for laughing and chattering with some of our friends, while somebody, I forget who—but I know it was no one of sufficient importance to be listened to—was singing."

"It was a young female," observed Bess, tears filling her fine eyes, "who, though not certainly possessed of the power or skill of the prima donna, sang with the most beautiful simplicity and feeling. She appeared timid—it was, I understood, her first appearance—and I confess I do think it was cruel and unjust to damp her exertions by your ill-timed conversation. Besides, dear Bell, I must tell the truth, I trembled at the observation that I saw was fixed on our party by the noise you made."

"You were afraid we should have been hissed, I suppose," returned Bell. "Oh, how I should have laughed—but you need not have been afraid, child. I don't suppose there was half-a-dozen people in the house who cared anything about it, or would not have laughed at your sensitive concern for the new singer, who was only a third or fourth-rate, if I recollect right, though really I paid so little attention at the time, that I do not know who it was, and should not have remembered the circumstance but that I was diverted at the observations that were made upon your indignant looks, when I refused to yield obedience to your entreaties to be quiet."

Bess made an attempt to laugh as she observed—

"This is really a very entertaining subject to discuss, for the amusement of Mr. Leicester, Bell. You will make him believe that I am quite a virago."

Mr. Leicester's eyes, however, expressed a very different impression. They said, as plain as eyes could say, that he honoured and admired the feeling that had actuated her indignation, and Bess was glad almost to find refuge from their animated expression in her mother's entrance, and a summons to dinner.

CHAPTER XI.

——A true knight;
Not yet mature, yet matchless; firm of word,
Speaking in deeds, and deedless in his tongue;
Not soon provoked, nor being provoked, soon calm'd.
His heart and hand both open, and both free;
For what he has he gives; what thinks, he shows.
Yet gives he not, till judgment guide his bounty;
Nor dignifies an impair thought with breath.—SHAKSPEARE.

R. LEICESTER'S visits to the cottage became now constant, and his intimacy with its inhabitants daily more warm and confidential. To Mrs. Leslie he appeared, as she frequently said, all that a young man should be, and the very being that she should have expected would have been formed by such a father and mother as his had been represented to her by her lamented husband. With Bell, he was on the best and easiest terms, on all but one subject. That, it may easily be guessed, was the Marquis of Ledbury. Of him, he would not hear her speak, without the most marked and positive condemnation; and Bell soon found the society of a gay handsome young man a great relief from the otherwise unvaried monotony of their lives, and his attendance on her and her sister in their walks and rides both pleasant and convenient. The last indulgence, indeed, being only procurable by his means, in occasionally borrowing horses for them. In reality, hiring them—though that they did not know, or suspect. These, and the numerous pretty presents he from time to time contrived to induce Mrs. Leslie to accept, but which were covertly intended for her daughters, were so many sources of gratification, that Bell would not hazard the loss of his favour by any indiscreet mention of the person who was so obnoxious to him. The name of the Marquis of Ledbury, therefore, ceased to be uttered, and Bess was almost inclined to hope that as nothing was heard of him, he had himself dropped all pretensions to Bell's favour.

And Bess—what were Bessie's thoughts of their new friend? Whatever those thoughts were, they were strictly confined to her own bosom. In his presence, she was even more silent and restrained than was natural to her disposition; and seldom, very seldom, in his absence, was his name uttered by her. At Bell's raillery on the conquest she had made—for from the first Bell insisted that her sister was the magnet that drew Mr. Leicester so frequently to the cottage—Bess became grave, and sometimes angry. It was a subject she did not like jesting upon, she would remark.

"No, because you feel it is becoming a serious affair," the incorrigible tormentor would reply.

Bess, however, would not acknowledge, even to herself, the source of those blushings and throbbings of the heart which would seize her even at the sound of Leicester's voice, or the sudden mention of his name; and to suppose that there was any foundation for Bell's assertions that she had made a conquest of his heart—oh, not for the world would she be guilty of such presumption.

"Presumption!" Bell's pretty lip would curl at the word, and then Bess would determinately refuse to hear another word on the subject; or, if her sister persisted, would seek shelter with her mother, who uniformly discouraged such suggestions on the part of her younger daughter.

Lady Jane Bevington returned to town, but no notification of her arrival reached the cottage, until Sir Matthew himself paid them a visit; and then, though his manner and expressions were as kind and cordial as ever to his sister and nieces, it became evident that Bell's predictions were correct. Not a word was said of either her or Bessie's return, as permanent residents at his house; but, he assured them, Lady Jane was very anxious to see them, and invited them all to a family dinner, on the next day but one, with the additional inducement that he would send the carriage for them early.

Bell bit her lips, and Bess trembled, lest she should expose herself to her uncle's displeasure, by some explosion of temper. Mrs. Leslie, of course, signified her acceptance of her brother's invitation.

"We cannot go very early, mamma," observed Bell, "because Bess and I are engaged for the morning. We cannot possibly be back before three, and then we shall have to dress for dinner."

"And, pray, what particular engagement have you and Bess made?" demanded Sir Matthew, good-humouredly, "that you cannot put it off to oblige your aunt, after not seeing her for two or three months!"

"Oh, it is a *very* particular engagement," replied Bell, with an air of indifference; "but I thought two or three hours' delay could not make much difference, as Lady Jane has not shown any extraordinary impatience to see us."

"You are not aware, perhaps, Bell," observed Sir Matthew, "but, if you had been attending to what I said, in answer to your mother's inquiries, instead of fondling and making that ugly cur so troublesome——" This was Leicester's dog, which Bell had taken a fancy to make a pet of, and which was therefore now oftener at the cottage than with its master——

"Ugly cur!" she repeated. "Dear uncle, how can you say so? I'm sure, it's the sweetest creature that ever was seen. Oh, my dear, dear Carlo, don't I love you?

Come here, you love of a dog, and sit beside me on the sofa. See, uncle, he understands every word I say to him."

Sir Matthew looked seriously displeased at this affected levity and indifference to his observations, and Mrs. Leslie and Bess were both alarmed and confused at the probable consequences of her folly, or rather determination to provoke her uncle.

A sudden thought, however, seemed to occur to Sir Matthew, and he good-humouredly observed—

"I suspect there is some reason for Bell's violent fondness for Carlo. Pray, may I ask, who introduced him here, for I recollect it used to be one of her pretty affectations to be frightened and scream, if one of the dogs found its way into the rooms at Bevington House."

Bell affected not to hear her uncle's question, but Mrs. Leslie saw that her brother expected a reply, and she therefore observed that the dog belonged to Mr. Leicester.

"A nephew," she hastily added, "of our neighbours, the Earl of St. Aldwyn." For she knew that to have mentioned Mr. Leicester merely as the son of an intimate friend of her late husband, would have called forth from her brother a thousand questions as to his situation, prospects, &c., which she was unprepared to answer, and would perhaps have induced Sir Matthew to have animadverted on the imprudence of encouraging the visits of a young man, and suffering him to be on terms of intimacy with her daughters, whose situation in life might be such as to render him a very improper associate for them. She judged correctly of her brother. The name of the St. Aldwyn family seemed to him quite a sufficient guarantee for Mr. Leicester; but Bess felt the colour mount into her cheeks, in spite of all her efforts to appear unconcerned, when Sir Matthew observed—

"So, then, I am to conclude that Bell has made another conquest? Why, Bessie, what are you about, girl, to let this saucy chit run away with all the beaux? Well, I suppose your turn will come some day, and perhaps, after all, you will get married first. There is an old proverb you know, Bell, about having too many irons in the fire."

"I really don't understand you, uncle," returned Bell, affecting confusion, but glancing mischievously at her sister, who returned it by a look which Bell knew well enough meant to implore her not to mention her name in connection with Mr. Leicester's.

"Well, never mind, child," replied Sir

Matthew, "I hope you will not find out my meaning by experience. However, with respect to your coming to us, the day after to-morrow, I suppose the angagement which is to prevent your coming early, is one in which Carlo's master is concerned, and therefore I should be unreasonable to expect you to give it up."

"Yes, uncle," returned Bell, with pretended simplicity and candour, but without offering any further explanation.

"Mr. Leicester has been kind enough to offer to drive the girls over to Chiswick, to see the splendid collection of flowers there," observed Mrs. Leslie, "and they have had so little pleasure of late, that—"

"There is no occasion for another word of excuse, sister," observed Sir Matthew, his good humour quite restored; "if you will appoint your own hour, I will send the carriage over for you. We dine at seven."

This point was settled, and Sir Matthew departed, perfectly reconciled to his volatile niece, who burst into a fit of laughing the moment he was out of hearing.

"Now, my dear uncle has gone away, full of his wonderful discovery," she observed. "I think I see Lady Jane and her toady forming a thousand conjectures, and laying their wise heads together, to ——"

"You have acted very foolishly, Bell," interrupted Mrs. Leslie, "and, but that I feared you would have given utterance to some nonsense that would have distressed your sister, I assure you I should not have suffered your uncle to have gone away with such a false impression of the motive of Mr. Leicester's visits here."

"Yes, I know, both you and Bess were afraid that I should betray the truth, mamma," replied Bell; "but you see, for once, I could be prudent."

"Prudent!" repeated Mrs. Leslie, with emphasis; "really, Bell, I cannot discover much prudence in your suffering it to be believed that you are the object of Mr. Leicester's attachment, and ——"

"Knowing all the while that he is over head and ears in love with my sister," interrupted Bell. "Well, never mind, Bessie. Time is the great tell-tale, that will set all things to rights, and so let me enjoy my imaginary triumph for a little while."

"I am sure you are welcome to enjoy it for ever, for me," observed Bess, but her heart smote her with the consciousness of insincerity, as she uttered the words, and her embarrassment was increased by Bell's incredulous look and significant shake of he head, and she made a pretext for leaving the room to avoid a continuance of the subject.

Lady Jane's reception of her nieces and Mrs. Leslie when they paid their promised visit was much more cordial than they had expected. She declared that they were both wonderfully improved in appearance, and observed that, after all, it was very evident that a quiet, regular life possessed advantages that more than counterbalanced the enjoyments of fashionable society. She was, indeed, so convinced of it, that she intended to shorten considerably her stay in London, and gradually contract the circle of her acquaintance. Her spirits and health, indeed, were, she had discovered, quite unequal to sustain the wear and tear of late hours, crowded rooms, and especially of public places, and she intended to become quite a domestic wife.

Bell could scarcely conceal her dissatisfaction at hearing this. She had secretly flattered herself that, although she could not hope, under the circumstances, to be fully reinstated in her former privileges, her aunt would have the kindness and consideration to invite her, occasionally, to share those pleasures and amusements to which the latter had been as much devoted as herself. But these observations completely obliterated these hopes and expectations, and placed before her, in all its *horrors*, the conviction that, unless rescued by some lucky chance or interposition, she was indeed inevitably doomed to waste, as she considered it, her beauty and accomplishments in the obscurity of her mother's despised home. The discovery that their dinner-party was strictly a family one, and the mortification of seeing Miss Moulsey considered one of that family, and indeed usurping almost absolute authority, under the pretext that Lady Jane was so extremely delicate that it was necessary she should be kept free from all cares and trouble, all added to Bell's vexation. Even Lady Jane's flattering remark as to her beauty, which, her ladyship said, had never been so brilliant as now, failed even to excite even a smile or a look of satisfaction; and Mrs. Leslie and Bess were both upon thorns, lest she should give vent to her dissatisfaction in terms that might seriously offend those on whom they were so unfortunately dependant.

Luckily, as they considered it, the discovery that Lady Jane saw company in the evening at once altered the complexion of affairs; and, once more, Bell was herself again. She was admitted, too, to the honour of a private conference with her aunt, at the toilette of the latter; and there, among various other matters, was fully discussed Mr. Leicester's constant attendance at the cottage, and the probable consequences.

Lady Jane was surprised to hear that it was Bess who was the attraction. She had concluded from what Sir Matthew had told her, as well as from her own conviction that *Miss* Leslie could never stand any chance of competing with Bell, that Mr. Leicester was avowedly the admirer of the latter; she acknowledged that she had already, *in confidence*, spoken of the probability, indeed, almost certainty of her younger niece's alliance with the St. Aldwyn family.

"Do not contradict it, then, dear aunt," said Bell. "I have reasons for wishing it to be considered as true. Besides, Bessie's delicacy is so excessive, that she would be ready to die if she were to hear her name mentioned in connection with Mr. Leicester's; while I have no objection, if they choose to assign me half-a-dozen more, provided they are all eligible matches."

Lady Jane looked earnestly in her niece's face, as if to penetrate her real meaning for this observation. That she did so, was plain from her subsequent remark.

"I understand you, my dear," she observed, "but I am afraid our hopes in that quarter are all——"

"Not if they are still *your* hopes, dear aunt," interrupted Bell, quickly, (this was the opportunity she had sought for). "If you still took as great an interest in that affair as you used to, my hopes would be realized."

"I do not understand you, Bell," replied Lady Jane, coolly.

"I will speak out plain, aunt," replied Bell. "Had I remained with you, instead of being banished, without any offence that I am aware of, everything by this time would have been in a fair train for my marriage with the Marquis of Ledbury. There," she continued, putting a letter into Lady Jane's hand, "there is what I received from him the week after I left you. Fortunately it came direct into my hands, instead of mamma's, for I saw the postman deliver it to the gardener at the front gate, and somehow, from the seal and look of it altogether, it struck me it was from him, and so I flew down stairs and intercepted it."

"I do not know, then, that I am exactly doing right," observed Lady Jane, gravely, "in encouraging a correspondence that Mrs. Leslie——"

"Do, dear aunt, read the letter," interrupted Bell, impatiently, "and then I

shall be guided by your decision. As to mamma, really she is more absurd, if possible, on the subject of morals than Bess; but read, and you will see whether I am wrong or presumptuous in my belief."

Lady Jane did read the inflated epistle, in which the marquis expressed his disappointment, his *despair* at not meeting the object of his most ardent love and admiration, as he had hoped to have done, at Sir Matthew Bevington's. He could no longer exist without seeing her. The world seemed a blank to him in her absence, and he now most passionately solicited leave to wait upon her, and be introduced to Mrs. Leslie, for whom he professed the greatest respect. He had called repeatedly, he said, in Portland Place, but Lady Jane was invisible. Once he had seen Miss Moulsey, but it was quite useless to hope to learn anything from Miss Moulsey which it did not suit her inclination to tell, and she pleaded entire ignorance of the "whereabouts," of Mrs. Leslie's residence. By the kind and friendly interposition of Sophia Balcombe, he had, at last, however, discovered the address, and should await with the greatest anxiety the answer on which depended his happiness, namely, whether Mrs. Leslie would admit him to her domestic circle.

"Well, my dear, and how did you reply to this?" demanded Lady Jane. "Surely Mrs. Leslie could never be so obstinately blind to her own interest, (for, of course, your interest is hers), as to refuse to admit the marquis's visits."

"I have never said a word to either her or Bess on the subject," replied Bell; "for I well knew it would be to no purpose, only to excite suspicions and give rise to perpetual quarrels between us. You can have no idea, aunt, of their extreme folly. I do believe actually that my mother would rather see me reduced to the necessity of getting my own living than see me Marchioness of Ledbury. She looks upon him, in fact, as a sort of monster who ought to be proscribed and driven out of society."

"Psha! the woman is a fool," said Lady Jane, angrily. "But, my dear," she continued, "what is it you would have me do in this case? You are aware, of course, that my situation has inevitably made a great alteration in your position in society, although it is undoubtedly Sir Matthew's wish and mine to advance your interests and promote your settlement in the world; but——"

"Now, dear aunt, 'but me no buts,'" interrupted Bell, assuming her most cajoling, coaxing manner. "I know I may

speak freely to you from the bottom of my heart, for I am still your own dear Bell, who ever loved you for yourself and not for any profit or interested motives."

"Well, my dear, I do not dispute it," returned Lady Jane, although evidently not with the warmth which Bell anticipated from her flattery. "I have ever," continued her ladyship, "believed that you were affectionate and grateful to me, and though, of course, other and nearer claims have supervened——"

"Yes, dear aunt, and nobody in the word, I am sure, can rejoice more sincerely than I do in the prospect of your happiness. I say little about it," she continued, with an appearance of great emotion, "because I know there are many little-minded people who would accuse me of hypocrisy, and think it quite impossible that I should feel any satisfaction at the event which has, as you say, greatly changed my position in the world. But I will not believe that you do me such injustice. I am sure you know my heart too well, and——"

"Well, well, I do believe it, my dear, and even if you did feel hurt and disappointed, I should not feel angry; for it would only be natural," replied Lady Jane. "But now, Bell, tell me how I can assist you; and if it can be done without compromising my character, as having been concerned in any clandestine proceedings, I——"

"I only ask to be reinstated for a few weeks, dear aunt, in my former privileges. Let me once more appear to the world as your favourite niece, though no longer the co-heiress of Sir Matthew Bevington. Only, in short, let me have the opportunities which I should have had if nothing had happened and I had remained with you; and if I do not make a good use of them (I need not explain any farther), I will be content to relinquish my ambitious hopes, and retire to the obscurity which my mother and sister consider, I believe, only a degree below Paradise."

Lady Jane did not immediately reply. She was evidently inclined to accede to Bell's request, but was withheld by, as the latter suspected, some engagement with Miss Moulsey, who, it was evident, had gained much greater power with her ladyship than even Bell, with all her talents for cajolement and flattery, had ever possessed.

"I know what you are thinking, dear aunt," she observed, with a winning smile. "You are afraid that I shall be gay and giddy, as usual, and that my high spirits will be too much for you, in your delicate situation; but I will promise to be as quiet and demure as even Bess could be, or Miss Moulsey herself; nay, more, I will put myself under her tuition, and it shall be hard indeed if I don't learn to be useful to you, while I am trying to serve myself. You don't know how I am already sobered down by the humdrum life I have lived with mamma and Bess."

"If I thought that you and Martha (Miss Moulsey) would agree, I would—"

"Oh, dear aunt, I will be so humble and submissive to her, that she shall not have an excuse for finding fault with me," interrupted Bell, eagerly; "only do not let mamma suspect that anything but your unbiassed inclination has led you to invite me. Oh, if you knew what I have suffered, and how I have been taunted and sneered at, under the impression that my aunt had totally discarded me from her favour,—I must tell the truth, dear, dear aunt—mamma has always been jealous of my affection for you, and she and Bess are so angry that I do not enter into their feel-

ings; but I still feel, as I have ever done, that to you I am indebted for everything, and that I have a right to rejoice in everything that can contribute to your happiness and pleasure, that—but I ought not, I know, to say anything about this, only it will show you what a miserable life I lead, and how anxious I must naturally be to free myself from——"

"Say no more, Bell—I do see it—I understand fully Mrs. Leslie's feelings on the subject—but no matter, I will do all in my power, child, to assist your views."

That Bell's insinuations of her mother and sister's selfish feelings were without the slightest foundation, need not be said; but she had long learned, under Lady Jane's own tuition, to disregard all conscientious scruples; and, in this instance, the lessons she had learned were practised with complete success. Lady Jane determined to exert herself to the utmost to forward her niece's views, and triumph over what she called and considered absolutely insane and ridiculous objections, on the part of Mrs. Leslie, to her daughter's aggrandisement.

The crowded rooms, the heat and dazzling lights, the vapid conversation, the disjointed observations and rejoinders of the fluttering groups, who never remained more than a few minutes stationary, and then passed on to seek some other excitement—all, in fact, in which Bell delighted, and which restored her eyes to all their brilliancy, and to her manners their most fascinating vivacity—overwhelmed Mrs. Leslie with lassitude and fatigue, and she longed for the hour that should dismiss them to her quiet cottage.

But music was proposed, and that, she knew, was an enjoyment to Bess, as well as a relief to her, who, though little acquainted with it as a science, was well able to appreciate the charms of harmony. The mother's maternal pride, too, was gratified when, after the execution of two or three fashionable airs, *Miss* Leslie was led from her side, to take part with Bell in the favourite duet of "Together let us range the fields;" and the deep breathless silence, which had succeeded to the noisy hum that had scarcely for a moment before ceased, proved how powerful were the charms of their finely harmonised voices. The most rapturous plaudits attended its conclusion, and Bess returned blushing to the side of her mother, who could scarcely command her feelings to bow her thanks to the numerous compliments that were addressed to her.

But where was Bell? She sought not her mother's side, nor shrank from observation; but yet, at that moment, she was totally indifferent, or rather too completely pre-occupied, to pay any attention to the admiration she and her sister had excited. Her eyes were, indeed, apparently cast down and veiled by their long dark lashes, as she retired from the pianoforte, and, complaining of heat, sought a seat in one of the recessed windows, to which, however, she did not retire unaccompanied. Three or four of the most distinguished young men present followed her, all eager to gain a look, a word, or a smile, and contending with each other to be employed in administering to her comfort and accommodation. But Bell's thoughts were not with any of this circle, though see bowed and smiled her thanks for their attentions, and replied with vivacity to their remarks. No, she was assiduously watching a gentleman who had entered the room just before her sister and self had concluded their performance, and who, although he had stood as if transfixed in admiration, and afraid, even by a breath, to interrupt the harmonious sounds, had not at their conclusion attempted to approach the singers, or even to join in the rapturous burst of applause that followed, but had taken advantage of the general movement to make his way to where Lady Jane Bevington was seated, and now stood leaning over the back of her chair, chatting with the greatest ease, gaiety, and unconcern, with her ladyship and her shadow, Miss Moulsey. This was the Marquis of Ledbury—and it was this movement of his which had decided Bell to seek a seat at a distance, instead of joining, as might have been expected, either her aunt or mother. The same policy made her affect not to see the sudden change that took place in the marquis's looks, as he listened with deep attention to some communication from Lady Jane. At first, he assumed a smile of incredulity, but her ladyship's earnest assurances were evidently enforced by Miss Moulsey, and Bell saw with inward exultation his countenance become clouded, and his eyes turned with increasing uneasiness towards the part of the room where she was seated. Carefully she avoided meeting his glance. Her eyes sparkled with malicious pleasure, and her vivacity kept a throng of delighted admirers around her. In a few moments, the marquis was at her elbow; but Bell concealed her exultation, and received him with a coldness strikingly contrasted with her previous liveliness and freedom to those who were comparatively strangers. But was the marquis deceived by this? Alas, no—he had too successfully studied the feelings, and (he would have said) the caprices of womankind. He played, indeed, to admiration, the neglected—the despairing lover, and Bell gloried in her supposed triumph, while, in reality, he was but rivetting his power over her. Had she been sincere in her desire to avoid him, would not she have sought shelter with her mother, who would have been an effectual protection? But no, Bell fluttered about the room, and chatted and laughed with every one, apparently unconscious that the marquis attended her like her shadow, though she still avoided those who alone could have relieved her from his apparently unwelcome attentions.

Bell believed that she was now secure— "C'est une affaire faite," she whispered to her aunt, as she threw herself by the side of the latter on the couch; but her eye at that moment caught her mother's looks, fixed upon her with an expression of deep solicitude, and her heart for a moment sunk. See knew not why, but it seemed as if in that look she read a prediction of future misery, and it was some time before she could rally her spirits.

Bell's mind, however, was not one to be depressed, even by real misfortunes, much less by those which were, as yet, only in anticipation. The marquis, encouraged by Lady Jane's easy address and conversation, renewed his attentions. Bell's reserve and coldness towards him gradually thawed, and, when he led her down to supper, they were upon as good terms as ever. The gentleman had vindicated himself successfully from the charge of neglect, and the lady had condescended to assure him that, whatever might be Mr. Leicester's hopes or intentions, she had not, nor was disposed to give them any encouragement; and, where each are disposed to accept concessions from the other, a breach between lovers is easily closed. Bitterly did Mrs. Leslie regret her acceptance of her brother's invitation, for she foresaw that, from that night, Bell's apparent contentment with their quiet domestic life at the cottage would exist no longer.

"It shall be the last time, though," she murmured to herself, "the very last time. I should be wanting in duty to myself and to her, if I were passively to submit to her being thrown in the way of that seductive, dangerous man."

The carriage was ordered to convey Mrs. Leslie and her daughters home, but Bell took no notice of the intimation given her by her sister, "that mamma was ready." Parties were forming for quadrilles, and to Bessie's surprise and consternation, Bell at that very instant allowed the marquis to lead her out. No opportunity was allowed Bess to remonstrate, and hurt and embarrassed she looked round to Lady Jane, who with a smile beckoned her to approach.

"What is the matter, Miss Leslie?" she inquired. "You look displeased."

"I am hurt, aunt, at seeing my sister show such an utter disregard of my mother's wishes," returned Bess, gravely.

"I do not understand you, my dear," returned her ladyship, sharply; "but it will perhaps lessen your sister's grave offence in your eyes, if not in Mrs. Leslie's, if it be her dancing you allude to, when I tell you that it was my wish that she should do so."

"But the carriage is announced, and my uncle does not like the horses kept waiting," replied Bess.

"They need not wait, my dear, if Mrs. Leslie wishes to go. I intend to keep Bell with me for a week or two, perhaps longer—that is, with Mrs. Leslie's permission."

Bess returned with this message to her mother. Her lips quivered with agitation as she delivered it, though she tried to conceal it, and treat Lady Jane's invitation to her sister as a matter of course, which would relieve them from any difficulty as to waiting.

A passing glance, however, which Bell bestowed upon her at that moment, as the dance brought her near where Mrs. Leslie was seated, convinced Bess that it was a pre-arranged affair, and that Bell's motive in having so pointedly shunned her mother for the last two or three hours had been to avoid any objection on the part of the latter.

"I cannot consent to it, Bess," observed Mrs. Leslie. "My dear child, I cannot leave her here. My heart misgives me. I will speak to Lady Jane myself, and tell her——"

She caught Lady Jane's eyes, however, at this moment fixed upon her with an expression almost contemptuous, and afraid of exposing herself and Bell to the animadversions of the company, or, as her ladyship would have herself expressed it, of making a scene, by betraying the agitation she even now could scarcely conceal, she gave up the attempt to dissuade her sister-in-law from her resolution to keep Bell with her, and quietly retired, Bell bestowing only a passing nod and smile, by way of adieu, and Lady Jane merely a stately bow, as Sir Matthew led his sister and niece to the carriage. Aware that her brother, though not disposed to entertain a very favourable opinion of the

female sex in general, and sometimes differing rather positively from Lady Jane's opinions, was yet apt to take offence very quickly at any observation that tended to impugn her ladyship's judgment or discretion, Mrs. Leslie checked the impulse which induced her to confide to him her objections to Bell's again becoming a resident in his house, and being thus thrown once more in the way of the marquis. When, therefore, Sir Matthew observed, rather dissatisfiedly, that he was sorry to see her in such low spirits, and apparently so far from comfortable, she only replied by pleading her habits having unfitted her to enjoy indiscriminate society, adding—

"I had expected, indeed, to enjoy a quiet, domestic evening with Lady Jane and yourself, and was disappointed to find myself among so many strangers. In fact, I have been so long out of society that——"

"Ay, ay, that is it," observed Sir Matthew, hastily, "but you must wean yourself from those habits, sister, for, as Jane says, how can you ever hope to establish the girls advantageously in life, if you keep yourself and them mewed up for ever at your own fireside? You must come among us oftener, and you will soon overcome that shyness which I was sorry to see kept you aloof this evening from many who, I am sure, would have been glad to form an acquaintance, and invite you to their houses, if it were only from respect to me."

Mrs. Leslie would fain have observed that she had no wish to cultivate acquaintance with those whose style of living she neither had the means nor the wish of emulating; but her brother's positive dogmatic manner disheartened her from speaking her opinion, and tears filled her eyes as she bade him good night. The carriage was driving off as he observed—

"Lady Jane desired me to tell you to send over Bell's clothes to-morrow."

And thus she again lost an opportunity of speaking on the subject nearest her heart. A night's sleepless reflections, and Bessie's dejected look and swollen eyes, when they met at the breakfast table in the morning, evinced how deeply she shared her mother's fears and presentiments, and determined Mrs. Leslie not to delay what she felt was her duty—to point out to Lady Jane the dangerous position in which Bell was placed, in being allowed to encourage the attentions of a man whose very name in connexion with hers was, as Mrs. Leslie said, enough to blast the character of a young female, especially of one who had so little pretension as Bell to an alliance with one whose birth and fortune, were it not for his vices, entitled him to seek a wife among the highest and proudest in the land.

"To suppose that Bell, even allowing that a partial mother's opinion of her beauty and accomplishments are not exaggerated," continued Mrs. Leslie, "with no other dowry but them and an unblemished name, would be considered a suitable match by Lord Ledbury, would, I feel, be presumption. I do not, I assure your ladyship, for a moment indulge the idea—No, though a blush of shame and indignation dyes my cheek as I write it, I must candidly avow that I do not believe a thought of such an alliance even enters the mind of the marquis; but that the attentions he so publicly displays towards her are caused by a very different motive. I do not distrust Bell. God forbid that I should believe that it is in the power of even that 'bold bad man' to banish from her bosom those principles it was her dear father's and my principal care to engraft there! But I trust your ladyship will agree with me, that it is not enough for a young female to be incapable of doing wrong, it must not appear possible that she has done wrong; and who will say that such is the case of any one who is the selected object of the Marquis of Ledbury's public attentions? You will think, my dear sister, for such I may call you, that I am prejudiced against the marquis; but I could 'a tale unfold' too long for a letter, but which I will repeat to you whenever you may feel disposed to honour me with a hearing, and which would, I am sure, instantly convince you that I do him no injustice when I say, as my poor departed husband once in his indignation said of him, he is a wretch whom every honourable man should despise, whom every virtuous woman should loathe and contemn. Could you have known the agony I felt last night, when I saw Bell's hand clasped in his, and her eyes beaming with delight, as he breathed his honied venom in her ear—could you have suspected, I say, what I was suffering, your kind heart would, I am sure, have prompted you instantly to have dissolved the spell he was wreathing around her, and have compelled her to return home with me, where she would have been safe from his contaminating influence."

Much more to the same effect Mrs. Leslie added, giving at the same time all due credit to Lady Jane's supposed ignorance of the marquis's real character, and the purity of her intentions towards Bell. The letter was sent with the clothes which Bess had selected as necessary for her sister's intended stay of two or three weeks; and Mrs. Leslie, satisfied with having, as she hoped, put Lady Jane on her guard as to the real character and intentions of Lord Ledbury, and convinced in her own mind that her ladyship would take effectual means to put an end to his correspondence with Bell, in a great measure recovered her usual composure, and returned with a delight increased by the temporary interruption to her quiet domestic enjoyments. A long morning visit from Mr. Leicester, whom they had not seen for two or three days, contributed to banish from the minds of both mother and daughter all that had occurred to disturb their tranquillity. He was in uncommon good spirits. Had brought some new music which he had before recommended to Bessie's favour; and it was, perhaps, no drawback to his perfect enjoyment that Bell was absent, though he was rather puzzled to account for the cloud that for a time obscured Bessie's sunny features, when in reply to his inquiry for her sister, she replied, that Bell had gone to pass two or three weeks with their aunt, Lady Jane. Mrs. Leslie's deep sigh, too, was evidently an echo of her daughter's uneasiness on the subject of Bell's visit; but, as in their intercourse with Mr. Leicester, confidential and frank as it was, they had ever been cautious of saying a word that could detract from Lady Jane's merits, or raise an idea that she was not altogether the most eligible protectress that could have been chosen for her nieces, not a suspicion entered his mind of the true state of the case. As if too, by mutual consent, both mother and daughter refrained from mentioning the Marquis of Ledbury as having formed one of their party, and as, after a time, Bess resumed her smiles, and Mrs. Leslie her usual placid look, the memory of their temporary discomfiture wore away. Scarcely, however, had the sound of Leicester horse's hoofs died away, as he galloped up the road to keep an appointment which, as he said, imperatively obliged him to leave them—and just as Bess, the smile of pleasure still lingering on her lovely face, at the *manner* of his parting with her, was sitting down to practise the songs he had brought her—the noise of a carriage was heard, and the bell at the gate gave notice of the approach of visitors.

"Who can it be, Bessie?" exclaimed Mrs. Leslie, "and I in this deshabille. I had better run up stairs and put on another gown and cap——"

Bess did not answer for a minute. She

had turned the Venetian blind, and was anxiously looking at the coming visitors ; but soon turned away, and, in a voice that betrayed some alarm, replied—

"You need not mind your dress, mamma. It is my uncle's carriage—and, if I mistake not, Bell alone ; but I will run down and see."

Quick, however, as were the movements of Bess, they were, it appeared, slow compared to her sister's; for, before the former had reached the bottom of the stairs, Bell darted past her, repelling, with vehement scorn and indignation in her looks, Bessie's outstretched hand. She rushed into the library, the door of which had been left open, and threw herself with violence on the floor, almost across her mother's feet.

"My dear child, my dear Bell, what has happened?" were the simultaneous exclamations of the mother and daughter.

"Go—go !" raising her head, and with difficulty uttering the words, from the passion that was choking her—"go and send those fellows away, who are, no doubt, laughing at me—at me !" and she raised her voice almost to a scream, "whom they would have scarcely dared raise their eyes to, unbidden, a few hours ago. Go, I say, Bess, and send Sir Matthew Bevington's carriage away. They asked me if they were to wait for orders. They knew, well enough, I should never order them again. Yes, they knew I was turned out —a degraded ruined outcast—to be the sneer, and scorn, and mockery of the world."

"Have you deserved to be so, Bell ?" uttered Mrs. Leslie, in tremulous accents. "If you have, it is well that you should thus humiliate yourself, your mother, and sister. But if——"

"Deserved !" repeated Bell, starting to her feet, and fire flashing from her eyes. "No, I have deserved nothing, mother. It is you that have brought it all upon me. You that have caused me to be sent home —and my clothes, too ! As if I were a poor miserable servant, who for some heinous fault is discarded at a moment's warning. 'Stop—stop!' screamed that little odious malicious wretch, Miss Moulsey, from the top of the staircase, as the carriage was rolling away with me. 'Robert, James—stop. Miss Leslie's box is forgotten, and it is your lady's orders——' I put my hands on my ears, that I might not hear the rest of the sentence, but I was compelled to sit quietly, while the box was brought out and strapped behind. Oh, I could have killed her with a look, when she bowed her farewell with mock humility. This is just what her

black malignant heart has been so long plotting against me, and now she is gratified. And you, mamma, what could you have written ? what could you have said to my aunt, to occasion her to treat me in this manner ?"

"Do not ask your anxious mother what she has said, in her tenderness to you, Bell," observed Bess, who had returned to the room, having calmly discharged the servants with an intimation that there was no occasion for their further attendance, which had been received by them with their usual respect, thereby convincing her that there was no foundation for her sister's violent and overcharged remarks as regarded them. "Sit down quietly, Bell, and listen to the explanation mamma will——"

"Yes, quietly !" she repeated, "quietly. That is always your hypocritical canting word," exclaimed Bell, scornfully. "Even my aunt—even Lady Jane herself—henceforth she is no aunt to me—but even she laughs at and ridicules your affected quietness. But I hate and detest it. I only want to know what I have done, that I should be included in Lady Jane's displeasure. But I forgot—I have a note here to mamma. It is not Lady Jane's hand-writing. I suppose she would not condescend even to write her imperious mandates."

Mrs. Leslie took the letter in her trembling fingers and tried to break the seal, but her hands shook so she was unable, and she handed it to Bess, desiring her to read it.

"Before I do so, my dear mother," observed Bess, "I entreat you to call to your memory the letter you wrote to Lady Jane and ask yourself whether any fear of her displeasure, or its consequences, could have induced you to say otherwise than you there said."

"No, my dear—my dear child, certainly not," returned Mrs. Leslie. "I could not consistently with my duty, and under the impression I was, from what I saw last night. No, Bell, it is you, and not I, should be blamed for——"

Bess made a motion to restrain her mother's reproaches, which had only the effect, she saw, of lighting up Bell's eyes with a blaze of defiance and rage.

"Stop, Bell, let us hear this letter before you speak," observed Bess, "there will be time enough then to vindicate, if you can, the conduct which has brought this unexpected blow upon your mother."

For once Bell appeared awed by her sister's calm and impressive manner, and Bess proceeded to read the following note:—

"Lady Jane Bevington's sudden indisposition and distress of mind, in consequence of Mrs. Leslie's ill-judged and most uncalled-for letter, compels her to make use of another hand to inform Mrs. Leslie that she relinquishes at once and for ever all charge and interest in Miss Bell Leslie, who she begs to assure Mrs. Leslie shall never again be exposed to the chance of contamination under her (Lady Jane Bevington's) roof. Lady Jane begs to say that she requests any future communication from Mrs. Leslie, or her family, may be addressed to Sir Matthew Bevington, who, her ladyship doubts not, will be greatly surprised when he hears the narrow escape Miss Bell Leslie has had from the horrid connexions to whom she has been introduced while under Lady Jane's protection.

(Signed) "MARTHA MOULSEY,
"For Lady Jane Bevington."

"There! and by this time my disgraceful exit from my uncle's house is being trumpeted in every circle that hateful, deformed, venomous little wretch can get admittance to," exclaimed Bell, throwing herself on the sofa, and hiding her face with her handkerchief, while she gave way, for the first time since her entrance, to a passionate burst of tears. Mrs. Leslie dried the big drops that had fallen silently down her cheeks while Bess read this insulting note.

"I am now ready, Bell," she mildly observed, "to give an explanation of the motives that induced me——"

"I want no explanation, mamma," interrupted Bell. "It is all quite plain. I am entirely ruined for ever with my aunt; and you, no doubt, will also feel the ill-consequences of what she truly calls your ill-judged letter. It must be ill-judged, indeed, to bring such consequences upon us all. But you have the consolation, as you observe, and as my *wise* sister observes, who never in her life did or said a foolish thing—the great consolation of knowing that you have done your duty, while I, of course, am to bear the blame of having excited you to it by my imprudence."

"And truly, most truly, Bell," observed Mrs. Leslie, with a severity she had never, perhaps, in her life before assumed towards her daughter. "Whatever be the consequences either to you, myself, or your sister, remember, Bell, and let it be a lesson to you to restrain you for the future, that to your imprudence and open defiance and disregard of my counsel, all these evil consequences are to be justly attributed."

Bell's heaving bosom and hysterical sobs evinced that her mother's words were not unheard or unheeded; but not a single word betrayed the existence or conviction of her fault, or penitence for its commission. In the same attitude she remained, until Rachel, who aware that something unpleasant had occurred, but, knowing Bell's haughty disposition would not brook her interference, had waited till her patience was exhausted for a summons to the library, and at last entered uncalled, to remonstrate that the dinner had been ready to be served up for more than half-an-hour—not until then did Bell, for an instant, relinquish her audible sobs, or even bestow a look upon her distressed mother, whom Bess was, in a low voice, endeavouring to comfort by the assurance that Sir Matthew would not be biassed to withdraw his countenance and favour from his sister and her children, by the representations of his weak and imperious wife.

"You do not know him as well as I do, my child," was Mrs. Leslie's only reply. "If Lady Jane persuades him to put the same construction on my letter that she has herself done, and his pride is aroused by the conviction that I considered himself and her incompetent guardians of my children, I know, too well, what will be the consequence. But we will not anticipate evil, but pray to God to avert it. At all events, I know myself guiltless of any designed offence, and if I have acted foolishly, or rashly, it will be my consolation to know that it was from a motive that might excuse even greater folly than mine."

"Goodness, goodness me!—What has happened, my dear mistress? Bessie, Miss Bell, do speak!" exclaimed Rachel, standing in surprise and consternation, as she looked at the tearful and agitated countenances of the two former, and the still more strongly marked distress which was evinced in the position and uncontrollable sobs of Bell.

"Nothing, Rachel, nothing has happened, or will happen, I hope," returned Mrs. Leslie, with her usual frank confidence to her valued domestic, "except," she continued, "that I have unintentionally given offence to Lady Jane Bevington, and Bell is in consequence—"

Bell started up with violence from the sofa.

"I have suffered enough, I think, already, mamma," she observed; "you may at least spare me the mortification of having my misfortune made a subject for kitchen gossip."

"Kitchen gossip, Miss Bell?" repeated

Rachel, angrily; "your poor dear papa, nor your mamma, ever thought me one who was capable——"

But Bell was already out of hearing of Rachel's self-vindication. She had rushed up the stairs, and the violent slamming of her chamber-door, after she had entered it, proved how much impression the mild forbearance of her mother, or her sister's gentle attempts at consolation, had made upon her.

"Dear, dear," was Rachel's ejaculation, with uplifted hands and eyes, as she followed her mistress and Bess to the dining-room. "Who can that poor child take after? Her dear father was hasty, to be sure, but he never said a harsh word to anybody in his life, that he was not the next minute sorry for, and would make amends to the poorest creature that ever stood before him; and her mother—bless her dear heart!—*she* knows I would die before I would make her or hers the subject of kitchen gossip."

CHAPTER XII.

Since thy gay morn of life's o'ercast,
    Chill came the tempest's lower;
(And ne'er misfortune's eastern blast
    Did nip a fairer flower.)

Since life's gay scenes must charm no more,
    Still much is left behind;
Still nobler wealth hast thou in store—
    The comforts of the mind!

Thine is the self-approving glow
    On conscious honour's part;
And, dearest gift of heaven below,
    Thine friendship's truest heart.—BURNS.

RS. LESLIE'S anticipations of the consequences of Lady Jane's representations of her sister's imagined insult to her ladyship, proved but too correct. Two or three weeks passed, and not a word reached the cottage at Highgate from Portland Place. Bess saw, with deep concern, the uneasiness that had taken possession of her mother's mind. She (Mrs. Leslie) avowed, indeed, in secret to her anxious daughter, that she dreaded more from Sir Matthew's silence than she should had he given vent to his indignation in the most violent reproaches. For how many years during the childhood of her girls had a similar unbroken silence proved his resentment of the only offence she had then ever given—her marriage to Mr. Leslie! And now, the same fears that had then weighed down her spirits, again pressed her to the earth. Her children, her dear children would be left at her death unprovided for. For the income which he had fortunately secured to her for her life, was little more than adequate to their expenses, in the style they now lived. Bess resolved to make a bold step, at least, to try to relieve her mother's anxiety. Under the plea of hoping to relieve a nervous headache, with which she had been for some days sadly afflicted, she told her mother that she would try a longer ramble and a different air to that she had lately enjoyed, and taking Susan with her as a protection, she set out immediately after breakfast, and instead of turning off, as Susan expected she would, towards the heath, hastened with her to the house from which the coach to London started, and was in a few minutes on her road to Portland Place. How many thoughts rushed into her mind as she found herself again in that humble vehicle, which her sister so despised. How had Leicester congratulated himself on the fortunate chance which had brought him in sight of the "leathern conveniency," just as it was drawing up to the gate of their residence on that memorable day, and thus enabled him to place himself *vis-à-vis* to the sweet face that had so often passed him in his rambles without having betrayed the slightest consciousness of having attracted his ardent admiration. How could she? her thoughts had always been much occupied, or her natural retiring modesty too prevailing, to allow her to

gaze on the mere passer-by, be they who they might.

"But are you sure," she would observe, with an arch smile, when he tried to recall his meeting with her, previous to his introduction to her in the stage-coach. "Are you quite sure that it was not Bell who first caught your roving fancy? I think it was more likely to be her, and that you did not discover, until since, the difference."

"I must have been blind, indeed, not to discover the difference," Leicester would reply. "No, no, Bessie, to the common observer—to the eye that cannot discriminate—the heart that cannot feel the difference in the expression of those faces, it may be difficult to discover the difference, where the features so strongly resemble each other, as do yours and your sister's. I confess, indeed, the resemblance is most striking, and were not my heart interested, it is possible I might mistake the one for the other; but a single glance of your eye—that glance which it was my happiness to observe, as you bounded from your mother's side to pick up the stick which had fallen from a poor old man's hand as he was slowly labouring up the hill with a heavy basket on his head—that glance, and the crimson blush that suffused your cheek, as you caught my earnest, admiring look—it was so, I know, though involuntarily—but that glance established your identity with me for ever. I saw your sister many, many times after, and was struck with the surprising resemblance between you; but never once led by it into mistaking her for you. It was the heart —the soul, and not the beautiful casket in which it was enshrined, worthy as it is of all admiration, that had won my ever-enduring regard."

But to return to Bess, now again a passenger in the Highgate stage, with only Susan opposite to her as a substitute for the gay, the gallant Leicester, whose former seat the pleased and surprised housemaid now unwittingly filled. Bess, as she thought of Leicester, rejoiced that there were no other passengers to disturb her thought from dwelling upon him whom she had first beheld here, and whose image, as she thus recalled every particular of that meeting, served to banish from her sundry qualms and fears, which almost made her "blench from her high resolve," as they conjured up to her view the stern an angry countenance of Sir Matthew Bevington, and the harsh tones in which she knew he *could* reprove those who offended him.

"But I have never offended him," thought Bess. "He was ever kind and indulgent towards me, and I cannot believe that his partiality—he was used to call it love—can be entirely banished by his unfounded anger against my mother."

Notwithstanding all her resolution, however, Bessie's knees trembled under her as she drew near her uncle's stately dwelling. She had taken Susan into a pastry-cook's shop in the neighbourhood, and directed her to wait there until her return; but as she came in sight of the dwelling, her strength so signally deserted her, that she almost repented she had not still the assistance of Susan's arm, and it was not till she had crossed the wide place, and was within a few yards of Sir Matthew's mansion, that she observed unusual appearances, which increased her alarm and terror. The street was thickly littered with straw, and the shutters of the whole of the upper windows closed. The knocker was portentously muffled with leather; and when, after a moment or two of hesitation, she ventured to pull the area bell, even that returned a deadened sound.

"I must know the worst," she desperately exclaimed, as she listened with beating heart for the accustomed sound of the porter shuffling from his easy high-backed chair to obey the summons. But no sound disturbed the stillness that seemed to chill her very blood; and when the door opened, it was so noiselessly that she started back, unable to control the expression of her alarm.

The old porter gazed at her with astonishment, but respect; and threw the door wide open as in "days of yore" to admit her.

"My uncle—Sir Matthew—Mr. Wilson," she said, unable to utter any further inquiry.

"Yes, miss, he is up at breakfast, I believe. I saw his man carry breakfast into the back library a few minutes ago. Shall I——"

"No; I will go to him," returned Bess, anticipating his offer of announcing her; "but (and she paused) tell me, Wilson," and she glanced again at the ominous indications, "is Lady Jane ——"

"Very bad, indeed, miss, I'm sorry to say. There's two doctors been with her all night and most of yesterday, and Sir Matthew is in a desperate way, for they do say, the women folk ——"

The door of the back library, which exactly faced the part of the hall to which Bess had advanced, at this moment was opened from within by a man servant, who was about to close it after him when his eye caught the anxious expression of Bessie's face, as she bent forward to catch a view of her uncle, and with a low bow he threw it open for her admittance.

"Who is it, Robert—Dr. Simmons?" interrogated Sir Matthew.

Bess stepped hastily forward.

"No, uncle, it is I," she said, extending both her hands in the manner in which he had been used so cordially to meet her after a short walk.

"Bess," he exclaimed, in a tone that reassured her; but the word was no sooner uttered, than he appeared to repent the involuntary expression of cordiality and kindness, and sinking back into his chair, sternly added, "What has brought you here, pray? Has your mother already learned the probable disappointment of all my hopes, and sent you here to triumph over me? But, no, *you* would not, I know, come on such an errand. No—no, she has determined to take time by the forelock, I suppose, and sent you to try to wheedle yourself into favour again.

She thinks, I suppose, the *old fool*, her brother's heart will be so desolate at this double loss ——"

Sir Matthew hid his face with his hand, his arm resting on the elbow of his chair, and Bess saw with surprise and deep commiseration the big tears trickling through his fingers.

There is something in the tears of a man —especially of one whose heart seems in the general events of life to be composed of even sterner stuff than the usual materials—there is something in such tears that excite even a deeper sensation than sympathy or pity. Bess felt awed at the unusual sight, and for some minutes she dared not utter a word even of consolation.

"I hope," she at last faltered, "I do, most sincerely hope and pray, that your fears will prove unfounded, that my aunt will recover, and—and—you may yet be blessed to the full amount of your wishes."

Sir Matthew shook his head despondingly, but without attempting to interrupt her; and Bess, gaining courage from his silence, proceeded—

"But, indeed, dear uncle, you wrong my mother, if you believe her capable —"

"Do not mention your mother," interrupted Sir Matthew, with a look of the fiercest anger. "I will never see or speak to her again. She knew well what she was doing, when she sent that cursed letter. She knew how sensitive my wife's mind was, and she reckoned upon the effect it would have upon her. And she was right—Lady Jane has never been well since, though, as Miss Moulsey says, she concealed, poor woman, the effect it had taken upon her, because she did not wish to hurt my feelings. But, depend upon it, Bess, it shall not answer your mother's purpose. I am sorry that you should suffer for it, but I would rather give the whole of my fortune to public charities, or to build almshouses, than that it should enrich the children of one who has behaved so cruelly and ungratefully to me as your mother has."

"And you really believe, then, Sir Matthew, that my mother wrote that letter deliberately to injure Lady Jane ?" said Bess, her eyes flashing with indignation.

"Believe it?—yes, certainly I do. What other purpose could she have in view ?" returned Sir Matthew, evidently surprised and startled at Bessie's energetic look and manner.

"Then I must tell you that the conclusion is most unworthy of you, uncle—most cruel and unjust to my dear mother. But I will not believe the idea ever origi-

nated with you—you must—you *do* know my mother incapable of such baseness, and I am only sorry to think that you should be so misled by artful and interested people, as to suffer such an idea to enter your mind. My mother," she continued, tears forcing themselves from her eyes, "may perhaps be over anxious for the welfare of her children, and—But in this instance I do not consider she was over anxious," she added, with sudden recollection. "She was justified in all she said, by her knowledge of circumstances with which it is but fair to conclude Lady Jane was totally unacquainted ; and I am sure, had her ladyship exercised only her own judgment, in judging of that letter, or had you not been influenced and misled by false representations, such a thought as that it was not dictated by the purest and most praiseworthy motives, would not have entered your mind."

If there was any one subject on which Sir Matthew was more tenacious, or could be galled and irritated sooner than another, it was that of being deemed capable of being misled and influenced by conclusions drawn by another, and that other a woman, too—the sex upon whom he looked down with such immeasurable superiority. Bessie's decisive manner of asserting that he had in this instance been so misled and influence, was an offence that at once aroused every irascible feeling in his nature, and he burst upon her with a storm of passion and invective that completely terrified her.

Bess was ordered to quit his house instantly, and never to dare intrude again upon one whose study, henceforth, would be to forget the very name and existence of those who had behaved with such base ingratitude to him.

The bell was rung for the servant to show her to the door; and, before he came, Sir Matthew had retreated from the room by another entrance. Bess exerted all her fortitude to appear calm and composed to the footman who answered the summons. Gentle and complacent as were her general manners to the servants of her uncle's establishment, she shrank from the thought of being considered by them as an object of pity ; and she left the house, and replied to the servant's bow with an air as complacent and independent as though she had still been the acknowledged favourite of its master.

It was not until she had walked a considerable distance, however, that Bess became conscious that in the distraction of her mind she had taken a different direction to that by which she should have rejoined Susan. It was the first time she had ever been alone in the streets of London, and although that part was much less crowded and busy than the principal thoroughfares, she felt some alarm at the novelty of her situation. Two or three times she stopped to look around her, and try to recollect the way she should have taken—but in vain. She was convinced that the streets through which she had passed were not the same as those by which she had entered Portland Place; and what was worse, in the full conviction that she should easily find her way back again, she had forgotten, when she had left her companion, to notice even the name at the pastry-cook's shop, or that of the street in which it was situated. What was to be done? Had she been alone, the remedy was easy enough—she would have gone into a shop, and paid some one to get a hackney-coach to take her home to Highgate; but Susan, who knew nothing of London, what would become of the poor simple girl, thust left alone, if *she* deserted her? The thought increased tenfold Bessie's perplexity and uneasiness, and with quickened step she hurried on, hoping every turning she took to meet with some object that would recal to her the way she should take, and blaming herself most severely for her thoughtlessness, or rather for having suffered herself to have been so deeply engrossed by thought as to have neglected to take proper precaution to secure herself and her attendant from the present dilemma. More than half-an-hour had already passed—to Bess it really appeared hours—and still she was wandering in as much uncertainty as ever, as to the course she should take, when she became conscious of a new source of annoyance. Two gentlemen passed her, as she was momentarily waiting to allow a carriage to pass before she crossed the street, to pursue a different direction, having discovered that the one she had previously been pursuing terminated in a square, which she knew did not lie in her way. Bess had dressed herself with studied plainness, and her large bonnet and thick veil almost defied the gaze of idle scrutiny, while the ample folds of a black silk cloak equally, as she believed, concealed her figure; or at least prevented her from appearing remarkable or conspicuous. Whether, however, it was her hurried, uncertain, and timid manner, or that the treacherous cloak and veil failed to obscure the beauty of her face and form—whichever was the reason, it is certain that the attention of one or both of the gentlemen was drawn to her, and

suddenly their studied lounge along the pavement was interrupted, and they stood, one on each side of her, as if waiting like herself to cross the street, but endeavouring at the same time, most offensively, to catch a fuller view of her features. Scarcely did Bess allow the carriage to pass, before she darted over. The gentlemen both followed with a step as quick as her own, but she put her foot on the curb of the pavement, and the next instant she would have fallen to the ground, had she not been dexterously caught in the arms of one of them. She had trodden on a bit of orange peel, and although she was saved by the activity of the stranger from the severe fall that threatened her, she had not wholly escaped injury; for when she would, with brief thanks, have released herself from his grasp, she discovered that she was unable to stand on one of her feet. She had violently sprained her ankle, and overcome with the severity of the pain—the awkwardness of her situation—her previous excitement in the interview with Sir Matthew—and the harassing uncertainty she had suffered in the attempt to discover the shop where she had left her attendant—she burst into tears, and was thus saved from fainting.

"By Jove, this is real!—It is not put on," observed one of the gentlemen. "What is to done? The poor girl is really hurt."

"She is a——fine creature," drawled the other, " and I would rather have broken one of my own legs, than that such a lovely-turned ankle should have been injured. Lean on me, my dear, or shall I carry you? I will do it with all my soul, upon my honour, until we can get assistance."

"*You* carry her," observed the other, who was the person who had saved Bess from absolutely falling, and who still supported her, although she tried hard to release herself. "Why, you can hardly carry yourself. No, no—it is I who am the knight to achieve this adventure, and you have nothing to do with it, but to envy me and look on. You will allow me to support you," he continued, addressing Bess, with rather more respect and less of levity than he had hitherto shown. "There is a surgeon's, I know, just round the corner, in Oxford-street, and it is necessary you should have immediate assistance. But, perhaps, you live near. If you will allow me——"

"Oh, no, sir—I am a considerable distance from my home. But, if this is Oxford-street, there is a tradesman's where I am known, and if I can reach it—"

"Psha! I thought so," observed the other *gentleman*, in an audible whisper to his companion. "Your usual luck, Cheverton, some milliner's girl, or——"

"Are you Mr. Cheverton?" exclaimed Bess, joyfully addressing her supporter, but almost instantaneously shrinking back from the expression of his eyes, as he gazed at her with a look of pleased surprise.

"My name is Cheverton," he replied, finding she did not proceed. "May I inquire——"

"If you are Mr. Cheverton, the son of the Earl of St. Aldwyn," she observed, blushing, but gathering resolution from what she had heard Leicester say of his younger cousins, "I may venture, I am sure, to claim your kind assistance to enable me to reach some house, from which I can get a coach to convey me to my mother's at Highgate."

"Highgate!" he repeated, with animated surprise. "You live there, then? By what strange accident does it happen that you are wandering here alone? And how blind I must have been, or how unlucky, never to have discovered my fair neighbour until now."

"I can very easily explain, sir, how or why I am here, as you say, alone," returned Bess, passing over the latter part of his speech, and replying only to the former. "I came from home to visit my uncle, Sir Matthew Bevington, with a servant, and have by accident——"

"Sir Matthew Bevington!" interrupted the young man, quickly. "Pardon me, your name is Leslie. What a blind, stupid fellow I must be, not to discover—But you must allow me to support you to the surgeon's I was speaking of. You are in dreadful pain, I see you are. Do let me carry you, or—Dallaston, what are you thinking of?" he added, turning to his companion, who had stood slapping his boot with his walking stick, and staring in Bessie's face with a look of stupid vacuity. "Give Miss Leslie your arm, and between us she—Do you know who it is?" he added, in an impatient whisper, as the other still stood immovable. "Miss Leslie, you know—the twin rose—Ronald Leicester."

The words fell disjointedly on Bessie's ear, but she heard enough to recall the crimson tint to her cheek, which pain had banished. She saw, too, the supercilious, and almost insolent expression of Dallaston's face as he slowly moved to her side, at his companion's indication, to offer her the support of his arm, and she instantly and decidedly rejected it.

Several persons had seen the accident—had heard the colloquy between her and Mr. Cheverton, and were still lingering to see how it would terminate. Bess selected with her eye from the group a decent-looking young woman, and beckoned her to approach.

"If you will be kind enough to allow me to take your arm," she observed, "with this gentleman's assistance, I shall be able to reach—What part of Oxford Street are we near?" she inquired, recollecting herself. "Mr. Wilson, the upholsterer, has been lately employed by my mother, and is one of Lady Jane's tradesmen. If I could get there——"

"Oh, you are only a very little way from Mr. Wilson's, miss," observed the young woman, who had very civilly accorded her assistance. "I work for Mr. Wilson," she continued, "and am going there now; and I'm sure he'll be very happy to do anything in his power."

"But you must have surgical assistance," observed Mr. Cheverton, who seemed rather chagrined at the turn affairs had taken. "Leicester will never forgive me," he added, in a lower tone, and with an expression Bess could not mistake the meaning of, "if you be the Miss Leslie—May I ask which of the far-famed twin-roses whose celebrity——"

Bess interrupted him with grave dignity.

"I am under great obligation to you, Mr. Cheverton," she observed, "for the very opportune assistance afforded me. Do not, I entreat you, give me other cause to regret our meeting than the pain I am suffering from the accident."

"If I were capable of adding to your pain, I am sure I should be a brute," he observed, with warmth; "but I really did not intend the slightest offence. I was only anxious," he added, with a smile, "to know which of the young ladies, whom I have so often heard spoken of, but never before had the pleasure to meet, I have now the honour—But we shall meet again," he added, with vivacity, "and then I shall find out—though I fear, very much fear that I have already discovered—Ah, that blush and averted eye speaks volumes. It tells me there is no hope for me—Happy Ronald!'"

Bess turned a deaf ear to these observations, and continued to speak to the young woman whose arm she leant upon, while Mr. Cheverton supported her on the other side. The girl knew the name of Lady Jane Bevington, as one of Mr. Wilson's most liberal employers, and she appeared quite rejoiced at having the opportunity of being of service to the niece of her ladyship, whom she recognised as having seen repeatedly in the carriage at Mr. Wilson's door.

Bess explained to her the manner in which she had missed the servant she had brought with her, and her anxiety, for the poor girl's sake, to find her out; and the young woman, who professed herself acquainted with every *crick and corner* of that neighbourhood, and was sure she could already guess where the pastry-cook's was that Bess described, promised to go in search of Susan, so soon as she had seen the former safe at Mr. Wilson's.

"You'll be glad enough, I can see, miss," she whispered, "to get away from these gentlemen, though this one does pretend to know all about you; but it was all along of their *imperdent* staring and following you that you slipped, so it's no great credit to him, whatever he may do to help you. As to that other pale-faced Jessamy——"

Bess pressed her arm to enforce silence; but the girl had very truly guessed her feelings. She was, indeed, heartily desirous of being freed from the presence of Mr. Cheverton and his friend; for the latter, though his arm had been so decidedly rejected by her, still kept close to her side.

"Thank goodness, this is Mr. Wilson's," said the young woman, and Bess instantly recognised the shop, and the very civil attentive master of it, who now came hastily forward, quitting rather abruptly a tall, thin, sallow young man in deep black, to whose instructions he was apparently attending at the moment Bess and her supporters entered the shop, Mr. Dallaston still following.

A few words on the part of Bess, with some explanatory notes as to the share she had in the matter from Mary Wilding— as the young woman was called—put Mr. Wilson in possession of the whole affair. Bess had been placed in a chair, and there she remained while Mary went to fetch Mrs. Wilson and her maid, to assist in removing the young lady to a room upstairs —one of the young men being sent off, by the express desire of Mr. Cheverton, to request the immediate attendance of a surgeon, though Bess strongly opposed it, observing that she was convinced she had only strained her foot, and that it would be time enough for any application when she got home, which would be as soon as her mother's servant whom she had brought with her from Highgate could be found, and a coach procured for their conveyance. But, if she was annoyed and confused by

Mr. Cheverton's ardent and persevering entreaties, or the silent supercilious attentions of his friend Dallaston, she was still more so by the looks and manner of the stranger (Mr. Wilson's tall, sallow customer), whose piercing black eyes, whenever hers met them, were fixed upon her with the most intense earnestness and admiration. With the habitual coolness of a London tradesman, to whom business is the one all-absorbing idea, Mr. Wilson having seen the relative of his great customer, Lady Jane Bevington, accommodated as far as was in his power, would have returned to the discussion of the order which the tall, sallow gentleman was giving him, when the former entered, or rather was led into the shop.

"I beg your pardon, sir," observed the upholsterer, with a low bow, "the curtains, I think you said, you wish to be blue damask——"

"Not now—not now," interrupted the gentleman, with extreme impatience, "blue, red, green, anything you like," he added, turning to his contemplation of Bessie's beautiful features, and evidently regarding, with anger and uneasiness, Mr. Cheverton, who was bending over her chair, and addressing her with an air of ease and familiarity which she appeared desirous to discourage.

Mr. Wilson drew back a step or two, with a low bow of deference. His customer's sudden indifference to the colour of the curtains was a mystery he could not fathom, as, previous to the interruption, the gentleman had appeared rather fastidious and difficult to be pleased, and had only been brought to something like a decision in favour of blue as the colour of his curtains, by the upholsterer having remarked that green—the colour first proposed by the gentleman—was very unfavourable to pale complexions, and that there were few ladies who would venture upon it.

Whether there was a lady's taste to be gratified in this case, Mr. Wilson failed even by this observation to ascertain. The gentleman was quite a stranger to him, and had been recommended to him by a merchant in the city; and the upholsterer, from the stranger's observations and inquiries, previous to Bessie's entrance, anticipated a large order, including ottomans, couches, &c., &c., for a drawing-room—chairs, tables, &c., &c., for a dining-room—and, in fact, all the usual furniture for the residence of a person of wealth and taste. It was therefore a matter of no small surprise and disappointment to Mr. Wilson, that his new customer seemed all at once to have totally forgotten the purpose for which he had come to the shop; and, instead of proceeding with his instructions, in which he had appeared before to be very deeply interested, was now totally occupied in contemplating Miss Leslie's feautures, and watching, with no very pleasant expression of countenance, the proceedings of the gentlemen, her companions. Once or twice the tall, sallow, and melancholy-looking stranger appeared on the point of addressing the young lady; but mingled with his dignity, which approached to haughtiness, and overpowering even the very evident interest she had excited, there was a sort of nervous bashfulness in his looks and manners, that appeared to restrain him; although, when Mr. Cheverton's saucy eyes met his, with a look that said, as plainly as eyes could say, his interference would be unwelcome, the stranger returned that look with a frown of defiance.

Bess felt even more uncomfortable and confused from the piercing gaze of this stranger, than she had previously done from the unwelcome familiarity of Mr. Cheverton, or the unaccountably supercilious looks of Dallaston, his companion; and most heartily did she rejoice when Mrs. Wilson, a formal, precise old lady, and her assistants, at last made their appearance.

Mary Wilding, it appeared, had already given the old lady a full detail of the particulars of Miss Leslie's accident, and while professing her readiness to assist the young lady, the old one took care to intimate, by looks as well as plain hints, that there was no further occasion for Mr. Cheverton and his companion's services. Bess also intimated her desire to get rid of them, by formally thanking Mr. Cheverton for the assistance he had rendered her, and observing that she was sorry to have so long trespassed upon his time and attention.

"But you do not surely imagine that I am going to leave you, Miss Leslie," he observed, "without having heard what the doctor says? Do you think Leicester would ever forgive me? By-the-by, I shall meet him almost directly. He is to be in town this morning, but I suppose you know that."

Bess felt irritated at this impertinent pertinacity in connecting Leicester's name with hers, and with visible anger she turned from him to Mrs. Wilson and observed—

"I will try, ma'am, if you please, to accompany you, if you will kindly give me shelter until my mother's servant arrives."

"Oh dear, yes, miss, to be sure," returned Mrs. Wilson. "Sally, Jane, here do help the young lady. If you can put your foot at all to the ground, you will find it better to use it; and I have got an embrocation upstairs that's a certain cure for sprains, if you do not wish a surgeon to be sent for."

Bess assured her that there was not the slightest occasion for it, and resolutely and coldly rejecting Mr. Cheverton's entreaties to be allowed to assist her, she took the arms of the two young women, and, in spite of the most excruciating pain, followed Mrs. Wilson out of the shop.

"I wonder," observed the old lady, after having administered her infallible embrocation, bandaged up the ankle, which was already frightfully swollen, and related to Bess half-a-dozen similar cases which *she* had cured without the intervention of a doctor—a class of people who seemed in very bad odour with her, and who, she observed, if they once got a footing in the house, there was no getting them out of it again—"I wonder whether Mr. Wilson has got rid of those bold-looking men, whose impertinence, Mary Wilding told me, was the cause of the accident. Dear me, I can't think how gentlemen can demean themselves so to follow and persecute ——"

Bess interrupted her by expressing a hope that they *were* gone, and the old lady instantly proposed to go down and ascertain, observing that she knew Mr. Wilson was busily engaged in attending on a gentleman, who was come to give a large order, and she was sure he would not like to be interrupted by *them* wild young men.

She returned, in a short time, with the welcome intelligence that they had departed—Mr. Cheverton leaving word with Mr. Wilson that he shoud do himself the pleasure of calling at Mrs. Leslie's cottage, and hoped he should meet Miss Leslie perfectly recovered.

"The new customer is there still," observed the old lady, addressing one of the young women. "We must work away, Sally, to make up for lost time, and clear off the job that's in hand, for he seems one of them sort of gentlemen that wants everything done in a minute, and I expect we shall be all hurry-scurry. I hope Mary Wilding isn't going to make a day of it, looking for that young woman."

Her hope was realised at that moment, for Mary entered with Susan, whom she had found at the pastry-cook's, in a state of great perplexity at her young mistress's protracted absence.

There was now no impediment to Bessie's immediate return home; but she again became conscious how particularly she was the object of attention to the tall, sallow gentleman, Mr. Wilson's customer; for he once more broke from the conversation with the upholsterer, to gaze upon Bess, as she was assisted to the coach which had been sent for, and seemed to be drinking in every word that she uttered, as she warmly returned her thanks, and pressed into Mary Wilding's and the other young women's hands a more substantial proof of her gratitude.

"Laws! what an ugly gentleman that was, Miss Bess, and how he did stare at you," observed Susan, the moment the coach was in motion.

Bess smiled.

"He is a singular-looking one," she replied, "but it is only his complexion, Susan, that makes you think him ugly, I suspect. It struck me he had very fine features. His eyes, too, are remarkably bright and intelligent, though he certainly makes rather an unpleasant use of them."

The subject was dropped; for Susan, whatever she thought, would not have ventured to have differed from Miss Bessie's opinion, who, in her sight, was infallible; but in her retrospection of the events of that day the image of that singular-looking man occurred to Bessie's memory.

Mrs. Leslie had felt considerable uneasiness from Bessie's long absence; but the accident she had met with now so completely engrossed her care and attention, that she forgot to make those particular inquiries which would have elicited from her daughter where she had been; and as Bess had paid the coachman before they stopped, and had cautioned Susan that, unless the question was directly asked, she should not mention their having been in London, the vexatious and mortifying result of the visit to Sir Matthew remained confined to her own bosom.

"I forgot, in my alarm at your accident to tell you, my love," observed Mrs. Leslie, some hours afterwards, "that Mr. Leicester called on his way home, and seemed greatly disappointed at your absence. I could not give him any idea which way you had taken, or I think he would have tried to overtake you, though he said he had been travelling all night, and had not yet seen any of his friends, though he had made an appointment to meet one of his cousins in London on some busines, but they had, he supposed, missed each other, and he was now going on to the earl's."

Bessie's looks betrayed her confusion at this intelligence. It recalled to her mind the recollection of Mr. Cheverton's expressed intention of calling at the cottage, and convinced her that it would be hopeless to expect that the circumstances under which she had met with that gentleman could eventually be concealed from her mother.

"It is odd enough, mamma," she observed with a smile, "that I was the cause of Mr. Leicester's disappointment in not meeting with Mr. Cheverton."

"You, Bessie?" returned Mrs. Leslie, with surprise, while Bell, who seldom now betrayed any interest in what was passing, laid the book she was reading on her knees, and looked up in her sister's face for an explanation.

"Yes," returned Bess, looking on the ground for her pocket handkerchief, which she had purposely dropped to afford her the opportunity of avoiding Bell's piercing look. "Yes, Mr. Cheverton was the gentleman who assisted me when I slipped, and, indeed, saved me from falling; and I heard from him that he was on his way to meet Mr. Leicester."

Bell looked still more amazed and suspicious.

"How could Mr. Cheverton know who you were, Bess?—and where could you be when the accident happened?" she demanded; "for he, of course, must have been going to town."

"I cannot tell, exactly, where I was, Bell," replied Bess, "for I had missed my way, and——but as to how Mr. Cheverton knew me, I told him myself, or at least—— I cannot explain very well how it was, for I was in very great pain at the moment, and very much alarmed at finding myself in such a situation, so far from home, that I scarcely knew what I said or did; but I know that Cheverton signified his intention of calling here. So you will have an opportunity, Bell, of gratifying the curiosity you expressed one day, as to Mr. Leicester's cousin."

And Bess smiled, in the hope of diverting her sister from the embarrassing questions she had asked.

Bell, however, was not so easily eluded. She saw from her sister's manner that there was something Bess wished to conceal, and, though she did not then press any farther questions while her mother was present, the moment Mrs. Leslie quitted the room she again threw down her book, and looking steadfastly in her sister's face, observed—

"Pray, Bess, what was the romantic expedition in which you were engaged today, and what is the reall secret of your

acquaintance with Mr. Cheverton? Leicester, I am sure, knew nothing of it, or else he must be much more artful than I think him."

"The real secret, then, as you style it, Bell, is no secret at all, for it is exactly as I stated it," returned Bess, "except that which I did not like to mention before mamma, that it was Mr. Cheverton and his companion's impertinent curiosity, in following and staring me in the face, that occasioned me to be so careless as not to observe what ↓ was stepping on ; and I will tell you still further, Bell, that though he was very attentive and obliging afterwards, and appeared very much concerned for the accident, there is something in his manner, an assumption, or at least a disposition to familiarity in his manner towards me, that made me feel very uncomfortable, and very, very glad to get rid of him, and would also induce me willingly to dispense with his threatened visit. I hope, indeed, that we shall be able to persuade mamma, without exciting any unpleasant feelings in her mind, to receive him alone. Her retired and reserved manners will not, I am sure, suit so gay a gentleman; and as it will be easy to be denied, if he should repeat his visit, we shall thus get rid of him without appearing ungrateful for his attention."

"All very proper and prudent on your part, no doubt," returned Bell, ironically; "but I think I read the true secret of this, my dear—you are afraid of exciting the jealousy of a certain grave gentleman, who suits your taste better than this bold, dashing Mr. Cheverton, who, however, I suspect, is worth twenty of his sentimental cousin. But now there is another question I want answered, and which I observe, in your very explanatory explanation, you have hitherto evaded. Where were you going, when you encountered Mr. Cheverton?"

"I was returning home, Bell," replied Bess, gravely.

"That may be," observed Bell, quickly, "but where had you been, for I can see there is some secret in the affair, and I really cannot understand why I am not as eligible a confidante as Susan?"

"Susan has never been my confidante, Bell," returned her sister, "and be assured," she continued, while tears started to her eyes, "if the result of my romantic expedition, as you called it just now, had been such as could give you pleasure, I should not have hesitated an instant to have communicated it. I have been vexed, grieved, mortified, I may say insulted, more than ever I was in my life, Bell," she continued, observing that the latter still regarded her with curiosity and suspicion, "and now, there's a dear girl, do not ask me any more questions."

Bell, however, was not of a disposition to rest satisfied with this half-explanation. She had half persuaded herself that Bessie's secret was an appointment the latter had made with Mr. Leicester, previously to his leaving the country; and, unlikely as this was, and totally inconsistent with her sister's conduct and character, she could not divest herself of this idea, and was thus prevented turning her thoughts in the direction she would otherwise have done, and of course the right one, that Bess had been to Portland Place.

It was long before Bess comprehended the meaning of her sister's sarcastic hints, that if *she* had so committed herself it would have been nothing surprising; but that Bess, who was so delicate and fastidious, should have hazarded such a step,

was indeed surprising; but the truth at last became obvious, and hurt, indignant, humiliated beyond measure, that Bell should have believed her capable of such a step, Bess, in a burst of passionate tears, revealed the truth—that she had been to Portland Place, and had been treated by Sir Matthew in a manner that had made her bitterly regret that she had done so.

"And it was for you, Bell, almost wholly on your account," she added, reproachfully, "that I hazarded an appeal to my uncle. For myself, I could not, would not have done it. But I saw you pining, fretting, and discontented—I knew that nothing but your restoration to Lady Jane's favour, and the advantage, as you consider it, of being again admitted to her circle, would make you happy, and—Oh, Bell, that you could be so cruel, so unjust to me as to believe me capable ——"

"Psha, Bessie, what a little fool you are," interrupted Bell, coaxingly. "It was only my own wicked imagination that put the thought into my head. It was just such a wild foolish trick as I might have played myself."

"God forbid!" murmured Bess, but Bell affected not to hear this and went on—

"Come, now, dry your eyes, and forgive me, and tell me what Sir Matthew said to you. I suppose the heir has made his appearance, and the amiable pair are so puffed up ——"

"No—no, I wish it were so," returned Bess, hastily, and shuddering at the reflection that perhaps, even now, all her uncle's hopes were extinguished in the death of his wife and child. Bell looked at her with surprise, as Bess, in a low voice and faltering accents, proceeded to relate what she had heard of the dangerous situation of Lady Jane.

"And are you so ridiculous as to grieve at that?" demanded Bell, with sparkling eyes. "Well, I confess I am totally unable to comprehend such romantic disinterestedness."

Shocked beyond measure at her sister's unfeeling selfishness, which could lead her thus to hear, not only without emotion, but actually with exultation, of the danger and probable death of one towards whom she had formerly professed such unbounded affection, Bess proceeded hastily to repeat Sir Matthew's closing denunciation, that he would, in the event of Lady Jane's death, bestow the whole of his wealth for purposes of charity, rather than his nieces should profit by it; but Bell seemed little affected by this. She knew, she said, that Sir Matthew was too much bent on the aggrandisement of his own family to persevere in such a resolution.

"No—no, Bess," she concluded, "if she dies, I have no fear that we shall yet be his heiresses, unless he should be mad or rash enough to marry again, and that we must try our best to prevent, if, as I have no doubt we should be once more restored to his favour."

Every word that Bell uttered on this subject served to give additional pain and uneasiness to her sister, and to convince her that the latter had indeed thoroughly imbibed the cool, unfeeling, selfish spirit of calculation, which so eminently distinguished Lady Jane herself, and was now turned against her; she therefore gladly availed herself of the opportunity of her mother's return to the room to drop the subject, though she could not but remark, with increased dissatisfaction, that for many hours afterwards her sister was in better spirits than she had seen her, ever since the certainty had been made known to her that she was no longer to consider herself as a part of Lady Jane's establishment.

Bell's hopes and expectations, however, soon received a mortal blow.

"Thank God!" exclaimed Bess, in a tone of unaffected gladness.

She was reading the morning paper, which Mr. Leicester had brought with him, and left during a hasty call he had that morning made at the cottage, having promised to pass the evening with them on his return.

Mrs. Leslie looked from her work in surprise at her daughter's exclamation, and Bell, who had been languidly yawning over a fashionable novel, in a reclining posture on a couch, started up with a look of eager expectation.

"What is it you have met with there, my dear, to excite such an ardent expression of gratitude?" demanded Mrs. Leslie.

Bess cast a deprecating look towards her sister, and proceeded to read—

"Yesterday, the 17th, at his mansion in Portland Place, the lady of Sir Matthew Bevington, M. P. for ——shire, of a son and heir. The lady and infant are both doing well.'"

"My dear brother!" ejaculated Mrs. Leslie, tears stealing down her cheeks.

Bess remained silent. She dared not give further utterance to her feelings, lest she should afford her sister an opportunity of breaking forth into the storm of passion with which it was plain to see her bosom was labouring. Mrs. Leslie, however, unacquainted with what had previously taken place between her daughters, did not observe how different were the feelings with which Bell had received this intelligence.

"Place my desk on the table, love," she observed. "I will write to your uncle, and tell him how sincerely we rejoice in the consummation of his hopes. God forbid that he should believe us indifferent to an event which, I am well aware, has made him a happier man than ever he was before."

Bess trembled lest this act on the part of her mother should elicit fresh insults from Sir Matthew—but then again, she thought to herself, he will see that this, the pure dictate of her feelings, cannot be the result of any views of self-interest or mercenary calculations. He will know that I have concealed from her the cruel and bitter remarks he made in our last interview, and I hope convince him of their injustice. Lady Jane, too, will perhaps, now that all doubt and suspense is at an end, feel softened towards those who have never in reality given her the slightest cause of offence, and we shall be once more a united family. All Bessie's pacific hopes and anticipations were, however, quickly put to flight.

"Did you hear what I requested you to do, Bell?" demanded Mrs. Leslie, who had been surprised by the latter's walking contemptuously away, and seating herself at the piano, where she began to turn over some music books, instead of placing the desk as her mother had requested.

"Yes, mamma, I did hear very well," she replied, her eyes lighting with indignation; "but, if Bess chooses to allow you to humiliate yourself, and be betrayed into a repetition of Sir Matthew's insults, I will not. I would die," she passionately added; "before I would feed their pride and insolence. And, after all, they cannot—will not believe that you really feel any pleasure in an event that reduces your children to beggary and ruin."

An explanation was no longer avoidable. Bess was compelled to relate the particulars of her interview with her uncle, and Mrs. Leslie, hurt and distressed beyond expression, relinquished, with tears, her intention of writing to her brother; though bitterly regretting that she had not been allowed to remain in ignorance of what had passed.

Bell had now full opportunity to give vent to the anger against Sir Matthew and Lady Jane which she had hitherto suppressed. Mrs. Leslie was too much dejected and overwhelmed by the conviction that the breach between herself and her brother was not likely to be easily repaired, while Bess, convinced that her arguments and remonstrances would tend rather to exasperate than induce Bell to refrain from the expression of her resentment, remained silent.

Bell's frequent repetition, however, of the expressions "beggary, poverty, and ruin," as applied to their own situation, at length provoked her to speak, and Bess mildly observed—

"This is cruel, Bell, to your mother, and it is also untrue. It will be our own fault, or we must be indeed peculiarly unfortunate, if we should be reduced to distress and misery."

"And what, then, do you call our present life but misery?" exclaimed Bell. "To you, indeed, it may be all very well to drag on existence in this petty, obscure, humdrum style, but I am not content, nor ever shall be. Oh, how I wish I had died before I knew the difference—before I had been fooled, betrayed, despised, and made the laughing-stock of those who ——"

She was interrupted by an exclamation of alarm from Bess, who, unable to stand upon her swollen foot, had in vain tried to prevent her mother's fall from her chair.

Mrs. Leslie, overcome with the anguish she had suffered from the unexpected discovery of her brother's apparently irrevocable renunciation of her children, and still more grieved and distressed by the exposure of Bell's violent and ungovernable disposition, had fallen in a fit upon the floor.

I was long before she returned to sensibility, or even the appearance of life, and when she did so, her heart-rending lamentations and expressions of utter despair were such as defied all consolation from Bess, and even alarmed and confounded the conscience-stricken Bell, who, too late, repented having given such an unbridled sway to her passions.

"I will try, indeed I will, mamma, to be content, and to forget all I ever hoped for, and was encouraged to believe would be my lot in life," she observed, with tears, "if you will forget what I have said, and try to smile and look happy again. See how you have frightened poor Bess. For her sake, then, if not for mine, say that you will forget and forgive my waywardness. But, indeed, if you did but know how I have been petted and flattered, and what brilliant visions of future greatness and distinction I have been encouraged to indulge—And then, dear mamma, you must yourself acknowledge that the continual round of pleasure and amusement that I have been accustomed to, while I was living with Lady Jane ——"

"Ay, indeed," sighed Rachel, who having been summoned to the room by Bessie's affrighted screams, still remained hovering around her beloved mistress, and mingling her tears with hers.—"Ay, indeed, Miss Bell," she repeated, "it is a thousand pities that you ever knew anything of such a life, which, as far as I can see, never does anybody good, but only hardens their hearts, and makes them care for nothing that they ought to care for. And yet, I don't know how it is, our dear Bessie has never been corrupted, nor ever seemed to have any longing after amusements, as they're called. If you would only take pattern by her, and study, as she does, to make everybody happy about her ——"

Bess contrived gently to interrupt Rachel's warm unstudied eulogium by observing, that she thought a little warm wine and water would be beneficial to her mother, and the good old woman hurried away to procure it. But the mischief was done. Bell's haughty spirit had taken fire at what she considered the unjustifiable presumption of her mother's servant, and when Rachel quitted the room she warmly observed—

"That is another cause I have of complaint, arising from the manner we live in. Would any family but ours submit to the interference and dictation of an ignorant, self-opinionated old woman, who thinks herself privileged to give her opinion upon every subject, just as if she were a part of the family?"

"I consider her as such, Bell," observed Mrs. Leslie, who seemed restored by this remark to something like her usual composure, "and if I and your sister do not feel ourselves degraded by Rachel's—degraded, did I say?—No, Bell, honoured would be a better word to use, for the warm, sincere, unselfish devotion of a heart so pure and upright, so correct and unsophisticated as Rachel's is. I honour the feelings that inspire it, and have for many, many long years profited by it."

"Profited!" repeated Bell, satirically. "I should really suppose, mamma, that the profit has been on Rachel's side. She has not served you for so many years, of course, without being well paid for it."

Mrs. Leslie's countenance at this observation assumed a severity that made even Bell blush and look confused.

"I should, indeed, be hurt, Bell," she observed, "if I thought that mean, mercenary sentiment originated in your own mind; but I trace it to the same source which has destroyed so much of your natural feeling, which," she added, in a broken voice, "has robbed me of my child—my once dutiful, affectionate child, and returned to me, in her place, a cold-hearted, self-sufficient, presuming girl, whose mis-directed, paltry ambition, and mistaken views of happiness, will render her miserable, and poison my few remaining years of life."

The faltering, tremulous accents in which this was pronounced drew tears of anguish from Bess, but her sister's heart was closed against all gentle impressions by that overweening pride, which spurned all counsel, and induced her to consider herself injured by even the mildest reprehension. Taught by Lady Jane to consider Mrs. Leslie as a weak, narrow-minded being, whose long seclusion from the world and unaspiring dispositon rendered her a most unfit person to advance the interests of her children, Bell in secret entertained an utter contempt for her mother's opinion and advice, while her own self-conceit and vanity, fostered as it had been by the adulation she had received from her aunt's circle, contributed to render her impatient and resentful of the slightest contradiction or reprehension. In silence, therefore, she beheld her mother and sister's tears, and listened, or rather turned a deaf ear to the efforts Bessie made to console the tender parent, whose heart was throbbing with agony for her wayward and thankless child, for whose happiness she would, if it could have been required, have sacrificed her very existence.

CHAPTER XIII.

To me no more the breathing gale
Comes fraught with sweets: no more the rose
With such transcendent beauty blows,
As when Cadenus blest the scene,
And shared with me those joys serene,
When, unperceived, the lambent fire
Of friendship kindled new desire:
Still listening to his tuneful tongue,
The truths, which angels might have sung,
Divine impressed their gentle sway,
And sweetly stole my soul away.
My guide, instructor, lover, friend,
Dear names, in one idea blend.—ANON.

SCARCELY had Mrs. Leslie and Bess recovered the agitation they had suffered during the morning, or rather had been able to subdue the outward and visible signs of that agitation, before Mr. Leicester was announced, in accordance with his previously expressed intention of passing a quiet evening with them. Bell was not visible. She had retired to her bedroom immediately after dinner, and when, on Mr. Leicester's arrival, Susan had been sent to summon her to tea, had excused herself with that convenient plea, so often substituted by ladies for the real motive—a violent headache. Mr. Leicester looked grave—more grave, Bess thought, than she had ever seen him. Mrs. Leslie's hands trembled so that she could scarcely manage to do the honours of the tea-table; an office which Bess, who usually officiated, was compelled to decline, from the awkward position she was obliged to submit to, in consequence of the accident she had met; and both mother and daughter, though they exerted themselves to appear easy and unconstrained in their efforts to entertain their guest, were conscious that he regarded them with more than common curiosity and interest, while at the same time his own mind seemed labouring with depressing thoughts, which checked his usual free and confidential intercourse with his companions, and induced frequent pauses of gloomy and thoughtful silence on his part—a silence that neither Bess nor her mother could muster spirits to break.

"You have, I hope, taken my advice of this morning, Miss Leslie?" he at length observed, after one of those long awkward pauses.

Bess looked up in surprise. She had forgotten for the moment what advice it was that he had proffered.

"I mean," he continued, "that I hope that you have had medical assistance."

Bess shook her head, and forced a smile.

"I do not like doctors," she observed, "and have great faith in Rachel's skill. Indeed, I am getting on so well, that it would be quite a shame to deprive our good Rachel of the credit of the cure. I hope to be able by to-morrow to get rid of my gouty shoe. Indeed I think, if I were to try, I could now, though I am obliged to submit to orders and keep quiet. If mamma wouldn't tell tales," she added, "and get me a scolding from Rachel, who is very tenacious of her authority over her patients, I would try whether I could not manage to creep up stairs and see Bell, who I am afraid is very dull there alone."

Mrs. Leslie, however, strongly objected to her making this exertion.

"If your sister's headache be really so bad as to disable her from coming down to tea, my dear," she observed, "quietude is the most potent remedy, and certainly it is not fair to trespass so far on Rachel's injunctions."

"But if it can do no harm, mamma," said Bess, who longed to try to persuade her sister to come down, in the hope that the presence of Mr. Leicester, towards whom she invariably showed a deference that few others could boast of, would have the effect of restoring harmony between her and her mother. "If it can do no harm," repeated Bess, "and Mr. Leisester said this morning that it is better gently to exercise the sprained foot, than to keep it in a constrained posture—Did you not say so, Mr. Leicester?" and she looked up smilingly in Leicester's face.

Good Heaven, what could she have said or done? How could she, by any possibility, have excited such resentment in Leicester's bosom, or what could be the meaning of the stern frown with which he was at that moment regarding her, and the effect of which was not diminished by the manner in which he replied to her question.

"I believe I did say so," he observed, with evident confusion, "that is, I know I have heard or read that—but, really, you must excuse my having taken the liberty of offering my opinion on a matter of which I know so little."

And with an air of indifference that was evidently intended to disguise an emotion he could not control, he stooped to caress Carlo, who was lying at his feet.

The strangeness of this remark—so unlike the usual tender earnestness of his manner on any previous occasion, where Bess was interested, or, indeed, his general feelings of kindness and friendly interest towards herself and family, could not fail to excite Mrs. Leslie's surprise, though she had not caught that stern expression of his features which had made Bess absolutely start. Depressed already by the morning's occurrences, Mrs. Leslie fancied she saw in this sudden coldness of Mr. Leicester, to whom she was warmly and sincerely attached, a prelude to a new misfortune.

"He has heard, I suppose, from Bessie," she thought, "the result of her interview with her uncle, and, like all the world, is desirous of retreating from those whose fallen fortunes—and yet can it be possible that Leicester is so mercenary—that the noble, exalted sentiments he has so often given utterance to, and which seemed the spontaneous dictates of his heart—can these have all thus suddenly disappeared, from the conviction that my dear ingenuous child—she whom I have often thought was the only being worthy of him—and he, how often has almost unconsciously and involuntarily the conviction entered my mind that, had I the power to choose from the whole world, Leicester would be the only man to whom I would entrust the happiness of my dearest child? How have I been mistaken!"

Mrs Leslie, however, was wrong. Bess had not confided to Leicester the circumstances of her recent interview with her uncle. In the few minutes he had passed with her alone, during his morning call, she had told him only briefly that she had met with the accident, which she represented as very slight, while out upon business, with only Susan for her attendant, and he had been too much engrossed by his tender sympathy, and his entreaties to have better assistance and advice than Rachel he feared was capable of giving, to make any particular inquiries where the affair had happened, concluding from his knowledge of her general habit of never going any distance from home, unless in the company of her mother and sister, that it had taken place in the immediate neighbourhood of their residence. Why it was that Bess felt an unwillingness to relate her rencontre with Mr. Cheverton, she could not herself explain—but so it was. She did feel an unaccountable reluctance to mention that gentleman's name to him, although she knew that Leicester would inevitably hear of the circumstance, even should Mr. Cheverton, as she earnestly hoped he would, relinquish his expressed intention of calling at the cottage.

How often does it occur that trifles,

which appear light as air in our estimation at the moment, produce the most serious and enduring consequences. Bessie's total omission of the name of Mr. Cheverton, in her explanation of the accident which, as she had laughingly said, when he had seen her in the morning, had chained her by the foot—a prisoner to the sofa—had, combined with other circumstances, raised a storm in Leicester's bosom, that momentarily, from his first entrance into the drawing-room, threatened to break the bounds that prudence imposed. Too proud and too angry to ask for an explanation, which it appeared to his jealous fancy Bess cautiously avoided, he had waited, with what he considered exemplary patience, for some observation either from Bess or Mrs. Leslie, which might lead to the subject on which his heart was racked; but both Mrs. Leslie and her daughter's thoughts were pre-occupied with their recent domestic discussion, and that which Leicester considered as coldness, reserve, and a desire to conceal from him his cousin's introduction to Bess, and his expected visit, was in reality the dejection and melancholy occasioned by Bell's violence and afflicting observations, confirmed still more by her obstinate determination to remain in her own room.

Bessie's first sensation, as she met Leicester's stern frown, and observed his equally unintelligible assumption of indifference, had been that of alarm and sorrow; and these feelings her beautiful eyes had, for an instant, most palpably expressed; but pride, natural feminine pride came the next moment to her relief. The pure blood, which had retreated from her cheek, returned in a deeper dye, and observing with a smile that, after all, she should do as the world in general did, whether the advice was gratuitous or paid for, receive it with all due thankfulness, but follow only so much as suited their own opinions, or convenience—

"Don't tell Rachel, though, dear mamma," she added, as with the help of the chairs she contrived to reach the door.

In spite of all his previous resentment and pretended indifference, Leicester could not resist the impulse to fly to her assistance, when he beheld the difficulty with which she walked; but Bess gracefully and calmly declined it, and having opened the door for her, he was about to return to his chair, when a sudden recollection seemed to overcome him, and laying his hand upon her arm to detain her, he whispered—

"Bessie, do not leave me in anger.

This may be, perhaps—I fear this may be the last evening that I may pass with you for years. I am going to leave England, Bess—to be torn from all, every one that I hold dear. I came with a resolution to spare myself the misery of telling you this. I meant to write to you an explanation of my situation, my thoughts—feelings, but——"

"Going—leave England!" repeated Bess, gasping almost for breath as she uttered the words; but she was recalled to recollection by her mother's anxious and astonished look at her, and making a strong effort to resume her self-possession, she added: "mamma, our friend, Mr. Leicester says, he is about to leave England."

Mrs. Leslie uttered an exclamation of surprise and sorrow, and Bess suffered herself, without any attempt at opposition, to be led, or rather supported by Leicester, back to her seat on the sofa.

It was some time before Leicester could command his voice to enter calmly and coherently upon his promised explanation, the feelings which had been so long pent up within his bosom overpowering all his attempts to appear calm and composed.

He began by speaking of the circumstances under which he had been first introduced to Mrs. Leslie.

"From that moment," he continued, "I became more anxious than ever to shake off the state of dependence in which I had been kept by my uncle, the Earl of St. Aldwyn. I need not, I dare say, tell you, my dear Mrs. Leslie, that my inheritance from my father was comparatively trifling, but to my uncle's kindness I was indebted for an education that placed me on a footing with his younger sons. I was their companion at school and at college, and their home was mine, both during the vacations and when we quitted our studies. So far the earl's conduct has been unexceptionably kind, and perhaps I have no right to complain of it in any other point of view, though I now feel the evil consequences of being allowed to waste two or three years in idleness. My uncle is not rich for his station, and it is well known to us all that his eldest son's expensive habits had considerably embarrassed him. It was necessary, therefore, that the younger should embrace some profession—Lewis chose the navy; and a rich living, which is the gift of the earl, determined the choice of his brother, who entered the church. I, with still greater necessity of determining the course I should pursue, still remained undecided. My wishes, indeed, pointed to the navy, but all the interest the earl possessed in that direction was exhausted in forwarding Lewis's interest, and I was dissuaded from following the bent of my inclination. I am ashamed almost to acknowledge it," he continued, " I know I ought to be so, but in the society with which I had been accustomed to associate, I had been learned to despise trade. My dear father, indeed, I knew had been happy, respected, and useful in a superior degree to his fellow creatures, though holding only a junior partnership in a mercantile house. I would have indignantly resented any personal reflection upon him, who was in my eyes the most exalted of human beings, and yet I was weak enough to despise the situation he had held. I might have entered into the same house, when I first returned from college, under the most favourable auspices, but the haughty contempt with which the St. Aldwyn family treated the proposal induced me to reject it. For these three years, then, I have been leading the life of a mere idler, though longing to exert myself, and with the unpleasing consciousness that I was hourly diminishing the little capital my father left me. But the earl had great prospects for me. He was partial enough, too, to think, or at least to say, that I had talents that would advance me to a much higher station in life than either of his sons. If the ministry were changed, and his friends came into power, he had sufficient interest to open a path for those talents—I tell you all this, I know, only as an excuse for my supineness—But I must hasten to a conclusion. Circumstances—why should I disguise the truth?—my feelings towards your daughter, my dear Mrs. Leslie, have, within the last few weeks, opened my eyes more completely to the folly of continuing to lead this life of idleness. Did I possess thousands, I would lay them at her feet, and implore your blessing on our union. Am I presuming, Bessie, in believing that with your mother's sanction, I might have hoped ——"

Bessie did not reply, but though the beautiful eyes, which had been so intently fixed on him during his narrative, were withdrawn and downcast at this observation, there was no token of discouragement in her eloquent silence, nor was the hand withdrawn which he had clasped in his. In Mrs. Leslie's looks, grief and pleasure were blended, as in a faltering voice, she observed—

" I will not deny, Mr. Leicester, that I have in part anticipated this explanation, nor will I hesitate to confess that to no one living would I with such perfect con-

fidence entrust the happiness of my dear, my affectionate, and dutiful child, as yourself ; though, at the same time, I will acknowledge that I *have* feared that there were circumstances that might prevent—"

" Not prevent," exclaimed Leicester, eagerly. " Delay only," he added, in softer accents, " the happiness which I trust our dear Bessie, as well as you, will allow me to hope will be mine. Speak, Bessie, let me hear from your own lips that I am not too presumptuous in believing that, should fortune smile upon me, you will not refuse to bestow upon me the gift without which all her favours would indeed be worthless"

Bess tried to speak, but the words died away on her faltering lips. It was very evident, however, that such as did reach Leicester's ear conveyed no discuragement, and Mrs. Leslie, smiling through her tears, observed—

" It is scarcely fair to press Bessie now, Mr. Leicester, for a more explicit acknowledgment, but she will, I know, let her mother answer for her that should you feel yourself in a situation to claim her as your wife (and I can, I am sure, depend upon your prudence not to do so until then), she will interpose no obstacle. Do you not ratify these conditions, Bessie ?"

" Certainly, my dear mother," returned Bess, who had in some measure recovered from her confusion and timidity at this unexpected avowal on the part of Leicester. " I will say more," continued the blushing but smiling girl, raising her eyes to his, but almost instantly casting them down as they met his impassioned gaze ; " I will acknowledge," she added, " that I shall look forward to the period—the time Mr. Leicester speaks of, with every hope and confidence that my happiness, too, will be secured, and that my dear mother will have no reason to regret having sanctioned ——"

Bess looked round, but Mrs. Leslie had vanished. She had considered it proper to leave the lovers alone to their mutual confidence, their pledges of constancy to each other, &c. &c., and we shall imitate her prudence and forbearance, by not seeking to penetrate further into those mysteries of the tender passion, which, deeply interesting as they are to the parties concerned, are seldom capable of being portrayed so as to excite pleasure or sympathy in the bosom of the reader.

There was one point, however, in which Leicester's explanation was as yet deficient, but on Mrs. Leslie's return to the room, he hastened to repeat to her, what he had already confided to Bessie—That was, his

precise situation at the present moment, and the nature of his hopes for the future. It was very evident, however, that he had some reserves, even now, with those with whom as he said he should consider his future interests were all identified; for he did not disclose what had been the subject on which the Earl of St. Aldwyn and himself had differed. Differed, however, they had, as he was compelled to acknowledge, and that had brought this affair to a crisis. Leicester had avowed his deter-

mination to remain no longer prom.ise-crammed. He blamed, he said, himself rather than the earl for his long supineness, and—

"But I will compress the whole in as few words as possible, my dear madam," he concluded, in the repetition he made to Mrs. Leslie of what he had already explained more fully to Bess. "I have relinquished for ever all the supposed advantages of my position, as nephew of the Earl of St. Aldwyn, and am at liberty henceforth to seek my own way to wealth and independence. Fortunately, my dear father's character still avails me, though not under such favourable circumstances as it would have done had I been wise enough to have embraced the offer made me by the liberal-minded man, his senior partner, who was the executor of his will, but whom I foolishly deserted for the privilege of becoming the recognised relative and protegee of the Earl of St. Aldwyn. Mr. Ashton, my father's friend, is dead, but the firm is still in existence, and I have succeeded in forming arrangements with them which eventually—It was not, however, until yesterday, within a few hours of my return to London, from the country residence of the principal partner, that it was decidedly concluded that the first few years of my probation must be passed in Canada, where they have an establishment. This, I confess, was an unexpected blow to the hopes I had ventured to form," he continued, looking tenderly at Bess, "and even now, when I reflect how many circumstances may arise during my absence—Even but yesterday—I will make a candid confession of all my faults—even yesterday, I was almost driven to madness by the boasting assertions of Lewis Cheverton that he had gained an introduction to the lady whose name, he knew, had been of late the subject of altercation between me and his father ——"

Bess started with surprise and concern.

"I did not mean to tell you this, by-the-bye," continued Leicester, looking conscious that he had committed himself, "but it is better, perhaps, my dear Bess, that I have no reserves. Well, then, the truth is that my uncle and I *have* differed as to the means which were best calculated to secure my happiness, and that I am henceforth free to follow my own ideas on that subject. As to Lewis Cheverton—"

"I will never see or speak to him again," interrupted Bess with warmth.

Leicester's looks expressed his gratitude; and Bess, as if she felt that some qualification was necessary for her unguarded warmth, added—

"Even if I knew nothing of Mr. Cheverton—if he were a perfect stranger to me, his manners were such as would induce me to avoid a second interview; but——"

"He did not dare to treat you with levity?" exclaimed Leicester, his fine eyes darting fire. "He told me, that in spite of his natural indolence, he exerted himself to the utmost to repair the injury which he acknowledged his indiscreet curiosity had occasioned, but he said it was very evident that the attentions of a gentleman, with whom he suspected you had some previous acquaintance, were preferred to his, and that he had therefore yielded his pretensions and left you to *his* care."

Bessie's cheek crimsoned at the recollections that were forced upon her mind at this observation, which was enforced by the keen glance of Leicester's eye, in whose mind the incipient jealousy of his nature had been rekindled by the accidental allusion to the circumstances attendant on Bessie's meeting with his cousin, Lewis Cheverton.

A moment's reflection, however, restored Bess to her usual composure.

"When I tell you," she observed, "that the gentleman Mr. Cheverton has so misrepresented was a total stranger to me, that I do not even now know his name, and that he addressed not one word to me, except such as any man of common humanity might be expected to do to a young female under similar circumstances, I trust, Mr. Leicester, I have said enough."

"Too much, my dear—dear Bess," he replied with earnestness. "It is too much that you should waste one precious word or thought on such an unworthy subject; but forgive me—do forgive me, if in the whirl and confusion of my thoughts—Can you blame me, Bess, that, estimating so highly as I do your every thought, word, and look, I should be fearful of——"

"We are, if I understand you aright, Leicester," observed Bess, "to be separated for many years——"

"Oh, no, no—do not say many," returned Leicester, "long, tedious—wretchedly tedious will they be to me, but——"

"Whether they will be many or few," interrupted Bess, "seems at present dependent on too many contingencies for us to decide; but I would ask you, with what confidence——"

"Oh, yes, I see—I know it all," interrupted Leicester. "It is madness, folly in me to doubt. Henceforth, farewell suspicion! Yet—but I cannot, dare not ask it."

"All that with propriety—not the cold, selfish feeling that the world calls propriety," observed Mrs. Leslie, "but such as is consistent with her own feelings and character, I am sure Bess is proposed to grant. Further than that, I am sure Mr. Leicester will not ask or wish."

Leicester bowed his head in silent acquiescence. He dared not now breathe one word of the wild wishes which would have prompted him to implore that Bess should have been secured to him by those holy rites, which would have effectually barred all pretensions to her favour; but he felt that he in some measure deserved the purgatory he was doomed to suffer, and the remainder of the evening was passed in discussing in full and perfect confidence their separate views for the future, which were to end in the blending of their views and interests in one.

During these deeply interesting discussions, Bell, though not forgotten, was but occasionally alluded to, although, in the mother's thoughts, she was the most prominent object. Mrs. Leslie, however, considering it finally concluded that Leicester was to become her son-in-law, no longer saw any objection to make him acquainted with that which now seemed her only source of uneasiness—Bell, her pride, ambition, and present cause or imaginary cause for discontent, not excluding or concealing the recent ebullitions of passion which had banished her to her chamber, and prevented her from being a sharer in their happiness.

For happiness it was. Yes, in spite of all that opposed their immediate union, both Bess and Leicester felt that it was happiness to be assured that their views, their wishes, their hopes, were all in unison; while Mrs. Leslie was equally satisfied, that however the full fruition of her beloved Bessie's happiness might be delayed, it was still certain. As certain as the mutability of this mutable world could render it.

"For Bess I have no fears," she observed, "but for my poor Bell."

Strange that the very unworthiness of the beloved child should but render it more near and dear to the heart of a mother. Yet so it was— Mrs. Leslie's thoughts seemed totally diverted from the difficulties that lay in Bessie's path, to dwell on those which beset that of the unworthy Bell. Was it her entire confidence in Leicester? He almost hoped it was; yet still he felt that it was an injustice to his spotless, blameless Bess, that the ungrateful, rebellious, and headstrong Bell should occupy so large a share of Mrs. Leslie's maternal anxiety.

Midnight surprised them, and still no definite plan had been proposed or adopted with respect to her who, from the moment the subject had been started, had at least been the most prominent subject in their confidential intercourse, and Bess started as though the idea was new to her, when Leicester, on taking leave, whispered—

"A few hours more and I shall be parted for—I dread to reflect—to name how long, from her whose image will be my consolation in my painful exile. Oh, Bess, if you are ever tempted to forget— to desert me—think what I shall be in a strange land, without a friend, a motive—"

"Never, never!" replied Bess, for the first time giving free vent and scope to her feelings. "Never, Leicester, while you remain true to your present—I will not say professions, for I feel they are more than professions. Never, then, while you remain true to me, will I desert you; and as I keep this oath, may I prosper, or ——"

Leicester clasped her passionately to his bosom, and prevented the deprecation she would have uttered; and Mrs. Leslie, who had considerately affected not to see this little interlude, observed—

"You will breakfast with us, my dear Mr. Leicester?"

Leicester looked his thanks, but appeared undetermined.

"Come," rejoined Mrs. Leslie, kindly, "I see how it is—you are afraid of trespassing on our regular hours; but Bessie is a very early riser, and she has during her attendance on me, as well as her aunt Lady Jane, accustomed herself to do with so little sleep, that I know, late as it is, she will feel it no punishment to make our coffee, be it ever so early. Say, then, what time you will be here?"

Leicester's expressive eyes spoke his thanks. He had appointed to be on the road to Portsmouth by eleven the next morning, but he could not resist such an offer, and accordingly seven was fixed on for the social meal, "which was to be the last he could hope for in England for—"

Leicester's quivering lips refused to conclude the sentence, and they parted till the morning.

Mrs. Leslie would have resumed her seat, and her discussion with Bess of the prospects which had thus unexpectedly opened to the latter; but Bessie's feelings were too deep for words. She was, in reality, also uneasy lest her mother's health should suffer from the agitation the latter had endured, and the breaking in upon her regular hours.

"I cannot talk to-night, dear mother," she observed, lighting Mrs. Leslie's bed-candle, which Rachel, by way of hint, had, an hour or two previous, placed on the sideboard. "God bless you, and grant you may sleep."

And, without another word, she retreated to her own room. Before she reached it, however, she was startled by the sight of Rachel, whom she supposed to have been for the last two hours in bed. Bess was about to give utterance to a kind reproof to the old woman, for being so inattentive to her own health as to be up at that hour, but Rachel raised her finger in token of silence, and Bess, surmising in vain what she could have to say that required secrecy, followed Rachel to her room.

"I have had something on my mind for several days, my dear child," she observed when the door was closed, "but, as I never like to speak before I am quite certain, I have been silent. Don't frighten yourself, dear child, but do you not remember that I remarked to you, a few days ago, how very condescending Miss Bell had become of late to Susan?"

Bess breathlessly assented. Her heart throbbed already with dread.

"Well, my dear," continued Rachel, "my mind misgave me that it was for no good such a great alteration had taken place, for Miss Bell was never Susan's friend before. She had no patience, she used to be always saying, with the simple girl's awkwardness and stupidity; and not more than three weeks ago, she told me one day that she was astonished how her mother could think of keeping a creature that was half an idiot. More shame for her, Miss Bess, to have taken advantage, as she has done, of the foolish creature."

"But now, dear Rachel? Do not keep me in suspense," exclaimed Bess.

"I won't, love—but I could not go to my bed without telling you that I have discovered to-night that the grand secret of Miss Bell's sudden kindness to Susan, and her giving her a heap of ribbons and net for caps, and a black silk apron, and a parcel of other frippery, that, as I told Susan, wasn't at all becoming in her situation, and—I see you're impatient, my dear. Well, then, the truth is, your sister is carrying on a secret correspondence, and Susan has been drawn in to be her tool."

"And does Bell know that you have made this discovery?" demanded Bess, after a pause of grief and surprise.

"No, love, not yet," returned Rachel, "for I thought it best to consult you, as to what is to be done, before—But I will tell you the whole story, as it happened," she continued. "As I said before, I have had my suspicions for a week or two, and I kept a sharp eye on Susan; but, of course, I was no match for Miss Bell, though I think she had an idea that I suspected her, and whenever I caught Susan and her in such deep conversation, I gave the girl a good rating, and insisted on knowing what was going on; but she was put up to all manner of artful evasions,

and no longer ago than yesterday I had almost made up my mind to speak to you about it, but, as I said, I cannot bear to accuse any one without I am certain. Well, my dear, to-day, you know, after Bell had gone up stairs in the sulks, your mamma kept me a long time talking in the parlour. Susan had been sent out, you know, for tea-cakes and two or three other articles. She was a long time gone, but I was too full of the subject my poor dear mistress was talking about to think about Susan's staying so long of her errand, though it's a fault she has been greatly given to lately; but at last I heard the front door shut, and I knew she had let herself in with the key, though I had ordered her never to take the key, but to ring the area bell. Well, I was very angry in my mind, but I wouldn't worry your poor mamma by saying anything about it; but, as soon as I could get away, I hurried down to the kitchen to give her a good scolding, when, to my great surprise, what should I see but Miss Bell coming running up the kitchen-stairs as fast as she could run. I have known the time when she wouldn't have set her foot over the threshold of the kitchen-door—no, hardly to have saved her life.

"'Dear me,' says I, 'Miss Bell—what could have brought you down here?'

"She was as red as fire, but she muttered something about a glass of water.

"I knew I had put fresh water in both bottles and ewers in her chamber, not two hours before, so that I knew this was only an excuse, and so I went straight to Susan. She was trembling like a leaf, and couldn't look me in the face. So says I, 'Mrs. Susan, this is your gratitude to your kind mistress, is it? You're plotting and planning against her, and striving to bring distress and misery into the house that's sheltered you, and would make a woman of you. But it shan't go on any longer—I've found you out at last, and I shall speak to my mistress, and you shall be packed off back to your mother in the country, without a character. We'll have no traitors here, I can tell you.'

"Susan began to cry—she couldn't tell how much I did know, or what I didn't, I took her so at a nonplus, and so at last, under a promise that I would not let Miss Bell know that she had betrayed her, she owned to all. That Miss Bell had first employed her to carry letters to the post-office and fetch the answers, and then watch for a gentleman whom she let in at the side-gate, and then contrived to give Bell the signal that he was there in the garden, and then Bell left you and her mamma, and pretended to go into the library to fetch books, and instead slipped out into the garden to him. Three times, it seems, this trick has been played within a few days, and Susan had now brought a letter from the post-office, by which she supposed he was coming this evening, for she was told, if she was sent up with Miss Bell's tea, to say that she was in bed ; and if she heard her mamma or me talk of going up stairs, to run out to the box-hedge and give her notice, so that she might get up to her room before she was missed."

"And did he come ? Did you see him, Rachel ?" demanded Bess, with trembling anxiety.

"No, my dear child," she replied, "you know Mr. Leicester's being here of course kept me occupied, so that I couldn't keep watch, as I would have done; but I thought, at any rate, I would disappoint him for to-night, and when the gardener was going home, I told him I would give him some supper if he would stay an hour or two; and then, when Susan was out of the way, I told him that I had found out she had made an acquaintance I did not approve of, and that the person was coming that evening, at seven o'clock, and I wished he would keep a look-out, and if he saw anybody come up to the gate, to go out and ask him if he was waiting for the young woman ? 'And then do you tell him, Richard,' said I, 'that it's all found out, and that it will be best for him not to come any more till he hears by letter.'

"You see by this, my dear, I saved Miss Bell from being mentioned at all in the business. Well, it all fell out just as I had wished. Susan was waiting at tea when the clock struck seven, and Richard had just finished his cold meat and beer.

"'I suppose it's time now, Mrs. Rachel,' said he. 'I hope Susan's sweetheart arn't as passionate as I was, when I went courting, or else, perhaps, he'll give me something more than thanks for my ill news.'

"I pretended to laugh, though, goodness knows, my heart was almost bursting, to think that Miss Bell should have lowered herself so. However, away went Richard, and it was not above a quarter of an hour before he was back again.

"'It's all right, Mrs. Rachel,' said he, rubbing his hands. 'I've sent him off, with a fly in his ear. But, gracious me, whatever could such a dashing chap as that see in our little Susan to fall in love? She's but a plainish body, in my eyes, and he's a fine, tall, swaggering fellow; and, if I didn't know better, I could have been

sworn was a real gentleman, though it's very unlikely, if he was, he'd take the trouble to be parading up and down in the dark and cold. I was afraid, at first, to speak to him, for I thought he couldn't be the right person, but he tried the side-gate. I'd left it open, on purpose, and in he came tiptoeing, and then he stood stock-still, and looked up to all the windows. So I knew, then, he was no right sort of a visitor, so I stepped forward—and, law, how he started when he saw it was a man instead of a petticoat.

"'I think I know, sir, who you be looking for,' said I.

"'Indeed,' said he, with a voice as grand as if he had been a nobleman. 'Have you brought me any message, then?'

"'Yes, sir,' says I—I couldn't help sirring him, somehow, though in course I know he's no great things, or he wouldn't be stealing about the house in that manner. So then I up and told him just what you said. He seemed taken all aback, as the sailors say.

"'Then I can't hope to see her even for a minute?' said he, lingering like, though he'd made his way to the gate the minute I told him all was up.

"'Lord love you,' says I, 'it's as much as her head's worth, for Mrs. Rachel's on the look-out. Goodness, begging your pardon, Mrs. Rachel—but how he did swear ! It was awful to hear the names he called you, between his teeth. However, I comforted him that he would hear from Susan as soon as possible, and with that away he went, though not till he'd slipped this sixpence in my hand, that showed, you know, he was no gentleman, because the least he would have given me would have been——'

"Richard happened at this minute to cast his eye upon the sixpence, as he called it, and sure enough I saw, as well as him, in a minute that it was half-a-guinea.

"Poor Richard was quite thunderstruck. At first he thought it must be a mistake, and that the man would come back for it, but I, of course, knew better, so I told him he might safely call it his own, but that if the person who gave it him was a gentleman, as it appeared he was, he could have no good motive in coming after a poor girl like Susan, and, therefore, I hoped he wouldn't let himself be bribed into having any concern in the affair.

"'No, no,' said Richard, 'I'm a father myself, Mrs. Rachel, so he's mistaken if he thinks to get me to do any of his dirty work, and so I should tell him, in spite of his half-guinea.'

"I told the gardener that I hoped we should hear nothing more of him, as I had been talking very seriously to Susan about it, and I charged him not to let her know that he had had any concern in the matter. But now, my dear child, what is to be done? I thought I would let you know all about it at once, that you may think over, before morning, what is for the best."

"Does Bell know that you are acquainted with all this, Rachel?" demanded Bess.

"No, and that was what I wanted to tell you, too," returned the old woman. "I took care not to let Susan go near her, so she knows nothing. Twice she rang her bell, and I could see disappointment in her look when she found it was I that answered it."

"'Send me up some toast and water,' she said, the first time. Of course, I carried it up myself. Your mamma went up, you know, to see if she would have some supper, 'No,' she said, and then a few minutes after she rang again. This time she would have some gruel, when I went up; and she looked as if she could have eaten me instead of the gruel, she was so vexed. But I pretended not to see it, and answered her so calmly that I think she had no suspicion, for she said, when I was going out of the room—

"Send Susan with the gruel, Rachel. I don't want to trouble you to come up stairs.

"No—no, thought I, it is Susan you want, I know, and not the gruel ; but I made it, however, and carried it up, and then she began to scold. She wouldn't have asked for it, if she had thought she should give me so much trouble. Where was Susan, that she couldn't come ? She looked at me, as if she would look me through, when she asked this question. I saw she was determined to find out, if possible, whether anything had happened—but I was as determined she should not, if I could help it, and so I said Susan was busy, for Mr. Leicester was going to stay to supper.

"'And, indeed, Miss Bell.' said I, 'I wish you were down stairs with them, for I don't believe moping up here by yourself will cure your headache.'

"'Oh, indeed, they don't want me with them, I am well aware,' said she, with a toss of her head, 'and I beg, Rachel, if Bessie or mamma ask any questions about me, you will tell them I am gone to bed, as I shall be indeed in a few minutes, and therefore you need not trouble yourself to come up again.

"Ah, thought I, Miss Bell, I wonder how long it is since you thought before anything about giving people trouble. But still, I must own the truth, my dear child, I couldn't help pitying her, she looked so miserable. Not but what she's greatly to blame, to be carrying on such an affair unknown, and—but, my dear child, don't look so distressed. All will end well yet, I hope and trust ; but what I want you to turn over in your mind is, what is to be done—whether it is best to let Miss Bell know that she has been found out—or whether my poor mistress could not be kept from knowing anything about it, it Bell would only give her promise—but I ought not to pretend to advise you, who are always so capable of judging what is for the best."

Bess, however, in this instance, felt little capability for deciding, as Rachel said, what was for the best. On one point only could she come to a decision, and that was to conceal, at least for the present, from Bell that *she* was acquainted with her imprudent and disgraceful conduct. This determination was easily kept, for Bell either was or affected to be buried in profound sleep when Bess went to her chamber.

That night was, indeed a night of sleepless misery to Bess. Leicester's recent avowal, so gratifying to her feelings in one respect, was yet a fertile source of uneasiness. How often had her mother spoken in strong reprobation of the folly and misery of young people pledging themselves to engagements, the fulfilment of which must inevitably be deferred for a long, a perhaps indefinite time. How many circumstances, too, might arise to prevent those engagements in the present instance from *ever* being fulfilled. For herself she could never, never change. No, it was impossible—for she could never meet with one who could be worthy of holding that place in her heart that he now occupied. There was but one Leicester in the world. But, though thus certain of herself—though thus convinced that neither time nor space could alter her attachment to him, was she equally assured of the stability of Leicester's affections towards her ? Man's inconstancy was proverbial. He would, in his intercourse with the world, encounter many, many much more deserving of his love. It was hardly an impeachment of his merits to consider it probable that he would yield to some one of the temptations that would assail him, and she should be forgotten. But even if it were not so—even if he remained faithful to his promises, what a gloomy prospect presented itself! Years of separation, of uncertainty—and, if he should not succeed, should not be as prosperous as he anticipated, *she* could be content to share his poverty—that which he called poverty would be to her comparative wealth, if it were shared with him, but Bess blushed for the thought that intruded itself upon her ingenuous mind.

"And yet it is too true," she reflected with a sigh, "that my—my attachment to him exceeds his, even now; for he could not evidently resolve to give up any of the advantages of wealth and distinction for my sake, while I could be content to share with him the humblest lot."

Could Bess have read Leicester's heart, she would have confessed how deeply she wronged him. It was for her sake—to shield her from even the slightest sufferings—to place her in a situation in some measure commensurate with her merit, in his eyes, that Leicester had suppressed the ardent feelings which would have prompted him to make her is under all disadvantages. No—he would toil and struggle—he would endure every privation and difficulty with patience; but he would not expose his beloved to share those difficulties and privations, even though her society, her smiles, would have lightened every care, and rendered the comparatively rude and uncivilised home that awaited him—a Paradise.

CHAPTER XIV.

Her tears fell with the dews at even,
  Her tears fell ere the dews were dried,
She could not look on the sweet heaven,
  Either at morn or eventide.
After the flitting of the bats,
  When thickest dark did trance the sky,
  She drew her casement curtain by,
And glanced athwart the glooming flats.
  She only said, ' The night is dreary,
    She cometh not,' she said:
  She said, ' I am aweary, aweary,
    I would that I were dead !'

And ever when the moon was low,
  And the shrill winds were up an' away,
In the white curtain, to and fro,
  She saw the gusty shadow sway.
But when the moon was very low,
  And wild winds bound within their cell,
  The shadow of the poplar fell
Upon her bed. across her brow.
  She only said, ' The night is dreary,
    She cometh not,' she said ;
  She said, ' I am aweary, aweary,
    I would that I were dead !'—A. TENNYSON.

 HE result of hours of sleepless anxiety and deep reflection, on the part of Bess Leslie, was very visible in her pale cheeks and heavy eyes, when she met Leicester at the breakfast-table next morning ; but those appearances were too flattering to him to excite regret in his bosom, though, in the progress of a long and confidential conversation, he endeavoured to cheer and dissipate her gloomy thoughts, by the most cheerful and brilliant anticipations of the success of his efforts, and the eventual happiness that awaited them. The plan, too, for their frequent communication with each other was settled. Leicester even hoped, or said he hoped that if the period of his exile were not considerably shortened, he might be enabled to visit England for a limited time. A voyage to North America was even then becoming a much less formidable undertaking than it had been years before, and Leicester tried to represent it to her " as a difficulty so slight as not to be worthy of consideration, should circumstances prosper so with him, in other respects, as to render it feasible. Events also might occur—her sister might marry, and——"

But there Leicester paused, for the agitation that shook Bessie's whole frame was by him interpreted into a full understanding of that which he hardly dared hint at, but which Mrs. Leslie's delicate, and indeed gradually declining health, rendered but too probable. If Bell *were* married, and Bess, as he feared she would be, deprived of her mother, he should then feel justified in pressing for the immediate fulfilment of her engagement—for where, then, could she be so safe, so happy, as with the man who adored her, even though his lot in life were so inadequate to her merits, so infinitely below what his wishes would have conferred on her?

Little did Leicester suspect the true cause of Bessie's agitation, when he spoke of the probability of her sister being settled in the world. Bess, perfect as was her confidence in Leicester, and unreserved as were her communications to him on every other subject, could not bring herself to mention to him her recent discovery of Bell's imprudence.

Leicester had on all occasions spoken of the Marquis of Ledbury with undisguised condemnation, and had latterly more than once delicately hinted to Bess his satisfaction that Bell, towards whom he ever evinced the most brotherly kindness and affection, was removed from the sphere in which the marquis's wealth, titles, and personal advantages, occasioned him not only to be tolerated, but a halo of meretricious brilliancy thrown around his vices. That Bell had felt any real attachment to the marquis, he never for an instant believed; nor could he believe that, vain, weak and ambitious as he saw she was, she had been weak enough to imagine that she had made a serious impression on the heart of a man so notoriously, so *professedly* callous. He who made a jest of love, and scoffed at marriage as a tie that could bind only fools, or serve the purposes of knaves, he could never believe that Bell, who with all her faults was still in his eyes innocent, delicate, and refined in manners, and he was firmly convinced pure and uncorrupted in heart, could have been so dazzled and blinded to the true character of that "bold bad man," as to have "set her young hopes upon him," or to have believed that she had power and influence to fix one whose boast was to keep himself free, and turn the efforts of wit and beauty to enslave him into weapons of destruction against themselves.

Knowing, therefore, so well Leicester's feelings and sentiments on this subject, Bess, though she felt how competent he was to advise her, and how confidently she might have relied on the prudence of the course he might recommend, abstained even from a hint that might compromise her sister in his eyes; and Leicester, attributing her agitation, when Bell's future prospects were alluded to, to a very different subject, immediately changed the topic of conversation.

Mrs. Leslie's *real* indisposition, considerably increased by the exciting events of the preceding days, prevented her from rising at the early hour agreed upon for the last social meal in which Leicester could hope to share, for many a weary month, or it might be years. She considered too, perhaps, that Leicester would have much to say to his betrothed, which her presence would have restrained; but, in reality, neither of these causes operated to prevent Bell's appearance at the breakfast-table. She was not aware of the perfect understanding that now existed between her sister and Mr. Leicester, and she listened with perfect apathy and indifference to the intelligence which Bess, with forced calmness, communicated while she was dressing herself, that Mr. Leicester was going abroad, and that the period of his return was quite indefinite.

"It is a farewell visit, Bell," continued Bessie, her voice faltering, in spite of all her resolution. "Surely, you will come down and say, 'Good-by, God speed you.'"

"I hate farewells and leave-takings, and fuss of all kinds, you know I do," returned Bell, petulantly; "and, besides, my headache is as bad as ever, and you can say everything that's proper for me; I daresay he will be much better pleased to hear them from your mouth than mine."

"I do not believe it, Bell," replied Bess. "I am sure he has ever shown the kindest feeling towards you. No brother could be more sincerely anxious for——"

"Oh, I am infinitely obliged," returned Bell, hastily, "and I beg you will make my acknowledgments for his condescension, though I really thought, Bess, that his *brotherly* affection had a somewhat deeper foundation than mere words. However, if you are satisfied with such a lukewarm attachment, I have of course no right to complain, though I do hate your platonic sentimental affections."

Bessie replied to this only by a smile, the reflection of which Bell caught in the toilet-glass, at which the former was standing, opposite the foot of her sister's bed.

"I tell you what it is, Bess," resumed Bell, sitting up in the bed, and apparently provoked at her sister's calmness, and her

quiet smile. "I tell you what, I really believe, from the bottom of my heart, that Mr. Leicester's going abroad so unexpectedly—for we have never heard a hint of his intention before—is merely a subterfuge, to break off, quietly and conveniently, a connection that he began to feel troublesome. If we—that is to say, you had remained presumptive heiress to Sir Matthew Bevington—had not that brat of Lady Jane's come into the world, 'to push us from our stools ——'"

"Oh, Bell, now can you?"

"And how can you, Bess, be so blind or so passive as not to see such conduct in its true light?" interrupted Bell. "Mr. Leicester, after all his fine professions, is, like all the world, deserting our fallen fortunes, and how you can, even with the milk-and-water (as Lady Jane used to say) that circulates in your veins, submit without resentment to such behaviour, passes my comprehension. Here has been Leicester for weeks and months laying himself out to gain your affections—his every word and look betraying his deep devotion to you—and now he comes quietly and deliberately to bid you farewell, and I will be bound will mingle his brotherly counsels and admonitions with his devotion to his toast and chocolate, and pour out the one as smoothly as the other, and you, poor simpleton as you are——"

Bess, who had finished her toilette, threw her arms around her sister's neck, with mingled smiles and tears.

"Come down with me to breakfast, Bell, and Leicester will convince you that he is not quite the apathetic nor interested being you believe him," she whispered.

Bell looked surprised. She could not misunderstand the deep blush that dyed her sister's cheeks, nor the expression of mingled pleasure and pain with which the latter uttered those few and simple words in Leicester's vindication.

"Yet he is going to America, and you know not when he will return," she observed.

"It is but too true, my dear sister," returned Bess, sighing, "but you know," and she forced a smile, "we have the authority of our favourite poet that 'the course of true love never did run smooth,' and we are doomed to verify the axiom."

Bell seemed for some minutes lost in thought—but, when her sister renewed her invitation to come down stairs to breakfast, she coolly declined.

"No, Bess, I confess that I am not fit society for you," she replied. "I cannot comprehend your high flights of sentiment, as my aunt—Lady Jane, I should say—was used to call what was indeed incomprehensible to her."

"I agree with you there," returned Bess, smiling; "to Lady Jane everything is incomprehensible that is in opposition to her selfish system. But you, my dear sister, however you may quote her sayings and opinions ——"

"I wish I had never seen, never known, never heard that such a person existed as Lady Jane," said Bell, passionately, and her sister, from the bottom of her heart, re-echoed the regret, though probably with very different feelings to those which prompted her sister's expression.

We pass over the parting-scene between Bess and her lover. Accustomed, as both were—and in no trait of character did Leicester and his betrothed more strikingly resemble each other than in that fortitude and resolution which enables the possessor to subdue and control the expression of feelings which must enhance the sufferings of others—accustomed as they were to

bear and forbear, where others would give free vent to passionate exclamations, and all the outward and visible signs of grief and despair, neither Bess nor Leicester could see the moment arrive which was to separate them—it might be for ever—without intense and heartfelt regret and sorrow.

Again and again Leicester returned to add some tender, some "more last words" to his parting injunctions. He had been previously admitted for a few minutes to Mrs. Leslie's bedside, had received her heartfelt blessing, and in Bessie's absence had solemnly pledged himself that, in the event of her death, which she in secret to him acknowledged she contemplated as much nearer than was suspected by her friends or children, he would instantly return to England, to become the protector of those who then would, indeed, be orphans and desolate.

"For Bessie," observed Mrs. Leslie, amid her streaming tears, "I have no fears. Under any circumstances, her rectitude of heart and principles, her personal and mental activity, her calm, equable, and contented disposition, will secure respect, esteem, and friendship from all who are capable of appreciating her worth. She will be happy and make others happy, even if you—But I trust in Providence that you, especially, will experience the full value of the gem beyond price which I now bequeath to you. But Bell—oh, Leicester, it is for her that the mother's fears as well as tenderness are awakened. Be to her a protector, a guardian, a brother—in the fullest sense of the word. She will need all your care, your vigilance, and—and your indulgence. From none else but you could I hope or expect that her faults would meet at once indulgence and firmness to correct and restrain them. I feel, even now, that I have much to blame myself for, with regard to my poor Bell. I have suffered worldly interest to overcome the dictates of reason and of conscience, I know that I speak it in confidence to you, Leicester, as my son. I knew that Lady Jane Bevington's school was one in which, without extraordinary firmness and strength of mind, my children's principles would be frittered away—their simple and pure habits corrupted—corrupted by senseless glare and frivolity, and yet—But your own excellent understanding and acute observation render it unnecessary to say more. One of my children has passed the ordeal, and has come out, like gold from the furnace, more valuable for the trial; but Bell—it is not her fault but her misfortune, Leicester, that she possesses less strength of mind than her sister. Watch over, then, and protect and guide her in the right path, and the blessing of a dying mother rest upon you."

Leicester was, indeed, deeply affected by this pathetic appeal. To most young men, scarcely arrived at years at which the law of the country acknowledges the right to decide and direct their own actions, such a charge as Mrs. Leslie now devolved upon him would have been, however they might have been affected at the moment by the pathos and impressiveness of her words and manner, a subject of light consideration for the future; but Leicester felt the full importance of the sacred charge committed to his care, and in words as heartfelt and sincere as her own did he promise that the interest and welfare of Bell should be dear to him, as his own or his beloved Bessie's.

Many hours had passed after the departure of Leicester, before Bess could recover her self-possession or even the appearance of serenity, necessary as she felt it to her own peace, or the comfort of those around her—a motive which ever had much greater influence with her than any selfish consideration. She had, as yet, formed no decision as to how she should act with regard to the discovery that had been made by Rachel of Bell's clandestine intercourse with the Marquis of Ledbury. She knew, indeed, that she could depend on Rachel's vigilance to prevent any immediate renewal of it; but it was alike degrading to her sister, and most revolting to herself and to the kind open-hearted Rachel, to be practising a system of *espionage*, under all circumstances so revolting to a well-constituted mind.

The pains which Rachel took to prevent any secret communication between Susan and her young mistress could not long escape the observation of the latter. Bell saw that she was detected, though she knew not how far the discovery extended. That Bess was aware, as far as it went, of what had occurred, she could not doubt. Not that the latter betrayed by her manner any resentment towards her sister; on the contrary, she was if possible kinder, and more gentle and indulgent; but, more than once, Bell caught Bessie's tearful eyes fixed upon her with an expression of the deepest sorrow and regret that was quite intelligible, but which, unfortunately, produced little effect on Bell's mind, except to irritate and provoke her with a conviction of her sister's superiority.

There was nothing, indeed, in Bell's manner that evinced any sense of shame at having been detected, or sorrow for what she had done. Anger and vexation were the only emotions she betrayed, and the fear of exciting one of those violent bursts of passion to which Bell had lately shown such a propensity, and thus betraying to her mother all that had taken place, kept Bess silent, even when her sister, by her contemptuous expressions, appeared to court an explanation.

Affairs at the cottage were in this state when its inmates were surprised by a visit from Mr. Cheverton, whose name had ceased to be mentioned, and indeed had been almost forgotten, even by Bess. Mrs. Leslie, whose languor and indisposition had increased considerably since Leicester's departure, had not left her room, and Bess was in attendance on her, when Mr. Cheverton was announced by Susan to Bell, who was alone in the usual family sitting-room; and the former, glad to be relieved from an interview with one who had left no very favourable impression on her mind, left to her sister the task of excusing her absence, and returning her acknowledgments for his assistance on the occasion which had introduced Mr. Cheverton and her to each other.

The gentleman's visit was extended much longer than usual in such circumstances, and the sound of Bell's voice and the piano-forte betrayed that she was already on terms of familiarity with their visitor, which was not likely to effect Bessie's wishes that he should not be encouraged to renew his visit.

Mrs. Leslie sighed as the latter made a remark to that effect.

"I foresaw it would be so, my dear," she observed, "for unfortunately our wishes and opinions have little influence with Bell. It is, however, of little consequence at the present minute, since I have come, after the most serious and calm reflection on the subject, to a resolution which will have the effect of at once putting an end to any hopes Bell may, and I know does entertain, as to my altering my mode of living, for one more congenial to her views and wishes. I have never ceased," she continued, "to reflect on Bell's observations that you and her would be left to beggary and destitution; and although, literally, that would not be the case, were I to die to-morrow, since there still remains untouched the slight provision your father had it in his power to make—my dear child, do not interrupt me—I am right, I feel I am, in the view I take of the case, and this is a good opportunity to explain what I mean to do. The sum your uncle fortunately settled on me is, in the

way we now live, little more than sufficient; yet even out of that, Bess, I contrived to lay by something, to add to the
provision for you and your sister. But
Rachel and I have consulted together, and
we are agreed that much more could be
done by taking a small, low-rented house,
in a cheaper part of the more immediate
suburbs of London. Rachel, with a little
occasional assistance, will be able and is
perfectly willing (indeed it was her own
proposition) to do without another servant,
and it will not be difficult to get another
place for Susan. Her wages, those of the
gardener, and other incidental expenses,
together with the difference of rent, will
be scrupulously reserved from my income,
and added to the fund for your future provision. My mind will then, Bessie, be relieved from the intolerable weight that has
pressed upon it ever since your sister's remarks awakened me——"

"Oh, do not—do not say so, my dear
mother," exclaimed Bess. "Do not let
me endure the misery of thinking that I
am in part the cause of your enduring
privations that——"

"There will be no real privation, my
child, in what I propose," interrupted Mrs.
Leslie. "On the contrary, I shall have
more real enjoyment than ever. My life
will become more valuable to me, under
the conviction that the longer it is extended, the more certain will be the provision that will be made against those
evils which Bell anticipated. Her words,
Bess, were ringing in my ears from the
time she uttered them until I came to a
decisive resolution to adopt the course I
have pointed out; but I feel already
happy and relieved, and I trust that the
all-wise and merciful God will spare me
many years, to enable me to perfect the
work that is begun. In ten years, Bess,"
added Mrs. Leslie, smiling, "I reckon
that with our new system of economy, I
shall have doubled your and your sister's
little fortune. Long before that, however,
I trust you will be placed beyond the want
of it; and then, should Bess still remain
unmarried, you I know will feel it no injustice that I appropriate the whole of the
additional fund to secure her comfort and
independence."

Bess tried, in vain, to speak. Her tears
choked the expression of her feelings, for
they were excited, even to agony, when
she reflected how little worthy Bell was of
the maternal anxiety that led Mrs. Leslie
thus to break up her establishment, and
retire to comparative privation and obscurity.

"There will be another advantage

attendant on this change," resumed Mrs.
Leslie. "Bell can no longer indulge any
hopes or expectations of entertaining company, or launching into expensive habits
of amusement and pleasure, as she considers it. Her pride will, I know, second
my wishes of living in quiet and domestic
comfort, when there will be no longer any
means of making a display; and, however
painful it may be to her at first, I do hope
and trust that she will gradually renounce
her propensity to show and company, and
learn to find her happiness in the comfort
and quietude of our own little circle, especially when she reflects that every year
that passes will tend more effectually to
confirm her future independence and happiness."

"God grant that she may!" fervently
ejaculated Bess. "That she may value,
as she ought, the sacrifice that you make
for her. But I fear, my dear mother, that
with her present impressions——"

"I anticipate all that you can say on
that subject, my dear," observed Mrs.
Leslie. "I know that, at first, it will be
a heavy blow to her pride, and her habits
of self-indulgence; but what you and I
can submit to, without regret, she must
learn to bear. Yes, I have foreseen that
my plan would meet with opposition from
her, and, therefore, I have, and am, taking
all my measures in secret. To Mr. Leicester alone I confided my intentions, and
was gratified, not only by his approbation,
but through his means have been able to
take some important steps in their realisation. On the very day that he left London,
he employed a person in whom he could
confide to procure a house suitable to my
plans, as well as to put in train my getting
rid of this, which you know I took on a
lease. So expeditious and successful have
been this person's exertions, that both
objects have been already attained. I have
received a note this morning from him to
say that he only waits my approbation, to
conclude for a house at Islington, which
he thinks every way answerable to my
wishes, at little more than a third of the
rent I pay for this; and that there is a
party ready, if my present residence
answers the description Mr. Leicester left
with him, to pay the premium I require
for the lease, and to take off my hands any
part of the furniture I wish to dispose of.
This is a good beginning, therefore, dear
Bess, for my plan; and I trust even Bell
will be disposed to view it with more indulgence, when she sees that it already,
when all expenses of removal, &c., are
paid, will leave between a hundred and
fifty and two hundred pounds to commence

our reserved fund, as I shall call it. But, of all this, not one word to Bell, my dear child, till everything is finally concluded. It will be time enough, then, to encounter the opposition I expect from her."

Bess could not, indeed, encounter this opposition, as her mother mildly called it, even in thought, without alarm. Knowing what she did with regard to her sister's clandestine correspondence with the Marquis of Ledbury, she trembled lest the proposed alteration might have the effect of rendering Bell even more desperately resolved on encouraging his addresses. She felt, indeed, that it was her implicit duty no longer fo conceal from her mother Rachel's discovery, and, softening it as much as possible in the relation, she proceeded to detail what had passed, and the means Rachel and herself had taken since to prevent any further collusion between her sister and Susan.

Mrs. Leslie was indeed astonished, hurt, and alarmed, the more so as she had been fully convinced in her own mind that even Bell herself had renounced every idea of the marquis renewing his addresses, and had become convinced that the splendid fortune it had been expected she would inherit from Sir Matthew Bevington had been in reality his (the marquis's) object. That he might have raised her to the station she so ambitiously coveted, with that desirable addition to her beauty and accomplishments, Mrs. Leslie never doubted; but now that she was notoriously cast off by her uncle and Lady Jane, and returned to her original obscurity and insignificance, could she be so vain, so blind, as to believe that he, in secret, intended that which he shrunk from publicly avowing?

"No—no, Bess, be assured," continued the agitated mother, "he will have no views, no intentions towards your sister, but such as will end in our dishonour, and her eternal ruin and misery. Blind, infatuated, unhappy girl, rushing thus madly on a course which must entail everlasting infamy and disgrace upon her friends, as well as herself, even at the moment when my sleepless nights and anxious days have all been given to mature a plan that should secure her even from the shadow of suffering hereafter!"

Bessie's cheeks crimsoned with shame and indignation at the no doubt true and correct view her mother took of the marquis's views, in his clandestine correspondence with her sister. She had herself feared that which her mother did not hesitate to avow, but her innocent pride in her sister, her inexperience of the world,

or at least of that world of which the Marquis of Ledbury was so distinguished a member, and above all her confidence in Bell's purity and delicacy, which she was sure would shrink from the slightest attempt to contaminate it—all had combined to make her unwilling to admit the idea that the marquis would dare to indulge dishonourable intentions towards her sister.

Gentle and forbearing as she usually was, under all provocations, Bessie's feelings were roused to a degree of agony which could only find vent in a torrent of bitter and heartfelt invectives against the wretch that could dare to behold in her sister an intended victim to his lawless passions. She would write to him—she would go to him—she would tell him that his infamous intentions were discoved, that her sister as well as herself scorned him—beheld him with horror and detestation. She would dare him ever again to think, of—to even mention the name of one whose purity and innocence had raised her above suspicion of his guilty——

Mrs. Leslie's melancholy and incredulous look suddenly arrested Bessie's vehement exclamations, and with lips still quivering and faltering from the excess of her feelings, she threw herself on her knees by the side of her mother, and hiding her face in her lap, tremulously observed—

"My mother, my dear mother, you do not, you cannot suspect that Bell is a willing instrument in her own dishonour? That she knows—suspects that the wretch does not mean to marry her? That—that——Oh, no, do not say that you believe this of your poor child, with all her faults."

"God forbid that I should be the first to condemn your unhappy sister," murmured Mrs. Leslie; "but, oh, Bessie, how is it possible that she can be deceived, knowing as she does the character of that man? The very circumstance of secret intercourse—his degrading himself and her by corrupting a poor ignorant servant, and making her the medium of their correspondence. Tell me, Bessie, has he not, even when Bell was moving in the same circle with himself, and by her expected inheritance of her uncle's fortune was placed, as I may say, on an equality with him—even then, Bess, it was your own observation that he acted neither openly nor honourably towards her—that he never applied, as he ought to have done, to her friends or guardians for their sanction to his addresses, and that his apparent devotion to her, in public, appeared to you to arise more from the gratification it afforded to his vanity to appear a favoured lover, and to keep others at a distance, than the result of any violent attachment to her. Even my brother felt uncertain as to his intentions; and Lady Jane, I know, from Bell's own confession, manœuvred in a way that I should have considered most degrading to draw from the marquis a direct avowal—such as they considered he could not retreat from. And if these were then his sentiments—if he were then reluctant to form the indissoluble tie of marriage with your sister, possessing the advantages of fashion and wealth to excuse the folly, as he calls it, of marrying, is it likely that now——"

"Oh, no, no—I see but too plainly what his intentions are," interrupted Bess in a tone of deep anguish; "but I must—I do hope that Bell is innocent—that she does not suspect——"

Mrs. Leslie shook her head incredulously.

"We will hope so, my child," she replied; "but, at the same time, we must take every precaution, and use every possible means, to break off the correspondence altogether; and, as one step towards it, we will conceal altogether the intention of removing, and prevent, as far as possible, his tracing out our new residence."

Bell's cheerful laugh was heard at this moment. Mr. Cheverton was taking leave, and Mrs. Leslie sighed still more deeply, and Bess felt more than ever indignant, at the too-evident levity of her sister, whose vivacity, it was plain, had suffered no diminution by the serious and painful enthralment in which she had placed herself. In a few minutes Bell entered the room, her eyes sparkling and cheeks glowing with pleasure.

"Well, Bess," she exclaimed, laughing, "I do not know whether I am to congratulate you or myself upon the conquest of Mr. Cheverton's heart; but he has been making desperate love to me for this hour, under the impression that I am the same young lady who was the heroine of the Oxford-street adventure. You did not tell me though, you sly thing, that there was a rival hero in the case. At any rate you can give up one of them. It is not fair you should monopolise all, is it, mamma?"

"I do not understand what you are talking about, Bell," replied Mrs. Leslie, who could scarcely disguise her anger at her daughter's thoughtlessness.

"You do not mean, Bell, that you allowed Mr. Cheverton to remain under the mistake?" observed Bess, a thousand vexatious and distressing thoughts and fears rushing into her mind.

"Certainly I did, my dear," returned Bell, with a provoking laugh. "It saved, you know, a world of explanations, and all the awkwardness of self-introduction, et cetera. Besides, it let me into some pretty little secrets, which I should not otherwise have heard. For instance, you never mentioned a word about the rich East Indian, 'the Nabob,' as Cheverton calls him."

"I have often told you, Bell," observed Mrs. Leslie, reprovingly, "that I dislike the familiar habit you have of speaking of persons without prefixing any title to their names. Cheverton, for instance, applied to a man whom you have never seen till within the last hour or two."

"Oh, but we are as well acquainted as if we had been bowing and curtseying to each other for a twelvemonth," returned Bell. "Mister Cheverton, if I must call him so, is one after my own heart. But I could not help laughing so heartily at his evident surprise at finding me so different at home, to the timid, blushing prude of his out-doors' adventure. I was afraid, once or twice, that he would find me out, especially when he accused me of having put on those pretty blushes and gaucherie to captivate the Nabob. 'Well, but do you think it succeeded?' I demanded, pretending of course to know all about it, though I was puzzled to understand what he alluded to.

"'You ought to know that,' he replied. "I expected, indeed, that by this time you had received a formal proposal; and, I assure you, I came with a throbbing heart, fearing I should encounter his tremendous frowns, or be thrown down stairs by some of his formidable suite. Seriously though, I do believe, if my friend Dallaston had not almost forced me out of the upholsterer's shop, the East Indian and I should have come to a quarrel; for he looked at me as if he could willingly have annihilated me, when I declared my determination to wait and see you safe home; and I had the best mind in the world to knock him down, by way of letting him know that he was in a land of liberty, where every man had an equal right to make himself agreeable to the female sex.'

"'A very pretty way, really, of recommending yourself to a lady's favour,' said I, laughing, 'to break the heads of your rivals. But, pray, do tell me—for I acknowledge I am dying with curiosity—Who or what is he? Where does he live? Is he rich enough to deserve the title of a Nabob, and above all is he——'

"I was just going to ask a question, Bess, which would inevitably have betrayed me; that is, he would have found out that there were two Dromios—that you were not I, nor I you—But I checked myself, as I was uttering the inquiry of what sort of creature the Nabob was in person.

"He shook his head at me. 'What would Leicester say or think, I wonder,' he observed, 'if he had seen those eyes, and heard that eager ——'"

"Oh, Bell, you have not been so cruel," interrupted Bess, "to suffer Mr. Cheverton to believe ——"

"That you could bestow a thought or word upon any living being but Leicester?" returned Bell, maliciously. "I acknowledge, my dear, I was cruel enough to let him think so; and, what is more, I suspect that it would be quite as well if Mr. Leicester thought so himself; and I declare to you, Bess," she continued, with more apparent seriousness than she had yet spoken, "I had nothing but your honour and interest in view, when I presumed, as your representative, to assure Mr. Cheverton that his cousin, Mr. Leicester, had no more right to assume any control over my looks or actions than he had."

Mrs. Leslie and Bess exchanged looks of vexation and anger.

"You have presumed a great deal more than you had any right to do, then, Bell," observed the former. "Fortunately, however, it is of little consequence to your sister what Mr. Cheverton may think on the subject."

"I don't know that, mamma," returned Bell, evidently designingly mistaking the meaning of her mother's observation. "Mr. Cheverton," she continued, "acknowledged that if he had not heard that assurance from my own lips, he should have considered himself bound, in honour to his cousin Leicester, to have suppressed the feelings of admiration (I won't be sure he did not say adoration) to his own bosom, and ——"

"Pray do not let me hear any more of this nonsense, Bell," interrupted Mrs. Leslie, with severity. "I am indeed truly sorry that you should indulge in such levity, especially at your sister's cost; but I shall take care to see Mr. Cheverton myself, and explain the whole affair to him."

Bell sat silently looking at her mother and sister for some minutes.

"I hope I have not done any serious mischief," she at last observed, with an affected air of contrition. "But really," she continued, "you have yourself to blame, Bess; for you have been so extremely reserved and uncandid, if I may be allowed the expression, with regard to Mr. Leicester, that I believed I was only asserting what was strictly true, in assuring Mr. Cheverton that his cousin was on no other terms in our family than a friend, for whom my mother had a great regard, on account of my father's former intimate connection with his parents. I was, indeed, I confess," she added, after a pause, during which her mother and sister had both remained silent, "I confess I was considerably startled and surprised when I learned from his observations that Mr. Leicester and his relations, the Earl and Countess of St. Aldwyn, had seriously quarrelled on the subject of Leicester's visits here. That the earl had formally demanded what his nephew's intentions were as regarded Mrs. Leslie's daughter, and that he had at once avowed that he intended nothing short of marriage, as soon as convenient. I own, Bess, I was provoked at hearing the gentleman had expressed himself so confidently that Mrs. Leslie's daughter, be it which it might, was at his disposal, and I replied, perhaps rather hastily and harshly—"

"'That if Mr. Leicester thought that, like the Grand Turk, he had only to throw the handkerchief, and it would be eagerly caught up by the ladies whom he might honour with such a mark of his favour, he was quite mistaken; for that I could assure him, on my own part, and I was certain I might answer for my sister, he was not at all the sort of person who would be acceptable in such a serious affair as matrimony.'"

"Go on, pray go on, Bell," observed Bess, coolly, though in reality greatly agitated and provoked at this recital. "Do not be angry, mamma. Bell has, of course, been actuated by the best intentions, and perhaps, as she says, I have been to blame in not telling her that I was engaged to Mr. Leicester; but I could explain that omission," and she looked hard at her sister, "though it might not be very satisfactory."

The hint was not entirely lost upon Bell, and her quick glance at her mother assured her it was fully comprehended by the latter; but she soon recovered from her momentary confusion.

"I am sure I am very sorry, Bess," she observed, "if I have done mischief; but, as you say, I had no evil intention in what I said, and I really was taken quite off my guard by what Mr. Cheverton told me, that Leicester had been actually discarded by the earl, and absolutely abused by the countess, but more especially by the old maid, the countess's sister, who had said all manner of spiteful things about us—that is, you and I, Bess. Mr. Cheverton, indeed, in his own droll language," continued Bell, "told me that there was a regular *row* with the two and Leicester, who manfully defended his intended and her sister, and that it ended in the countess's sister declaring that she would instantly send for her attorney, and erase Leicester's name from her will, and would never see, speak, or even think of him again, if he persisted in marrying against her will. Mr. Cheverton then proceeded to say, that if he were not himself the most disinterested fellow in the world, and very sincerely attached to his cousin Ronald, who was one of the very best and most warm-hearted fellows that ever existed, he should have felt that he was greatly indebted to Miss Leslie for ousting (that was his word) the said Ronald out of his place in the old woman's will; for it had been pretty well known to them all, that her nephew Ronald, as she called him—though in fact he was no relation to her—being only her sister the countess's nephew by marriage—still he was, Cheverton said, so decidedly her favourite, that the family firmly believed he was destined to inherit the bulk of her large fortune. Fortunately for me, he added, next to Ronald Leicester, your humble servant, Lewis Cheverton, holds at present the post of honour in the old girl's estimation. My brother, the heir-apparent, I suppose you know, my dear Miss Leslie, is *tout à tois et travers* with his family, and the younger one is at present not upon terms with my mother and aunt, for an offence somewhat similar to Leicester's, that of choosing with his own eyes, instead of two old women's, the lady to whom he pays his devotions. My name, therefore, I suspect, is destined to cut a pretty respectable figure in the last will and testament of my honourable aunt; that is to say, if she does not live long enough to find out that, after all, Ronald Leicester is not the chosen of Miss Leslie, although his obstinacy and pride, I suppose, would not permit him to own it."

Neither Mrs. Leslie nor Bess made a single observation when this detail, given with such apparent candour and thoughtlessness of evil, was concluded. Bess, indeed, was so absorbed in reflecting with mingled pain and pleasure on Leicester's generosity, in not only for her sake relinquishing his succession to a fortune which would have rendered unnecessary years of toil, anxiety, and banishment from his native country, and the society he was so calculated to ornament and to enjoy ; but also, in having so entirely concealed from her that he had made that sacrifice—that all Bell's taunts and sneers, for such they evidently were meant, at her engagement with Leicester, were lost upon her, and she felt that, however in one point of view her sister's interview and imposition upon Mr. Cheverton were vexatious, the result upon the whole was satisfactory, for it had convinced her, even more firmly than ever, how well-founded was the reliance she placed upon him, were they both spared to each other to meet again, for the happiness of her future life.

Again and again Mr. Cheverton renewed his visit, but Mrs. Leslie had come to a resolution on that subject, which neither Bell's pouts and sullenness, nor her open anger and vituperation of conduct, which she said was calculated, on her mother's part, to deprive her (Bell) of every pleasure or opportunity of improving her situation in the world—all; indeed, that she could say or do could not shake Mrs. Leslie's determination to decline any farther visits from Mr. Cheverton, and in consequence he was told, candidly, by Rachel, in her own homely and straightforward way, that her mistress and daughters thanked him for his attentions, but having resolved to receive no company, declined his future visits. Mrs. Leslie had at first determined to see him herself, and explain to him the deception Bell had practised ; but on a further conference with Bess, it was agreed that this, perhaps, would lead to observations and remarks as regarded Leicester, which it would be difficult to evade, so as to avoid betraying more, after what she had heard was willing should be done, respecting her engagement to him.

Rachel, therefore, as has already been said, was deputed to represent her mistress, when Mr. Cheverton came the next time, he having, on the preceding morning, been told that Mrs. Leslie and the young ladies were engaged—a denial which he had received with a very bad grace, for the more fashionable "Not at home," would be probably thought less significant of their wish not to receive him.

Rachel returned from her task evidently fluttered.

"He is a saucy upstart, ma'am," she observed, "and I'm very glad I had an opportunity of mortifying him. I don't think he has had such a set down, for many a day, as I gave him."

Bell tossed her head contemptuously.

"A fine opinion, indeed, Mr. Cheverton must have of our domestic establishment, when a servant is allowed to consider herself on an equality with the son of a nobleman, and to talk of setting him down. But it is of no consequence—he will know, I am sure, that I am no party to the insulting treatment he has received."

"It would be a good deal better if you had given no opportunity to him to insult you and your family, Miss Bell," returned Rachel, angrily; "but I must speak if I die for it," continued the old woman, "and I would die rather than hurt your mamma, or your dear sister. You, if you persevere in your present conduct, are more likely to bring disgrace——"

"Rachel, my dear good Rachel," interposed Bess, who dreaded the result of an exposure of Bell's conduct, as likely to drive her to throw off even the little influence her mother had over her actions.

Rachel burst into tears.

"I will not say another word, my dear,"

she observed, "but when I think that the child I loved as dearly as if she had been my own—ay, Miss Bell, you may toss your head as contemptuously as you like —I know very well that you have been taught to think that servants have no business with feelings or affections—that they ought to be mere machines. But I have done—You will know better, I hope, some day. I hope you will, at least, learn the difference between them that would lay down their life for you, and them that would serve you only while you could pay their wages."

Bell's countenance betrayed a desire to answer this observation in a manner that would still further have irritated poor Rachel, whose tremulous voice betrayed how deeply she felt the ingratitude of her former favourite, but Mrs. Leslie's decided manner, as she observed—

"I insist, Bell, that this altercation, which reflects only disgrace upon you, is ended here"—prevailed over even her assumption and pertinacity; and, to Bessie's infinite satisfaction, prevented any further exposition of her sister's conduct. Some observations of Rachel's respecting Mr. Cheverton's impertinence during her interview with him, had raised a feeling of uneasiness in Bessie's mind, which led her to seek, on the first opportunity, an explanation from the faithful old servant.

"Don't ask me, my dear," replied Rachel, with a look of evident dissatisfaction at the remembrance which Bessie's question awakened. "It would have served Miss Bell right, though," she added after a moment's pause, "if I had told her all he said about her. But no matter, it is done with now, and I don't think, with all his bold impudence, Mr. Cheverton will make another attempt to force his company where he is not welcome."

Rachel's refusal to repeat what had passed between her and Mr. Cheverton did not tend to remove Bessie's uneasiness, especially when she reflected that the mistake into which he had been led by her sister's almost undistinguishable resemblance to herself, and the wilful levity of Bell in encouraging that error, had not been explained to Mr. Cheverton. It was not that Bess wished to vindicate herself, at her sister's expense, that she felt thus dissatisfied and uneasy, but a vague, and scarcely to herself intelligible suspicion of future evils that might arise from this mistake dwelt upon her mind, and added considerably to the already existing causes of gloomy and painful forebodings that weighed upon her spirits.

In less than a week after the preceding events, Mrs. Leslie, without apparently exciting any suspicion of what was passing in the mind of Bell, concluded all her arrangements for vacating the cottage at Highgate, and taking possession of the much humbler, though still respectable, and, for every purpose of comfort and convenience, desirable residence that had been taken for them at Islington. Fearful as Bess was of the consequences of her sister's mortification and resentment at the discovery of the intended change in their style of living, she yet felt that her mother and Rachel's plan of concealing that intention to the last moment was by no means a desirable one. Bell would, she pleaded, "consider it an additional provocation and insult, and——"

Bessie's farther remarks were arrested by Rachel's significant look and shake of her head. What it meant, indeed, Bess could not entirely comprehend; but, whatever it was, she dreaded the effect of an explanation upon her mother, and therefore abruptly though reluctantly relinquished her opposition, convinced at once that Rachel, if she were urged upon the subject, would be able to give quite sufficient reasons for her adherence to the proposed plan. It was not, therefore, until the evening preceding their removal from the cottage that Mrs. Leslie entered upon the painful but necessary explanation of her intentions and motives.

In perfect silence Bell listened to her mother. There was neither surprise, regret, nor resentment in the expression of her countenance; but when, in conclusion, Mrs. Leslie remarked that no selfish motive could have influenced her resolution, and that she trusted her children would feel that she had acted to the best of her judgment for their interest and advantage, Bell bent her head down over her work, and two or three silent teardrops that fell upon it proved that she was not quite insensible to the voluntary sacrifice her mother was making for her and her sister's sake.

"Thank God!" murmured Bess, with pious fervour embracing her mother, when Bell soon after quitted the room. "Thank God, her own right feelings—her good heart is, at last, triumphing over the mistaken doctrines she has been taught, and we shall yet be happy and united, as we were before she learned to fix her happiness in splendour and show. Why do you look so mournful and incredulous, dear mamma?" she added, reproachfully. "Has she not behaved wonderfully well, considering all circumstances, and did not her tears prove that she felt deeply the value of the sacrifice you are making for her—for our sakes?"

"I hope and trust that she, at least, was convinced I can have no motive but for her happiness, my dear child," returned Mrs. Leslie, "but whether she is satisfied as well with the means as the end, time only can show. There is one point, at least," continued Mrs. Leslie, after some moments' silence, "which, though it has escaped you, Bess, was very visible, and, I confess, very unsatisfactory to me—that was, that it is plain Bell felt no surprise at my announcement. That she had been previously aware, in part at least, of the intended change, I cannot doubt, however she has acquired the knowledge; and it augurs, I fear, no good that she has so completely dissimulated her knowledge up to this moment, while at the same time it proves how insufficient has been all our watchfulness, since it must have been from Susan she has learned what was in agitation."

Bessie's ingenuous countenance betrayed how much she was grieved and mortified at this discovery of her sister's dissimulation, for she could not doubt that her mother's observations were correct. She had, indeed, herself been unable to account for the total absence of even a look of surprise from Bell, but believing as she (Bess) did in Susan's professions of sorrow and penitence, it had not occurred to her as possible that there had been any renewal of the secret correspondence between the latter and her young mistress. Susan, however, was to be left behind. The family who had taken the cottage, consisting only of an elderly lady and gentleman, had agreed to retain her as housemaid, on Mrs. Leslie's recommendation, the latter observing to Rachel, when the subject was discussed whether it would be preferable to sending the girl back to her mother, that as there could not exist any temptation in the new family to a repetition of the only fault she had to lay to the poor girl's charge, she should feel herself warranted in recommending her, especially as she considered Bell was principally to be condemned in having tempted the silly, good-natured girl into the error she had committed. It was a source, therefore, of satisfaction to Bess, though she blushed at the thought how degrading it was to her sister, when she reflected that, in their new habitation, Bell would have no coadjutor in folly and imprudence, and she prevailed on her mother, for Susan's sake, to be silent to Rachel as to the additional breach of trust the former had committed.

"How inevitably does the commission of one fault lead to others," thought Bess, observing the perfect indifference with which their late attendant, who was left to give possession, beheld the departure of the family with whom she had been so long domesticated, and by whom she had been treated by the kindest consideration. "A few months, or rather weeks ago, Susan would have been all tears and sorrow to have parted with us, and now she looks as if *she* had a right to feel offended."

The removal to the new habitation—the arrangements which were proposed or carried into execution, to make it as comfortable and convenient as possible, and in which Bess exerted herself with the utmost good-will and good-humour, were all beheld by Bell with silent indifference. She betrayed neither sorrow at quitting their old residence, nor expressed either satisfaction with the new one. Even the absence of the latter was, however, a source of gratification to her anxious sister, who, though herself perfectly contented with the change, had anticipated with much alarm Bell's discomfiture at the comparative meanness and confinement of their new residence. Even Bess herself, accustomed to apartments of large and lofty dimensions, had been rather startled at the first view of the two small parlours which were to be their only sitting-rooms, and somewhat annoyed by the total want of that accommodation which she knew Bell considered indispensable—a dressing-room. It was, therefore, a cause of nearly as much surprise as gratulation that Bell seemed neither to care for one or the other, though it would have been pleasanter still, if the latter had appeared to take the slightest interest in the arrangements which Bess was working at with such hearty goodwill.

The bustle of removal passed over, and Bess had leisure to observe and to think more of Bell and her sentiments, as to the change that had taken place in their situation and mode of living; but those observations were unfortunately, anything but satisfactory; for Bell's reserve and silence seemed to increase rather than diminish with every hour that passed, and she spent as little as possible of her time in the society of her mother and sister. That she might feel as little inconvenience as possible from their change of habitation, a pleasant, airy, and cheerful room, on the second floor, had been appropriated entirely to Bell's occupation by her thoughtful sister, who had taken care that it should be fitted up with everything she could command to give the former pleasure. The books that

Bell called her own were arranged on light swinging shelves, her embroidery frame placed near the window, china vases were every day supplied with such flowers as the long slip of ground behind the house, which had been cultivated with some taste by a previous tenant, enabled Bess to command; and, in fact, nothing spared that the latter could do to induce Bell to forget the inferiority of her present home to that they had given up.

"She will pass her mornings here, I daresay," observed Bess to Rachel, who was assisting her in making these preparations for Bell's reception, "and then, you know, we shall be able to get through all our domestic employments down stairs, without inconveniencing her, or giving her the opportunity of making comparisons that would annoy and mortify her."

Rachel looked at the smiling and animated face of the speaker with tears in her eyes.

"It ain't right, though, my dear child," she observed, "that all the care and toil should fall upon you. I must speak the truth, Bessie. It is *not* right that Bell should be encouraged in her pride and vanity, and that you should fag yourself to death with your exertions to pamper her and wait upon her, as if ——"

Bess, however, would hear no remonstrance on the subject. It was a pleasure to her, rather than a pain, to contribute in every way possible to the comfort of her mother and sister; but she could not help feeling sometimes that Bell's assumption and exclusiveness were carried rather too far, when the latter passed whole days alone in her own room, retiring the moment she had taken her meals, appearing totally absorbed in herself, and avoiding as much as possible all conversation with her mother and sister. There was, indeed, as Bess keenly felt, an apparent determination on her sister's part to consider herself not as a member of what would otherwise have been a happy family circle, but rather as one whom circumstances compelled to submit to a mode of life which was anything but pleasant and satisfactory, and from which she would willingly secede, if it were in her power. It cannot be supposed that Mrs. Leslie was either blind or indifferent to this conduct on the part of her daughter, or that she did not feel its injustice towards Bess; but the entreaties of the latter, and her sanguine predictions that Bell would gradually of herself become more domesticated, and bear with a better grace the change in their situation, succeeded in prevailing upon Mrs. Leslie to indulge the wayward girl in the way

of life she had chosen for herself—for the present.

"Only for the present, dear mamma, depend upon it," Bess would conclude, "for I know that Bell's natural disposition revolts from silence and solitude. She will become tired of being so much alone, and the monotony of her pleasant employments, and then she will of herself become one of us. Nay, I would not wonder," Bess would add with a smile, "if she should become convinced, as I am, that active exertion for a few hours in the day enhances all the enjoyment of the evening's leisure; and she will lay aside the last lingering remnants of foolish pride, deprive me of half my employments, which I assure you are becoming every day more easy and pleasant to me. Now, do not shake your head, dear mamma, for Bell has already taken the first step in domestic economy. These two days she has made her own bed, and put her own room to rights, instead of sitting and looking listlessly at me while I did it, as she used to do, and that I am sure augurs well, does it not? Oh, yes, I know she will by degrees get over all the fiddle faddle notions she acquired from Lady Jane, and will be convinced that there will be no degradation, even to the most refined and delicate, in learning to be useful, and contributing to the comfort of others as well as her own."

Poor Bess! how little did she suspect that what she was adducing as a proof of her sister's improvement was in reality the result of the most unworthy and disgraceful artifice. Bell had reasons, or rather motives for excluding her sister, as far as possible, from her own apartment—far, far more degrading than the employment she had taken upon herself; but the denouement was approaching—that it had been so long delayed was, perhaps, owing to some latent, lingering remains of principle in the bosom of the unhappy Bell; but certain it was, as was afterwards discovered by her distressed relatives, a correspondence had been regularly carried on between the Marquis of Ledbury and his destined victim—the opportunities for which had been unfortunately facilitated by the very means Bess had adopted for her sister's comfort and happiness. More than one of the inhabitants of —— Street had been amused by observing the constant visits of the tall military-looking gentleman, with whom (when she thought herself secure by her mother and sister's occupation) the beautiful girl at No. 31 was seen exchanging signals and smiles; and more than once they had observed, at dusk, the lady lowering a letter by the aid of packthread from her window, or receiving in the same way the answers to those epistles. A variety of conjectures were, of course, set on foot respecting this evidently clandestine intercourse, but no one knew anything of Mrs. Leslie or her family, or considered themselves privileged to interfere in an affair that did not concern them; and thus the proceedings of the lovers (a title, by-the-bye, very inapplicable to the feelings of either of the parties) remained a profound secret to those most deeply interested. There were one or two servant-maids, indeed, belonging to the houses opposite, who would willingly have indulged their gossiping propensities by making Rachel acquainted with what they had discovered, and learning, as they hoped, the whole history of the family, and all the mystery of the love affair in which they had become interested, but Rachel shrank with undisguised pride and resentment from their proffered familiarities, and gave such a sharp and snappish answer to the very first question respecting her mistress and the young ladies, that they were instantly discouraged from proceeding, and mutually agreed that it would be a pity to thwart the lovers, especially as it was very plain the poor young lady was cruelly treated, if not absolutely a prisoner in the room which, from the many hours she passed there alone, it was almost believed she was.

Bell's motive, therefore, for excluding her sister for the last few days from her chamber, it was afterwards but too evident, was to prevent any chance of the latter discovering the final preparations she was making for quitting her despised and detested home for ever.

A violent cold and sore throat compelled Bess most reluctantly to submit to a few days' confinement to her chamber, which was a little back-room adjoining her mother's sleeping apartment, and this facilitated the fatal step which Bell, though she had resolved upon it even before she had left the cottage at Highgate, had still with trembling apprehension delayed. But nothing could be more opportune for her purpose than the indisposition of her sister. Mrs. Leslie's whole thoughts and attention were devoted to her beloved child, whose bedside she never quitted for more than a few minutes at a time; and Bess was suffering too much to be as observant as usual of her sister's looks or manners, during the short visits the latter made to her chamber. Bell, indeed, did not scruple, for the furtherance of her purpose, to hint a fear that the disorder might be infectious; a fear which the medical attendant—a stranger who had been called in—did not decidedly contradict; and though Mrs. Leslie positively refused to listen to Bessie's entreaties, and leave her to the care of Rachel, who had attended all sorts of fevers without catching them, and was convinced she never should—though Mrs. Leslie resisted, as has been said, every entreaty to leave the sick chamber, Bell was much more passive. She acknowledged, indeed, that she had a secret dread upon her mind that she should take the disease, and she yielded, though with apparent reluctance, to her mother's injunction and Bessie's tearful request that she would keep her own room until all danger was over.

How could that tender mother, that devotedly attached sister, suspect that Bell's assumed fear was but artifice to secure more certainty for the execution of that project which was to entail upon them years of suffering, and, upon herself, eternal misery and disgrace? How could they have believed that when she closed the door of that chamber, followed by looks of tender anxiety and affection, she had quitted them for ever? Yet it was so—and cruel, callous, and selfish as she had become, even Bell trembled with agitation as she returned to her own chamber with the conviction that in all probability she should never again behold those o whose affection she was so unworthy.

"Poor girl!" sighed Mrs. Leslie, as soon as she had left the room, "how little calculated is she to meet the real difficulties and dangers of the world, when she is thus ready to take alarm at what I am convinced is only imaginary."

"I believe—I hope so, my dear mother; indeed, I am convinced that there is no serious cause for apprehension, for, in spite of all the doctor says, I am sure I have no complaint but a common cold, which Rachel's gruel, and a little warmth and care, would cure, without his assistance; but I have heard and read that persons have often terrified themselves into fatal diseases, and Bell's alarm was too real and evident not to render every precaution necessary. I could see that she trembled so she could scarcely stand or speak; but a few hours will, I hope, convince her that there is no real danger. If she hears, to-morrow, that I am getting well, as I hope I shall be ——"

"God grant it!" ejaculated Mrs. Leslie, fervently.

"I wish, though," resumed Bess, anxiously, "that she would be persuaded to take some wine whey, before she goes to bed. Perhaps, Rachel, she will, if you persuade her."

"I will try, my dear child, if you wish it," replied Rachel, "though I am very sure that, if anything should ail her, it will be fright that is to blame, and not any infection from your illness. It is a pity, indeed, as your mamma says, that she should be so ready to take alarm at fancied dangers."

"And so selfish," Rachel would have added, but that she knew the remark would have hurt and vexed Bess, who was ever the last to see her sister's faults, and the first to find excuses for them. So it proved, indeed, in the present instance, for Bess gently observed that Bell was indeed to be pitied, for she had imbibed her dread of catching diseases from her aunt, Lady Jane, who avowed her horror of sick rooms, and if she knew that one of the servants was ever so slightly ill, would torment herself, and worry everybody about her, with her alarms lest it should prove to be a fever, or some other infectious disorder.

"I remember once," continued Bess, "that I observed mademoiselle, as her ladyship's French maid was called, looking dreadfully pale and her eyes very heavy, although she had evidently put on a more than usual quantity of rouge, as if to disguise it; and at last I asked her, before Lady Jane, if she was ill, and was surprised at her vehement manner of denying it, and declaring she was never in better health in her life; but when my aunt left the room, the poor woman turned to me, and in her broken English, exclaimed—

"'Oh, Miss Leslie, I am die almost with the head-ache, only I must not tell you so before my lady; but I would give my life to lie down for two three hours.'

"I was, of course, surprised, and I told her I was sure Lady Jane could not, would not be so unfeeling as to deny such a trifling indulgence if she knew that she was suffering so. But the poor woman shook her head, and told me she would not for the world own to her ladyship that she was so ill, though it was only a sick headache, to which she was constitutionally subject; but she knew that Lady Jane would immediately take alarm, and insist that she herself was in danger. 'And perhaps,' continued mademoiselle, 'send me away in a minute to the hospital, as she did the poor house-maid, who had nothing the matter with her when she was sent off but a pain in her limbs from rheumatism, through kneeling to whiten the steps in a bitter cold day, but that

Lady Jane would persist was a fever, and they should all catch it, and all the doctor could say wouldn't convince her; and so,' she said, 'poor Sarah was hurried out of bed, and sent off, in the frost and snow, in a miserable crazy hackney-coach, to some hospital that her ladyship subscribes to, that she may secure admittance for her servants in illness; and there, it appeared, she *did* take a fever that was raging in the ward where she was put to bed, and in less than a week the poor creature died. But that,' mademoiselle observed, 'had not cured her ladyship of her whims about illness, but rather confirmed them; for she persisted that she was right, and that Sarah had the fever before she was sent out of the house, and for two or three weeks there was nothing but misery and consternation, Lady Jane worrying herself into hysterics, the house fumigated, from the cellar to the attics, as if,' said mademoiselle, 'we had had the plague, or some dreadful thing among us, and my lady never believing she was safe till Sir Matthew yielded to her terrors and went off for a month to Brighton.'

"This, it seemed," observed, Bess, "and one or two similar instances, occurred while Bell was with my aunt, and it is scarcely to be wondered at, though greatly to be lamented, that my poor sister has acquired some of her ladyship's unreasonable fancies and terrors."

Mrs. Leslie sighed.

"She has, indeed, acquired much that I fear will neither conduce to her happiness or ours," she observed. "Would that the evils were all as likely to be as speedily eradicated as, I trust, her present unfounded terror will be."

Bessie's predictions of her own speedy recovery seemed, in the course of a few hours after the preceding conversation, to be in a way to be realised. At ten o'clock, Mrs. Leslie yielded to her entreaties, and retired to her bed in the next room; and Rachel, having first, in compliance with Bessie's wishes, carried up some whey to the door of Bell's chamber, but failed in getting admittance, the latter declaring she was undressed, and could not take it—stretched herself on a couch by the side of her beloved charge for the night; and, relieved in a great measure from her anxiety on account of the latter, was soon in a profound sleep.

Bess, however, did not sleep for some hours. She was better—quite free, indeed, from pain or fever; but she could not dismiss the anxiety that Bell's very palpable agitation had occasioned. Once or twice she fancied that she heard a noise in her sister's room, as if some one were walking about in it, and she sat up in bed and listened with apprehension, lest Bell were really ill. But then she knew the disposition of her sister too well to believe that she would hesitate to call for assistance. It would be cruelty to wake Rachel, who had been up all the preceding night ; and Mrs. Leslie, too, by her gentle and regular breathing, was sleeping. By degrees Bess argued herself into the belief that her fears had been unfounded, for all was now quiet, and she lay down and yielded to the drowsiness which had succeeded to many hours of pain and feverish restlessness, nor did she awake until Rachel, who had stolen softly from the room at her usual hour of rising, smilingly withdrew the bed-curtain to invite her to partake of the coffee she had prepared.

"Have you seen Bell, my dear Rachel?" she inquired. "I was rather uneasy for an hour or two, in the first part of the night, for I could not help fancying that I heard her walking about her room, and I began to apprehend that her fears were verified, and she was really ill."

"That, then, accounts for her sleeping so sound this morning," returned Rachel. "I knocked softly at her door, a few minutes ago, to ask whether she would come down to breakfast, or I should bring it up to her, but she did not answer, and I thought it was a pity to disturb her out of a sound sleep. As to her being up, long after we are all in bed, that is nothing new; for I have been surprised, two or three times since we have been in this house, by being waked from my first sleep by her moving about the room, or some noise that showed she was not in bed."

Bess sighed at this proof, as she thought, of her sister's uneasiness of mind and discontent with her present situation ; but as was usual with Bess, on all occasions where Bell's faults or follies were concerned, all was referred to the habits the latter had contracted by her association with Lady Jane Bevington.

"She has been so long accustomed, you know, to turn night into day at my aunt's," she observed, "that I dare say, poor girl, our early hours are irksome to her."

Mrs. Leslie entered, and in her joy at seeing Bess so much recovered, and her thankfulness, as she observed, for the quietest and most refreshing night's repose she had experienced for many weeks, Bell was forgotten, or at least not mentioned for some time.

She was not absent, however, from Bessie's mind, although she would not speak of her, lest she should disturb Rachel from the comfortable breakfast she was enjoying with so much apparent zest, observing with a smile at Bess—

"I am eating and drinking to make up for lost time, my dear ; for, ever since you have been ill, the victuals have seemed as if they would choke me."

Bess returned a smile of gratitude, and the breakfast was quite finished before she remarked that she dare say Bell would be glad of hers now.

"Yes, I will make her some fresh coffee, and carry it up," returned Rachel, "for I suppose, although you are so much better, my love, we must not venture to ask her to come down ?"

"She is a silly girl, to give way to such nonsensical fears," observed Mrs. Leslie, and Rachel bustled away to make the intended preparations for Bell's breakfast.

In a few minutes Rachel's foot was heard on the stairs hurriedly descending from the upper room, but she did not, as Bess expected, come in to tell them how she had found her charge. Bess heard door after door open below with a haste and noise so unlike Rachel's usual sedate and noiseless manner, as to denote that something unusual had occurred ; but Mrs. Leslie did not appear to notice it until Bess observed—

"What can be the matter, mamma? Rachel is running about from parlour to parlour—she has been in the kitchen—down the garden, as if——"

Before she could conclude the sentence the bed-room door opened, and Rachel, her face and lips as snow-white as her spotless cap and apron, stood before them, her eyes staring wildly as if she had seen some horrid sight.

"My sister—my sister !" screamed Bess, the most dreadful presentiment taking possession of her mind. In a moment all her own weakness and previous sufferings were forgotten, she threw herself out of bed, and would have flown to Bell's room, but was restrained by Rachel, who now recovered her voice.

"No—no, you must not kill *yourself*, dear Bess ; and you can do no good," she exclaimed. "She is gone beyond our reach."

"Gone !" repeated Bess, in wild amazement. "Oh, speak, Rachel, what is it you mean ?"

"That your cruel, wicked, unfeeling sister has deserted her home," replied Rachel, bursting into tears.

"Oh, no—no, she will return, Rachel, she will come back to us. Oh, I thank

God she is living! I feared—I dreaded—dear, dear mother, speak to me, our dear Bell is not dead," continued Bess, throwing her arms round Mrs. Leslie's neck, who sat motionless and apparently completely paralysed by the unexpected blow.

"Would that she were dead—that I beheld her lifeless," murmured Mrs. Leslie, in a hollow tone, "rather than——" Her voice failed, and a paroxysm of hysterical tears prevented her further utterance.

"How blind and foolish I must have been not to have sooner discovered what has happened," observed Rachel. "I was indeed surprised when I found this morning that the street door was unchained and unlocked; but then I thought that in my anxiety last night about you, Bess, I must have neglected to fasten it. Do not, my dear child, run the risk of bringing back your illness (for Bess was hastily dressing herself.) You can do no good by going up stairs. She is gone, and that she does not mean to return is plain, for her drawers are empty of everything of value."

Bess, however, would not be restrained from going up. She should find something explanatory of the step her sister had taken. Bell could never have been so cruel as to have left them for ever without one word, one single line, one expressive hope of returning to them. She could not, she was sure she would not have rushed voluntarily on destruction; and if she had been hurried away under the pretext of a secret marriage, surely—surely she would have left some assurance to her unhappy mother and sister that she was less guilty than she appeared.

Bess was, however, mistaken. The most diligent search proved unavailing. Some nearly consumed scraps of paper were indeed scattered in the fire place, but the few letters that remained perfect—for there was not one whole intelligible word—were evidently not Bell's writing, but a masculine hand, and Bess threw them from her with horror, for she doubted not that it was the handwriting of the wretch who had robbed her of her sister.

All that day and the next night both Mrs. Leslie and Bess remained as it were stupified with horror and despair, incapable of collecting their thoughts or concerting any measures that might lead to a discovery of their unhappy relative's retreat; and the poor mother, with clasped hands, and in a tone of voice that would have melted a heart of stone, repeated again and again—

"Not one friend, not one living being to direct, assist or, guide me. God help me—God help us—my child, my child, for we have indeed none else to help."

Even, if it were possible, Bess was more deeply wounded and distressed than her mother, or from her recent illness and consequent weakness was less able to bear the shock, or show that fortitude and presence of mind which hitherto had in all circumstances of trouble or affliction enabled her to be the counsellor and consoler. Hour after hour she sat, her eyes fixed on the door, and intently listening to the slightest sound, while the only words that escaped her lips were—

"She *will* come back. Oh, yes, yes, she *will* come back, mother. She cannot have left us for ever, without one word—one word."

Rachel, however, though scarcely less grieved and distressed for the misfortune that had fallen upon those to whom she was so devotedly attached, was more collected and capable of reflection. She was aware that means might be adopted to trace the fugitive, and ascertain where she was, although she was herself too little versed in the ways of the world to know how to set about employing those means; but she had noticed that the next-door neighbours were steady, elderly people, living in respectable style. They had once or twice had trivial opportunities, which they had with readiness adopted, of showing civility to her as a stranger in the neighbourhood, and she (Rachel) had also observed other proofs of their kind and charitable disposition. To Mr. and Mrs. Lorton, as they were called, Rachel, in her present grief and uncertainty, determined to apply for advice and assistance to carry into execution the plans that were floating in her mind for the recovery of the lost, unhappy Bell.

She found them as she expected, plain, kind-hearted, sensible people, ready to afford all she required, and to her great surprise, fully acquainted with particulars relative to the recent elopement, which Rachel knew nothing of.

"The fact is," observed Mrs. Lorton, "that though we never trouble ourselves with our neighbours' affairs, one can't always shut one's eyes and ears to what is going on, and in this quiet street anything at all out of the usual way is sure to attract attention, especially among the servants. Mine is a decent young woman, and a good servant; but, as I tell her sometimes, rather too fond of a bit of gossip, and equally as fond of repeating the news, as she calls it, which she hears at the grocer's or cheesemonger's, which, being one at the corner, and the other a

few doors off, are pretty generally frequented by the inhabitants of the neighbourhood. You had not removed here many days, before Margaret brought home a long story from one of the gossip shops, as I call them, about a gentleman who had been seen parading the street for some time, and looking up at all the windows; and at last it was discovered that the person he was in search of was one of the widow lady's daughters, meaning, of course, your mistress. Margaret, herself, I believe, saw him—at least, I know she described him as a very fine, dashing-looking gentleman, though he was muffled up and—but I won't tire you with all the nonsensical talk there was about the young lady and gentleman, and the many different reasons that were given why Mrs. Leslie prevented the young people coming together. However, when our maid went for some chocolate, this morning, she came back with a look that meant she had heard something of particular importance that she was eager to tell. So she began by saying—

"'Did you hear the noise of a coach, ma'am, this morning, driving into the street, a few doors from the corner?'

"I replied I did not remember to have noticed it. There had been often coaches lately at all hours, because there are several musical people, that play at the theatres, that have come to live in the street.

"'Yes, ma'am,' replied Margaret, 'but it wasn't them I meant. I expect there'll be a pretty piece of work when it's found out—but the poor young lady that's been kept prisoner, in the two pair next door, is off this morning. How she got out of her room, I don't know—for they say her mamma always kept the keys, both of her own room and the street-door, under her own pillow; but 'Love laughs at locksmiths' ma'am, as Mr. Daniels says, and so, as he tells me, he'll take his oath he heard the coach draw up right under his window, and that made him jump up and look between the curtains, and who should get out but the very gentleman—him there's been such talk about—and in a minute or two the young lady's window was thrown up, and out she popped her head; but Mr. Daniels said he was quite thunderstruck when he saw her walk out quite composed at the street-door, with a large bundle—her clothes, of course—the gentleman took it from her, shut the door, as softly as he could, and then the young lady and he ran and jumped into the

coach, and off they drove as fast as they could go. Mr. Daniels says he does not think it's found out yet, for the young lady's prison-window that she opened is still standing open as she left it, and that, as he says, is a proof, poor thing! how cruelly she must have been treated, for the family's been all up and about these two hours or more, and it's plain there's been no breakfast carried up to her yet.'"

Rachel's surprise was only equalled by her indignation at these mistakes and misrepresentations; but it cost her very little trouble to convince these good people (the Lortons) that Mr. Daniels, who it seemed was the grocer, and his contemporary gossips were entirely in error as to the young lady's situation and treatment; and Mr. Lorton, an active and intelligent old man, proceeded systematically not only to arrange, but put into execution every means that could be adopted to trace the fugitive. The result of those means—the advertisements in the newspapers of the day, and all the other methods which Mr. Lorton's knowledge of the world suggested, have been related in the commencement of this history, as well as the melancholy termination of all suspense—of every hope indulged against hope—in the discovery of the mutilated remains of the lovely and blooming Bell Leslie in those waters which have entombed many a victim of similar error and imprudence—but, perhaps, few more pitiable than the once-admired Twin Rose of Arundale.

CHAPTER XV.

Sincerity! Oh, let no mortal leave thine onward path—
No, though earth gape and hell destruction cry—
To take dissimulation's winding way.—HOME.

ROM the dreadful shock she had sustained in the loss of her daughter, Mrs. Leslie never recovered either her health or spirits; but although Bess had at first yielded, as it appeared, without a struggle to such utter despair that her mother and tender-hearted attendant, Rachel, had trembled for her intellects; and though the name of her lost sister, at one time connected with the most pathetic prayers

for her return, at others with the tenderest lamentations for a loss which she now considered utterly irreparable, still broke involuntarily from her lips, her mind gradually strengthened with her physical powers, and she became again her mother's most assiduous and affectionate attendant and friend. Each, indeed, strove to subdue the outward expressions of grief, for the sake of the other, and thus unconsciously acquired a command over themselves that, in reality, produced a greater degree of resignation than could have been otherwise hoped for. The society of their benevolent friends, the Lortons, too, though at first irksome—for true and heartfelt grief like theirs shuns even the best-meant and most delicate attempts at consolation—yet by degrees that which had at first been looked upon by both mother and daughter as a positive affliction, became absolutely necessary to their comfort. Mrs. Lorton brought in her knitting, and sat for hours by Bessie's bedside—for some weeks she was unable to rise from her bed—and was silent if her patient, as she called her, was not disposed to listen, or endeavoured to beguile the recollection of their griefs from both mother and daughter, by anecdotes and reminiscences of her own early life, which had been singularly chequered with good and evil; and who could refuse to listen to, or fail to be interested in, tales which were enforced by the smiles or tears of a countenance that beamed with candour, benevolence, and feeling? Then, too, she was so unostentatiously busy in preventing even a wish on the part of the invalid, or her scarcely less suffering mother, and contrived, without letting even Rachel herself see it, to save her so much personal exertion, that all felt, even more than they could express, the inestimable value of her friendship. The old gentleman, too, for he was one of "Nature's gentlemen," though he had filled only an humble and subordinate station in the map of life, was fully worthy of his kind-hearted and unassuming wife, and, from his superior acquirements, even more calculated to be a pleasant companion to Bess and her mother, so soon as the health of the latter was sufficiently re-established to allow him to join their circle. He brought his books or a newspaper to read to them, if he met with anything likely to interest or amuse them. The best flowers in his little garden were gathered for Bessie—the nicest delicacies that could tempt the sickly appetite of Mrs. Leslie were procured for her, and always, as he delicately contrived to insinuate, at a cost so trifling that it was not worth speaking of, and even Rachel could not feel the obligations she was under to the worthy pair oppressive, because they made it plain to her that they were not obligations. They were both getting old, and perhaps should, some time or another, require a great deal more assistance from such a useful friend as she could be, and, therefore, it was only policy in them to bespeak her kindness.

"You have not brought in your newspaper, dear sir," observed Bessie one evening when the old gentleman came in at dusk. Mrs. Lorton had been that morning suddenly indisposed, and Rachel had been with her all day—Margaret, *their* servant, supplying her place in attending on Mrs. Leslie and Bess.

"No, my dear Miss Leslie," he replied, "there is nothing in it that is worth reading to you, to-night."

Mr. Lorton's voice was so tremulous as he uttered this, that Bess instantly took alarm.

"Something has happened, sir. I know there is something of importance—pray tell me!"

Margaret brought in candles at that moment, and Bess saw that Mr. Lorton was pale, and looked fatigued and distressed, and again she repeated her anxious question.

"Nothing, my dear, immediately concerning myself," he replied, "has occurred, I assure you; but a circumstance, relative to some of the nearest and dearest friends I have in the world, has just come to my knowledge—I have had a long walk, too," he added, wiping his forehead with his handkerchief, but, as it struck Bess, more to conceal the agitated expression of his features, than from necessity. "Come," he continued, forcing a smile, "you are going, I hope, to give me some tea, my dear; for I was too late for Mrs. Lorton's tea-table, and so came away in a pet to you."

"How is Mrs. Lorton now, sir?" demanded Mrs. Leslie, who had but just entered the room. "I shall come to see her after tea, if Rachel will come in and sit with Bess till I return. I should not, indeed, have stayed away so long from my kind friend, only that Rachel sent in word by your Margaret that I had better delay my visit till the evening, as Mrs. Lorton had taken a sleeping draught. Is she subject to these sudden nervous attacks, Mr. Lorton?"

"No, madam—no," returned Mr. Lorton, tremulously, ' only two or three times in the course of her life, as I remember."

There was a mystery in all this, and in the manner in which the old gentleman avoided Bessie's eyes, that did not fail to excite her observation. She saw, almost imperceptible as it would have been to an ordinary observer, that there was some reason which rendered Mrs. Leslie's promised visit to Mrs. Lorton by no means acceptable.

What the secret could be, of which Rachel was the chosen confidante, but Mrs. Leslie and herself to be excluded from, it was impossible for Bess to divine;

but an indefinable impulse assured her that it was so, and convinced in her own mind that Mr. Lorton's motives could not be wrong, she determined to assist him in keeping her mother from intruding upon it. This intention succeeded. A very slight intimation from Bess was sufficient to induce Mrs. Leslie to postpone her visit until the next day, and Mr. Lorton, after a vain attempt, as Bess could see, to rally his spirits, or rather to conceal their deep depression, pleaded the unusual fatigue he had undergone during the day as an excuse for leaving them early.

"Our good friends, I fear, have met with some serious affliction," observed Mrs. Leslie with a deep sigh, when the door closed after him. "I did not like to press him on the subject, but we shall hear, I expect, from Rachel, when she comes in."

Rachel, however, did not come in, that night, nor the whole of the next day; and Margaret, by whom she sent a message excusing herself by the necessity of still attending to Mrs. Lorton, betrayed so much embarrassment in her manner of delivering it, that Bess became more than ever convinced that there was a deep mystery connected with the whole affair. Her suspicions were more than confirmed, when by accident she discovered that Mr. and Mrs. Lorton, with Rachel, had all left home in a hackney-coach which had waited for them at the corner of the street.

It need scarcely be told that the object of this mysterious journey, and indeed the secret of the whole affair, from beginning to end, was the discovery of the unfortunate Bell Leslie's wretched termination of her short career of guilt and infamy; and the identification of her mutilated remains by Rachel, whom her kind friends had accompanied, to support her in her melancholy task. The result of this has been already related, and it would be tedious to dwell upon the various stratagems by which Mrs. Leslie's kind and considerate friends (the Lortons) contrived to conceal from the already deeply afflicted mother and sister the actual fate of their unfortunate relative. Bess, indeed, was not wholly deceived on the subject; for, although before Rachel returned from her attendance on Mrs. Lorton the latter had acquired sufficient command of herself to avoid betraying what she had suffered, Bessie's acute observation was not so entirely baffled as to believe implicitly the tale that had been concerted between the faithful affectionate servant and the kind friends who had thus studied to save Mrs. Leslie and her daughter from the dreadful shock of learning the miserable end of

the unhappy Bell. Bess, indeed, felt quite as forcibly as Rachel and her other friends that in Mrs. Leslie's present precarious health any additional grief to that she was already enduring would in all human probability prove fatal; and this consideration—this dread, continually present to her mind, compelled her to yield in appearance her belief to the narrative by which Rachel strove to account for Mrs. Lorton's indisposition, and her own employment during the three days that she had been in attendance upon them.

A near friend of Mrs. Lorton's, Rachel said, had been lost to her relatives for years—having married imprudently; and it had been discovered, on the morning that Mrs. Lorton had been taken ill, that the poor woman way dying in a hospital, deserted by the man for whom she had sacrificed her friends. Rachel had been employed as the representative of Mrs. Lorton, to seek her out, and do all that was necessary for her comfort. But it was too late—the sufferer was dead before she reached the place, and she (Rachel) and Mr. Lorton had since been engaged in performing the last melancholy duties towards their poor friend.

"God reward them!" murmured Bess, in an agony of tears, which Mrs. Leslie attributed only to the same natural sympathy with the unfortunate that occasioned the silent drops to steal down her own cheeks, but which Rachel felt arose from a deeper source.

"Tell me—tell me all, Rachel, you see I can bear it," exclaimed Bess, the moment she found herself alone with Rachel. "Yes, for my mother's sake," she continued, "I can bear to hear that *she* is dead—that I must never, never hope to behold my sister again. It *was* her—oh, yes, my heart told me it was—and she did not live to see you—to know——"

"She did not, my dear child," replied Rachel, struggling with her own feelings of horror at the recollection of the dreadful truth, which she dared not disclose to the already agonised girl, whose whole frame shook with anguish.

"But you saw her, Rachel?" resumed Bess. "You beheld that sweet face, which I shall never, never see again! Oh, that I could but once have looked upon it—that I could have kissed her cold lips! Oh, Rachel, why did you not contrive that I should see her? I could, you know I *would* have borne it with fortitude, for my mother's sake."

Rachel shuddered at the recollection of the awful spectacle which even she had revolted from—the swollen form—the discoloured, mutilated features, in which every trace, not merely of beauty or comeliness, but even resemblance to human nature, was lost.

"Yes, if ever deception," thought Rachel, "was not only allowable but praiseworthy, it is this—this by which my poor child is saved from the misery of knowing—of even imagining that horrible reality which will never be absent from my thoughts!"

Bess removed the handkerchief that had concealed her face, and looked up earnestly at Rachel for an answer; but Rachel could not answer, and Bess, again hiding her face, with quivering lips observed—

"I see—I see what you mean! She was changed—disfigured! Oh, my sister—my sister! Dreadful—dreadful! And none but strangers near—Not one to soothe. Oh, why did she not come to those who would have received her with outstretched arms! Oh, Bell, could you, did you doubt your mother and sister? Did you think that they——"

"My dear child," observed Rachel, gently, "you must not, indeed you must not give way to these thoughts and vain regrets. Consider the consequences, if your poor mother should suspect——"

"Yes, yes—oh, yes, I know," exclaimed Bess, raising her head and dashing the tears wildly away that were streaming from her eyes. "Oh, yes, I must conceal it all from her. I must hide it for ever in my heart. It would kill her! Oh, Rachel, I know I am wrong—I ought rather to rejoice that her sufferings are for ever hushed in the peaceful grave. Yet I cannot but grieve that she did not seek the arms and the forgiveness of her earthly parent, before she sought——"

Rachel could bear this no longer, and her sudden heartfelt sobs created a new subject of interest in Bessie's bosom. She was startled, alarmed, and bewildered; for Rachel had hitherto preserved a calmness which the former had considered arose from the conviction that it was better that they should know the worst, than that Bell's fate should remain in perpetual uncertainty. Her mother herself had said, at the period of her daughter's desertion, that the knowledge of her death would be easier to bear than the harrowing reflection that her child was living a life of infamy, which must—for, even in this world, that particular error seems with few exceptions doomed to meet retribution—must terminate in misery and despair; and Rachel, she knew, partook of this sentiment. Why, therefore, she should now, even when she had a few minutes before reprehended Bessie's indulgence of sorrow—why she should thus suddenly give way to such apparent hopeless agony, Bess could not understand. Could there be anything hidden from her? And yet what could be worse than death? Death! which cut off every hope.

Bessie's silence, her look of utter consternation, and then her terrified expression of—

"What can this mean? What have I said? Oh, Rachel, speak—is there yet something horrible concealed?" roused the latter to recollection.

"No—no, my dear," she hurriedly replied. "Our poor girl—the child who was as dear to me as if she had been my own—is in her grave. Is that not enough to the victim of a—but I am weak, dear Bessie, I have suffered a great deal, and been harassed, too, with fears of the consequences to you and my mistress. But it is all over now—I will not give way again. Come, my child, let me prevail upon you to try and get some rest, as I shall do, that we may be able to meet your poor mother in the morning, without betraying that anything has happened."

It was a hard task, after a night of tears and anguish, such as few at Bessie's age had ever experienced, to meet Mrs. Leslie at breakfast, without exciting suspicion in her mind; but the latter had been too long accustomed to melancholy looks, the traces of tears, and sleepless hours, since Bell's desertion, to notice it farther now than by a tender regret, expressed more in manner than words.

It was a beautiful morning, and as she stood at the window of their little breakfast-room, looking into the garden which Bess had never visited since the loss of her sister, Mrs. Leslie observed—

"You must, indeed, my dear child, conquer the reluctance you feel to get out into the open air. It will do you so much good and restore your strength and appetite."

"I mean to go out soon, mamma," replied Bess tremulously, and with a look at Rachel, who was removing the breakfast things, that the latter instantly comprehended.

"Why, then, not at once, love?" returned Mrs. Leslie. "There cannot be a better opportunity than now, while the weather is so fine."

"Not to-day—oh, no, not to-day. I—I am not strong enough yet," returned Bess, "and Rachel, too, is fatigued and wants rest; but in a few days, when she is better——"

Rachel shook her head mournfully, for

she was now quite aware of what Bessie's observation tended to. It was impossible, however, for her to resist Bessie's pathetic entreaties, and within a week the latter, leaning on Rachel's arm, stood by the side of a mound of earth, covered with fresh green sods—the grave of Bell Leslie, in the burial-ground of the parish in which the body had been found. It would be vain to attempt to describe the feelings which, now that she dared give vent to them, agonised the heart of the attached and afflicted sister. Again and again did Rachel express her regret that she had so weakly yielded to wishes that had produced such an effect, but her observation that their long absence could not fail to alarm Mrs. Leslie, and lead to explanations which would have the effect of raising suspicion, and disturbing the comparative calm she had attained, roused Bess from the indulgence of her sorrow. She suffered Rachel, passively, to lead her to the hackney-coach which waited for them at the gate of the burial-ground, and exerted herself so successfully to subdue all trace of recent agitation, that Mrs. Leslie, though she observed that she feared the exertion of walking, as she supposed they had, a considerable distance, had been too much for her, and gently blamed Rachel for not having persuaded her to be content at first with a shorter excursion, had no suspicion that anything had occurred to distress her. It is a common observation, but not less true for being common, that suspense is worse to bear than the reality of misfortune. Bessie's gradual recovery of health and comparative tranquillity, after the first agonising grief at her sister's death, was a proof of this.

She could never cease to regret and mourn the loss of one so dear to her as Bell had been, but she was no longer harassed with conjecture as to her fate—no longer felt the burning blush of shame on her cheek, at the thought that her sister was living in guilt, and it was possible, nay, even highly probable, in infamy and misery, too dreadful to be thought upon. Bell was at rest for ever, and her faults, her errors, were expiated by her sufferings, and buried (Bess fondly hoped) in eternal oblivion in her early grave.

But Bess, though she herself became thus resigned to the dispensation of Providence, which she piously believed had in its mercy thus rescued her unhappy sister from the evils that must have beset her onward path—still dared not communicate the truth to her mother; for Mrs. Leslie's health still remained in a state which required the utmost care, and as her medical attendant observed, the only chance of preserving life was the absence of all sudden and violent emotion.

To Rachel, indeed, and their friends the Lortons, the physician, who had been recommended by the latter, had avowed the truth, that Mrs. Leslie's disorder was an affection of the heart, under which life might be preserved even for years, but that sudden death would almost inevitably be the consequence of any violent exertion, either of body or mind. From Bess this was carefully concealed. There was no necessity to guard her against anything that could produce the dreaded effect; and no utility, as her friends observed, in rendering her miserable by constant anticipation of the fatal event, which they fervently hoped might yet be far distant.

It is natural to suppose that in the distressing events which had followed so quickly Ronald Leicester's departure from England, Bessie's thoughts had not been so often devoted to him as they would have been under more prosperous circumstances. Yet it was true, also, that often, in her first grief, when her mother had so pathetically lamented they were alone in the world, without a friend to counsel or direct them, his name, on whom they could with the most implicit confidence have relied, was often on her lips, and uppermost in her thoughts. Mr. Lorton, indeed, was a friend, and proved himself worthy of all confidence by the exertions he made at the period of Bell's elopement. He exposed himself even to insult from the pampered lacqueys of the Marquis of Ledbury, by the pertinacity with which he pursued his object of gaining an interview with their master; and when he at last succeeded, he spared not his denunciations against the titled seducer. The marquis, however, had been impenetrable to all Mr. Lorton's solicitations, and laughed to scorn his threats. He had descended, at the very first, to the meanness of denying that he was the person who had deluded the unfortunate girl from the protection of her natural guardians, although he was told by the venerable old man that his person was well known, and could be identified by many in the neighbourhood of Mrs. Leslie's residence. "But what hope," as Mr. Lorton said, "could there be from a man who could thus boldly utter a deliberate lie?"

Bess, indeed, felt that there was no hope; and yet, though the next moment she reproached herself for ingratitude, the thought involuntarily would intrude that had Leicester been there he might have succeeded where her aged, and of course less energetic friend had failed. Now, however, that neither hope nor fear remained respecting her unfortunate sister, Bess found reason to rejoice at what she had formerly regretted, that Leicester had not been at hand, had known nothing of what had occurred. She had received one letter from him, as soon, indeed, as a letter could by possibility reach her ; but it was not until after the certainty of her sister's death she replied to it.

Leicester's letter was full of hope and cheerful anticipation. His voyage had been prosperous, and he had arrived at a season of the year when everything bore a smiling appearance. True, the habits of living, the occupations in which he was engaged were in striking contrast with the luxury and idleness in which the former part of his life had passed away ; but, as he said, the little inconveniences of the one, were more than compensated by the feeling of independence they conferred ; and for the other, incessant occupation was, as he felt, not only the most certain remedy against all *heart* diseases, but became a positive pleasure, when the reward was, as at present, so certain.

"I am indeed," he wrote, "so busy, dear Bessie, that I have no time to be miserable, and if, after the day's occupation is concluded, sometimes, as I sit down to my solitary cup of coffee, a distressing sense of my utter loneliness in a stranger-land will intrude, I drive it away by picturing to myself that dear family circle of which I am one day to form a part. If it were not for that certain definate prospect, Bessie, if I did not see in perspective the certain reward of my labours in not only *our* mutual happiness, but our dear mother's (for so I may now, I trust, without presumption call her) relief from all anxiety and care. Bell, too, will not, I trust, refuse to smile a welcome to the wanderer, whose fervent wish is to be able to prove by deeds, not words, how sincerely he has her happiness at heart. But of this hereafter. I am going now, in true business-like terms, Bessie, and by the aid of figures, to show you that I am not too sanguine in believing that *our* probation need not extend even to the term I at first assigned for my residence in this country. Need I say that not one instant beyond what absolute necessity requires will I delay that return, upon which my every hope of happiness depends ? I think of it, Bess—I see, 'in my mind's eye,' that bright smile, those radiant eyes of confidence and love—yes, I may (I know without incurring your censure for my pre-

sumption) say, of love—fixed upon me until I almost forget the thousands of miles, the formidable ocean that divides us, and start at the thought that even they are not the only obstacles, but that not only days, months, years, the rolling seasons with all their changes, must pass over before I can hope to realise the delightful picture."

With what anguish, what desponding feelings did Bessie read again and again this transcript of her lover's feelings, before she replied to it. How fearful was the void already in that picture of domestic felicity which Leicester had so feelingly drawn ! Bell was in her grave — her mother trembling on the verge of it—and Bess herself, where were now the bright smiles, the radiant eyes, which had helped to win his love?

"He would not know me," thought Bess, as she raised those still beautiful though sunken and tearful orbs from the paper on which she was writing, and beheld her pale and care-worn features in an opposite mirror.

It was a task, indeed, which recalled, almost with all their pristine force, the anguished, the agonised feelings she had at first endured, to commit to paper the heart-rending fact that her sister was no more. But she could not write to Leicester, without communicating the mournful intelligence, although she felt it to be impossible that she could reveal, even to him, the dreadful circumstances attendant on that event.

"He must know it," she observed to Rachel, from whom alone she could seek counsel on this subject. "Oh, yes, it will be plainly my duty, if we should meet, and he should still retain his present sentiments and intentions—I must not suffer him to ally himself to — to disgrace and——"

"It will be time enough, then, my dear child," returned Rachel, who had many reasons — many, iddeed, that even Bess knew nothing of—for wishing as little as possible to be said on the subject of poor Bell's death —"It will be quite time enough, when Mr. Leicester returns to England, to explain what has happened. And it will become better, then, from some friend, than that you——"

"Oh, no, I could not—I could not tell him that she—that my once pure, innocent sister——"

Bess could not finish the sentence, nor was it possible for many hours that she could command her feelings sufficiently to proceed with her letter.

"When I tell you, my dear Leicester,"

she wrote, "that I have lost my dear, my beloved sister—that the beautiful blooming creature, towards whom your letter expresses such feelings of genuine love and kindness, is in her grave—you will not be surprised that I am totally unable to reply to that letter in the manner it deserves. My heart, indeed, seems dead to every emotion of pleasure. Do not blame me when I acknowledge that I try in vain to rejoice even in your happiness. I am not so weak as to think that I am wedded to grief, for I know that it is a merciful dispensation of the all-wise Providence that, however keen and overwhelming may be our sorrow and regret, time will calm and soften those feelings. I pray, indeed, in all fervour and in sincerity to my God that I may be resigned to the decree which has—Oh, Leicester, the tears which blot this paper will, I fear, tell you how far I am yet from attaining that calmness and fortitude with which I ought, I know I ought, to receive this affliction. I cannot now enter into the circumstances. If we ever meet, you shall know all. My mother—you who know my mother's disposition — her natural affection — her devoted attachment to her children, will readily imagine—but no, even you can form no conception of what she has suffered. Her health, always as you know precarious, has, I fear, received a fatal blow. I cannot conceal it from myself, that she is gradually sinking beneath its effects. Perhaps, even before this letter comes into your hands, she, too, may be taken from me, and I shall be indeed an orphan and destitute.

"Sir Matthew and Lady Jane Bevington—I should not have mentioned their names, for I strive to forget their existence, lest I should give way to a bitterness of feeling for which I blame myself, yet can scarcely control—but you mention them in your letter, and therefore I tell you what otherwise I would conceal. In the very height of our distress, Leicester, a kind-hearted man, a Mr. Lorton, who with his equally benevolent wife have to the utmost of their power soothed and consoled my poor mother, having learned that Sir Matthew was her nearest, and indeed almost only relation, waited upon him, in the natural hope that he would, under such circumstances, forget all that had occurred to divide the brother from the sister. As Mr. Lorton told him, nothing was required from him but counsel, and—but I cannot bear to go on with the subject, Leicester. It is sufficient to tell you that it was *refused*. I have never heard the particulars of the interview from Mr. Lorton—I did not then know the application was made, and from my mother it is a secret, even now, for it could only serve to add to her distress; but the indignation with which the good old man glowed, when I one day alluded to his visit to my uncle, and the manner in which he said, 'My dear, you have no uncle. Sir Matthew Bevington disclaims all alliance with you. He is not a man of flesh and blood, but of stone, or he could not, in the hour of affliction such as had fallen on your poor mother, have replied to me as he did. Let it be your study, my poor child, to forget him as he has forgotten you. It would have been, indeed, fortunate for you and your family if he had never, as he boasted he had, taken you and your sister from obscurity, and—but let us never again speak of the man whom I, humble as I am, despised even in the midst of all the grandeur and display in which he contrives to smother all natural feelings.'

"I did not, of course, Leicester," continued Bess, "seek for any farther explanation, and the name of Sir Matthew would never again have escaped either my lips or pen, had you not appeared anxious to know whether there was any prospect of a reconciliation, if, as you properly say, the term could be used as to the existing causes of our separation. I must, in reality, confess that I do not believe Sir Matthew to be so utterly callous as Mr. Lorton evidently thinks he is. But it is of little consequence *now* what is the real secret of his indifference. She, for whose sake only I regretted my uncle's desertion, is no more ; for myself, I want not, I would indignantly reject any favours which he or Lady Jane could bestow. Happily, my mother is placed beyond the necessity of humiliating herself to them, and I will dismiss the subject by saying that I sincerely hope that their new-found happiness —the child in whom now is centred, as I am well aware, all their cares, hopes, and wishes, may live to repay them. And now, dear Leicester, I must bid you farewell. I need, I think, hardly tell you that in the troubles and afflictions I have undergone since your departure — afflictions more severe, more heart-rending than you can imagine or conceive—it has been no trifling aggravation that I could not seek advice, assistance, and sympathy from you. My heart has, indeed, incessantly turned to you, as the only one who could fully appreciate its feelings and share its sorrow. Do not think, dear Leicester, that dead as I seem to be to all emotions of joy or pleasure, I am indifferent to your success,

or ungrateful for your tenderness. Write to me again as soon as possible, and let your letter be of yourself. On one point only be silent. I could scarcely refuse to show your letter to my dear mother, for to you, as she frequently observes, she looks for the only ray of comfort and consolation that can reach her in this world. Her health, her mind, is so shaken, dear Leicester, that the slightest reference to our lost one brings on attacks which make me tremble for her life. When you reply to this, then, avoid, I entreat you, all direct mention of my poor sister. She knows that I intended to write, but did not ask to see my letter. Why should I conceal from you, Leicester, that there are circumstances worse even than death, connected with our loss, and that render the utmost caution necessary towards my poor mother. If we meet again, all will—all must be explained to you; but I cannot trust to paper that which will weigh me to the earth with shame and sorrow, to breathe even into your ear. Write again, I entreat, write without delay, but let your reply to my letter be general. I cannot well explain my meaning; yet I think you will understand me and be cautious. Adieu!—adieu! in the full sense of the word, for to God's holy and merciful keeping I commit you, my *dear*, perhaps soon, alas! my *only* friend!"

From the period of the discovery of her sister's wretched fate, Bess had lived in continual apprehension that some untoward event would one day or other disclose what had occurred to Mrs. Leslie. Kept in ignorance, as she was herself, of the real circumstances of Bell's lamentable death, and believing implicitly the statement of Rachel and the Lortons, that her sister had died of natural disease (a fever was the cause they assigned), she, after the first violent natural burst of grief, became gradually able with calmness to reflect upon the consequences of the deception, or rather at present concealment, practised towards her mother.

Truth itself, in word and deed, Bess had a perfect horror of everything that resembled even dissimulation or equivocation in any shape; but, putting aside the painful efforts it cost her to suppress the natural emotions of her grief for the irreparable loss of her sister, so as to prevent Mrs. Leslie's suspecting that anything had occurred subsequent to their first shock—that of Bell's elopement—Bess felt, deeply felt the additional burthen imposed upon her by the secret which she dared not share with her mother. Again and again did her heart whisper that this secrecy was wrong. Rachel's tears and Mrs. Lorton's arguments prevailed, especially when their advice and admonitions were backed by the opinion of the physician who had been called in to Mrs. Leslie, that the almost certain result of any violent emotion to his patient would result in her sudden death.

Mr. Lorton's opinion, he did not disguise, leant to that of Bess; that *if* it

could be communicated without fatal consequences to Mrs. Leslie, it ought not to be concealed that her unfortunate daughter was at rest for ever, from all the misery her conduct had been calculated to bring upon her.

"For my own part," observed the good old man, "I will confess that death, in such a case, appears a merciful dispensation—an evil far more easily to be borne than the horrible suspense, the——"

"I have heard my mother say so," murmured Bessie's trembling lips, "and yet——"

"Ah, my dear, it is easy to say so," interrupted Mrs. Lorton. "A mother, in her first distraction at the ruin of her child, will perhaps think that it would be better that the child had died; but while there is life there is hope, and even now it may be that poor Mrs. Leslie is in secret buoyed up with the belief that her daughter will return a penitent to her arms. I myself should, I know——"

"Hush—hush, my dear," gently interrupted Mr. Lorton, "we can form very little—very imperfect notions of a mother's feelings in such a case, and we are only distressing our poor young friend by these remarks. After all, Bessie must be the best judge of her mother's feelings."

Mrs. Lorton was a good woman, a kind-hearted woman, but she was rather tenacious of her opinion—her judgment. On this subject she had a strong auxiliary in Rachel. Poor Rachel had besides so thoroughly imbued with the impression that Mrs. Leslie would inevitably sink beneath any accession of grief, that no argument could convince her that it might be possible gradually to prepare the unhappy mother for the truth; and Bess, wavering and unhappy, and afraid to incur the fearful responsibility, as her friends called it, at length yielded implicitly to their counsel, still to keep secret the death of her sister, and thus, it is not improbable, paved the way to many additional sorrows and sufferings.

CHAPTER XVI.

Down from her hand it fell—the scroll
  She could no longer trace;
The grief of love is in her soul,
  Its shame upon her face.

Her head has dropp'd against her arm,
  The faintness of despair;
Her lip has lost it red-rose charm,
  For all but death is there.

And there it lies, the faith of years,
  The register'd above:
Deepen'd by woman's anxious tears:
  Her first and childish love.

Like a fair flower beneath the storm,
  Is bow'd that radiant brow;
But pride is in that fragile form,
  It droops not aye as now.

'Tis not the lover that is lost,
  The love, for which we grieve;
But for the price which they have cost—
  The memory which they leave.—L. E. L.

LENGTH of time passed over, without any new event disturbing the comparative calm of Mrs. Leslie's and Bessie's life. The health of the former still remained precarious; the natural result of time, in softening the bitterness of Bessie's regret and grief, had restored the bloom to her cheek and the brilliancy to her eye, although the expression of her features was still saddened and subdued, and the light step, the vivacious reply, and the merry ringing laugh, which had once rendered her the life and delight of her friends, was exchanged for a thoughtful, pensive tone and manner, that, although it detracted nought from her beauty, completely changed its style. To Mrs. Leslie, the death of Bell still remained a profound secret, and to Bess it was frequently a source of unmitigated grief, amounting to agony, to discover that her mother, even yet, in secret indulged the hope that her erring and guilty child would one day return a penitent to her arms. It was under this impression that Mrs. Leslie frequently spoke of Bessie's marriage with Ronald Leicester, as an event which she most ardently wished could be accelerated.

"I know, indeed, my dear child," she would observe, "that in parting with you, I should lose the only prop, the only remaining joy of my existence; but on the other hand, I should be left free to act as my heart would dictate. Neither you nor the world could then blame me for opening my arms with joy to receive your unhappy sister. While you are still unmarried, I feel that it would be an injustice to you, and might, indeed, be ruinous to your future prospects. My own conscience, indeed, tells me that it would be cruel and unjust to make one so fallen, so guilty, the companion, the associate of innocence and purity like yours. Yet I could not'—Oh, Bess, I could not see that still dear, though degraded, child suing to me for an asylum against the miseries she has brought upon herself, without—Nay, nay, Bessie, hear me out. It is but seldom I speak on this subject, though, believe me, it is never for a moment absent from my thoughts. We know not how soon I may be placed in the situation I speak of; and which I cannot help praying for, even though I dread it, as it may affect you. No, no, here she must never come, be the consequences what they may, I say to myself. And yet, Bess, were I to see her—if I but heard her say, in the words of the prodigal, 'Mother, I have sinned against Heaven and against you ——'"

Bessie's agony was no longer to be controlled. The fatal secret was already upon her lips. What, indeed, could be worse than that her mother should (as by her own confession appeared) be perpetually suffering in silence from this contention between her reason and her maternal affection for her fallen child? Would it not be better, at once, to set all at rest, by saying, "Your poor Bell has already found an asylum, even more lasting than a mother's love could confer. She has hidden her shame and sorrow, and, let us trust, expiated her offences in the eternal grave." But, before Bess could command her voice to utter this, Mrs. Lorton entered the room.

"I see you have heard it all," she observed, looking from the mother to the daughter, and discovering that both were pale, agitated, and in tears. "But, my dear Mrs. Leslie, I really must blame you for suffering yourself to be thus agitated at an event so natural. I have known it for some time, and should have mentioned it, but——"

"My mother knows nothing, madam," interrupted Bess, surprised and bewildered at Mrs. Lorton's observations and manner. It could not—surely it could not be the death of her poor sister that the latter thus alluded to, with so much composure as a natural event. "Neither my mother nor I," repeated Bess, looking earnestly at Mrs. Lorton, "have any suspicion what you allude to."

"Pray speak, my kind friend," added Mrs. Leslie, observing the good woman looked puzzled and embarrassed at Bessie's observation. "If it is any 'natural event,' in which I have an interest," continued the former, laying strong emphasis on the words Mrs. Lorton had used, "you will find that I am too inured to grief and disappointment now, to shrink from any infliction."

"This is no grief, my dear Mrs. Leslie," returned her friend, "neither, under all circumstances," (and she paused and looked at Bess) "can I call it a disappointment, since I am well assured you have long ceased to indulge any hope connected with the person to whom it alludes. I will not keep you in suspense any longer—I imagined that you had heard of the marriage of the Marquis of Ledbury, which I saw announced in the papers last week."

Mrs. Leslie's lip quivered, but Bess, relieved from the suspense that had for the last few minutes oppressed her almost to fainting, breathed more freely.

"You are right," observed the former. "The event you speak of, can be of little consequence now to me, except——" and her eye lightened up with an expression of hope to which it had long been a stranger, "except, indeed, that it may lead to the restoration of my child sooner than I could otherwise hope. Yes, I will now confidently trust that she will return to me, for, guilty as she is, I cannot believe but that this will——"

The deep emotion that overcame her prevented the completion of the sentence, and Bess turned despondingly away. The opportunity she saw was now lost to reveal to her mother the truth respecting her sister, and in silence she was compelled to hear, day after day, her mother's hopeful allusions to that meeting which she (Bess) knew could never take place in this world.

One only source of consolation, it might be said, of happiness unmixed and unalloyed, remained to Bess Leslie. Leicester wrote by every opportunity, and always in the same strain of hope and unlimited confidence. All with him was prosperous, beyond his most sanguine hopes, and every letter was fraught with fond and tender anticipations of the period when he should return to claim, as he said, the rich reward of all his privations and exertions. He had not extorted—as we were about first to write, seeing that on that subject young ladies generally make such difficulties as render their hardly-gained consent rather an extortion than a gift—but from Bess he had frankly received the promise he had as frankly required, that she would not throw a single obstacle in the way of their nuptials, but that they should be united the day month that he should arrive in his native land. "And with that blessed certainty to cheer me on, my own dear affianced wife," he wrote, "I have only to pray for patience, or some lucky chance, to shorten the interval of my probation."

On this point, therefore, Bessie's heart was perfectly at rest; or, if ever a sombre thought did intervene to cloud the prospect, it was when she remembered the dangers of the voyage which Leicester had yet to encounter. But youth is the season of hope. Bessie was still in the blush and bloom of girlhood, and in spite of all her sorrowful experience of the instability of human happiness, hers was not a disposition to despond. Even Mrs. Leslie's pale and faded features would lighten up with a ray of pleasure, as Bess read to her passages from Leicester's letters, in which he spoke of the happiness to come, and in which she (Mrs. Leslie) was never forgotten. "*Our* mother's taste; *our* mother's inclinations," were ever to be consulted, even in the choice of their future residence. Even Rachel, her wishes and comforts, were not forgotten; and, while Mrs. Leslie's deep sigh and silence seemed to express rather gratitude for his intentions than hope to benefit by them, Rachel, in a faltering tone, and with tears streaming down her cheeks, would ejaculate—

"God bless him! He is worthy of my own dear Bess!"

But soon "a change came o'er the spirit of their dream." A change as unlooked-for, as undeserved and incomprehensible.

"Another letter, my dear child," said Rachel, hurrying into the little parlour, after answering the well-known double-rap of the postman at the front door. "It is a double one, too, this time," added the old woman, as she put the parcel into Bessie's trembling hand; and then, as if she felt she had a right to share in the pleasure she had no doubt it contained, although she wished to avoid the appearance of improper curiosity, she turned away from the contemplation of her favourite's glowing and animated countenance, and busied herself sweeping up the hearth, and replenishing the fire. Mrs. Leslie had not yet left her room, and Bess, after a moment's contemplation of the well-known handwriting, broke the seal.

There was a long silence—Rachel listened in vain for some cheering word, some tenderly breathed exclamation, such as she had before heard on similar occasions, that should tell her all was well with him on whom all *their* hopes of happiness now rested. Still all was silent, and Bessie's face being turned towards the window, prevented its expression being seen. Rachel saw, however, that the letter lay on her knee, and that she appeared in deep thought.

"My dear child—my dear, *dear* child!" exclaimed the old woman, unable any longer to bear the anxiety and suspense created by this silence. "There is nothing the matter, I hope? Mr. Leicester is well —is he not? That is his writing, I know," and she glanced at the letter which lay open, while Bess held in her grasp a second paper, which appeared to have been enveloped in the former.

"*His* writing!" repeated Bess, with an hysterical laugh that terrified Rachel. "Yes, it is his writing. If—if I am not mad, or he—Read it, Rachel, read it, and let me be sure that I am still in my senses."

At any other time Rachel would have found it necessary to seek for her spectacles, and even then, perhaps, would have found some difficulty in deciphering the hasty and scrawled lines which were thus presented to her. But fear and surprise seemed to have lent her new powers, and she read as follows:—

"When you have read the enclosed letter, you will perhaps be able in some measure to appreciate my feelings. Oh, Bessie, what can I say? What can I think? It has thrown me on a bed of sickness. For days I have been in the delirium of a fever, which has left me so utterly prostrated in bodily strength, that I am unable to rise from my bed. Had it not been so, I should before this be on my way to England, by the same vessel which conveys this to you. As it is, weeks must elapse before another opportunity will offer. And I must bear this galling, torturing suspense! Suspense!—is it suspense? Is it not certainty, maddening certainty? Would any one, the veriest demon in human shape, dare to write what I have been condemned to read, if it were not true? My head throbs, my heart feels as if its very chords were broken. If I live, Bessie, I will see you —will hear from your own lips—Yet what could I hear that would —Bess Leslie, I am literally distracted. I cannot write, I cannot even think coherently. I have been reading over, for the thousandth time, the letters you have written to me. Not one word but breathes of truth and purity and innocence. And then I turn to the portrait, sketched in these horrible lines, and ask myself if it be possible? And I, then, was to be the victim of your infamous artifices? Did you hope it? Did you believe that—Yes, you might well agree so willingly to become my wife, the moment I demand 'the fulfilment of your promise,' those are your words. Your only hope, of course, was not allowing me time to discover your infamy. My God! my God! is it the chosen of my heart—to her whom I loved—*loved!*—still love to idolatry, that I address these lines? Bess, if you are innocent, a whole life of penitence, of contrition, on my part cannot atone for this. If—dare I hope?—I will try to be calm and reasonable; I will entreat of you to write; write *immediately*, though if I live—if my physical strength does not utterly sink under the tortures of my mind —I shall be on my way to England before a letter from you can reach me.

'RONALD LEICESTER.'

"There must be some dreadful mistake," muttered Rachel, as she gently withdrew from Bessie's grasp the other letter.

"Mistake!" repeated the latter, in a tone of bitterness. "But read that—read that, too, my dear Rachel," and again Bess leant her head on her hand, and resumed the posture of deep meditation, or rather stupefaction, in which she had appeared ever since she herself had read its astonishing, overwhelming contents.

Rachel turned first to the signature. It was "Lewis Cheverton."

"Cheverton," repeated the old woman, "that is the bold, saucy——"

"Yes, yes," interrupted Bess, impatiently, "read on, Rachel."

"I cannot, my dear, my eyes fail me, and the handwriting—but I will get my spectacles, and——"

"No, I will read it to you," returned Bess, in a voice unnaturally calm. "To you only," she added; "for no other eye shall ever—Listen Rachel."

Bess rapidly glanced over the first page, which contained, it appeared, nothing personally interesting to her, and then she commenced reading, in a low tone—

"You have seen, of course, in the English journals, which I have regularly transmitted to you, the account of the tragical death of one of the Leslies—one of the Twin Roses of Arundale, as they were so sentimentally called. It was a shocking affair, and even I, whom you have often lectured for my want of principle, as you were pleased to call my free and *liberal* opinions where the fair sex are concerned, would not have been in Ledbury's place for any consideration. I have never heard the rights of the story, but the marquis was on the Continent at the time the poor girl destroyed herself."

Bess paused, and lifted her eyes to Rachel's with an expression that made the latter tremble,

"My poor child!" murmured the old woman. "Oh, Bessie—Bessie, try, for your poor mother's sake, to——"

"Yes, yes, yes—you are right," interrupted Bess, in a choking voice. "It *would* kill her, I see it all now. You are right—she could not outlive *that*. Yet I do—I——"

Again she turned to the letter, and read on—

"There are a great many different tales told, or rather were told, for the nine days' wonder is, of course, long since over, and the fate of the Twin Rose forgotten in the circles in which she bloomed and blossomed. But there were, as I said before, numerous immediate causes assigned for her 'committal of the rash act,' as the newspaper editors call it. By some it was said that the marquis had actually deceived the poor girl by a sham marriage, and that her despair, at discovering this deception, induced her to take the fatal plunge into eternity; while by others it was alleged that Ledbury had found out that he was not the only one on whom the lady's favours were bestowed, while they were in Paris. That they had consequently parted, and she had returned to London with her new paramour, who turned out to be nothing but a swindler; and, having robbed her of all that the marquis's lavish bounty had bestowed, had left her in the most abject poverty. I believe, however, that very few know anything of the real story. As to Ledbury, I should say, any girl must be worse than a fool to trust to his bare promises; for it's very well known that, though he will stick at no expense to gratify his fancies, he is the meanest fellow living to those who have outlived his liking. One or two of the dashing belles of the day have contrived, by address and cunning, to wheedle a tolerable settlement out of him; but, on the other hand, I could point out half-a-dozen, at least, who owe their introduction into *gay life* to him, but who could not get five pounds from him, if it were to save their lives. However, I am not going to say this was the case in the present instance; and, indeed, to tell the truth, I am rather inclined to think that the fault was on her side, whatever it was that led to their parting so quickly; and I'll tell you why I say so. Because I know Ledbury's vanity leads him to take a pride and pleasure in exhibiting his conquests, and the notoriety of being talked about as the seducer of the beautiful and fashionable Twin Rose of Arundale, in my opinion, was quite as gratifying—but I am, I dare say, tiring you, and uselessly occupying my own time, on this worn out subject. Only this as a prelude to what I am about to communicate to you. I must say that I suspect the world, in general, gave the Leslie girls credit for the possession of a much greater degree of innocence, simplicity, rectitude, and all that sort of thing, than they deserved.

"Don't start, Ronald. Perhaps *you know* I am correct. If so, you will not be surprised at my observation. But if you do not—if you were really deceived by their apparent respectability, and was seriously attached—I mean, in what the world calls an honourable way—to the other sister, I am truly sorry for you; for, I must tell you the truth, you have been most wretchedly duped. You never thought me worthy of your confidence, and perhaps you were right; but *n'importe*. If I had known all the circumstances of your *liaison* with the lady in question, I might have been less free and unshackled in speaking my mind than I am at present; besides, honour would then have interfered, perhaps, and withheld me from following up *la bonne fortune* that has fallen in my way. After this introduction, you will of course understand that I have recently seen the remaining rosebud—she who, as Moore says, is

'Left blooming alone.'

"But you shall have the whole story, chapter and verse. You remember, of course, my first accidental rencontre with the charmer, just before you left England. I was comparatively new, then, to the gay scenes of London life; but, among the set I had even then got among, I had frequently heard the two Leslies, the Twin Roses, spoken of in terms of the most rapturous admiration, as to their personal beauty. At the same time, I must acknowledge, I had heard remarks connected with them very inconsistent with that respect which their situation in society demanded. They were represented as regular husband-hunters; to say the least, putting up their charms to market for the best bidder. But that was nothing, for I knew many other girls, far their superiors as to birth, &c., whom our fellows, that is to say, Dallaston, Peters, Philipson, and the rest of the set, represented in the same light. But, with regard to the Leslies, other insinuations were not spared. It was said that the young ladies would not be over scrupulous as to such an old-fashioned unnecessary ceremony as marriage; though their mamma and their aunt, Lady Jane Bevington, to whom they were indebted for their introduction into society, and the *eclat* that had for a short time attended it, were, of course, inclined to prefer the permanent tie, if they could manage to inveigle any body into it. You know, I dare say, what lengths men such as those I have mentioned will go to on such subjects; but still, thou h I might have been inclined to have doubted as to the truth of their general observations, I certainly believed there must be some foundation for the levity with which they spoke of the Leslie girls, as they affectedly called them. At this time I had never, however, heard your name in any way connected with them, and was, therefore, as you may suppose, greatly surprised, when only a few days before my accidental introduction to Miss Leslie, Frank Peters, in the course of conversation after dinner, when about a dozen of us were present, observed—

"'Is it true, Cheverton, that Ronald Leicester has been suddenly converted from the wicked ways of the world, and, renouncing 'the devil and all his works,' as the little boys say in their catechism, he is over head and ears in love with Bess Leslie, one of the Twin Roses that there was such a clatter about last winter?'

"I replied, of course, that I knew nothing about it. I had never heard you mention her name.

"'But how did you hear it, Frank?' I demanded.

"Peters could not or would not explain, then; but I saw he knew more on the subject, and on remarking so to Dallaston, when we were alone together, the latter observed—

"'You may depend upon it, he heard it from Ledbury, who is on the very *best terms* with the other sister.'

"I could not misunderstand his expression, and I immediately replied that, if that were the case, I was very sure Ronald Leicester was not likely to have any *serious* attachment to the lady in question.

"'Serious?' returned Dallaston. 'I don't suppose Leicester is fool enough to marry a girl, whom he may have on easier terms, even if she had the beauty of an angel.'

"'Do you know the Miss Leslies?' I asked.

"'No; you know I was abroad when they came out, and they were going down before I came back; for Lady Jane Bevington has brought an heir to her husband, in his old age—the girls, his nieces, are thus cut out of their chance for his fortune, and I believe they have not so much of their own as would pay for their satin slippers and French gloves.'

"'Poor girls,' I observed, 'it is rather hard upon them, too, after being brought out with such expectations.'

"'Oh, yes, my sister Augusta told me there never were such flourishes of trumpets as attended their *debut*. Nothing was talked of but the heiresses, the twin roses, &c., &c. It was thought, at first, that Ledbury even was seriously caught; and Lady Jane, who, Gussy says, is the vainest, weakest fool that ever existed, did not scruple to talk openly of the match between the marquis and her niece as a settled thing.'

"'Where do the Leslies reside?' I asked, for I confess, Ronald, I had become interested by what I had heard; 'I suppose, though,' I added, 'with the Bevingtons?'

"'Oh, no, the poor devils were sent of, *sans ceremonie*, to make room for the young heir,' he replied. 'I am surprised though, Cheverton, that you should not know where they live; for I heard, a week or two ago, that your cousin passes half his time with them. I know, Ledbury complained that Leicester was in his way, for the one he is after is mighty desirous to keep up appearances, for the sake of her sister. Of course, it would spoil the match, if Leicester were to find out the *liaison* between Ledbury and his intended sister-in-law.'

"I said nothing to this, Ronald, but determined within myself to try and find out what terms you really were upon with Miss Leslie, and prevent your being imposed upon by telling you what I had heard respecting the marquis and the other sister. You were then absent from London, and before you returned the accidental rencontre took place between Miss Leslie and myself, in Oxford-street. You resented so violently the levity, as you called it, with which I spoke of the Leslies, that you compelled me either to drop the subject, or quarrel with you. You know how unwilling I should be to let anything break the friendship that has grown with our growth, and strengthened with our strength. Besides, you were going to quit England, perhaps for ever, and thus convinced that there was no fear of your being seriously entangled by your passion for the young lady, I considered it of no consequence that you should be enlightened as to her real character. Some observations, however, that have at times fallen from my father, as to your motive for leaving England, have led me to believe that I reckoned wrongly upon the effects of absence in your particular case. I hope, sincerely hope it is not so, but—never mind my reasons, I will at once relate an occurrence, as yet only a few days old. I was riding in the park, on Sunday last, with Dallaston, his sister Augusta, and two or three more, when a female passed on horseback, attended by a smart groom in livery. A thick green veil (they are the ugliest things that were ever invented) concealed, in a measure, her features; but her figure—the most symmetrical and elegant I ever saw—and the masterly manner in which she rode and managed a fiery and peculiarly beautiful Arabian horse, attracted all eyes. 'Who is she?—Who can she be?' were questions that I heard from many besides our own party. Lady Augusta herself, no despicable horsewoman, looked at the graceful stranger with no small degree of envy.

"'It is a beautiful creature,' she observed, confining, of course, her admiration to the animal.

"'And a beautiful rider,' added Philipson, with enthusiasm. 'By Jupiter, I never saw a woman sit a horse so admirably in my life.'

"Lady Augusta pouted—Philipson is her *cavalier servante*—but he seemed to forget everything but the equestrian, who, as if conscious of the admiration she excited, at that moment just touched the neck of her steed with her light whip, and away he flew with his graceful burthen, at a pace that carried her out of sight of our admiring eyes in no time.

"Lady Augusta's *nez retroussée* became more *à la Roxalane* than ever, as she turned disdainfully to her dear friend, Emily Philipson, who, though she sits like a sack of flour on a horse, always rides with her ladyship.

"'How unbecoming such exhibitions in public are,' she observed. 'For my part, I ride because I consider horse-exercise beneficial to my health; but I should sink with shame to exhibit in the manner that girl does.'

"'Oh, yeth,' lisped Miss Philipson, 'the rideth for all the world like the woman we thaw at that horrid plathe over Wethminther Bridge—Athleyth, they call it, I believe, where Captain Peterth perthuaded my brother and I to go one night.'

"I confess, Ronald, though I laughed at the girl's envy, I did think there was rather too much show-off in the lady's riding. However, not to keep you in suspense, she passed us a second time—not now alone—for there were not less than half-a-dozen men with her, all apparently contending for a smile, a look, or some mark of preference. You know, as well as I do, how many (ay, and men of rank, too) there are who disdain to bestow any attention on a woman, will devote themselves, without a particle of shame, to all the whims and airs, and caprices of a fashionable one of no—or, rather, I should say, notorious—character. I had very little doubt, in my own mind, this was the case in the present instance; but, imagine my surprise, my astonishment, when, at the very minute she was passing me, in laughing conversation with a gentleman who rode on her right hand, she threw back the veil that had before concealed her face, and I beheld Miss Leslie's beautiful features. She recognised me instantly, I saw; for her colour heightened, although she was evidently rouged; and I saw, too, that the recognition was mutual between her and Lady Augusta, for the latter turned her head away with a look of horror, which Miss Leslie returned with proud disdain.

"Had I been disposed to entertain a doubt, it was soon dispelled. Dallaston fell back behind his sister, and rode close to me.

"'Don't you know who it is, Cheverton?' he whispered.

"'Yes,' I replied.

"'By Jove, what an escape Leicester had,' he continued. 'Why, she was very near drawing him in to marry her, was she not?'

THE WATERMAN CONVEYING THE CORPSE OF BELL TO THE DEADHOUSE.

"The subject made me very uneasy, Ronald, for, but a few hours before, my father had told me, speaking of you, that he believed you were under a positive engagement to marry the niece of Sir Matthew Bevington.

"I got rid of Dallaston and his party, as well as I could, and then I rode after her. I was determined to learn all I could about her, for your sake. She left the park, but the men I mentioned still attended her, or I should have spoken at once to her, and reminded her of our former acquaintance. I haven't told you that I visited her once at her mother's cottage at Highgate, and had no reason to complain of my reception, but was denied admittance, for some reason, when I called again. Well, the conclusion of this long story is, that I traced her to a house in the neighbourhood of Brunswick Square, which was evidently her own residence. Two of her companions alighted and entered with her—the others rode off; and

I, of course, was obliged to do the same, resolving, however, to return to the neighbourhood the next morning, and learn what further particulars I could respecting her present situation. A circumstance, however, not worth relating, prevented my going as I intended, though the subject was never out of my mind ; and, as if fate willed that she should fall in my way, I went the same evening to Drury Lane, to see Kean. The house, of course, was crowded, but I had scarcely looked round me before I again beheld, shining in all the brilliancy of beauty, and dressed in the utmost extreme of fashionable display, in an opposite box, the fair vision of the preceding day. This time she was attended by a plain and rather elderly man, of not very prepossessing features. He appeared very attentive to her; and, unlike the bold levity she had displayed in the park on the preceding day, her smiles seemed studiously reserved for him alone. I confess I envied him those sweet smiles. She evidently did not see me, but I was still gazing at her when our old schoolfellow, Percival, tapped me on the shoulder.

"'Don't fall in love with the modern Cleopatra,' he observed, laughing; "for you may sigh your heart out in vain, unless you can lay down thousand for thousand with Harcourt, and let the covetous gipsy rule with sovereign power, as she does over him.'

"'I don't understand you,' I replied. 'Who is Harcourt?'

"'Harcourt! I thought everybody knew him,' he replied. 'He is one of the richest men in London. As rich as a Jew, if he is not one, which I wouldn't swear for.'

"'And the lady?' said I, affecting ignorance.

"'Oh, the lady,' he replied, with a significant smile, 'she is the favourite sultana who condescends to scatter his money for him, with the most enchanting grace possible. The old fellow is positively in his dotage! Look, how she smiles upon him, and he believes those smiles are all his own. It would be a sin, worse than all she ever committed, if they were. They say, too,' he continued, 'that she is as accomplished as beautiful, and belongs to a very respectable family, though for 'Gold she has sold herself to shame,' as the poet has it.'

"'But perhaps he intends to marry her,' I observed.

"'Marry!' repeated Percival significantly. 'No—no, there is no question of marrying in the case, even if there was not an effectual bar in the person of a fat jolly, respectable old lady, the mother of half-a-dozen grown-up sons and daughters,

rejoicing in the name of Harcourt, and being the legitimate heirs of the old moneylender.'

"'A married man!' I exclaimed with a look that betrayed, I suppose, that I was shocked, for Percival laughed and rallied me on my *moral* scruples.

"'You have not told me yet the lady's name,' I observed.

"'She passes by the name of Lawrence,' he replied, 'but all these *sort of women* have *noms de guerre*. I have heard that her real name is Leslie, and that she is the niece of a baronet; but whatever she is, or may have been, she is a beautiful creature.'

"I had heard enough now, of course, Ronald, and I fear you will say too much; but I cannot forbear telling you the conclusion of the adventure was that I contrived to place myself in the way, as the old money-grub was conducting her to the carriage that waited for them, and was honoured with a smile from Mrs. Lawrence, that told me she had not forgotten old acquaintance, nor would be sorry to renew it, time and place fitting."

We have omitted to notice Rachel's indignant exclamations, or the frequent pauses which Bess was compelled to make to recover breath, and force submission on the feelings that seemed to threaten almost suffocation, while she read this elaborate tissue, as she believed, of the most unfounded and infamous falsehoods. There was one agonising truth, indeed, which it conveyed to her knowledge, for the first time; and Bess clasped her hands, and fixed her eyes on Rachel, as if she would look into her soul, as she said—

"Now, then, Rachel, I am prepared for all. Tell me—tell me the truth—my sister——"

Rachel burst into an agony of tears, that rendered her words unintelligible.

"I am cruel—yes, I am cruel to ask it," articulated Bess, with difficulty. "One—one only question, dear Rachel. You saw her—you will not deceive me now—you did see her yourself—dead?"

Rachel did not comprehend the purport —the full force of this question. The recollection of the dreadful spectacle she had beheld rushed with all its force upon her mind, and she hesitated.

A glow of life for a moment illumined Bessie's face, as she beheld what she thought a look of doubt on the poor old woman's face.

"Tell me—tell me the truth—is it possible that she still lives? That——" and Rachel's desponding look, the melancholy shake of her head, spoke volumes—

but Bess had been once, as she said, deceived, and she had, as it were, now wound herself up to a desperate determination to hear the whole truth.

"Rachel," she observed, "it is mistaken kindness on your part to withhold the circumstances of—of *her* death. You see—you must see that I have now fortitude to bear anything. I *do* feel, indeed, that I am past suffering—look, how calm I am."

"Calm," repeated Rachel, gazing with agony on the ghastly, corpse-like features of the poor girl, "calm—oh, my poor—poor child, this will kill you! Do not look at me so, Bessie. Your mother—my dear good mistress—how will she support this blow? No—no, she cannot support it—she will sink under it; and I, miserable, unhappy wretch that I am, shall be left in my old age alone in the world. Every creature that I have loved gone before me to the grave. Oh, Bessie—Bessie, have pity on me, on your poor mother. For her sake—for mine, who have always loved you as my own——"

Rachel's pathetic remonstrance—the anguish that almost convulsed her time-worn features, effected a sudden revulsion in Bessie's feelings, and melted her into tenderness. She threw her arms round the old woman's neck, and laid her head upon the bosom which had so often been her refuge in infancy, and had never beat but with kindness and sympathy towards her —and tears, warm gushing tears, not of sorrow for her own misfortunes, but the unselfish tenderness for her humble, but most true and faithful friend—came to her relief.

"Thank God! thank God!" murmured the old woman, who had trembled for the life or intellects of her beloved charge. "Yes, yes, *He* is gracious and merciful," she added, with fervour, "and as He has hitherto supported, so will the Almighty give her strength to bear even this heavy burthen."

And Bessie felt that she had strength; for, although her lips remained silent, her heart was lifted up in fervent prayer to her Creator, "who tempers the wind to the shorn lamb," and calmness and resignation took the place of that wild and frenzied feeling which had before threatened the extinction of both body and mind.

From Mr. and Mrs. Lorton Bess heard the real circumstances of her unhappy sister's death—for the remembrance of those circumstances was still so agonising to Rachel that she could not acquire sufficient command of herself to relate them.

The half-formed hope that had glimmered in Bessie's mind, that the unfortunate Bell might yet be alive, was of course entirely extinguished by the mournful narration of her kind and benevolent friends, which was further confirmed—if, indeed, it could be said to require any confirmation—by the details of the newspapers of the day, which Mr. Lorton had preserved, and now (though reluctantly) placed in Bessie's hands.

It would be vain and useless to attempt to describe Bessie's anguished feelings as, alone and in secret, she read again and again those records of her sister's sorrows and shame—before which her own present and, it may be said, personal misfortunes seemed to shrink into nothingness. It was long, indeed, before Bess even recurred to Leicester's letter; but it was absolutely necessary to assign some cause to Mrs. Leslie for the grief and agitation which it was impossible for her to subdue entirely; and as the former knew that a letter had been received from America, her suspicions were naturally led in that direction, although too delicate to press for an explanation which her daughter appeared desirous to avoid.

From Rachel, however, Mrs. Leslie soon learned sufficient at once to account for Bessie's despondency, and, as the former sighingly observed, put an end to all her long-cherished hopes of seeing her beloved and only remaining child happy in the protection and affection of the only man in the world she (Mrs. Leslie) had considered deserving of such a treasure. Kind and affectionate as she was, and fully acknowledging Bessie's merits—appreciating as she did, to its fullest extent, the devoted filial attachment of her daughter—it must be confessed that Mrs. Leslie's heart was too pre-occupied by her lost child to allow her to dwell, so exclusively as she would otherwise have done, on the disappointment of Bessie's hopes and her own, as regarded Ronald Leicester.

The fortitude, which it cost poor Bessie so hard a struggle outwardly to attain, served, too, to lessen the acuteness of the mother's feelings. Little did she suspect the anguish—the almost utter despair, which lay hidden under that apparent calmness and quiet resignation. But Rachel saw it all—she knew that Bessie's nights were sleepless; and that, except when engaged in active duties, in administering to her mother's comfort, or trying to beguile her into temporary forgetfulness of her maternal sorrows and anxiety, her (Bessie's) days were passed in hopeless, blank despondency; and the good old woman felt sometimes angry at what she considered absolute injustice, on the part of her mistress, in thus lavishing all her maternal affection and anxiety on one who had proved herself so undeserving of it, and remaining blind, as it were, to the sacrifices and sufferings of her exemplary daughter.

CHAPTER XVII.

She never told her love,
But let concealment, like a worm i' th' bud,
Feed on her damask cheek ; she pined in thought,
And, with a green and yellow melancholy,
She sat like Patience on a monument,
Smiling at Grief.—SHAKSPEARE.

ESS LESLIE has nothing to reply to Mr. Leicester's extraordinary letter, or rather to the letter of his correspondent, Mr. Cheverton, since she feels it would be degrading herself to enter into any refutation of the vile tissue of falsehoods it contains. Mr. Leicester is, of course, free to act as he pleases ; but Bess Leslie considers that it would be quite unnecessary that Mr. Leicester should inconvenience himself by prematurely returning to England, since he may rely upon it that she would disdain to enter upon any personal discussion of the charges (if she may so call them) to which Mr. Leicester has so unequivocally given credit—in opposition, as it appears to her, to common sense, candour, or humanity ; and, certainly, in direct opposition to the whole tenor of her life and conduct, and the opinions which it has so often been Mr. Leicester's pleasure to express regarding her.

"Miss Leslie certainly hopes and trusts that Mr. Leicester has, if not exaggerated his very serious illness (which she should be very sorry to think him capable of doing), at least mistaken the source of it, when he attributes it to his wounded feelings on her account. Judging from herself, she should say, that where a *real* attachment existed, it would have been quite impossible to have given one moment's credit to such a fabrication as that on which Mr. Cheverton has expended so much ingenuity, for what purpose is best known to that gentleman. At all events, Miss Leslie is convinced that Mr. Leicester is quite right in the inference which he evidently intends to be drawn from *his* letter ; and she therefore encloses, with this, all those previously received from Mr. Leicester ; and requests, in return, that he will have the goodness to forward, by the first opportunity, those which, under a mistaken view of his character, Miss Leslie has addressed to him. She begs to assure Mr. Leicester that he has her best wishes, both for his recovery, and his future happiness.

"P. S. As it is very possible that Miss Leslie may have left her present residence before the papers she solicits to be returned to her can have arrived in England, she will be obliged by Mr. Leicester addressing the parcel to the care of Mr. Lorton, No. —, —— Street, Islington, near London."

Such was Bessie's reply to Leicester's communication ; and a world of tears, of trouble, and of reflection it had cost her, to frame that reply so as to convey her resentment at his unqualified belief of Cheverton's base calumny against her, without degrading herself by an appearance of eagerness to contradict it. Pride, indeed, the pride of conscious innocence, supported her in her determination to enter into no details, to bring forward not one argument, to offer not one single proof how deeply she was wronged—how utterly void of the slightest foundation was the tale which Leicester had credulously suffered at once to dissipate all his confidence in her.

"No," she observed to Rachel, who would have suggested a different course. "No, Rachel, my own heart tells me that were the case reversed—that if it were he who was traduced, I should have spurned the base calumny with utter contempt. I have read and re-read Mr. Cheverton's ingenious tale—for such it certainly is— and each time I have said to myself, with increased surprise and indignation, 'Is it possible that any one who has known me—who has seen my conduct—could believe that I had become all at once, and without any temptation, except the vilest, grossest, most degrading of all motives, the sordid love of gold—could, I say, one living creature believe that I had thus sunk into infamy, the very thought of which brings the fever-spot upon my cheek, while the blood seems to freeze into icicles at my heart? But that *he* should believe it—he, to whom my every thought was confided—who knows beyond what any human being can know, the most secret impulse of the heart that rested on him as upon a second self—for him to receive this most improbable tale as truth—to dare insult me by sending it to me, as if demanding either a refutation, or a confession that it is true—No, Rachel, even if I were sure that a simple denial on my part would efface his belief in the vile calumny, and bring him a penitent to my feet, I would not utter that denial. What I have written has not been written for his satisfaction, but my own. I thought, at first, that I would not write at all—that I would treat his communication with silent contempt; but, then, again I considered that my silence would perhaps be interpreted as a confession that I was guilty, and though I know a time must come that will overwhelm him with a conviction of his injustice, yet——"

"Oh, yes, yes," interrupted Rachel, "it must, it will come—but, oh, Bessie, will it not be more for your happiness—I am a foolish old woman, I know, my dear, and not a proper judge, may be, in such matters; but it seems to me as if the note you have written seems too—too—I don't well know how to express what I mean, but I am afraid that, after such a letter as that, there can be no explanation, such as there ought to be—though I don't blame you for showing proper pride, but——"

Bess smiled, but it was a bitter smile.

"You would wish me to leave Mr. Leicester an opportunity to reply—to vindicate himself—to apologise," she observed. "No, never, Rachel, never. Even should he, after this, write again, which I think very improbable—but should it happen so, depend upon it, I would not even read it. I should enclose it to him unopened."

"Then you would act very unjustly," returned Rachel, warmly. "Yes, Bessie, I must tell you that I think it would be cruel and shameful not to allow him an opportunity of vindicating himself. If he was not sincere, it would not have taken such an effect on him. But never mind,

I won't say any more—only, perhaps, while you are giving way to such angry feelings towards him, instead of the wretch that has imposed upon him—even, I say, at this very minute, who knows what he is suffering? He may even be dead and buried, and then how sorry you will feel."

Bessie's cheek, before crimsoned with indignation and resentment, became pale as the marble it resembled in purity. The image of Leicester dying, lonely, deserted, and believing her on whom his every hope had rested not only false to the solemn vows she had pledged, but guilty, degraded beneath even compassion, was too painful. She hid her face in her hands and wept long and bitterly, and Rachel believing that she had made an impression that could not fail to be beneficial to the cause she had at heart, namely, the reconciliation of her darling child to the only man who was deserving of, or could make her happy, stole softly out of the room, leaving it, as she would have said, to work its way, and induce, as she hoped, Bess to adopt a gentler tone in her reply to Leicester.

Rachel, however, was mistaken. A calm and cool review of all the circumstances which succeeded to the first gush of tenderness and feeling towards him whom she had so long "nurtured in her heart's core," convinced Bess that she acted justly and rightly in writing so as to convince him that nothing could ever atone for his insulting conduct and want of confidence in her. The letter, or rather note, therefore, was despatched without any alteration or amendment, and Bess considering now that the affair was finally settled, exerted all her energy to subdue even the appearance of regret or sorrow. But although neither sigh nor tear betrayed her suffering—although she relaxed not in her exertions to render her mother's declining days peaceful and happy, if such a term as happiness could be applied to one who was ever occupied by one regret, who was constantly pining for the realisation of hopes that were unattainable — although Bessie's sweet smile was ever ready to reply to her mother's interrogating looks, and enforce her appearance that she was " quite well," that she was not conscious of any ailment, yet her failing strength—the rapid alteration of her before rounded and symmetrical form—the hectic spot that at times glowed upon her cheek, and gave almost supernatural brightness to her eyes, or when absent, left those eyes dull and heavy, and the fair skin faded to a ghastly hue, —the sleepless nights that could not always be disguised or denied, and the total failure of appetite, which could not with all her efforts be concealed, at length aroused Mrs. Leslie to the alarming fear that her beloved child, the only hope and stay left her, was gradually sinking under some hidden and devouring disease. To Rachel, and their friends, the Lortons, the fact had long been apparent. Almost on her knees had the former implored of Bess to have medical advice, to try the effect of change of scene, of amusement; all was met by a steady denial that there was any occasion for her friend's alarm. She was quite well. No change of scene could afford her half the happiness she felt in the society of her friends.

"As to amusement," and her bright though hollow eyes filled with tears as she looked up in Rachel's face. "What amusement could *now* interest, or indeed would not be a painful infliction to bear with? No, no, dear Rachel," she continued, "do not needlessly alarm yourself. I do not deny—you cannot, I know, expect me to deny that I am far from tranquil, or happy. I cannot at once conquer my feelings, and, of course, the body will in some degree suffer with the mind, but reason and resolution will eventually triumph, and I shall learn that hardest lesson of all—to forget."

"Yes, in the grave," murmured her almost heart-broken friend. But Bess would not, or did not hear the reply, and all her efforts were directed to convince her anxious friend that she had overrated her danger, and that in reality she was rapidly attaining that happy state of forgetfulness which was to restore her to health and happiness. Mrs. Leslie's maternal fears, however, once awakened, were not to be lulled or pacified by anything Bess could say, and the latter was compelled most reluctantly to submit that the physician should be consulted, who had formerly upon Mr. Lorton's recommendation been called in to her (Mrs. Leslie's) assistance. The doctor's numerous questions, and grave and concerned looks (although Bess tried to parry them with assumed cheerfulness and protestations that her mother's alarm was quite unnecessary and unfounded), were quite sufficient to convince the anxious parent of the truth of her suspicions, even before he gave his decided opinion that, although there was no immediate danger, there was great reason to apprehend it eventually, unless his recommendations were followed. These were, frequent change of air and scene—removal, if possible, of any cause of mental disquietude—moderate exercise —cheerful society—and, in short, any means that could be adopted to prevent

her mind from dwelling on the subject of uneasiness, whatever it might be.

The doctor anticipated the objection Bess was about to make to this view of the case.

"It is of no use, my dear young lady," he observed, "for you to attempt to persuade either yourself or others that the seat of your disorder is not in the mind. I do not seek to know what it is that is thus preying upon the very strings of life, but I tell you, that were you even in appearance prosperous and happy—in seeming possession of all your wishes—I should say, as I do now, that some mental affliction is turning all your blessings into curses, and that it is the duty of all who wish to preserve your life to adopt my recommendation, and yours to second it by exerting your good sense. I will say no more on this subject, for I see you understand me, and I trust you will, for your own sake, as well as your friends, be guided by my advice. Remember it is criminal to neglect the means of restoration to health, which a merciful providence has placed at our disposal."

Bess blushed deeply, for the doctor's penetrating eye seemed to read her very heart; and certainly there lingered there no very keen desire to live. Doctor Beaumont's observations, however, failed not of their due effect, and she expressed herself perfectly resigned to adopt any means that would not interfere with her mother's comfort or convenience. To Mrs. Leslie, indeed, all places were, as she observed, now alike, except that a removal would separate them from their kind friends, the Lortons. But both Mr. and Mrs. Lorton were too sincerely anxious for their young friend to suffer any selfish regret to interfere, and they warmly seconded the doctor's advice, not to delay the remedies he proposed. A short consultation between the friends decided upon Dover, as combining many advantages for a residence of some months, with the peculiar one of an introduction from Mr. Lorton to an old friend, and, indeed, relative of his, a maiden lady, who added to her slender income by letting a part of her house during the season. Fortunately her apartments were now vacant, and Mrs. Leslie, her daughter, and Rachel were soon established to their own complete satisfaction in a neat house, combining all the advantages of an extensive land and sea view. Bess had never before beheld the "deep, deep sea," and Mrs. Leslie saw with pleasure that the apathy and indifference with which the latter appeared to behold everything around her yielded to the novel, grand, and impressive scene that now presented itself. Bessie's eyes lighted up with somewhat of their former life and spirit, and a faint blush stole over her pale cheek, as she leant from the window of the post-chaise, which conveyed them to their new residence on the South Pier, to catch a view of the blue waters, now calm and smooth, and sparkling in the bright sunlight of an almost cloudless day in June; but "a change came o'er the spirit of her dream," as her eye rested on the white sails of a vessel gliding majestically over its glassy bosom—tears, so long a stranger to her eyes, stole down her cheeks, and sobs, in spite of every effort to restrain them, shook her whole frame, and betrayed the source of her emotion.

"My dear, dear child, I ought to have foreseen and avoided this," observed Mrs. Leslie, "but——"

"No—no. It will do me good. I shall be better—be quite well, presently," returned Bess. "It is a weaknes of which I ought to be—I am ashamed of. Oh, how beautiful, how very beautiful—and look at those small boats coming home—how light and gracefully they skim along. Ob, dear mamma, how glad I am you decided upon coming here, instead of going to an inland place. Nothing can be compared with the sea."

The animation with which she spoke was evidently forced; but it was a great point to see her capable of making the effort, after the long—long dreary apathy in which her every feeling had seemed enveloped. Both Mrs. Leslie and Rachel would have persuaded Bess to have chosen a bed-chamber in the front of the house, which looked towards the heights on which the castle is situated; but Bessie's election was immediately made for a diminutive room, looking out upon the sea, and from which, in clear weather, the opposite coast was distinctly visible. Here, with a book upon her knee, but seldom occupying her eyes, Bess would have been content to have constantly sat inhaling the fresh breeze, and gazing with never satiated delight on the calm, yet moving panorama before her. But although, even with this, her health and spirits evidently mended, Mrs. Leslie felt that it was not likely this means would effectually restore her, since it was but too evident what were the nature of the contemplations which absorbed her whole attention. How, indeed, could it be otherwise, while she gazed continually on the ocean, and watched with such deep interest its various fluctuations, but that her thoughts should continually revert to him who was now,

in all probability, wending his trackless way through its boundless space towards his native home.

Bess did, indeed, think of Leicester. She trembled for his danger, and prayed, fervently prayed for his safety; but her fears and prayers were alike unselfish; for she had brought herself to consider him as much lost to her as though he were buried beneath the waves. But her assurances to her mother that she had triumphed over every remaining weakness, and that her silent meditations were not of a nature that could impede her restoration to perfect health, failed to convince the anxious parent; and Bess was compelled to yield her solitary enjoyments, and join the former in the excursions which she considered necessary, fully to carry out the system Doctor Beaumont had recommended. By degrees it became evident that these rides and walks, in which Mrs. Leslie participated, as far as her strength would possibly allow, had effected a good which had been but little calculated upon, for the mother's health as well as the daughter's began to show signs of visible amendment; and the belief that the fatal nature of Mrs. Leslie's disorder had been mistaken, and that she would eventually surmount the symptoms which had impressed her anxious friends with the fear that it would terminate in her dissolution at no great distance of time, contributed perhaps more than all the remedies employed to restore to Bess the bloom of her cheek and lip, the springiness and elasticity of her step, and if not the natural light and sunny expression of her smile, at least a calmness and placidity that spoke a mind comparatively at peace.

"We are all, I think, growing young again," observed Rachel, with a smile, after having surmounted the steep ascent to Shakspeare's cliff; "and certainly," she continued, "if anything could restore youth and health, it would be this beautiful view and these pure gales, so cool and refreshing. I should not like, though, to lie so near the edge of the cliff as that gentleman is. It must be a steadier brain than mine that would not grow giddy; and, after all, it is very foolish, for he can see nothing more than we do here in perfect safety."

Bess looked carelessly towards the person in question. It did not appear to her that he was in the dangerous situation Rachel apprehended, though it was evident he was leaning over to observe some object immediately beneath the spot on which he lay, and she was passing on to join her mother, who was some paces in advance, when he suddenly arose from the ground and turned towards her, revealing the well-remembered features and form of the tall sallow stranger, whose scrutinising observation of her, at the upholsterer's in Oxford Street, on the day she had met with Mr. Cheverton, had rather added to than decreased the annoyance she had felt from the free and easy manners of the latter. The recognition was evidently mutual, for the gentleman stood for a minute, as if fixed to the spot; but Bessie's eyes were instantly turned away, and, although it was plain his first impulse was to have spoken to her, her look seemed instantly to discourage the attempt.

The look which had passed between him and Bess had not escaped Rachel's quick eyes; and, before they came up with Mrs. Leslie, the latter whispered with a smile—

"If I did not know it to be impossible, Bessie, I should say that is a discarded lover of yours."

"You would say wrongly, then, Rachel, for I never saw the gentleman before but once, and that on an occasion that I have no wish to recal to memory."

Rachel looked surprised, but in a few minutes she observed, after looking back,

"The gentleman does not, however, seem equally desirous of forgetting your meeting, my dear, for he is following us, as if desirous of renewing your acquaintance."

Bess made no reply but by hurrying on, and taking her mother's arm, as if for protection; and the stranger, seemingly discouraged by this action, and perhaps by Rachel's keen glances, as she turned round from time to time to look at him, slackened his pace, so as still to keep some paces in the rear.

Bessie's grave and no longer confused looks prevented Rachel's making any further remarks on the subject, and the presence of the stranger was not noticed by Mrs. Leslie, although he still continued to keep their party in sight, stopping whenever they stopped to enjoy and remark the beauty of the scene, and sauntering on when they moved, at so slow a pace as never actually to come up with them, though he was all the time near enough almost to hear every observation that was uttered.

Anger was the only emotion Bess now felt at this intrusive conduct. A thousand harassing and painful remembrances had been recalled to her mind by his first appearance, for with her accidental meeting with him was connected all that had since poisoned her happiness; but now Cheverton, Leicester, and all that appertained to them, was for the moment forgotten in her resentment at his pertinacity in following and watching her.

"You are heated and exhausted, my dear child," observed Mrs. Leslie, for the first time discovering that Bessie's cheek was flushed, and her manner hurried. "How foolish I have been," continued the anxious mother, "to lead you so far. Let us return home. Lean on me and Rachel. How strange it seems that I, who have been such a poor, weak creature for so long, should have recovered my strength so as to be able to support you. Yet I am, for I did not discover that we had walked so far, until I saw your look of fatigue."

Bess smiled; but she did not undeceive her mother, although she felt that fatigue had very little to do with the appearance her mother had remarked.

The descent of the cliff was, of course, much easier, and more quickly accomplished than the ascent had been; but Mrs. Leslie again and again repeated her entreaties to Bess not to hurry herself, for the latter's quickened pace very little accorded with her supposed exhaustion. She was anxious, indeed, to show the intrusive stranger, who still followed, that she was desirous of avoiding him; and as they approached nearer their home, Mrs. Leslie discovered that there was some other motive for the manner in which she hurried her and Rachel along, than she (Mrs. Leslie) had as yet discovered.

A few words from Bess explained the mystery in reply to the latter's earnest and alarmed exclamation of—

"What is the matter, my dear child? Why are you so extraordinarily anxious to get home?"

"Only to avoid impertinent intrusion, dear mamma," she replied. "A person is following us, whom I have once seen before, and have felt annoyed by his particular observation."

Mrs. Leslie was satisfied with this explanation, and Bess was rejoiced that she did not seem to think it necessary to ask for any farther particulars. The good lady, indeed, simply imagined that her daughter had recently encountered the impertinent stranger in her walks on the pier, or the beach, which she had sometimes taken alone, or with Rachel; and therefore, beyond some general remarks on the folly and idleness of mere loungers, who, as she observed, frequently take a pleasure in annoying modest and delicate females, to whom they see their attentions are unwelcome, and an injunction to Bess not to hazard going out again alone, she

PREPARING THE FINAL HOME FOR UNFORTUNATE BELL.

paid no farther attention to the subject; and the latter was thus spared the mortification of recurring to her former interview with the person in question.

It had not escaped Rachel's observation, however, that the stranger had followed so closely as to ascertain their present residence; and she could not repress the desire to mention to Bess, when the latter retired for the night, the fact, adding— "I don't wish, my dear, to pry into anything that you wish to conceal, but I am much mistaken if this strange man has not something more in view than mere idle curiosity to find out where you live, and you will forgive me, I know, for pointing out to you that it will have a strange appearance to your mother if—"

"I have no concealment on the subject, dear Rachel," returned Bess, "but I do wish, as much as possible, to avoid speaking of one who has so cruelly injured and insulted me as Mr. Cheverton, and as it was in his presence I first saw this——"

"My dear, dear child, forgive me," interrupted Rachel, "you have said quite enough to explain all; and I will take upon myself to prevent your being annoyed with this man, if he should be bold enough to make the attempt I suspect he will."

Painful recollections, however, were excited in Bessie's mind by this accidental rencontre, that effectually banished sleep from her pillow, and she arose in the morning, more languid and unrefreshed than she had felt for a considerable time past.

It was yet early when she left her room. Mrs. Leslie had not yet risen, and Bess was surprised to see on the breakfast table a basket of the finest and loveliest fruit of the season, and by its side a large bouquet of choice and hot-house flowers. It had been a matter of frequent regret to them that in their home they enjoyed personal not the slightest approximation to a garden, and their kind-hearted, good humoured landlady had expressed her sorrow, more than once, that she had not a single friend or acquaintance who were better off in that respect to enable her to gratify Bessie's longing for flowers. The few they had been enabled to procure had been purchased in the market, and were of the commonest sort; but here was a choice and tasteful assortment, many of which were the most valuable products of a green-house, while the grapes, nectarines, &c., it was equally certain, must have come from a hot-house. Bess was still examining, admiring, and wondering, when Rachel entered; but, though she smiled significantly, in reply to the former's eager inquiry, she professed herself equally unable to solve the mystery. A man on horseback, who looked like a servant out of livery, had delivered them to Miss Watson's maid, after inquiring for Mrs. or Miss Leslie's servant, and had immediately ridden off, without saying whence he came, or indeed uttering another word, except a request that they should be placed on the ladies' breakfast table.

"They are intended, therefore, as a present to you, my dear," observed Rachel, "and a very delicate and handsome way it is of showing attention and kindness to an invalid, though who it comes from, whether a gentleman or lady, you may be a better judge than I am."

Bess, however, disclaimed all knowledge on the subject, though the blush that crimsoned her cheek certainly betrayed something like a suspicion which she was unwilling to acknowledge.

Mrs. Leslie's opinion was that it was a mistake. That they were intended not for them, but some one of the same name; but she had not finished relating an anecdote of a similar error that had occurred some years back, before the question was set at rest by Rachel's discovery of a small embossed card, attached to the string which bound the flowers together, on which was written—"Miss Leslie, Miss Watson's, South Pier." There could no longer be a doubt that this was the tribute from some unknown admirer to Bessie's charms, but Mrs. Leslie and Rachel both abstained from the raillery they were inclined to indulge, when they saw that it distressed her; and the former readily complied with her daughter's request that Anne (Miss Watson's maid) should be instructed not to take in any similar presents that might be sent. Notwithstanding this injunction, the very next day a basket of game was left under the same circumstances. "What could Anne do? The moment she opened the door, there stood the basket on the step, and the man was off like a shot, before she could speak." Again and again this occurred. Every delicacy that could be procured was placed at Miss Leslie's disposal, and Bess was not only vexed and humiliated by these extravagant proofs of silent devotion, but provoked by Miss Watson's half-laughing and half-serious apologies for the stupidity of her maid, who, according to her own account, was always tricked by the dexterity of the messenger into receiving the presents. Nothing makes a more favorable impression on common minds than an appearance of reckless generosity. Miss Watson already bedecked the unknown bestower of such expensive gifts with every desirable attribute under heaven, and the only source of regret to her was that he did not come forward to reap the benefit she imagined he must have gained, in Bessie's eyes, by so many proofs of delicate attention. Difficult as, according to her own account of herself, she had found it to make a selection from her numerous admirers, and had thus remained single up to the ripe age of thirty—(the gray locks, which were straggling beneath the well-curled and glossy auburn ringlets that were attached to her smart cap, betrayed that their owner had made a trifling mistake in the register of her birth, for they proclaimed her, at the least, ten years older)—but, even prudent and cautious as she had always been, she declared that she did not believe that she could have been so cold and insensible as Miss Leslie seemed to be. At any rate, she should be dying with curiosity to find out her unknown admirer.

"But suppose your heart was already engaged, Miss Watson?" replied Rachel, to whom these observations were addressed. "You would not, of course——"

"Oh, dear, dear, I never thought of that, I declare," returned the spinster, gratified at being thus made, as she thought, the depository of a love secret. "Certainly, in that case, it is a very awkward affair, and I don't wonder at the young lady's being vexed and uneasy; however, she may depend upon it, I will try my best to find out who the gentleman is, and then, of course, Mrs. Leslie will take proper means to let him know his attentions are not acceptable. I have already ordered Anne never to answer the door without first looking out of the kitchen-window to see who it is; and, if it is the man on horseback, to let me know, that I may go and see him myself."

Chance, however, or rather an accident that might have ended fatally to both Bess and her unknown admirer, at length revealed the secret. From her first arrival the former had been desirous of an excursion on the water. Day after day she had seen parties embark in the small sailing boats that were always ready to be hired at the pier. She had watched them dancing lightly over the waves until they were out of sight, and had again gone to see them come in, and always heard expressions of pleasure and gratification, and as frequently had she longed to partake of the amusement. Naturally timid, and totally unused to the water, Mrs. Leslie at first turned a deaf ear to Bessie's hints on the subject; and even Miss Watson's assurances, that the boatmen were so skilful and attentive that there was not the slightest probability of accident to be apprehended, failed to reconcile her to the experiment. But habit does wonders, and the daily sight of parties going and returning began at length to induce her to regard with more favour her daughter's wish, though she could not be induced to join in it herself. Not that she any longer apprehended danger, but that she was convinced she should become giddy, and sick with the motion of the boat, and thus mar all enjoyment both to herself and Bessie. A favourable opportunity at length presented itself for the latter's indulgence of this coveted pleasure. Miss Watson was invited to join three or four of her acquaintances, who were going to dine on board a vessel that was lying off Deal, some miles distant. They were all steady, married people, her neighbours;

the two boatmen were noted for their carefulness, and the party would have the additional gratification of passing close to one of the largest men-of-war in the service, which was lying at anchor in sight almost of Bessie's chamber-window. It was the same from which a foreign ambassador had landed a few nights past, and the salute of which, from the guns at the castle, had so startled them all. Miss Watson's friends would feel themselves highly honoured by Miss Leslie's company; they would return quite early; and, in short, the voluble and good-humoured spinster held out so many inducements and temptations, independent of Bessie's well-known wishes on the point, that Mrs. Leslie, in spite of her still lingering reluctance, at last gave her consent that the latter should go.

"There couldn't be a finer day, my dear Miss Leslie—no, not if it was made on purpose for us," observed Miss Watson, as they walked down to the pier, where her friends were already waiting for them. "And see," she continued, "the water is as smooth as glass. How I do wish your mamma and Mrs. Rachel had come with us. They would have so enjoyed it, after they had once got aboard; and there won't be any tossing up and down to make anybody sick; and really, you have confined yourself so to the house this last week or two, that you look almost as pale as when you first came down from London. But the fresh sea breeze will soon bring your colour back again. I had a young married lady at my house last summer, for some weeks, and the physician ordered her to go on the water every day that the weather was favourable, and I declare she went home quite hearty, and a colour like a rose in her cheeks, though she was as pale as a lily when she came to me. I do, indeed, wish Mrs. Leslie would have ventured, for she would soon have got over her fear of the water, when she found how delightfully pleasant it is."

Bess wished so to, and, in spite of the enjoyment she expected, she almost repented that she had been so selfish as to leave her mother, for she knew that, if not actually alarmed, the latter would feel considerable anxiety until her return. It was too late, however, to retract—the boat was waiting, and Bess and her companion were received with such a hearty welcome, that she had not courage to avow at this, the last moment, that she felt any reluctance; and yet at the very instant she took her seat, her heart reproached her for indulging a selfish gratification, at the expense of her mother's peace. The novelty, however, of all she beheld—the delightful and renovating breeze, which carried them smoothly along on the bosom of the waters, which they seemed to skim with the easy motion of a sea-bird, scarcely ruffling the surface, and the light-hearted and cheerful, if not over-refined conversation and remarks of her companions, gradually banished her uneasiness. The utmost attention was paid to her comfort, and everything worthy of notice pointed out to her. The different vessels they passed were named by the boatmen, with the ports which they had lately arrived from, or where intended to sail for, and Bessie's heart palpitated with a thousand different sensations as they approached near to one, and the old boatman remarked—

"That's the 'Adventure' from Quebec, Canada; she came up yesterday, and will sail next tide for London. She's had a rough passage, and been sadly knocked about. My son went off to her this morning, to fetch a gentleman passenger, and he said, when he landed, that a week or two ago he never thought to see the white cliffs of Dover again."

The "Adventure" was the vessel in which, nearly three years before, Ronald Leicester had sailed for Canada. It belonged to the merchants with whom he was associated, and what could be more probable, if he where still living, and adhered to his exressed determination of returning to England, than that he had taken his homeward passage in the same vessel? It was not impossible, or even improbable, that the very passenger who had that morning landed was Leicester himself. She would have given the world for an opportunity to ask the old boatman a few questions, with a view of ascertaining the fact; but the latter had already found some other subject to talk about, and draw the attention of her companions to; and, besides, it would naturally excite their surprise and curiosity, if she were to betray any interest, and how could she help doing so, if his answers should at all confirm her suspicions? As long as it was possible to discern it, her eyes were fixed on the vessel which had been pointed out as the "Adventure," but they were now getting among a whole fleet of ships that were waiting for a favourable wind, and she lost sight of the only one that possessed any interest to her.

All the pleasure of the excursion was now lost to Bess. Her thoughts were all absorbed by the solitary passenger from Quebec. Even if he were not Leicester, there was no doubt that the "Adventure"

brought tidings of him. Perhaps of his death—or it might be there was a letter for her. He might have repented of his insulting belief in Mr. Cheverton's shameful and improbable narrative. But, no—no apology, no penitence could atone for what he had written on that subject. She would spurn him with scorn, if he were at that moment kneeling at her feet.

The account Miss Watson had previously given of Miss Leslie's affability, sweetness of manners, her superior understanding, which placed her above all pride or affectation, and made her society so delightful, even to those over whom her birth and station elevated her, certainly appeared very overstrained and undeserved to her present companions, for poor Bessie's thoughts were so abstracted from all that was passing, that she frequently did not even hear what was addressed particularly to her. As to entering into their rather boisterous mirth, or even often comprehending its subjects, it was impossible; and the general opinion of her was, no doubt, that which one of the ladies whispered in Miss Watson's ear, "that Miss Lessie was a very yea-and-nay sort of young lady, much too fine and finikin for plain people like them, though she dare say she was well enough among her own sort of folks, who have neither heart nor soul to enjoy any real pleasure, and think everybody low and vulgar that dare give vent to their feelings, and be happy in their own way."

Miss Watson was sadly disappointed and hurt. She could not, as she said, at all account for the striking change that had taken place in Miss Leslie. If the party she had introduced her to were really low, vulgar people, she should blame herself only, and think the young lady quite right in being so reserved and silent, but it was not so. An officer's widow and her son and daughter—a dissenting clergyman and his wife, and the captain of the vessel on board of which they dined, and his family, were people not to be despised even by Miss Leslie. No, there must be some other reason for her strange manners; but, with all Miss Watson's penetration, she could not discover what was the reason. Whatever it might be, however, it soon ceased to be regarded by all but Miss Watson herself. The party had come out determined to enjoy themselves, and they very probably resolved that the whims, caprice, pride, or whatever might be the cause of Miss Leslie's silence and abstraction, should not disappoint them of their promised pleasure. Bessie, therefore, was soon left to follow her own inclinations, unmolested by any remonstrances or attempts to engage her in their amusements, nor were they inclined to shorten their stay on board, by what they considered her very unreasonable impatience to return, though that impatience was only betrayed by an occasional gentle inquiry, "What hour it was? and whether they were sure they should have light to reach home?" At last came the (on her part) long-wished-for hour of departure. They had considerably exceeded that originally appointed, for the captain's entreaties to take coffee with him had been quite irresistible, and all this time the two boatmen, who had brought the party, had been enjoying themselves unrestrainedly with the sailors in the forecastle. Unused to such persons, Bess saw nothing in their manners to give her any suspicion that they were less steady than in the morning; and her companions, all cheerfulness and jollity themselves, were in all probability as little observant as herself of their situation; but the adieus, "God bless you's," and waving of handkerchiefs to the captain and his family (who were left on board), and which were continued so long as they could distinguish them on the deck of the vessel, had no sooner ceased, than some uneasy whispers and anxious looks among the females of the party betrayed that they were not quite satisfied as to the condition of those on whom their safety depended. The gentlemen, however, at first made light of their companions' fears. There was scarcely a breath of wind, as they remarked, and what there was, as well as the tide, was all in their favour. They had still plenty of light, and they should be no time hardly going. The boatmen had passed their lives almost on the water, and, of course, for their own sakes, they would be careful. Such a thing was never in their memories heard of, as a Dover boat meeting with an accident, in fine clear weather, and open daylight, too. Such were the arguments at first used to tranquillise the timid females, but the boisterous and noisy disputes that continually recurred between the two men—the obstinacy, or what appeared obstinacy (for, of course, his passengers knew not whether he was right or wrong) of the old man, and the apparently reckless and provoking inattention to his orders of the younger one, which never failed to call forth a storm of oaths and curses from his mate, as he called him, soon produced its effects on the male party, who, though they concealed their uneasiness as far as possible, showed by their silence, and the anxious look-out they kept, that their confidence in their conductors had failed. Unfortunately, neither of the gentlemen knew anything of the management of a boat, and it had never occurred to any of the party, as Miss Watson whispered to Bess, who sat silent and pale as marble by her side.

"It never came into our foolish heads," she observed, "that, though we should be quite safe with Captain Thornhill, in going out, we should not have the same security coming back."

"My mother—my poor mother," was the only sound that escaped Bessie's tremulous lips. She knew less of the danger they were exposed to than any of her companions, but the boatmen's looks and expressions were enough to chill her blood, and when she turned from them to her companions, she read there only alarm and anxiety. It seemed as if the younger boatman comprehended, and maliciously exulted in heightening their alarm. More than once he contrived, by a mischievous manner, that the boat should ship so much water that a faint scream from one or two of the elder females betrayed the fears they could no longer suppress, while the younger ones, with more anger than alarm, deplored the injury done to their dresses, and the soaking of their silk stockings and their kid shoes—observations which drew forth a saucy chuckle from the offender, and a volley of execrations and threats from the old man, who, though excited and unsteady, from the effects of the liquor he had swallowed, was still civil and attentive to his passengers. The sun went down behind a thick bank of clouds, and a rising gale swelling the hitherto smooth waters into a rough sea, would have greatly increased their apprehensions and added to their discomfort; but now they were almost at home. They were within the harbour—there were crowds of well-dressed people and others on the beach and on the pier, watching their progress. Bessie's heart whispered that her mother and Rachel were there, and that heart beat still higher at the thought that there might be other eyes fixed upon that boat, though little suspecting that it contained any one in whom they were particularly interested. Already they were within a few yards of the landing-place, and numerous ejaculations of thankfulness for their safety, and determination never again to risk a similar peril, had broken from Bessie's companions, when either from a sudden and violent gust of wind, the mismanagement of the boatmen, or the precipitancy with which the greater number of the party sprang to their feet, in their eagerness to reach *terra firma* once more, or probably from all these causes combined, the boat was upset, at the very moment when both those on board, and those on shore, who with considerable anxiety from the indications of a coming storm had been watching their progress, were rejoicing in their safe arrival. Bess remembered nothing after the wild shriek that burst from the spectators. In that shriek, as she arose to the surface, she fancied she distinctly heard her mother's frenzied voice calling upon her child, but the waters again closed over her, and all was darkness.

CHAPTER XVIII.

I saw him beat the surges under him,
And ride upon their backs; he trod the water,
Whose enmity he flung aside, and breasted
The surge most swoll'n that met him, his bold head
'Bove the contentious waves he kept, and oar'd
Himself with his good arms in lusty strokes
To th' shore, that o'er his wave-worn basis bow'd
As stooping t relieve him.—SHAKSPEARE.

STRANGE sounds and voices were buzzing in her ears, and strange forms seemed flitting around her, when Bessie once more opened her eyes upon the world. The light pained and oppressed them, and she closed them again, with the consciousness only of intense pain in her head, a weakness that seemed to chain every faculty, and obliterate all memory of what had happened to her, and rendered her perfectly passive and unresisting to all that was passing around her. But this dreaminess and half-consciousness of existence soon yielded to more definite impressions. She was raised up in bed by the supporting arm of a female, and there were many anxious eyes fixed upon her, but they were those of strangers—no, not all—Bessie's earnest scrutiny lighted at last on one pale expressive face that she had seen before, whose ardent looks were fixed upon her with mingled fear, hope, and tenderness. It was the tall stranger, who had been the source of so much vexation and unpleasant feeling to her, and Bess, little suspecting the debt of gratitude she owed to him, hastily averted her eyes from him, while her lips faintly murmured an inquiry for her mother.

"You shall see her presently, my dear, dear child," whispered the well-known voice of Rachel, who was supporting her in her arms, while the doctor, who had been called to her assistance, held a warm cordial to Bessie's lips, and gently entreated her to swallow it.

The effect was almost instantaneous. The blush of life revisited her pale lips and cheeks, and the remembrance of the danger from which she had been rescued rushed into her mind. With clasped hands she uttered a pious ejaculation of thankfulness, and then the consciousness of her strange situation occurred to her, and she hid her face on Rachel's shoulder.

"You are convinced, now, my dear sir, that the young lady is living—thanks to your noble exertions," observed the medical attendant. "Let me then prevail upon you to retire, and take some precautions against the effect of remaining so long in your wet clothes."

The gentleman made some reply in a low voice; but Bess now comprehended the whole affair. She owed her life to Mr. Hastings, the tall stranger, and could she be so ungrateful as to let him leave the room without some acknowledgment? Timidly she raised her head from Rachel's shoulder, but her eyes met his, and in vain her tremulous lips essayed to utter a word. She stretched out her hand to him, however, and as he passionately pressed it to his lips, Mrs. Leslie, whose frantic entreaties had at last elicited the truth from the person who had been sent by Miss Watson to her servant for a change of clothes, and had insisted on being conducted to the house to which her daughter had been taken, rushed into the room.

It would be impossible to describe the

feelings of either the mother or daughter, as they remained long clasped in each other's arms, but the doctor's remonstrances at length prevailed. He represented the danger of fever to his patient, unless she was left to repose, and then he solicited Mrs. Leslie's interference with Mr. Hastings, to prevail on him also to take the necessary means to counteract the effects of his having remained so long without having changed his lower garments. His coat, it appeared, he had thrown off, at the moment he leaped into the water.

Warm and heartfelt, indeed, were the expressions of gratitude and thankfulness which the agitated mother poured out to the preserver of her child's life; but she did not forget or neglect the doctor's hint of the danger of Mr. Hastings's present situation, and at her earnest request he retired to his room, having received Mrs. Leslie's promise to see him in another apartment, as soon as she could leave her daughter.

"That will be immediately, madam, if you take my advice," observed the doctor, who overheard this brief conversation. "So far, I mean, as to leaving the young lady, for I fear there is little probability of her sleeping while you are present, and I cannot answer for the consequences, I assure you, if my directions are not attended to."

Mrs. Leslie was compelled to yield, and Bess was left to the care of Rachel, who, though perhaps little less agitated than her mistress, possessed more command of her feelings.

Bess had been conveyed by her preserver to the nearest hotel, and Mrs. Leslie, on leaving her daughter's chamber, was shown into a handsome drawing-room, where she was told Mr. Hastings would wait upon her, as soon as he had changed his clothes. A few questions to the servant who attended her, previously to his entrance, informed Mrs. Leslie that the humane man to whom she was indebted for the preservation of her child's life was a gentleman of fortune, who had resided at the hotel for some weeks. That he had several servants, a carriage, saddle-horses, &c., &c., and, although rather eccentric in his mode of living, avoiding all company, and shunning the amusements by which most visitors to a watering place contrive to kill time, he was liberal even to extravagance; and to use the young woman's own expression, "spent his money like a prince."

The talkative maid was apparently about to relate some striking proofs of Mr. Hastings' disregard for money, a *trait* which is apt to make a more favourable impression upon people of that class than any other; but she was interrupted by the entrance of the mistress of the hotel, who apologised for not having before waited upon Mrs. Leslie, by the confusion which had been created by the recent accident, in a house that was at the present time crowded with company. She had come now, by Mr. Hastings' desire, to beg that Mrs. Leslie would consider herself perfectly at home, his apartments were entirely at her disposal, and he would give immediate orders for everything conducive to her own comfort and that of the young lady.

"I assure you, ma'am," observed the landlady, after delivering the message with which she was charged, "that I am so anxious to oblige Mr. Hastings, that I have been compelled to get apartments in the neighbourhood for a family who have been here some days, in order to have two bed-rooms for you and the young lady. He is a gentleman that won't bear the slightest contradiction to his wishes; but then, as I say, he pays so liberally for any extra accommodation, that——"

Mrs. Leslie interrupted her by expressing her regret that her daughter's accident should have occasioned any inconvenience. She trusted that the latter would in the morning be sufficiently recovered to be removed to her own home; and, for herself, she could very well pass the night in the same chamber. Indeed, she would prefer doing so; for rest in the present state of her feelings was quite impossible. As to refreshment at present——

But the objection she was about to utter was interrupted by the appearance of the tea equipage, followed by Mr. Hastings himself.

That Mrs. Leslie felt more than favourably disposed towards one to whom she was under such an inestimable obligation, may be readily supposed, and the extreme respect and deference of Mr. Hastings' manner towards her, as well as the anxiety he expressed for Bessie's entire recovery, increased still more this impression. But when she spoke of her gratitude, and expressed her hopes that he would not feel any ill consequences from having been in the water, she felt rather surprised at the enthusiastic manner in which he replied, "that he should regret no personal suffering in such a cause, and should ever consider his having been the means of rescuing Miss Leslie from danger the happiest event of his life."

Mrs. Leslie's countenance probably expressed some astonishment, for her counpanion appeared, for a few moments, rather confused and embarrassed, but the good lady's surprise was considerably increased, when, after trifling with his teacup and saucer, her new friend observed—

"I can scarcely flatter myself that Miss Leslie has any recollection of our having met before, and yet, I can assure you, my dear madam, that her image has never from that period been absent from my memory. I should, I acknowledge, have devised some method of getting an introduction to her at that time, but, from the result of the inquiries I then set on foot, I was induced to believe that she was already engaged. Since then, I have tried to forget her, in change of scene and place. I concluded, of course, she was married. How, then, was I surprised at meeting her here with you, on the cliffs, a short time since. My hopes immediately revived. I thought she seemed desirous to avoid me ; but even that was flattering, for it seemed to say she had not wholly forgotten me ; and the circumstances under which we had met were so unpleasant to her, that, without any reference to myself, she might not wish to recal them. I found, by inquiries in the neighbourhood, that she was still Miss Leslie, and——"

"It is to you, sir, then, I suspect," interrupted Mrs. Leslie, "my daughter and I are indebted for——"

"Not a word of that, my dear madam," returned Mr. Hastings, hastily. "If you could know what a gratification I have derived from having it in my power, even thus clandestinely, to contribute in the slightest degree to your and Miss Leslie's comfort, you would, I am sure, feel as I do—that the favour is conferred on me."

Mrs. Leslie bowed, and Mr. Hastings proceeded.

"You cannot, my dear madam, conceive the anxiety with which I have, day after day, waited for some favourable opportunity to introduce myself, or get introduced to you or Miss Leslie. It seemed as if the very fates conspired against me ; for I have never seen either since the time I met you on the cliff. This evening, however, my good genius prevailed. I strolled accidently to the sands, and heard that considerable anxiety prevailed among those who were there collected, for the fate of a boat which ought to have been in some hours before. The indications of an approaching storm were too obvious to be mistaken, and the general opinion seemed to be, that the persons on board the boat in question were exposed to great danger. I felt, of course, much interested in the different remarks that

were made on the subject ; but just at the very moment that I was attempting to offer consolation to some persons who, I understood, had relations in the boat, and were in a dreadful state of alarm, my eye rested on the countenance of an elderly female, whom I immediately recognised as the the person whom I had seen with you and your daughter.

"I could not mistake her fixed look of agony and apprehension, as she gazed over the distant waters ; but at the very moment that I was about to address her, and learn from her what my heart foreboded was true, a general shout was raised. 'There she is—there she comes—thank God ! She will get in safe, at last !' and similar exclamations. No one, however, seemed to regard or even notice your friend, amid the general joy, and I ventured to address her. She was greatly agitated, but tears came to her relief, and I prevailed on her to accept my arm, and lean on me for support, while I assured her that there was no further occasion for alarm or anxiety. The boat was already in safety—indeed, it was already so near that there was no occasion for me to ask a question as to whom it was for whose fate she was so deeply interested—for I could distinctly see Miss Leslie's beautiful features, and her eyes turned with earnestness towards the crowd that was collected on the very edge of the water. With an impulse I could not restrain I disengaged myself from your friend or attendant, and rushed forward to be the first to receive your daughter, and conduct her to the arms of her friend—but, oh, my God, what were my sensations when, the next moment, I beheld her struggling in the water, and heard that despairing shriek that rose above all others ! I take no credit to myself, my dear madam, for what I did—I should probably have done the same for a stranger—but I felt that my very existence depended upon my saving hers, and, thank God, I succeeded !"

That this detail considerably heightened Mrs. Leslie's feelings towards her companion, may be easily imagined ; but other thoughts had also arisen in her mind, from the very candid and ardent explanation of his sentiments ; and a long and confidential conversation ensued, in which the former acknowledged that her daughter had, at the period mentioned by Mr. Hastings, as to his first interview with her, been engaged to a gentleman ; but that his circumstances not having allowed of their marriage, he had gone abroad, and all intercourse between them had long since ceased. She would also have entered into an explanation of her circumstances,

and her inability to bestow any fortune upon her daughter; but on this subject Mr. Hastings would not hear a word, though he readily entered into a detail of his own position in the world. He was, he said, the illegitimate son of a gentleman who had been high in office in the East Indies, and who had recently died there. Mr. Hastings had been sent to England for education, but had been deserted, or at least very slenderly provided for, by his father, who had married a lady of fortune, and had two children by her, while Mr. Hastings was still a boy. Cast thus, as it were, on the world, he had contended with many difficulties, he said, which were increased by a spirit that shrank from obligations, or that subservience which, as he observed, he found was expected from one who hesitated not to own that he was poor and friendless. He had, indeed, he acknowledged, no one requisite to enable him to advance himself in the world, and, unfortunately, possessed feelings that were ill-calculated to endure the constant struggle with adversity. For some years he had ceased to have any communication with his father, and would have perished, he said, rather than have sued to him, as a favour, for that assistance which, as a parent, he ought voluntarily to have conferred.

"I had been long," he continued, "earning a poor and precarious subsistence by writing for a magazine; but some weeks' serious illness had thrown me out of even this miserable pittance, and I was reduced to almost absolute despair, when I most unexpectedly received a letter from my father, who, I imagined, had long since forgotten there was such a person in existence. Some numbers of the periodical for which I had written had fallen into his hands. He thought much more highly of those that bore my signature than they deserved, and one paper especially, I believe, found its way to his heart—for in it I had spoken freely the sentiments of mine—and in a tale, part truth and part fiction, had painted the misery too often resulting from such love, if that could be called love, which condemns its object to infamy, and brands the innocent offspring of such connexions with indelible disgrace.

"Whatever had been his feelings, my father now appeared sincerely desirous of compensating for his long neglect of his son. He wrote to me, through the publisher, placing at my disposal a larger sum than ever I had before possessed, and expressed, in warm terms, the pleasure it would give him to see me once more. There existed no longer, he said, those causes which had prevented his acknowledging our relationship. It was now too late in life for him to think of returning to England, in which, he said, he knew not that he possessed a single tie, besides myself; and he concluded in a strain that awakened, at once, all my long dormant feelings towards him—lamenting that, after forty years of toil and struggle to acquire riches, he now found himself alone in the world, and without the enjoyment of that, for the attainment of which he had sacrificed so much. His children had both died in the prime of life—his wife had recently followed them to that 'bourne from whence no traveller returns.'—'And I,' he concluded, 'am fast sinking into the grave, without a single friend—one of my own 'kith and kin'—to close my eyes. If you, Clement, feel but half as warmly as you have forcibly portrayed the misery of being alone in the world, you will hasten to one who has now

no other hope or object but to die in your arms.'

"I am wearying you, I am afraid, with my long story, my dear Mrs. Leslie," observed Mr. Hastings, "but it is nearly concluded. I answered my father's letter in person, and my reception exceeded even my most sanguine expectations. My attentions and society seemed for a time to rekindle his fast-declining energies; but my hopes that his life might be prolonged soon faded, and he died, happily, as he wished, in my arms, before I had been two years resident in India. With the exception of a few trifling bequests, the whole of his large property was bequeathed to me, and it might naturally be supposed, my dear mother, that with the uncontrolled possession of upwards of five thousand a year, I must be a happy man—but such was not the case. I was again alone in the world—an unconnected, isolated being; and, most unfortunately for myself, my experience of the world had been of a nature to jaundice my feelings towards it. For the luxuries and pleasures which wealth only can command, I had no relish; and still less was I inclined to derive any pleasure from adding to my hoards. But I will not weary you with my ineffectual pursuit of the shadow of happiness, which seemed constantly to recede, when it was apparently within my grasp.

"It was my father's earnest desire and recommendation to me to marry; but whether from my own fastidiousness, or that I had really been unfortunate in the limited circle of families to whom I had at different times been introduced, I know not; but never, until the moment I beheld your daughter, did I see one who at all resembled the portrait my fancy had sketched of her to whom I could willingly devote my existence.

"You will, perhaps, think me foolishly romantic, but it is nevertheless true, that from that moment her image has been the worshipped, cherished idol of my imagination. Yet it was not so much her beauty, as the extreme modesty and innocence, and the exquisite sensibility that her every look and motion betrayed, that impressed her image so deeply on my heart. The dignity with which she repressed the impertinence of those two fops of fashion, who accompanied her to the shop, and who I afterwards learned, when too late, had been the cause of the painful accident she had met with—gave me assurance of her superior understanding. The crimson blushes which checked even my own, perhaps, too ardent gaze—her voice—her smile—but *you* are smiling, I see, at the lover's rhapsody, although none so well as you can know that the object of it is deserving all, or more than I can say in her praise."

Mrs. Leslie's smile, however, was rather that of pleasure than raillery of the ardent lover. Truly, indeed, she felt, as he had said, that Bessie deserved his praise; but it was not for her to descant upon the merits of her daughter, and she only, therefore, expressed a hope that a farther acquaintance would confirm Mr. Hastings' favourable opinion of Bess.

"So far, indeed," she added, "I may be allowed to say, that as a daughter her conduct has been irreproachable. Never has a word or act of my dear Bessie's cost me a tear or even a sigh. She is, indeed, the only hope, as she has been the only support of her widowed mother through scenes of distress and suffering which must have crushed her to the earth, had she not had this one prop to lean upon."

The expressive countenance of Mr. Hastings evinced at once his satisfaction at the unaffected tribute to the domestic virtues of the lovely girl who had made so deep an impression on his heart, and his sympathy with those sorrows, the remembrance of which shook every fibre of the agitated mother's frame, and drew forth a flood of tears from her eyes. By degrees he succeeded in drawing from her the contemplation of the heavy affliction which had befallen her, and once more the future, which he trusted and hoped to make a happy future to her, engaged her attention.

"How easily do we believe the things
We wish were true."

Already prepossessed most powerfully in Mr. Hastings' favour, not only by the strong tie of gratitude, but from his candour—his manners—the respect and tenderness which he evinced in every word and action towards her, Mrs. Leslie believed it impossible that Bess could be long indifferent to the passion he avowed for her. She (Mrs. Leslie) had never properly understood the circumstances of the rupture that had taken place between Ronald Leicester and her daughter, but she had learned from the latter that their engagement was finally dissolved; and as she was well convinced that the fault, whatever it might be, did not lie on Bessie's side, she had naturally arrived at the conclusion that Leicester's constancy had not stood the test of absence—that touchstone of true affection, and that he had voluntarily broken the pledge between himself and Bess. It was impossible for her to

be blind to the sufferings the latter had endured on this account—sufferings which spoke, with more eloquence than any language could have expressed, the depth and sincerity of her affection for her (supposed) ungrateful and faithless lover. And yet, although Mrs. Leslie knew this—knew that Bessie's life had nearly been the sacrifice of her pure and ardent attachment, she was already beginning to indulge the pleasing and flattering anticipation that the void which Leicester's treachery and desertion had left in her daughter's heart would be more worthily and more advantageously filled by Mr. Hastings. Advantageously—shall we confess the truth—yes, for we aim not to draw

"Such faultless monsters as the world ne'er saw;"

but poor human nature, with all its mixtures of vices and virtues, strength and weakness.

"Virtuous and vicious every man must be,
Few in the extreme but all in the degree;
On life's vast ocean diversely we sail,
Reason the card, but passion is the gale."

We are then, as faithful historians, constrained to confess that Mrs. Leslie was but too susceptible of the worldly advantages of the marriage of her daughter with the possessor of upwards of five thousand a year. The kind-hearted but weak mother was dazzled with the prospect of seeing her beloved child elevated beyond what, in their present comparatively humble situation, she could have dared to hope; and though, from her knowledge of Bessie's character, a fear sometimes intruded that Mr. Hastings would meet with greater difficulties than he seemed to anticipate, she could not bear to damp his hopes by acknowledging those fears.

True love, it is said, is ever diffident and distrustful, but it must be acknowledged that, at present, these qualities seemed to enter very little into the complexion of Mr. Hastings' passion. He felt he had secured Mrs. Leslie's warm interest. She had assured him that Bessie's heart was at her disposal. Perhaps she herself believed this assertion, for could she for a moment suppose that her high-minded, noble-spirited daughter would still indulge, and secretly cherish, an affection for one who had renounced her? At all events it was certain, for Bessie's own lips, and they were truth itself, had assured her so. The tie that had existed between her and Ronald Leicester was severed, and her only study henceforth would be to forget that it had ever existed.

"Do not ask me, my dear mother, to enter into any detail of the cause that had produced this," Bess had observed on the only occasion that she ever spoke on the subject. "You will, I know, believe that it is no light cause that has induced me to release Mr. Leicester from his engagements. It is for his happiness, as well as mine, that we part for ever."

It could not be supposed then or expected, argued Mrs. Leslie with herself, that Bessie was to condemn herself to a single life, and her friends to the mortification of seeing her reject an opportunity of establishing herself in the world, if an advantageous offer were made to her, and what offer could be more unexceptionable than the present one? Five thousand a year—a gentlemanly person—superior education and accomplishments—and, above all, passionately devoted to her. Oh, no, Bess could not, would not be so blind to her own interest and happiness, so indifferent to her mother's comfort and peace, which, as far as she was concerned, would be permanently secured by this alliance, as to reject Mr. Hastings, from a foolish, girlish attachment to one who had renounced and deserted her.

Mrs. Leslie fancied that she had argued herself into the belief that all would finally accord with her now most earnest wish and desire—yet, that she was not quite so well assured on the subject, as she tried to be, and to appear to be to her elected son-in-law, was evident from the hints she frequently contrived to throw in, in the course of their long and confidential conversation, to check his impatience, and prove that it would be advisable not to act with too much precipitancy in making his proposals. A piece of advice which, although he promised to be guided by it, was evidently not very acceptable or agreeable. An obstacle, however, presented itself to the speedy fulfilment of their mutual wishes, that neither Mrs. Leslie nor her new friend had anticipated.

Even before he retired for the night, Mr. Hastings was seized with shiverings that showed he was not likely wholly to escape the natural consequence of his imprudence, in having remained so long in his wet clothes; and Mrs. Leslie's inquiries for him, in the morning, were answered by his servant, that his master had been so restless and feverish all night, that he was unwillingly compelled to excuse himself from breakfasting with her, as he had intended; but he should be able, he trusted, to join her at the dinner-table. Dinner time, however, found his illness much increased, and Bess and her mother both sincerely regretted at hearing from the doctor who had been called in to see him,

that there was every reason to fear that Mr. Hastings would have a severe illness. Fortunately for Bess, her accident was followed by no serious consequences; and, had she been allowed to follow her own inclinations, she felt herself, before the next evening, quite well enough to return to her own home. This, however, was strongly opposed by Mrs. Leslie. She had visited Mr. Hastings in his bed-room, and had given her promise to him that she would not leave the house, until he was able to leave his chamber; and, though she did not think it expedient to tell this to Bess, she represented to her that it would appear ungrateful to her friend and benefactor to hurry away the moment they were able to leave the house, when he expressed so anxious a wish that they should stay until he was sufficiently recovered to accompany them.

To this reasoning Bess was compelled to yield. How, indeed, could she for a moment oppose her own wishes to those of the preserver of her life? She had heard from Rachel the whole account of the danger he had encountered for her sake; for, though her companions in the boat had from their vicinity to the shore been speedily got out of the water, without any mischief beyond the fright and a complete wetting, she had drifted a considerable distance, and twice sunk, before Mr. Hastings reached her, and, but for his exertions, must inevitably have perished.

Bess could not bear this, it may be supposed, without a thrill of gratitude to her preserver; and yet she was uneasy and discomposed at the manner of both her mother and Rachel, when they spoke of him; and this uneasiness was greatly increased by her observing how well satisfied her mother appeared to be at remaining the guest of Mr. Hastings.

For herself, every hour seemed painfully to add to the obligation she was under to him, and she felt almost angry with her mother for making so light apparently of her scruples on that point. But that anger was increased when Mrs. Leslie observed, with a smile, that it would be insulting to Mr. Hastings, possessing an income of five thousand a year, to suppose that he would even think, for an instant, of the additional expense of their residence there.

Bess gazed for a moment at her mother with utter astonishment, but Mrs. Leslie affected not to see it, and continued—

"To convince you, my dear, that Mr. Hastings is not very likely to regret the burthen that seems to weigh so heavily on your mind, I must tell you that I have discovered a little secret, that——"

"Mamma, I do not wish to hear any secret connected with Mr. Hastings," interrupted Bess, hastily.

The tone of raillery which Mrs. Leslie had assumed, evidently to disguise deeper feelings, was instantly checked. She looked vexed and disappointed, and then, as if suddenly recollecting herself, observed—

"I believe, Bess, that my feelings are quite as tenacious as your own, as to subjecting myself or you to obligations which I have no prospect of repaying, and I, therefore, request that you will rely on my judgment in the present instance."

Bessie's eyes were cast down, and she made no further attempt to renew the subject, though she could not divest herself of the uneasy feeling that her mother had stronger reasons than she had avowed for her ready acceptance of the hospitality of Mr. Hastings.

The increasing and soon alarming illness of Mr. Hastings, however, banished all selfish feelings and anticipations from Bessie's bosom. He was, indeed, dangerously ill, and her sorrow and regret were unbounded that she should have been the cause of his sufferings.

Rachel had now transferred her attendance to his sick bed. For nearly a week she did not leave him, day or night; and Mrs. Leslie herself, who passed hours by his bed-side, seemed to have forgotten every other subject of regret or sorrow in her anxiety for the result of his illness. It was impossible for Bess to misunderstand the expression of his eyes or words during the brief visit she paid him on the third morning of his confinement to his room, at his earnest request, that he might convince himself, as he said, by his own eyes and ears, that she was indeed so perfectly recovered as her mother and Rachel represented her to be. But the crisis of the fever approached, and the two physicians who had been called in suggested the propriety of his being made acquainted with his imminent danger, in order, as they observed, if he had any friends whom he wished to be summoned, or any wordly affairs to settle, it might be done ere it was too late.

It was Rachel who, in broken and tremulous accents, communicated this to him. She had become so attached to him, during the few days that she had been his constant and almost his only companion, that she was overwhelmed with grief at the probability of his death being so near.

"Friends," he repeated, with a placid smile, "friends—my kind, good Rachel, I have none beside yourself and——but, for

their sake, I must not delay what, indeed, I ought to have done at the commencement of this illness. I have been very thoughtless and forgetful, but, thank God, it is not too late to repair that fault. My will can soon be made, for I have but few instructions to give. Will you ring and request Mrs. Houseman will direct one of my servants to summon an attorney? She can, of course, recommend some professional person to execute the necessary document."

Rachel, drowned in tears, hesitated for a few moments, and he closed his eyes, as if to collect his thoughts.

"It is hard, too," he murmured, "to die just at the very moment that I seem to have that happiness within my reach which has so long eluded me. But His will be done. I shall not—" and he opened his eyes and looked up with a momentary flash of their wonted brilliancy—"I shall not die amid strangers, nor quite unwept and unlamented. Yes, *her* beautiful dove-like eyes will——Rachel, you still here? I thought I was alone. Do not, my kind friend, delay a moment longer. I shall be happier and easier when this, perhaps the last act by which I can prove the sincerity of my respect and love, is concluded. Go to Mrs. Houseman yourself, but do not agitate Mrs. Leslie, or my beloved Bessie, by letting them know what I am about to do."

Rachel obeyed, and before two hours had passed, Mr. Hastings had placed his signature to the will, which constituted Bess Leslie heiress to the whole of his wealth, with no other exceptions than handsome legacies to his servants, whom he recommended also to her future favour. A thousand pounds to Mrs. Leslie, as a token of respect and friendship, and three hundred a year for life to Rachel Myton, as a proof of the testator's gratitude, at the same time expressing an earnest hope and desire that she would not, under any circumstances, separate from her and his beloved friend, Bess Leslie.

Rachel's audible sobs interrupted the stillness of the sick-room repeatedly, while the cold and formal man of law read over, in a monotonous tone, this princely testimony to the regard in which she was held by Mr. Hastings—he alone was calm and unmoved; but when the business was concluded, and he and Rachel were left alone together,

"Thank God," he observed, as she removed the pillow on which he had been raised in order to affix his signature. "Thank God that I have nothing now on my mind, if I must die—but I will tell you candidly, my kind friend, that I still hope—Yes, long that I may live. It seems, indeed, that with such a prospect of happiness before me——"

A heavy faintness, however, at this moment came over him—it was the consequence, probably, of the exertions he had made; but to Rachel it appeared a sad foreboutement that his hopeful anticipations with you and Leslie. In a few minutes he again opened his eyes, and would have resumed his observations, but he yielded to her earnest request to try and take some repose.

"I will—I will, Rachel," he replied, and calm, tranquil, and docile as a child he lay down, and closed his eyes. Suddenly, a painful thought seemed to arouse him. "It may be that if I sleep, it will be the sleep of death! Tell me, I do not fear it, but do you think that there is a probability that I may not awaken again to consciousness? If it be so, let me see Bessie once more. I would not distress—I will not even utter a word, if you desire it—but let me have the satisfaction of gazing once more upon her, that she may be the last object—my eyes are very heavy, Rachel, and soon, perhaps—do not deny me."

Rachel could not resist this entreaty, though, from what the physicians had said, she considered this heaviness rather a favourable symptom than otherwise; and she hastened to the drawing-room, where Bess was sitting with her mother. Their first glance at Rachel's agitated countenance occasioned both to start up in alarm, but Bessie's look betrayed reluctance when informed of Rachel's errand.

"If I could do him any good," she observed, "I am sure I would not hesitate, but it is so painful to see him——"

Rachel interrupted her with the most bitter reproaches for her cruelty and ingratitude to one whose last act had been to prove his devoted attachment to her; and Mrs. Leslie, who fully understood the meaning of what appeared to Bess a mystery, added to the alarm and astonishment of the latter, by exclaiming—

"Bess, I command you, on your duty, to comply with the wish of Mr. Hastings. For your own sake go, my dear child," she added, in a milder tone, "for you will, I am sure, bitterly regret your refusal, if—"

Bess did not wait to hear the conclusion of the sentence, but glided, with a quick step that left even Rachel behind, to the chamber of the invalid, and when the latter entered she beheld her, pale and trembling, bending over him who was unconscious of her presence.

Rachel stole softly to her side, and her heart throbbed with apprehension. Bess grasped her arm, as she whispered—

"He is not dead? Oh, no, Rachel, do not say that he is dead!"

But it seemed that her voice, gentle as it was, could pierce even the death-like heaviness of the slumber that enchained his senses. He opened his eyes, and recognised the lovely face that was leaning over his—he smiled tenderly, and stretched out a hand attenuated almost to a shadow. Bess could not resist this. Her own trembling hand was placed in his, and for hours that he remained silent and motionless, she did not withdraw from the position she had unconsciously assumed, on her knees by his bedside.

It was midnight before Mrs. Leslie, fearful of the consequences to Bessie's health, still so precarious and delicate, gently disengaged the hand of the latter; and after having stood a few minutes by his side to ascertain that he was not disturbed by this movement, gently led her daughter to her own room, to seek repose. But Bess was too powerfully excited to sleep, and Mrs. Leslie, who felt some explanation was due to her daughter for the unwonted harshness with which she had herself spoken, and the vehemence of Rachel's reproaches, proceeded to relate to the former all that she had heard from Rachel, as to Mr. Hastings' disposal of his property. Bess turned first red, and then pale. It was evident she was more distressed than gratified by the information. In a low tone, as if speaking to herself, she observed—

"God in his infinite mercy grant that he may live to release me from——"

She paused, for she saw her mother's eyes were earnestly fixed upon her, as if she would read her very heart.

"I hope, indeed, he will live, my dear child," she observed, with emphasis.

"And you think he will—do you not, dear mamma?" returned Bess, hastily.

"There is a probability of it, my dear, I think; but a few hours will decide it; try, then, and sleep for a short time, that if he should awake again to consciousness he may have the satisfaction of seeing you by his side. Gratitude, Bess, must suggest to you that——my dear, dear child, why do you clap your hands, and look so despairingly?"

"Because I do indeed despair, my dear mother," returned Bess, in a voice of anguish; "because I see," she continued, "whither all this gratitude, that you lay such stress on, is driving me. I am grateful, truly grateful to Mr. Hastings, for risking his life to save mine; but it is a poor gift, indeed, if in return he requires that I should sacrifice my every hope of happiness—that I should falsify my own conscience and feelings by uniting myself to a man that I cannot love. Mother, I cannot—I could not marry Mr. Hastings. I have no heart to give him, and I——Oh, if you knew, feeling as I do towards him, how oppressive is even the thoughts that I should be indebted——"

"There is time enough for this discussion, Bess," returned Mrs. Leslie, gravely. "You are foolishly excited, and I will not talk to you now. Do, pray, go to bed."

Bess was, indeed, excited—she was more than excited. For the first time in her life she felt that her mother's wishes and sentiments were in direct opposition to her own. And Rachel, too, even she was arrayed against her; suspicions, that brought a blush of shame to her cheek, entered her yet pure and unsullied mind. She suspected that both her mother and Rachel exaggerated the danger of Mr. Hastings, to take advantage of her feelings, and draw her into concessions from which she could not, upon his recovery, retreat. At one moment she reproached herself with ingratitude, and at the next shrunk with horror from the thought that her mother, and Rachel, too, should be so dazzled by the riches of Mr. Hastings as to wish her to dissemble her feelings towards him.

"Willingly would I give my life to save him, if it were possible," she exclaimed; "but I cannot sacrifice my own—I cannot forswear myself—I cannot, no, I cannot forget!"

Bess was wrong in her suspicions. Mr. Hastings was really in imminent danger; and although both Mrs. Leslie and Rachel without doubt considered that a marriage with him was calculated to ensure Bessie's happiness, they were actuated by no other motive than kindness towards him in their present conduct. They saw that the happiness of this romantic and enthusiastic being depended upon Bess, and they considered that gratitude demanded of her that at such a moment she should lay aside every consideration, or feeling of reluctance, for his sake.

To Mrs. Leslie, indeed, Bessie's opposition appeared quite to wild, as she could not but acknowledge to herself Mr. Hastings' ardent passion was for one of whom he had seen so little; but Bessie's violent agitation on the subject alarmed her, and she resolved, whatever might be the result, she would not again urge her daughter into any concession that was contrary to her feelings.

CHAPTER XIX.

At that sweet voice wild passion's thrill
    Is chained 'neath reason's holy sway,
And thought, though all unfettered still,
    Moves calmly on his sober way.—ANON.

If we stand still,
In fear our motion will be mocked or carped at,
We should take root here where we sit, or sit
State statues only.—ANON.

BESSIE'S presentiment that Mr. Hastings would live proved correct. He awoke from his long sleep, calm and refreshed, but it was with difficulty Mrs. Leslie evaded his earnest inquiry for her daughter. The assurance, however, that she had remained with him many hours, and in fact had not quitted his bedside until convinced that his profound sleep assured his anxious friends that his disorder had taken a favourable turn, at length reconciled him to her absence; but, when hour after hour passed away without his seeing her, his impatience became so evident, that his careful attendant, Rachel, began to fear the irritation would have the effect of bringing back his fever, and entreated Mrs. Leslie to use her influence to persuade Bess to visit him, if it were only for a few minutes. It had likewise occurred to Rachel's mind to consider Mr. Hastings' attachment to Bess a very extraordinary occurrence, viewing her in the light she did, as the loveliest, the best, and most attractive of human beings, it was quite natural in her eyes that Mr. Hastings should have the same opinion of her merits; but now, as she watched the expression of his eyes, and saw that it was impossible to divert his attention from the one object that seemed to engross every thought or care, a fearful thought stole into her mind that this all-absorbing passion was rather the effect of mental derangement than the attachment of a rational being. Such an idea, once aroused, is of all others the most likely to find corroboration even in the most trifling incidents. During the first part of her patient's illness, Rachel had attributed most of his passionate expressions and incoherencies to the delirium of fever. But the physician had now pronounced him quite free from fever, and yet the same fire was kindled in his eye, and the same romantic and exaggerated language was used, whenever he spoke of Bess. He seemed to have no suspicion that it was possible the object of this ardent passion might reject his addresses, and the only subject of his uneasiness appeared to be the fear that she had not entirely recovered from the effects of her late accident.

Rachel, too, now recalled the various hints that had been dropped by the servants of their master's eccentricity, or as they termed it, "odd ways." Even Mrs. Houseman, the mistress of the hotel, though lauding to the skies his generosity, had said that he was very whimsical, and had strange out-of-the-way fancies. But then, as Rachel's good sense suggested, everything that differs from their own selfish common-place ways is looked upon by narrow-minded, vulgar people, as proofs of madness.

All Rachel's reasoning and reflection, however, failed in enabling her to come to a satisfactory conclusion as to Mr. Hastings' perfect sanity, although it must be confessed that the bare suspicion had the effect of greatly diminishing the warm interest she had felt in his success with Bess, and rendered her very cautious in saying anything to her patient that could have the effect of encouraging the hope he evidently indulged, that his proposals would be accepted by the object of his devoted affection.

Rachel, however, determined not to be guided in her decision by her own fallible judgment, hinted her suspicion to one of the physicians; but the doctor, after listening to all she had to say, smilingly reproved her for giving way to such ungrounded suspicion.

"It is very natural," he observed, "that to you and I, my good lady, (who have long passed the hey-day of youth) the vagaries of a passionate lover should appear more like madness than the dictates of sober reason, but I would certainly advise you not to mention your suspicions to the young lady or her friends. It would, indeed, be an act of injustice to Mr. Hastings to do so, and might hereafter be productive of much uneasiness. It is a suspicion, in fact, that ought never to be spoken of, unless you can produce the strongest confirmation; and really, in this instance, I cannot discover the slightest proof of the truth of your suggestion."

Rachel was certainly far from being desirous that its truth should be proved; for, though as far removed from a mercenary disposition as possible, and quite as well convinced as Bess herself that Mr. Hastings' five thousand a year could not alone confer happiness, she saw too many advantages to her darling in a union with him, not to be anxious that it should be brought about. In her eyes, indeed, (that one impediment removed which she was willing to believe originated only inly in her own foolish imagination), her interesting patient possessed every requisite to ensure happiness to the fortunate object of his choice.

Among all the chances and changes of her chequered life, as Rachel would sometimes smilingly say, it had never happened to her to fall in love. She did not pretend to assert, like many old maids, that she had never met with a man whom she considered worthy of her virgin heart; but, as she would laughingly observe, "It was so ordained that those on whom she could have bestowed her preference were not inclined to prefer her, and, on the contrary, those who had taken it into their heads to bestow their good will upon her, were precisely the sort of persons whom she could not *fancy*." Never having, therefore, been silly enough, as she would have said, to fall in love, Rachel could not be supposed to have any very accurate ideas on the subject of that mysterious passion. She had been a witness, indeed, of the struggles which Bess had endured between reason and passion, before she could finally resolve to dismiss Ronald Leicester from the place he had held in her heart; but having at length, (so she had repeatedly assured Rachel), conquered, and being fully determined to forget him, she could see no objection Bess could make to one who in her (Rachel's) opinion, was in every respect, except a handsome face, infinitely Mr. Leicester's superior.

Having, therefore, made up her mind that Bessie's happiness would be secured by this marriage, and having, from Doctor Stanfield's assurances, become quite convinced that the only impediment, as it seemed to her, to that happiness was merely the suggestion of her own foolish imagination, she became almost as anxious for Bessie's re-appearance at the bedside of the invalid, as Mr. Hastings, and willingly yielded to his request that she would go and ascertain herself what was the cause of her young lady's absence.

Bess cou'd assign no cause, but that she had before given to her mother, namely, her disinclination, or rather determination, not to mislead Mr. Hastings as to her sentiments towards him, as it was repugnant to her ingenuous character to act a part she did not feel. She was now cool, calm, and much more rational than she had been in the former discussion with her mother, but she persevered in her declaration that no consideration could ever bring her to regard Mr. Hastings with any other feelings than those of gratitude and respect; and that, until he was convinced of this, and was content to receive her only as a friend, she thought it advisable that she should abstain from visiting him.

Rachel, however, contended that the present was not the time to communicate such unwelcome information; that it was more decided that her dear Bess could ——— ——— dictates of common humanity ——— would say nothing ——— ——— common humanity ——— ——— her refusing ——— ——— on which he ——— ——— who ever ——— ——— hovering on the very brink of the grave—and for her own too.

——— overborne ——— prudent ——— ———

Mrs. Leslie's and Rachel's hopes revived —but they had now learned caution in the expression of them; and Bess no longer distressed by reference to the ——— more on their parts, or obtrusive declarations of passion from Mr. Hastings, gave free scope to the natural kindness and humanity of her disposition, and became the most active and efficient of the invalid's attendants.

Happiness is a most powerful restorative. Mr. Hastings's expressive countenance evinced that he was now perfectly happy; and, though his recovery was slow and tedious, it was no longer doubtful. Whether that as his mind grew "stronger with his body," he became aware that his former passionate expressions and declarations were not likely to make a favourable impression on Bessie, or that Rachel's gentle hints to the same purpose had taken due effect—certain it was that his manner had become much less impassioned, more consistent, and, to Bess, infinitely more pleasant.

She was no longer treated as an idol, whose worship was to engross every thought and look, but as a rational, sensi-

ble, and agreeable companion. Every hour, indeed, enhanced the value of Bessie's society in his estimation, and rendered him more solicitous to secure her ———; while Bess no longer harassed and distressed by declarations of a passion which appeared to her as irrational as ——— ——— awarded full justice to ——— ——— of his sentiments ——— ——— and unworldliness of ———.

As a brother and friend she should esteem—love ——— but him ——— she avowed ——— belong to her mother, but in no ——— to him; and Mrs. Leslie, with perhaps a better knowledge of the human heart ——— could ———.

Mr. Hastings recovered sufficiently to ——— began to ——— on the property of their ——— apartments which ——— day to day, at his ——— now, how——— against it, ——— caused by ——— Watson, their ——— accident ——— introducing Mrs. ——— her daughter into their present ———.

——— inmates ——— to them ——— Hastings ——— that ——— more ——— quite un——— conversation that ——— passed between the sister and her mother.

On the morning, however, that Mr. Hastings was, for the first time, to dine with his friends, out of his own chamber, Miss Watson was announced as a visitor to Mrs. and Miss Leslie, and was shown into the drawing-room, where Bess was sitting alone, her mother being walking in the garden belonging to the hotel. After the first usual salutations and inquiries, Miss Watson congratulated Bess on the fortunate results of an accident which threatened so different a termination.

There was a meaning in the look that accompanied these words, that puzzled Bess to comprehend; but it was soon explained by the spinster's adding—

"Now, my dear Miss Leslie, I hope you won't think I am taking too great a liberty in asking you to let me be bridesmaid. Do you know that I have never yet had the good fortune to be asked to a wedding, and I have such a desire, you can't think, and, as I said to my friend Mrs. Holmes, this morning, I know Miss Leslie can't be engaged, and she is so kind, and so free from pride, that I am certain she will not refuse me, if I speak in time; and I have got a beautiful lavender silk dress, not made up, and my white satin bonnet can be made up again, as good as new, for it's very little the worse for the wetting it got the other day; and that, with a blonde veil and my lady scarf, will be the very thing for a wedding dress, you know. I shan't have a shilling to lay out, except for a veil, and that I've been promising myself for a long time—they're so useful, and look so dressy, don't they?"

Miss Watson's arrangements and opinions had been delivered with so much volubility and self-satisfaction, and Bessie's astonishment and, it may be added, vexation had been so great that she had in vain attempted to interrupt her, until the former at length paused for want of breath, and an answer to her question.

"My dear Miss Watson," she at last observed, "I really cannot imagine what has put it into your head to make such an application to me, for I assure you, most sincerely, I have no thoughts of matrimony. I hope, indeed, the disappointment will not very seriously affect you," she continued, forcing a laugh, "for if your wearing your pretty bridal dress depends on my marrying, I suspect it will be by till it is faded, or gone out of fashion."

"You can't be so serious, Miss Leslie," replied the spinster, staring incredulously at Bess, "or, perhaps, you mean to be married in London, but——"

"I am quite serious, my dear madam, when I assure you that I have no intention of marrying at all," returned Bess, gravely; "nay, more, I will, if it be any satisfaction to you, give you my word that it is at present my firm determination never to marry; and now I hope, in return for my candour, you will tell me what has induced you to think there was a probability——"

"Probability, my dear," sharply returned Miss Watson, "how could I or anybody think otherwise, after—but I assure you, I heard, from Mrs. Houseman herself, that everything was settled; and indeed how, my dear, to speak plainly, could anybody think otherwise, when you have been living in such a sort of way? Upon my word, I must speak the truth. I think your mamma has not been so prudent as could be wished, for there are always people ill-natured enough to take advantage—and, as I said to a friend of mine this very morning, when she repeated a scandalous story she had heard about your

former acquaintance with Mr. Hastings in London, and your coming down here after him—I told her that in the first place I did not believe a word of it—though it might be possible that you and Mr. Hastings had met before in company—as I knew, whatever your present circumstances might be, that you had very genteel connections, and had at one time lived in very different style to what you do now; but as to your having ever been a light character, I was very certain it was an abominable falsehood, because not only your own conduct and manners contradict it, but that I had the best of recommendations of you from my cousin Lorton; and so far from your having thrown yourself in Mr. Hastings' or anybody else's way, it had often been surprising to me to see how close you kept at home. Never going to show yourself at the libraries, or any where else, where you would be likely to meet with company. No, I said, Mrs. Holmes, I would not believe——"

"Pray who is Mrs. Holmes, madam," demanded Bess, suppressing all appearance of anger or agitation, "and by what authority does she take upon herself to judge of my conduct, or rather to impute conduct to me that——"

"Mr. Holmes, my dear?—bless me, don't you remember she is my neighbour, that I told you was so envious and jealous when you first came down, because her apartments had been standing empty for near three months," replied the voluble spinster. "It seems," she continued, "that Mrs. Holmes has got a single gentleman and his servant, now, and a very good lodger he is, too—at least, so she says; but they are all good lodgers at first, till they find out her mean ways, and how she imposes upon them, and turns they're everything that's bad, and——"

Bess, however, did not want to hear the history of Mrs. Holmes's speculations, or her disputes with her lodgers, and she therefore hastily interrupted her visitor.

"But what has all this to do with me, Miss Watson, or why should this Mrs. Holmes interfere with——"

"I will tell you, if you will allow me, Miss Leslie," returned Miss Watson, evidently angry at the hasty and somewhat haughty tone Bess had assumed. "This gentleman (I forget his name, though I've heard it so often, for Mrs. Holmes can talk as usual of nobody but her new lodger) happened to see you, it seems, in my garden, the very day before that unlucky excursion that had like to have ended so fatally for us all. He asked her, it seems, a good many questions about you, and when

Mrs. Holmes said that you were a Miss Leslie, who had come down from London in ill health with your mother, who was a clergyman's widow, he laughed and said, 'Indeed,' very significantly, as much as to say, as Mrs. Holmes observed, 'It was a very fine story, and he knew better.' Mrs. Holmes, of course, asked him if he had ever seen you before, and he made answer, 'Certainly not, if the lady's name is Leslie, and she is the respectable person you represent her.'

"Mrs. Holmes, however, was not the person to be put off with such an answer, because, as she said, she saw there was some mystery in it, and so she said she knew nothing about you herself, and wouldn't answer for your respectability, and that she should be very sorry to see me imposed upon, as I was a single woman, who had always borne an excellent character—I am sure, by the by, I am surprised if she did say so, for she is the most scandalising, ill-natured, envious—"

"Do, pray, go on, Miss Watson: was there anything more said about me?" interrupted Bess.

"Of course it's very natural you should be anxious, Miss Leslie, on such a subject," returned Miss Watson, greatly offended; "but really I am not used to be catechised, or talked to as if I were a child, or a servant. If you'll let me go on, I'll tell you the rest."

Bess apologised, and the lady proceeded, though in a very sulky tone.

"All Mrs. Holmes could say or do, she couldn't get any explanation from the gentleman then, except that he certainly had seen you in a very different situation to what you were in now, and under a different name, too; and Mrs. Holmes had made up her mind, as she said, to come and tell me how I was imposed upon at the first opportunity. But the very next day, the accident happened, and you know I caught such a cold, and that and the fright together confined me to my bed for several days, and Mrs. Holmes, for a wonder, was considerate enough not to worry me by telling me what she had heard, though she threw out some hints how strange it was that the gentleman who had saved your life should have been an old acquaintance of yours, although you appeared to be so totally a stranger here. This, it seemed, she had learned from somebody who saw the whole affair, and who had told her that Mr. Hastings was in conversation with Mrs. Rachel, and evidently anxiously waiting for your landing; and the same person repeated every word Mr. Hastings uttered, both before he

jumped into the water, and after he got you out, and that showed that, far from being a stranger, he was violently attached to you.

"Well, Miss Leslie, it came into my head, then, where all the presents came from that had seemed to be such a mystery to you and your mamma; but I did not say anything to Mrs. Holmes about it, though I certainly thought it very sly of you, for I couldn't doubt you knew all about it, though Mrs. Leslie might not."

"You were mistaken then," observed Bess, hastily, "I knew nothing of——"

"Stop a bit, if you please, Miss Leslie," interrupted Miss Watson, "it will be time enough, when I've told you all, for you to defend yourself, or prove that——"

The sharp impertinent tone in which this was uttered roused all Bessie's pride and natural spirit.

"You do not suppose, madam," she hastily interrupted, "that I am going to enter into any vindication of myself against the slanderous assertions of Mrs. Holmes and her nameless lodger?"

"Her lodger is a gentleman, Miss Leslie, or rather was, for he's gone now," returned Miss Watson, with increased sharpness, "and as to his being nameless, that's only my forgetful memory. I don't believe that he had any reason to deny his name, or to take another than his true name, to suit his convenience as some people do."

This was too pointed an insult for Bess any longer to feel the slightest wish to convince or conciliate her visitor. She was desirous, indeed, of hearing whether any further remarks respecting her had been uttered by the unmanly slanderer, who had thus, without any apparent motive, attempted to ruin the fair fame of an innocent girl; but it was, she felt, a degradation to listen for another minute to Miss Watson's insolent insinuations, and she therefore, with as much calmness as she could assume, arose from her seat and rang the bell, observing,—

"As the motive of your visit to me is quite sufficiently apparent, madam, and I do not wish to prolong a conversation so dissatisfactory to both parties, I shall take the liberty of wishing you good morning."

Miss Watson, who had at first also risen from her seat, in some confusion at Bessie's haughty and dignified manner, seemed suddenly to recover her self-possession, as Bess moved towards an inner door, which communicated with her mother's bed-room.

"Oh, but I'm not going to be put off, ma'am, in this manner, for all your lady-like airs, I assure you," she replied, seating herself again on the sofa. "I shall insist on seeing Mrs. Leslie, and having some explanation, because, if she thinks, by keeping on my apartments——"

Rachel entered the room in answer to Bessie's summons, and stood for a moment in utter surprise at the expression of rage which was so visible in Miss Watson's hitherto smiling and complacent countenance, and of ill-suppressed agitation in that of Bess.

"What is the matter, my dear child?" she demanded, looking from one to the other.

All Bessie's pride and self-command vanished at this question.

"Only that I am again doomed to be the victim of unmerited—of the most inexplicable slander," she observed. "That I am accused of——"

"No, no, Miss Leslie, don't say that I accused you of anything," interrupted Miss Watson, evidently softened by Bessie's tears and emotion. "On the contrary," she continued, "I have taken your part through it all; for, as I said to Mrs. Holmes, was it likely that if you were a young woman of no character, you should be going to be married to a gentleman of such fortune as Mr. Hastings, and——"

"Bessie, my dear, you had better leave me to hear what Miss Watson has to say," interrupted Rachel. "Dry up these tears, for which I am sure there can be no real cause, and go to your mamma in the garden; I do not wish, and I am sure you would not, that she should be distressed and made uneasy by——"

Bess vanished before the sentence was completed, for all the consequences that might result from her mother's becoming acquainted with what had passed between herself and Miss Watson flashed across her mind. It was very evident that the latter had relied upon Bessie's marriage with Mr. Hastings to silence all observations and reports injurious to the reputation of her lodgers; and it was probable, that but for the decided manner in which Bess had repudiated all intentions of marriage, Miss Watson would not have mentioned a word of the reports on which she had been so diffusive. Bess could not forget that the first exclamation of disappointment and dissatisfaction, on the part of the astonished spinster, had conveyed the impression that the failure of the expected marriage would subject Mrs. Leslie, as well as her daughter, to the imputation of imprudence in having remained so long the guests of Mr. Hastings, and to tell this to her mother now, would be undoubtedly to furnish the latter with a new

and incontrovertible argument in favour of the alliance, which it was very evident was still Mrs. Leslie's cherished wish and desire should take place, but which Bess was equally anxious and determined to avoid. Constraining herself, therefore, to appear calm, though inwardly distressed, and agitated to the greatest degree, at this second instance of unprovoked misrepresentation and unfounded calumny—the first, it need scarcely be mentioned, being the falsehood propagated by Mr. Cheverton, which had proved so fatal to all her hopes of happiness with Leicester—and Mrs. Leslie saw nothing more than usual in her daughter's manner, when the latter, passing her arm through hers, observed—

"Let us walk round the garden again, mamma, for Rachel has got Miss Watson with her, and I know you are not more partial than I am to her gossiping habits."

"No, but I am glad she is come," replied Mrs. Leslie, sighing; "for, of course, if we are to return to her apartments, it is necessary she should be made acquainted with it."

"Did she not, then, expect we should return, mamma?" demanded Bess, who began to suspect that to some disclosures made by her mother respecting Mr. Hastings, was owing the confidence with which Miss Watson had spoken of her (Bessie's) intended marriage.

Mrs. Leslie's reply, much to her daughter's dissatisfaction, confirmed this impression.

"I confess, my love," she replied, "that, at the time of my last conversation with Miss Watson, I was so impressed with the belief that you would confirm your own happiness and mine, by accepting Mr. Hastings's offer, that I was, perhaps, less unreserved with her than I ought to have been, considering, as you say, her gossiping propensities. However, Rachel will, of course, explain everything to her, and as you are determined on leaving here——"

"But I do not see, mamma, any necessity for our returning to Miss Watson's," observed Bess, hastily; "on the contrary, the term for which we agreed to take her apartments is expired. She has already been paid for a week over, though we have given her no trouble for the last three weeks; and, I candidly confess, it would be much more satisfactory to me to leave Dover at once, than to return to Miss Watson's."

Mrs. Leslie looked, as she felt, surprised and disconcerted at this expression of her daughter's wishes; but it did not occur to her that the latter had any particular objection to return to their late residence, but only that Bessie wished, by suddenly quitting Dover, to put a final termination to Mr. Hastings's hopes that time and a further acquaintance might induce her to lend a more favourable ear to his proposals.

"You are very whimsical and capricious, my dear," she observed. "When we first came here, you remarked that you hoped you should never be compelled to live in London again; and that you were sure, if anything could make you well and happy again, it would be the fresh sea air, the beautiful scenery, quiet and comfort——"

"I think still as favourably as ever of the place, dear mamma," returned Bess, despondingly, "and certainly, both your health and mine have been benefited by our residence here, beyond even my hopes; but there are circumstances——"

"What circumstances, Bessie?" demanded Mrs. Leslie. "You cannot, my dear child, be so ungratefully disposed towards Mr. Hastings as to wish me to reject all friendly connection with him? Remember, Bess, his health is far from established. I refer it, then, to your own feelings, whether we ought, from mere whim and love of change, and I am sure I know not any other or more reasonable motives I could give, desert him entirely; and leave him to strangers and hirelings. He is already more hurt and mortified at my—or rather, I should say, your determination to return to our own residence than I can describe; and I really cannot consent to hurt his feelings still more, by announcing your capricious dislike to that spot which, within a few weeks, you pronounced the most delightful you had ever seen, not even excepting your own dear native Arundale."

"Oh, that we were still there!—that we had never quitted Arundale!" exclaimed Bess, with impassioned fervour, as the recollection of all that she had endured—all that threatened her future peace, rushed upon her mind.

Mrs. Leslie, too, sighed—for with the remembrance of the peaceful retreat of Arundale, came the conviction that the happiness and calm content, in which her years had there glided away, like weeks or days, had vanished for ever. The husband who had been her never failing support and protection, was in his grave—a victim, as she could not conceal from herself, to the cares, the unregarded responsibility, and ill-requited sorrows that had resulted from that change of place and station which was looked upon by a misjudging world, and which she herself hailed, as a promotion due to his merits.

Her dear Bell had forfeited every hope of happiness, and repayed all her maternal care and anxiety by deserting her for ever.

And that, too, whispered "the still small voice" that will be heard in the ear of the dejected mother, was the result of the same foolish ambition, the same craving for worldly aggrandisement, that induced me to rejoice in my poor husband's removal from the place and station in which we had found as much—nay, more happiness than usually falls to the lot of frail mortality. "Yes, yes," she continued, in mental reflection, "had I been content with the station unto which it had pleased God to call us, he might still have been living—the humble, but happy and contented curate—my children, now parted for ever, the still united, beloved and admired, Twin Roses of Arundale."

Mrs. Leslie's melancholy reverie of the past had absorbed all thought of the present, or the future. She had totally, while recalling the happiness of those departed years, forgotten the subject she had been previously discussing with her daughter; and Bess, equally absorbed, though with reflections of a very different complexion, was by no means disposed to break the silence that prevailed between them, as they paced the spacious and well-laid out garden of the hotel, until they were joined by Rachel, who came to meet them.

"You have got rid, then, of our gossiping visitor, Rachel," observed Mrs. Leslie, as they returned to the house. "Have you mentioned our intention of taking possession of our apartments—though I suppose, of course, there was no need of preparation, for she is always so neat and attentive to comfort and regularity, that there is no fear of finding her unprepared."

"Certainly not," returned Rachel, "and, therefore, I did not come to any decisive arrangement respecting your return, my dear madam; but I have promised to take my tea with Miss Watson, this afternoon; and then, of course, if you decide——"

Bess slipped away, for she foresaw her mother was about to report to Rachel her supposed capricious objections to return to their former residence, and she determined to trust to the latter's good sense and calm decision, to suggest the course she thought most proper. The presence of Mr. Hastings at the dinner-table, when she next met Mrs. Leslie and Rachel, prevented any observation respecting the subject which still occupied all Bessie's thoughts. He was silent and dejected, though still most kind and attentive, and Bess readily conceded to the feeling that she supposed prompted both her mother and Rachel to be silent on the subject of their intended separation. The announcement of Rachel's intended tea-visit, however, brought a flush into his pale cheek; and when Bess hastily arose to accompany her, to make some change in her dress, he tremulously remarked, that he hoped Miss Leslie was not going to deprive them of so many hours of her company.

"Oh, no, I am only going to help Rachel to make herself smart, for her visit," replied Bess, with assumed spirits, though in reality trembling with anxiety to hear from Rachel the result of her confidence with Miss Watson, with which, she naturally concluded, the former's intended visit was connected. Her conjecture proved correct—Rachel acknowledged that she was going expressly to meet Mrs. Holmes, and hear from her own lips the detail of what had passed between that busy lady's gentleman-lodger and herself, respecting Bess.

"It is no use vexing you, my dear, with what Miss Watson related to me this morning, until I hear what this Mrs. Holmes has to say on the subject. She has, perhaps, greatly exaggerated the story, by her desire to mortify Miss Watson, between whom and herself there evidently exists a strong jealousy and rivalry. Miss Watson, too, acknowledges that she, on a former occasion, made herself very busy in exposing the character of a lady-lodger of Mrs. Holmes's, who came down here with a person she called her husband, but whose conduct was anything but what it ought to have been, if she was what she represented. Lodging-house keepers, my dear, in all watering-places, are liable to be imposed upon by pretended respectability; but, of course, all who wish to keep a reputable character, will immediately get rid of people whose conduct appears even doubtful. In this instance, according to Miss Watson's story, Mrs. Holmes was paid so well, that she did not like to be convinced that her lady-lodger was not what she pretended; and the consequence was, that Miss Watson's indefatigable determination to expose her true character, and force Mrs. Holmes to turn her out, brought on what she calls a civil war between the rival houses of Holmes and Watson, that has never been properly healed. I am ashamed to repeat all this rubbish to you, Bess, but I do think and hope that in this bad feeling, on the part of Mrs. Holmes, has originated in a great measure the falsehoods and misrepresenta-

tions—but we shall see, Bessie. Depend upon me, that full justice shall be done to you, as far as it is possible to secure justice in this corrupt and misjudging world. I have given your mother a hint on the subject, and she leaves it entirely to me, whether we return at all to Miss Watson's; and I shall certainly decide against it, without she declares herself fully satisfied, and makes a proper apology to you, for having so cruelly wounded your feelings. You shall not be, if I can help it, a victim to another plot, the motives of which are so mysterious, that, as I recollect you said on a similar occasion, I am doubtful almost whether I do not dream, or am in my proper senses."

It was late when Rachel returned from her visit. As she avowed to Bess, who was waiting up alone, in the drawing-room, she had purposely delayed, though she longed to get home, in the hope that, as it proved, Mr. Hastings, who was still very weak, would have retired to his room.

"I hardly expected," she observed, "that your mother would have gone to bed, though it is much past her usual hour; but I am thankful it is so, for we shall have now time and opportunity to consider what we shall say to her, or whether we shall tell her at all."

"Oh, no more concealments, dear Rachel, for Heaven's sake! I am miserable enough already, under the burthen of the secrets I have kept from my mother."

"If you think it would increase your mother's happiness to tell her all you know, my dear, I do not blame you," returned Rachel, gravely; "but I very much doubt——"

"Oh, no, I am selfish, I know I am," interrupted Bess. "Do not be angry with me, my best friend, but tell me—I can see that you are vexed and disappointed."

"I am more than vexed, my dear child," returned Rachel, "I am so confounded—so utterly unable to comprehend——"

"Answer me one question first, dear Rachel, and then tell me the particulars. Do we—are we to return to Miss Watson's?"

"No—not, at least, if I have any influence with my mistress," replied Rachel.

"That is enough—I am prepared now to hear anything," observed Bess, calmly, "for I foresee that your evidence has been insufficient to clear me from the malevolence of those who seem determined on my ruin."

"And yet what motive," observed Rachel—"but I will not detain you with my remarks, but relate what I have heard. Mrs. Holmes, who had been, at my particular request, invited to take a friendly cup of tea with our late landlady, without being prepared to meet me, is, as I had expected, a little mean, bustling, ignorant woman, not in any way to be compared to Miss Watson—silly and narrow-minded as *she* certainly is. She (Mrs. Holmes, I mean) was cringingly polite to me, and as I said nothing at all during tea-time of the purpose for which I had given her the meeting, she was equally obsequious in her inquiries after Miss Leslie, and poor Mrs. Leslie, whom she had seen, it seemed, at the moment that the intelligence had been brought her by Miss Watson's stupid servant-maid that you were just taken out of the water, and she believed was dead. I answered her as civilly as I could, but at last she gave me the opportunity I was waiting for, by observing what a fortunate thing it was that Mr. Hastings was present at the time of the accident; but I need not repeat, my dear, all that was said, and indeed, to tell you the truth, I have only told you so much because I am still so confused and surprised that I am, all in a flutter, and can hardly collect my thoughts to go on straightforward with my story. I can hardly tell you how I broke in first upon her fawning hypocritical professions; however, I know I said I was surprised that she should express so much kindness towards a person whom I understood she had represented in such a disreputable light as Miss Leslie.

"'Oh no, not me, I assure you, ma'am,' she replied. 'I never took upon myself to say anything about Miss Leslie, farther than to repeat what Mr. Harcourt, my lodger, told me; but which, as I said to him, I was sure must be some mistake.'

"I begged she would repeat to me what this Mr. Harcourt had said, hoping, dear Bess, that it would prove she had exaggerated what had passed ; but, guess my surprise, when, after telling me, exactly as Miss Watson told you, her lodger's remarks when he first saw you in the garden, she proceeded to state that this Mr. Harcourt was one of the crowd that were collected on the sands at the time of your accident.

"'He seemed mightily concerned about the young lady,' continued Mrs. Holmes, 'when he came home; and, next morning, when he was at breakfast, his servant came down to tell me that his master wanted to speak to me. He was a mighty free gentleman in his ways, and always would stop, if he saw me, to have a bit of chat; but he was rather particular and trouble-

some about trifles, and I expected he had sent for me to find some fault or another; but, instead of that, it was to ask if I had heard how the young lady (Miss Watson's lodger) was, and whether she had returned to her home. I told him, of course,' continued Mrs. Holmes, 'that she had not, and that her mother, Mrs. Leslie, was at the hotel with her; but I supposed they would come home, as soon as she was sufficienty recovered. He smiled—I must say, for a gentleman, he had a nasty, sneering, malicious sort of smile, when he meant to say he did not believe what you were saying, and it often used to provoke me, when I was telling him what things came to that I'd been buying for him—for he was rather mean, and seemed to think that people took advantage of him—however, as I was saying, he smiled now in that sort of way, and I said, "You don't seem to think, sir, that Miss Leslie *will* come back to my neighbour's?" "I should think it very probable that she will prefer the superior accommodations of the hotel," said he.

"'I knew he meant this as a fling at me, Mrs. Rachel, because he was always, when we were disputing about prices, hinting that he wished he had gone at once to a hotel instead of private lodgings. "I don't know, sir," said I, "about preference ; but I should suspect the expences of living there wouldn't suit Mrs. Leslie's income."

"'He laughed again in his sneering way, and observed, "Oh, but Mr. Hastings is very rich." "Mr. Hastings, sir?" says I; "you don't suppose Mrs. Leslie would condescend to live at Mr. Hastings's expense, hardly? And, another thing, what would the world say, if she and her daughter were to leave private lodgings like Miss Watson's for the most expensive hotel in Dover?" "What will you bet me that they do not stay there as long at least as Mr. Hastings does?" said Mr. Harcourt.

"'I could not help laughing, ma'am, to think of a gentleman offering to bet with *me*. But I suspect Mr. Harcourt was a good deal given to betting and gambling, and all that sort of thing, from what his man-servant let out in the kitchen, and I fancy that was the reason he was down here so quiet and retired like ; and, indeed, the man as good as owned that his master was out-at-elbows, as they call it, when they've got in debt, and obliged to keep out of the way of their creditors.

"Well, Mrs. Rachel, there was nothing more said at that time, only I told him I never betted, but time would show whether

he or I was in the right. Every day, after that, he used to ask me if my neighbour's lodgers were come back, or what news from the hotel, or something; and, I believe, as much out of contradiction as otherwise. I used to stand to it that they were coming, as soon as Mr. Hastings was better; but at last Miss Watson told me that she had heard from Mrs. Leslie herself that her daughter was going to be married to Mr. Hastings, as soon as he could get about. It happened that night

Mr. Harcourt stayed out late, which he had never done before, and when he came home he had plainly been drinking. I was sitting up in my parlour, for, though his man stayed up to let his master in, I didn't choose to go to bed till he was in, and I could see to the doors being locked. To my great surprise he walked into the parlour, instead of going to bed, and then he began to talk about the young lady again —"Miss Leslie, as you call her," he said, with his usual sneer. I told him I did n't know her by any other name ; but, let that be as it might, she would soon have a lawful right to another name, for she was going to be married to Mr. Hastings. "Psha," he said, "you don't believe that stuff, do you? The fellow will never be such a fool as to marry a girl whose character is notorious. He must know well enough who she is, for I heard from a friend that I have been dining with, at the same hotel, that Hastings knew her in London, and Mrs. Houseman told my friend that he had been sending presents of game, and fish, and fruit to Miss Leslie and her mother ever since they've been in Dover."

"'Well, I knew that was correct, Mrs. Rachel, ma'am, because I'd seen the man with my own eyes bringing basket after basket. However, I stuck to my text, that the young lady was going to be married, and indeed I told him what I'd heard, that Mrs. Houseman would have insisted on their returning to their own lodgings, as soon as Mr Hastings was able to leave his room, only that she had been let into the secret of the intended marriage, and, moreover, that the wedding was to be kept there, in the grandest of style, and she knew that would put a pretty penny into her pocket; and I even went further, for I told him Miss Watson was to be bridesmaid, and was to go up to London with the happy couple.

"'Well,' ma'am, he laughed quite rudely in my face, and at first he said he didn't believe a word of what I'd said, and then he laughed again, and said, "The girl," meaning Miss Leslie, "deserved to get a husband, for having played her cards so cleverly," and then he said if he was a relation of Hastings, he would take out a statute of lunacy against him, and shut him up in a madhouse, before he should make such a fool of himself. So then, of course, I took the young lady's part, and said I didn't believe she was any such character as he represented, and so at last he told me he would take his oath that he was intimately acquainted with a gentleman that Miss Leslie lived with, under the name of Lawrence—Mrs. Lawrence.'

"Ay, Bessie," observed Rachel, "you start, and so did I start when I heard that name, for I recollected directly it was the name that villain Cheverton wrote to Mr. Leicester——"

"Go on, dear Rachel," interrupted Bess, faintly; "let me hear all."

"Well, my dear, Mrs. Holmes went on to say that this Mr. Harcourt told her that you had lived in the utmost dissipation and extravagance, having spent enormous sums, and that the man's folly and infatuation had induced him entirely to desert his wife and children, and that he had even gone so far as to make a will, leaving all his fortune to Mrs. Lawrence; but, luckily, his family had found it out, and laid a plot so as to open the old man's eyes to her true character, and the consequence was, that Mrs Lawrence was turned out of the house in which she was living with this man, and he was gone back to his wife and family again.

"Mrs. Holmes added," continued Rachel, "that she still persevered in saying that Mr. Harcourt must have been mistaken in thinking that Miss Leslie and the Mrs. Lawrence were one and the same person, and at last he got quite in a passion, and then he said he had the misfortune to be the eldest son of the foolish old man he spoke of; that he had himself been one of the persons who turned Mrs. Lawrence, by actual force, out of the house his father had taken for her; and that, determined to be convinced that Miss Leslie and Mrs. Lawrence were the same person, he had contrived to make acquaintance with a gentleman lodging here, and had not only had an opportunity of seeing you repeatedly, and hearing you speak, but had managed to meet you face to face on the staircase, and that you shrunk from him in the greatest confusion, and retreated to the room from whence you came."

Bess recollected, instantly, having met a person on the stairs of the hotel, who regarded her with a peculiar insolence of look—so much so, that as he stood, as if inclined to address her, she had turned back, and rejoined her mother in the drawing-room, instead of going, as she had intended, to breathe the fresh air in the garden.

"Yes, my dear," observed Rachel, when Bess repeated this, "but this don't clear the mystery. This man saw you, and he must know that you were not Mrs. Lawrence, if there ever was such a person. Oh, I forgot, I asked Mrs. Holmes whether her lodger, this Mr. Harcourt, had said anything about the way his father became acquainted with Mrs. Lawrence, or who or what she originally was, and she said— "Yes; he told her that he understood she was a French lady's maid, or governess, or something, but she was a noted bad character before his father met with her."

Bess was lost in a whirlwind, as it might be said, of surprise, confusion, and conjecture. Hitherto she had considered the whole of Mr. Cheverton's detail to Leicester as a fabrication, for which he had no foundation but his own malevolent ingenuity, and no purpose but that of effectually separating her and Leicester; but the coincidence of this Mr. Harcourt's story—the names, too, of Lawrence and Harcourt—and his positive assertion that she was the very person who, under the former name, had been the source of disgrace and uneasiness to his family, seemed a convincing proof that it was not with Mr. Cheverton the tale of falsehood had originated. Could it be possible that it had been all built upon some unfortunate personal resemblance between herself and this abandoned woman, Mrs. Lawrence, as she was called? And yet this supposition was contradicted by Cheverton's assertion that the friend, from whom he had learned the particulars of Mrs. Lawrence's situation, at the time he saw her at the theatre, had expressly spoken of her real name as being Leslie, and that she was niece to a baronet; while Mr. Harcourt, on the contrary, represented her as a Frenchwoman, &c. This inconsistency had not escaped Rachel's observation either, and it confirmed her in the view she took of the affair, and which eventually she persuaded Bess in believing—namely, that the whole originated in the malicious invention of Mr. Cheverton, and the determination of Leicester's relatives to prevent his marriage.

"I have never told you before, my dear child," observed Rachel, in conclusion, "because I considered it not worth while to vex or mortify you, and I knew too, that Mr. Leicester would be involved in a quarrel with his cousin, if it came to his knowledge how shamefully he had behaved; but you recollect that when Mr. Cheverton paid his second visit to the cottage at Highgate, your mamma desired me to see him, and tell him plainly that his company was not welcome; that, in fact, if he came again he would not be admitted."

" I do remember it well," observed Bess, sighing deeply; "and I remember, too, that though you succeeded in putting a stop to his future intrusion, you were very vexed and dissatisfied at what passed in that interview."

"I was vexed, my dear," replied Rachel, " and yet, if I were called upon to repeat all that passed, it would not seem of any very great consequence. But there is a manner, Bess, which may convey a great deal, though the words uttered are nothing, and that was the case with Mr. Cheverton. I do not wish—God forbid I should lay any blame on our poor unfortunate Bell, but you know how she gloried in having imposed herself upon him, in his previous

visit, as the person he had met with in Oxford Street; and I do suspect, from what he said to me, that she had acted towards him with great levity, disclaiming any idea of a serious engagement with Mr. Leicester, and giving him every encouragement to think his attentions would be far more acceptable than Leicester's, whose gravity, and particularly delicate notions about females, she ridiculed and laughed at. In short, my dear, I hardly know how to express it, but it was plain to me that he had formed very degrading ideas of you, or rather, I should say, of—but this is such a painful subject, I do not know how to express myself. This I must tell you, that when I angrily hinted that Mr. Leicester would not feel much gratitude to him for his impertinent insinuations, he laughed in my face, and asked me whether I really had the confidence to imagine that Mr. Leicester's family would suffer him to be drawn into a marriage with a female who avowed that she was glad to get rid of him, and that, if she ever had him, it would be only that she could get nobody else. I know very well, my dear, that poor Bell was only enjoying a good joke, as she thought it, in speaking her own sentiments of Mr. Leicester in your character, for I know she did not like him; but I was not aware, then, how she had imposed upon Mr. Cheverton. I was very sure you would not have spoken so of Leicester, and I at once told him that he was putting expressions into your mouth that you would not have uttered. In fact, we so completely misunderstood each other, my dear Bess, that we came to absolute high words. He told me he pitied the poor girl for being under the tuition of a cunning old woman, who was evidently bent on making a market of her, and more than insinuated that my reception of him was only put on, for the purpose of getting a handsome bribe, and then he threw out a hint about the Marquis of Ledbury that drove me almost frantic—I do not know what I said in my rage—but I will not say any more on this subject, it is too distressing—only I have often thought since that Mr. Cheverton's malice towards you, and his eagerness to do you all the harm he could with Mr. Leicester, took its rise from that time."

Bess, whose cheeks had glowed with shame, vexation, and distress, during this retrospection on the part of Rachel, sighed heavily, as she observed that it seemed, indeed, but too probable that the latter's conjecture was correct.

"And yet," she observed, " one would imagine that his object once answered in raining me in the estimation of his cousin, he might have been content, and not sought, as it appears he is still doing, to degrade me even in the eyes of strangers. What interest, too, this Mr. Harcourt can have in abetting such an infamous plot——"

"That is what has puzzled me more than all, my dear," observed Rachel, hastily. "There is only one thing that can explain it, and that is, that it is possible, though he called himself Harcourt, that Mrs. Holmes's lodger might be Mr. Cheverton himself. The description she gives of him, as to age, height, and even manners, is very like him —his being in debt, and out of the way of his creditors, as his servant hinted, might account for his taking a false name, and what more likely than that he should fix upon the name of Harcourt, seeing that he had already used that name for a false purpose?—I mean in that abominable letter, my dear."

Rachel's explanation, or rather surmise, seemed so probable, so likely to be the truth, that Bess unhesitatingly adopted it as such. It was, indeed, rather a consoling idea than otherwise to attribute to Mr. Cheverton the whole of the wrongs she had suffered, and was suffering, than to suppose there was another being wearing the form of a man, and claiming the distinction of a gentleman, capable of joining in so nefarious a plot to injure the reputation and crush the prospects of an innocent and unoffending female. It was not until long after Rachel had concluded her detail of what had passed, including all the previous surmises and conjectures, that Bess thought of asking—

"And what conclusion did Miss Watson and her friend come to respecting these calumnies, my dear Rachel? And yet, now I remember, you said——"

"Yes, I did say, Bess, that until Miss Watson acknowledges, unequivocally, that she is convinced—but what matters it what such a silly narrow-minded woman as she is, says or thinks? I do believe her disappointment at not being bride's-maid— though what put such a ridiculous idea into her head, I cannot imagine—but I do really think that has influenced her more than anything. Mrs. Holmes, cunning, low-minded, and mercenary as she is, appeared much more reasonable, and better disposed to believe my representations than Miss Watson, though I could not succeed in convincing either of them that you had refused Mr. Hastings, and that your motive in so doing was merely that you did not feel towards him that preference that was necessary to make the marriage state happy. Miss Watson did

not, indeed, scruple to hint that she suspected the intended union (which they seemed to have made themselves quite certain of) had been broken off by Mr. Hastings himself; and she had the impertinence to tell me, that after the remarks that had been made about Miss Leslie's remaining in the house with Mr. Hastings, and passing hours by his bedside, nothing but a marriage could save her character, even though there was no truth in Mr. Harcourt's story, which few people would believe, if Miss Leslie left Dover unmarried. I feel, indeed, now, Bessie," continued Rachel, "that both your mother and I acted very foolishly in opposing your wish to return home as soon as you were sufficiently recovered; but how could we foresee how matters would turn out, or suspect that people would be so wicked and malicious as to put an evil construction on your visits to a dying man, and such, I am sure, Mr. Hastings appeared at that time."

Bess remained silent. This was a new subject for vexation and uneasiness, which even she, in her objections to remain in the same house with Mr. Hastings, had not foreseen. How, indeed, as Rachel had properly said—how could she, in the innocence of her heart, have suspected that her grateful attentions to the preserver of her life could subject her to such vile imputations. She felt, indeed, that the heart must be most depraved who could see in those attentions anything to condemn, or to offend the most rigid propriety. Her only motive in wishing to leave the hotel, had been the uneasiness she felt at incurring further obligations to Mr. Hastings, and, as she now observed to Rachel, she blushed for those who were capable of so misconstruing her intentions.

"Yes, my dear child, and so do I," returned Rachel, sighing, "but unfortunately, however our own hearts acquit us, the consequences will be the same as if——to be sure," she continued, after a long pause of reflection, "Mrs. Holmes hinted that she considered her friend Miss Watson was rather too particular, and laid too much stress on what people had said and would say, and I have no doubt that she would be very glad, and would set all scandal at defiance, if your mother would take her apartments instead of Miss Watson's for the rest of——"

"Oh, no, no," exclaimed Bess, shuddering with disgust at the thought. "For Heaven's sake, dear Rachel, do not let us have anything more to do with either Miss Watson or Mrs. Holmes. Mamma is not bound to remain here a moment longer than is pleasant to her and, for my own part, so far as I am concerned, I quite hate the place now."

Rachel shook her head.

"I hope, nevertheless my dear," she observed, "that you will reconcile yourself to stay some time longer. To leave it so hastily, will be to give these people the opportunity of saying that you were driven away by the discoveries they fancy they have made. But go to bed, Bessie, and try to sleep. We will talk over, tomorrow morning, what is best to be done. I am so excited and irritable now, that I am not fit to discuss the point, or suggest anything. Go to bed and sleep, my child, in the blessed consciousness that if the whole world condemns you, there is One above who knows the secrets of all hearts, and will not withdraw His gracious protection to innocence like yours."

CHAPTER XX.

But let harsh care the lover's peace destroy,
And roughly blight the tender buds of joy,
Let reason teach what passion fain would hide,
That Hymen's bands by prudence should be tied.
Venus in vain the wedded pair would crown,
If angry fortune on their union frown:
Soon will the flattering dream of bliss be o'er,
And cloy'd imagination cheat no more.—LYTTELTON.

ITTER tears watered Bess Leslie's pillow that night, although she tried, in the spirit of Rachel's parting admonition, to draw consolation from the conviction that the heavy load of calumny and falsehood, that seemed destined to crush her every hope, was totally undeserved. To say that she did not feel anger and resentment against her calumniators would be to give her more than human endurance and equanimity. But it is certain, Bess thought less of those immediately concerned—less even of the unmanly, mendacious Cheverton, than of him who had so readily yielded his belief to a fabrication that, it appeared to her, would so easily have been detected had he acted differently.

"Yes, even at that distance," thought Bess, "had he acted with that coolness and good sense, of which he always appeared to possess so large a share, he might have effectually baffled all Mr. Cheverton's assertions, and proved their utter falsehood. But his perfect success with Leicester has no doubt encouraged my bitter enemy—and yet, why should he be my enemy? Why, having succeeded in his first—in perhaps his only view—that of breaking the tie between his cousin and myself, why should he still pursue me with this inveterate malice?"

How often had this question arisen in her mind, during Rachel's narrative, and how often did it recur during this long and sleepless night, without her being able to assign a probable motive for the supposed Cheverton's renewed persecution. Yet, despicable and cruel as she felt his conduct to be, Leicester's appeared infinitely more inexcusable.

"He knew me," she exclaimed, "knew every thought, every sentiment that arose in my heart, and yet in an instant, without a single inquiry, he condemned me. No, no, it matters not what the world thinks, if he believes it."

Bess, however, though she tried to persuade herself of the truth of the last assertion, could not think with indifference of the probability of Mr. Hastings becoming acquainted with the scandalous reports that, according to Miss Watson and her friend, were already in circulation. She could not hope or expect, indeed, that either of the ladies would keep secret the falsehoods they had heard respecting her former life; but painful as was the idea of being regarded by him as an impostor—as one totally unworthy of the regard and esteem in which he held her—it was yet a satisfaction that he could not accuse her of having taken any undue advantage of his sentiments towards her.

"What would he now think of me, if I had acted otherwise?" she observed to Rachel, when talking over the events of the preceding evening. "If I had yielded to my mother's wishes and his, could I have then asserted, as I now can do, my innocence—no, he would have looked upon me as a mercenary wretch, to whom money was the only object, and who would have made him my victim. Now, at least my disinterestedness in rejecting his offers, will induce him to hesitate before he gives entire credence to the degrading character given me by enemies."

"God forbid he should believe one word of it," exclaimed Rachel, "if it should reach his ears, but I trust it will not. This I am sure of—that both Miss Watson and Mrs. Holmes would rather do anything to forward your marriage with Mr. Hastings than to prevent it."

"I am sorry to hear it," observed Bess, with emphasis. "Sorry, indeed, to think so meanly of them as to believe that my marriage, and the possession of wealth—for that, I suspect, would be the principal object, could induce them to alter their opinion of me. If I am what they believe me, I should only be ten times more guilty and despicable, in having taken advantage of the foolish romantic passion of an honourable man, to hide my infamy under his name."

Rachel did not reply to this. She was thinking, indeed, how more desirable than ever was the union against which Bess appeared more than heretofore resolved. Under the protection of Mr. Hastings' name and station none would dare assail her reputation, thought Rachel, and even if the calumnies of the past were renewed he would not rest until they were satisfactorily refuted, and her enemies silenced for ever. What Rachel only *thought*, however, Mrs. Leslie ventured boldly to *say* to Bess, when, in pursuance of the latter's determination to have no more secrets from her mother, Rachel related to her the real motive of her visit the night before to Miss Watson, with the addition which Rachel had suppressed in her previous conversation with Bess, that Miss Watson had positively declined receiving Mrs. Leslie and her family again into her house, under the present circumstances.

"That is to say," added Rachel, "in Miss Watson's own words, that, setting aside all that had been asserted by Mrs. Holmes' lodger, she considers nothing can save Miss Leslie's character but her marrying Mr. Hastings."

Bess was, of course, not present during this mortifying explanation, and Mrs. Leslie did not attempt to disguise her earnest wish for this union. Much as she was surprised, grieved, and irritated at the disclosures made by her confidential domestic, it appeared as if she would scarcely

have regretted the means, if it might have forwarded the end to which all her hopes and wishes were directed, that of uniting her daughter to Mr. Hastings, and Rachel was happy to see that the hope that Bess would be awakened to a proper appreciation of the advantages of the union, for which Mr. Hastings was more solicitous and impatient than ever, absorbed in a great measure the distress Mrs. Leslie would have otherwise felt at the unmerited persecution of her unoffending and innocent child. Leicester's desertion of Bess, indeed, which was now explained to have arisen from similar false representations on the part of Cheverton, excited Mrs. Leslie to the most vehement anger. Like Bess, she considered his credulity unpardonable. It was insulting alike to her as to Bess, and, as she observed, removed at once her last lingering scruple against promoting by every means in her power Bessie's marriage with Mr. Hastings."

"I own, Rachel," she observed, "that I have once or twice forborne to say as much to Bessie as I should have done, because, in spite of her assurances to the contrary, I have fancied that it was possible that the breach between her and Leicester might be healed, and that she still entertained hopes of marrying him. I was afraid her ardent attachment to him was stifled but not obliterated, and though she has never admitted me to her confidence as she has you, I believe that it was this hope that rendered her so unwilling to listen to the proposals of Mr. Hastings. But, after what you have told me, I consider it utterly impossible she can entertain such a hope. She would be, indeed, wanting in self-respect, in duty to me, who am equally insulted with herself, if she were ever even to listen to any apologies on the part of Leicester, or consent, if he were ever so willing to fulfil his engagements, to connect herself with a family by whom she has been so cruelly injured. But he will never seek to renew those engagements, depend upon it—he has been but too glad to have an excuse for breaking off a connexion so little to his interest; and Bess must be mad, infatuated, indeed, if she suffers her attachment to him to render the remainder of my life and hers miserable.

Rachel heard all that her friend and mistress had to say, without interruption. She saw, quite as plainly as Mrs. Leslie herself, how desirable it was that Bess should marry Mr. Hastings; but she was much less sanguine than the former, that the discovery of the injury her character had suffered, would operate as a recommendation of the measure she so decidedly opposed. She was about to quit the room at Mrs. Leslie's request, to send Bess to her mother, when she recollected that one of the chief purposes for which the latter had requested her to consult Mrs. Leslie, was as yet undecided.

"We have lost sight of that which requires immediate decision," she observed, returning to Mrs. Leslie's side. "If all that I heard last night be true, it will be very unadvisable to remain in this house even another day, to subject Bess and yourself to the possibility of insult; since, if Miss Watson is to be believed, the mistress of the hotel has declared that nothing but the certainty of Miss Leslie's intended marriage has induced her to bear in silence the remarks that have been made by other inmates. I am sorry, indeed, very sorry, that our persuasions prevailed over Bessie's earnest desire to return home."

"I am not," returned Mrs. Leslie, whose hopes of a favorable termination of her plan, it was plain, triumphed over all pain and regret from other sources. "Leave it all to me, Rachel; I will take care, now that I am admitted to your secrets, that neither Mrs. Houseman, or any one else, shall insult Bess with impunity. Why do you hesitate, Rachel—you must, I am sure, agree with me that it would be the height of folly to quit this place suddenly. Besides, were we to go to Miss Watson, you say——"

She turned at a slight noise, and beheld Mr. Hastings listening to her with a look of surprise and anxiety, and he instantly came forward to require an explanation of the expression she had last used.

Rachel regretted much that Bess had not seen her mother before this interview between the latter and Mr. Hastings, for she very much doubted whether, in Mrs. Leslie's present excitement, she would not say much more to him than would be prudent, or than Bess would wish communicated to him. She could not, however, pretend to misunderstand Mrs. Leslie's intimation that she wished to be left alone with Mr. Hastings, and she therefore hurried away to find Bess, who she expected was in her favourite resort—the garden.

"The young lady is just gone up to her own room, ma'am," observed one of the housemaids, as Rachel was crossing the hall on her way to the garden. "Miss Watson's maid has just brought her a letter," continued the girl, "and I took it up to her."

"Miss Watson write to Bess," thought Rachel. "I hope she has not been taking the liberty to intrude her ridiculous narrow-minded advice upon her."

Bessie's looks, however, betrayed a much deeper interest in the letter she was perusing, when Rachel entered the room, than any letter from Miss Watson was likely to create; but the mystery was in part explained when Bess, with raising her eyes from the paper, observed,—

"It is from our good friend, Mr. Lorton."

This was of itself satisfactory, but not so satisfactory was the agitation which was visible in Bessie's trembling frame and changing cheek as she proceeded with the letter.

Twice it was read over before a word was uttered by either—and then, just as Rachel was about to hazard the expression of a hope that nothing had happened to their friends, the Lortons, Bess folded the letter, and in a tremulous voice observed—

"It seems as if the whole world were conspired against me."

"My dear child, what new cause have you to say so?" demanded Rachel, with her usual tenderness.

Bess burst into tears, and hid her face with her handkerchief, while she observed,—

"You will think me weak and foolish, I know, for regretting—but read Mr. Lorton's letter, dear Rachel, and you will understand my feelings."

Mr. Lorton commenced his letter by gently reproaching her for her neglect in not having written to him since the first week of her arrival at Dover, when she had given him a lively description of her journey, and the favourable impression her new residence had made upon her. She had spoken also very gratefully of Mr. Lorton's relative, Miss Watson's kind attentions and anxiety to make her mother and self comfortable and at home; and, at the former's particular request, she had mentioned that Miss Watson intended soon to write, and thank him and Mrs. Lorton for not having forgotten her. Mr. Lorton, therefore, after playfully animadverting upon Bessie's having already broken her faithful promise of writing often, proceeded;—

"Fortunately, however, I have found that some ladies will keep their word even to an old fellow like me, for I have had two letters from my cousin Watson, and therefore am acquainted with all your goings on. Tell my good friend, Rachel that I have not forgotten the wager between us, and that I shall claim the stockings accordingly, as soon as ever she comes to London, whether she has knitted them or not. But I suppose there is little chance of that, as I understand my nose is put quite out of joint by a new favourite. Don't let him quite steal your heart, Bessie, from your old friend, though he did pick you up out of the water. Pooh, a good Newfoundland dog could have done that, and would have been quite content with a pat on the back, and a "Well done, old fellow," for his reward; and now this great, tall, two-legged animal expects, I understand, that you are to repay his services with the gift of your pretty person and invaluable heart.

"To be serious, dear Bessie, Mrs. Lorton and I did not get over our fears and trembling for many days after we received Cousin Watson's account of the danger from which you had such a narrow escape; and Mr. Hastings, as I understand he is named, has had a thousand blessings attached to his name ever since, both by my good old dame and myself, your humble adorer; and I can assure him, stranger as he is, we both most anxiously and earnestly prayed for his life, while according to cousin Watson's account, in danger from his gallant achievement.

"I will give my old lady, however, credit for more sagacity and foresight than I claim for myself; for it never struck me how the affair would end, though she says that she foresaw that if Mr. Hastings did not lose his life, he would his heart, and that you could not do less than give him yours in return for the obligation. I do not think anything in the world could have given Mrs. Lorton and myself more heartfelt pleasure than the prospect of your happiness, dear Bess, and your being restored to that station in life which you are formed to ornament and give value to, which I understand, from my cousin's account of Mr. Hastings, is the case. God bless you, my dear child, for well do you deserve every good that can befall you, and I hope and trust I shall live to see you and your dear mother enjoy many, many years of comfort from this alliance.

"Mrs. Lorton was sadly cast down and low-spirited after your departure. She misses friend Rachel especially, and when she was seized one night, with her old disorder, nervous spasms, did nothing but cry and lament that Rachel was not with her. I have been obliged, indeed, to turn quite rakish, to keep her from giving way to low spirits, and we have been twice to the play, and had several excursions a few miles out of town, just to drive away the blue devils. Indeed, I began to think seriously of packing up bag and baggage, and coming down after you. We have

lost our old maid, or I think I should have put this plan in execution, rather than see my old dame continually in the pouts after her friends; but it would not do to trust the house to a stranger. Our maid, Margaret, I should have told you, has, after keeping company as she called it, for ten years, rewarded her swain's constancy with her hand.

"This was a sad blow to our comfort, for we were used to her habits, and she to ours, and it will be some time before we feel quite at home with our new maid, though she is not quite a stranger, having lived two months with us while Margaret was ill some two or three years ago.

"By the by, I have something to tell you concerning yourself and this new maid, though you will wonder, I dare say, what she can have to do with you, or you with her. Nothing, my dear, for unfortunately she had never heard your name mentioned, although we were talking of you every hour of the day, when, while we were absent one day on one of the excursions I spoke of (I think we were at Greenwich), a gentleman called at our house, and inquired for me. Kitty, our new maid, of course told him I was out, and as she had received *no end* of cautions, as Mrs. Lorton would say, as to not letting any stranger inside the door while we were absent, she thought this answer quite sufficient, and would have closed the door; but the gentleman would not take such an abrupt answer. He wanted to know where I was, when I should return, and in fact asked, according to Kitty, a *power* of questions; and at last, when they were answered, he inquired if she could tell him where Mrs. and Miss Leslie, or either of them, were living. Of course, Kitty knew nothing about any such persons. There was nobody of that name ever come to *our* house, nor she never heard her master or mistress mention such a name.

"'Pray, how long have you lived with the family?' inquired the gentleman.

"'Off and on, going on for three years,' was Kitty's reply.

"'Three years, and you never saw any one of the name of Leslie here,' observed the gentleman.

"'Never,' returned Kitty.

"'Do you know a lady named Lawrence,' was the next question.

"'No;' that name was equally a stranger as Leslie to Kitty, 'and the gentleman appeared,' she said, 'quite discontented and unwilling to go away.'

"'Perhaps you have been told not to answer any questions?' he observed.

"Kitty, who was thinking only of her

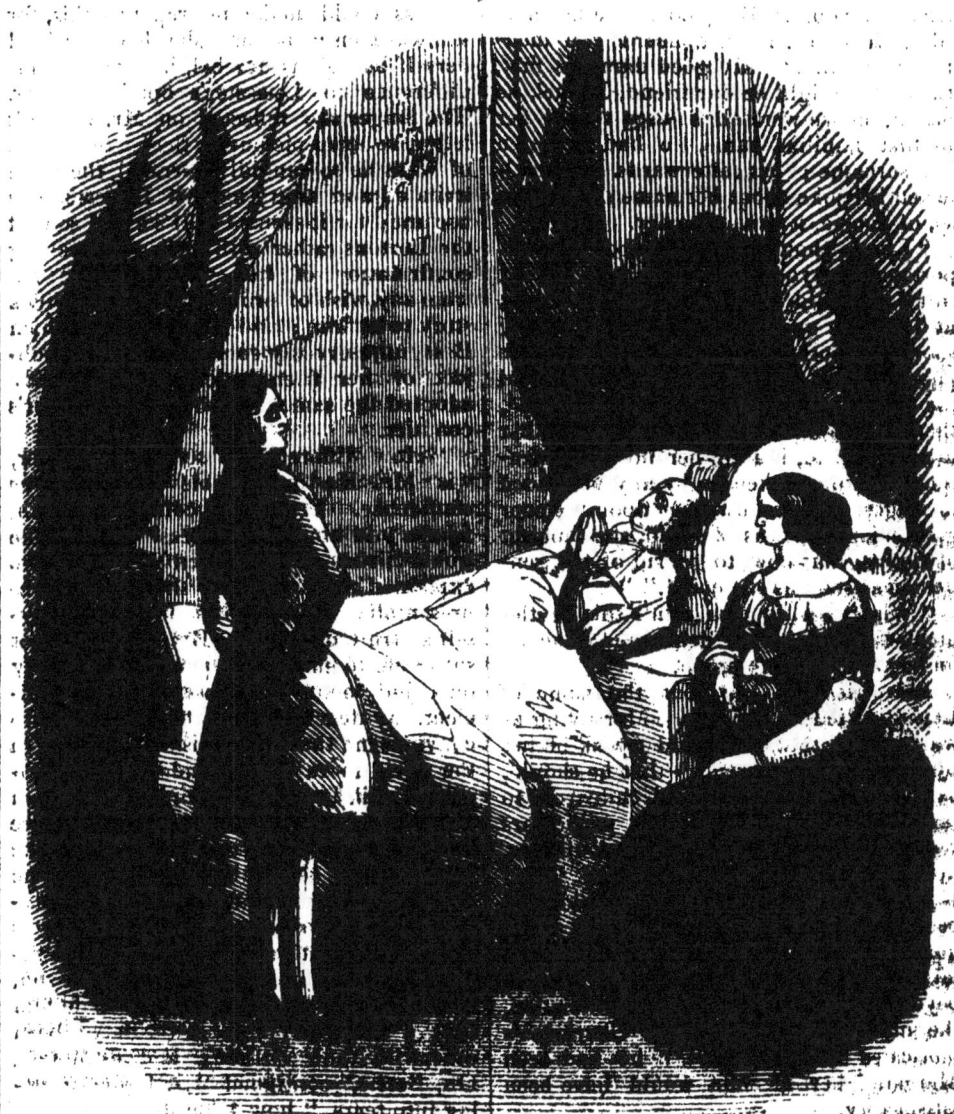

mistress's prohibition to her to hold any converse with strangers, replied,—

"'Yes, sir,' and then added, 'that she hoped he'd please to go away, for that she should get anger from her mistress, and, perhaps, lose her place, if it was known that she stood there talking to him for so long.'

"'Then your master and mistress do know Miss Leslie,' he observed. 'Come, my good girl, speak out and tell me where I can find either that lady or her mother, and I will give you this,'—holding up a half-crown piece, which he intended as an inducement.

"Kitty, however, assured him that he was mistaken; she had never said she knew Miss Leslie, or anybody belonging to her, and as to being bribed into telling anything, she was but a poor girl, but yet she scorned the action.

"The gentleman, it is very plain, my dear Beaste, could not make anything of the simple girl, and at last he went away, observing, that he should call and see Mr. Lorton himself. He has never been, however, Bessie, and this is more than a fort-night ago, and I have been sadly vexed to think I was out of the way, if it was any friend of yours. But who did he mean by Mrs. Lawrence, I never heard you mention that name? My good dame, at first, thought it might be our friend, Rachel, he meant, for we were all so used to call her by that familiar name, we had forgotten her surname; but afterwards we recollected her joke about her name of Mytton, so, of course, it cannot be her.

"I hope, though, it was nobody of importance to you. And yet, if it were, I think he would have come again. I was, at first, very angry with Kitty for saying she knew nothing about you; but, as the poor girl said, she really never had heard the name of Leslie or Lawrence, and, therefore, she could not give any other answer. And, indeed, her mistress's caution's not to be taken in by any pretended messages, etc., had dwelt so upon the poor girl's mind, that, as she said, she thought of nothing but how to get rid of the gentleman as soon as she could."

"Who then do you think this gentleman was, my dear?" demanded Rachel, folding the letter up again.

Bess tried to reply, but the name of Leicester died on her lips. Mortifying as was the idea that *he* should speak of her by the name of Lawrence—that he should, as it was plain to her he had, endeavour to learn from a servant any particulars respecting her, still she did not, could not, doubt that it was Leicester himself. And if he had seen Mr. Lorton, all would have been cleared up. He could not have doubted the old man's assertions, and certain he, (Mr. Lorton,) could have proved, beyond the possibility of contradiction, the utter falsehood of Mr. Cheverton's fabricated story. Even if he had seen Margaret, her answers would have been satisfactory.

"And now," as she observed to Rachel, "he has gone away convinced, from this girl's pretending not to know me, that there is some disgraceful mystery attached to the Lortons' knowledge of me which he does not think worth his while to attempt to penetrate."

Rachel could not offer any consolatory arguments against this, which she thought was but probably the truth. She ventured, however, to hint, that she was sorry to see that Bess still attached so much importance to Mr. Leicester's opinion, adding—

"I had begun to hope, my dear child, that what you have so often asserted was true, and that you had ceased to consider it desirable that he should be convinced

how cruelly he had wronged you in so readily crediting Mr. Cheverton's false-hoods."

Bess could make no reply to this, for she was conscious that she had deceived herself as well as Rachel, in affecting indifference to Leicester's opinion of her. The longer she reflected on Mr. Lorton's letter, so unsuspicious of the consequences of what he so candidly narrated, the more irritated and angry against Leicester she became; for it seemed as if he had sought the Lortons rather with a view of seeking confirmation of her worthlessness than from any wish of proving Mr. Cheverton's story to be false; and Mrs. Leslie, to whom Bess unreservedly communicated the subject of her friend's letter, immediately adopted the same view of Mr. Leicester's conduct.

"How different," observed the latter, "is Mr. Hastings' noble and generous confidence. Yes, Bess, I confess the truth, I have told him all—at least so far as he would listen to me—when I would have explained the cruel and shameful misrepresentations that have made you and myself so truly unhappy. But he would not suffer me to enter into particulars. 'My own judgment and observation is sufficient, my dear madam,' he observed, 'to convince me that there exists not a being in the world more noble-minded, more innocent of evil, in thought, word, or deed than your daughter; if the whole world were combined against her, they would not shake my opinion.' And then, dear Bessie, he paid me the handsome compliment of saying that my own principles and sentiments were a sufficient guarantee for my daughter; and, even if he had not known you, it would have been hard to persuade him that a child of mine could have been otherwise than virtuous, and estimable. Oh, Bessie," continued Mrs. Leslie, bursting into tears, "how little did he suspect that those words wrung my heart. I had made up my mind before to conceal nothing from him—to tell him that I have one child, who——but I could not do it, after what he said. He thinks, I know, that your sister is dead, and it is, perhaps, as well he should do so. Hereafter, per-haps——"

Bess did not attempt to seek into the meaning of this unfinished sentence. The subject was, indeed, too painful for her to wish to dwell upon it. She was, indeed, quite as much impressed with what her mother had truly called Mr. Hastings' noble and generous confidence in her integrity, especially contrasted as it was at that moment, with Leicester's apparently ready belief of everything that could tend to confirm the degrading opinion he had formed of her, and she met Mr. Hastings at dinner with less reserve, less determination to repress his warm attentions and expressions than she had ever shown before. Too delicate, and too anxious to avoid giving the object of his devoted affection the slightest cause for uneasiness, Mr. Hastings did not, in the most distant manner, refer to the subject of her mother's confidential communication to him, and this enhanced Bessie's gratitude towards him. She was, in fact, just in the state of mind that her mother could have wished; indignant in the greatest degree towards Leicester, and disposed, in contrasting his conduct with that of his rival, to do even more than justice to the superior qualities of the latter. But still, it must be confessed, as not very favourable to Mr. Hastings' wishes, that she was the more pleased with him, and the more inclined to do him justice because he forbore to press his suit with the warmth and passionate earnestness he had formerly evinced. While he did not speak of love, Mr. Hastings was, indeed, all that Bess could wish; but from that subject she still shrunk. She could not, would not think of him as a lover.

"Friendship in woman is akin to love," so says the poet, and so said Mrs. Leslie, when she smilingly assured Mr. Hastings that all would end happily. Could she have read Bessie's heart, have seen how torn it was with contending feelings, she would have been, perhaps, less sanguine. But the time was fast approaching which was to put to the test the hopes she had so assiduously encouraged of seeing Bess united to Hastings. We have forgotten to state that Mrs. Leslie, yielding in part to Bessie's wishes, quitted the hotel where she had so long been Mr. Hasting's guest. A small furnished cottage at Charlton, a pretty rural village a short distance from Dover, offered on reasonable terms, and was altogether an unexceptionable residence, that Bess was compelled to give up her wish of leaving the place altogether; which both Mrs. Leslie and Rachel opposed, on the ground that it would have the appearance of being fearful of the misrepresentations of their *ci devant* friend, Miss Watson, and her friend Mrs. Holmes' misrepresentations.

At Lavender Cottage, as it was called, they were now comfortably and most pleasantly settled. Mr. Hastings was their daily visitor; and Bess tried to forget there was a world beyond its wal's. Of this, however, she was destined to be painfully reminded by another letter from Mr. Lorton.

Cousin Watson had again written to him, and written in a manner that had surprised and pained him beyond all measure. He could not, would not believe one-half of what she had asserted. How, indeed, could he believe any part of it was true, after what he had seen and known of his dear young friend and Mrs. Leslie, and Rachel, too, that worthy, upright, single-hearted woman, on whose sincerity and integrity he would venture his life. Oh, no, he was sure there must be some dreadful mistake; and, yet, Miss Watson had written to him, reproaching him for having recommended to her people of no character, or rather, such character as had already brought disgrace upon her. She, who, in the difficult position of a lone unprotected *young* woman, had hitherto defied the tongue of scandal.

"She goes on to say," continued Mr. Lorton, "that you, Bessie, instead of being married, as she had been persuaded and willing to believe you were about to be to Mr. Hastings, are openly living in defiance of the opinion of the world, and that your mother and Rachel—but no, I will not, cannot repeat half the abominable things she asserted. I know, I am sure, they must be false, and yet, from my knowledge of my cousin Watson, I can hardly believe that she is the originator of the scandal. Who is this Mr. Harcourt, dear Bess, that she talks about as being acquainted with your whole history, and having opened her eyes to the injury that was likely to result to her character if she suffered you to return to her house from the hotel where you had been residing with this Mr. Hastings, and been, she says, turned out in disgrace. Good Heavens! I can scarcely believe this of Bess Leslie, and it is to Bess Leslie that I am writing this. And yet I know it will turn out to have all originated either in misrepresentation, or some cruel and deliberate enemy. Though what, or who can be *your* enemy, is a mystery I cannot unravel, I should not have thought it possible that there was a living being who felt a spark of enmity towards you, my dear child. I have been so hurt, bewildered and vexed by my cousin's letter, that I should certainly have come down to see if I could not have set matters to rights on the spot, but my poor wife has had a terrible attack of her old complaint, the spasms, which are sure to seize her whenever her mind is disturbed, and I scarcely remember any circumstance of our lives that has given her more uneasiness and vexation than this. To think, as she says, that we should be accused of imposing upon my cousin Watson, and should be told in plain terms that the only friends she has made for years are——Well—well, we must bear it all patiently till we receive your explanation, dear Bessie, for, I am sure you can explain it to our satisfaction, and then I shall write to Miss Watson, and tell her very plainly what I think of her suffering herself to be imposed upon with such an improbable story, and to join in circulating such scandalous falsehoods.

"Do write, immediately, my dear child, and believe me, nothing but Mrs. Lorton's continuing so ill and weak could keep me from coming down to Dover; for I would rather spend fifty pounds than not be satisfied that all Miss Watson has written is utterly false. God bless and protect you, prays your sincere friend,

"R. LORTON,"

"P.S. What puzzles me and Mrs. Lorton most, dear Miss Leslie, in this business, is the stranger, who I mentioned before as having called during our absence, having mentioned the name of Lawrence; and, from what I can learn of our servant, spoke of it as if Miss Leslie and Mrs. Lawrence were one and the same person. I know it is quite impossible that you can ever have had any reason for taking a false name, and yet what a strange coincidence it is, that he should mention it. I hope your letter will explain this satisfactorily, for I confess it gives me more uneasiness than anything else."

A second postscript to her friend's diffuse letter considerably increased the pain and vexation with which Bess had perused the preceding.

"I had just, as I supposed, finished my letter, and was going to seal it, when I was interrupted by a visit from a distant relation of mine, whom you may have heard me mention as having behaved very ill and ungratefully to me some years ago, since which time I have never heard of him; and, indeed, did not know whether he was living or dead. It seems, however, that what he has suffered from his bad conduct in his youth, has at last made him a wiser, and I hope a better man; and, though his situation in life is a very low and humble one to what it might and ought to have been, from his education and early prospects, it is better than I had any reason to expect from his former idle and profligate courses.

"He has been, he informed me, for the last four years, coachman in a gentleman's family, and has behaved to the perfect satisfaction of his employers. You will naturally say, 'What is all this to me?'

and you will, perhaps, be as much surprised as I was, when I learnt that the name of his master and mistress is Harcourt. But this is not all, Miss Leslie—for, though under any other circumstances, I should have scorned to have listened to any tales of the family he is living with, I could not help asking some questions which led to his owning that his mistress, and her sons and daughters, of whom, it seems, there are several, had been for a long time at variance, as he expressed it, with Mr. Harcourt, the husband and father. In James's own words, he hardly knew there was a master when he first went to live in the family; for old Mr. Harcourt was abroad in France, or somewhere on the continent; and though he heard afterwards, it might be a year or more after he went to live there, that the old gentleman had returned to England, and was living in London, he never saw him, but he heard from the young ladies' maid, with whom, it appears James is upon intimate terms, that Mr. Harcourt, though quite an elderly man, was a shocking profligate, and had deserted his wife and family to live with a female of bad character, whom he had taken abroad with him.

"The news came, James said, some time after this, that this woman was dead, and James's sweetheart (as I suppose this ladies' maid is) seemed to think it likely that Mrs. Harcourt and her husband would be reconciled, and he would return to his home, but this supposition turned out wrong, for they (meaning the servants) heard nothing more of him for a long time, except, James says, that when he has been waiting at table, as he does occasionally, he has heard the sons speak of having seen 'the old man,' as they called their father, but they were always checked by their mother, who said she did not wish to hear anything about the unworthy wretch.

"Well, the upshot of all this appears to be, that some months ago this Mr. Harcourt returned home in a very bad state of health, in which he has ever since remained, and James learned from his manservant, whom he brought with him, that his master had had a lady, a *Mrs. Lawrence*,—though that was not her real name—living with him; that the old infatuated profligate, though naturally miserly and avaricious, had let her get such an ascendancy over him, that she had lavished away thousands, and would in the end have ruined the family had not his sons laid a plot by which her worthlessness and treachery was proved to their father, and he consented to part with her.

"I was so struck with the coincidence of names and circumstances in this story," continued Mr. Lorton, "that I could not rest until I saw this man-servant of Mr. Harcourt's, and accordingly I took a hackney-coach, and went back with my nephew to his master's or rather his mistress's house. James introduced me to the man as having some reason to be anxious to hear all I could about Mrs. Lawrence, and he very readily answered all my questions; but judge of my grief and surprise when he described, at my request, his master's late companion, and in every respect (*except the conduct*) it answered to that of one whom I had so dearly loved and esteemed under the name of Bess Leslie. There was only one thing more necessary to make me give up every hope.

"'Have you ever heard what the real name of this Mrs. Lawrence is,' I asked.

"I am not sure what her real name might be,' he replied, 'for women of that kind change their names as easily as their gloves; but I did hear that she was formerly a Miss Leslie, and that she belonged to a very respectable family; and, indeed, I know there was a sad piece of work one night at the Opera, where a lady in the next box, that was said by some to be her mother, but at any rate was some near friend, went into fits at seeing her, and our lady, Mrs. Lawrence, was brought home by master in hysterics. Poor foolish old man, she frightened him to death by threatening to cut her throat, and actually did get a razor out of his dressing-case; but she knew better than to use it, and in a few days it all blew over, and she went on as if nothing had happened. However, they do say that when she left my master, or, rather, he left her, she did return to her mother; and so, as it's never too late to mend, it's to be hoped she may lead a better life for the future.'

"I have now, Bessie, set down everything as I have heard it, but my mind is in such a state of perplexity that I can't come to any conclusion. Sometimes I think —but no, I know that it is impossible— that this Mrs. Lawrence and my dear young friend are the same person : I know —I think, I know it is impossible. Mrs. Lorton, who has just been reading my now double letter, observes, 'To be sure it is impossible, for has she not been continually under our own eyes, at the very time she is represented as living this shameless life. It is then, it must be, all a mistake.' And then she reminded me how many instances we had read of people being taken and even sworn to for other people, or what the newspapers call "mistaken identity." This must account for it all, dear Bessie ; but it's a sad—a very sad thing we can't hit upon some way of clearing it all up, and proving how shamefully you have been misrepresented. I have felt so angry with Miss Watson, and yet so stupefied how to contradict her effectually, that I have not answered her letter yet, but I shall do so now, for I see very plainly that it is all a mistake. To be sure, I cannot contradict what she says about Mr. Hastings, and so, upon second thoughts, I shall defer writing till I have a letter from you, my dear young friend ; and, in the firm trust that it will prove satisfactory, I conclude once more.

"Your anxious and true friend,
"R. LORTON."

"*Another* P. S., dear Bessie —I forget to say that my good dame has taken it in her head that the air of Pentonville does not agree with her, so we are looking out for a little house at Greenwich, or that neighbourhood, as she has taken quite a fancy to the river-side. We shall not remove, however, for some time. She desires me to say how much we both wish we could have you and Mrs. Leslie and Rachel for our neighbours again ; and, indeed, if you are not going to be married, I should think it might be managed. So pray write at once, and tell us whether there are any hopes."

Agitated, vexed, and mystified as Bess felt at the contents of this letter, she could not restrain a smile at the vacillation of mood in which it had been written. At first it was evident that the old gentleman had begun to write in the full impression of Bessie's innocence. Then, again, he had been perplexed with doubt, and at last so completely led away by the seemingly perfect evidence against her, as to have arrived almost at the conclusion that she was really the person against whom such terrible charges had been brought ; and then, when he was at the very point of avowing his belief that he had been imposed upon, and of accusing her of the deception she had practised towards him, a simple remark of Mrs. Lorton's had convinced him of the utter impossibility that she (Bess) could be the person represented; and he had hastened to make the *amende honorable* by expressing his perfect conviction that the whole of the charge was false, as it related to her.

A second time Bess was reading over, and reflecting upon this voluminous epistle, when Mrs. Leslie entered the room.

As yet Bess had not considered whether she should make her mother acquainted with this new subject for surprise and uneasiness; but, whatever might have been her determination, had she had time for reflection, there was now only one course to be pursued. Mrs. Leslie had seen the letter, and Bess could not, if she had wished it, conceal its contents. With considerable anxiety she watched her mother's countenance while the latter was reading; but her alarm and consternation may be conceived when Mrs. Leslie, letting the paper fall from her trembling hands before she came to the conclusion, in a voice of agony, exclaimed—

"My child, my child! Wretched, miserable, unfortunate Bell. It is but too plain how this all originates. Oh, Bessie, it is your unhappy sister! It must be her, who—Oh, that she had died, that I had seen her in her grave, rather than this."

Bessie's emotion was so violent that for some moments she was unable to utter a word; but she saw that the time at length had arrived when it became impossible longer to conceal from her mother that the child, whose supposed depravity she thus deplored, was no more, and yet she trembled to utter the fatal truth.

"No—no, you are wrong, dear mother," she at last faltered, in tremulous accents. "I could—I could convince you that you are wrong, but I fear to——"

"Fear what?" exclaimed Mrs. Leslie, with vehemence. "Oh, Bessie, what can equal the misery, the agony of believing that my child, that your sister is—but you know something of her that you conceal from me, I see you do. Speak, I charge you, tell me the truth. Your sister is——"

"Dead!" uttered Bessie's pallid, quivering lips, and then sinking on her knees, and hiding her face in her mother's lap, she gave way to a fit of convulsive sobbing which prevented the utterance of another word.

"Dead!" repeated Mrs. Leslie, at last, in a tone of such bitter anguish that it roused Bess instantly from the indulgence of her own feelings. "Dead! my child dead—and I—where, when, how did she die? Tell me. You see I am calm, Bess—quite calm. I prayed just now that she were dead, rather than the wretched vile thing this would make her. Yes, I can bear her death now."

Bess, however, was terrified at the ghastly expression of her mother's countenance, and the hollow, unnatural tone in which she spoke, even more than if she had given full vent to the violence of her feelings.

"My dear, dear mother, for my sake

try to bear it with resignation," she began, but Mrs. Leslie interrupted her.

"Do not keep me in suspense," she exclaimed. "Tell me the whole truth; or are you inventing this to save me from the misery of thinking——"

"My dear mother, I have told you the truth," replied Bess, with solemnity. "My poor sister has been released from all her sorrows many, many months. Rachel will tell you all—she knew it long before I suspected it, and——"

Mrs. Leslie uttered a deep groan, and fell back in her chair; and Rachel, who had entered the room just as Bess commenced her last reply to her mother's interrogation, flew to her assistance.

"You have killed her. Oh, what can have induced you to do this, Bessie?"

"I will explain all," murmured Bess, hurriedly. "Do not blame me, Rachel. It is better that she should know the truth and——"

"Yes—yes, it is better—better," exclaimed Mrs. Leslie, who, though she appeared lifeless, still retained her senses. "Bessie is right—she is always right. All is over now—fear and hope—all is buried in her grave. And she died, then, without seeing her mother, without feeling that she was forgiven. Oh, it was cruel to keep me from her. You knew that I forgave her——"

A violent burst of tears came to her relief, and it was long before either Bess or Rachel even attempted to interrupt them.

The latter had learned from Mrs. Leslie's exclamation that she was still unacquainted with the real circumstances of her daughter's death, and it gave her time to reflect upon the explanation she could give. The same fear that had hitherto induced her to conceal from the unfortunate mother that Bell was dead, now operated to restrain Rachel from confessing the manner of the death; and when Mrs. Leslie recovered sufficient calmness to listen, Rachel, whose look had imposed silence on Bessie, proceeded to relate the same tale which had at first imposed upon the latter, as to the cause of her unfortunate sister's death. It soon became evident, however, that Mrs. Leslie's apparent calmness was rather the stupefaction of intense grief than the effect of resignation. The blow had, as it were, stunned her for awhile, but it was succeeded by a paroxysm of grief that terrified her anxious attendants. Poor Rachel bore in silence the reproaches she wildly heaped upon her for the secresy she had observed

"If I had only seen her once—once more, before the grave hid my child for ever from my sight," she exclaimed. "If I had only gazed upon her sweet face, peaceful in death—Oh, tell me, tell me, Rachel, did she look——"

Rachel shuddered with inexpressible horror at the remembrance this question brought to her mind. Those swollen distorted features scarcely bearing even the resemblance of humanity, still less any traits of their pristine loveliness, how often had she prayed to be delivered from the awful recollection of them, that haunted even her slumbers for days—weeks after she beheld them, and now recurred in all its loathsomeness.

"She was changed, then, before you saw her?" continued Mrs. Leslie, comprehending instantly Rachel's expressive gesture. "But she would still have been beautiful to her mother," she added, "and it was cruel—cruel to deny me that last satisfaction. But you saw her, Bessie? You did not shrink and shudder at your sister."

Bess tried in vain to speak. She could not utter a word, for Rachel had, in answer to her importunities at the time she (Bess) became acquainted with the true circumstances of poor Bell's death acknowledged the dreadful truth, as to the loathsome state of decomposition in which the corpse had been found. Even the beautiful hair, once so glossy and silky, was changed by the water, and the long tress which Rachel had herself severed after the body had been placed in the coffin and still preserved, had lost all its original beauty, though it still retained nearly its original colour.

The lock of hair—the purse—and a small cornelian heart, of little intrinsic value, but had been prised by Bell as the last gift of her father, and which was found suspended by a black riband round the neck of the corpse, were the only memorials that remained of the unhappy girl. Rachel had hitherto concealed the possession of them from Bess, for the fear the effect that the sight of them would have upon her feelings; but Mrs. Leslie's vehement inquiry whether she (Rachel) had not preserved a single relic of her poor lost child, amounted to bitter reproach for supposed carelessness or thoughtlessness on the part of the former, and drew the acknowledgment that she had some slight memorials in her possession. Fain would she have persuaded Mrs. Leslie to delay seeing them until she was better able to bear the sight; but she would not be restrained, and Bess and her mother wept tears of bitter agony over them. The little cornelian ornament

was an especial object of interest, for it recalled the tender father who placed it round the neck of his darling child. A similar one, except that the material was coral, he had given at the same time to Bess, and it had never left her neck from that time. However splendidly she might have been dressed, this valued gem retained its place, though, while under her aunt's government, she had frequently been compelled to conceal it. Lady Jane having pronounced it vulgar and old-fashioned; and this decision had so far influenced Bell, that hers had been laid aside, and apparently forgotten. That her sister should have resumed it again, at such a time, spoke volumes to Bessie's heart. How many tears of agony must have been shed when her unhappy sister returned it to that once pure and hallowed sanctuary from which it had been banished by the dictates of vanity and frivolity. Perhaps the last agonising throbs of that heart which was now for ever silenced, had beaten against this memorial of a father's love. Not for the costliest diamond that ever gemmed a monarch's diadem would Bess have exchanged this simple tribute of affection that was now laved in floods of anguished tears.

But she was recalled from the thousand thoughts and recollections that crowded upon her memory by an exclamation from Rachel. Mrs. Leslie had not spoken from the moment that she drew from the little morocco case in which Rachel had enshrined these "fond memorials," the long tress of hair which the latter had carefully cleansed and plaited before she placed it there. Twice she essayed to raise it to her lips, while she passed her other hand over her eyes, as if to clear away something that impeded her sight; but, the next moment, the precious treasure fell from her grasp; her hand dropped powerless on her knee, and Rachel saw, with indescribable terror, that her features had not only assumed the ghastly hue of death, but were drawn and distorted in a manner that betrayed that it was not a mere fainting fit that had attacked her, and rendered her alike insensible to the past or the present.

Too soon were all the worst apprehensions of Bess Leslie and her attached friend Rachel confirmed. Her disorder was pronounced by the physicians who were called in, to be paralysis; and, although they tried to disguise their opinion from the distressed and agitated daughter, to Rachel they candidly avowed their conviction that the attack would be fatal.

"She may linger some time," they observed. "It may be days, weeks, or even months—for occasionally we see such cases—but her constitution is too completely broken to afford a hope that she can eventually rally and overcome a disease which is most frequently fatal, even when it attacks those of robust frame, and inevitably so those who have suffered so long, both bodily and mentally, as it appears this poor lady has. It is, therefore, necessary that Miss Leslie should be prepared for the worst.

Prepare! How was it possible for Rachel even to hint this decision to the affectionate and devoted daughter, whose own life seemed so bound up with that of her adored mother that Rachel scarcely believed it possible she could survive her loss. But there was a strength beyond her own that did support Bessie through this trial, and enabled her to say, not merely in that cold lip-service which too frequently belies the heart, but with the true resignation of a Christian, "Lord, thy will be done."

Never had Bessie seemed to rise so superior to the weakness of frail mortality as now, when, suppressing every selfish sigh or murmur, she devoted even every thought to cheer and soothe that which her heart too truly told her was the death-bed of her beloved mother. Fortunately, she was spared the anguish of seeing this cherished parent evince any indication of acute pain, or suffering; and she checked even the wish that she might return from the calm unconsciousness in which the former now lay, lest that return to sense might bring with it sufferings from which happily she now seemed free.

"And yet," she murmured, "it would be a blessing hereafter to reflect upon, if I once more hear that voice that never uttered but the accents of kindness, acknowledge her child."

And Bessie's wish was fulfilled. Five days had passed since Mrs. Leslie had lain in that state of living death, insensible alike to the sorrow and filial tenderness of her daughter, or the anxious cares of those by whom she was equally beloved and revered. Night or day, Bessie had never quitted her side, and to Mr. Hastings' or to Rachel's tender remonstrances she returned a gentle, yet firm denial, that she would leave her mother to their care, while she took the repose so necessary to maintain her own strength.

"I am strengthened and refreshed, more than you can imagine," she would observe. "Even last night I slept whilst kneeling by her side, with her hand in mine, and dreamt, too, as calmly and peacefully as

if, indeed, the happy child I thought I was; but if I were to leave her, I should have a thousand dreadful fears to keep me from sleeping; and if she were to awake suddenly, as the doctor told me she may, probably, for a short time, never should I cease to reproach myself, or to regret, if I were not here to receive her first, it may be"—and her voice became almost inaudible—"her last look!"

Bessie's presentiment that her mother would awaken to consciousness was fulfilled. On the fifth day from the first attack, a faint, life-like glow revisited her pallid cheek. She opened her eyes, and looked around her, as if recovering from the oppression of a heavy dream, and her features gradually resumed their usual placid composure. Bessie's tremulous lips could scarcely utter the words, but she bent over her, and in the faintest tones, lest she should disturb the growing consciousness, whispered—

"Mother, dear mother, do you know me?"

"Know you? Yes, my own child," returned Mrs. Leslie, in a clear, though low voice. "What has happened?"

Rachel and Mr. Hastings, who were sitting together at some distance from the bed, both arose, and Mrs. Leslie's countenance beamed with an angelic smile. She beckoned them to approach.

"Raise me, dear Rachel," she said. "I know all now—I am dying, but I die happy, happy for—not such was *her* death bed! Yet, she is in Heaven, and there—Bessie, my child, my dutiful child, I have but one wish in this world. You will not refuse your mother?"

Bessie's heart throbbed with agony—she anticipated that wish, but she suppressed the anguish that seemed to swell her bosom even to suffocation, and in a firm voice, replied—

"Your wish is sacred, my dear mother. I will not affect not to understand it. If Mr. Hastings——"

She stretched out her cold and trembling hand to him, and he bent low over it, as he raised it to his heart.

"Nearer—nearer—my children, both—both now my children," murmured Mrs. Leslie, and she pressed both their trembling hands in her already cold grasp, and raising her eyes to Heaven, while her lips faintly murmured a petition to the throne of grace for their happiness. "Rachel, dear Rachel," she added, smiling upon her, "you—you will be now their——"

Her voice faltered, and she faintly indicated her wish to lie down. The light of intelligence faded again from her eyes, and Mr. Hastings would have withdrawn Bess,

but she gently repulsed him, and he drew back a few steps. But death was not so near as his fears predicted. Not a sigh or sound disturbed the solemn silence, but, from time to time a faint murmur broke from the lips of the dying mother, but they spoke rather of pleasure than of pain. Those murmurs ceased—but her arm still remained round the neck of her daughter, and her cheek rested on hers. The arm became heavier, the cheek more icy cold— she was dead !

CHAPTER XXI.

MANY weeks passed away after Mrs. Leslie's death, without restoring Bessie to that calmness and resignation to her irreparable loss which might have been hoped and expected from her previous fortitude and self-command ; but, with the motive for exertion, had apparently ceased the power to control her feelings, and although she did not sorrow as one without hope—although she acknowledged the mercy of the Divine decree which had removed her mother from a scene of suffering to that in which "sorrow cometh not, neither have tears a place," she felt in its fullest force her own bereavement.

Perhaps, indeed, her present sufferings were rendered more acute by their previous long restraint. The bow had been overstrained, and its present relaxation therefore threatened to render it useless. There were moments, indeed, when Bessie was startled from the heavy, aimless, almost hopeless monotony of her present grief, by the recollection that she still had painful duties to perform; that she dared not, even now, resign herself entirely to the indulgence of her own feelings. She could not forget that there was one living who looked to her for that happiness which she felt could never be her own lot. She could not forget, and she dared not repent the promise she had made to her dying mother; and though, with most commendable delicacy, Mr. Hastings forbore to utter a word that could recall it to her memory, she could not look in his face or listen to the tender accents of his voice, and hope that he would forget or forego his claim.

Mr. Hastings, indeed, acted, as Rachel said, like an angel; and to suppose that her darling child would be or could be otherwise than happy with such a man, when those natural tears were shed, which were the just tribute to the loss she had sustained, never entered into Rachel's thoughts. Little did Rachel suspect the bitter struggle in that rebellious heart, of which she fancied she knew every movement. Little did she suspect that time, so far from smoothing over every difficulty, and obliterating every obstacle that lay in the path to that perfect happiness which she imagined was to be the result of Bessie's union with Mr. Hastings, that time was but increasing her aversion to the projected alliance.

Mr. Hastings had among the other duties which he had taken upon himself at the death of Mrs. Leslie, and which saved Bess from all those details so inexpressibly painful to the survivor, whose grief is too deep to be soothed with the magnificence of funeral arrangements, or all the solemn trappings and "paraphernalia of woe"—he had written to Sir Matthew Bevington, to inform him of the decease of his sister, modestly requesting to know, as Mrs. Leslie had left no will, and consequently no directions as to the disposal of her funeral, whether Sir Matthew wished, as her nearest friend, to make any suggestions on the subject. He mentioned, too, that Miss Leslie was overcome

by the irreparable loss; that he (Mr. Hastings) felt it impossible to apply to her, and that the only wish she had expressed was one which he believed Mrs. Leslie had herself entertained, namely, that she should be buried with her husband at Barton Regis. The answer to this had been such as to create no little surprise and indignation in the bosom of the sensitive Hastings, who had, in the conclusion of his epistle hinted that though, at present, only entitled to address Sir Matthew as a friend of the family, he hoped at a future period to claim Sir Matthew's notice under another title.

Sir Matthew in his reply, after a mere common-place expression of sorrow for Mrs. Leslie's death, disclaimed all right or inclination to interfere in the arrangements spoken of by Mr. Hastings.

Time wore on, and Mr. Hastings did not relax the least in his assiduous attentions to Bess, and at the expiration of the term set aside by the customs of the world for mourning, he gently but respectfully reminded Bess of the promise made to her beloved parent on her death-bed.

A promise so made, Bess had not the slightest intention of breaking, yet she sincerely wished it had not been made; for should Leicester return and find out the errors into which he had fallen, as she felt assured he would, and crave her forgiveness she was convinced she could not repulse him. If she married Mr. Hastings, she felt certain Leicester would not seek an interview, for his nice sense of honour would prevent such a thing, besides it would be impolitic and unwise in her to grant him one, therefore all chance of healing the unfortunate breach that was between them must be totally abandoned.

To the earnest entreaties of Mr. Hastings and Rachel she at length consented to the marriage taking place in Ramsgate, where they were then stopping; and a grand one it was, for Mr. Hastings was diffuse in scattering some of his immense wealth on the occasion, not only on the equipage and the necessary appendages to a wedding, but to the charities in and near the town, by giving them donations of large sums, and he and his beautiful bride won golden opinions from all, for all, more or less, were sharers in their bounty.

After the ceremony had been performed, the carriage, containing the bride and bridegroom had not left the hotel door more than half an hour, on its route for the splendid mansion Mr. Hastings had provided in London, than to Rachel's surprise she was solicited to attend a gentleman in a private room of the hotel who had a desire to say something to her; she readily acquiesed in the request, though who it could be that wanted to see her she could not guess. Judge her surprise when in the stranger she beheld Ronald Leicester, Bessie's former lover. She clasped her hands in thankfulness that the ceremony was over, for had he made his appearance before she, Rachel, could not say what the consequences would have been. In all probability Bess would not have gone to the church with Mr. Hastings in spite of the immense wealth by which he was surrounded.

How altered was Leicester from when Rachel last beheld him. A foreign climate and mental anxiety had made themselves apparent on his careworn and haggard features.

He commenced the interview with Rachel by putting questions to her as fast as he could put them, relative to the manner in which Bessie had spent her time during his absence; and when he heard the innocent, simple, artless manner in which Rachel accounted for the whole of the time he had been absent, and every particular with which the reader is acquainted, he became frantic, and bitterly accused himself for believing the reports that had reached him. And but that he knew that Lewis Cheverton would not wilfully deceive him, he would immediately have taken summary vengeance on the authors of the base calumnies that had been uttered against his beloved Bess - no longer his. The thought was maddening. He felt convinced that there was some gross mistake in the whole affair, and he determined to set himself to unravel it, though that could not bring him back the lost one, yet it would be some gratification to him to be able to clear her name of the vile aspersions so malignantly cast upon it.

He left Rachel and the hotel immediately after their conversation, to the infinite relief of the former, who was fearful that he would remain till the return of the newly married pair, who purposed fetching Rachel in a short time.

* * * * *

Mr. Hastings and Bess were at length established in their new mansion, with Rachel as their mutual friend, surrounded by every requisite for a well-ordered house, carriages, servant, etceteras, and there seemed to be a prospect of long continued harmony and happiness; but this was soon put an end to by its being discovered that Mr. Hastings was a violent maniac, and had been so for years, at intervals, but that he resumed his reason after a time; his old and attached servant was the only person cognisant of the fact; but it soon became apparent to everybody, for he behaved with such violence to his household, and especially to poor Bess, who on two occasions narrowly escaped being murdered. At length at the earnest request of the physicians, his old servant, and two neighbouring magistrates, she consented to his removal to a private asylum where she could frequently see him.

The winter succeeding Mr. Hastings affliction, which had made so material a change in his wife's situation, proved a very severe one, and the only alleviation of the melancholy that preyed upon her, arose from the opportunities that presented themselves of administering to the distress which was forced more particularly on the notice of the rich and fortunate by the inclemency of the season. The state of comparative apathy into which she had fallen, at first confined Bessie's exertions in this praiseworthy purpose to the mere act of bestowing munificent donations of money wherever it was suggested that it was required, and would be properly applied for the benefit of the sufferers; but although these gifts were for the most part bestowed anonymously, and always without any ostentatious parade of her name, it soon became known that she possessed not only the means, but the inclination to befriend the unfortunate; and, in a short time, Mrs. Hastings found the former monotony of her life completely broken up by the applications that poured in upon her for relief and assistance—a great many of which were of a nature that required personal investigation, and forbade her referring them to those whom she had, in a measure, constituted the distributors of her bounty. Many, many were the scenes of distress she visited and relieved, and in the contemplation of them, learned resignation to evils which she was compelled to acknowledge were comparatively light. Truly, indeed, did she feel that it is easy for the rich to underrate the physical sufferings of poverty, but when she saw families pining and weak with hunger, and shivering with cold; children appealing in vain to their parents for bread; and parents driver, by despair, even to pray for death to relieve them, she was compelled to own that there were sorrows to which those she endured were as nothing in the scale. Among the numerous written applications she received was one which added curiosity to the other sensations with which she perused it. It was evidently the production of an uneducated person, and purported to be from a female who had brought up a large family with credit, except in one instance.

"One of my daughters, indeed," continued the writer, "turned out badly, and was the cause of great trouble to her poor father and myself. But I need not say any more on that subject, madam, because I am sure you had good cause to know as well as me, that all the good counsel and good examples in the world are thrown away, when once a young w man takes a contrary way, and listens to the persuasions of bad people. It was a long time, indeed, before I could believe that my child, that was once so good and kind, had taken to bad ways; but, thank God, it's my consolation that she never had but the best advice and example from her own family, and it was not our fault if she did not do as well as her sisters, who, though they are poor, too poor to be much help to me or their father, are honestly married and settled in the country, which I wish we had never left, nor my poor Susan either; for I can't help saying, though I mean no offence, God knows, to you, ma'am, that it was coming to London that was the ruin of her as well as us."

The writer went on, in the same rambling style, to state that her husband and herself had been induced to come up to London to take possession of a little business and a small sum of money, which had been left to them by a brother; but, after struggling for some years, and meeting with many unforeseen troubles, they were compelled to relinquish their shop, and were now, in their old age, quite destitute, and unable to work as they had done. She went on to say that the parish, to which they had applied, wanted to pass them down to their own parish in the country, but that they would rather die than be sent back like paupers to the place where they had lived so many years in credit. That they had accidentally discovered that Mrs. Hastings—the lady who was doing such a deal of good to the poor in the neighbourhood—was the Miss Leslie whom they had formerly known in such different circumstances, and had therefore taken the liberty to write to her, &c., &c.

The letter was signed Thomas and Susan Barnard, and Bess read it twice over before she could recal the name, or the writers to her recollection.

"God Heavens! it is the mother of Susan, the poor girl whom we brought up with us from Upton Barton," she at length exclaimed; "but what does she mean by Susan's having done badly? You never told me—did you know, dear Rachel, that—but read this letter. I will go to the address they have given as soon as possible. Poor creatures, little did I think—but tell me, Rachel, were you aware what had become of Susan? I thought she was respectably settled."

Rachel was aware, and she now confessed she was, that Susan had quitted her place very abruptly, and that there was too much reason to fear discreditably, very soon after they (the Leslies) had left Highgate; but Rachel did not reveal, even now, what had come to her knowledge, that there was too much reason to fear that the unfortunate girl had been induced to take the foolish step she had done, in order to share the fate of Bell Leslie, who had promised to take her as her own servant, whenever she should be free to do so, and had fulfilled her promise immediately upon leaving her mother and sister. So far Rachel had learned from one of the fellow servants of the misguided and unfortunate girl, who had, in confidence, boasted to her of the advantages she had expected to reap from having been her young mistress's confidante in "the love affair" between the latter and the Marquis of Ledbury. The young woman, to whom Susan had confided her expectations, had according to her own account, remonstrated with her that she would totally forfeit her own character, by going to live with a person in such circumstances as Miss Leslie; but Susan was deaf to persuasion. She was sick, she said, of hard work and confinement, and she would have neither with Miss Bell. Then, too, there would be no restriction as to her dress, and what was the use of having all the smart things Miss Bell had given her, if she were not allowed to wear them, which was the case in her present situation; the lady whom she now served being even more particular and precise as to the appearance of her servants than Mrs. Leslie had been. In short, Susan had made up her mind to run all risks to become Miss Bell Leslie's companion, which she evidently expected to be, rather than servant; and, accordingly, upon the receipt of a letter, which of course, was surmised to have come from her late young mistress, quitted at a moment's warning her really kind and respectable mistress, to plunge, it was much to be feared, into a life of infamy.

Rachel had learned this soon after Bell's elopement from her home, but she naturally considered that it would add to

Mrs. Leslie and Bessie's affliction to know that Bell had thus cruelly involved the thoughtless and simple Susan in the ruin she had brought upon herself; and she, therefore, prudently, as she conceived, concealed from them all she knew respecting their former attendant, whom they thus believed comfortably provided for. Even now, although she foresaw the probability that the truth would be revealed by the unfortunate parents, and Bess would thus become aware of the shameful part her sister had acted, Rachel could not bring herself to disclose all she knew on the subject, but tried to persuade the former to suffer her to see old Barnard and his wife, and inquire into their present circumstances before she (Mrs. Hastings) saw them. For a wonder, however, the latter was deaf to her persuasion. She longed to see the poor old people—any one, indeed, would be welcome whom she had known in former and happier days, and they had known her dear father, too. She remembered how often he had spoken in praise of poor old Thomas, his industry, sobriety, and the decent pride he felt in his rising family, and it would be such a gratification to converse with the poor old man, who, she was sure, would remember his former pastor and friend with regret.

"No, dear Rachel," she continued, "I must go to them myself. They will think else that I am lifted up too high by my prosperity in worldly affairs. Alas," she added, "they little think that I am, in reality, scarcely less unhappy, and, indeed, I may say, less unfortunate than themselves."

The only concession, therefore, Rachel could obtain, was that she should accompany Mrs. Hastings, and trusting that she might find an opportunity of giving the old people a hint on the subject which weighed so heavily on her mind, Rachel followed the former to the carriage, which was ordered to drive to an obscure street in Somers Town, to which Mrs. Barnard's letter had directed them.

Within the last few weeks Bess had become pretty well familiarised with the abodes of poverty, yet not one that she had visited appeared to her so completely destitute of common comforts as the residence of her old friends. But, though thus struck with the miserable appearance of the room in which she was conducted, Mrs. Hastings was more surprised by the cheerful looks of both Barnard and his wife, who were conversing, when she entered, with an appearance of interest that prevented them apparently from noticing who their visitors were. The mystery,

however, was soon explained, for Mrs. Barnard scarcely allowed herself time to utter a welcome to her visitors before she exclaimed—

"Oh, dear ma'am, we are so happy that we hardly know what we are about; but we may thank you for it all, for as Thomas was just saying, it's very plain the gentleman did it all out of respect for you, and so we ought to be as thankful to you as if the money had come out of your pocket."

"What gentleman?" was of course Mrs. Hasting's immediate inquiry. "What had he done—and how did they know that he knew anything of her?"

Mrs. Barnard's explanation was confused and circumlocutory, but her attentive and interested auditor at length comprehended that the former had, previous to her writing to her (Mrs. Hastings), been persuaded to make their situation known to a gentleman of fortune, who was known to be charitable and benevolent.

"He has done a world of good among the poor in this neighbourhood, ma'am," continued the old woman, "and so, as Thomas said, there could be no harm in our trying, though it was hard enough to look like beggars to one we knew nothing about, and who could not be expected to feel for us like them that had known us in better times; and, indeed, to tell the truth, if we had known then where to write to you, ma'am, I don't think we should have applied at all to Mr. Leicester."

"Mr. Leicester!" repeated Mrs. Hastings, a bright blush suffusing her cheeks as she uttered the name so long a stranger to her lips and ears.

"Yes, ma'am, that is the gentleman's name that is just gone, and has behaved so handsome to us," returned Mrs. Barnard. "I am sure he was a friend of yours, for he told us so himself, and he asked a thousand questions about you, when we knew you at Upton, which I wish we'd never left, for we've had nothing but ill-luck and misfortune, as I told him, ever since; and he knew our poor Susan, too—he told us he did, when she lived with you and your mamma at Highgate. Oh, Miss Leslie—I beg your pardon, Mrs. Hastings, I mean—but he called you Miss Leslie, though he said he knew you was married. Somehow, I thought he did not like to hear you called anything but Miss Leslie, and——"

"But Susan—Mrs. Barnard, you were speaking of Susan," interrupted Bess, anxious to divert the old woman from the subject she was inclined to animadvert upon.

"Ay, that was the beginning of our misfortunes," replied Mrs. Barnard. "Oh, ma'am, could I ever have thought that my child would have turned out a disgrace to her father and mother, and all that belonged to her; and yet, as my poor old man often says, why should we be surprised that a simple girl like her should be led astray, when one that was so much her betters, and had everything, as one may say, that she could wish for in the world——"

The old woman caught at the moment Rachel's discouraging look, and suddenly stopped, but she had said already sufficient to excite the most painful suspicions in Mrs. Hastings' bosom, and the latter immediately remarked—

"I know nothing of Susan's conduct, Mrs. Barnard, since she quitted my mother's service at Highgate. I know that she was then provided for to her own satisfaction, and ours, with a situation in a respectable family, and at wages much better than my poor mother could afford to give her. If, therefore, she left it, and has since acted wrong, as you insinuate, I hope and trust that you do not reflect upon——"

"God forbid, ma'am, that I should reflect upon anybody," interrupted Mrs. Barnard, hastily. "Susan was old enough, as I told her, the only time I ever saw her, quite old enough to know what she was about, and judge between good and evil, and though she wanted to lay all the blame on Miss Bell, and declared that if she hadn't believed that she was married, or going to be married to the gentleman she ran away, she (that is, Susan) would never have left her place to live with her, still——"

"Bell—my sister!" ejaculated Mrs. Hastings, with horror pourtrayed on her features. "Do you mean, Mrs. Barnard, that your daughter left her service, to——"

"Yes, ma'am, but I beg your pardon for mentioning it—I don't mean, I'm sure, to throw any reflections upon your family. You must have suffered enough, I'm sure, in having such disgrace brought upon you, though my child was as dear to me as the young lady could be to you, and as I said to Thomas——"

"And where is Susan now?" demanded Bess, who had hoped through this means to learn something decisive respecting her sister.

Mrs. Barnard shook her head with a mournful look.

"I wish I could answer that question, ma'am," she replied, "but I never heard anything of her since she came to us, soon after we took possession of the shop that's been our ruin. She was dressed up then like a lady, though she said she had been out of place for many months, and had lost her character, and wasn't likely ever to get a place again, for Miss Bell was as bad, if not worse off than herself, and indeed she hadn't seen anything of her for a long time, for she had quarrelled with the gentleman she run away with from home, and he'd turned her off, and—it's no use to conceal the truth, ma'am," continued the old woman. "We made out from Susan's own account, that her mistress and her had been leading a shameful life together; and Susan, it seems, had been latterly setting up for a fine lady, as well as her mistress, and so Miss Bell's high spirit, it seemed, wouldn't put up with being made companion where she used to be mistress, while it was but natural that Susan, seeing she had given up everything for her, should take liberties, and think she had no right to be kept under by one that was now no better, as it might be said, than herself. However, I'm not going to say who was in fault, or who was not; but, it appears, Susan and Miss Bell quarrelled and parted, and Susan had been living how she could for some time, parting with one thing and another till pretty well all was gone but what she had on her back. It was not in nature, ma'am, not to be angry to see a girl that had brought herself to destruction, and was a disgrace to herself and all her family, and now come to us, when everything was gone, and she could find no other friends. Thomas was in a sad passion with her, and told her as she had made her bed so she might lie in it, for he was not going to be burthened with an idle, good-for-nothing hussey, that set herself above working for an honest livelihood. Notwithstanding," continued Mrs. Barnard, after pausing, wiping her eyes, and looking at her husband in a manner that convinced her hearers that his presence restrained her from saying all that she would have said, "Notwithstanding," she repeated, "I know her father would have given her a home, and have tried to have got her into service again if she had been humble, as she ought to have been, and owned she was sorry for what she had done; but, instead of that, she took a many airs upon herself; and said she wasn't the only one in the world that had been misfortunate; and, indeed, her father and her came to such high words that she walked out of the house, and said she'd put an end to herself rather than ever ask him for a bit of bread, or have her 'sul thrown in her face in that manner, no so," continued the poor old woman, bursting into tears, "I have never seen her since, and whether she is living or dead, God knows !"

Mrs. Hastings felt that any consolation she could offer on this subject would be of little avail. She was dreadfully shocked at this proof of her sister's recklessness and folly, in involving the poor simple girl, Susan, in ruin ; but she endeavoured to turn the mother's thoughts from the subject, by making further inquiries into their present situation.

"Mr. Leicester," the old woman said, "had behaved most liberally and generously to them. He had given them five pounds for present necessities, and had promised, as soon as they settled whether they should go down to their native place, or attempt some way to get their living in London, that he would advance money sufficient to set them forward in the world.

"There was only one thing," the old woman observed, "that made her unwilling to leave London, for she knew they could do better in the country, where they should be among friends and relations, and respected by everybody that knew them. If I could only know what has become of my poor girl," observed Mrs. Barnard, "I should be glad to turn my back upon London to-morrow ; but, somehow, I can't bear to leave the place when I know she hasn't got a friend in the world besides ourselves."

"And how, I should like to know, would it be any service our staying here," demanded the old man, "when she couldn't know where to find us. If she didn't seek us out when she knew were we were, it's not very likely that she would take the trouble to trace us through the half-dozen places that we've lived in since we've been going down in the world."

This was a subject that Mrs. Hastings felt she could not interfere in, and accordingly, having made the old woman a handsome present, and requested her to call upon her in Grosvenor Square, and let her know which way she decided, whether to remain in London, or to return to their native place, she departed.

Much as she had wished to hear more of Leicester from the objects of his bounty, she had scrupulously abstained from asking a single question respecting him, and had only, by her silence, admitted to Mrs. Barnard that she had formerly been acquainted with him ; yet, with all her determination to forget, if possible, all that had ever passed between them, she could not drive him from her thoughts, now that he was thus again, as it were, brought before her. Mrs. Barnard's observation that he seemed unwilling to speak of her as Mrs. Hastings, which had brought the colour to her cheek at the time, again recurred to her memory—yet she tried to forget it, tried to believe the woman was mistaken.

"No, no," she softly murmured, "it is sufficient that one of us is miserable—he, I hope and trust, is happy."

Some days passed, and Mrs. Hastings, busied in her voluntary labours, had almost ceased to think of the Barnards, or aught connected with them, when she was informed the old woman requested to see her, and gave orders to the servant to show her into the breakfast-room, where Rachel and herself were sitting.

"You have come, I suppose, to tell me that you have decided on going down to Barton," she observed to the old woman.

"Yes, ma'am, I have," she replied, with a mournful look, that seemed to express anything but satisfaction at the decision.

"I am glad to hear it," observed Mrs. Hastings, "for I confess that I think your staying in London could answer very little purpose, unless you had some clue to poor Susan's——"

"Do not speak of her again," interrupted the poor woman, bursting into tears. "I shall never, never see her again."

"You have heard something, then, since I saw you," rejoined Mrs. Hastings, in a compassionate tone. "I will not distress you by asking, but——"

"Oh, no, do not ask me anything," exclaimed Mrs. Barnard, wildly. "I have solemnly promised not to tell you; but I shall never, never see my poor girl again."

Mrs. Hastings felt surprised. A thousand confused thoughts darted into her mind as to who could have enjoined secrecy to her, and how was she interested further than mere compassion for the unfortunate girl. She would not attempt, however, to question the woman, or persuade her to break the solemn promise she had given, and again she applied herself to endeavour to soothe and console her.

"If the poor girl is dead, as I suppose by your observation, my poor woman," she observed.

"Oh, don't speak of it, don't talk of it," exclaimed the old woman. "I shall never be happy again. I shall never have her out of my eyes and my thoughts—and her father—oh, I shall never forgive him. He might have saved her, if he had only spoken a little kinder to her—if he hadn't thrown all her faults in her face as he did. And he knew, too, that from her childhood she was like himself—obstinate and determined. She would always be led, but never driven, and—but it is all over, and I shall never see her again. Oh, my Susan, my poor child, who was once so good, and honest and industrious, and would have been still if it had not been for bad example and temptation, as I told——"

She suddenly paused at the moment. Bess was regarding her with the most anxious expectation, and Rachel's countenance expressed, if possible, still more intense interest. The old woman, however, the burst of violent grief having subsided, began to speak more calmly and collectedly of her present situation.

Her husband, she said, was bowed down to the earth with grief and bitter repentance for the harshness which, he could not conceal from himself, had driven his unfortunate daughter to despair. He had resolved on accepting Mr. Leicester's proffered assistance to return to Upton Barton immediately. They were to leave London in two days. And then Mrs. Barnard congratulated herself that "Thank God, none of her old friends and neighbours would know the wretched end of her poor child. I could never look them in the face if they knew it," she added, " and as I was told, when I learned the truth, that is another reason why I should keep the secret, and let everything remain as it is."

"If that secret concerns Mrs. Hastings, Mrs. Barnard," observed Rachel, with peculiar significance, "I must tell you that I think you act very cruelly and ungratefully towards her, not to speak out plainly what you know."

Bessie's cheek became deathly pale. She did not clearly see what Rachel's observations tended to, but she knew, from the agitated look and voice of the latter, that she (Rachel) was convinced that Mrs. Barnard could, if she would, throw some light on the mystery that had so long occupied both their minds.

"My dear child," observed Rachel, "let me prevail upon you to leave Mrs. Barnard and me together for a short time, and endeavour to compose yourself. Hope for the best, dear Bessie," she whispered, as with gentle force she led the latter from the room, "I foresee that this woman has it in her power to explain all that has hitherto prevented my indulging the hopes that I considered contrary to reason and my own experience. Be guided by me, dear child, I cannot put the questions in your presence which I will force her to answer before she leaves this house."

Bess reluctantly yielded, but as she was quitting the room, she suddenly recollected herself, and turned again to Mrs Barnard, whose looks expressed considerable uneasiness at what was passing.

"If I have understood your hints and observations correctly," she observed, in a tremulous tone, "you consider that you have a right to attribute your unfortunate daughter's ruin to the example and persuasions of—of one who certainly ought to have known better than to involve a simple ignorant girl in the distress and disgrace she brought upon herself and her family?"

"But which might, perhaps, have all been prevented, had Susan done her duty in the first instance," interrupted Rachel, with warmth. "I do not wish to hurt Mrs. Barnard's feelings. It is natural for a mother to say and think all that can excuse her own child ; but still, in fairness and justice, I must speak the truth, but for Susan's duplicity and artful contrivances, the clandestine correspondence that ended in her own ruin as well as——"

"I've heard enough of that, ma'am, before," interrupted the old woman angrily "Yes, it was thrown in my teeth that Susan's artfulness and contrivances had—but no matter, she's gone now, and can't defend herself. She can't tell us of the temptations thrown in her way, and the persusions of them that she looked up to as her betters. God forbid I should try to throw her sins upon the shoulders of them that's got plenty of their own to bear, but she was a poor, weak, simple girl. Nobody knows it better than you, Mrs. Rachel, for I remember well, that when first it was proposed that she should go to London with the family, I didn't hide it from you that her greatest fault, and that which made her father and her quarrel so that I was glad to get her out into the world, was that she was vain, and fond of dress and finery. But as you said that was a fault many girls at her age fell into, and after all it was no sin, though my poor husband, who was always, as you know, strict and religious, thought it the greatest of sins, and always prophesied it would bring her to ruin if it wasn't checked. Poor man, he little thought, when he rejoiced that she was going with those who would keep a strict hand over her, and take care that she shouldn't launch out

beyond her station—he little thought that she was running into the lion's mouth, and that a few cast-off silk gowns, and——"

"These are painful retrospections, that cannot improve either your feelings or ours, Mrs. Barnard," observed Mrs. Hastings, mildly, though her tremulous lips and agitated look betrayed how deeply she was distressed by the old woman's remarks, "what I wish to say is," she continued, drawing her purse from her pocket, "that as far as money can contribute to restore you to comfort and happiness——"

"I shall never be happy again," sobbed the old woman, bursting into a fresh flood of grief.

"I hope and trust you will, at least, enjoy many years of comfort," returned Mrs. Hastings, "and as I feel it to be my duty to secure that object, as far as it be possible, I will give you sufficient now for your present purpose, and will take the necessary means to settle a yearly sum upon you and your husband, so as to prevent your incurring any obligations to any other person. You understand me, do you not, Mrs. Barnard? Mr. Leicester—" her voice faltered as she pronounced the name, " has, of course, many claims upon his benevolence."

" He is an angel if ever there was one upon earth," murmured Mrs. Barnard, with a warmth that brought a smile upon Rachel's countenance, and a faint blush to Bessie's cheek, which was still further heightened when the old woman added—

" God for ever bless him for his kindness to me and mine, and make him as happy as he deserves to be. And I'm not the only one, by hundreds, that has reason to pray for him. Don't think, ma'am, that I am not grateful and thankful to you for your kindness. No, no, I feel it more than I can say, and I know, too, that had my poor Susan listened to your good advice and Mrs. Rachel's, though she seemed angry with me just now, for taking my child's part——"

" No, no, not angry, Mrs. Barnard—God forbid that I should feel anger on such a subject," observed Rachel.

" She told me," continued the old woman, again bursting into tears, at the recollections that rushed upon her mind, " she told me, that evening that she came to our little shop in Clerkenwell, that if she had been guided by Miss Bessie's good counsel, and Mrs. Rachel's, too, who had been like a mother to her, she should never have been brought to ruin and misery. Oh yes, she was not ungrateful, poor thing, and she said that she knew, too, if she could conquer her shame for having betrayed the trust reposed in her, and apply to you, ma'am," addressing Bess, " she knew you wouldn't see her want. Oh, that I had but acted as my own heart told me I ought—that I had insisted on her father's giving her a home till she could do something for herself—and yet I won't be unjust—he wouldn't have refused her, if she would have humbled herself, as she ought, and listened to him with penitence ; but instead of that, she turned upon him with such violence I could hardly believe my own ears, and told him he had never behaved like a father to her ; that his strictness, and his whims about her dress had made her hate religion, and —but I can't tell half she said. She must have been mad. My poor husband would have it that she had been drinking, and that made him ten times worse. God knows if it was so. She was so altered in many respects that I scarcely knew my own child. I have heard since that that

was one of the consequences of the way of life she had got into. It might be so— but, as I said, it wasn't for them that had been the means of seducing her into that horrible life to be the first to turn round upon her, and——"

" Do not let us again get upon this subject, Mrs. Barnard," interrupted Rachel, who saw that Bess shuddered with horror at the thoughts that these observations suggested. " Have you anything more to say, my dear child, respecting what you intend to do for Mrs. Barnard? It is as well there should be a thorough understanding on the subject."

" Yes," said Mrs. Hastings, and she named a yearly sum, certainly quite sufficent to prevent the old people being compelled to incur obligations to any one else. That they should not do so was the only condition she wished to impose. It seemed as if she considered it a personal humiliation that they should be indebted to Mr. Leicester ; and though she did not again directly name him, Mrs. Barnard fully understood her wish, and promised compliance; not, however, without a secret reservation which Mrs. Hastings was far from suspecting—though, had she known more of the woman's character, she might readily have guessed at—namely, that she (Mrs. Barnard) did not by any means feel herself bound by this compact to return what she had already received from Mr. Leicester; but only to assure him that Mrs. Hasting's bounty rendered all further assistance from him unnecessary. This she readily promised, and intended faithfully to fulfil, although she carefully concealed the fact that what she had already received from Mr. Leicester rendered Mrs. Hastings's present gift quite superfluous ; and, with the forty pounds a year which the latter had promised to settle upon them for life, would render the Barnard's richer people than they had ever been, or ever had hoped to be.

Rachel's experience of the world enabled her to detect the reservation the cunning old woman had made, but whether she thought it was too much to expect one of Mrs. Barnard's class to give up money actually in possession, or whether she (Rachel) considered Bessie's scruples, as regarded Mr. Leicester, overstrained delicacy, she did not hint to the former her suspicions, and Mrs. Hastings gladly withdrew from the expressions of Mrs. Barnard's gratitude.

" I will come to the point at once on which I wish to speak to you, Mrs. Barnard," observed Rachel, when she was left alone with the old woman, who showed considerable uneasiness the moment the door closed upon Mrs. Hastings, and would gladly have taken her leave immediately, on the pretext that her old man would feel uneasy at her long absence. "You cannot deceive me," she continued, looking fixedly at her, and trying to speak with calmness, though her own bosom heaved, and her whole frame trembled with impatience for the answer which was at once to prove the error of her own hitherto firm belief, and solve the whole mystery which had been productive of such serious mischief to her beloved Bess. "You have seen one who I have for years believed in her grave. Do not deny it. It was Bell Leslie from whom you received the intelligence of your daughter's death!"

Mrs. Barnard looked for a moment confused, but the next she recovered her confidence.

"You are wrong—quite wrong, Mrs. Rachel, I do assure you," she replied.

Rachel, however, was not to be so easily deceived. This was an equivocation, if not a direct falsehood; and, without hesitation she told Mrs. Barnard so. What, however, was her surprise when the old woman, pressed on the subject by questions she could not evade, acknowledged that it was from Mr. Leicester she had learned the particulars of the event which had deprived her of every hope of beholding the unfortunate Susan again.

"Mr. Leicester! how was it possible— Mr. Leicester was thousands of miles distant when that event took place," exclaimed Rachel; "but if you have any feeling, any gratitude to Mrs. Hastings, you will not conceal anything from her. You must know, by your own experience, the misery of suspense. Tell me the truth. You do know that Bell Leslie is living?"

"Mr. Leicester can tell you all about it, Mrs. Rachel," replied the old woman, after a few moments' hesitation. "It is not right of you to ask me to betray what I have given a solemn promise not to mention."

"Then I must seek an explanation of Mr. Leicester," observed Rachel, deeply disappointed, but now fully convinced her suspicions were correct; since nothing could be easier, or would have been more natural than that the old woman should instantly have disclaimed all knowledge on the subject.

Mrs. Barnard's countenance betrayed considerable uneasiness and hesitation for some minutes, but at length she observed that she had one particular favour to request. It was, that Rachel would defer any inquiries till after she (Mrs. Barnard)

and her husband had left London, which would be at the latest in two days.

Rachel could not comprehend the motives of this delay on a point which she was, of course, desirous of having explained as quickly as possible; but Mrs. Barnard pleaded so earnestly that she had reason to think Mr. Leicester would be offended with her for having betrayed what she had been enjoined silence upon, and that she was under such deep obligations to him that she could not bear the idea of seeing him after he had discovered that she had disobeyed his injunctions, that the required promise was given, and the old woman departed.

It was, of course, no cause of surprise to Mrs. Hastings that Rachel, at last, confessed that she was a convert to the opinion she had herself so long avowed, namely, that Bell Leslie was still living. She knew that, sooner or later, Rachel must be convinced of a fact which her own senses witnessed; for that it was her unfortunate sister, whom she had beheld in the Park with Captain Kennard, she had all along been thoroughly convinced, much as various circumstances, and even the declaration of the supposed Mrs. Lawrence, militated against it; but the hopes she had entertained of an immediate explanation of the seeming mystery, through the means of Mrs. Barnard, were grievously disappointed when Rachel avowed that she had learned nothing from her, but had gained a clue, by which she hoped, in a few days, to ascertain the truth. What were Rachel's motives for concealing the name of Mr. Leicester, as connected with the delay, which was so painful and unsatisfactory to Mrs. Hastings, was known only to herself; certain it was, that she gave no hint even that it was through Mr. Leicester that she expected to gain the desired information, and the former was again condemned to suffer in silence the misery of suspense, while Rachel employed herself in devising how she should proceed in gaining an interview with that gentleman, an unexpected and unforeseen obstacle to which having presented itself in her own thoughtless omission in having neglected to inquire of Mrs. Barnard his present residence.

To remedy this, after having in vain attempted to devise some means of seeing Mrs. Barnard, previous to her departure, without the knowledge of Mrs. Hastings, Rachel was at last compelled to acknowledge to the latter that she had a strong motive for wishing to see the old woman once more, and the former immediately proposed to accompany her to the house they had before visited. Rachel would willingly have dispensed with her company, and her countenance betrayed this feeling, though she hesitated to avow it."

"I will not seek to penetrate your secret, whatever it may be, dear Rachel," observed the former. "I know you think you act for the best, yet I entreat you to recollect how mistaken—how injurious, I may say, has in many instances proved your system of concealment, merely from the wish of not inflicting pain. Forgive me, my dearest, best of friends—I know you always mean right, but——"

"In this instance, at any rate, I know I am right," observed Rachel, with warmth, "but you are mistaken if you think I am concealing from you any intelligence that could set the matter at rest."

"I will not press you further, dear Rachel," exclaimed Mrs. Hastings, hurt that she had aroused the feelings of the latter; "nay more," she continued, "to show you how implicitly I rely upon you, I will not even see Mrs. Barnard, but remain in the carriage during your interview with her."

Bessie's promises were, however, needless—the Barnards were gone. They had left London early the same morning, and Rachel had only, as she thought, to blame her own carelessness for an oversight which would now delay to an indefinite period the explanation she had hoped to expedite. In pursuance of her resolution, Bess forbore to ask a single question, though she read extreme vexation and disappointment in her companion's looks.

"Home," was the order given to the coachman as soon as Rachel re-entered the carriage, and homewards they were proceeding in silence when, in passing down a street from the New Road, Bess uttered an exclamation, and drew back in the corner of the carriage. Rachel bent forward as eagerly as her companion had withdrawn herself, but it was too late to accomplish her purpose; for the persons who had attracted the attention of the former had already disappeared; though not so quickly but that they had distinctly been recognised by both. Yes, not a doubt remained on the mind of either Mrs. Hastings or Rachel.

The gentleman whom they had seen knocking at the door of a shabby, suspicious-looking house was Leicester—the person who opened the door to admit him so hastily as to show that she had been anxiously expecting if not watching for him, was Bell Leslie.

She stood in the full light of the sun, unconscious of the eager eyes that were fixed upon her. They saw even the faint smile that struggled with a look of confusion and extreme dejection on her still beautiful features. They could almost hear the words of welcome that her lips uttered.

Bessie's hand tightly grasped Rachel's arm as the latter eagerly threw herself forward, exclaiming—

"My God—it is she—it is herself—my own dear child, my dear, dear Bell!"

"Not now—oh, not now," gasped Bess, withholding her, "not while he is present. Oh, no, this is too much."

Rachel instantly comprehended her feelings.

"My poor Bessie, this is what I wished to save you from knowing," she observed. "Yes, my heart foreboded the meaning of Mrs. Barnard's secrecy. It was that which prevented my telling you—"

"It is all over now," murmured Bess, a burning blush of shame suffusing her countenance, and banishing the death-like paleness which had overspread it at the first sight of Leicester. "Oh, God," she continued, "can it be possible? Can he, too, be so lost to every feeling? Thank God, he did not see me—he did not know that I beheld this most mortifying, humiliating, and—"

She was interrupted by her companion pulling the check-string.

"Oh, no—not even if I were sure I should never behold her again, would I seek an interview with her at this moment," she exclaimed. "Let us at once return home."

Rachel explained. She was only desirous of ascertaining the name of the street, lest they might mistake its situation.

The servant looked surprised at the inquiry, and his mistress felt as if she shrunk even from his eyes as he replied to it. It was evident from his hesitation that he knew the disreputable character of the place, and was wondering what interest his mistress could attach to it? And this was the abode of her sister!—and here, regardless even of appearances, destitute of all shame, the once delicate-minded, refined, and strictly moral Leicester—

"Oh, how I hate, detest, despise, scorn him at this moment," she exclaimed, scarcely conscious that she was uttering her thoughts aloud, "and Bell, too, if but one spark of proper feeling, of pride, existed in her bosom——"

"There is one consolation, at least, my dear," observed Rachel, "Mr. Leicester must be now convinced how cruelly you were wronged. He must know how the mistakes have originated from which you have suffered. There cannot be a doubt now that Bell's supposed death, and your striking resemblance to each other has occasioned it all. I do not wonder at Mr. Cheverton, or any one else being deceived, for as she stood this morning, with her beautiful curls falling round her face and neck, I said to myself, 'Had not Bessie been by my side, I would have sworne it was her.'"

Bess felt there was little matter of congratulation to her in a vindication that now came too late, and was achieved at the expense of her unhappy and degraded sister.

"I would have been content that he should still have believed me the guilty creature he once represented me, rather than that I should have been thus vindicated. And, after all, perhaps he still believes me guilty. If Bell has been so cruel and unfeeling as to profit so long by the belief that was spread of her death, to my condemnation, it is not probable that she will have feeling enough for me now to confess——"

"Leicester has long, long been convinced of your innocence, dear Bessie," interrupted Rachel. "He had done you justice long before even the suspicion had arisen how the mystery which has puzzled us all originated. Yes, if he had never seen Bell, never known that she was still in existence, he would have been—he *was* as firmly convinced that you were innocent as I who knew every movement, every thought of your heart."

Bessie's surprised look demanded an explanation of this positive assertion, and Rachel, glad of anything that could divert her companion's mind from dwelling on the painful scene they had just witnessed, proceeded to relate the particulars of her interview with Leicester on the morning of the marriage—his bitter despair and self-condemnation.

Bessie's expressive countenance—the breathless earnestness with which she listened to this detail—and the silent and mournful reverie into which she sank at its conclusion, all told how deep were the sensations it excited.

It was a triumph to know that Leicester's heart had done her justice—that the web of guilt and mystery which had been woven around her had never alienated that heart entirely from her—and that to the plain and simple voice of truth, in the person of Rachel, he had instantly yielded his entire conviction, in spite of all the appearances that had militated so strongly against her. They were sweet and pleasant tears which she shed to the memory of that affection which had once united them, as it were, in one soul. They were tears of gratified pride with which she repeated to herself, in gentle aspirations:—

"He knew I was innocent. Thank God, he knew, though too late for our happiness, he knew that I had never deserved to forfeit his love, and that we were both victims of his rashness, not of my deceit and inconstancy."

It was the first time since she had become the wife of Hastings that Bessie had ever voluntarily yielded to the recollections of her first and only affection, and she now started from her deep and almost unconscious reverie as if she had committed a crime, for Rachel, who had been looking at the superscriptions of two or three letters which were lying on the library-table, having arrived during their absence from home, uttered in a tone of surprise the name of Hastings.

"It is his hand-writing, my dear—I should know it anywhere," she observed, as she put the letter into Bessie's hand.

It was the first time since he had left his home that her unfortunate husband had written to her, and Bess trembled with agitation as she opened it.

The letter was short—but in a calm and collected, though melancholy strain.

"The delusion," he said, "which rendered our separation necessary has, thank God, passed away. I have become conscious that there existed no foundation for my suspicions, and I trust that you will yield to my ardent request and prayer that I may return to die at home."

Many expressions of ardent affection towards his wife, and regret and sorrow for the affliction and trouble he had caused her, concluded this letter, which was accompanied by another from the physician under whose care Mr. Hastings had been placed, and who, although he did not so positively confirm the recovery of his patient from his mental malady as might have been expected from the calm and reasonable tone of the latter's epistle, informed Mrs. Hastings that he no longer considered it necessary or advisable to restrain Mr. Hastings from being visited by his friends, and especially her whom he expressed great anxiety to see as soon as possible.

"The state of Mr. Hastings's health," added the physician, "certainly rendered every possible indulgence necessary and advisable, and although he did not wish to alarm her, he considered it would be better not to delay her visit."

All that had previously agitated and occupied her mind was instantly dismissed. Leicester, her sister, though not forgotten

—how was it possible to forget?—but at that moment every thought but of her suffering husband was thrown aside. She reproached herself for having indulged, for an instant, thoughts and feelings which were inconsistent with her duty to one, who, whatever had been his faults and weaknesses, had given many, many proofs of a noble and generous nature, and had regarded her with the warmest and most disinterested affection.

Before two hours had elapsed she was seated by his bedside, suppressing all the natural fear and horror which the recollection of his former violence and unjust suspicions of her could not fail to have excited at the sight of him, and intent only upon contributing to his present comfort.

Greatly altered as he was in person, he was even more so in manner, and apparently in disposition. The one, indeed, was for the worse, the other for the better; his looks were almost ghastly from the effects of his disorder and confinement, while all the harshness, the proud irritability and superciliousness of his manners seemed to have vanished as if by enchantment, and he seemed as if only desirous to live that he might atone for the injustice and violence of which he seemed, to Bessie's great astonishment, to retain a clear and complete recollection.

Had she listened only to the dictates of her own feelings, she would not have returned home without his accompanying her ; but she, and, indeed, he yielded to the earnest persuasions of the physician that he should remain a few days longer, and that, in the meantime, Mrs. Hastings should make every necessary preparation for a visit to the South of France, the climate of which was considered likely to restore, if anything could, his bodily health.

The kind manner in which he inquired after Mrs. Mytton, emboldened Bess to tell him that she had been living with her ever since he had been from home, and to her great satisfaction he seemed pleased that it had been so.

"I have often thought," he observed, "when I have been capable of thinking, how miserably solitary must be your life ; but then, again, I imagined that the Ellisons would not suffer you to be much alone, and their gaiety and liveliness—"

"Would not at all have agreed with my feelings and habits," returned his wife, with quickness. "I have seen scarcely anything of them. They are good girls enough," she continued, "but their friendship is only suited to the holidays of life—

it will not stand the storms and gloom of affliction."

The expression of Hastings's eye showed that he was rather pleased than grieved at this remark, and Bess, as she observed this, drew from it an inference not altogether satisfactory. It argued, she thought, that he still retained sufficient of his former weakness to be jealous, and suspicious that she had enjoyed too much pleasure during his absence ; and, while she sighed at the thought, she felt rejoiced that her answer, which was even less than the truth, should have removed for the present this lingering of selfish and ungenerous feeling. His answer, however, after a few moment's consideration, banished all unpleasant feeling from her mind.

"I feel now," he observed, "how very wrong has been my system of seclusion and distance from the world, for although, perhaps, had our circle been much larger, you would have found but too many like the Ellisons, mere holiday friends, as you say, there would have been a chance of meeting some one who could advise, assist, and soothe the hours of affliction. I know you would say that you had all you wished, my dear girl, in Rachel, and I am willing to do all justice to her merits, but still I feel I have not done you justice in my selfish love of quietness and solitude. If I live to return, I will try to amend this, and especially, I have been thinking, that we ought to take some means to endeavour to conciliate the only member of your family who is, I believe, living."

Bess turned pale and trembled, her thoughts naturally turned to her sister, yet she could not imagine how he could possibly know anything, and if he did, it was not within the bounds of probability that he should thus speak of one who had forfeited all claim to be considered an eligible companion.

Mr. Hastings soon, however, dissipated all doubt on that subject.

"I allude, my dear Bessie," he continued, "to your uncle, Sir Matthew Bevington, and Lady Jane. If I have understood you rightly, the cause of your alienation from them was very slight on either side."

"I know nothing, on my part," observed Bess, coolly. "The birth of their son and heir was the only cause of estrangement——"

"And that can no longer operate," observed Hastings, quickly, "as their fortune, they must know, can be no object to you, who will—who do, indeed possess one infinitely superior. But, as I was going to observe, Bessie—it is certainly from you an overture to reconciliation ought to come, and I blame myself much for not having enforced—recommended the measure, I should say."

Bess half smiled at the hasty correction of the word, but the smile was soon changed for a look of deep emotion and gratitude as he continued—

"I have thought much, my dear girl, of the circumstances you would be left in at my death, totally unprotected and desolate, and I feel how desirable it would be to secure to you the assistance and protection of your own relatives. I will write to Sir Matthew myself, and you shall—will, I know, at my request, endeavour to conciliate Lady Jane."

Bess knew not how to object to this certainly reasonable proposition, which was evidently the result of the most disinterested anxiety for her welfare; but she thought of her sister at that moment. How great would be her relief if she dared to entrust to Hastings the secret of that sister's existence and present situation, but she feared the effect it might have on his proud and sensitive nature. The physician had enforced strongly the necessity of his patient being kept from excitement—"On that alone," he had said, "depended his perfect recovery"—and she remained therefore silent, determining, however, to have no concealment from Sir Matthew Bevington, should he respond favourably to Mr. Hastings's letter, but at once to reveal to the former the whole mystery from which she had suffered so severely, not only in the eyes of her own family, but of nearly all who knew her.

From the renewal of intercourse with Lady Jane, she foreboded little pleasure or satisfaction, but her eyes filled with tears as she recalled to her memory her uncle's former kindness and affection towards her, and she felt that she would willingly bear infinitely greater inconveniences and unpleasantness than were likely to result from her restoration to Lady Jane's favour.

For two days her necessary attendance on her husband postponed Bessie's intended measures as regarded her sister, but it had been settled that Mr. Hastings was to return to his home on the following Saturday. It was now Thursday, and, as the former observed to Rachel, it became imperative there should no longer be any delay. Whatever was done, must be done before Mr. Hastings' return.

And what was to be done? To see her sister once more, face to face. To hear her speak, to hold her to her heart, and tell her, guilty and degraded, and fallen as she was, that she was still dear to her. To

offer to her—to force her to accept the means of rescuing herself from a life of misery and disgrace, and to plan the course that should be pursued to effect this was all easy enough in perspective. There was one, only one obstacle, one difficulty that presented itself. Should she (Bess) encounter Leicester in that interview, so ardently desired. Oh, with what inexpressible loathing and terror did she turn from the thought.

"Anything but that," she exclaimed to Rachel. "I could bear anything but that."

Rachel, however, very rationally observed that there was not the slightest probability of such an occurrence; because, in the first place, it was not likely that Mr. Leicester passed much of his time at such a place as that where they had seen Bell—a house of the shabbiest, not to say most miserable appearance; and, in the second, it was certain he would be even more eager to avoid such a meeting than she (Mrs. Hastings) herself.

The strange appearance a visit to such a place might have in the eyes of the servants decided the friends to walk until they reached a coach-stand, from whence they took a hackney coach to S—— Street. Rachel had taken sufficient note of the exterior of the house to point it out to the coachman, and in a few minutes his thundering rap at the door announced them.

"You will wait, if you please," observed Rachel, as she assisted her trembling friend to alight.

"Yes, I'll wait, in course," returned the coachman, in a saucy tone, "but you'll pay me my fare first, ma'am. I've been done, too often by the ladies hereabouts to——"

Rachel put a stop to his mortifying harangue by putting half-a-crown into his hand; and his tone instantly changed to extreme civility.

"Let me help you, miss," he observed, offering his arm to Bess, who had sunk back, trembling and irresolute.

A wretched-looking, dirty, emaciated old woman had by this time opened the door, and was regarding the visitors with a scowling look of surprise and curiosity. Bess made a resolute effort to suppress the terror and dismay which had almost deprived her of power to stand, and rushed into the passage, while Rachel whispered an inquiry to the old woman for Miss Leslie.

"Don't know such a person," replied the woman, her eyes fixed on Bessie's pale face with a look of astonishment.

"Mrs. Lawrence, then," said Rachel.

"Ay, I thought so," muttered the old

woman. "Yes, yes, you're right enough. I thought it was her you wanted. My gracious, she's the very moral. As like as two peas to one another, if I didn't—"

"Pray let us see her immediately," added Rachel, pressing some silver into the old woman's hand.

"She aint up yet," returned the woman, whose eyes glistened with pleasure as she looked at the money; and then turning, as if to look that no one was watching her from the staircase, which was at the extremity of the passage, she hastily drew a dirty rag from her pocket, wrapped the money in it, and thrust it into her bosom.

"Who's wanted, Nance?" interrogated a coarse female voice from the top of the stairs, and a bloated ill-looking face, enveloped in a profusion of dingy frillings, was seen over the balusters, reconnoitring the party.

"Oh, Bella—Mrs. Lawrence," was the laconic explanation.

"Can't you ask 'em into the parlour, and call her, then, without such a fuss, keepin' the front-door open, and the wind comin' up the stairs enough to cut one in two?" was the answer.

The old woman threw open the door of the room denominated the parlour, and Bess sank down on the first chair that presented itself.

"Bella!" Oh, how had her heart sunk lower and lower as she heard her sister spoken of with this degrading familiarity by the revolting being that stood before her.

"Shall I tell her who it is wants her?" inquired the woman, as she was about to leave the room. "She'll be in a precious ill humour, I reckon, at being woke up, for she didn't come home till five o'clock this morning."

"Cannot we go up to her?" said Rachel, reading Bessie's wish in her countenance.

"Oh, no, missus'll be angry, maybe," was the brief reply.

The sight of a piece of gold which Bess drew from her pocket would evidently have reconciled Nance, as she was called, to a much greater evil than the anger of her mistress.

"If you'll step softly after me I'll show you the way," she observed, eagerly grasping it, and consigning it to the same depository as the silver. "If missus comes out and sees you, you must say you followed me without my leave."

Rachel nodded assent to this, and the woman led the way up the dark and narrow staircase—the former supporting Bess, who could scarcely stand. A loud knock at the door by their conductor was at first unattended to; but, at the second, the well-known voice of Bell Leslie was heard, exclaiming—

"Who is there?—what do you want?—why don't you come in?"

In another instant Bess was at the bedside. She rushed from Rachel, and clasped her sister in her arms, unable to utter a word.

"What is the meaning of all this nonsense?" exclaimed Bell, who, evidently just awakened, and apparently in a state of great confusion, did not recognise the intruder. The old woman, however, who seemed to feel a great curiosity, if no better feeling in what was passing, threw open the window-shutters, and Bell's eye, resting on the face of Rachel, who stood with clasped hands by the bed-side, discovered at once in whose arms it was she was thus strenuously and closely embraced.

"My sister—my own dear sister, dear sister," murmured Bess, raising her head, and gazing fondly and earnestly on the features which were almost convulsed with conflicting passions.

"No, no," she at last exclaimed in a tone of bitterness. "Do not call me sister —that tie has long been broken between us. I have no claim upon you—I make none—I want none. Leave me to my fate. You are happy, prosperous, respected— why do you come here to triumph over me? To make me feel what a wretch I am?"

"Oh, no, no, do not say so, dear Bell," exclaimed Rachel, eagerly, "your sister is wholly incapable of such——"

"Oh, I know it, full well I know it," interrupted Bell, with almost fierceness. "My sister always was and is immaculate, while I——but why should you interfere with me? I have never troubled you—I have never asked any favour of you. No, I would die, starve, rot, perish piecemeal before I would humble myself to those who I know despise me—who look upon my very existence as a disgrace to them."

"Do not say so, oh, Bell, do not think thus of one who would sacrifice her very existence to restore you to happiness," exclaimed Bess, bursting into tears. "Oh, if you knew how I have mourned for you, when I believed you lost for ever. If you could have seen what I felt when I first discovered that you were living. Oh, Bell, Bell, for the sake of that dear mother, who to the last moment of her life—"

"Do not speak of her," interrupted Bell, with vehemence. "If you do not wish to drive me to desperation, do not mention one whom it has been the study

f my life to forget. I have tried to forget you all, to think, as you did of me, that——"

"And how cruel," exclaimed Rachel, with warmth, "oh, Bell, how cruel have you been to suffer your friends——"

"Friends—I have no friends, I want none," returned Bell, with increased violence. "No, leave me to myself—I will never live to be the object of your pity, your contempt. No, I could bear anything—anything but that."

"Do not say so, dear Bell. Are you not my own dear sister?" exclaimed Bess. "Dear to me, even more dear than—than——"

"Than before I had brought ruin, destruction on myself—disgrace and infamy upon you. Is not that what you would have said—what you hesitated to utter?" returned Bell, with bitterness. "Yes, that or something nearly approaching to it, was in your mind—but hear me, Bess. Is it possible that you now speak the pure dictates of your heart?"

"Possible! Can you be so unjust as to

doubt it?" exclaimed Rachel, indignantly. "If you could have seen, as I have seen, the agony your sister has suffered—"

"I do not doubt it—I need not your testimony to tell me that she has bitterly lamented my departure from the path which she has pursued, so fortunately for herself," replied Bell, haughtily. "But what I have done, I have done. It cannot now be recalled, nor am I disposed to listen to *your* strictures on my conduct."

"Oh, Bell, do not speak thus harshly to one who has ever proved herself the truest, best of friends," observed Bess, with generous warmth. "Deeply, sincerely has she lamented your supposed death. That death which is even now wrapped in a mystery that——"

"There was no mystery in it," returned Bell. "The person who I have since learned was committed to the grave in my name was the girl who lived with us at Highgate, and who requited all my kindness and generosity to her by the vilest ingratitude, deserting, and finally robbing me of the last article of value that I had preserved. But as to my gratitude towards Rachel, you must excuse me if I acknowledge that I must doubt that I am very deeply indebted on that account. It suited her to believe that I was removed beyond the power of inflicting farther disgrace on you; but that she was really deceived, I can never for a moment believe. The difference between me and Susan was rather too striking, I should suspect, to deceive anybody. I took it, however, as it was intended, no doubt, as a forcible hint that I was henceforth dead to those whom I had quite as little inclination to make any claims upon as they had to acknowledge me. It was a foolish, romantic scheme, such as could only have originated with those who knew nothing of the world, because a word from me at any time would have——"

"Gracious Heaven," exclaimed Rachel, whom amazement had up to this moment deprived of speech. "Gracious Heaven, is it possible that you mean to accuse me of such a heartless deception upon your mother and sister, I—who——"

She burst into tears, and Bess, who had not been less astonished, and, indeed, horrorstruck at such a cruel and unfounded accusation, for the first time relinquished her warm and affectionate embrace of her sister, to press to her bosom and console the kind hearted and excellent being to whom she felt she was indebted for years of unwearied kindness and attention.

"Bell cannot seriously believe what she has said, dear Rachel," observed the latter. "She must, she does know—and, if she does not, I do—how earnestly, how deeply, how sincerely you lamented that event which caused us all such unspeakable horror, and which, even now—"

"Ay, even now I cannot recal to my recollection without shuddering," returned Rachel, in a low tone. "It would need little argument on my part to prove to you" she continued, turning to Bell, "how natural and likely was the error into which I fell, in mistaking the disfigured remains of that simple and unfortunate girl—"

"For one who ought, perhaps, to have followed the example she set me," returned Bell, with bitterness.

"Oh, no, no, dear Bell, my dear sister, do not say so," exclaimed Bess, with shuddering horror. "God be thanked you are saved to—"

"To repent of my crimes—to linger out the rest of my days in solitude and penitence—to depend, in all due humility and thankfulness on my exemplary sister for the means of existence," exclaimed Bell, with vehemence. "To see her courted, caressed by the world, enjoying wealth, and honour, and distinction, while I—I——"

She burst into a fit of hysterical and passionate weeping that choked the words she would have uttered. Bess flew to endeavour to soothe and console her, but she pushed her away with a violence that completely terrified the former, who clung to Rachel in an agony of sorrow and alarm.

The old woman, who had still lingered in the room, unnoticed by any one, now came forward.

"Don't frighten yourself, miss," she observed, addressing Mrs. Hastings, "your sister, if she be your sister, is oft n in this way ; but it'll soon be over. Come, come, my dear," she continued, shaking Bell by the shoulder with an assumption of authority that made her appear even more revolting to the former than before—"come, don't let's have any more such nonsense as this. I'm sure your sister speaks very fair and kind to you, and what's the use of putting yourself in such figaries. You'll bring all the house presently, and missus ain't in the best of humours, I can tell you."

"Oh, no, no—do not let any one come in," exclaimed Mrs. Hastings, who felt the utmost disgust and alarm at the specimen she had already witnessed of the person the old woman denominated missus. "Leave her to us—pray do. She will be better left with us."

And again she thrust some money in

the hand of the old woman, who seemed about to offer some objection.

"Well, if you think you can manage her, I'm sure I don't want to stay," she replied, "but you'd better let me get her something—a drop of brandy will do her more good than water,"—Rachel had poured out a glass of water, and was holding it to Bell's lips. "Lor' bless you I've seen her often in these tantrums, after she's been having too much overnight, and nothing but a drop of brandy brings her round again."

Bess shook her head—she could not speak, for every word the woman uttered increased her horror and disgust. She had been, from the first moment, impressed with the idea that there was something uncommon and unnatural in Bell's looks, and voice, and manner ; and it was now but too evident, from the old woman's remark, that the former was still under the excitement arising from the previous night's intemperance.

And this was her sister? The twin sister, who had lain in innocence with her on the bosom of her sainted mother, who had shared—almost more than shared—the fond affection, the wise counsel of her adored, lamented father.

Bess sank on her knees by the side of the bed and hid her face, while she raised her heart to heaven, in fervent prayer for the lost, unhappy being in whom every trace of the sister she had so loved, except in feature, seemed changed.

Rachel succeeded in getting the half-stupid and troublesome woman out of the room, and locked the door, to prevent any further intrusion, and then patiently awaited the return of reason, if such it could be called, to the unhappy Bell.

A few words only had passed between Bess and her (Rachel), but the latter fully comprehended the most pressing wish of her beloved Bess ; and when Bell, at length, sunk down on her pillow, silent and exhausted, she calmly addressed her.

"You do not, I am sure, dear Bell, wish your sister to remain any longer in this house, and she will not leave you here. Rouse yourself, then, dear girl. Tell me what shall I do to assist you in getting ready?"

"Oh, yes, yes," exclaimed Bess, eagerly. getting up. "Let us go. Let us leave this horrible place."

"Go where?" returned Bell, languidly raising her head, and smiling incredulously. "Do you know what you are saying? Do you think that the outcast, despised, degraded Bell Leslie could be received as a guest in the proud mansion of Mrs. Has-

tings, or do you think she would enter it as a miserable beggar — the object of charity? No, no, no—I tell you, Bess, once more, leave me to my fate, I want not to intrude upon your happiness—I ask no favour of you—I will never, never stoop to——"

Again she burst into a passionate fit of weeping, and again Bess renewed her tender and affectionate endearments and entreaties that her sister would forget the past, and look forward to a happy future.

"Only leave this place dearest Bell, and trust to my affection, to my love for you, which has never been shaken. Never shall a word or thought from me give you pain," she continued "I will remember you only as the dear sister who shared with me the love of those who are now angels in heaven, and who——"

"No, no," exclaimed Bell, resentfully, I never possessed an equal share in their affection. You were always the favoured, the faultless one. It was you whom I was ever bade to copy. Your example that was always held out to me. No one ever did me justice but my aunt. She for a time, indeed, till her own selfish nature interposed, saw that I was not fairly treated, that—but what is the use of talking of these things now? You have triumphed over me at last. I am scorned, despised, shunned, as a disgraced, degraded, debased creature, while you—."

"Oh, Bell, my dear sister, do not give way to these mistaken feelings," interrupted Bess, shocked at the discovery of how long the former had treasured in her secret heart feelings of jealousy and resentment against her—a jealousy, too, so unfounded and unjust, and which she could only attribute—as, indeed, she did every fault of her misguided sister—to the influence of the weak-minded Lady Jane Bevington. "Never, I am sure, dear Bell," she continued, "can I accuse myself of having, in any respect, assumed superiority over you."

"You had no right, *then*," observed Bell, with asperity.

"No, nor now, dear Bell, nor *now*," returned her sister, with marked emphasis. "In the eyes of the world," she continued, her voice trembling with emotion, "that world, ever prone to mark with severity every deviation from—"

"I do not want to hear from *you* what the world says of me," interrupted Bell. "I know it—I feel it, every hour, every moment of my miserable life, I am made to feel how scorned, how lost, how despised a wretch I am become !"

"Then leave it, Bell. Fly from the

world that can treat you so cruelly, to the arms of those who will shield you from every suffering," exclaimed Bess; "whose whole study it shall be to render you happy, to banish from your mind every distracting thought and care. To teach you to forget the past, and look forward in hope and trust."

"Yes, to mourn in sack-cloth and ashes—to brood, in humble penitence over my horrible crimes, and humbly acknowledge the goodness and generosity of my pure, virtuous sister, in bestowing upon me the means of living," interrupted Bell, with a smile of bitter irony. "No, I will starve first."

Bess burst into tears. This was, indeed, a cruel addition to the affliction she had already suffered from her sister's misconduct, to find her thus perversely determined to misconstrue her feelings, and reject her affectionate offers.

"I know who it is I am indebted to for this visit," suddenly observed Bell, starting up with an expression of anger and vexation. "I knew his hypocritical pretences that he held no communication with you were false. But take care, Bess—do not trust to his affectation of morality. They are all alike—all false, deceitful, treacherous towards women. There is not one among them, be they as honourable as they may in their dealings with their own sex—no, not one who will scruple to lie, and flatter, and deceive a woman. Look upon them, Bess, as I do, as the natural enemies of our weak sex. Treat them as such. Suspect, distrust them, and the more so when they make the pretentions Leicester does, to superior principles, a higher code of morality. Believe them, then, the most dangerous—for they add hypocrisy to their other vices. They dissimulate, only the more certainly to effect that which guides and dictates the indulgence of their own selfish passions, and the destruction of all who are foolish enough to believe in them. Oh, yes, I knew, with all his plausibility, his affected horror at vice, his eloquent eulogiums on the beauty of virtue, his insinuating persuasions to me to renounce the path I have chosen for myself—"

"Oh, no, Bell, not chosen," interrupted Bess, with tenderness. "Do not say, my own dear sister—do not say that you have voluntarily abandoned the principles our dear father and mother implanted in our hearts. You have strayed, indeed, from the paths in which they guided our steps, but it is not yet too late to return, to retrieve all—"

"Psha, teaze me no more, Bess. If you are really disposed to do me any good, give me the means in my own hands of acting as I think proper," observed Bell. "In fact," she continued, "I have a right, I believe, to demand my share of what was left at my mother's death—that is to say, if she did not deprive me of it by a will."

She looked anxiously and penetratingly at her sister for a reply. Bess was too much shocked, for a moment, to speak. That Bell could speak thus coolly and systematically on such a subject was, indeed, astonishing and revolting to her warm-hearted and noble-minded sister; but the latter, suppressing as far as possible all emotion, the moment she could collect her thoughts, replied—

"I cannot believe, Bell, that your heart could do such injustice to our dear mother as to suppose that she would have suffered any conduct on your part to obliterate her tender feelings towards you. It seems, however, that you have forgotten that she died in total ignorance of your existence, and—"

"I do not want to hear anything on that point," interrupted Bell, with violence. "You can, I suppose, give a direct answer to my question—have I, or have I not, a right to share what was left at her death?"

"It is all yours, Bell," returned her sister. "Fortunately, Mr. Hastings' generosity has left me unconditionally mistress of much more than that sum. It is, therefore, yours."

"I want no more than my proper share," muttered Bell, apparently somewhat ashamed of the light in which her precipitancy had placed her in her sister's eyes.

Bess still lingered—she would have renewed her entreaties to her sister to leave, at once, the connexions she had there formed; but Bell's manner was so repulsive and so determined that she (Bess) trembled to renew the subject. The remainder of their conversation, therefore, was confined to merely the arrangements necessary to transfer to the former the sum of several hundred pounds which had constituted all the late Mrs. Leslie's property. The amount was evidently satisfactory to Bell, who had, probably, considerably underrated it; but Bess was far from being satisfied, and would have greatly increased it, but for the energetic remonstrance conveyed to her privately by Rachel, who very properly observed—

"It will be always in your power, my dear child, to prevent your sister's feeling the pressure of want, and to bestow more upon her now, in her present frame of mind, would, depend upon it, be injurious. Reserve, therefore, your generosity until she stands in need of it, and may be, I hope, better disposed to make good use of it."

Bess yielded to this advice, and having made the necessary arrangements for her sister to receive the money, whenever she chose to apply for it to the banker in whose hands it was deposited, nothing remained but to bid her farewell; and the former, though reluctantly, quitted the room, almost broken-hearted at the coldness, apathy, and obstinate determination to persist in her evil course of life evinced by her unworthy sister.

CHAPTER XXII.

The lichen clingeth to the rock,
  The ivy to the tree—
Yet, oh ! more fond, more close the bond
  That linked this soul to thee.

The form that twined about thy neck
  In happy infant play ;
Once more is bowed above thy shrowd,
  And bends beside thy clay.

Once more I press the gentle hand
  I ever loved to hold ;
It does not strain my hand again,
  Ah ! no, 'tis dead—'tis cold !

Once more I kiss thy whitened lips,
  But, hark ! the tolling bell ;
Once more—the last—away, 'tis past—
  Sister, farewell, farewell !—*Anon.*

MANY months had passed —Mr. Hastings had returned home, restored in a great measure in mind, but gradually sinking in bodily health. Bessie's whole attention was absorbed in administering to his comforts and happiness. Yet was not her unhappy sister forgotten. Repugnant as it was to her feelings, Rachel contrived to establish a communication with the old woman, the drudge of the house in which Bell had resided at the period of the interview between the sisters, and from her she not only learned many particulars of Bell's history, from the time she left her mother's protection, but also contrived to keep her eye upon her present career. The former part of her history would but little interest our readers, and we, therefore, proceed to that which came to the knowledge of her amiable and tender-hearted sister, subsequent to the latter relinquishing to her the money left by Mrs. Leslie.

"She's dashing away as usual, ma'am," observed the old woman, whom Rachel met, by appointment, at the house of a tradesman in the neighbourhood. "She's living away, as she always does when she's got a little money, in the very height of extravagance; and, I suppose, will go on so till every farthing's spent, and she's as bad off as ever. Nobody, indeed, never can do her any good, she's so wilful and——"

Rachel mildly put an end to these comments, and having amply satisfied the woman for her trouble and information, which included not only Bell's present residence, but many particulars of the thoughtless course she was pursuing, returned to communicate, in as softened terms as she could, to Mrs. Hastings, the intelligence she had acquired. Bitter, very bitter, were the tears Bessie shed at this confirmation of her sister's unworthiness; and they were not ameliorated, when soon after, she was one day summoned from the bedside of her husband to receive a visitor in the person of her uncle, Sir Matthew Bevington. He had lost his heir—the child whose birth had effected such a change in the prospects of his nieces—and, as Bess felt, had originated all the troubles and errors into which her unfortunate sister had so desperately plunged herself. His own health was visibly fast declining, and Lady Jane's situation was pronounced to be hopeless.

A thousand mournful and tender recollections rushed upon Bessie's mind as her uncle, with evident shame and sorrow at his past conduct, affectionately embraced her. A long and interesting conversation ensued, and much was discussed and cleared up which had contributed to alienate the uncle and niece from each other, although it was but too evident that Sir Matthew would never have sought these explanations, had it not been that his hopes were blighted by the loss of his son, and the consciousness that all his worldly prospects were fast drawing to a close. Bessie, however, was too generous and kind-hearted to retaliate for the cruelty and neglect from which she, as well as her mother, had so deeply suffered, and to which, she felt, was clearly attributed the ruin of her unhappy sister ; and although she took the first opportunity, afforded by an observation of Sir Matthew's, as to the eventual disposition of his fortune, to assure him that as far as she was herself concerned, it was a matter of perfect indifference to her to whom it was bequeathed, and that it would be far more satisfactory to her that he should be convinced that no mercenary considerations prompted her in the wish for a perfect reconciliation, and a renewal of the intercourse between himself, Lady Jane, and her; she considered it her duty to take advantage of his present favourable disposition to secure, if possible, a provision for her unfortunate sister, which would effectually place the latter above all temptation to renew the dissolute course of life she had led.

The simple mention of Bell's name, however, which Sir Matthew had hitherto cautiously avoided, roused from him a storm of passion. He would, without pity or remose, see her (Bell) perishing for want in the streets rather than she should enjoy a shilling of his money ; and then came a list of grievance, insults, and mortifications, evidently studied on the part of Bell, towards himself and Lady Jane, but more especially towards the latter, which proved that revenge on her part was predominant over every other feeling; and that exposure and disgrace were nothing in her mind, compared to the satisfaction she derived from the gratification of her resentful feelings towards those to whose injustice she attributed her ruin.

Bess was, therefore, compelled to relinquish her hopes of being, through the means of her uncle, enabled to make a permanent provision for her sister, which would place her above all temptation to vice ; nor, indeed, under the circumstances, did she dare acknowledge to him what she

had recently done for Bell, and the ungrateful return the latter had made for it, in withdrawing herself, as she supposed, entirely beyond the reach or knowledge of her sister. It was, in that respect, fortunate for Bess that Mr. Hastings's situation necessarily confined her to her home, for she was thus spared the misery of encountering Bell, which must have been the case had she visited any public places of amusement. She heard, however, sufficient to convince her that every hope of her sister's reformation was vain and futile ; for, as if setting all appearances at defiance, Bell was squandering the money she had received in a manner that must speedily reduce her again to utter poverty and dependence.

Suddenly, however, the information which Rachel from time to time received respecting her was brought to a close, for Bell disappeared from her residence, without leaving any trace wither she had gone; and Rachel then learned from the old woman, her informant, the truth of what she had once before heard hinted, that Bell was in reality a married woman. What had been her motives for marrying one who, it appeared, possessed so few recommendations to her favour, the old woman could not pretend to say ; but she knew that Bell was the wife of a man named Lawrence, and that she had been dreadfully ill-treated by him during the short time they had lived together. That, for some time, the unfortunate girl had not known what had become of him, but that, within a few days of the time that she (the old woman) communicated this intelligence to Rachel, Mr. Lawrence had suddenly re-appeared, and had called at Bell's former residence in search of his wife.

The woman concluded her information by observing, that there was no doubt that Bell's knowledge of this was the cause of her sudden flight ; as she knew, from his character, what she had to expect if he found her in possession of any money, &c. This, of course, was a further source of uneasiness and sorrow to Mrs. Hastings, but much of her attention to her sister's unhappy situation was at this time withdrawn by Mr. Hastings' death, which took place after a long period of suffering, comforted and consoled to the last moment, by the undeviating tenderness and constant presence of the wife to whom he was so passionately attached. All that had ever occurred to disturb his mind, or prompt a suspicion of her entire innocence and devotion to him, had long since been fully explained, and the most entire confidence on his part restored towards her ; and Bess e found herself, by his death, the sole and undisputed heiress to the whole of his immense wealth, and placed in a situation to follow up every dictate of her kind and benevolent disposition towards her fellow-creatures, while she was equally free to consult her own happiness in any mode of living she might choose to adopt.

Bess, however, as the rich widow of Mr. Hastings, was still the same simple and unassuming being she had ever been ; and, in accordance with those retired and domestic tastes and habits, which had ever distinguished her, she, as soon as possible, relinquished the splendid establishment of which she had so long been the mistress without enjoyment, and having secured a beautiful, though small estate in the immediate vicinity of Arundale, the scene of her happy childhood, retired thither to enjoy, as she hoped, the remainder of her life in peace, if not perfect happiness. That, indeed, was forbidden by recollections of the past, and, above all, by the uncertainty that still existed as to the fate of her unfortunate sister, which still eluded every means that could be devised to ascertain it.

And did Bessie, in this retirement, never think of him who had once occupied so large a share in the thoughts and hopes, and wishes of her pure heart? Was Ronald Leicester entirely forgotten, now that it was no longer a crime to remember him—now, when all had passed away that once embittered his remembrance, and had dictated the strong, the arduous effort to forget that such a person had ever existed ?

The truth must be told—Bess had not forgotten him. His image was still treasured in her "heart of hearts"—his words, his thoughts, the pure and noble sentiments which had fallen from his lips during the happy though brief period when, sanctioned by her mother's approval, they had been all in all to each other, were constantly recalled to her mind, and brooded over in secret. Even his refined and peculiar tastes were though almost involuntarily, her guides in the alterations and decorations of her lovely little retreat. Even in the choice of furniture, in the arrangement of her gardens and shrubberies—in all, in fact, that could contribute to the beauty and comfort of her secluded residence, she constantly recurred to the plans which he had been used to sketch ; and whenever she was in doubt as to the effect of any proposed alteration, " Would *he* approve of it?" was the question she endeavoured to solve.

More than twelvemonths passed away, without any incident occurring to break in upon the quiet uniformity of Arundale Cottage, as Mrs. Hastings had unassumingly named her delightful retreat. She had renewed her acquaintance, not only with every one who retained a recollection of their regretted and respected pastor, the Curate of Arundale and his family, but with every spot and scene which had been hallowed by his or her dear mother's presence.

Every plan which her beloved father had suggested, and, as far as his circumstances would allow, practised, for the benefit of the humbler inhabitants of the Vale, was now scrupulously followed out ; and the poor had already learned to bless the day that had restored to it her whom they still remembered as one of the " Twin Roses of Arundale."

And yet, though thus blessed, though still in possession of youth and beauty that fully entitled her to the appellation which still distinguished her, possessed of wealth sufficient to gratify every wish, and especially that—the dearest to her heart—of removing, from all within her sphere, the semblance of poverty or suffering, Bess was not happy.

It was in vain she sought, by constant occupation in the service of others, to shun the memory of the past. Her sister was ever present to her memory, and Rachel began almost to repent having agreed with her in fixing upon Arundale as her settled residence, where everything combined to remind her of Bell.

The death of Lady Jane Bevington, which took place at this time, seconded Rachel's wish that she would for a time leave the spot which, endeared as it was by so many circumstances, seemed but too much calculated to confirm the pensive and melancholy turn of her mind. On this occasion Bess received a letter from her uncle, in which he most pathetically entreated her to visit him in London; and, accordingly, once more Bess quitted her beloved seclusion, and returned to the metropolis, which she believed she had quitted for ever.

It was a dark and gloomy evening when the travellers entered London, by the way of Knightsbridge. Bessie's spirits were even more than usually depressed, and the bustle and gaiety which presented itself, from the lighted and splendid shops, and numerous carriages rolling in all directions, seemed even more oppressive to her than had been the silence and gloom of the roads.

Bess threw herself back in the corner of

the carriage, and closed her eyes, as if to shut out that which was so repugnant to her present feelings ; but she was speedily aroused by the sudden stopping of the chariot ; and, on looking out, she found that it was prevented proceeding by a dense crowd of people who were pressing forward towards a large building on her left.

"It is some accident, probably," observed Rachel, leaning forward. "That is St. George's Hospital."

The next moment she almost forcibly drew her companion back ; for, passing the carriage, so close as almost to touch it, was the object which was the cause of so much interest and curiosity.

A human form, stretched on a shutter, and borne on the shoulders of several men, the light covering that veiled it from the eyes of the spectators concealing only the head and shoulders, and leaving exposed the slender form of a female of apparently delicate and elegant proportions.

A cold shudder ran through Rachel's blood. It was not that she could, in that transient glance have had any recognition of the form which met her eyes ; but close behind it she beheld a well-known face. It was that of the old woman, the miserable drudge of the house in which Mrs. Hastings and herself had last beheld the unfortunate Bell Leslie, or rather Mrs. Lawrence.

There was an expression of horror and bewilderment on the usually stolid and inexpressive face of this miserable creature, that showed she was not a mere casual spectator, drawn thither by that which in all probability actuated three-fourths of the crowd—that morbid curiosity and interest which is ever excited in some minds by any case partaking of the horrible.

The woman, too, was supported on each side by two persons; one a man, the other a female of rather decent appearance ; and, in short, Rachel saw quite sufficient to convince her that the ghastly form that had passed, so like a dreadful vision, was one in which the wretched old woman was peculiarly interested.

"What is the matter?" demanded Bessie, whose surprise now amounted to alarm, as she saw, by the bright light of the gas lamps at the turnpike close to which the carriage had drawn up, the deadly paleness of her companion's face.

"Oh, speak—what is the matter?" repeated the former, more loudly, on finding that Rachel did not reply. She was unable from terror.

"It's a poor young woman that's been murdered by a wretch of a husband, ma'am," replied a woman, who was standing close to the carriage, and who seemed to imagine that Mrs. Hastings' inquiry had been addressed to her. "They're taking her to the hospital," continued the woman, "but I don't know what's the use of it, for she's dead enough, and they can't bring her to life again there, I suppose, any more than any where else."

"Do not ask any questions, dear Bessie. Let us go on," faintly articulated Rachel.

But her companion's alarm had been too powerfully excited. A vague idea that it was not the mere sympathy of compassion that could have been excited by a stranger in such circumstances that had produced such an effect upon Rachel, had already been excited in her (Bessie's) mind. She leaned eagerly forward to restrain the coachman, who had heard Rachel's eager command to drive on, and was about to obey.

"Stop ! stop ! I must—I will know what this means !" she exclaimed. "Rachel, for Heaven's sake, tell me !" and then, suddenly recollecting herself, she beckoned to the woman who had given her the voluntary information as to the cause of the excitement she beheld, and who, though she was moving away, still kept her eye upon the ladies in the carriage, probably surprised at the agitation she there beheld.

"Tell me, pray tell me who was it you spoke of, just now? Do you know the person, the—the young woman you spoke of. Her name—her——"

"Oh, I knows nothing about her, ma'am, I do assure you," returned the woman, "only I was passing by the house that they brought her out of, and I just asked a question or two of the people that was about, and they told me she was a beautiful young creature, but had married a desperate brute, and they'd been parted two or three times, and now he'd found her out, where she was living with another gentleman, and——"

"Where is the house ? What is the name of the street? No, I will go at once to the hospital. I cannot bear this suspense,' exclaimed Bess, attempting to open the door of the carriage.

Rachel would have restrained her. She tried to persuade her that the terror that had seized her was without foundation ; but Bess was not to be deceived, and although she could not comprehend how Rachel could have so immediately divined the fact, she was not the less convinced that her presentiment would prove correct —that the murdered woman would prove

to be her sister,—her lost, regretted Bell. Finding it useless to attempt to alter her determination, Rachel gave the necessary order to the servants. The horses' heads were turned, and in a few minutes Mrs. Hastings, trembling and pale with agitation, was with Rachel admitted into the hall of the hospital, the doors of which had been closed upon the admission of the body, to prevent the indiscriminate entrance of the crowd—but were immediately opened upon the announcement, made by some officious bystander, that two ladies in a carriage, who were relations of the murdered woman, required admittance.

"That's her sister, I'll swear," ex-claimed a voice among the persons who were standing in the hall. "Lord bless you, they are as like as two roses on one stalk. She was a beautiful young creature as ever my eyes were set upon."

"Beauty is as beauty does," replied another speaker; "but I suppose that is the poor mother. She is to be pitied but as for young women that desert their lawful husbands——"

"God break hard fortune before every poor mother's child," observed a clean, decent-looking Irishwoman. "Sit down here, darling," and she kindly took Bessie's trembling arm, to place her on the bench she had herself vacated. "An here's room for you, too, poor lady," she continued, dropping a curtsey to Rachel. "Heaven comfort ye both—I'm the mother of childer meself, and my heart bleeds for ye, it does."

The question which had quivered on Bessie's lips, ever since her entrance, but which she had vainly looked around for some one competent to answer, was now on the point of escaping, when it was prevented by the old woman before mentioned, who rushed towards her and Rachel, from the listening group who had collected around her.

"Oh, Lord, you have heard it all already," she exclaimed. It is but this minute that I was saying that the poor soul had no relations in the world but one sister, and I didn't know where she was to be found."

"It is her, then," ejaculated Rachel, while Bess sank down fainting upon the seat which had been offered her. It was not long before she recovered sufficiently to understand what the old woman was rapidly relating to Rachel, but hope suddenly sprung anew in her bosom, and she started up with renewed strength, when from the speaker's disjointed remark, "If she should recover," she comprehended that her sister was still living.

With agonised earnestness she now entreated to see her. The officials, however, to whom this entreaty was addressed, were too scared and callous by the frequent sight of misery to depart from the general usages on such occasions.

"You must wait till the doctors have done, and the young woman's put to bed ; and then, if they think proper, you will be admitted," was the reply given to her earnest supplication.

Oh, how dreadful was the interval which, though in reality not more than twenty minutes, appeared to Bess protracted for hours; and then, when the appointed time was come, when the buzz around her announced that it was "over," for "the doctors were coming down stairs," a new impediment arose. They had given orders that the patient was not to be spoken to, or disturbed. The slightest excitement would probably prove fatal, and the nurse, who, with an air of kindness, and an attempt at soothing, informed Bess of this, assured her that she would be taken every care of, and she could, if the doctors gave permission, see her in the morning at ten o'clock.

"A night—a whole night of misery and suspense, and she may die ! Die, without a friend near her !" exclaimed Bess, wringing her hands in agony.

The tone in which this was uttered caught the ear of a gentleman who was passing hastily through the hall. In another instant he was at Bessie's side. She gazed upon him with a look of bewilderment. It was Ronald Leicester. All that had happened to keep them so long estranged from each other was in that moment forgotten. He was a friend —the only friend who could enter into feelings—who could sincerely sympathise in her present distress, and clinging to his arm, as, in that tone of tenderness that had so long been a stranger to her ear, he implored her to let him conduct her from a scene so painful she implored him to let her see her sister—her own unhappy sister.

Leicester was for a moment paralyzed, as it were, with astonishment. He had come, as it afterwards appeared, on an errand of kindness and mercy to a poor wretch who was dying in the hospital, and though he had heard the bustle and buzz occasioned by the arrival of the poor woman, who it was said had fallen a victim to the vindictive passions of her husband, he dreamt not who that victim was—how deeply he was concerned in the case. A brief explanation ensued from Rachel as to her and Bessie's appearance there, and, imprudent as it might appear, he entered fully into the feelings which prompted the latter in her entreaty to be allowed to see, to watch by the bed of her sister. Committing Bessie again to the care of Rachel, having previously succeeded in getting her removed from the gaze of curiosity into a private room, he sought and obtained an interview with the principal surgeon at once, to learn the real situation of the unhappy Bell, and to procure the necessary permission to see her. He learned that there was scarcely a possibility she could recover from the injuries she had received ; but she was in a state of stupor, which would prevent the possibility of her recognising any one, and if the sister could be depended upon, that she would keep perfectly quiet, and not disturb the unfortunate woman by any ill-timed grief and lamentation, she might be allowed to remain with her.

Leicester gave, and felt he could give with safety, the necessary pledge for Mrs. Hastings's prudence and forbearance ; but to secure it still further, he avowed his intention to remain near her. Rachel, too, upon a few further words of explanation, was included in the permission, and though trembling at the ultimate effects upon Bess of her fulfilment of this melancholy duty, he hastened to impart to her the grateful intelligence that he had succeeded.

All that long dreary night Bess remained upon her knees, silent and immovable, by the bed-side of the unhappy sufferer. She shed no tears—she uttered no sound—but the deathly paleness of her countenance, and the convulsive quivering of her lips, betrayed her inward suffering, as from time to time a feeble groan, or faint, and unintelligible expression from the wretched Bell evinced the intense agony she was enduring. Two or three times during the long and awful hours Leicester, who remained in an adjoining room, ventured to her side, to utter a whispered remonstrance on the injury she was doing herself, but an impatient wave of her hand obliged him to relinquish his effort to withdraw her from the bed-side. A visit from the surgeon, soon after daybreak, however, accomplished what his (Leicester's) persuasions failed to effect. She dared not dispute the doctor's authority, which, the nurse told her, required that everybody should be removed before he made the necessary examination of his patient ; and she suffered, passively, Leicester to carry her in his arms (for she could not walk) into the adjoining room, and even forced herself to swallow the wine and water which he held to her lips, when he whispered in her ear, in those well-remembered tones that had so long been a stranger to it—

"Bessie, for my sake, if not for your own, do not wilfully reject what is necessary to support you through this trying scene. Do not let me have the misery of losing you now when—"

The remainder of the sentence was not uttered, for he felt that it was wrong, at such a moment, even to hint at the possibility of his own future happiness. But Bessie felt all that was unsaid, and the first tears she had shed stole down her cheeks, as, raising her head from his shoulder, she whispered—

"Oh, Leicester—if she could live ! If she were but once more restored to us !"

"She will, my own, my only love ! God will hear our earnest prayers—I trust he will," returned Leicester, pressing her to his heart. "But, if she does not—If it be His will to remove her from all suffering now—"

"Yes, yes," murmured Bess. "I will, I will resign into his hands all hopes and wishes. His mercy is infinite, and—"

She was interrupted by the voice of her sister, replying in clear tones to a question from the surgeon, and Bessie's heart leaped in her bosom at what she thought so favourable an omen.

"Have you any friends ? Any one you wish to see ?" demanded the medical gentleman.

"Friends !" she repeated, with bitter emphasis. "Oh, no, no—where should the wretched find friends ? Not one—not one. I have driven from me all who loved me, and now I am dying among strangers. Oh, Bess, Bess, my sister, my sister, you would pity me, you would I know you would—"

"You must not excite yourself in this manner," interrupted the doctor.

Bess had flown to the door the instant she heard her name ; but he held up his finger to restrain her, and she stood motionless while he proceeded to prepare Bell for her appearance.

"Yes, I will be calm. I will be composed," she replied, "only let me see her. Let me hear her say that she forgives me for all the misery I have caused her."

"It matters little now," whispered the surgeon to Leicester. "Let the young lady come. No human help can save her."

In a minute after, Bess was again on her knees by the bedside—Bell's cold hands were grasped in hers, and the eyes of the dying victim lingered on her face until they were closed in death. It was not, however, until after many hours of bodily and mental agony, which wrung the heart of the affectionate sister, and made even her almost pray for death to release the sufferer, that the scene closed ; but

> "At length from her world-wearied heart,
> The fever and the flame depart.
> Then softness came, and gentler woe,
> Firm loathing of the hateful past,
> Efforts towards God's will to go,
> And yearnings to be pure at last
> Till, praying with her latest breat ,
> She brightened gently into death."

It need scarcely be said that all that had hitherto estranged two hearts, so born for each other, as Ronald Leicester's and Bessie's, was now obliterated, and they were happily united. Bessie was long indeed, before she could subdue the intense sorrow arising from the loss of the sister he so dearly loved; but time, the great soother of all human sorrows, has softened her remembrance into gentle and melancholy regret, while in the high and exhalted station she now holds, is buried, as far as the outward world is concerned, all recollection of the disadvantages that attended her outset in it and which followed her a long time.

> "And no one misses aught or knows
> The story of the blighted Rose."

THE END.

B. LLOYD, 12 SALISBURY-SQUARE FLEET-STREET, LONDON.

www.ingramcontent.com/pod-product-compliance
Lightning Source LLC
Chambersburg PA
CBHW080733250626
47170CB00010B/2814